BEN ANDERSON

W9-BIM-740

The McGunnegal Chronicles

Books 1-3 – The Strange Land Trilogy

Edition 3.1

Copyright (c) 2014, 2015, 2017 by Ben Anderson

Edited by BZ Hercules

For Sam, Luke, Rachel and Katie.

All my love.

– Dad

BEN ANDERSON

ACKNOWLEDGEMENTS

Thanks to everyone who helped me with editing, ideas, and encouragement, especially Frederica, Mary Beth, Sharon, Doris, Katie, Rachel, Julia, Jannie and others.

Thanks to BZ Hercules for their great editing help.

Special thanks to my dear wife, Janet, who has been so patient with me on the journey of writing The McGunnegal Chronicles.

And thanks to all my heroes of ages past, whose teachings whisper through these pages.

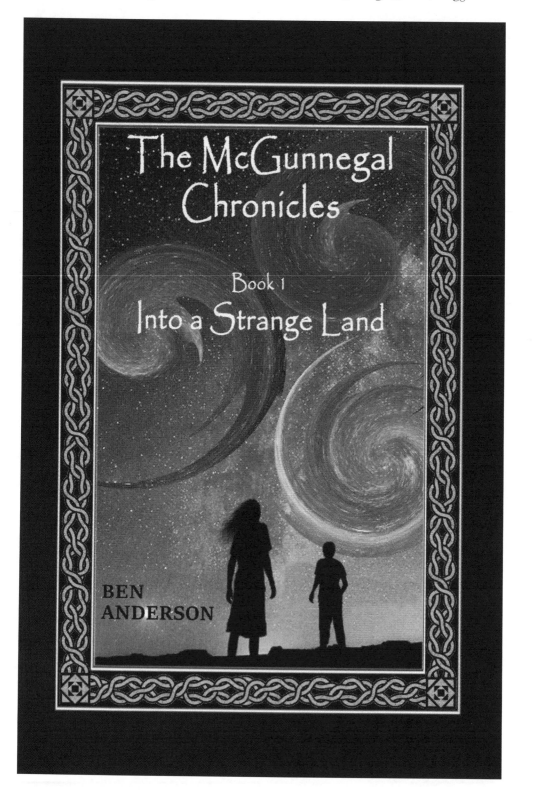

The McGunnegal
Chronicles

Book 1

Into a Strange Land

BEN
ANDERSON

Chapter 1 – Grandpa's Secret

Frederick glanced over at his cousin, Colleen McGunnegal, and did a double take. For a moment, the wind had whipped Colleen's hair into a golden-red frenzy, and with her form silhouetted against the sun, she seemed to be transfigured into some mysterious elemental with hair of fire. Then the gust died as they walked into the shadow of her great grandfather's hut, and she was just herself again – a thirteen-year-old girl, half-starved from the famine.

The old porch steps sagged and creaked as Colleen climbed them. She motioned for Frederick to follow, but he hesitated, eying the broken shutters, crumbling mortar, and the strange carving on the door – three interlaced spirals. A crow sat on the roof, ruffling its feathers, a black shape against the orange western sky. It squawked, a sickly croaking sound, as Colleen pushed the door open and rusted hinges groaned in protest.

"Come on, Frederick," she said, waving to him. "He won't bite, you know. He doesn't have enough teeth left. I've got to warn you, meaning no disrespect, but he's, well, a bit... old."

"You mean he's a bit corr in the head?" asked Frederick as he climbed the steps.

Colleen frowned at him, turned, and went in. He took a breath and followed. Inside, the hut was dark except for the glow of a fire on a stone hearth and the fading light of day filtering in through several draped windows. Scant furniture lay about the room – a wooden chair beside a small table, a lidded wooden box, a cot covered with thin blankets, and a rocking chair, in which sat a hunched old man smoking a corncob pipe. Frederick wrinkled his nose at the smell of bad tobacco.

"Grandpa!" said Colleen, her voice full of joy.

She went to him and gave him a hug and a kiss on the cheek, at which he waved her away and wiped his face on his sleeve. When he spoke, his voice reminded Frederick of walking through dried leaves – brittle and crumbling, crunching underfoot.

"You'll give me the *kootinanee*, girl, with all those kisses!"

"Oh, Grandpa, you know you love it," she said. "Look who I've brought to see you – it's our cousin Frederick. He's come all the way from Wales to visit Ireland with his family. His pa and Dad said they had business to discuss and for us to find something to do, so I told him we would come see you."

Grandpa McLochlan turned slowly in his chair. Frederick had never seen a face so wrinkled, a nose so large, or ears quite so stretched and drooping. The old man grabbed his shillelagh from beside the chair, a black stick with a knobby head and, with a grunt, stood and shuffled slowly over to Frederick.

Although Grandpa's back and neck were so bent that his chin nearly touched his chest, he still managed to hobble around Frederick, looking him over and sniffing, as if inspecting a piece of fruit. Frederick froze, following the old man with his eyes.

"Well, what's the matter, boy? Are you dumb or something? Cat got your tongue?" Grandpa prodded a gray cat that had appeared at Frederick's feet, and it meowed and ran under the rocking chair. The old man cackled with delight and looked Frederick over once again.

"Say, young feller, don't I know you from somewhere? Where ye be from?" he said.

"Uh, I'm Colleen's cousin, Frederick – Frederick Brendan Buttersmouth, as she's said, and I'm just now come from Wales. My father has business with Colleen's dad – your, uh, great son-in-law."

"Well, then!" shouted the old man. "What's your picture doin' on me wall?"

He lifted his cane and shook it at a faded oil painting hanging above the fireplace.

"Now, Grandpa, you know that's Mom and Aonghus, not Frederick," said Colleen. She had seen it many times, and now that her mother was gone, she often came here just to look at it.

"Ha!" he said, a note of victory in his voice, though over what, Colleen was not sure. "That's not yer mum nor yer brother! It's been hanging there since I was a lad, and when my grand was a lad, and before him as well. It's *him*, I tell ye, and you'll know it soon enough!" He shuffled back to his chair, plopped himself down, and stared into the fire.

"See," whispered Colleen to Frederick. "I told you, he's old - a hundred and three, actually."

She led him over to the fireplace, and they sat at her grandfather's feet.

"Tell us one of your tales, Grandpa, one about the olden days," she said.

He narrowed his eyes at Frederick, glanced up at the picture, and said, "Well, since *he's* here maybe I'll tell ye at last. No, I can *show* ye the *secret* where all the stories began. Follow me."

He rose once again and went to one corner of the room. "Franklin, move this here rug for me. Just shove it aside."

"It's Frederick, sir," said Frederick, but he grabbed one end of the round braided rug and pulled it away. There in the floor was a square trap door with an iron ring for a handle.

"I've not been down there for some time," the grandfather said. "Too old. 'Cept for once back when..." He mused for a moment then muttered, "Taters are probably all spoiled by now, though they might be better than those in the fields, what with the blight and all." Then, in a hissing whisper, he said, "But *it* was down there. Yer mum found it that night. That's why she's been away." His eyes grew wide, as if some memory suddenly became lucid to him.

"Mom found what?" said Colleen. Her mother had vanished without a trace eight months ago. She had come here to visit her grandfather, but he said she had gone down into the potato cellar and never came back. Something else had come in her place – something dark that the old man said he only *smelled* and caught a glimpse of before it dashed out the door. Not a day had passed by that Colleen had not thought about her mother, wondering what had happened.

"Go and see!" the old man said.

Colleen reached down and heaved on the ring. It moved a few inches, then fell back with a thud.

"Give her a hand, Farman," said Grandpa, and whacked Frederick on his backside with his shillelagh.

"It's Frederick, sir," he replied, his voice rising in agitation. But he bent down to help.

Together, they lifted the door and leaned it against the wall. A wooden ladder descended into darkness, and the musty smell of rotting potatoes wafted up to meet them. Frederick turned away and coughed.

"Grab a lantern, Frederick," said Colleen. "And hand it down to me, then come down yourself."

"I'm not going down there," he said. "Who knows what's down in that musty old cellar? It's probably full of poison spiders and rats and such."

"Oh, just hand me a lantern, then, if you're too scared. There's nothing down there but old sacks of potatoes," she said, although she felt a queer chill at the thought of going down into the dark cellar – the last place her mother had been seen.

Frederick retrieved a lantern from the wall and lit it while Colleen climbed down the wooden rungs. Halfway down, she paused and said, "Now hand it to me."

He did so, and watched as she descended the remaining few steps to the dirt floor. She paused, holding up the lantern and looking around. Then she looked up at him and said, "Oh come on, there are just a load of old sacks and such. Grandpa, what was it that you wanted me to see down here?"

"Under the blankets, girl, over to your left," he called down to her.

Colleen looked. A piled heap of crates covered in old, thin blankets lay against the wall. Frederick watched as she moved out of sight, and suddenly felt ashamed that he had not gone with her.

"Ye best git down there, Ferdinan," said Grandpa. "Ye wouldn't want her going *there* all alone, would ye?"

"It's Fred... Oh, never mind." He gulped, looked one last time down into the shaft, then got on his knees and slowly backed into the hole. The old man wore an eager toothless grin, and his deeply sunken eyes followed Frederick as he descended.

Off to the left, he could see the glow of the lantern sitting on a crate and Colleen's flickering shadow dancing about as she dragged boxes away from the wall.

He made his way over to her, and then turned to look back at the trap door. He jumped and yelled out – the old man was standing right behind him.

"How did you..." he began, but Grandpa moved past him to where Colleen had now cleared the debris away from the wall.

There, engraved on a single massive stone at least seven feet high and four feet wide, were three interlaced spirals.

"Why it's the same design as on the front door. When did you carve this?" asked Colleen.

He lifted the lantern in one hand and leaned heavily on his cane. He frowned, and his face looked eerie in the dim light. "Old, it is," he said. "Older than me. Older than the farm. Older than the Celts themselves. Much older."

"What is it?" whispered Frederick. He was getting a strange feeling in this place, as though something was watching him. He looked about, but could see nothing in the dim light other than vague shapes.

"A marker," replied Grandpa. "A marker to an *entrance*."

Colleen's eyes grew wide. She suddenly remembered another place where she had seen the triple spiral before. There was one on the passage tomb up at Newgrange. She had seen it several years ago when they had gone to visit her mother's cousin.

"It's a grave, isn't it, Grandpa?" she whispered.

He slowly turned his bent neck and looked sidelong at her. "Maybe. Maybe they're *all* dead."

"Who?" said Frederick.

"The *Others*," he hissed. "Maybe *it* was the last one – the one that came that night."

He paused, looked at Colleen, then at Frederick, as if considering something.

"*It* lives in the bog now. But some nights, it comes. I can *smell* it. It wants to go back – back to its place. Back to where the old tales all began."

Placing the lantern back on the crate, he fumbled for a moment in his sweater pocket. Removing a small box, he held it next to the light.

"This is the McLochlan family secret, child. *You* have to keep it now."

He glanced at Frederick and said, "Fandrick must help you. *It* must not get it!"

"Why, it looks like a tiny treasure chest," said Colleen.

"Yes. An ancient treasure."

The old man removed a thin chain from around his neck. On it was a tiny golden key that bore the triple swirl pattern. With this, he unlocked the box and opened it. Inside was a perfectly round crystal ball. Colleen looked up at her grandfather, and he nodded.

"Take it," he said.

She carefully lifted the ball from its red velvet seat and held it in her palm near the lantern. Inside the clear two-inch sphere was a tiny forest scene with perfectly formed trees that all appeared to be dead. A scattering of minute leaves littered the ground. In the midst of the hunched trunks, jutting upward from the forest floor, was what appeared to be a broken section of a stone wall. On one side, a large mirror was hung, and on the other side, a triple spiral design was delicately carved.

They all drew their faces close to the crystal, staring into its intricate depths, illuminated by the lantern's flame. Frederick's palms were beginning to sweat, and he wiped them on his pants.

"What is that?" he asked. "It looks like a haunted wood or something."

"Haunted?" whispered Grandpa. "Yes! Mothers whisper tales to their children about it. They say that dragons and poisonous beasts lurk there – all the treasures of evil! There are other things as well – beings and cities of light and marvel that men dream of seeing – all the treasuries of unstained kingdoms that the Haunts have never fouled. There are doors and paths that one must take – but one must first find an entrance. And it's said that if mortal folk dare to tread those lands, they find their true selves there."

"Sounds too deep for me," said Frederick, trying to push away a growing sense of dread.

"Deep calls to deep!" whispered the old man.

"That's just a bunch of fairy tales and superstitions," said Frederick. "My father is an archaeologist, and he says..."

He was interrupted by the sound of creaking floorboards above them. Dust sprinkled down on their heads.

The old man sniffed the air and wrinkled his nose. He snatched the crystal ball from Colleen's hand, and held it up for a moment in front of the spiral on the wall. He stared hard into its depths, then put it back in its box, locked it, and handed it to Colleen along with the key.

"Hide!" he whispered. "And no matter what you hear, don't come out, and don't tell anyone about the secret!"

"But why, Grandpa? It's probably just one of my brothers, Bran or Aonghus, come to fetch me," she said, putting the box in her pocket.

"Hush! It's none of the McGunnegals! Hide now, quick!" he said. "*It* is here."

"What?" asked Frederick nervously.

"A *superstition!*" said the old man. "Now hide!"

He turned once again toward the spirals on the wall and said, "Go on now, and close your eyes and count to a hundred before you come out."

Colleen and Frederick ran behind several large sacks that reeked of mildew. Frederick wanted to gag. He was getting a bit irritated with the old man's crazy antics and had a mind to say something about it all. However, something deep inside, whether fear or curiosity or some other instinct, also told him to stay put and see what would happen.

"No peeking!" said the old man, and he cackled as if he had made a marvelous joke.

They crouched down, listening intently. It sounded as though Grandpa was climbing the ladder. There was a bang that sounded like the trap door had been shut, and then a moment later, there was a grinding sound, like stone on stone. A rush of wind blew through the cellar, stirring up a cloud of dust. The old man laughed giddily, and then whispered, "Farewell! I'll send help." Something flashed, the grinding noise ceased, and all was still.

They sat frozen, hardly daring to breathe, when suddenly from the room above them came a good deal of scuffling and bumping. The muffled screech and hiss of the cat could be heard, and then there was a loud thud, followed by a shower of dust.

"That's it," said Colleen, jumping from their hiding place. The old man was nowhere to be seen. "Grandpa could be hurt!" she said, and she ran to the ladder.

"But, he said to hide!" said Frederick.

She ignored him and began to climb.

"Brilliant!" he muttered, and ran after her.

Colleen pushed on the trap door, but it barely moved. "I think something is on top of it!" she whispered.

They listened and could hear someone shuffling about, and then the sound of the iron ring being fiddled with.

They scrambled down, grabbed the lantern, and ran back to their hiding place, dousing the light just as the door in the ceiling cracked open.

Frederick shuddered as a bare, gray, misshapen foot stepped down on the first rung of the ladder. A second mottled, gray-green foot with bulbous toes followed, and a small figure, no larger than themselves, draped in a tattered and hooded black cloak, slowly descended into the darkness.

A smell that reeked like rotting meat filled the room, and the two children watched with wide eyes as the stinking creature stood swaying back and forth in the dim shaft of orange light that shone from the room above.

Every hair on their necks stood on end, and their hearts began to pound. A cold sweat broke out on Frederick's brow, and he felt as though he was going to be sick.

He looked at Colleen, and in the dim light, he could see her face was a mix of emotions, but whether fear or outrage and indignation, he could not tell.

To his utter surprise and terror, she stood up and shouted, "What have you done to Grandpa?"

She lifted the lantern and somehow it flamed to life. Frederick shielded his eyes from the sudden light, which for a moment appeared to spread all about Colleen, making her seem to be shining. The darkness that had been descending on his mind snapped and vanished.

The creature hissed and crouched down, spreading its arms across its hooded face. Gray-green clawed hands with dirty brown nails knotted into fists. It peered through its arms at them, then dashed up the ladder in a flurry of ragged black robes and was gone.

Colleen sprang from their hiding place and raced after it, leaping over the potato sacks, knocking one of them to the ground. Neither of them noticed that as she leaped up, the little box and key slipped from her pocket and fell to the floor, and the falling sack tumbled right on top of them, hiding them from view.

Frederick blinked, and then ran after her, but when he climbed up into the house, he found her standing in the living room, the lantern burning dimly in her hand. The furniture in the room was toppled over, and the gray cat sat on the shelf above the hearth, its fur all standing on end. It growled and hissed, then leaped down and ran out the open front door.

"Grandpa?" Colleen called. No one answered. She ran to the door and looked out. For a moment, she thought she saw a dark shadow run away southward, then it was gone. But an eerie wailing came floating across the field from its direction. "Grandpa!" she called again.

They searched the house, but the old man was nowhere to be found.

"I'm getting out of here," said Frederick, and he ran out the door.

Colleen paused for a moment, looking desperately around the room. Then she too ran from the hut and caught up to Frederick.

Together, they reached the farmhouse and burst through the door. Everyone inside turned and stared.

"It's happening again!" said Colleen breathlessly, her face terrified. "Just like before, when Mom disappeared!"

Chapter 2 – The Decision

"They're just downright unnatural," said Frederick to his rather portly, ten-year-old brother, Henry. "In fact, that old O'Brian fellow who lives down the way from them said this sort of thing has happened before – I overheard Dad talking to him in the pub last night."

Henry shrugged and took a large bite of chicken.

"There's more," said Frederick. "Get this – O'Brian also said that the McGunnegals have a bunch of giant grave mounds on their side of the farm, but the McLochlans – Colleen's mother's side of the family – they have no graveyard at all, and none of them are buried at the church either."

"So?" said Henry through a gulp of juice.

"So, isn't that weird? I mean, where do they bury their dead? That old geezer said the disappearances explain it – they're all cursed or something. And those McGunnegals – every one of them has something strange going on. It's just unnatural, it is, being so impish and all. O'Brian said that's what happens when a McGunnegal marries a McLochlan – their children all have this *strangeness* about them."

"Impish?" said Henry, now working on a melon.

"I mean, it's been four days since their grandfather disappeared and they've been out and about the countryside searching for him without a speck of sleep and barely eating anything. How do they do it?"

Henry stopped eating for a moment. His cheeks were covered with grease and jelly, and melon juice dripped down his chin. "You mean they haven't eaten or slept in four days?" he asked.

"That's what folk are saying. And what about that black creature?" said Frederick. "I've been thinking that it was probably some Irish kid who ate too many bad potatoes. They say people all over the country are sick and dying from eating them. I'm glad I'm not Irish. At least I'll never look like *that.*"

He was about to say more, when their mother, Mabel, poked her head in the door.

"Time to be going, boys," she said.

"But I'm not done eating yet!" complained Henry.

Mabel looked at the biscuits, pulled her considerable bulk through the door, and helped herself to one.

"Yes, yes, well, you can have a snack later. We have a meeting with the

McGunnegals. It shouldn't be long," she said.

With a heavy sigh, Henry pushed himself away from the table, grabbed a biscuit, and put it in his pocket.

Frederick followed his mother and brother out to a carriage where their father, Rufus, and their cousin, Helga, waited. Rufus was a short man with quick, intelligent eyes that took in everything at a glance, and Helga was a large German woman with a square jaw and a sour, distrusting expression. Both carried themselves with confidence and purpose, but did not smile.

They climbed aboard and, a moment later, were rolling down the bumpy dirt road toward the farm.

In the farmhouse, Mr. Adol McGunnegal had gathered his children in the living room and was studying their worried faces.

"The Buttersmouths and Helga should arrive shortly, children," he said in his deep, booming voice. "I was going to tell you this before, but then Grandpa disappeared and it just didn't seem like the right time. I've agonized over it for days, but now my mind is made up. Helga contacted my cousin Rufus in England some weeks ago, telling him of our plight, and he has offered to do us a favor."

"What kind of favor, Father?" asked Henny as she crawled up on his lap. She leaned her golden head against his massive chest and looked up at him with her strange violet-blue eyes.

He sighed deeply and said, "You all know that the farm is not doing well. The potato crop failed last year in the blight, and things are not looking good this year either. Our neighbors are going hungry, and some are sick. We've managed to sell some things to buy food, but it's not enough."

"Dad, what are you saying?" asked Colleen.

"We're out of money, children," he said, his voice cracking and his eyes growing wet. "And I have to do something to feed you. Rufus Buttersmouth has offered to take you all to Wales, and there pay for a full year of boarding school."

A chorus of protests filled the room as the children all spoke at once. Adol held up a hand and began to say more, but there was a knock at the door and it swung open. In strolled Helga, followed by the Buttersmouths.

"Hello, Helga, Rufus, Mabel, Henry, Frederick," said Adol. "I'm glad you're here. I'm just telling the children what we have been discussing."

When they were all seated, he took a deep breath. There was an uncomfortable silence for a moment, and then Colleen's sister, Bib, spoke.

"We'll make it somehow, Dad," she said. "We can all do odd jobs for the neighbors and such, and I hear the Brits will be sending corn over soon."

"The Brits!" said Helga, disdain in her husky voice and thick accent. "No offense to our kind cousins, but let us be frank about the situation. The British government cares nothing for the Irish. They say that this *Irish problem* will take care of itself one way or another. You are out of money, out of food, and out of things to sell. Your neighbors are starving to death, and you don't know how long this famine is going to last. Your countrymen are dying or fleeing to America or other shores, and now it is time for you all to do something as well."

She paused for a moment, looking them over, and then continued. "I recently came into an inheritance, and have enough money to pay the taxes for one year, and Rufus has been so kind as to offer to take you to Wales and give you a decent education. There really is nothing to discuss."

"Please, Helga," said Adol. "Let me explain our plan to them."

He was about to go on when Henry piped up. His voice whined and sounded as though he were holding his nose. "Father, this hut stinks and I'm very sleepy. We're not staying *here* tonight, are we? And I'm hungry!"

"Quiet!" snapped Rufus. "We'll be staying at the village Inn this evening, and we'll be done here soon enough!"

He looked at Adol and said, "I'm quite sorry about that. The boys have had a long day, and they're a bit cranky."

"Aye, that's all right. I quite understand," he said. "I have considered your offer, but I've hardly had time to discuss it with my children. I've only just now begun to tell them."

Rufus looked at the six children and then his eyes glanced about the room again, lingering for a moment on a picture frame hanging above the fireplace. "They will be well cared for, well fed, well housed, and well educated, Adol," he said. "My time is very precious, and I shan't stay and try to convince you that this is the best and only opportunity that you have to provide them with more than poverty and starvation. You recall my terms, I assume?"

Adol nodded. "Give me this evening to explain to them, Rufus. We'll meet with you in the morning."

"Early then," said Rufus. "The ship leaves at one o'clock. Come, Mabel, Frederick, Henry. Helga, how about spending the evening at the Inn with us? We could discuss... a few things."

"Certainly, cousin," she said. "Adol, we'll see you in the morning. Do consider our offer, hmm?"

With final goodnights, the lot of them left, and the children could hear the horse-drawn carriage drive away.

"Father," said Bib. "What did Cousin Rufus mean by his *terms*? What is he asking for? And what was that about a ship leaving at one o'clock?"

Adol looked at the floor, then at each of them. "He wants the farm as collateral for paying him back."

"The farm!" said Aonghus. "But, Dad, this farm has been owned by the McGunnegal family for generations! We can't give it up just because of one failed potato crop. We'll make it somehow."

"I've agonized over this for days and days," Adol said. "Think about it – if the potato blight ends and the crop goes well this year, we'll make enough to pay the taxes. We won't need Helga's money, and I think in six or seven years, I can pay Rufus back, and you all will have gotten a good year of schooling. If the blight goes on, though, we'll have nothing, and we'll lose the farm anyway. At least this way, it goes to someone in the family. Besides, what happened this week has helped me make up my mind. I can't risk any of you with that *thing* having come back. I'm sure it had something to do with your mother's disappearance, and now with Grandpa's – I won't risk losing any of you while it haunts our farm. This will give me a chance to find it and … take care of it."

There were more protests and arguments, with many reasons why they should not leave Ireland, and all sorts of ideas of how they might make money, grow other food, or do this or that. In the end, however, Adol shook his head and said, "I love you all, my precious children, and I would sacrifice anything, except you, to save this farm. You are more important to me than all the world, and I'll do what I must to save you first. The ship leaves tomorrow at one o'clock in the afternoon."

"Dad, why didn't you tell us sooner?" said Aonghus, a hint of anger in his voice. "We've got no time to properly pack, or say goodbye, or anything!"

"The ship wasn't expected to arrive until next week, but the captain's plans changed and he arrived yesterday. I'm sorry, children, but this is our last, best hope," he said sadly. "I need you all to help me with this. It tears me up inside to send you away! See here, now, let's all get to bed early and get up before the sun. We'll spend what time we can together."

They sat for a long moment, then Aonghus rose and walked away without a word. Adol could see the frustration on his oldest son's face. Then, one by one, the others got up and followed him upstairs.

16

In the girls' room, Colleen turned to her sisters and said, "Something is rotten about all this. It just seems wrong that all these cousins should suddenly show up and take such an interest in our farm, especially when it's in such bad shape. What are they up to?"

"I don't know," said Abbe. "But let's get to sleep. Father won't let us down. He'll do what's best for us."

"True," said Bib. "But I don't trust Helga or the Buttersmouths. Colleen is right – they're up to something."

"Well, I'm going to find out," said Colleen, and she slipped on her shoes. "I'm going to run to the village Inn and listen at their door. Maybe they'll be talking about the whole affair."

The three sisters watched as Colleen quietly opened the window, swung her legs out, and grabbed a branch of the tree that grew next to their house.

"Be *careful*," whispered Henny.

Colleen made her way toward the trunk and then climbed down to the ground. With a wave, she dashed into the night, down the dusty street toward the village, her long hair flying behind her.

She ran as quickly as she could down the dark road for a good ten minutes, and then, to her surprise, she rounded a bend and almost immediately came upon the carriage. It had stopped, and there were voices coming from it. She quietly slipped forward and hid behind a tree, straining to hear what they were saying.

Rufus was speaking. "... yes, but did you get the *map?*" he was asking.

Helga laughed. "Of course, I got the map. What do you think I've been doing all this time at that miserable hut?"

"Fine, fine," said Rufus. "And what does it show?"

"I have it here with me," she said. "Look!"

Colleen could hear the rustling of paper, and a bit of jostling going on.

"Let me see!" said the voice of one of the boys, which was followed by a howl. She could imagine Rufus pulling him back by his ear.

"Just sit still and you'll get your chance!" said Mabel, and the boys went quiet.

"Now look here!" Helga was speaking again, and the light of a lantern shifted inside the carriage. "This is only a copy of the map. The real one is hanging over the fireplace in the living room. I did not dare take that one – there was no chance to do it. Those children don't like me very much, and they were always watching me. However, I did manage to make a copy of it, a bit at a time. Look, here it is."

There was silence for a moment, and Colleen could imagine them all looking at the map – a copy of Father's map of the farm that hung above their fireplace.

"There is clearly a trail leading from the hut to this hill, just on the north end of the farm. Look here – here is the key to it all! There is a clue written on the map that I cannot read. That is where you come in, Rufus, you are the expert in ancient languages."

There was silence for a few moments and then Rufus spoke. "It seems to be written in a combination of ancient Norse and old Gaelic. One moment…"

Long minutes passed, and Colleen crept closer, just under the back end of the carriage. Standing on her tiptoes, she peered over the edge of the back window and could just see through the nearly drawn curtain. Rufus was scribbling on a parchment, looking at the map, and then scribbling more, until, after a long while, he spoke again.

"There, I've roughly translated it, and not too badly, I think. It's entitled *The Lathe of Atsolter.* Here it is."

"Under the hill lay eight doors.
Some lead to sun, and some to moors.
In one, you find the Little Folk,
With treasures hidden under oak.

There I found the lady sleeping fast,
And broke the spell that had been cast.
But, no princess prize was she,
Indeed, a witch turned out to be.

Oh, what treachery was this,
That I should wake her with a kiss?
Door two finds Trolls, their cruel hearts long
To rob and steal and do folk wrong.

Once architects and builders tall,
Now under bridges they do crawl.
A third finds gold and gems and ale,
And treasuries and spear and mail.

Magic ax and armor bright,

And carven halls of dwarven might.
Four is where the Giant roams,
Beware him lest he crush your bones

Into his bread and nasty meal
To feed his lusty gullet's zeal.
The fifth you must not pass, be sure!
For demons wait beyond that door.

Your soul they seek! From them I fled!
Do not open! This I have said!
The sixth leads home, remember it when,
You wish to return to the world of Men.

And there find rest and peace at last,
When you return from the looking glass.
The seventh finds Elf and tree and song,
Spells and laughter all day long.

Bright never-dying folk and friend,
And maids so fair your heart will rend.
Open eight and find sure gloom,
An ancient plague, the Goblin's doom.

And there the Worm that brought the blight,
Calling all into its pits of night.
Behind these doors such perils lie,
And lo, no keys to these have I!

Yet to these worlds I yet have passed,
Through a simple looking glass.
The portal to a perilous maze
Into which I have dared to gaze.

No simple trek around a wall,
But beyond it, I have placed it all -
A king's ransom, oh, and so much more!
Things of might and magic stored.

Things too great for mortal men,
Things so great that I, a brigand, send
Them far away from mortal lands
Into, I hope, far wiser hands.

Yet three things I dare not leave
Lest too our world become bereaved.
The first, this map to mark the place
That leads beyond our time and space.

The next an orb so small, yet rare!
With it you travel, but oh, take care!
And last, a looking glass to see
Wherever the traveler may be.

And at special places you may pass
And step through the looking glass.
What secret powers these things possess,
None have fathomed, none have guessed.

Yet with simple folk who have no cares,
I leave these things from wizards' lairs."

As Rufus finished, a cold wind blew from the woods, bringing with it a fog that snaked and swirled about the road. A chill ran down Colleen's spine and she shivered. She turned and looked behind her, sensing eyes upon her, but no one was there. The horses stamped their feet and neighed, and those inside the carriage must have felt it too, for they were all silent for a long moment, until Rufus spoke again.

"So there it is," he whispered. "The last of the riddles. But this one speaks of eight doors under a hill."

"Yes," said Helga. "Like the other maps, there is a hill. This must be the last one. The artifacts must be here. Once we have the farm, we can begin digging."

"How many years have we searched?" asked Rufus. "It seems a lifetime."

"Think of it!" said Helga. "The wealth and relics of a lost world! We must keep this secret!"

"Who is Atsolter?" whined Henry suddenly. "That riddle said there was buried treasure somewhere. Is that why you want to steal your cousin Adol's farm, Father?"

"Hush!" hissed Rufus.

"Now, Rufus," said Helga. "Let the boys in on our secret. They will be rich with us soon enough."

"Oh, fine," said Rufus, and his voice lowered so that Colleen had to strain to hear.

"Well, boys, before you were born – some twenty years ago – I was on an archaeological dig in Germany. That is where I met our friend here, Baroness Helga Von Faust. We were, with her permission, digging at a site around her family castle when we broke into an old vault. Actually, it was a tomb and, in a stone box in the tomb, we found a skeleton."

"A skeleton, as in a dead man?" said Henry.

"Of course, you ninny," said Frederick. "That's what a skeleton is!"

Rufus continued. "In the hand of the skeleton was an old parchment. It was so brittle that it nearly broke to pieces when we finally dislodged it from the bony hand. But it was the first piece of the map, and it spoke of the other three pieces and of fabulous treasure, and told a tale of a certain Viking commander named Atsolter, who somehow acquired an incredible amount of wealth and hid it somewhere that the whole map would reveal."

"Real treasure?" said Frederick, sounding in awe.

"More than that!" said Rufus, rather pleased with himself. "The riddles always mentioned things of *magic* and *might*. You know that I am not a superstitious man, but I have investigated many ancient legends and cultures, and they all speak of such things – relics that were revered by the people, and around which strange things happened. I, myself, have seen strange things…"

He paused for a moment, unconsciously touching a smooth blue ring on his right hand, and then seemed to come to himself, and continued.

"The scroll that we found said that one of Atsolter's men had gone to Norway, there to hide another piece of the map. Immediately, Helga and I entered into a partnership, and we have been searching for these twenty years for the other three parts. It took us nearly twelve years of excavations along the Norwegian coast and various ancient sites. Dig after dig, dead end after dead end, until finally, we found it. Again, it was at the ancient ruins of a castle on a hill, just as in Germany, and there, in a vaulted grave, we found a second skeleton gripping the second piece of the map."

"What did it say?" asked Frederick.

"Well," said Rufus, who was obviously enjoying telling the tale. "It pointed to a province in Spain for the third piece."

"But no treasure?" asked Henry, sounding disappointed.

"Some," he replied. "But not what we expected, so we kept searching. It took us nearly six years to find the third, and we focused our digs at ancient castle sites on hills. Once again, we found the grave, hoarded wealth, and a piece of the map. That last piece pointed to Ireland, to this province and, for the past four years, Helga has been here searching, while I pursued the site in libraries and old archives, looking for hints. We performed a number of digs, but found nothing, and it was only by chance that one night in a pub that I was inquiring of the locals about ancient sites and maps, and one of the men mentioned the old map over Adol's fireplace."

"That's the fourth piece, isn't it!" said Frederick.

"Yes!" said Rufus, barely able to contain himself. "How remarkable that it was my own cousin who owned it! After all these years of searching, it was right within my own family! Helga and I came up with the plan that she would pretend to be a long-lost cousin. I would confirm this, and she would befriend Ellie and Adol, pretending to have come here from Germany to escape poverty. Her real job would be to get the last piece of the map."

Then, he laughed. "Now we have it! It is the most important piece of all, because it pinpoints the location of Atsolter's share of the treasure that he had divided among his men."

Colleen's mouth dropped open and she almost let a cry escape from her lips.

"Father, why are you telling us all this?" said Henry. "You never tell us anything about your business ventures, and this one seems like a real doozy."

He paused, considering, then said, "I have a job for you two. I need you to make friends with those McGunnegals and find out as much about their farm as you can. They've lived here all their lives, and they no doubt know every inch of it. They might know about this key of which the riddle speaks. If there truly is some sort of door, we just might need such a key. Often, old things are passed down by families through the years and people have no idea what they were originally used for. I want you to start asking questions and keep your eyes open. Who can say what ancient relics lie buried under their land?!"

Helga laughed. "Your father is interested in relics. I just want the money!"

Colleen had heard enough. Her heart was beating so hard that she almost felt it would burst as she slipped away from the carriage and then sped back down the lane toward her house. She ran across the yard, then climbed up the tree, and back through the open window.

The girls were still awake and had been watching for her.

"Get Aonghus and Bran," whispered Colleen breathlessly. You'll never believe what I've found out!"

22

Chapter 3 – A Song on the Hill

"They want the farm because there's something valuable buried here, Dad," said Colleen as she and the family ate a breakfast of stale bread early the next morning. "We just can't let them get it. I think we should stay and catch a later ship. Maybe we could find whatever it is and be able to pay the taxes without Rufus' help."

Adol took a deep breath, considering, and then said, "No. I've made up my mind, and this doesn't change it. I'll keep my eyes open, you can be sure. That map over the fireplace is old – older than this house, probably. It's been passed down for generations and generations. I can see why Rufus would want it, being an archaeologist. But, all that about strange creatures and such... honestly, that's a bit much. At any rate, it's become much too dangerous for you to stay."

He paused, his brow furrowed, then went on. "Well, come on, then. We'll walk around the farm and up to the Hill and watch the sun rise, then we'll come back and get packed."

They left the house and walked together in silence as Adol led them across the quiet fields of their farm. Colleen thought how this place was all she had ever known. This land and their old house – these were hers and her family's, and somehow they had to find a way to keep them. But her father was right – they had little food left and precious little to sell. They were better off than most, though – at least they still had a home. So many were being evicted by greedy landlords, or were sick and dying. Rumors were spreading that disease was rampant in the south, especially in Skibbereen. What was becoming of her precious Ireland in this Spring of 1846?

After walking for some time, they neared the wall that bordered their property. It rose up before them in the darkness, six or eight feet high in parts, a jumbled mass of broken white and gray stone.

Colleen brushed her hand along a chunk of cold rock, and her fingers traced the edges of an ancient rune engraved into its surface. Even in the dim light of the stars, she could see many carvings like this one on the piled and strewn stones that had been carelessly tossed in this great heap that was the wall. No one could read them or guess what they meant, and no stories told of their origin.

Henny wrinkled her nose as they walked on. "I smell the bog," she said. "I wonder why it's here, right next to our good farm."

"That's how some things are," said Adol. "Even some people. Seems the bad grows up right next to the good at times."

He looked up, and Colleen followed his gaze. The Milky Way blazed above them, illuminating the long cairn that stretched from east to west.

"You know, now that I think of it," he said, "that old bog never has passed this wall, not in all my years. These stones seem to keep the foulness out."

"What do you mean, Dad?" asked Henny.

He picked her up, placed her on his broad shoulder, and pointed up. Thin tendrils of mist lingered at the top of the pile, reaching toward the farm.

"Do you see that?" he said. "The bog wants to come in, but this bulwark won't let it."

"What if it did?" asked Colleen. "Suppose the wall gave way? What would happen to our land?"

Adol glanced at the stones and then at Colleen. Her golden-red hair shimmered, and her eyes reflected a thousand shining stars as she looked up at him.

"Come on, I'll show you. You first, Henny. Let's climb up and have a look. I'll follow right behind."

Up they scrambled and sat at the top. Colleen waved her hand at the misty air. Thin wisps of slowly moving fog drifted below them among a dense collection of creepers and vines and twisted trees, colliding blindly with the wall, rising, curling about their legs and hands, and vanishing as they sought to pass to the other side.

"You see, lass, it's like this," said Adol. "Sometimes bad things will try to get into what is good. There's something about this barrier, though, that keeps the bad things in the bog from getting over it and messing up our farm. You just keep on being like this wall, Henny. Don't let bad things creep into your heart."

Colleen sat listening to the night crickets and strange croaking and bubbling sounds that the mists seemed to give birth to. *Bad things...* she thought. Was that black creature living in there? Grandpa thought it was. But what was it? He had called it a *superstition.*

"I went in there once," said Bran, interrupting her thoughts.

His face was blank, unreadable as he recalled the memory. Then he breathed deeply, frowned at the putrid smell rising around them, and continued.

"Some ways in, I found a hillock of sorts, with old ruins of a building or something on it. A terrible stench came from it – maybe the source of all the stink in the whole place. But more than that, it made all the hair on my arms and neck stand on end. It was as though something with terrible malice were watching me. I left that place and ran all the way back to the farm, and those invisible eyes were on me the whole way. I was never so glad to see this wall and climb back over and, when I did, that feeling was gone. It was the first time I ever truly felt... afraid."

"Yes," said Adol after a moment. "There's more than bad air and will-o-the-wisps in there, but what, I can't say. Whatever it is, it chills the heart."

How the mists swirl and move, Colleen thought. *As if something were flitting about beneath them.* Then she started, for she was sure that something *had* moved down there, and that she had caught a glimpse of two pale eyes peering through the gloom at them. She was about to say something, but Aonghus spoke first.

"Let's walk by the graves before we go to the Hill," he said.

The others began to climb back down to the farm, but she lingered, gazing into the haze. But the mists had returned to their lazy drifting, and the eyes were gone. At last, she too climbed down and followed them.

They walked along the long line of stones eastward for some way before coming to two great mounds that were nearly as high as the wall.

"I love this place," said Aonghus. "I feel a closeness to our kin here."

"Aye," said Adol. "Here are the graves of our ancestors – Geer, Laar's son, and his sister Aililli - the tallest people in Ireland, if tales be true. It's said that after Geer died childless, Aililli married the steward of their house, Aeden McGunnegal, and so here we are, their descendants, untold generations later, standing by their graves."

"I've sometimes wondered where Laar's grave is," said Aonghus. "If he was as tall as the legends say – nine feet – he would have been the tallest man in the world, much less in Ireland."

"There are other stories about big people – even in the Bible," said Bib. "Some called them the Nephilim."

"True," said Adol. "We really don't know how long ago Laar and his children walked the Earth, nor why they came to the Emerald Isle. It's said that Laar brought things of great magic to Ireland with him, and that his children buried most of them in his grave, save a few that they kept for themselves. Who knows what the truth of all that is? One thing's for sure, their descendants were always big people."

Colleen looked at her brothers and father. They were rather like giants, especially Adol, who towered above other men at six-foot-eight. Bran and

Aonghus, at seventeen and nineteen years old, were well on their way to matching him.

She walked over to the great mound of Aililli and ran her hand through the tall grass that covered it. *What is buried under this mound*, she wondered. *Just old bones from ages long past?* Or were the stories true, that they had possessed magic from the Old World, and took it to the grave with them? *Is that what the riddle on the map had spoken of? Could there be relics and treasures of the past lying beneath her feet?*

She looked out across the other graves, some marked with Celtic crosses, some with standing stones, and others with older blocks whose inscriptions had worn away long ago. The McGunnegals of untold generations lay here, now all silent beneath the eternal sky. A vision flashed in her mind of tall men and women working the fields, year after year, century after century, passing on stories and songs to their children's children, preserving the traditions of their fathers. It made her heart ache to think that she and her brothers and sisters might be the last generation of their family to live and die here. She bowed her head for a long moment, then turned to the others.

"Come on," she said. "Day is dawning, and I want to greet the sun from on top the Hill. Today may be our last morning in Ireland for a long time."

Leaving the graveyard behind, they headed back north, past Grandpa's hut, and toward the Hill that loomed in the distance.

As they came to its base, Aonghus said, "I wonder if this hill could be the grave mound of Laar. It is strange that so large a hill would sit on these flat lands."

"I've wondered that myself," said Adol as they climbed its steep green side.

At the top, Colleen climbed up onto a low branch of a great oak tree and stood facing east. The dawn was beginning to break and the stars were fading.

"This is where I first met your mother," said Adol. "We were youngsters then - just ten years old. I remember seeing her standing on this hilltop under this oak, and she was singing some love song about an Irish maiden. Fifteen years later, I married her, and we still came on occasion. She loved to sing songs on this hill. What a magical voice she had."

Colleen's thoughts drifted to her mother – her beautiful face, her golden-red hair, her slim form. She sighed and climbed down from the tree as the first sliver of red fire slipped above the horizon and flooded the world with light.

A deep red filled the sky, lining silver clouds with pink and orange. She walked to the edge of the hill, her slight frame silhouetted against the brilliant colors, and her long, golden hair fluttering in the breeze.

"My, Colleen, you do remind me of your mom," said Adol. "Would you sing us a song before we go back home? It would make me so happy."

She hesitated, but then decided to do it. She thought for a moment and then began to sing a song that her mother had taught her. Her voice was strong and sweet and, with perfect notes, she sang.

"Long ago from distant lands
A magic people came to see
The Emerald Isle so fair and old,
A land unstained by mortal feet.

There they lived in joy and rest
And wove their spells among the trees.
Until the mortal men did show
Bold faces on their shores of peace.

With happy hearts, they welcomed all
Until sad treachery was seen.
From their fair city they did go
And leave the Emerald Isle to me.

But in the blood of mortal men
Their fair semblance at times 'tis seen.
For one did choose a bride so fair
And wed her in that very Spring.

So if you see fair golden hair
Blowing softly in the breeze
That maid may have within her soul
The magic lost so long ago."

As her song ended, the morning rays sliced higher over the horizon and filled her golden hair with fire. They all stared, transfixed at the sudden transformation that had taken hold of her. For her voice had been that of their mother, only younger, and standing there, surrounded by the sun's radiance, she just seemed to *fit*. She was in her element somehow, as natural here as the tree and the grass and the stars and the morning light. Somehow, in this place, singing that song, she was changed from a simple girl to a young woman knowledgeable beyond her years, a master of song and nature, with a power and wisdom that lay hidden just beneath her slim frame. For several long moments, no one stirred.

Then, suddenly, a strange sound rose from the south – a shrieking, like a crazed animal that screams a menacing cry when threatened. The eerie sound rose to a desperate pitch as the sun crested the horizon and blazed in all its glory on the farm. The howl seemed to rise and blow across the hill, dispelling the magic of the moment and sending chills down their spines.

"What was that, Daddy?" asked Henny, clutching him tightly. "I saw a little black thing down by the wall a minute ago." She pointed south where, far away, the bog stretched out, a dark field beneath the brightening sky.

"You have sharp eyes, little one," said her father. "I've been hearing it now and then in the night since..."

Colleen thought he was going to say *since your mother disappeared*, but instead he said, "Oh, it might be that old fox down there. He gets cranky sometimes."

But they all knew that it was no fox. They knew exactly what it was – it was that *thing*.

"Let's go home, Dad," said Colleen.

They rose together in silence, Adol carrying Henny in his massive arms, and walked down the hill and through the fields, listening to the sounds of the morning. But they did not hear the strange cry again.

Finally, they came to the farmhouse and their horse trotted up to greet them as they came through the gate.

"Poor Badger," said Colleen. "Let me take you to your stall and get you some hay."

"I'll come with you," said Aonghus, and they led the old horse toward the barn.

"Don't be long," called their father. "Time is moving along and we need to pack."

"Yes, Father," they called, and walked on.

After a moment, Aonghus spoke. "You know, Colleen, you seemed different up on that hill this morning."

"How so?" she said.

"I mean, you were, well, I can't explain it. Just different, that's all. Not in a bad way, in a really good way - like you *grew* or something. You seemed a lot like Mom when you were singing out there. Something good is happening to you, Colleen." Then he gave her an unexpected hug, which he rarely did to anyone who he wasn't trying to crush in a wrestling match.

She led Badger into the barn and put him in his stable. There wasn't much hay left to give him, so she gave him a few mouthfuls, left the stable door open so he could wander back outside, and walked back to the house.

Before they went in, Colleen said, "Aonghus, I'm really glad we all spent the morning together. You know, I did feel different up there on that hill. I hope you're right. I hope something good is happening. We need something good for a change."

Chapter 4 – Departure

Adol bowed his head and sighed deeply. Then he looked up into the sky, and his heart cried out, *Why must it be like this?* But he knew there was no other way. So he steeled himself, went into the house, and called his children.

"Be quick now," he said. "We can't let you miss the ship."

A few moments later, all six of them had gathered in the living room, their few extra clothes tied in old blankets.

"Well, I guess this is it, then. We're actually leaving," said Bib.

Adol took her in his huge arms and hugged her. "Bib, my lass, even at fourteen years, with the mind that you have, you'll find yourself the smartest in the school. I'll be expecting great things from you when you return next year."

He smiled weakly and kissed her on the forehead, and then one by one, embraced each of his children.

"Come on, now, we don't want to be late. I've already hitched Badger to the cart – go and put your things in it. Aonghus, sit up front with me," he said.

For a time, they rode in silence, each absorbed by their own thoughts as they passed broken down huts, old men walking feebly down the road, young men meandering aimlessly, kicking stones and looking downcast, some hacking and coughing, beset with sickness. Sodden fields, ruined by too much rain, lay barren or unplanted, destined to become grazing land for foreign-owned cattle. Withered leaves of potato plants filled others, a portent of bad things to come at harvest. It seemed that the whole land around them groaned under the weight of the Great Hunger that had beset Ireland.

Ahead of them, Adol could see a young mother holding her little girl's hand. Both were barefoot, and the girl was thin. They walked with their heads bowed.

Adol recognized them and stopped the cart as they rode up beside them.

"Orla MacLeish, where are you and little Sarah going this morning?" he called.

Orla slowly looked up. Her face was dirty and streaked with tears. She opened her mouth to speak, but nothing came out. Then she stumbled and nearly fell. Adol leaped from the cart and steadied her.

"Orla, what's wrong? Where's Shane?" he asked.

"Daddy went to heaven," said the little girl. "Mommy says we've nowhere to go, so we're going to try to get on a ship."

"Come, both of you get up in the cart and ride with us. We're going to the docks as well. Bran, jump down, lad, and give them a place to sit," said Adol.

Bran jumped from the cart, and Adol lifted Sarah and put her next to Henny. He marveled at how thin and frail the little girl had felt.

"There you are, lass. Don't you worry, now. You're going to be just fine," said Adol.

"Thank you, Adol," said Orla as she weakly climbed into the cart, helped by Bran. She leaned back heavily and shut her eyes. Sarah laid her head in her mother's lap and, within moments, both were asleep.

Adol climbed back into the front seat and flicked the reins.

"Poor things," whispered Abbe to no one in particular as the cart started off again. "We've no room to complain about our lot. Loads of folk are far worse off."

Adol, overhearing her, smiled at his daughter. Then he leaned over and whispered to Aonghus.

"Son, you've seen the folk on the road. Look hard at these dear ones we've just picked up. Do you understand why I'm sending you all away for a time?"

Aonghus looked back at Orla and Sarah. Even in sleep, lines of care and grief were etched in their thin, hungry faces. He nodded, but said nothing.

An hour later, they arrived at the village and watched as a few dilapidated old carts rolled by, and various shopkeepers stood in their doorways, watching the seven McGunnegals as they made their way to the docks.

"'Ear you're sendin' 'em all away, Adol," said a thin, gruff-looking old man leaning on a lamppost. His face was drawn and emaciated, his eyes sunken.

"Shame. Real shame," said the man. "Too many of us leaving." He shook his head, looked down at his worn and broken shoes, then turned and shuffled away.

Adol did not reply, but continued on toward the docks. A single tear spilled down his weathered cheek, which he quickly wiped away.

"Here we are, Miss Orla," said Abbe, shaking her slightly to wake her.

Oral opened her eyes with effort, looked around, and said, "Wake up, Sarah. It's time."

She thanked them and weakly climbed from the cart.

31

"Is there anything we can do for you and Sarah?" said Adol.

"No, no," she said. "We'll be boarding the next ship to Canada."

"Well, good luck to you," he said. "I pray you'll find you way safely there and back again one day."

"Thanks, and you as well," she said.

She took Sarah's hand, and they walked slowly down the docks. The little girl looked back once, her face uncertain and fearful. She waved her tiny hand, then turned again and walked on.

Adol wondered if he would ever see them again.

"Ah, there you are at last!" said a harsh voice, interrupting his thoughts.

The large form of Helga appeared in the street in front of them.

"Hurry now, the ship is nearly ready to go. Come, come!" And she waved for them to follow.

"Go on, boy," said Adol, and the horse pulled them forward.

Helga turned down the next street and led them three more blocks through a row of old buildings, only two of which were not boarded up, and out onto the wooden docks where a large sailing ship was tethered. A rather rickety-looking gangplank stretched from the deck of the ship to the docks.

"Ho there, Adol, children, come aboard, come aboard!" called a man from the ship, and they could see Rufus Buttersmouth waving to them.

Adol tied Badger to a post, and the children all gathered their belongings, then they carefully walked single-file up the plank and to the ship's deck.

"Well, here we are at last," said Rufus, smiling broadly at the children. "A grand adventure is about to begin for you. I just know that you will love Wales. And see, you are to board a true sailing ship – one of the last of its kind, I dare say. They'll all be replaced by steam ships one day, you know."

But their sad faces and silence said that they certainly did not plan to have any grand adventures in Wales, and he stared at them awkwardly for a moment before saying, "Well, that is... Yes! And let me show you to your cabins now." He turned and walked toward a door that opened to stairs leading down into the lower parts of the ship.

All three of the McGunnegal men had to bend down to avoid hitting their heads on the low ceiling, and Adol's and Aonghus' shoulders were actually too wide to fit down the hall, forcing them to move sideways while ducking their heads. Henny giggled to see her father and big brothers squeezing through the hallway with such trouble. Her laugh lightened their hearts and they smiled.

The accommodations Rufus had arranged for them were certainly not the best and were rather crowded, with all four girls packed into one cabin, and Aonghus, Bran, Frederick, and Henry in another. Mabel seemed to have acquired a cabin of her own.

"Well, now, isn't this cozy!" said Rufus a bit too loudly. "You should all be quite comfortable here for a few days."

"I suppose it's not too bad," said Colleen, trying to make the best of it, and she dropped her sack in one corner of the room.

Four hammocks were arranged for them, two on either side of the room, which itself was not much larger than a good-sized broom closet.

"At least we'll be out of the open air," said Bib.

"Yeah," said Aonghus, poking his head in their door. "At least you'll fit in your hammocks. Ours are way too small for us. Guess we'll be sleeping on the floor."

He waved to them and they squeezed out into the hall and to the room opposite the girls. Peering into their equally small room, they burst into laughter as they saw Bran attempting to lounge in his hammock, his long legs draped over either side, his knees hitting one wall and his head leaning against the other.

"Well, at least I have a place to sit!" He grinned.

"You're all taking this quite well, children," said their father, who was now smiling.

"Well, I guess it's like you always say, Dad," said Abbe. "There's no sense in crying once the milk is spilled."

"Right!" he said, and continue to grin, though his smile didn't entirely reach his eyes, and they all knew that they were only making the best of a bad situation.

"And I do have some good news for you," he said after a moment. "Rufus has informed me that those old stones around the farm with writing on them might be worth something to collectors back in England and here in Ireland. He might be able to sell them for a few pennies each, and has already packed a few of them with Cousin Mabel's things. The museum in London might be interested and, if they are, they'll gather more and split the profits with us."

"That's ... really great, Dad," said Colleen, although her mind was racing. She simply could *not* let those stones get to anyone. What if they were old – really old? If they were, she was sure that an entire army of treasure hunters, scientists, and greedy land owners would descend upon the farm and find some *legal* reason to take it from them.

"Yes, and in fact," Rufus put in, "your father and I must be going. We have a meeting with the curator of the museum in Dublin quite soon. We're dropping off the horse at the farm and then meeting him half way. I sent a message to him some days ago, and he has agreed to come and examine some of the pieces himself."

Colleen and the others gave each other a knowing glance, and then Aonghus said, "Well, might we have a few moments with our father alone – to say goodbye?"

"Of course, of course," said Rufus. "Mabel and the boys are up on deck. Meet us up there, Adol, as soon as you can." He squeezed past them all and disappeared up the steps.

"Well, this is goodbye for a time," said their father. "I shall miss you all terribly. But do write to me when you can. And you can be sure I will write to you as often as I can buy the postage."

They all hugged him, doing their best to put on smiles, until Henny burst into tears and clung to his neck as he picked her up in his massive arms. But at last, he passed her to Abbe, and they all went back up on the deck.

With many waves and goodbyes, the children watched as their father walked down the gangplank after Rufus and Helga, got into the cart, and drove down the street, following a carriage that Rufus and Helga had gotten into.

Just before he rounded a corner and rode out of sight, he waved one last time. They heard his booming voice call out a last farewell, and then he was gone.

Chapter 5 – Captain Truehart

Colleen stared down the empty lane. Her father was gone, and even though she was surrounded by her five brothers and sisters, she could not suppress feelings of hurt and abandonment. She understood their need – the starvation they would soon face, the sickness that was spreading across Ireland, the lack of money – but her heart still ached. Soon they would sail away, leaving their home for an entire year. Beyond that, she feared for her father's well-being, and knew that when they left, he would have to deal with Rufus Buttersmouth's schemes all alone.

She wiped her eyes and turned away, thinking that she would go below deck, when a voice said, "Well, then, would you like to see the rest of the ship?"

She and the others all turned to see who had spoken, and Henny took a step back, reaching for Aonghus' hand. The appearance of the man before them was so striking, even disturbing, that for a moment, she forgot her grief and concern and, in spite of herself, simply stared.

His face was weather-beaten and pitted, and tanned dark from countless hours on the open sea. Terrible scars ran down the right side of his face, as if he had been burned, and the eye on that side was covered with a brown patch. Colleen could not help but follow the line of scars down his neck, to his right hand that was missing its pinky, and down to a wooden post where his leg should have been. He smiled at them, but only the left side of his face seemed to work – the other was frozen in a grim scowl.

"Truehart's the name," he said through the left side of his mouth. "Captain Truehart. It's a pleasure to have you all aboard."

His voice was rough, and the accent that of an English commoner, but somehow jovial in spite of his appearance.

Suddenly, a flurry of images danced in Colleen's mind – rough seas, blistering suns, long starry nights, dreadful storms, shipwrecks, battles with pirates, and high adventure – all this she read in a moment's time in the eyes of this man.

Henny also seemed to see something unusual in him, beyond his appearance, and she cocked her head to one side, looked him thoroughly up and down, and then walked up to him and took his mangled right hand.

"You had a bad accident, didn't you?" she said.

Truehart wrinkled his brows beneath his captain's hat, leaned down to her, and said, "Aye, lass. That I did. Years ago. But don't you be troubled by it."

"Oh, no," she said. "I see that the scars don't touch your heart."

"Do ya now?" he said, standing straight and raising his one eyebrow, "Let's hope that it's true. I wouldn't want me inner self wrestling with old wounds. Dealing with them in the flesh is trouble enough. But come now, let me show you around the ship."

He winked at Henny.

"I've owned the *Lady* for near twenty years now. Got her from me own dad, rest his soul. She's a mighty fine ship, and near dances across the water when the wind is full in her sails." He removed his hat and ran his thick fingers through his mop of brown hair that was streaked with gray, and beckoned for them to follow him.

He led them up a broad-stepped ladder to the upper deck, where a large steering wheel turned the rudder, his peg leg thumping on the wide rungs as he went.

"Now, you're a strapping young man," he said to Aonghus, who stood at least six inches taller than he did. "Do ya think you could steer the *Lady Wave* on the open seas? It takes a strong arm to hold her."

Colleen exchanged a knowing glance with her sister Abbe. Aonghus *strong* enough?

"I've never been on a ship," he replied. "But I'd love to try."

"All right then, when we set sail here shortly, you come up here with me and I'll teach ya to steer the *Lady*. Looks to me that you'd make a fine sailor."

He paused, looked at the rest of the children, and then walked in front of each of them, eying them up and down with his one good eye, as if inspecting them.

"Aye, a fine lot you are, fit for the sea!" he said.

Upon coming to Henny, he bent down to her with some difficulty, looked in her face, and said, "And how old might ya be, young lass?"

"I'm seven," said Henny.

"Seven!" he bellowed. "Why, you look at least ten, what with all that golden red hair and ... and ... well, the most unusual eyes I've ever seen."

He then glanced from one child to the next and, rubbing his grizzly brown and gray speckled beard, he said, "Well, you all have those eyes. Blimey if I've never seen eyes like you lot have! Blue and ... lavender, or I'm a bald parrot! Now where did you get those from?"

"From our mother," said Colleen. "She's been missing for nearly a year."

"Oh," he said, pulling himself back and frowning, and still scratching at his beard. "Yes, that's what Mr. Buttersmouth said. So sorry."

But then he smiled a half toothy smile at them and said, "But on the *Lady Wave*, you'll be my guests. And you can help me out for the next day while we sail southeast to Wales. I'll have some jobs for ya all, if you've a mind for it, even you, young... young... now what was your name?"

"Henny," said Henny.

"Henny, it is!" he bellowed again. "And for you, I think ya might need to help your big brother steer this ship tomorrow."

Henny grinned up at the captain, looking excited.

"Well, off with ya now. We'll be shoving off within the hour. Why don't ya have a look around? Just don't climb the masts or ropes and stay out of the cargo hold and the crew quarters. Other than that, you're free to go wherever ya like. But I would ask that you boys keep an eye on your younger sisters," he said.

This they promised to do, and as Truehart limped away, yelling orders at his crew to make ready for departure, Colleen wandered away from the others and over to the side of the ship. Some twenty feet below, waves lapped at the side of the ship, and in the sky, the sun had begun its westerly descent over Ireland.

Her thoughts returned to her father and their farm, and she looked out at the town for some time, until suddenly, a bell began to clang, and the gruff voice of the captain called for all hands on deck, and all ashore who were going ashore.

Not wanting to watch Ireland slip away, she found Aonghus and told him she was going below to her room. As she descended the steps, a thought struck her and she put her hand in her pocket. It was empty. She checked her other pockets and realized that it was missing – the little box containing the crystal ball that Grandpa had given her – it was gone.

Frantically, she thought where she must have put it. Was it in her room? No, she couldn't remember having it at the house. It must still be...

She dashed back up the stairs and nearly collided with a startled Frederick.

"Hey, what... I was coming down to..." he began, but she ran past him and back up on the deck.

Looking around, she saw Mabel, Henry, and all of her brothers and sisters on the upper deck milling about.

Henny spotted her and came running, climbed down the ladder to the lower deck, and said, "Colleen, Captain Truehart is quite nice. He's given us each a silver penny to spend when we get to Wales!" And she held out her hand, showing Colleen the silver penny that the grizzled captain had given her.

"Listen to me, Henny. I've got to get off this ship. I forgot something really important, and I've got to go and get it. Look, can you cause a bit of a distraction for me. I need to get off without being noticed. Can you play a bit of hide and seek, just like you do at home, so that no one can find you?" she said.

Henny nodded and said, "But you've got to come with us!"

"I'll come on the next ship with cousin Rufus and Helga. They're not coming on this ship, remember? It will be okay. Father will understand too. Now, can you keep this a secret until you're well out to sea?"

"Well, all right. But you have to promise to come on the next ship," she said.

"I promise," said Colleen. "On the next ship I'm able to board."

Henny climbed back up and looked about, thinking about what she might do. Then, walking past the huddled group, she climbed up on the rail of the upper deck and called, "Look at me!"

Captain Truehart stopped in mid-sentence and said, "Now see here, youngster, get yourself..."

But he stopped again as Henny had quite suddenly vanished. The entire group rushed over, expecting to see Henny tumbling into the water below, but upon reaching the rail, found her simply gone.

Colleen took the opportunity and ran down the deck, and, just as a sailor was about to pull the gangplank in, ran across it, down the docks, and up the street toward home.

What she did not notice was that Frederick, seeing her go, paused for only an instant, then darted after her.

Once again, the sailor, who had begun pulling in the gangplank, was interrupted by a second child running ashore and back through town. He shook his head, pulled in the plank, and went about un-tethering the docking ropes.

Henny, in the meantime, had re-appeared behind the group that was gazing at the waters below and said, "What ya looking at?"

Captain Truehart bellowed, "Whoa, there ya be! Don't do that to an old sailor! Now you stay with your big brother here for the rest of the trip and stay off those railings!" He smiled at her and winked at Aonghus.

"Now where was I..." he began, but a bell rang again, and he said, "Ho there, that's me first mate's bell. All's ready to go now. Unfurl those sails, lads, and shove off!" he bellowed.

Away they sailed for Wales, while Colleen dashed back toward the farm, with a panting Frederick running as fast as he could to catch her.

Chapter 6 – Swirls

Frederick, though several inches taller than Colleen, was having trouble catching her. He jogged down the road, holding a stitch in his side. *"How can that girl run so fast?"* he mumbled to himself through his panting breath. He was a fast runner, but he was barely keeping her in sight. *And where was she going?*

I've got to keep after her, he thought. *Maybe she's just scared and running home, but she might be going back for some old relic or something else valuable. Father would want me to follow her. But she's too far ahead!*

Then the thought struck him that if he cut across the fields to the old McLochlan hut, he might beat her back to the farmhouse. He had studied maps of the area with his father the week before and had memorized them. He turned abruptly off the road and ran through a number of barren potato fields until he saw Grandpa McLochlan's old house in the distance. He jogged up to it and bent over, breathing heavily, and then noticed that there was an outside entrance to the basement through two rather large wooden doors that lay at an angle to the ground.

He went over to them and hesitantly pulled on one of the handles. It lifted easily, and the moldy smell of old potatoes reminded him of that night that he and Colleen had seen the dark creature. A ramp went down into the cellar, and as Frederick pulled open the second door, he could see that it was larger than he first thought, and must have been used to let down carts for unloading.

Suddenly, a figure riding on a horse appeared, coming up the trail from the McGunnegal farm. It was Colleen, riding on their old horse. How could she have gotten to the farm so fast? He glanced about and then slipped down into the cellar to hide.

Looking around, he ran to the place where he and Colleen had hidden, then realized that she would see him. He was about to dash to another hiding place when he saw something shiny just sticking out from under a sack. He heaved it out of the way, and there, lying on the floor, was a small box and key – the very same that Grandpa McLochlan had given Colleen. *She must have dropped it,* he thought.

He grabbed them and ran over to the wall where the strange swirl patter was inscribed, stooped down behind the crates that Colleen had piled up that night, and waited, expecting Colleen to come in at any moment.

But she did not come in immediately, and he began to wonder about the little crystal ball inside the box. What was it, really? Could it be that this was the *orb* of which the riddle on the map had spoken? He put the tiny key in the lock and turned it, then lifted the lid. Taking the crystal between his fingers, he held it up to the light shining in through the open doorway. The perfect forest scene lay silent and still inside.

Suddenly, something in the tiny scene moved, startling him. Had it been his imagination? He stared into its depths harder, and then gave the ball a shake. To his surprise, tiny golden flakes swirled around in a circle. He stood, holding the crystal close to his face and watching as the little particles began to take on a pattern – a triple swirl.

His eyes grew wide as he realized what he was seeing. He turned to look at the wall behind him and, as he did, the huge block of stone that bore the same shape began to move. It rotated, a circle of the floor beneath it turning in place, revealing for a moment a black passage beyond. Then it had turned completely around, hiding the passage, and there stood a marvelous mirror as large as the stone block. All about its rim were shapes of branches and roots and trunks of trees. He stared at himself in the mirror for a moment and whispered, "It must have been on the other side of the wall. So that's where the old man went. He's probably hiding in some hidden room back there."

Suddenly, he jumped as someone spoke his name. "Frederick!"

He spun around and saw Colleen coming down the ramp, leading her old horse.

"What on earth are you doing here!" she demanded. "And... what's this?"

He backed away without thinking, right into the mirror, and before he knew it, he was falling backward, and landed with a thud, not on the dirt floor of the basement, not into the dark passage he had seen, but into a pile of *leaves*. He looked around, wondering what had just happened, for he found himself sitting in the middle of a dead-looking forest, staring at a broken piece of wall on which was hung a huge mirror. Or was it a mirror? It looked more like a window, for he could see Colleen coming toward him, leading the horse. She paused, looking puzzled, and then reached out her hand to touch something in the middle of the window. But she did not appear to see him.

Frederick looked at the crystal ball. The tiny golden specks had settled now and were still. He gave it a shake again, and again, they swirled into the triple swirl pattern.

Chapter 7 – Into a Strange Land

Colleen knew she had seen Frederick standing there a moment ago. But he had ... vanished! She thought he was going to fall into the big mirror. Where had it come from anyway? Wasn't this the very spot where the triple swirl pattern had been carved on the wall?

She led Badger over to it and reached out to her own reflection, touching its smooth surface. It was solid enough. What had just happened? She leaned against the glass surface and pushed. Still solid.

Suddenly, her image in the mirror began to shift and swirl like water into three whirlpools, which just as quickly vanished. There before her was not her reflection, but Frederick, sprawled in a bed of leaves and surrounded by great trees.

She reached out again, but this time touched – nothing. She stumbled forward, finding herself falling *through* what should have been the mirror, but was empty air. Grabbing Badger's reins for support, she fell forward and the old horse simply followed her and, before she knew it, the world around her changed.

Badger neighed, reared his head, and his eyes rolled wildly.

"Easy, old boy, easy!" she said, patting his nose and neck. "Easy there."

A confused and uncertain Frederick sat in the leaves before her. He looked about, unsure of what to say. Then his eyes focused, not on Colleen, but on something behind her, and a look of sheer terror swept over his face.

Colleen spun about, and there, hanging on an old ruined wall that stood in the middle of the forest, was a large mirror - a twin to the one through which she had apparently just stepped. But she could see clear through it into her grandpa's basement.

A curious smile crossed her face, and she took a step forward and reached out her hand, which easily passed through, as if there were nothing there at all.

"What good luck!" she said, and turned back to Frederick.

"Colleen," said Frederick. "Get away from that thing! There was something... something dark... I saw..."

"Whatever do you mean?" she said, turning and walking over to him. "It's a doorway of sorts, back to the basement, you silly goose."

But the same look of terror returned to his face as he looked beyond her. His mouth moved, but no words came out.

She smiled wryly at him, then turned back to the mirror – a magic mirror, she thought it must be, and was about to say so, but stopped short. Her smile vanished as a black shadow ran across the doorway and then disappeared.

Suddenly, a gray bony hand slipped around the edge of the brass frame, followed by a dark hooded face.

Colleen backed up a step, pulling Badger with her, and Frederick crab-crawled backward in the leaves until he hit a tree. A chill shot through her as the creature hissed and began to pull itself in front of the mirror, revealing a ragged black cloak covering a hunched form about four feet tall. A horrid odor came from it, making them want to retch. Then it began to inch its way forward, swinging its hooded head back and forth. *It* was back.

Colleen could hear Frederick panting, and she struggled to control her own mixture of fear and revulsion. Yet, she also had a sudden desire to rush forward and grab this thing and force it to tell her what it had done with her grandfather.

She was about to muster the courage to actually do something, when from behind her, Frederick cried out.

"Get out of here you, you... thing!" he yelled in a rather high-pitched voice.

Colleen glanced back at him, and there he was, splayed against the tree, gripping something in his hand.

The creature took a step forward, its mangled gray foot stepping into the leaves. Frederick shouted something unintelligible, then threw what he had in his hand at the creature.

Colleen watched in disbelief as her grandfather's crystal ball, its box, and the little key flew through the air, right at the thing's head. It hissed and jumped back through the mirror, and the little treasure continued its flight after it, disappeared into the darkness of the basement with a *plink* and a *ding*, and was gone.

The scene in the mirror swirled into a gray mist, and a moment later, Colleen was staring at her own reflection.

Chapter 8 – The Land of the Little People

For a long moment, Colleen stared at the mirror, unsure what had just happened. Frederick moaned, and she glanced over at him. He was standing with his back against a huge tree, gripping great flakes of bark with his outstretched hands.

"Wha... what happened?" he said. "That *thing*... it... it almost came through! And how did we get into this forest?"

Colleen looked around. The trees all about them were gigantic, with great gnarled roots protruding from the ground like knobby knees. Many seemed dead, or dried up, as though it were the middle of winter, though it was warm and stuffy. To one side of the broken wall stood an ancient trunk, its twisted branches reaching outward in frantic chaotic directions, and its rotted heart exposed by a ragged hole that dripped with black sap. A thin fog shrouded the wood, causing everything to fade in the distance into a gray haze.

Colleen leaned heavily against Badger's side. Her mind whirled with the possibilities of what was happening.

"So this is it," she said after a moment.

"This is what?" said Frederick, still gripping the tree. "Where are we? We've got to get out of here."

"Don't you see?" she said. "This is what my grandfather was talking about. We've come through the *entrance*."

"That's a load of rubbish," said Frederick, his voice a higher pitch than usual. "We've come through that revolving door thing in the cellar, and stumbled into a woods on the other side of a tunnel or something, and that sick child or whatever it was has shut the door on us. Yes, that must be it."

"No, Frederick, we just stepped through a magic mirror, I'm sure of it. That's the secret that my grandfather has kept all these years. He must have come through as well that night he disappeared. We're in the Land of the *Others*!"

"Rubbish!" he said again, but his eyes were darting to and fro, as though searching the mist for signs of any *Others* that might be lurking there.

"Now calm down, Frederick," she said. "It's no good going off like that. I'm sure we can't be far from home. But did you... did you just throw my grandpa's crystal ball at that thing in the mirror?"

He looked at the ground and shook his head. "I was ... well, it just happened, that's all. I didn't mean to do it. That was the key, wasn't it? It was our way home. Now it's lost, and that *thing* has it." His voice was growing more desperate now.

"What did you do, Frederick? How did you make the doorway open? Frederick – was it the crystal ball? Did that open this... *entrance*?" she asked.

"I don't know!" he moaned. "I'm sorry! I wasn't thinking. And I'm not sure how I opened it, if that's what I did," he said. "I just shook the crystal and all those little glittery things inside started swirling around in that weird shape and then it happened. It must be the key, Colleen – the key that the riddle..."

Suddenly, he realized what he had said and fell silent. He wasn't supposed to tell the McGunnegals what he knew about the map. He was supposed to get information from her.

"I know, Frederick, about your father's plan to steal our farm," she said. "We all know."

"But... but how?" he said.

"I followed your father's carriage the other night and overheard you talking. There's more to our farm than meets the eye – as we've just found out," she said.

"But the riddle spoke of eight doors, Colleen. *Under the hill lay eight doors.* Did we just find one of them? Which one do you think it is? Or maybe we just found the *looking glass* that it spoke of," he said.

Colleen sighed and didn't reply. Was Frederick right? He must be – the crystal ball must be the key to opening the looking glass. But Frederick had thrown it at that creature, and now it was lost.

A wave of panic threatened to take hold of her, but she consciously stilled her thoughts, forcing herself to think clearly. *Eight doors.* Had they found one? But which?

"Frederick, didn't that riddle say something about not having a key to the eight doors? If that's so, then how..." she began, but stopped suddenly.

A tiny flash of green and red, a small figure just four or five inches high, had just dashed behind a tree root, startling her. For a moment, she froze, unsure what she had just seen, but then slowly tiptoed toward the tree where the little form had disappeared.

"Wait!" said Colleen. "Wait, please don't run. I won't hurt you. We need your help!"

A little woman peeped over the root so that just her scarf, eyes, and nose were visible.

"I promise I won't... I mean, *we* won't hurt you. Please, do come out and talk to me!" said Colleen.

The little woman slowly came out from behind the root, and then dashed back again as Frederick came lumbering up behind Colleen.

"Who *are* you talking to, Colleen?" he said. "The roots of the trees? We've got to get out of here! We've already missed the ship, for sure. But my father is still in Ireland – we can sail on the next ship with him if we can just get back. Come on now, let's get going. There's got to be another way... what...!"

A plump little lady had climbed up onto the tree root and now had her hands placed firmly on her hips.

Frederick yelled and backed away, his hand in front of his face, as if he was seeing a thing of horror.

"Now, you just settle yourself for a moment, young man," said the little woman. "And sit down right there before you step on someone."

Frederick obeyed immediately and, in fact, not only sat down, but fainted dead away, falling into the leaves and there he lay still.

"In all my days!" said the little woman, and turned to face Colleen, who was glancing back and forth between the woman and Frederick.

"And now, young lady, who might you be, and for heaven's sake, how *did* you get here and what happened a moment ago?" The little woman seemed a bit brazen, but then her expression softened, seeing the look on Colleen's face.

Colleen was rather taken aback and, for a moment, she forgot that she had just landed in a strange wood after falling through a mirror. For there before her was what was obviously one of the little people that she had heard about in so many fairy tales and legends.

"My name is Colleen McGunnegal," she said, "and this is my horse, Badger. And that, well, that's my cousin, Frederick Buttersmouth."

Colleen tried not to stare, but simply could not help herself.

"A bit of a troublemaker at times?" asked the woman.

"Well..." she began. "I mean, he's not as bad as his brother, I don't think. But as to how we got here, we must have fallen through the looking glass! It has to be a doorway of sorts."

"You fell *through* the mirror?" the little woman asked. "But of course, that would be the only place you could have come from."

"But where *are* we?" asked Colleen. "And who are you? Are you ... are you one of the ... little people?"

"Well, first let me say that you are the *second,* or should I say *third* person who has arrived in a most curious way in the past year. The first... why now that I think of it, she looked very much like you! Could have been your sister, in fact. But, she didn't fare too well in these woods. Poor thing! She was taken away with my dear husband, Bhrogan."

The little woman grew silent and bowed her head.

"Taken away?" asked Colleen.

"Aye, taken by the goblins. She fought a good fight, though, and kicked one of them right through that mirror over there, and it plum vanished! I take it she had a bit of magic in her too, to do that trick! But there were five of those evil brutes left. They knocked her cold, tied her and my dear Bhrogan up with magic string, and stole them away through the forest."

At that, she sat down on the root and began to weep with great sobs. She soon recovered, however, and blew her nose on a hankie that she produced from a pocket in her dress.

"Forgive me, young lass, but it grieves me so to think of my dear Bhrogan slaving away for the goblins in their wicked pits. Slaving away with so many others! But here," she said, wiping her nose again, "that cousin of yours seems to be coming around."

Indeed, Frederick lifted his head, looked at Colleen, then at the little woman, groaned, and fainted again.

"Well, maybe not," said Colleen. "But please, what is your name?"

"Forgive me. My name is Mrs. Edna Sofia Wigglepox. I am, of course, one of the Tuatha de Dannan – a leprechaun, to be precise. And you are in Dannan Land – the Land of the Little People."

"You are a ... a Tuatha de ... a leprechaun?" said Colleen, amazed.

"Well, of course I am! What else would I be? Certainly not a gnome or pixie or sprite or ... but anyone can see that!" she said.

"And your husband, Mr. Wigglepox, he was a leprechaun too?" asked Colleen.

"Dear girl, of course he was, I mean, *is*. Those horrible goblins came and took him away, as I said, along with that lovely woman who fought so valiantly," she replied with a sigh.

"But I thought that leprechauns were all little, well, *men*. I've never heard of a leprechaun lady. Plus, I thought that they were all magic, and could disappear and grant wishes, and all of that. Why doesn't he just wink out of their dungeon and come back to you?" asked Colleen.

"It's a long story. Our world is under a dark spell that limits our magic. We don't understand where The Spell really comes from. Some say it comes from the Witch who lives in the South. Some say they have seen the source of the Spell in their dreams, and that it comes from someone they call The Gray Man – a shadowy spirit that dwells under the Witch's dungeons and is her dungeon keeper. Others say that something went terribly wrong in the last Great War against the Witch, and that the wizards are to blame. We only know that we are small and weak, and have been this way for a long, long time. Even most of our trees have fallen under this Spell. Why, there was a time when the trees were green and the sea was blue and we could grant a wish as quick as anything!"

She sighed and continued. "All of our pots of gold have been stolen, and now we're lucky to have enough magic to make our shoes, and even they're not what they used to be. Most of us have forgotten how to really wish."

She paused, looked sad, and then angry. "That's what those nasty goblins steal away our people for – to make them magic shoes and hats and cloaks and that sort of thing."

Then she sighed again and said, "As for us all being *men,* I assume you mean our *he-folk,* for we are most certainly not Men – humans, that is. And dear child, *of course* there are lady leprechauns, although now that I think of it, I can't recall any of our own tales speaking of our lady-folk going to your world as some of the he-folk did long, long ago."

"Amazing," said Colleen. "What was that you called yourself – *Tuatha* something?"

"Tuatha de Dannan," she said. "It means the *people of Danu.* Danu is the Lady of our land. She is very great and powerful, and if it were not for her, our forest would long ago have completely fallen under the dominion of the Witch and the goblins. She lives near, or some say *in,* a lake many days walk from here. I have never seen her myself, but I have heard that she is very beautiful and is one of the Big Folk, like you. But I fear her power has waned, and the power of the Witch grows."

"You mean this lady is human?" asked Colleen.

"I've heard tale that she *looks* human. But the tales say that she is far older than any human could be. Older than the Forest itself, and that is *old!*" she said.

Colleen pondered this for a moment and then a thought struck her. It was a wild, desperately hopeful thought.

"Mrs. Wigglepox, I don't mean to change the subject, but you said that a woman came here just like we did. Do you remember what she was wearing when she came?" she asked.

"Oh yes, it was a brown dress – like a work dress, and she had on a red apron with a beautiful pattern on it. I'll never forget it – it was like nothing I've seen before," she said.

Colleen reached into her pocket and pulled out her mother's scarf.

"The pattern on the apron – did it look like this?" And she held up the scarf.

"Why, yes, child! It most certainly did! In fact, a piece of her apron tore off in the scuffle and I saved it and made this little scarf I'm wearing now!" And she untied her own scarf and held it up. Indeed, it had the same pattern sewn into it.

"Mrs. Wigglepox, that was my mother! She's been missing for months! Someone must have looked into the crystal ball or something that night and activated it, and she must have fallen in through the mirror, just like I did. But the crystal ball was still on the other side – in my... in my world." She said the last few words slowly, thoughtfully.

"So," Colleen continued, "the mirror *is* a door of some sort. You look into the crystal ball, or do something with it – maybe shake it like Frederick did, and it can take you to the place that you see – you just walk through and you are there! I wonder... did Grandpa use it that night he disappeared? Did he activate this portal and come here, or go some other place? He might also still be alive! Have you seen an old man with a walking stick come through?"

Before Mrs. Wigglepox could answer, a voice from behind interrupted her.

"We've got to get out of here and get back home!" it said.

It was Frederick. He was rubbing his head and staring at Mrs. Wigglepox.

"This must be a bad dream," he groaned as he sat up.

"No, Frederick," said Colleen. "It's not a dream. We've come through a sort of magic doorway or something. And the same thing must have happened to my mother and grandfather! And now those – those *goblins* have her, and maybe Grandpa as well. We've got to save them!"

"No way," said Frederick. "We've got to get back and tell my dad about this."

He got up then, and Colleen whirled to face him.

"No!" she said, her voice full of anger. "You're going to come with me to find my mother and grandfather or you're going to stay here in these woods alone. Just how do you intend to go back? You threw the crystal ball on the other side, remember, and that *thing* that was coming through the mirror likely took it! You can wait around for it to follow us through, or we can move away from this place."

"Yes, *it* was likely a goblin," said Mrs. Wigglepox. "They are wicked creatures that roam the night, casting spells of fear and dread and plague. You mustn't face them alone."

"Let's not talk nonsense," said Frederick. He was trying to sound brave, and his father had always said that logic and clear thinking could solve every problem that one might face. "There's a logical explanation for all of this. And those things you're calling *goblins* are nothing but a bunch of outlaw thugs that have been roaming the countryside – or maybe the children of thugs, by the size of that one we saw. My father warned me of them – a band of homeless misfits who can't find jobs and are all in a huff because they've lost their land. They roam about stealing and robbing from anyone they can. That's what that thing was in the doorway – it was one of them. And I say it was one of them that stole away your mother, Colleen, and maybe your grandfather as well. Father told me about the whole thing before we came."

"Lawless misfits and robbers – yes, they are that, my boy," said Mrs. Wigglepox. "But they are not men. They are goblins. And they have dark powers, or at least some of them do. You would do well to stay clear of them. As for your grandfather, Colleen, I've not seen anyone else. I'm sorry."

Frederick sniffed and said, "Well, you can believe what you want, but even so, how do you expect to do anything about them? And, if they've kidnapped Mrs. McGunnegal or your grandpa, what can we do about it anyway... two kids and a ... a... a l...leprechaun!"

He stumbled over the last words, and began to mumble about not believing in little people. "Must have hit my head... that's it... it's all a hallucination... I'm imagining it all. Yes..." But he sounded most unconvincing, even to himself.

"Well," Colleen said slowly, "you may have a point - about us just being kids, I mean. I hadn't thought of that. But perhaps Mrs. Wigglepox can guide us, and we can rescue Mr. Wigglepox as well. We've got to try to do something!"

"Yes, in this place, you will most definitely need a guide. Those who know how to guide well are rare at every season, but in this time of darkness in our land, a good guide would be hard indeed to find," said the little woman. "I am certainly not fit for such a venture, and as for going to the strongholds of our enemies – that is far too dangerous. Why, it would take a troop of strong men and a wizard to break into the fortress of the goblins, and even then, you would have to face the Goblin King, Gruazard, and his Court Witch. I've never seen them myself, but it's said that the Goblin King is horrible and huge, and does things to his prisoners that just can't be mentioned. And the Court Witch – it would take a powerful wizard to face her. Plus, the goblins roam about these woods and try to snatch away what few of us are left."

"See there," said Frederick. "Now, let's just try to get home and... and, well, you can tell your father and big brothers all about it, and the police too, and bring them all back here to take care of this... king and witch and ... goblins ... if that's what they are. I suppose if there are really little people, there *might* be goblins. But really, Colleen, we're just kids! We have to get some adults to help."

Colleen started to protest, but Frederick was making a bit of sense. Surely Father, Aonghus, and Bran were more than a match for any goblins. Why, they were the biggest men in the whole territory, and were wonderfully strong and even a bit frightful when angry.

"But it seems," said Mrs. Wigglepox, "that you have lost the way back. You will need to find another way."

Colleen thought for a moment and then said, "If this mirror is a doorway, it might lead to other worlds as well. There's an old map over my fireplace back home that has a riddle on it. I think it speaks of other worlds where the maker of the map went to. Maybe there's a different key for each world or something. If we could find another key..."

They were all quiet for a moment, and then Frederick said, "It was the pirate."

"The Pirate!" said Mrs. Wigglepox.

"The map back at your farm mentions a pirate named Atsolter. He must have come here the same way. That means that the crystal ball *is* the key and he must have hidden the treasure *here* somewhere!"

Colleen noticed a strange gleam in his eyes when he spoke of treasure.

"Yes," said Mrs. Wigglepox. "There are tales of someone called the Pirate. But they are old, old tales, though not as old as the tales of the wizards, or even so old as the witches coming to our land. But yes, there are tales of someone called the Pirate."

"I think the crystal ball is the only key that there is," said Frederick. "At least if that riddle is right. And I'll bet *this* was the last place that Pirate went to – that's why we ended up here and not somewhere else. Imagine having the power to go anywhere in the universe right from your living room! Someone with the mirror and the crystal could..." He stopped mid-sentence, pondering where he might go and what he might do.

"But we came through a mirror on the other side, Frederick," said Colleen, interrupting his thoughts. "I think it will only take you through to another magic mirror. Whoever made these mirrors must have gotten here somehow in the first place to put them here. If we could figure out how they got in, maybe we could go back that way too. Mrs. Wigglepox, you mentioned the wizards - how did they ..."

But before she could finish her sentence, Badger gave a whinny and stamped his feet. Off through the mist came the distant sound of cracking branches and rustling leaves.

Mrs. Wigglepox gave a shriek and leaped from the root to the ground. "*Goblins!*" she whispered. "We must hide!"

Chapter 9 – Goblins

Colleen froze, squinting through the fog, trying to see any movement in the direction where the noises were coming to them. But the mists hid whatever it was.

"We can't just hide under the leaves," said Frederick. "We've got to get out of here."

"Badger," said Colleen, pointing at the horse. "Come on."

Mrs. Wigglepox looked up at the horse. "I'm afraid you'll need to carry me," she said. "Quickly now, put me in your pocket."

Colleen hesitated only a moment before carefully picking up the little leprechaun and sliding her into her dress pocket, then she mounted Badger.

"Frederick, come on. Climb on behind me," she said urgently.

"I'm no good at riding!" he said in a whisper. "I'll fall off!"

"Just get on the horse and hold onto me. Hurry now, they're coming!" she said.

Frederick glanced in the direction of the noise coming towards them and then ran to the horse. Putting his foot in the stirrup, he swung his leg over and nearly fell, and was only saved by Colleen steadying him.

"Now hold on around my waist and don't crush Mrs. Wigglepox – she's in my pocket!" she said.

She heeled Badger and off they went at a dead run. The sound and smell of the goblins seem to put speed in the old horse's stride. But the trees were close, and even as they started out, a long, hanging branch snagged Colleen's shawl and snatched it from her shoulders. She glanced back at it, but kept going.

Mrs. Wigglepox peered out from Colleen's pocket and said, "There's a path up ahead that your horse could run on better, and it leads down to the old bridge across the river. The goblins use it sometimes, but I think that's our best bet."

Within a few minutes, they were at the path, and Mrs. Wigglepox directed them to the left. Badger seemed to be enjoying the run, somehow, and Colleen hadn't seen him so lively in years. He galloped along at a good speed until they came to the bridge, and there they stopped.

For an instant, Colleen gazed in amazement at the structure – a massive bridge with intricate workmanship, although obviously quite ancient. Its huge stones were perfectly shaped and fitted together, forming a single span across the deep chasm. The path, however, did not cross it, but continued on along the side of the gorge.

Colleen began to move Badger toward the bridge, but Mrs. Wigglepox said, "No! Not that one! That was the Troll Bridge. I don't trust it. See, there, down the trail – the wooden bridge to the right – that's the one we're taking."

"But ..." began Colleen.

But Mrs. Wigglepox cut her off and said, "I'll explain later, Colleen. Just run Badger across the wooden bridge and up the trail a ways, and then ride back to the bridge."

"But why?" she insisted.

"We're going to try to fool them into thinking that we went up the trail. Be quick!" she said.

Reeds grew along the banks of the river in the chasm, and there seemed to be a small side trail of sorts on the far side of the wooden bridge that appeared to run off the main path and down to the riverside. The strong smell of rotting grasses and cattails reached their noses.

Colleen said, "Run, Badger, run!" And the old horse took off, a glint in his eyes, and clattered across the wooden bridge.

"Slow down!" wailed Frederick as he bumped up and down. "I'm going to fall off!"

"Just you hold on if you don't want those goblins catching you," said Colleen, and he clung tighter around her waist.

Up the trail they flew, then, after about a quarter mile, she turned and they raced back, but this time on the side of the road until they reached the bridge again.

"Now, quickly, we must get down and walk Badger down the side trail and under the bridge!"

Off the horse they jumped, with Frederick sliding down Badger's back side and falling on his own.

"Frederick, grab that bunch of ferns there and try to wipe out our footprints," she said.

Frederick obeyed, grumbling.

Colleen paid him no mind and led the horse down the embankment and under the bridge. Frederick threw the ferns into the brush to one side, looked anxiously across the bridge and down the path, and then followed where Colleen had gone.

They hurried into the shadows, and not a minute later came the sound of tramping feet and rough voices above them on the bridge.

"They came this way," said a gruff voice. "Look here, their trail goes on down the path. It's a bit confused, but they ran off that way, for sure."

"Maybe the Old Troll scared 'em off," grunted another.

"Or ate them," said another, which brought a chorus of harsh laughter.

"Maybe we should send Bones down there to check," said another.

"Yeah, go on, Bones," jeered a rather high-pitched voice. "You know you like to pick over the carcasses."

"On with it, you gloats, we're almost on 'em," shouted the first voice. "Get down the trail or I'll throw you to the Troll myself. Get on!"

Colleen listened as the voices faded in the distance, and then they were gone.

"That won't fool them for long," said Mrs. Wigglepox. "We've got to make our way back to my tree. We should be safe there. Come now, we'll stay in the river so that we don't make tracks. Hurry along."

Colleen mounted Badger again, and Frederick climbed unsteadily behind her.

"We'll have to go under that... Troll Bridge," said Frederick.

"Yes, we shall," said Mrs. Wigglepox. "The goblins will never suspect that we went that way. They fear the bridge."

In a few moments, Badger was nearing the massive structure. Its impressive arch loomed high above, and they stopped before entering its dark shadow.

Colleen looked where Frederick was pointing, and there in the mud were huge footprints, at least two feet long. Frederick opened his mouth to say something more, but Mrs. Wigglepox spoke first.

"Colleen, you must have Badger run for all he is worth under the shadow of this bridge. Do not let him stop!" she said.

Colleen didn't question why, but said, "Hold on, Frederick," and spurred Badger.

Badger took a step, then hesitated, neighing and tossing his head. But then there was a distant sound of harsh voices, and Colleen kicked him again and said, "Go boy!"

The old horse leaped forward, and as they passed under the arch, Colleen saw why the goblins feared the Troll Bridge. Beneath one side of the arch, a massive black shadow moved. She could not see it clearly for the darkness, but its muscled bulk sat hunched, and as they bolted by, it rose from its place and lunged at them.

Colleen's blood ran cold, and Frederick blathered something unintelligible as the great shape flung itself after them, its breath coming in harsh gasps with every step.

Just as they passed into the light on the other side of the arch, it stopped, a huge green-scaled hand reaching outward, but quickly withdrew with a dreadful cry of anguish and rage.

Colleen looked back as they ran on, and she could see the thing standing in the shadows, its great shoulders heaving, its breath labored.

"Was... was that a troll?" said Frederick, his voice weak.

"It was indeed," said Mrs. Wigglepox. "It was a very old troll. I thought surely it was dead by now. I am sorry."

"A troll!" he wailed. "A troll! We were nearly eaten by a troll!"

Colleen urged Badger on up the stream as quickly as she dared. When they had gone for some minutes, the river bed began to grow rockier. "I think we better slow down a little. It wouldn't do for Badger to break an ankle. But why did the troll stop? Why didn't it chase us?" she asked.

"I think they fear the sunlight," Mrs. Wigglepox replied. "But why that is, I don't know. Legend has it that it got trapped here long ago during one of the wars."

Colleen slowed Badger, and for a good hour, they made their way up the water course, until finally, Mrs. Wigglepox said, "This is where we need to leave the river. I think we'll be safe now."

They climbed the bank on the left and Mrs. Wigglepox said, "Now we've got to make it to my house before nightfall. It's not safe anytime, but it's especially dangerous after dark."

"Why do you say that? Will the troll come after us?" said Frederick.

"Maybe, but the goblins love the darkness too. Actually, I'm quite surprised to see them out even in the fading daylight. It's very unlike them. But they won't stay out in the day for long. I think it actually hurts them in some way. But at night – that's when they grow fierce and do terrible things. You mind yourself, young man, and don't go slipping away from us," she warned him. "There are worse things than trolls and goblins that haunt the forest when the sun goes down."

Chapter 10 – The Wigglepox Tree

Colleen rode on through the mists, guided by the little leprechaun perched in her pocket. They had doubled back on their trail several times to elude any goblins that might still be tracking them. Dusk was heavy upon the forest, and the great trees loomed before them like vast giants with outstretched arms.

Mrs. Wigglepox urged Colleen to ride faster.

"My tail bone is surely bruised," said Frederick with a moan.

However, they didn't slow, but rode on through the deepening gloom, until eventually, Mrs. Wigglepox said, "Here we are at last – the Wigglepox Tree."

Colleen drew Badger to a stop and gazed in awe at the most enormous tree she had ever seen. Great branches near the ground, as thick as Badger was tall, reached outward from the vast trunk and ran in crooked paths through the surrounding wood before raising themselves haphazardly toward the sky. Her eyes slowly followed the hulking growth upward, through a great tangle of massive gnarled arms.

Frederick let out a low whistle. "My whole house would fit inside that thing," he said.

Then he gripped her waist tighter, and she felt an involuntary shudder run through him.

"What's wrong?" she said.

"There are faces in that tree," he whispered.

She looked up again, and the many knobs and contorted twists and turns of bark seemed to cast the illusion of eyes and noses and great mouths frowning down at them.

Then, suddenly, another vision came to her. It was more than just a face, but a sense that something in this tree was deeply *aware* of them – a mind that gazed down and considered them with deep, slow thoughts.

"Please, Colleen, put me on the ground," said Mrs. Wigglepox.

Colleen blinked, and the vision vanished, but the feeling of watchfulness in this tree lingered on. She and Frederick dismounted, and she carefully placed the leprechaun on the ground.

Mrs. Wigglepox walked beneath the massive branches right up to the base of the tree. Cupping her hands against the bark, she appeared to whisper something.

With an earsplitting sound of creaking and grinding and thrashing of branches and leaves, the great tree began to change. Two of the huge branches nearest the ground began to writhe, moved apart, and formed a passageway through the tangle. Then a large opening appeared in the trunk between the branches, big enough for Badger to walk through easily.

"Welcome to the Wigglepox Tree," she said. "My family has lived here since before anyone can remember."

"You live in a rotted-out hollow tree?" said Frederick.

"My boy, this is *not* a rotted-out tree," she said sternly. "For your information, the Wigglepox Tree and its little people have lived in harmony, protecting and caring for each other, for ages and ages. The tree has *opened* itself up to us, and you're fortunate that it doesn't give you a good thrashing for such an insult."

Frederick took a step backward. "I didn't mean..."

"Never you mind," interrupted Mrs. Wigglepox. "But you just mind your manners, since we'll be sleeping inside it tonight. Come along."

Mrs. Wigglepox disappeared into the tree, and Colleen led Badger through the aisle of branches toward the opening. Frederick hesitated, looked around at the deepening darkness, and quickly followed.

As Colleen passed into the great tree, a dim light greeted her that seemed to come from the wood of the tree itself. As her eyes adjusted, she saw that, although the tree was hollow, the wood was not rotted at all, but rather clean and smooth, not at all like other hollow trees she had climbed into that were full of sawdust and ants and crickets and spider webs. This tree seemed more like a house – or at least the room of a house – and it was spacious, comfortable, and welcoming.

"Well, let me just check in," said Mrs. Wigglepox.

She hurried over to one wall and disappeared through a small hole.

A moment later, they heard her voice call from above them and they looked up. There she was, looking out a window of sorts about ten feet above their heads.

"Everything is fine, my dear, and word from the forest is that the goblins have lost our trail and have gone on south, back toward their holes, no doubt to report what they've discovered," she said.

She disappeared again and re-emerged at the base of the tree, and behind her came two even tinier people.

"Colleen, Frederick, I would like you to meet my two daughters, Lily and Rose," she said.

"How do you do?" said Colleen. Frederick grunted and nodded his head.

The two tiny girls, no taller than Colleen's fingers, curtsied and said in very small voices, "Fine, thank you. Very nice to meet you."

"And you," she said.

Meanwhile, Frederick had gone over to the far wall and was poking his fingers into more holes in the side, when he suddenly said, "Hey, see here, let me go!" and was pulling frantically at his hand. Apparently, his finger had gotten stuck in one of them.

"Help! It won't let me go! It grabbed me, I tell you!" he cried.

"Well, it serves you right," said Mrs. Wigglepox. "How would you like it if someone went poking their fingers in your belly?"

She watched him jump about, trying to pull his finger free, and finally, with a chuckle, said, "Lily, how about helping the boy? He's really got himself into a fix."

Lily walked across the floor until she was just a few feet from the struggling and now moaning Frederick.

"Now, boy," she said. "You must stand still. I shan't help you if you're going to dance all over the place like that. I do not wish to be stepped on!"

Frederick stopped his dancing and looked down at the little girl.

"Now be still," she said, and walked next to him and leaned close to the tree. She cupped her hands against the wall and said something that Frederick could not make out, but almost immediately, his finger popped out of the hole and he fell backward in a heap.

Lily giggled and walked over to him. She was a very pretty little girl with brown braided hair and tiny freckles across her nose.

"How old are you?" she asked him.

"Well, I'm... I'm fourteen," he said to her.

"I'm nine. And I think you're cute," she said, and she ran back to Mrs. Wigglepox.

Frederick actually blushed for a moment and then got to his feet.

To change the subject, he said, "Have you got anything to eat? It's well past tea time."

Mrs. Wigglepox frowned. "Yes, we do have food for folk our size, but one small meal for you would clean out our cupboards! I am sorry, but I'm afraid we're going to have to find you something in the forest in the morning."

She thought for a moment and then said, "There's a berry patch not far from here, least ways not far for your kind to walk to, and a few hickory and chestnut trees as well. That won't be much, but at least it should fill your bellies."

"Can't we go now?" asked Frederick.

"At night?" said Mrs. Wigglepox. "No, no, we mustn't wander about in the dark, not in this wood. The Haunts come out at night."

"What are the haunts?" asked Colleen, and she glanced at the open doorway.

Mrs. Wigglepox looked down at her daughters and said, "That's what we call a person who has fallen under the Spell. Ah, but let's not speak of it in the darkness. Bright morning is the best time for such tales. I'm sure you must be exhausted. Please, make yourselves as comfortable as you can. It's time to close up for the evening."

With that, she spoke to the tree, and Colleen watched as the entryway began to close with an echoing sound like thunder, grinding stone, and great creaking boards. Then the doorway was gone, and no crack or crevice could be seen in the place where it had been.

She turned to Frederick. His eyes were wide and his face was ashen.

"Well, we might as well settle in," she said. "Come on, help me with Badger's saddle."

He stared at the blank wall a moment longer, then said, "What? Oh, all right," and helped her unsaddle the horse.

"Best get some sleep," he muttered.

"Here, we'll share the saddle as a pillow. You sleep on one side and I'll take the other," said Colleen.

"You two sleep well," said Mrs. Wigglepox. "We'll see you in the morning."

She led Lily and Rose back to the hole in the wall, and they disappeared, but not before Lily lingered a moment longer, staring out at Frederick. Then, she too vanished.

Colleen lay on the soft pine needle floor of the tree, her head resting on one side of the saddle.

"How about this?" she said. "Who would believe it if we told them?"

"Not my family, that's for sure," replied Frederick. "I wouldn't have even a few hours ago."

"It's maddening and terrifying and, well, exciting, all at the same time," said Colleen. "Still, I do hope we can find another way back soon."

They said no more that night, but stared up at the high ceiling above them, each lost in thought about the strange things they had seen. It was a long while before they slowly drifted to sleep.

Neither of them noticed the little faces of Lily and Rose peering down at them from a high window, their tiny lips forming innocent smiles as they beheld their first glimpse of the big people. Mrs. Wigglepox joined them for a moment, then shooshed them to bed. Then, going to her own room and gazing out a knothole into the night, she made a wish.

"Let these be the ones," she said to the listening night. "The ones who will break the Spell and set us free."

Chapter 11 - Oracle

"Wake up!" said a little voice in Frederick's ear.

He opened one eye and jumped. Lily was sitting on the saddle right next to his head. She was dressed in a mottled brown dress that made her look remarkably like a leaf with a head.

"Don't scare me like that!" he said and sat up. "It's not every day you get woken up by a little person."

His stomach growled, reminding him that he had not eaten since lunchtime the day before.

Colleen was already up and looking as fresh and perky as ever, as though falling through magic mirrors, being chased by goblins, and sleeping in haunted trees with a family of leprechauns was something she did every day, and was of no account.

"Up at last, sleepyhead?" she said. "We've been waiting for you. The sun is up already."

He stood and stretched, then realized he was covered with pine needles.

Both Colleen and Lily laughed, and Colleen helped him brush himself off.

"Best be going for breakfast," said Mrs. Wigglepox as she came out of her tiny doorway. "Come on now, we'll show you the way. Colleen, will you carry us?"

"Mother," said Lily. "I want Frederick to carry me. Can't he, please?"

At this, Frederick looked quite surprised and even a bit taken aback.

"I, uh, well, that is, I..." he stammered.

Mrs. Wigglepox looked hard at him and then nodded to herself. She walked over to him, leading Lily by the hand.

"Frederick," she said. "Do you see my daughter here?"

He nodded.

"Do you know how valuable she is to me?" she asked.

He shook his head.

"She means more to me than all the treasures in Fairyland, more than all the pots of gold at the end of all the rainbows in the world. You've not shown yourself to be a very trustworthy young man. But I trust my daughter's judgment of you. Apparently, she thinks you worth trusting, so I put her, literally, in your hands. Mind you, I'll be watching, and if any harm comes to her, you shall have me to deal with, and I shall have this tree take hold of more than your finger to squeeze!" At that, she stepped back a few paces, leaving a beaming Lily staring up at him.

"But, but..." he began.

"Come on, Frederick," interrupted Lily. "It will be grand fun. You'll carry me and I shall tell you stories of the woodland."

He paused a moment, and then said, "Well, all right. Why not? It's not every day you get to carry a leprechaun in your hands." So he knelt down and held them out.

Lily stepped onto his palm and, with a care that Colleen thought him incapable of, he raised her up and held his hands close to his chest, where she sat down cross-legged and leaned back against him.

"Off we go!" she squealed happily.

Colleen carefully picked up Mrs. Wigglepox and then Rose and put them each in a pocket.

"Shall we ride Badger?" asked Colleen.

"Let the old boy sleep," said Mrs. Wigglepox. "He's had quite enough excitement for a while."

"What fun!" cried Rose. "I've never been carried by a giant before!"

"They are not giants," said Mrs. Wigglepox. "If you, a little seven-year-old leprechaun, ever came across a giant, you probably would not even know it, because his shoes alone would seem like a huge mountain to you."

She paused a moment, smiling at her daughter, then called out, "Open, please!"

The noise of the tree opening filled the room for a long moment, sunlight streamed in, and there before them was a pathway through the great branches. The fog of the previous night had vanished, but the sense of heaviness in the forest remained.

Still, the Wigglepox children giggled and called to one another as they walked along and, after a short time, they came to a large meadow where there was a spring and many berry bushes. In the center of the clearing was what appeared to be a broken tower of sorts, its stones crumbling with long years of disrepair.

At first, Frederick started to run toward the berry bushes, but at a scream from Lily, he remembered that he was carrying her and immediately stopped.

"Oh... sorry," he said in a low voice so no one but she would hear him, and he walked over to a berry bush that was laden with fruit.

He picked a particularly juicy one and popped it in his mouth.

"Mmmm," he said, and reached for another one.

"Frederick!" said Lily. "Doesn't a lady get any?"

"Oh, sorry," he said and, looking about, picked a small but juicy one and put it in his hand next to her.

She grabbed hold of one of the juicy knobs and twisted it free from the rest of the fruit, and then took a bite. Purple juice came squirting out and dotted her checkered dress. Frederick laughed.

"Uh, here," he said, and reached in his pocked, pulled out a hankie, and handed it to her. "It's not used or anything," he said. "Maybe you could use it like an apron or something."

She smiled at him and said, "I have a grand idea. Put me down in the grass here and we'll spread this out like a picnic cloth. You can get yourself a handful of berries, and I'll just have this one. It will be more than enough for me."

To Colleen's amazement, Frederick Buttersmouth, the boy of whom she had so many bad impressions, sat down in the grass, spread out his hankie, and piled a handful of berries on it, and sat eating and talking to a three-inch tall little leprechaun girl. He even went to the spring and drank deeply, then brought back a bit in his hand for Lily to drink.

"Would you look at that!" whispered Colleen to Mrs. Wigglepox as she put Rose down on a large toadstool, where she happily sat to watch. "Who would have thought?"

"Amazing what a little trust can do for someone," Mrs. Wigglepox replied. "Sometimes a person just needs someone to believe in them. But the proof's in the pudding, as it's said."

For a moment, Colleen munched on her berries in silence, and then said, "Mrs. Wigglepox, what's this old stone heap here in the meadow? It looks ancient."

"I believe it goes back to the time of the wizards," she said. "It was a tower or house of some sort once, but it has not been used in our living memory, and even the forest has forgotten how it was used. Some say that a beautiful princess with the most extraordinary hair was trapped in it once, but she escaped through some sort of magic and ran off with a prince. Others say that dwarves built it, and some that wizards lived here once, but no one knows for sure. It was long, long ago."

After they had eaten their fill, Colleen said, "Frederick, I'm going to climb to the top of this broken tower and have a look around. Want to join me?"

He looked up hesitantly, then nodded.

Up the pile of ruined stone they went and, as they did, Colleen noticed many strange runes and carvings on the rocks.

"Frederick," she said. "Look at these carvings. They look very much like ones I've seen back home. They're all over the broken rocks that make up the wall that borders our farm."

Frederick looked closely at the odd letters carved on a large stone block that he was leaning against.

"Could be," he said. "Father went walking about your farm while you were all looking for your grandfather. He brought a whole sack of them to the inn and had me look them over. He said I was to help him decipher them when we got back to England. He always makes me do that sort of thing. He says he's preparing me to take his place when he retires."

"He was taking stones from our farm without permission? Well!" she said.

She was exasperated at the thought of Rufus taking things that were potentially of great value without even asking, especially when they were so poor and needed money to save the farm.

"I suppose there's nothing for it now. So, can you read these things?" she asked.

"No, they're not in any language I've ever seen," he said. After a moment, he said, "Say, maybe Mrs. Wigglepox could read them."

"Let's see," Colleen replied. "But first, let's get higher. We're almost over the treetops now."

As they neared the top, Colleen could see a vast brown carpet that stretched in all directions, dotted only occasionally by a lonely green patch. Far to the south, she could barely make out a distant range of high hills that ran from east to west and beyond them a brown horizon.

"What's that?" asked Frederick, squinting as he peered southward and pointing. "That shiny thing way off in the middle of the forest."

Colleen looked where he pointed, and there was a tiny speck of something shining in the sun.

"Must be a lake or pond or something," said Colleen. "It certainly is shining."

"Colleen, this is pretty scary," said Frederick. "This forest must stretch for hundreds of miles all around us. There's no place like this that I know of anywhere in Ireland or England. We've *got* to be in some other land. And it looks like our only way home is going to be the same way we came."

Quite suddenly, there was a sound, and a very strange sound indeed, for a large round stone that was sitting on the peak of the mound began to speak.

"The spelpy forest strunes frightibly round. But farder lies the Landu ground. There brines the spectvelous light! The Leople's hope amid the night!"

Colleen and Frederick both jumped and nearly went tumbling down the rocky hill.

"What was that?" said Frederick.

Colleen looked upward at the gray rock, and realized that it was not a rock at all, but a small hunched man wearing a tattered gray cloak. He had been sitting very still on the highest point of the pile, with his back to them and his head bent down. Now he slowly uncurled himself and turned to meet their astonished expressions.

His face was neither old nor young, and he was rather bald with strands of gray-white hair strewn across his head. He had a short, scraggly beard but no mustache, and the clothes under his gray cloak were faded green britches and a tunic with a brown belt that had a dull brass buckle. He looked as though he might stand about two feet high in his worn, black, brass-buckle shoes if he were not so bent.

He squinted his large brown eyes at them and said in the same scraggly voice, "Helves and Smen, come to the Leoples land again!"

Colleen had no idea what he had just said, so she just stared at the little man, not knowing how to reply. After an awkward moment, Frederick spoke.

"Uh, please excuse us, sir, but we didn't quite catch that."

The little man closed his eyes and said, "Trechangers and frighty times may lie ahead, for Fredersmouth and Colligal shall besperience the dead."

Colleen and Frederick looked at one another, and then she said, "Please sir, what is your name? My name is Colleen McGunnegal, and this is my cousin, Frederick Buttersmouth. We've only just arrived in your land."

But the man picked up a cane that was lying next to him, stood up, and began slowly to descend from the mound, glancing at them as he passed them by.

They watched him as he made his way from rock to rock, grunting at times, but muttering a tune as he went.

"When chidescents of oldient king
Clascend the broashed tower again,
The time to rejelbate has come
For Leoples will get liberdom."

He kept repeating this, with an occasional laugh of glee between the verses.

"He's loony," whispered Frederick. "Maybe that Spell that Mrs. Wigglepox was talking about has gotten to him."

The little man seemed to hear this, for he stopped and turned, looked Frederick in the eyes, and shouted, "Imachievable!" then continued on down the mound singing his tune.

"Best follow him," said Frederick.

Colleen nodded, and they began to follow him down, being careful not to knock any of the loose rocks down on the little fellow as he picked his way toward the meadow.

When they finally reached the bottom, the bent man sat on a rock and called loudly, "Pigglewoxes!"

Mrs. Wigglepox, Lily, and Rose all looked up with a jump of surprise. They all dashed behind a large mushroom and peered out.

Frederick walked past the man and over to where they were hiding and bent low to talk to them.

"There is some sort of mad fellow here," he said. "We can't understand a word he says."

All three of the Wigglepoxes climbed up on the mushroom and looked across the meadow where Colleen was stooped down, trying to talk to the hunched man.

"Did he say who he was?" asked Mrs. Wigglepox.

"Just went on with a bunch of nonsense," said Frederick. "I was wondering if you might know him."

"I've never seen him before," she said. "My, but he is a big fellow."

"Big to you," he said. "Rather a midget to me."

"Well, at any rate, he's not a goblin, I can tell you. But my eyesight isn't what it used to be. Let's go meet him," said Mrs. Wigglepox.

They slid off the mushroom and made their way quickly across the meadow.

As they drew near, they could hear Colleen talking to him.

"Please, sir, won't you tell me who you are? What is your name? Do you live nearby?"

But the man didn't say anything in reply, and only watched as Frederick and the Wigglepox family made their way toward him.

When finally they drew near, Mrs. Wigglepox exclaimed, "Well, bless my soul! You are a leprechaun!"

"Coursitutely!" said the man, and he winked at her.

"If he's a leprechaun, how come he's so big?" asked Frederick.

The strange little fellow turned slowly toward him, pointed at the Wigglepoxes, and said, "Questery is, why's them so miniscuall?"

There was an awkward moment of silence before Colleen said, "Well, at any rate, won't you tell us your name?"

But the bent little leprechaun slid from his rock and hobbled over to the Wigglepox family, bent down even lower to them, closed one eye, and gazed at them with the other one, which he opened quite wide.

After looking them over, he nodded to himself and said, "You'll do."

"I say we call him The Oracle," said Frederick with a laugh. "He seems to say a lot of nothing in a rather mysterious way."

The little man rose from his examination of the Wigglepox family, hobbled over to Frederick, and whacked him in the shin with his cane.

"Ouch!" said Frederick. "What was that for?"

But the leprechaun said nothing, proceeded over to a berry bush, began to pick some low hanging fruit, and placed them in a shoulder pouch that he had produced from somewhere.

Colleen could not help but giggle at the sight.

"I think he's rather charming," she said. "But I do wish he would tell us something of himself."

"Well, at any rate, he does have a good idea - we best gather as much fruit as we can, and be getting back to the Tree," said Mrs. Wigglepox. "And Mr. ... Mr. ... well, if you won't tell us your name, then we *shall* call you Oracle. So then, Oracle, would you join us back at our tree?"

He paused in his berry picking, looked at her, winked again, and then continued picking berries and humming a little tune.

Frederick rolled his eyes, but Colleen wondered about this fellow. He was odd, but there was something about him that made her instinctively trust him.

Suddenly, a strange feeling swept over her, as though his frail frame and gray cloak veiled a hidden – *something*. But she could not put into words what she felt. Then he flicked a berry through the air, grinned, and hobbled down the trail.

"He's a loon," whispered Frederick as they followed him.

But Colleen was not so sure.

Chapter 12 – Another Night in the Land of the Little People

The mysterious little man lagged behind as Colleen and Frederick made their way back to the Wigglepox Tree. Soon they were back, where they found Badger still contentedly sleeping.

Oracle went up to the tree and gave one of its massive roots a hug. It gave a slight quiver, and then was still. Mrs. Wigglepox looked at the leprechaun and rubbed her chin for a moment, then shrugged.

"I guess you'll want to be making plans today, and spend at least one more night with us," she said.

Spend the night! thought Colleen. All the events of the prior day and night came rushing back to her, and she realized that they did need to get back home. Her mother was here, and she was being held captive by terrible creatures. She had to get back home and bring back her father and brothers, and then they all could rescue her. Besides, her family would be getting terribly worried by now... or would they? No, actually they would not be worried, not for some days at least. Henny would tell the others that she was home, and Father... he would not even know that she was missing. These and other thoughts whirled about in her head as she walked into the huge tree.

Mrs. Wigglepox interrupted her thoughts and said, "It's a mighty shame that you lost that crystal ball. I'd hate to think of a goblin having the power to move from world to world through that mirror."

Oracle grunted and looked very serious and, in a somber tone, said, "Hoblgobs and Witlcore mustn't get the keydloore, or Fredersmouth and Colligal shall see their middangeard go ill."

"What *is* he saying?" said Frederick.

"I think I actually caught that one," said Colleen. "I think he might have said that the goblins and the Witch mustn't get the key to the door or something bad will happen to our world."

Something bad will happen. Suddenly it hit her. Something bad *was* happening back in their world. The black blight had arrived in Ireland the very year that her mother had disappeared and the goblin had come through the mirror.

"Frederick, we have *got* to get that crystal ball back somehow, and get that goblin out of our world. I think it plans to turn Ireland into *this!*" she said, pointing out the doorway at the dead forest.

For a few moments, they all sat in a depressing silence, then she whispered,

"I think it's already started."

Frederick was not sure what to say. He had seen the sick and starving people in Ireland firsthand, but he had never stopped to think much of what was happening to them. He had overheard old O'Brian say that he had seen mortiferous vapors rising out of the swamp near the McGunnegal farm, and he speculated that those fumes might be to blame for the failed potato crop and the sicknesses that were spreading. Could it be that this goblin was somehow involved as well? And what if it spread to England?

The very thought of it made him feel sick and helpless, and so, to change the subject, he asked, "Mrs. Wigglepox, how is it that just the three of you live in this huge tree? It seems as though it would hold many more folk of your size."

Mrs. Wigglepox bowed her head and said, "Once there were more of us here. And... well... once we were... bigger, or so our legends say. Something like..."

She glanced over at Oracle, and then said, "But never mind that. The goblins have taken all the others. Once this tree was the home of quite a few of my people – a veritable village of leprechauns, and all related to the Wigglepoxes! My grandmother told me of the days when many a rainbow ended at this tree. But now all are gone, and all their pots of gold are stolen away. I suppose that one day, we will be gone too, and the old tree will close itself up forever."

"But I thought leprechauns were magic and all that. Couldn't you just zap those goblins with lightning bolts or something when they came near?" asked Frederick.

"It's the *Spell*, Frederick. It has robbed us of our gifts, and if they want, sometimes the Witch's people can actually *hide* within the Spell, sneak up on you, and catch you off guard," she said.

"But how could they hide inside a spell?" asked Colleen, joining in the conversation.

"It's hard to explain, but it seems that they can sort of blend in with it at times, like a fox hides in the grass until a mouse comes by, then it leaps out and gobbles it down," she said. "I'm afraid the Spell sometimes makes the Witch's folks rather hard to spot. They become like shadows, especially at night when the darkness deepens. They don't like the sunlight, you know. They can't seem to blend in with the Spell so much when the sun is shining on them. I think it might even hurt them somehow.

"But so many of us have been stolen away and cast in their dungeons because we just didn't see them coming in time. We wandered out at the edge of night among the lengthening shadows, and there we found them waiting for us. At first, we didn't know what was happening, but by the time we did, we were weak and had little strength to fight back."

"Blazight!" said Oracle from the place where he had seated himself. "Scalurns and healooths!"

"Loony," said Frederick under his breath. Then a thought struck him and he said, "Earlier, you said that there were stories here about the Pirate that came to your land. What do those stories say about him?"

"There are quite a few of such tales. They tell of a man who called himself a pirate who came long ago through that very mirror that you came through, and caused great havoc among the little people. He stole our pots of gold and they granted him wishes to get them back. With some of his wishes, he gained great treasures and wealth and power. But for his final wish, something within him changed."

"What did he wish for?" asked Colleen.

"It's said that he wished for great wisdom. He disappeared for some time after that, but returned later, bringing with him all the pots of gold he had taken and all the treasures he had wished for, along with a good many other things that he had taken from our land. He left them here, disappeared through the mirror, and was never seen again."

"So there is great treasure here somewhere!" said Frederick.

"Alas," said Mrs. Wigglepox. "The goblins have taken it all long ago. It was not long after the Pirate left that the goblins came in force. Some said that it was he who somehow led them here from their deep places under the Earth. They had come from time to time before, but now they began to come with greater numbers and with dark magic."

After a moment, Colleen asked. "Mrs. Wigglepox, tell us more about the goblins. I mean, why are they here in your land? Just what *are* they?"

"'Tis a sad tale, lassie," she replied, "but I suppose I should tell you at least some of it. Long ago, there were no goblins in the Land of the Little People. We all lived in peace and were quite content. All the leprechauns and fairies and gnomes and pixies and such – why we had such wonderful times! The grandmothers of our grandmothers used to tell us marvelous tales of the Good Old Days, as we call them, before the Great Wizard opened the Gates."

"The Great Wizard?" interrupted Frederick. "Who was that?"

"Ah!" said Mrs. Wigglepox. "That was Anastazi the Great. He comes into many tales, as does his daughter, Mor-Fae. He was a great Elf Elder, perhaps the greatest of them all, besides their king. And he built the Timeless Hall, as he called it, and in it made the Gates of the Worlds. And when he opened the Gates, the way to each other's worlds was open!"

"You mean that you had never seen anyone besides the little people before then?" asked Colleen.

"That's right, child," she replied. "No one except the Dryads and other such folk, and the Lady, that is. We didn't even know that anyone else existed until one day, a great silver gate appeared in the forest and through it stepped a giant! Or so we thought. It was the Great Wizard himself, all clad in shining blue robes. He had a crown on his head and a white staff in his hand. My people hid from him at first, but soon they found that he was friendly and good, and it was not long before we were freely visiting all the worlds, and learning from them, and they from us. Ah, those were the Good Old Days."

"So, is that how the goblins got here?" asked Frederick.

"Indeed it is," she said. "But the stories say that they were not evil at first. Something terrible happened to them. I don't know the whole story, but it has something to do with the Great Wizard's daughter. A sad tale, at least the part I know. But suffice to say, after Mor-Fae came, it was but a few hundred years before the evil goblins came too. Some say she let them loose from some awful place, and some say she cursed them and they became evil, while others say that she let loose something in *their* world that made them evil. I don't know what the truth is, but she is always in the tales when it comes to the goblins. She's all mixed up in it somehow. But now they are long gone - all of the elves and wizards that is, the Gate is closed, and we are left with the goblins and the Court Witch," she said sadly.

"Gone?" said Frederick. "But where did they go, and why did they leave?"

"Who can say where they went?" she replied. "Probably through the Gate, and they seemed to have locked it behind them. Some say the Gate was destroyed in the Last Battle, for it was supposed to have been at the Wizard's Castle that once stood far to the south of here."

"Do you think that castle is still there?" asked Frederick, a look of wonder on his face.

"Perhaps, but wherever the Gate was, or is, it's said that some of our people were on the other side when it disappeared. We never saw them again. I suppose they made their way to the other worlds and made homes there as best as they could."

"And some *must* have gone to our world," said Colleen excitedly. "Why, we have *loads* of stories of little people where we come from. Those tales must have come about long ago when your folk came to the lands of Men."

"Now those would be stories worth hearing," she said. "You must tell them to me some time soon."

"But what of the elves and wizards?" asked Frederick. "Why did they leave?"

"I think it was because of the Court Witch," said Mrs. Wigglepox. "She's in many a tale too. The elves and wizards fought against the goblins and the Court Witch for many, many years. Over a hundred years, I think! But somehow, in the last battle, a terrible thing happened. It's said that the Witch unleashed some dark magic that nearly destroyed the wizards. They fled for their lives, leaving behind a great many treasures, and after that battle, it was thought that the Court Witch was gone for good, for there was peace for a long while. The castle was laid desolate and was lost, though legends say that it now lays empty in the Burning Sands – a great desert that lies south of the forest. Few tales come out of those lands, but those that do say it's a mystical place. People that go there are *changed* by it. The Court Witch is powerful, but I guess she still couldn't *undo* all the magic that once dwelt there."

"That sounds *marvelous*," said Colleen. "A magic castle with a gate to other worlds!"

"Yes," the little woman replied. "It was, supposedly, a wondrous place. Anastazi the Great, and Mercurus the Wise Wizard, and all sorts of fair and terribly powerful folk all laboring there and inventing magic things and keeping the goblins away from the Forest... But, alas, now they are gone."

"Mrs. Wigglepox," said Colleen, "if we could get to that castle, then maybe we could find that gate and get through it. That could be our way home!"

"It could be, child, but that would be a very long journey. You would have to travel through the whole forest even to reach the desert's edge, and then somehow you would have to find your way through the Burning Sands to the castle. No one knows for sure where it is," she said.

"Do the goblins ever venture into the desert?" asked Colleen. "Where do they live?"

"Somewhere far to the south," she said. "No one goes there. It's far too dangerous."

Frederick didn't like the idea of potentially having to travel right into goblin territory.

"So is that when the goblins started coming into your forest and taking away your people – after the war, I mean?" asked Colleen.

"Well, it took a while and, as I said, we thought that the Court Witch was destroyed. The final battle was a dreadful one. It devastated the whole land south of the Great Hills. It wasn't even a desert before that war. It was green and growing – beautiful fields and meadows and hills and woodlands, and the Great Sea was not so wide. But the dark power that the Witch unleashed laid it bare – or perhaps it was the clash of the powers of the Witch and the wizards that destroyed it, and a great piece of the land just *sank*. It's said that a terribly huge wave swept across the land almost to the Great Hills when that happened. Perhaps it was from that dreadful wall of water that the wizards fled.

"After that, there was no sign of the Witch or goblins for a long, long time. And then the Pirate came, and that is when the Witch showed up again.

"But the goblins began to come slowly – and we were not defenseless, no! The little people had magic too! Why, whenever they would come, we would weave spells of forgetfulness on them and make them lose their way in the forest. We would lead them through paths that ended up back at the desert, so that they never found us or our trees," she said.

"But they are here now," said Frederick. "What happened to your magic?"

Mrs. Wigglepox sighed. "It's the Spell. It overshadows everything in the Forest, and our magic is ever so weak because of it. The goblins and cluricauns and gremlins came, slinking within it like ghosts and shades, and began to take away our pots of gold. That's when our magic began to wane.

"It's also said that she has done something to the Waking Tree, and because of that, all the forests in all the Land are fading. And her spell is spreading. It's like a slow-moving fog that creeps farther and farther year by year. One day, we fear that it will cover the whole world, from the Great Sea in the South to the Northern Ices and beyond."

"The *Waking Tree?* What's that?" asked Colleen.

"Ah!" she said. "The father of the fathers of the fathers of the trees. It was the first tree in our world, you know, and from it all the forests were born."

"Why is it called the *Waking Tree?*" asked Frederick. "Does it keep the other trees awake?"

"Well, not exactly," she said. "It was in that tree that our first ancestors *woke up*, you see. They awoke and found themselves there, inside it, much like we are inside this tree, and it spoke to them and they to it. It was from there that we and the forest spread out to cover all the land, oh so many ages ago. It is said that the Creator planted that tree himself, then made the first little people – two of each of our peoples – and placed them inside it. He placed wisdom and knowledge and power in that tree for us to learn from and use. From there, we and the forest spread across the world.

"But we have not seen the Waking Tree since the war, and we were afraid that it was destroyed. But we think now that it was not destroyed, only lost. We wonder if the Court Witch has found it and cast her black magic upon it. Some say that it was the Pirate who actually found it, sailing the South Sea, and it was from him that the Witch discovered its location. If that's true, maybe we could go and somehow free the Waking Tree from her spell, then our own magic might return. Then we would deal with these goblins!"

She made a fist and slapped her hand with it, looking defiant. But a moment later, a look of hopelessness washed across her face.

Oracle stood and joined their little group. He looked at each of them and said, "Wæcan it, Colligal. Bereofan the Sorcergic, and snatch, scratch the Leople's folclond from the hobgobles."

Frederick rolled his eyes, but Colleen looked hard at him.

"I do wish you could make yourself plain, Oracle," said Colleen. "You are rather hard to understand."

"Mph!" said Oracle, and then in a sing-song voice he chortled out a rhyme.

"Colligal and Fredersmouth!

Side and ring and sail far south!

Amid the sea, lies Witcherisle,

Place of doom and grief and mother's smile."

Having said this, he returned to his place and sat hunched, staring at his shoes.

Mrs. Wigglepox looked at him, sighed, and said, "I have heard tales of long ago that when the gate to *your* world was open, we found the magic of your world mostly faded too. Did some witch or evil sorcerer cast a spell there as well?"

"I don't know about that, but we have many tales of magic in our world. Most people think they are just fairy tales. But these days, some people believe in it, though I doubt that anyone has actually *seen* any magic," said Colleen.

"Never seen magic? Surely there is still *some* magic left in the lands of Men! Or perhaps some wicked witch did cast some vast sleepiness over your world too. How terrible a thing, to live in a world with no magic at all!" said Mrs. Wigglepox sadly.

"Most people think that magic is a bad thing," put in Frederick.

"Well, I suppose that may be true, if you're talking about the Witch's kind of magic – power for the sake of power, no matter its source, or for personal gain or glory. Some of that sort of thing comes from dark powers that ought never to be sought after," said Mrs. Wigglepox. "But the magic of the little people isn't *that* kind of magic. Maybe it ought not to even be called *magic* at all, since that seems to make folks think of the Witch's kind of power. It's more like the gifts that the Creator gave our people at the beginning – gifts to be used for the betterment of all of our people, never for our individual selves. I think that all of the races were given some sorts of gifts like that, though each one was likely of a different kind. But some of them went all wrong and turned what powers and gifts they were given into dark desires that ruined them."

"Do you mean that humans once had magic, and now it's gone?" asked Frederick.

"The Noetic Wolf huffed and puffed and blew their house down," said Oracle from his seat, shaking his head sadly.

They all looked at him, but no one knew what to say in response to his ravings. After a moment, Mrs. Wigglepox looked at Colleen and Frederick, and then said, "It is curious, though. We have not had humans visit our world in a very long time, other than the Court Witch – and we are not sure if she is human or not and, of course, the Pirate. But when humans did come, the stories say that they were powerful wizards. I wonder now if they were wizards back in the world of Men, or if they *became* wizards here? I mean, did the magic in our world awaken something in them that had long been slumbering, and they took that back with them? Or did they find their magic in some other source?"

"You mean," said Frederick, "that *we* might become wizards or something if we are here long enough?"

"I don't know," she said. "I don't think that is what your people were meant to be. But as I've said, our magic is fading too. Once the Wood was alive with magical trees and creatures and little people, and there were rainbows and ..."

They talked on and on through the day, and Mrs. Wigglepox told one tale after another of leprechauns, fairies, gnomes, pixies, goblins, and trolls, of wizards and the Witch. Frederick and Colleen in their turn told her as many tales as they could recall of the same people that appeared in the legends back home.

At last, Mrs. Wigglepox glanced out the door and said, "See here, I'm rambling on and it's getting late. Look, dusk is coming, and the mists are settling. We had better have a quick meal and drink from the spring, then get some rest."

They ate a brief meal of nuts and berries, and then went outside to drink from a small spring that ran near the Wigglepox Tree.

Then Mrs. Wigglepox said, "Lily, Rose, come along, off to bed with you. And you, Colleen, Frederick, get some rest. Oracle – rest well. Tomorrow promises to be a day of adventure!"

After many goodnights and with much fussing about wanting to stay up a little longer, the girls followed their mother through a tiny door and disappeared.

When they had been gone a few moments, Frederick said, "That's just amazing. I still can't believe it. I *wouldn't* believe it if I hadn't seen it with my own eyes. *Little people! Goblins! Wizards and elves and witches!*"

"And more than that," said Colleen. "We're in the *Land* of the Little People. It's all like a dream, somehow. But think of it! My mother is *here*. You can't imagine what that means to me. I've got to get back home somehow and bring my father and brothers to rescue her. I mean, what if those *things* - those goblins - are doing something awful to her? And that evil Court Witch... I just can't imagine what they..."

At this, she began to sob. The full realization of all that had happened to them that day and the knowledge that her mother was here and was in danger came rushing into her heart and mind all at once.

Frederick did not know what to do. He was not good at comforting people, and he knew it. In fact, he couldn't remember ever trying.

But it seemed to him that he ought to say or do *something*. Here was his cousin sitting across from him, crying her eyes out because her mom had been missing for months, and the very day she finds out she is alive, she also finds that she's in the dungeons of some horrible creatures that were apparently quite *evil*.

That word – *evil* – seemed new to him too. He had never really thought about what evil *was* before. But he now supposed that it was what *they* were – the goblins. They were brutish people who took advantage of others for their own pleasures or greed and didn't care, really, whether they lived or died, so long as they got control of them for their own purposes.

And then it dawned on him that *he* was that way. So was his whole family. They had always lived just like that – taking whatever they wanted without regard to what other people thought or needed. And now, somehow, he felt very sorry about it all.

He moved over next to Colleen and put his hand on her shoulder.

"Don't worry, Colleen," he said. "We'll rescue your mom somehow."

"I do hope so," she cried. "But I'm *so* worried about her. And I feel so *small*. We're just kids, Frederick. What can we do to help her?"

Oracle was at her side as well, his hunched form looking up into her lavender eyes.

"Courageroic Colligal must be," he said.

Colleen took a deep breath and nodded. She wiped her eyes and sniffed, steadying herself.

"I'll be okay," she said after a moment.

Frederick fidgeted with a pine needle, unsure what else to say. Then, to break the silence, he said, "Oh, look, Badger needs a bit of grass. Oughtn't we get him settled for the night?"

Colleen wiped her eyes once more, nodded, and together they went outside, pulled up tufts of dry grass, and gave it to the old horse.

"I guess we don't have a brush to brush him down with," said Frederick.

"No, I'm afraid not," said Colleen. "But he'll be all right for a few days. Hopefully, we'll be home by then."

They talked for a while more about their strange day, and Oracle sat quietly, listening. Soon they grew tired and lay down once again, sharing the saddle for a pillow. The tree creaked and groaned as Mrs. Wigglepox bid them goodnight one last time and closed the door. The ground was as soft as moss and both of them fell fast asleep almost immediately.

Late in the night, Frederick woke with a start, sat up, and looked around. But seeing nothing, he lay down again.

He did not know that, just outside, strange eyes glowed in the darkness, and a misshapen nose sniffed around the base of their tree, smelling something new, but finding only strange footprints.

Chapter 13 – Journey to Wales

Aonghus stood beside his brother and sisters on the aft deck as Ireland shrank away in the distance. He studied their faces, seeing the ache of their hearts in their eyes. This journey would be especially hard on Henny, he knew – no one so young should lose their mother and be forced to leave their father all in a single year.

He understood his father's reasons for sending them all away – good reasons – but everything within him cried out against the injustice of it all, and he wondered what kind of Ireland he would return to in a year.

"Say now, where's that other sister of yours... what was her name?" said a voice behind him.

He turned to see Captain Truehart coming across the deck toward them.

"Colleen is her name. She must still be below deck," said Aonghus.

At this, he noticed that Henny looked at the boards on the deck and pretended to study them.

"She's missing a good part of the trip, she is. Why don't you go below and fetch her up here? Perhaps she could steer for a while," said Truehart.

"I'll get her," said Abbe.

"I think I'll come along too," said Henny.

Aonghus watched them go to the door that led below deck, where Henny stopped Abbe and whispered something in her ear. Abbe's eyes went wide and her jaw dropped. They rushed below deck and returned a few moments later without Colleen. Abbe beckoned for Aonghus, and he hurried over to them.

"Henny has something to say," said Abbe, a worried expression on her face.

Henny folded her hands in front of her, shrugged her shoulders, and rubbed her shoe on the deck.

"Well... Colleen isn't on the ship. She got off just before we left," she said quietly.

"What?" said Aonghus rather loudly. "What do you mean, she got off?"

"She told me not to tell," said Henny, her eyes a bit fearful. "She said she had forgotten something and that she would catch the next ship to England with Cousin Rufus and Helga. She promised me she would."

Aonghus stared at her, disbelieving. "Are you sure?" he said.

"Yes, I watched her go. And Frederick followed her too," she said.

"Frederick too? I wonder if Mabel knows?" said Aonghus, worried. "We better go tell her. But first, let's tell the others."

He waved to Bran and Bib, and they excused themselves from Captain Truehart and joined the others.

"What's wrong?" said Bran. "Is Colleen sick or something?"

"No, not sick," said Abbe. "She's not on the ship!"

"What!" said Bib.

"That's right. Henny says she got off just before we left, and Frederick followed her. She said she'd catch the next ship with Rufus and Helga because she forgot something," said Abbe.

"That's just like Colleen," said Bib. "Father is going to ground her for a month!"

"No, he won't," said Aonghus. "I think Colleen had a good reason for going back. What was it, Henny? What did she go back for?"

"She didn't say," said Henny. "But it was really important. I know it was."

"Well, Colleen can take care of herself. It's not that far from the docks back to the farm – just a few miles. But Frederick is another matter. He's liable to get himself lost or something. We better go tell Mabel," said Abbe.

"Right," said Aonghus, and they all headed out to find her.

After looking about the decks, and just double-checking to be sure Frederick was nowhere to be seen, they decided to check her cabin. Upon knocking on the door and hearing Mabel's drawling voice call "Enter!" from within, the five children piled into the room.

Mabel's room was much larger than theirs was, and she was not lying on a hammock, but on a large bed that was adorned with a fluffy-looking mattress and several large pillows. Lovely paintings of sea birds and lighthouses adorned the cabin walls, and a bowl of fruit sat on a lace-covered table, several half-eaten pieces of which lay on a dish of blue china. Mabel herself was eating another piece as she lounged comfortably on the bed.

"Ooh, it's you, children," she crooned. "Come in, if you must. What can I help you with?" She took another bite of her fruit.

"Thank you, Cousin Mabel," began Aonghus. "We need to talk to you about Frederick."

"What has he been doing now?" she said, her mouth still somewhat full. "Is he climbing the masts or swinging from the ropes? I hope not. He's like that, you know – the adventurous type like his father. Why, I remember when..."

"He's not on the ship," cut in Abbe.

For a moment, Mabel looked shocked and stopped chewing. She swallowed, looking hard at their faces, and then chortled. "Don't be silly, of course he's on the ship. Why, I left him up on the deck some hours ago."

"We've looked up there, ma'am," said Bib, "and he's not to be found. Colleen is gone as well."

"Whatever are you saying, child!" Mabel said, a bit more loudly. "Quickly now, spit it out."

"Henny said that the two of them left the ship just before we set sail," said Aonghus.

"Henny, come here, child. Tell me what you saw, quickly!" Mabel's voice was quite aquiver now, and she listened intently as Henny told her that Colleen had forgotten something and said she was going back to get it, and that she would come on the next ship with Cousin Rufus.

"Those little rats!" said Mabel, growing angry. "I'm sure Colleen egged Frederick into leaving the ship. Why, when I get my hands on them, I'll give them a tanning!"

She rolled from the bed, squeezed out of her room, stomped up to the upper deck, and fairly shouted at the captain that both Frederick and Colleen had gotten off the ship and that she would have his commission if he didn't refund her entire fare.

"They both got off the ship?" he replied, coming over to her. "Why, we surely would have noticed that. What say we have a look about the ship? I'll have my men look below deck. Maybe they've wandered into the crew quarters or into the cargo hold. I'll have a bit of a scolding for them if that's where they are. I told 'em not to..."

"Yes, you just do that!" interrupted Mabel.

"Right, then," said the captain, and he walked over to the bell hanging from the center mast and rang it.

The men on the deck gathered 'round.

"Now see here, men," he barked. "Miss Mabel here seems to have misplaced her boy, Frederick, and that little golden-haired girl Colleen as well. Have a look about the ship, down below and all, and see if you can find them. Off you go now."

The group of men started to disperse, when one of them spoke up.

"Was the girl about this high," he held up a hand to his chest, "with long reddish-gold hair, and the boy a bit taller with dark hair?"

"That's them," said Aonghus.

"Well, there were two kids like that who dashed down the gangplank just as I was pulling it in. I figured they were supposed to be going ashore, since you had just called for it," the sailor said. "Anyway, they were in a big hurry. Ran like jack rabbits, down the docks and into the village."

Mabel narrowed her eyes and frowned. "What kind of irresponsible crew do you have, Captain, allowing children to run wild. You shall indeed refund my fare and pay a fee for my trouble."

"Now see here, Miss Mabel. Isn't your husband still there? He's supposed to come on the next ship in a few days. Surely your boy and Colleen can come with him then?"

"That's true, Cousin Mabel," spoke up Henny. "Colleen did promise that she would come on the next ship with cousin Rufus and Helga. Frederick can come too."

Mabel blew heavily through her teeth and said, "I suppose that will have to do, but I shall be reporting this incident to the port authorities!"

"Come, let's go down to my cabin and we'll discuss this," said Truehart. "Back to work, lads!" he shouted to his men, and they all turned, shaking their heads and talking among themselves.

He led her away and through the door which led to his cabin. "You children come too," he called, and they followed.

Truehart's cabin was neither as large nor as comfortable as Mabel's was. Its walls were lined with maps and nets and odd driftwood and starfish and other dried sea creatures. An odd assortment of round glass balls dangled from one net in a corner.

He led Mabel to a chair at a small table and sat in an adjacent chair.

"If Frederick misses the next ship, Truehart, I shall hold you personally responsible!" she said, sitting heavily.

"Don't worry, Mabel," said Aonghus. "Colleen knows the way back to the farm, and the town folk know her. If Frederick is with her, they'll be just fine."

"But why would they leave the ship!" she snapped.

Everyone was silent for a moment.

"Well, no matter," said Truehart. "No matter. We can't turn back now, in any case. I'm on a contract that I have to keep. No way around it, ma'am. If I'm late with this shipment, I could lose me ship. And if your boy is safe, as these good folk say, I think there's no reason to sail back. And besides, with the winds the way they are, it might take us twice as long even to make the attempt. Why, it could be eight or ten hours just getting there, maybe more. By then there'd be no tellin' where those kids would be."

Mabel harrumphed and said, "You most certainly shall *not* turn back. I do not wish to be late to the ladies' ball in two days!"

"Don't worry, Cousin Mabel," said Bran, although Mabel looked anything but worried. "Colleen will take care of Frederick and make sure he gets to the farm safely. Then Rufus will bring them both along on the next ship."

With many more words, and not a few promises of decent food and repayment, Mabel finally calmed down and said that she would retire to her cabin. Captain Truehart said he would send her an extra meal that evening, along with some wine and brandy, and deliver it himself, and this seemed to settle her considerably.

After seeing her to her room, Aonghus gathered his brother and sisters in the girls' room to discuss the situation.

"There's nothing for it," he said. "We'll just have to trust Colleen to get them both safely to the farm and to come on the next ship like she promised. The captain won't sail back, and there's no way we could swim back, or even row back in the dingy – we just aren't good on the sea."

"But what if something happens and she and Frederick don't show up with Rufus?" asked Bib.

"We'll just have to cross that bridge if we come to it. If they're not here in a few weeks like they're supposed to be, then I'll sail back on the next ship to Ireland myself and find out what's going on," he said. "But we'll just have to trust in Colleen's good sense and pray she and Frederick will be all right."

They talked on for some time until Aonghus turned the conversation to what they might discover in Wales.

"I hear the headmasters of the schools are very strict," said Bib, "but that they have wonderful libraries."

"And they have great sports, such as rugby," said Aonghus. "I wonder if our school will have a team."

"Do they beat their children at their schools?" asked Henny.

Aonghus picked her up in his massive arms and looked her in the eyes.

"Now don't you worry about that, Henny. If anyone lays as much as a finger on you, they will have me to deal with," he said seriously.

"And me," said Bran.

"And us as well," agreed Abbe and Bib.

"We'll all stick together," said Aonghus, "and have no secrets. Agreed?"

"Agreed," they all said.

After a bit more talk of what lay ahead, Aonghus and Bran headed to their room, leaving the girls to lie in their hammocks.

They found their room much less comfortable, and after unsuccessfully attempting to sleep in his hammock, Aonghus finally curled up on the floor to wait for the dawn. It didn't come too soon.

Chapter 14 – Morning in the Wigglepox Tree

Morning came, and with it, Colleen heard Mrs. Wigglepox singing an opening song. The tree opened with a creak, and sunlight streamed in, waking Frederick as well.

He yawned and sat up, and Colleen giggled at him.

"You have pine needles in your hair again," she teased.

"So do you," he said, grinning.

They both laughed and helped one another pick them out.

"Oh my," said Colleen. "I have no comb with me. I'm sure my hair will look like a rat's nest soon."

"It's fine," said Frederick.

Her hair fell across her shoulders as if she had not slept at all, and he shook his head.

"Wish my mop would behave like that," he said, running his fingers through his tangles.

Colleen only smiled.

"Well, children," said Mrs. Wigglepox. "I can't offer you any hot cakes or muffins, but I suppose there are still some berries and nuts left from yesterday. You had best eat something before we set out."

"Yes, I suppose we should eat something. Badger will need something too," said Colleen.

She and Frederick led the horse outside to where a small patch of grass grew by the spring and set him to graze, and there she found Oracle, standing some ways off on a large, flat stone, facing the rising sun.

"How did you get out here?" asked Frederick.

The old leprechaun ignored him and continued to gaze silently east.

Colleen and Frederick shook their heads, sat down, drank from the spring, and washed their faces.

Then a thought struck Colleen, and she said, "I wonder how that crystal ball ever came to be a family heirloom? It's a *magic* thing, and like we were saying, there's not much of that back home."

"Maybe there's more than we know," said Frederick. "I mean, it's not logical or anything, but maybe a long time ago there was more of it, and some seems to have lingered on from that earlier age – like that mirror and the crystal ball, and those – what did your grandpa call them – *entrances*? Maybe that big stone with the swirls on it really was a marker. It marked the place where the mirror stood."

"And other things seem to have lingered on too," said Colleen. "Just think about where we are! The old legends talk about these things, and here we are walking among them. Little people and goblins!"

"And a nasty lot they are," said Mrs. Wigglepox, coming outside. "They've put a plague on our land, what with their black ooze and all. They spread disease and death wherever they go."

Colleen was thoughtful for a moment and then said, "I've been thinking about it – it was shortly after Mother disappeared that the famine started. Loads of people have been starving since then."

"Oh, dear," said Mrs. Wigglepox. "No doubt it was a plague put on the land by that creature, or it stirred one up that had already started. It must have been a goblin chieftain to have such dark magic. They are horrible creatures, all misshapen and distorted, and terribly cruel, and they carry in their very bodies some disease or evil."

Images of the goblin running about Ireland, cursing the land and its people flashed through Colleen's mind. It was still back there – still performing its mischief. She knew she had to get home somehow and warn everyone – to tell them what had happened, and make them believe her somehow. But she also somehow had to get help for her mother.

"We've got to get to that castle," she said. "We just have to. It's our only hope."

"It will be a hard and dangerous journey, child," said Mrs. Wigglepox. "You will need to find shelter each night for both of you and your horse... and for us."

"You mean you'll go with us?" asked Colleen.

"Well, I could not let you go off on your own. I know these woods as well as any leprechaun around. In fact, we may be the only leprechauns around to help you out, at least for some days' walk."

"Thank you, Mrs. Wigglepox! How can I ever repay you?" said Colleen.

"No thanks are necessary. I've been sitting in this tree hiding long enough. My daughters and I will come along and do what we can. At least we can be your guides, and perhaps you can help us find my husband as well," she said.

"Now, let's talk a bit about the journey," she continued. "If I'm not mistaken,

I'll bet your horse could make it to Nidavellir, just south of here, by this evening."

"Where?" said Frederick.

"Nidavellir. Some call it the Dark Fields, or the House of Mysteries. It's was built ages ago, during the time of the wizards, but it's been long abandoned. I don't think even the goblins go in there. It's said that it's haunted by the spirits of the wizards who once dwelt there, imprisoned in it by the Court Witch. But I don't know if that's true or not. But it is a huge house – a mansion, really, and legends say that it had dark tunnels far, far beneath it – the Dark Fields that are now haunted. Since the goblins fear it, it just might be the place to head to today."

"Then that is where we must go first," Colleen replied. "If there's any hope of rescuing Mother – and Mr. Wigglepox – then we might as well be on our way."

"Brilliant," said Frederick, not fully convinced that a haunted house was better than a forest full of goblins.

"I'm with you, Frederick," said Lily.

"And me too!" said Rose, clapping her hands.

Colleen and Mrs. Wigglepox looked at them and smiled.

"Well, now, here we are - an old horse, two human children, two little people children, and an old little people woman off to fight goblins and a wicked witch! But maybe we'll have a few tricks up our sleeves as well," said Mrs. Wigglepox. "The magic of the little people may be down, but it's not gone yet. And there are other little people in this forest who have not yet been captured, or so say the birds that are left. Perhaps we will meet some of them along our way."

"What about Oracle?" asked Colleen.

She turned to the little man and said, "Oracle, I can't ask you to come with us. Perhaps you could stay here in Mrs. Wigglepox's tree. You would be safe here."

Oracle was silent for a moment and then turned, climbed from the rock, and hobbled over to them. Then he gazed at them with his deep-seated eyes and waited.

"Does that mean he's coming with us?" asked Rose.

"I'm not sure," said Lily. "But he is an unusual old chap. I think he's quite dear and his company would be grand."

So it was decided. For a long time, they sat and discussed their plans and Mrs. Wigglepox spoke with a bird that happened by and landed on Oracle's head, and with a fox that had silently slipped into their circle, and nuzzled against the old leprechaun. There wasn't much news from the forest. But before long, they had gotten together a plan, of sorts, although they still did not know what chance they might have of succeeding at it.

First, they would go south toward the House of Mysteries, which Mrs. Wigglepox thought they could reach in a single day if they rode Badger hard enough.

From there, they would keep on toward the south, toward the Valley of Fairies, where it was said that the Lady Danu now dwelt, and she might be able to give them some aid, or at least advice. But that would be a three-day journey, and they would need to find help along the way. "We had better," said Mrs. Wigglepox. "We don't want to be caught outside after nightfall."

"And what if this Lady can't help us?" Frederick asked.

"Then we keep going," said Colleen.

And to keep going meant going through the Great Hills, and from there, across the desert of Burning Sands, where the Wizard's Castle was said to be. If they could find this magical Gate of Anastazi and get home, then they would. But if not, they would cross the desert to the sea, where the Island of the Waking Tree and the fortress of the goblins were both said to be.

If there were some way to find the Waking Tree and break the dark spell that enchanted it, then perhaps the Witch's hold over them would be broken. Then they would not be alone, but have all the magic of the little people to aid them. This was Mrs. Wigglepox's one hope, for, she said, there was no way to enter the goblin fortress alone.

"It's a slim chance," said Colleen, "but at least it's a chance."

Frederick said little, but wondered how they were going to get to those hills off in the distance, or how they would ever cross a desert. Even if they did make it to the sea, how in the world would they find a boat and then somehow explore the sea, searching for some lost island? And then, even if they found it, how that was supposed to help them find Colleen's mother, he couldn't imagine. But he kept these thoughts to himself, and gave a practical suggestion.

"We had better map out our whole journey," he said, "so that we can find our way back to the Wigglepox Tree. At least here, we can live on nuts and berries for a while if we have to."

To this, they all agreed. Fortunately, there had been an old parchment in

Badger's saddlebag as well as a quill and ink that Mr. McGunnegal kept there to keep track of his bartering. One side of the parchment was blank and, on this, Frederick began to draw his map, beginning with the Wigglepox Tree.

Chapter 15 – A Foreign Land

Abbe opened one eye and looked up, sensing someone watching her. A small gray mouse sat perched on the rope that secured her hammock to the wall. It twitched its nose, sniffing the air as it stared at her.

"Hello there," she said to the mouse. "Come here, let me have a look at you."

The mouse scurried down the rope, hopped onto her leg, and ran onto her outstretched hand. It stood on its hind legs, squeaked, and pawed at the air.

"What a handsome fellow you are," said Abbe.

"Who are you talking to?" groaned Bib.

"This mouse," she replied. "I think we're getting near the shore. He's seems to think the air smells different."

Bib popped open both eyes and looked over at Abbe holding the mouse.

"Ugh, how can you do that?" she said.

"What?" said Abbe.

Suddenly, there was a knock at the door. Henny, who had been watching quietly from her hammock, got up and opened it. Aonghus poked his head in the door.

"Breakfast bell just rang," he said.

The mouse looked over at him, squeaked loudly, and scampered away.

"Thanks, Aong. We'll be there in a minute," said Abbe.

"See you there," he said, and left.

Abbe and Bib climbed from their hammocks, stretched, and combed out their long, red locks.

"Get any sleep, Henny?" said Abbe as they walked down the hall.

"Plenty," she replied, "but those mice woke me up a few times. They kept running up and down your hammock ropes and sniffing you."

Abbe smiled. "I like mice," she said.

The ship's mess was a large room with wooden tables and benches lined with rough-looking sailors who glanced up at them as they entered. They paused, unsure of the hard looks they were getting, until a weathered old man who sported a wide scar across his forehead rose from his seat and approached them.

"Cap'in told us you'd be joinin' us this mornin'. See that there ugly feller by that big pot?" he said, pointing to one corner of the room. "That's Onion, the ship's cook. He's stirred up some mean gruel if you care for it. Just go over and introduce yourselves."

Abbe noticed the wry smile on the man's face and the sniggers that passed among the sailors. "It's good stuff!" called a gruff voice from one table. "Put hair on your chest, it will."

Laughter erupted around the room, and the tension that had hung in the air vanished. The men went back to their meal, and Abbe led the others over to the man who was stirring the pot.

"Good morning," said Aonghus. "Might we have a bite to eat, please?"

"Don't do it," called a skinny sailor. "We never know what he puts in that pot." The men laughed again.

"Yeah, look what it did to Skinny," called another rather round man, pointing at the first.

"Doesn't seem to have hurt you, Plumps," said another. "You seem to thrive on it pretty well."

"Pay 'em no mind," said the cook, a big man with thick forearms and a broad face. "They've no appreciation for fine food."

He smiled, showing a gap in his brown teeth, then grabbed a bowl from a rack beside him. He wiped it out with his apron, filled it with a white mush from the pot, and handed it to Abbe.

"There are spoons," he said, pointing to a barrel filled with wooden spoons, which looked none too clean.

"Thank you," said Abbe, looking down at the gruel. "I'm sure it's … delicious."

"'Course it is!" shouted another man from the tables, prompting groans and gags and more laughter. As the cook served Bib, Henny, Bran, and Aonghus, the sailors struck up a song about eating the cook's food, singing in loud and raucous voices.

Oh, life on the sea is quite a boon,
The waves and the wind can make you swoon.
Lucky are we to be so free,
And eat from Onion's fine galley.

Onion is fat and his food is fine,
He scrapes off the worms and peels off the rind.

And rarely a rat or beetle is seen,
Swimming in Onion's fine cuisine.

If waves make you sick and spray makes you sneeze,
It's nothing compared to Onion's rare feed.
Colors so rare and smells so unique,
If you can down it, we'll know you're a freak.

Then they started over and sang it even more loudly than before, then lifted their cups in the air and shouted, "To Onion!" then laughed all the more.

"Quite a crew," said Aonghus as they sat eating their breakfast.

"The food's not that bad, though," said Bran, tasting the mush. "Better than some we've had this year."

"True enough," said Aonghus.

They had no sooner finished their meal when a bell clanged and the crew rose from their benches and tossed their bowls and spoons and cups in a great heap on one table.

Abbe looked at the mess, then saw two boys who couldn't have been more than her own age of fifteen come out and begin to pile the dirty dishes onto wooden carts.

One of them with blond hair and blue eyes glanced over at her, removed his cap, and bowed slightly.

"Hello, ma'am," he said, smiling broadly.

His partner elbowed him and they went back to work, but she noticed that he kept glancing her way.

"Come on, Ab," said Bran, pulling her after him as they left the mess.

Abbe followed behind the others, but had a strange urge to go back to the dining hall and help the boys. But as she climbed to the upper deck and looked out over the water to the southeast, she could just make out the outline of land on the horizon.

"I see it!" said Henny excitedly. "Is that England?"

"Wales," said Bib.

"Looks like we'll be there soon," said Bran. "Perhaps this afternoon."

"Aye, aye," said a voice behind them, and they turned to see Captain Truehart coming toward them.

"Won't be long now," he said cheerfully. "And I suppose you youngsters will be going off to school. Even you, Aonghus?"

"Yes, sir," said Aonghus. "My father would like for me to take the opportunity to study agriculture and bring back some new farming techniques to Ireland."

"Ah, a fine, fine thing farming is. Me own uncle is a farmer, one of the best in England," said Truehart. "And what of you, lad – Bran, isn't it? What will you be studying?"

"Well, seeing that I'm a fair hand at hunting – much to my sister's chagrin," he replied, winking at Abbe, "Dad thinks I might look into learning both the blacksmith and weapons-making trade. He says that to make a plow and a bow and use them both will take me far. But I can already do both. Dad thinks that these English folk might have some ideas that we haven't heard of, though," said Bran.

"And what of you, young Abbe, what will you be looking into at school?" the captain asked with a smile.

"The veterinary trade, to be sure, sir," she said. "I love animals." She stuck out her tongue at Bran, but then smiled at him.

"And I will be studying the sciences," piped in Bib.

"And I'm going to learn to read better!" said Henny.

"Good, good for you all," said Truehart heartily. "I think you'll find your time in school just grand." He gave them all a big toothy smile. "And I hear it's the Ismere school that you're off to," he continued. "I know one of the teachers there. Professor Atlas McPherson is his name. A fine old chap... if a bit odd. One of his boys went sailin' with me some years back." The bit about the professor being a bit odd he said rather under his breath so that only Henny, who was nearest him, heard what he had said.

"How's he odd?" asked Henny, her innocent eyes looking up at him.

"Well, now!" he replied. "Nothing in a bad way, you know. It's just that he collects odd things, you might say. Has all sorts of trinkets and oddities in his office."

Truehart then bent down low and whispered, forcing the lot of them to lean in close to hear, "And he's got a door in that office of his where his boy, Charlie, told me he keeps even stranger things – old things that come from ancient civilizations and castles and graves and things like that. I suppose he's some sort of archaeologist, like your cousin Rufus. Come to think of it, that's probably how Mr. Buttersmouth got you all into the school – had a contact there in old McPherson. And, oh! He owns a ship! A bit of an old dumpy ship, mind you, but a ship nonetheless!"

Then he stood straighter with a slight groan and said, "Well, anyway, you say hello to him for me, right? But if he asks about Charlie, tell him that I haven't heard hide or hair of him since he sailed away for Bermuda."

"I've heard strange things about that place," said Bib.

The captain glanced around, and then leaned down again, an odd look in his eye.

"Aye," he said in a hushed voice. "Bermuda is a piece of ocean that gets 'em, it's said. Strange things happen there. Whole ships get swallowed up and are never seen again."

Truehart grinned, glanced about once again, and then continued, "Once, when I was just a lad, and was a deck hand on a ship sailing in the waters somewhere southwest of Bermuda, we spotted something floating in the ocean. We sent out a row boat and found it was a piece of ship, and there was a man floating on it!"

"Was he dead?" asked Henny, her eyes wider than ever.

"No, lass, he was alive, but his clothes were torn to shreds, and he was baked near to death from the salt and sun. We took him aboard and they found he was gripping a stone chest in his arms. Wouldn't let go of it! Kept mumbling about some great door and a throne and a dead man. At times, he would seem to speak in gibberish. We figured he was out of his mind from the sun and the sea.

"But one night, I slipped into the cabin where the man was sleeping and hid behind a barrel to watch him."

"What happened?" whispered Henny.

"Well, quiet as a mouse, I slipped over to the bedside and found that the chest was unlocked. I peeked inside and saw some scrolls and a compass and a dagger. I pulled one of those scrolls out and had a look. It was real strange – written in a funny language with all sorts of symbols, and it was a map of a land I've never sailed to before. Big place, and far as I can remember, it was situated right there between Africa and South America. Must have been some old map made before folk got good at making maps. There's no island there that's that big today.

"Anyway, that's when the man woke up and grew angry. I ran out the door right quick and up on deck again.

"But it was after that the man seemed better and was able to tell his tale. He said that his ship had been sailing to South America, but had lost all wind for three weeks and they sat drifting day after day. In all that time, it never rained and their supplies began to run low. But one night, a frightful storm suddenly blew up and drove the ship like they were in a hurricane. They never saw the rocks that they hit until they were well-nigh upon them, and then it was too late. Their ship was smashed to pieces, and he was swept overboard into the sea."

"And what happened to the crew?" asked Bran.

"He never found out. Never found any of 'em. But he said that he was driven by the waves to the island - was washed right into a rocky cave. He crawled inside to escape the storm and waited through the night, half dead from exhaustion," said Truehart.

"But you said you found him in the ocean," said Bib. "How did he get off the island?"

"Ah, now that's a tale! He wouldn't tell anything about this treasure he had been mumbling about, nor about the door. A huge door in the cave, he had said in his madness. And he wouldn't say much about the chest – said that he had saved it. When they asked him his name, he said it was ..."

But before he could finish, there was a loud clanging of a bell, and the captain straightened himself with a grunt and looked about.

"Ah, sorry, lads, lasses. It's time for inspections. We'll talk more in a bit. A tidy ship gets better trade prices, you know."

With a wink, he limped away toward his first mate, who was waiting for him by the main mast.

"That's quite a tale," said Abbe to Aonghus. "I'm going to ask him what that man's name was just as soon as I can."

"I was thinking the same thing," he replied.

But the chance to speak to Truehart never came. As land drew steadily nearer, the crew busied themselves with cleaning the decks and coiling ropes and folding nets and making the ship look generally neat. Each time Abbe thought she might have a chance to speak to him for a few moments, he spotted something or other that needed doing and was barking orders to his crew.

When at last the port was in sight and it would only be a few minutes before they docked, Abbe took Aonghus by the arm and said, "Come on."

They climbed to the upper deck where the captain was at the wheel, still calling out this or that command.

"Captain," said Abbe, "that shipwrecked sailor you were telling us about – the one you rescued by Bermuda – who was he? Is he still alive today?"

"Of course he is. Didn't I mention it? He's your professor – Professor McPherson," said Truehart.

"McPherson!" said Abbe.

"Aye, the very same," he replied.

"Does he still have the stone chest and all that?" asked Aonghus.

The captain looked sidelong at them for a moment and then said, "Well, that I don't know. His son, Charlie, may have taken it with him. At least, he had a copy of that map I was telling you about when I saw him last. But if you talk to old McPherson about it, mind yourself. He loved his boy very much, ever the more so since his wife passed on some fourteen years back giving birth to their second son, God rest her soul. And when Charlie decided to sail to Bermuda to look for that island, he was at odds with the old man about it. I don't think they parted on very good terms."

"We'll remember that, sir," said Aonghus. "Thanks very much for your kindness."

He extended his hand, which the captain took and shook vigorously.

"My, but you've got a powerful grip, lad!" said Truehart with a grin, rubbing his hand. "You'd make a fine sailor. If you ever want to join my crew, come and look me up!"

"Thank you, sir. Thanks very much!" said Aonghus.

"Well, now, best be getting to business. Look here now, we're bringing her in to dock," said Truehart.

Two dinghies had been let down over the side with ropes fastened to their sterns and tied to either side of the ship. Four strong men in each were slowly rowing, towing the ship toward the docks, where Aonghus could see the dock men waiting to tie her to tall wooden posts.

Captain Truehart busied himself with barking orders and the ship drew nearer and nearer. When they were close enough, several sailors threw thick ropes to the waiting men, who caught them and pulled hard to inch the ship closer.

"I'm going below to get my things together," said Aonghus. "Want to tell the others?"

"Right," she said, and went down to her brother and sisters on the lower deck.

"You'll never believe what we found out," she said to them. "Professor McPherson, who we're going to have at the school, is the sailor that Captain Truehart rescued."

"Brilliant!" said Bib, "What a story he'll have to tell!"

"Well, at least going off to school isn't turning out so bad after all. I just hope Colleen gets here soon enough," said Abbe. "Come on, then, let's get our things together."

She led them below and they gathered up their belongings and then went to Mabel's room to see if she needed any help. They found her sitting in a padded chair directing two sailors who were struggling to haul a sizable trunk toward the door.

"What have you got in this thing, ma'am?" asked one of the sailors, a big brawny man. It feels as though it's packed full of rocks!"

"Those are my personal effects," said Mabel in her drawling voice. "Please be careful with that."

The two men, huffing and puffing, carried the trunk through the door, and the McGunnegal children moved aside to let them through. As they began to struggle up the steps toward the deck, the contents of the chest shifted, and the sailor on the bottom lost his footing and began to fall backward, grimacing with fear and letting out a yell as the heavy box came crashing down on him.

In that moment, Aonghus, seeing what was happening, leaped forward, catching the chest with one hand and the man with another.

"Are you all right?" asked Aonghus as the man stood up and looked at him in amazement.

The other sailor had put his end of the chest down on the steps and gawked at Aonghus as well.

"Here, let me help you with that," he said casually. Taking the chest, he lifted it easily, and the sailor quickly moved out of his way. Up the stairs he went and placed it on the deck while the other children, Mabel, Henry, and the other sailor followed behind.

"Why, lad!" said the man who had slipped. "I've never in all my days seen anyone as strong as you! Name's Jones, Harry Jones, and I'm indebted to you." He held out his hand to Aonghus.

Aonghus took his hand and shook it. "Aonghus McGunnegal," he said.

Harry Jones, who prided himself among the sailors as having as powerful a grip as any man, withdrew his hand and rubbed it. "Good Lord, son! Where *do* you get your grip from?"

"My father, I suppose," he said. "He's a bigger man than I am."

"If I didn't know better, I would swear I've met a hero from the past – like someone who walked out of a legend!" said Jones, laughing. "I've never felt such strength!"

Aonghus looked down, embarrassment rising in his cheeks. "It's just from working the farm all day long."

"Well, listen here, Aonghus. The boys and I are going to the Gull this afternoon for a few rounds after we finish loading the ships. That's the pub right down there on the wharf," said the sailor, pointing to a gray building some distance away that had a chipped and flaking painting of a sea gull on a large sign above the door. "How about you join us? They always have arm wrestling matches, winner take all that's bet. I'm sure you could beat any man, even Bob Watchford, who's never lost a match."

"I'm traveling with my family here," he replied, "and we're heading to school after we leave the ship. I suppose we will be traveling on now."

"No, no," said a voice behind them. It was Mabel. "After that horrid trip, we will be staying the night at the Five Springs Inn, a fine establishment. You *will* need to earn your room and board for the night. So go and wrestle with the ruffians and earn a few silver pennies. It's that or sleep in the barn."

"The Five Springs!" said Jones. "That'll be a pretty penny for the lot of you to stay at! But if I don't miss my guess, you'll earn that and more if you come down to the Gull. I'll keep an eye out for you."

He winked and bent down to pick up an end of the heavy chest. The other sailor joined him, and together they heaved it up and struggled carefully down the gangplank with their burden and, to their dismay, found that they had to lift it onto the top of a coach.

Aonghus followed them down and, with his help, they easily placed it on top of the coach, which creaked and sagged under the weight.

"What *is* in that chest?" whispered Bran to the others as Mabel and Henry waddled down the plank toward the coach, watching as other bags and chests were loaded on top and in the sagging vehicle.

"Probably stuff they stole from the farm," whispered Abbe. "I'll bet it *is* filled with rocks – rocks that have all those runes and carvings on them. Dad said he took some. My guess is that they're pretty valuable to people like Rufus or he wouldn't have packed away so many of them."

"I don't remember that big chest coming on board with us," said Bib.

"She must have sent it on ahead so that we wouldn't be suspicious," said Abbe.

Mabel heaved herself into the coach, barely squeezing her large belly through the door, and Henry followed behind. Aonghus poked his head in, frowned, and motioned for his brother and sisters to come. He lifted Henny aboard and she climbed in among the bags next to Henry, who scowled.

"Looks like the rest of us will have to ride on the outside," he said, but then saw that there was only room for two.

"Ladies first!" he said to Abbe and Bib, and he helped them climb up next to the driver. "We'll just run alongside."

"It's quite a ways, lads," said the driver. "You can hang onto the back if you like. Only, be careful."

"I'd rather walk," said Bran. "I've been cooped up on that ship too long."

"Aye," said Aonghus. "And I say we race!"

Placing their belongings on top of the carriage, and seeing that everyone was ready, the driver cracked his whip and the four-horse team surged forward, straining at first, but then pulling easier as the carriage moved.

"Where is this Five Springs Inn?" Aonghus asked the driver as he and Bran trotted along beside the horses.

"It's clear across town. You follow this street to Center Circle, then take Roadham Road until it leaves town. The Five Springs is about a mile outside of town," he said.

Abbe watched as Aonghus and Bran looked at each other, nodded, and took off at a run. Seeing the boys speed ahead, she let out a low, fluttering whistle, and all four horses immediately began to gallop at full speed. The road they were on was straight and paved with smooth cobblestones, and Abbe laughed as her long, red hair flew behind her in the wind.

From inside the carriage came a muffled cry from Mabel and a giggle from Henny.

Now the horses were running full tilt and caught up with Aonghus and Bran.

"We're right on your tail!" shouted Bib to the boys, who both looked back in surprise, then looked at each other and, with a great surge of energy, ran even faster.

The surprised coach driver had by now gotten a grip on himself, but could not rein in the horses. He shouted at them and pulled, but they raced on, spurred ahead by some unseen force. For several moments, they ran, until Abbe, seeing that they would not catch her running brothers, whistled again and the horses slowed to a trot.

The driver eyed her suspiciously as he regained control, but she only smiled at him and looked about innocently.

The boys had now disappeared from sight and, for a good while, the coach rode on quietly. When they reached the edge of town, the boys came racing back down the road at a dead sprint, flying past them, with Bran beating Aonghus by a step.

They both trotted back beside the moving coach, breathing heavily but smiling. "Beat you again, big brother!" laughed Bran.

"Only by a step!" he said. "We'll have a rematch in the morning!"

"Whatever you say," he laughed.

"Do they always run like that?" the driver asked Abbe. "They're incredible!"

"It comes from running over the farm all the time," she said. "When you have six children and only one horse, you end up doing a lot of running."

"Still!" said the driver. "They outran the horse team, and I've never seen these horses run so hard!"

Abbe just smiled and shrugged, but that night the driver, over his pint of ale, told of the two boys who outran his team of horses, and many a townsman said that he had seen them racing through the streets like no horse or deer or fox had ever run.

Chapter 16 – Five Springs Inn

Aonghus jogged next to Bran and the carriage carrying their sisters and cousins. He glanced at his brother and shook his head.

"Don't you ever sweat or get tired?" he said, mopping his forehead with his sleeve.

"Can't say I ever have," said Bran, grinning.

"You are a freak," said Aonghus with a laugh.

"Would you look at that?" said Bib from her seat, pointing forward as they pulled from the street onto a smooth, multicolored cobblestone pavement that ringed an ornate marble building.

In the middle of this wide circle were five pools lined with white stone.

"Guess that's why it's called the Five Springs Inn," said Aonghus.

As they pulled up to the front door, a butler, dressed in coat and tails, walked up to the coach, opened the door, and put his nose in the air. Mabel squeezed herself backward out of the coach.

"Welcome to the Five Springs, Ms. Mabel, Henry, and..." he paused, eying the McGunnegals' shabby clothes, sniffed, then said, "and guests. Lunch will be served within the hour, ma'am."

"Good, good. And I need a large bath prepared as well. That ship was wretchedly dusty," she drawled.

"Very well, then. And will your... your guests be joining you for lunch?" he asked.

"Oh. Well, I had not thought of that," she said. "Children, did you bring anything to eat with you?" she asked in a sickly sweet voice.

"No, ma'am," said Abbe.

"Careless of you," she replied, dismissing them with a wave of her hand. "I suppose they could eat with the servants at a reduced fee?"

The butler rolled his eyes and sighed. "Yes, ma'am. I will make arrangements."

"Thank you, my good man," said Mabel, and slipped him a coin.

"Now!" she said more sternly to the children. "Help unload the coach and bring my things to my room for me. There now, that's right."

They all loaded their arms with as much as they could carry, with Aonghus and Bran easily handling the huge chest. It was locked with a large iron key lock, and Bran whispered to Bib, "Do you think you could unlock this thing and get a look inside?"

"No problem," she whispered back, and pulled an old hairpin from her hair. Shifting her load of bags to one arm, she walked beside the trunk on the side with the lock.

"Slow down!" she said as she fumbled to get the hairpin in the lock keyhole. They did, and within a moment, there was a click as the big lock fell open.

By now, Mabel had made her way inside with the butler and, seizing the opportunity, Bib lifted the lid and looked inside.

"Clothes!" she whispered.

"No way," whispered Bran back. "This thing must weigh a couple hundred pounds! Dig around in there, quick!"

Bib handed her bags to Abbe, who was now quite overloaded, and dug beneath the clothes in the chest. She pursed her lips, narrowed her eyes, and pulled out a heavy brown sack.

"It's rocks from our farm, all right," she said, opening it and pulling out a white chunk of stone. "And they all have those runes on them."

"So, we were right," said Abbe. "He took more than a couple of them – he took loads! But quick, shut the lid!"

The butler had appeared at the door, and Bib, not having time to put the sack of rocks back in the chest, quickly locked the chest, and cradled the heavy bag in her arms.

"Lazy child," snorted the butler at Bib. "I can see that you will amount to nothing. You should take a lesson from your sister here, who is carrying at least three times what you are."

Then he looked them over, sniffed again, stuck his nose in the air, and said, "Follow me. And you boys, clean your shoes before you enter."

He led them up a flight of stairs to Mabel's rather luxurious room and said, "Leave the lady's effects here, and then go down to the kitchen. It is in the back of the Inn. The chief cook has jobs for you to do to earn your supper." Then he left.

"Earn our supper?" asked Henny. "What do we have to do?"

Aonghus knelt down next to her and pushed her long golden hair out of her eyes.

"Now don't you worry, little sprite. I'm going to take care of you. It might just be a few dishes or something. It'll be fun, you'll see." And he winked at her and the others.

Following the sumptuous smells of cooking food, they soon found the kitchen, where a very fat cook bustled from pot to pot, mixing, tasting, adding spices, and guiding several other cooks in making lunch for the rich guests who were visiting the inn.

"Ah!" he bellowed as they entered. "Stay out of the way until cleanup time. Over there by that wall will be fine." And he waved them to a far wall away from the stoves.

Soon, plates and dishes, heaped with chickens and roast beef and succulent vegetables were loaded onto carts by servers and rolled out to the dining area.

Henny's eyes were wide, and they all licked their lips as the wonderful smells rolled by. An hour passed, and the carts began to return, laden with dirty dishes and silverware. These were unloaded in the sinks, and re-loaded with plates full of pies and cakes and teas.

"To the dishes now!" bellowed the cook a moment later. "And see to it that you don't chip any of the tea cups! Come on, now, move along!"

"Come on," said Aonghus.

They gathered around the two massive sinks, with Henny standing on a chair, and washed and dried dishes until their hands were wrinkled and their clothes soaked and soapy. As they worked, Bran struck up an old song that their mother and father had taught them, and they all sang together as they worked.

A long ago stranger did visit our land,
Her name, fair Orlaithe the Gold.
No man had ever seen such a maid,
For her beauty was beyond what can be told.

Long did she walk on the Emerald's fair shore,
Greeting many a folk as she went.
She found that war made them glad, but their songs were all sad,
And the maiden she wept when they sang their laments.

Now the Gold One she spied a tall, red haired man.
'Twas Cian, whose strength was renowned.
'Twas love at first sight, and they married that night,
And in that same year, their fair Lucy was born.

But one dark night came a band from the sea,

Forty pirates stole Orlaithe away.
And Cian pursued and did slay all but three,
But mortally wounded he lay. But mortally wounded he lay.

On bloody sands he did watch his fair maid,
As they stole from the shore to the sea.
And the pirates did carry his true love away,
And left him to die as he called out her name.

But Cian did crawl to his home that same night,
And fell by his little lass' bed.
And with his last breath, he did cry out and bless
Little Lucy with all of his remaining strength.

Now Lucy was taken by friends and was raised
And ne'er was so fair a green-eyed maid.
Her golden hair shone in the sun like its rays,
And Lucy McLochlan ran like a deer in the glade.

Lucy could sing and make grown men just weep,
Her voice filled with magic and power.
And all men would stop to hear her fair songs,
And women and children would all sing along.

But Lucy's stepparents told her one day,
How her father was slain and her mother away'ed.
And Lucy did run to the sand and the sea,
And gazed out and wondered where her mother might be.

Then one lonely day, she did sail away
In search of her mother, long lost to the sea.
And the Emerald Isle lost its fairest of maids
To a life of long wandering, hoping, and dreams.

As their song ended, Aonghus noticed that the kitchen had grown silent, and even the fat cook was wiping his eyes on his apron.

"Come, come now," he choked. "Eat something and leave the rest of those dishes for later."

He went over to them, took Henny in his round arms, and carried her over to a table where leftovers had been placed.

Aonghus gave thanks, and they all hungrily ate, thanking the cook again and again.

"I've never heard voices like that before," the cook said after they had eaten for several minutes. "Why, you children could sing for a living and make a mint!"

"You should have heard our mother sing," said Abbe. "Now she could *sing*!"

"And our sister, Colleen, too," said Bib through a mouth full of green beans.

"I'll tell you what, little friends," said the cook. "You sing for the Master here tonight, and you can bet that there will be no sleeping in the barn for you! You just finish up your lunch there right quick and I'll go speak to him."

He smiled a huge grin and waddled out of the kitchen. Slowly, the other kitchen staff went back to their tasks, whispering and talking among themselves.

"Now *that* was a meal," said Aonghus when they were done.

"Amazing," said Abbe.

"I've never eaten like that before," agreed Bran.

Seeing them finished, the cook came over and said, "The Master of the Inn has agreed to hear you sing tonight, and in exchange to give you two rooms for each night that you sing, if you please him and his customers," he said.

"Well, it would be nice to sleep in a decent bed, just for one night, I mean," said Bib.

"Aye," said Bran. "And a bit more of that mince pie wouldn't hurt either!"

"Pie it is!" said the cook. "And tonight you sing! Be sure you are ready and cleaned up and here in the kitchen at six!"

Then he bustled off, humming the tune they had sung.

Chapter 17 – Supper

Aonghus sat on a stone bench outside the Inn, looking at the lush gardens of roses and carpeting flowerbeds. The fragrance was intoxicating, and the late afternoon summer sky was bright and clear. Birds sang in the shade trees, and honeybees buzzed in a blue and white flowering bush beside him. Women in silk dresses and pink umbrellas walked along the path, holding the arms of gentlemen dressed in coats and tails.

"How strange," he said to his sister, Abbe, who was seated next to him.

She looked at him inquiringly.

"It's like a paradise here," he said. "There's food and riches and good clothes – everything you could possibly need and more. Yet just across the Irish Sea, our whole nation is starving. Do these people even know?"

"Maybe," she replied. "Bib says the government knows, but they're so busy planning how to help that no help is coming."

"Not the government, Ab. I mean these folks right here, walking along happily arm in arm and chatting about the sunshine and whether they'll have lamb or steak tonight. I'm not faulting them, mind you, I just wonder if anyone has told them – if they might organize some relief or something if they only knew."

Abbe didn't reply, but only looked at her dingy and worn dress, then at the rich ladies in their ornate gowns.

"You could ask them," she replied.

"I just might do that," he said, and rose.

At that moment, a young freckle-faced boy came running and said, "Master Ted bids you come down to the kitchen and have some supper early. We have roast lamb and potatoes and greens, and pie for dessert!" he said cheerfully.

Spying Bran, Bib, and Henny in the next garden, Aonghus called to them, and they all followed the lad inside and there found five plates all prepared for them.

They all hungrily ate the meal set before them, and Bran especially noted that the pie had been excellent.

When they were done, the cook said, "The guests will be finishing up and wanting some song before bed. Hurry now, quick – off to get your best things on, and be back here in ten minutes! Ten minutes, mind you!"

They hurried off and put on their Sunday best, and when they returned, exactly ten minutes later, the cook eyed them up and down, tsked, and shook his head.

"It's the best we have," said Abbe, looking down at her faded dress.

"I suppose it will have to do," he sighed, and then brightened. "But with your voices, the clothes won't matter a bit. Let's go now. You all will stand together in the middle of the hall and sing us the songs of Ireland!"

As they walked out into the dining room, Aonghus surveyed the guests. At least fifty, he thought, and all of them dressed like noblemen and women. The ladies wore wide dresses made of satin and silk, and carried fans or umbrellas, and the men wore dark suits with red vests and white shirts and carried black canes with golden goose heads.

"I feel like a rotten potato in a pot of golden apples," whispered Bran to Aonghus as they took their place, and Aonghus could see by the look on the other children's faces that they felt the same.

But the Master of the Inn was speaking now, and Aonghus held a finger to his lips.

"My dear ladies and gentlemen," he was saying. "I present to you, all the way from Ireland, the band of singers whose voices will bring tears to your eyes. I give you the famous, no, the legendary, Singing McGunnegals!"

He bowed a deep bow, and passing by the children, he hissed, "You better sing well, young ones!"

"Thank you, kind sirs and ma'ams, for your attention," said Aonghus. "Let me introduce to you the McGunnegals! I am Aonghus, strongest lad in Ireland. This is Bran, the swiftest of foot, and Abbe, our sister, who can tame the wildest Spanish stallion in a moment. And Bib, who can fix anything broken, our youngest, Henny, who can... who can never lose at hide and seek!"

The faces in the crowd were stern, and the women began to fan themselves and whisper. Aonghus caught sight of the Master, who frowned and mouthed the word "Sing!"

"In addition," continued Aonghus, "we all can sing like no one you have heard before!"

Then he whispered to the others, "Follow my lead, just like we do back home at the Old Inn."

He began to sing then, in his deep baritone voice, a song of lovers and war and life and loss, and the others joined him on the chorus, each singing a different part, their voices blending with such perfect harmony that the room grew silent, the ladies stopped fanning themselves, and began to dab their eyes with their handkerchiefs.

When the song was finished, there was a pause of silence and Aonghus whispered something to Henny, and she began to sing in her clear little girl's voice. Like her sister Colleen, Henny too had inherited something of her mother's spellbinding voice, and though only seven, her perfect pitch and sweetness captivated the room. It was a simple song of springtime and rains and flowers and bees, but visions of clear blue skies and green fields filled the minds of her listeners as she sang, and when the others joined her in hushed voices on the chorus, all leaned closer to hear what they sang.

"Oh the green shores of Ireland are calling to me,
To away, far away, to my home 'cross the sea.
Where children are happy and brave and so free.
On the green shores of Ireland that one day I'll see."

Through the evening they performed, with each of them leading a song, and all of them joining in the chorus, and then all of them singing together, or a solo and, as they sang, Aonghus watched the faces of the men and women in the room, noticing their hard expressions soften, and canes laid down on the floor, fans put away, and many a handkerchief wiping a wet eye or blowing a nose.

When they had sung for over an hour, and Henny began to yawn, Aonghus took her in his great arms and sung a few lines of a farewell song, which they all joined in as the five of them slowly walked across the floor toward the kitchen, where they bowed, sang the final line, and left the hall.

For a moment, there was absolute silence, and then a sudden thunderous applause with many a "bravo!"

The Master of the Inn waved to them from the door to come back out into the Hall, where the applause continued. The children shyly bowed again and then retreated to the kitchen. The cook motioned for them to follow him and bustled them to the back door.

"We have not had songs like that in this inn since... well... well we've *never* had songs sung like that here before!" he said, his face glowing. "And did you hear them clapping? *Clapping!* Children, those sour-faced nobles have *never* clapped for *anyone* before tonight, I can tell you that. There's something real special about you youngsters, real special. You keep together, you hear? And Aonghus, you watch over that little Henny there."

Aonghus handed Henny to Bran as the cook took his arm and led him a few steps away.

"You be sure you *do* watch over her," he said. "There's some bad or downright evil folk that dress in those top hats and fancy dresses out there. They'd as soon steal away a little gem like Henny and sell her talents for a pound as look at you. Mind you, watch them all."

"Thank you, sir," Aonghus replied. "No one will touch my brother and sisters as long as I'm around."

The cook looked at Aonghus' massive muscles and said, "No, I don't expect they would. But you watch yourself and them nonetheless. By the way, my name is Corry - Ted Corry the cook. And if you're down this way and need anything, you look me up, see," he said. "But come on, now, I'll show you your rooms."

He led them up the back stairs to a pair of large rooms that had several wide beds with soft pillows and clean sheets.

"It's not fancy, but it's clean and comfortable. You lock the doors tonight and don't answer them if anyone knocks until morning," he said, smiled at them, and waddled away, humming one of the tunes they had sung that night.

Chapter 18 - Breakfast

Aonghus stretched and bumped his head on the headboard.

"They don't make beds for McGunnegals," he said to himself.

His brother, Bran, lay curled up in the bed across the room. He opened one eye, yawned, and proceeded to bump his own head.

Aonghus laughed. "You see?"

Bran rose and stretched his lean form to its full six-foot-six height.

"Might as well get washed and wake the girls. Do you think the cook is up this early?" he said.

"Let's find out," said Aonghus, rising.

He went to the washbasin, splashed water on his face, rinsed his hands, then looked in the mirror and stared. They had sold all the mirrors in their house back in Ireland to buy food, and it had been months since he had seen himself. Even though he was powerfully built, his face was gaunt, even somewhat grim. Hunger had taken its toll. He looked over at Bran, and realized how thin he had grown over the past six months as their food supply had diminished.

"What's wrong?" said Bran, seeing Aonghus staring at him.

"Nothing," he replied, drying his face with a towel. "You should wash."

Bran did so, combed out his hair with his fingers, then said, "Come on, the cook must be up. I smell breakfast."

Stopping at the girls' room, Aonghus knocked, but when no one answered, they went down to the lounge and found them all sitting at a table, talking.

"Slept in, I see," said Bib with a grin as they approached. "Soft mattresses making you lazy?"

Just then, the cook came bustling in with plates and cups and silverware in hand and set the table for them.

"Breakfast will be right out," he said.

"We would like to work for our meal, sir," said Abbe as he put a plate before her.

"No need, no need," he said. "It'll all be paid for."

"But, we have no money," said Bran. "Is Cousin Mabel paying for it?"

The cook looked at him for a moment, and then said, "You talk to your

112

cousin Mabel about that," he said. "It seems you'll be staying here a day or two more, and singing for us again."

"Singing..." began Bib, and then she added, "Mabel decided this, didn't she?"

A cart bearing ham, eggs, cakes, and fruits was rolled out by one of the kitchen hands, and heaping platefuls were placed on the table.

"I only heard a rumor that she and the Master of the Inn talked quite a bit after your performance last night, and I was given instructions to feed you well and tell you to be ready to sing again tonight," said the cook.

Then, in a lower voice, he said, "One of my table servers said he saw the Master hand her a silver coin, but I suppose that's between you and her," said the cook. "Enjoy your breakfast, and call if you need anything."

He bustled back to the kitchen, and when he was gone, Abbe said, "So that's it – She's getting *paid* for us to sing!"

"Well," said Aonghus, "remember that we are under her care for a time and things may not be as they seem."

"Oh, you can be sure that Mabel Buttersmouth is in it for money if money is to be had," said Bran.

"Bran," said Abbe, "you mustn't talk about Mabel like that. We *are* going to get a good education, and we wouldn't have it without her and Rufus."

"Maybe so," he said grudgingly, "but I still don't trust her. She just seems... well... all wrapped up in herself, if you know what I mean. Both her and Rufus, and Henry and Frederick seem to be like that."

"Bran!" scolded Abbe.

"That's just how I see it, Abbe," he replied. "Meaning no harm, mind you."

Abbe was about to say something more, when in through the door came the Master of the Inn. He was dressed in a green smoking jacket and a tall hat and had a black cane in his hand.

"Ah, children!" he crooned, his deep melodic voice filling the room. "I am so pleased to hear that you will be staying another day or two. Apparently, your cousin, dear Mabel, needs rest from her journey from Ireland and has decided to stay on for a bit."

His large dark eyes swept their faces, and a large smile revealed his unusually white teeth.

"You know what white teeth mean," whispered Bib to Abbe.

"What?" she hissed back.

"He probably gargles ur..." she began, but Aonghus' strong hand on her shoulder cut her off.

"That's just fine!" said Aonghus. "But we would like to work to pay for our stay. We can work the barns and the kitchen if you would like."

"No, no," he said. "Your voices this evening will be quite enough. In fact, I have sent word all about to the nearby towns that the, well, the famous Singing McGunnegals will be performing tonight. I'm sure we will triple our crowd. In fact, you can keep any tips that you receive."

"What are tips?" asked Henny.

"Money," said Abbe.

"Oh. You mean you're going to pay us to sing tonight?" she asked, her innocent eyes looking up into his.

The Master's grin broadened, but still the smile never reached his eyes. "You might say that, little one. Why, with your young voice, I'm quite sure the coins will be showering down."

He patted her on the head and then turned to go. "This evening at seven, my Singing McGunnegals. Be ready then. Eat heartily. And do wash properly. And comb your hair." Then he turned and walked away.

Aonghus watched him go.

"Stay together today," he said. "Something feels wrong about this."

Chapter 19 – The House of Mysteries

"It's time," said Mrs. Wigglepox.

Colleen studied the little leprechaun's face, trying to read what she was feeling. A sense of many, many summers living in the Wigglepox Tree washed over her. Memories of bygone years, of generation after generation coming and going, moving on to other trees. Of goblins and darker creatures stealing them away. Fear. All this came to Colleen in a moment as she gazed into Mrs. Wigglepox's eyes, and then it was gone. She wondered how old the tiny lady actually was.

"You don't really want to leave, do you?" said Colleen.

"It's hard, you know," she replied. "This will be the first time this tree will have been without someone living in its heart for many thousands of years. The trees need us, you know. We live in them and care for them, and they for us. A living thing is only half alive when it doesn't have someone else to care for. It's just the way we're made."

"I suppose so," said Colleen.

"Well, let's hope we're not gone for long," said Mrs. Wigglepox, wiping her eyes. "Would you and Frederick mind stepping outside for a few minutes while we say goodbye?"

"Of course," she replied.

Colleen and Frederick led Badger from the great tree and sat down in its shade.

"Can you believe it?" said Frederick after a moment. "I mean, being here – in the Land of the Little People and all. I'm having a hard time getting a grip on it."

"Why's that?" asked Colleen.

"I mean it's not logical," he said. "My father has always said to think things through logically and not believe in superstitions. 'Rational thought will solve all man's problems,' he's fond of saying."

Colleen thought for a moment.

"I don't think there's anything wrong with logic," she said. "But I don't think it's the only thing that can guide us. Sometimes, my heart tells me something different than my head, you know?"

"Now you're sounding like a girl," said Frederick.

"No, not that way. I didn't mean emotions. It's more like... intuition.

Sometimes I *sense* things about people. I can't explain it, really, it just *is*. Maybe the whole universe is like that – maybe there are things that we can't see and hear and touch, but are still real, and we still experience them somehow. They're magical."

"Like this place?" said Frederick.

"Maybe. I wonder what other passageways one might stumble through, and what magic those worlds hold? Maybe something totally, well, *different* from what we experience in our world, or even here. The legends back home do call the fairy people the *Others*," she said.

"Hopefully, they're not too much different from us," replied Frederick. "I wouldn't want to meet something with no head or covered in eyes."

"Better watch out." She laughed. "You just might."

Just then, Mrs. Wigglepox, Lily, and Rose walked from the tree, turned toward it, and stood silently for a moment. The tree trembled once, then slowly began to close its great opening. The sound of it was like a deep moan of sorrow.

Oracle appeared from behind the tree, placed his hands on a huge root, and closed his eyes. The tree seemed to sigh as the last bit of the doorway disappeared, and then all was still.

They stood for a long moment in silence before Mrs. Wigglepox said, "Let's be off, then. I suppose you children have enough food for a day or so?"

"We'll be fine," said Colleen. "We still have some berries, and I'm sure we can scavenge roots or something along the way. Let's ride Badger for a while."

Colleen mounted first and said, "Frederick, can you lift Oracle up to me?"

"If he's agreeable," said Frederick.

Oracle hobbled over and allowed himself to be hefted up, and Colleen sat him in front of her. Then Frederick handed her the Wigglepox family and she placed them in her pockets, then helped Frederick up behind her.

"Easy now," said Colleen to Badger. "Let's go, boy."

With that, the old horse stepped forward.

"Off at last," said Frederick.

Oracle chattered on quietly in his nonsensical way, talking to Badger, who seemed perfectly content to listen to the little hunchback.

Frederick reached into his pocket and pulled out a blackberry. "I think that I may never eat another berry pie again if I ever get back home," he said. "My stomach aches already from eating so many!"

"At least we have food to eat. We ought to be thankful for that," said Colleen. "Better a stomach full of nuts and roots and berries than an empty one."

"I suppose so," said Frederick.

On they went, always southward, and passed by an occasional meadow or glen in which birds sang and rabbits and squirrels scampered. Each of these had a flowing spring in it, but these were few and far between, and all the trees in the forest were bare, save a few of the old giants that held sleepy green leaves near their tops, and these also, as Frederick pointed out, had springs nearby.

There was a thickness in the air most of the time that made them drowsy, and after riding for some hours, Frederick said, "Can we stop and take a rest? I feel as though I could fall asleep sitting here."

"Lily and Rose are already asleep," said Mrs. Wigglepox with a yawn.

"We better reach the House of Mysteries soon," said Colleen. "It's getting late, and I feel so very sleepy."

Mrs. Wigglepox looked worried and said, "We better quicken our pace a bit. We need to reach that house before sundown."

Colleen urged Badger along a bit quicker, but kept having to do so, as he slowed down every few minutes.

The afternoon lagged on, and the ground began to rise and fall. Finally, they came to a deep forest glen that was wild and lonely, the bottom of which was filled with broken rock fallen from the cliffs that surrounded its shady depths.

They were about to pass by when Colleen thought she saw someone down in the gully, leaning against a large tree.

"Oh my!" she said, and backed Badger away from the cliff.

"What is it?" asked Frederick.

"I thought I saw someone down there," she whispered.

"Not one of those black things, I hope," said Frederick.

"I don't know – it looked as though it was resting against that large tree," she said, pointing to an aged giant whose top protruded from the ravine. "Come on, let's have a look."

Dismounting and putting Oracle and the Wigglepox family on the ground, she crawled to the edge of the cliff and peered over the edge. Frederick slid off of Badger, flattened himself on the ground beside her, and squinted into the deepening gloom.

"I don't see... wait, yeah, there is somebody down there. He's got his head on his chin, and he's got a long gray beard. But he's got no legs, or else he's sticking right up out of the ground," he said.

"Do you think he's dead?" asked Colleen.

"Could be," said Frederick. "He doesn't look too alive, that's for sure."

"Oh, dear," said Mrs. Wigglepox, coming up behind them. "What is he wearing? Is it a black robe?"

"No," said Frederick. "He looks more like a man than a goblin, if you ask me. He's got a long gray beard, anyway."

"Well, he's not a goblin, then," said Mrs. Wigglepox. "They haven't got beards."

"I suppose we better go down and see if he needs help," said Colleen.

"But what if it's a trap of some sort – you know, an illusion or something set by the Witch?" said Frederick.

Colleen thought for a moment and then said, "Trap or not, if that fellow is in trouble, we can't just leave him lying there. He could be hurt, or worse."

"See here, Colleen," said Frederick. "It's none of our business who he is or what he's doing down there. What if it *is* a trap set by those goblins? They could be waiting right in those shadows, ready to jump out at anyone passing by. This poor fellow could just be a bit of bait, and then where would we be? I say we leave well enough alone."

"No, Frederick. I'm going down there. Come if you like or stay. But it's just not right to leave someone lying by the side of the road if you can help it."

"Good for you, child," said Mrs. Wigglepox. "Good for you."

She rose and went back to Badger, where Oracle sat leaning against one his legs.

"Let's go, boy," she said. "Oracle, are you coming?"

She took the reins and led the horse along a thin rabbit trail that went down into the ravine.

"Come along, Frederick," said Lily. "Pick us up and carry us down there."

Frederick sighed and did so, then followed Colleen, with Oracle trailing along behind.

Down the slippery path she led them, watching the figure that lay against the tree to see if it stirred and watching even more carefully the shadows along the cliffs that now began to surround them.

"It's scary down here," said Rose.

"And the air is so heavy!" whispered Lily, with a yawn.

When at last they reached the bottom, Colleen could now clearly see the figure lying against the tree. It was a small man whose aged face was covered with stringy gray hair and whose gray and white beard covered his chest. Fallen leaves lay on his broad shoulders, and one sat unceremoniously on his head. He appeared to be half buried, but in a moment, Colleen realized that he was simply covered in leaves up to his waist.

She quietly inched her way forward, watching the gathering shadows, until she stood right before him. Frederick tiptoed up behind her and peered over her shoulder.

The man wore an old tattered leather brown coat that was quite weathered, and a dirty tan shirt beneath that. But the oddest thing was a jumble of sticks and grass that lay intertwined in the beard on his chest.

"He looks dead," hissed Frederick. "Look, there's a bird nest right in his beard!"

They stood absolutely still for a moment, until Colleen got up her courage, cleared her throat, and said, "Sir, are you all right?"

The man lay there, making no sound, not stirring in the least. His face wore a stern, troubled expression.

"Sir?" she said a little louder, but still he did not move.

"He's dead," said Frederick. "Now let's get out of here."

But Colleen went closer, bent down, and very gently touched his face.

"He's warm," she said and, even as she said it, his chest rose and fell with a single breath.

"Oh!" said Colleen. "He's alive!"

She began to brush the leaves from on top of him, and found that they lay at least a foot deep over his short legs.

"He is a small fellow, isn't he?" said Frederick, who had gotten up the nerve to help her.

"But he's in some sort of trance or something – this sleeping wood has gotten the best of him," he said. "And just look at him – he's not very happy, even in his sleep."

"You've nailed it on the head there," said Mrs. Wigglepox. "It's this cursed Spell of the Witch. Some who succumb to it sleep on and on, but they get no rest. Even their dreams are full of trouble, or so it's said. You can see that plain enough by the look on this dwarf's face."

"A dwarf?" asked Colleen. "You mean a *real* dwarf?"

"I'm fairly certain of it," said Mrs. Wigglepox.

Colleen paused, looking at the old face of the dwarf, his grim frown, the lines and creases in his forehead and behind his eyes. Then she moved to dig him out again.

"Come on, Frederick, help me get him uncovered. Who knows how long he's been sleeping here. He'll catch his death of cold if we don't get him to some shelter," said Colleen.

Frederick began brushing leaves aside, but then stopped and stared at the dwarf.

"Colleen, wait," he said.

She stopped again and looked at him.

"Wait. I think we'd better cover him back up," he said.

"Cover him back up! Why?" she said.

"Look at him, Colleen. Look at his hair and beard... Colleen, he's got a *bird nest* in his beard! He's been sleeping here for a really long time, I think. What are we going to do with him anyway? It's pretty obvious that *we're* not going to wake him up if he's slept through years of everything that Mother Nature has thrown at him."

Colleen stared at the old dwarf and then gently shook his shoulders. She called to him, shook him harder, and even tried shouting, at which Mrs. Wigglepox reminded them to keep still for fear of attracting attention to themselves from unwanted eyes.

But the dwarf slept on, a crooked frown on his hard, old face.

"No," said Colleen. "It wouldn't be right to just leave him."

She dug on. Frederick shook his head, and then went on helping her. At last, after much heaving and hauling, they managed to pull him out of the deep pile of leaves and twigs and branches that had covered him, and gently laid his head on the ground.

"I wonder how many years he's been sleeping," said Frederick.

Oracle climbed up on his chest and poked him with his cane.

"It's been many, many years since there were dwarves in these woods," said Mrs. Wigglepox. "And I do mean *many* years. I must say that this dwarf is under more than one enchantment. He sleeps under the Spell of the Witch, but he *lives* under some other magic."

"And now that we've got him out of that living grave, what are we going to do with him? We can't put him on Badger – he's much too heavy for us to pick up, and he'd fall right off anyway," said Frederick.

"We'll have to make a litter for Badger to pull," said Colleen. "Go find a couple of long, strong branches. We'll have to use Badger's blanket for the litter."

After they had found two sturdy limbs and laid the blanket across them, then tied them to the branches with a bit of rope that was in Badger's saddle bag, they carefully hauled the dwarf atop it and, with great difficulty, managed to lash the ends of the poles to the horse's saddle.

"There's no way I can ride now," said Frederick. "I don't think the old boy could carry us all and pull this contraption behind at the same time. I'll just walk."

"Me too," said Colleen. "I need to lead Badger and carry the Wigglepoxes anyway."

Oracle, however, climbed up on and sat perched on the bird nest that the dwarf's beard still sported. This made Lily and Rose laugh until Mrs. Wigglepox shushed them.

Slowly, they pulled the litter out of the gully, with Frederick on the downhill side, steadying the dwarf as he threatened to roll off.

But, at long last, they made it to the top and, with a great sigh of relief, started south again, the litter bumping along behind them.

Twice the dwarf would have slid off had it not been for Oracle's warning cry of something unintelligible, and so finally, Frederick lashed the last bit of rope under the sleeping dwarf's arms and to either pole to keep him from slipping.

Before long, the sun was low in the west, and the trees cast long shadows across the brown forest floor. Colleen looked back at the strange little man behind her. She wondered again how long he had been sleeping under that tree and what dreams he must dream in his long, deep, and troubled sleep. What magic or curse was this world under that could preserve life and yet condemn it to eternal nightmares? How could such a world even continue to exist?

But as she looked around, she realized that this was a dying land. Everything was slipping away into an eternal night, withering beneath the unrelenting power of the Spell. The whole world had nearly given up, succumbing to its dreadful weight. Colleen suddenly felt as though she was sloshing through thick muck, as if the very air were resisting her movements. She looked back at the others, and saw that Frederick's head was bowed, as if he were walking against a great wind. She turned and pushed on.

"Badger is really getting tired," she said after they had walked in silence for some time. "How much farther do you think it is?"

But even as she said it, Frederick stopped, rubbed his eyes, and stood blinking stupidly. After a moment, he seemed to come to himself.

"Look, there, just up the next rise. What's that?" he said thickly.

The ground rose sharply before them and, at the crest of the hill, they could see an old stone building looming through the trees.

"That must be it," said Colleen. "Come on, one more go and we'll be there."

She led Badger up the hill, which seemed to go on and on, higher and longer than seemed reasonable.

"I don't think we're getting any closer," said Frederick after a time. "It looks just the same as before."

"Hold on," said Colleen. "We've not been walking up this hill at all – we've just been going round and round it. See here, I remember this old tree stump. In fact, I've seen it twice, now that I think about it. Something strange is going on."

She strained her eyes, looking up at the distant structure, then saw it – a thin trail that she had missed before. But as soon as she looked straight at it, it disappeared.

"The trail is hidden, Frederick. Don't look straight at it. Just sort of narrow your eyes and look to one side."

Frederick squinted as well.

"Say, yeah, I see it now," he said.

Colleen turned and followed the trail up, not looking directly at it, and as soon as she did, it opened up before them, a clear path curving upward toward the summit.

The building loomed larger and larger as they approached, until they passed through the remnants of a stone wall and stood before massive stone pillars that supported the slate tiled roof of a large front porch, behind which was the most massive house that Colleen had ever seen.

"It looks like a castle," whispered Frederick. "Do you think anyone still lives here?"

Colleen said nothing, but craned her neck to gaze up at the towering walls and ornately carved but weathered windows that faced them. Marble steps led up to the porch, and a pair of dark ironbound doors stood tightly shut, with many of the now-familiar runes and symbols carved on them. They were the biggest doors Colleen had ever seen, at least thirty feet high.

"It looks spooky," whispered Colleen.

"Do you think the door is locked?" said Frederick.

"Only one way to find out," said Mrs. Wigglepox. "Let's try it."

Colleen tied Badger to a post and started walking up the steps to the huge front door.

But as soon as her feet touched the bottom step, there was a rumbling sound, as if deep under the ground something massive was moving.

She took her foot off the step and backed away, and as she did, the rumbling quieted and stopped.

"What was that?" hissed Frederick.

Colleen put her foot back on the first step, then on the second. The rumbling under the ground began again, deeper this time.

"Something doesn't want us to go in there," said Colleen. "First that hidden trail, now this."

Frederick glanced nervously about. Out of the corner of his eye, he thought he glimpsed a dark shape run behind a tree.

"Colleen, there's something in the woods..." he said, his voice cracking with fear.

Colleen stepped down again and the ground ceased its trembling. The wood grew still and nothing moved. She was about to turn around again when she also saw something. Her sharp eyes could see a black-hooded head peeking out from behind a tree, still as a stone, but there all the same, a darkness against the shadows.

"Maybe I was just imagining it," said Frederick.

"Hush!" she breathed. "I see it now. We've got to get in this house and shut the door behind us. When I say 'run,' we all run up these steps and push open that door!"

The shadow moved.

"Run!" she said, and they bolted up the steps, dragging Badger behind them.

"Ho!" called Oracle, who tumbled off the sleeping dwarf and began to roll away.

"Stupid leprechaun!" Frederick cried, but ran down the steps, grabbed the leprechaun unceremoniously by the belt, and then ran back up again.

The ground began to shake fiercely. The forest around them, and the whole house shook. Colleen watched as Frederick nearly lost his balance, stumbling to one side. The deep rumbling became an audible grinding of stone on stone.

"It's an earthquake!" shouted Frederick as he mounted the porch and put Oracle down.

Colleen turned to the doors. "There's no doorknob!" she said desperately, and reached out and gave them a push. Nothing happened. "There must be a latch or something," she yelled above the rumble that was now becoming like thunder.

"I don't see a key hole," yelled Frederick. "It must be hidden somewhere. All doors have locks."

He gave the doors a shove, then leaned his shoulder against one of them and pushed with all his might. But the doors held fast.

Then suddenly, Mrs. Wigglepox yelled, "Look out – it's a goblin!"

They all turned and could clearly see now a black-hooded figure stumbling toward them across the shaking ground. It seemed to *flicker* from reality to shadow and back again.

Colleen turned back to the doors, desperate and more than a little scared.

"You've got to OPEN!" she yelled.

Oracle poked the doors with his cane and, immediately, there was a clicking sound and they swung silently open, revealing a dark hall within.

For a brief moment, they all stared in amazement, but before anyone could speak, Lily cried out from Frederick's pocket.

"Mother!" she called. "I saw a face in the upstairs window!"

They looked up at the window that she pointed to, but there was no face to be seen, only ancient curtains that hung trembling behind the rattling glass.

"No time!" said Frederick, and pointed. The goblin was trying to run toward them now, and making a good show of it.

A boulder went careening toward the creature, barely missing it as it rolled away.

Colleen looked at Frederick and he nodded. She ran into the dark house, pulling the horse with her, and Frederick followed closely behind.

As soon as they were all inside, the door swung shut, surrounding them in darkness.

All at once, the quaking ground grew still and all was silent.

"I think we're going to need a light," said Frederick, and even as he said it, yellow torches sprung to life on the walls.

Colleen looked around. They were standing on a great slab of white stone, and a long, wide tiled hall stretched before them, with numerous shut doors on either side. The ceiling soared upward to a high peak, and a balcony stretched out on either side where she could see more doors. Ancient dusty tapestries hung from the balcony, depicting various forest scenes with many little people in them.

At the far end of the long hall appeared to be a broad stairway that split to the left and right, and between the two stood a tall stone statue of a great forbidding centaur holding a spear in its right hand. Its onyx eyes stared coldly at them.

"What is this place?" whispered Frederick.

"No one knows for sure," said Mrs. Wigglepox. "But it's said that it was built by the wizards, or perhaps by dwarves, back before the Great War. Some say that an old wizard hermit lived here, and other stories speak of this being a place where Anastazi the Great himself came from time to time. The dwarves held this as someplace special, and there were other houses like this once, but this is the last one that still stands."

"Well, we'd best move on," said Colleen, and she took a step forward.

But as soon as she did, the tiled floor seemed to shift under her feet and she nearly fell.

Stepping back onto the door's landing, she watched in amazement as all of the tiles down the long hall shifted places with one another like some giant children's puzzle, and then grew still again.

"Now I know there's magic here," said Colleen in a whisper.

"Yes," said Mrs. Wigglepox, "and it's still active after all these years."

"It's easy enough to guess that someone doesn't want us here," said Frederick, and he touched his toe to the tiles.

Again, they shifted and slid about, then grew silent again.

Suddenly, a deep booming voice broke the silence. Both Colleen and Frederick backed against the door in fright.

"The path is always treacherous when you do not know the way," it said.

"Who said that?" whispered Colleen.

She turned to look at Frederick, and saw that his eyes were wide and staring down the long hall. She followed his gaze and gasped, for the stone centaur at the end of the hall seemed to come to life. It shook itself and stretched, as if it had just wakened from a long sleep.

Slowly at first, and then more quickly, and then at a gallop, it charged down the hall, its great spear held out before it.

Badger whinnied and reared, sensing the danger. Colleen gasped, and Frederick could say nothing but "Oi!"

As the stone creature approached, Colleen could see that it stood at least seven feet high at the haunches. Its great stone, muscled upper body of a man towered another four feet upward to a stern, rough face with dangling stone curls.

It charged forward on thunderous hooves that echoed loudly as stone met stone.

Badger reared again and kicked wildly at the air. Colleen screamed, "Stop!" as the terrible spear drew up, ready to pierce her horse through the chest.

She covered her eyes and turned away sobbing, knowing what was about to happen next.

But the awful moment never came. Instead, she heard Badger snort in defiance, and Frederick collapse to the floor beside her.

A dreadful thought seized her mind as she uncovered her face and saw him sitting hunched against the door behind him.

But he was staring up, unhurt, and Colleen turned and saw why.

The great stone beast had stopped abruptly, its shining silver spear tip inches from Badger's neck. It was staring down at them with great black eyes.

Then, it spoke again. Its voice was like thunder and stone grinding on stone.

"Why does the daughter of the daughter of the Great One not speak the Words of Passage!" it roared. "Speak them, for you shall not pass until they are uttered!"

It was staring at Colleen now, and she did not know what to say.

"Speak!" it demanded in its rocky voice.

"I... I... don't know them," said Colleen. "What words?"

"I think that was the wrong thing to say, Colleen," whispered Frederick in a trembling voice.

"What she means, sir," began Frederick, "is that... that..."

There was a grinding sound as the centaur turned its gaze on Frederick and its eyes narrowed to black slits.

"And you, son of the son of the Great One - will you speak the words of passage?" it asked.

Colleen looked at Frederick. He seemed uncertain as to what he should say to this terrifying thing before them. He glanced at the door, then at her, then back at the centaur.

"We have..." he began, but his voice broke and he had to start over. "We have traveled from the world of Men," he began, and he tried to compose himself and sound important. "... and are here to destroy... er...uh, to defeat the Witch and her goblins and set free the little people from her ... uh... dominion."

The centaur looked back and forth between them and said, "I shall give you a riddle. Answer it rightly, and live. Fail, and I shall know that you are false!"

"Right then," said Frederick, and he swallowed hard. "A riddle it is. But first, uh, can we ask you a riddle so that we know that you are, well, uh, the proper guardian of the, uh, thing."

Oracle, who had tumbled behind Frederick, peered out from behind him, a strange grin on his face.

Colleen took a deep breath and steadied herself. Frederick didn't seem to be handling the situation very well, and she knew that she had to do something quickly.

"Sir, we are here to help, although it would seem that we came by fortune or providence. I hear that the Witch has taken my own mother, and I must find her and rescue her if I can, or at least return home to my own land and bring back my brothers to help me."

"First, the riddle!" thundered the statue, and bent down, its face toward Frederick. "I have never been defeated by any riddling. Only the true son of the son of the Great One could surpass me. I will permit you to speak first. If your riddle foils me, then you may pass. But these others must guess my riddle or they shall die!"

"What are you doing, Frederick!" whispered Colleen.

"Don't worry, I've got one that nobody has ever guessed," he whispered back.

Frederick cleared his throat, then spoke.

"Motherless, fatherless, born without skin.
Speaks once and never speaks again."

The centaur frowned and creases formed in its stone forehead. It rubbed its chin and looked thoughtful for several moments.

"See," whispered Frederick, "that riddle's been passed down in my family. Nobody else knows the answer! Besides, a stone centaur would never guess it."

"What's that!" boomed the centaur. "A hint! What would a stone centaur not know about – something beyond its experience? Hmm."

For several minutes, the centaur mumbled loudly, guessing this or that to itself, until with a frustrated grinding of its stone teeth it conceded. "Very well, son of the son of the Great One. Your riddle has surpassed my knowledge! Never before has anyone out-riddled me! Therefore, you may pass. But now, I shall give you my riddle."

The centaur raised itself to its full height and began to chant.

"Source of grief and pain and fear,
Home of love and hate and tear.
Place from which the song doth flow,
Home of dragons, lies, and woe.
Yet amid its raging storms is found,
A quiet little knocking sound,
Of one who stands outside its door,
And longs to enter its depths once more."

Then it glared down at them, waiting.

"A moment, please, if you will," said Colleen, and she looked at Frederick, who seemed to be rather absorbed and was quoting the whole riddle back to himself.

"What do you suppose it is?" Colleen asked him after a moment.

"One moment," he said, and he quoted back the riddle again in a whisper, thinking as he did.

"I thought for a moment it was something like the pits of the Witch that Mrs. Wigglepox was telling us about," he said, "but I don't think so."

Just then, Mrs. Wigglepox peered out from Colleen's pocket and stared up at the stone centaur, which now was standing still as a statue again, its great spear pointed down at them.

"I think the answer is something much deeper than any pit the goblins could dig and something with much more woe than they could ever bring and more joy than any gift a leprechaun could give," she said.

"What could it be then?" asked Frederick.

"I grow impatient!" thundered the centaur. "But since you gave me a hint, I too shall give you one. This too is something that is beyond a stone centaur's experience."

A sudden thought struck Colleen and she said, "Mr. Centaur, may I touch you?"

"Touch me?" he said, and then looked thoughtful. "It is permitted."

Colleen took a slow step forward and put her hand on the great creature's side, closed her eyes, and began to hum.

For a moment, Frederick thought that his vision had blurred, for Colleen appeared to turn to the same gray stone as the centaur. He rubbed his eyes and looked again, but Colleen had removed her hand, and she appeared normal again.

"The answer is *heart*!" she said. "A stone centaur has no heart!"

And as soon as she said *heart*, the great centaur bowed once, turned, galloped down the hall, and stood back in his place at the base of the stairs.

"That was scary," said Lily from inside Frederick's pocket. "What do you think would have happened if we got the riddle wrong?"

"Who knows?" Colleen replied. "Let's just get past this place. We'll need to find a room that we can all stay for the night – someplace that's big enough for Badger too," she said.

"Frederick," said Lily, "what was the answer to your riddle?"

He blushed slightly and said, "Well, I don't think it's proper to say it in front of ladies."

"Come now, Frederick," said Mrs. Wigglepox. "Is it that bad?"

"Well, not really, but let's just say it rhymes with the answer to the centaur's riddle," he said.

"It rhymes with *heart*?" asked Colleen.

"Yes," he said.

Lily and Rose looked at one another and giggled. Mrs. Wigglepox looked perplexed, and Colleen put her hand over her mouth to hide her smile. Oracle only thumped down the hall, although Frederick thought he saw a twinkle in his eyes.

"Right, then, best get going," he said, trying to change the subject, and he followed after Oracle.

At the first door, Colleen stopped. It was like the big entry doors to the house – with no keyhole and no doorknob, and no amount of pushing would open it.

"Remember what you did outside, Colleen? Try saying 'open' and see what happens," said Frederick.

She stood in front of the door, and said, "Open!" Her voice echoed down the hall.

All at once, every door in the hall clicked and swung open, both downstairs and on the balcony upstairs. Some doors were small, not more than three feet high, and some were gigantic, nearly forty feet tall.

"Sheeeww," said Frederick. "You've really got a talent there! If there are any closed doors left in this house, let me give it a try!"

Colleen grinned at him and said, "Right. Now let's see what's been opened for us."

Chapter 20 – A Doctor of Stone

Frederick peered into the room. Torches with bright blue flames sprang to life on the walls, casting an odd light about the room. Tapestries depicting wizards and armies and princesses and a black dragon hung about the place, dusty, but not moth eaten or rotted with age. Against the walls stood suits of silver armor that gleamed dully in the blue light.

In the center of the room was a round table with a dozen seats around it, and above the table hung a fabulous crystal chandelier, the crystals of which glowed with a white light that radiated downward to illumine the table, and outward to mingle with the blue light of the torches on the walls.

"Amazing!" said Frederick.

"It's beautiful!" said Rose.

"It looks like some sort of meeting room," whispered Colleen, "but I don't think anyone has been here in ages."

Dust and spider webs covered everything, and it appeared that the room had not been disturbed for many years.

Frederick walked about the room, examining the armor and weapons lining the walls. They seemed just about his size, or smaller.

"They must have been small folk to fit into these things," he said, and he lifted a coat of silver ring mail that had an attached ring hood from its hanger on the wall.

"Why, this is amazingly light!" he said and, dusting it off, slipped it over his own shirt.

"And it fits too!" he said, smiling broadly.

There was a belt and short sword as well, and he buckled it around his waist and pulled the sword from its sheath. He held it up and it sparkled in the blue light of the torches.

Colleen giggled and said, "Hail, Sir Frederick the Knight!" She curtsied.

He laughed, swung the sword over his head with a flourish, and bowed in return.

"You might as well borrow it," said Colleen, growing serious. "I think the owners are long dead by now."

"Yeah, I guess so," he said. "But I wonder who made these things. They're marvelous!"

"Elves, likely, or dwarves," said Mrs. Wigglepox. "Not men, I think. They're too small."

Frederick saw that there was also a pair of blue boots and leggings, and these, he found, fit as well, and the boots were far more comfortable than his hard black shoes that he had been wearing.

There was a blue cape as well, and soon he had dressed himself completely in the outfit, and spread his arms wide, saying, "Well, what do you think, Colleen?"

Colleen stared at him for a moment.

"You look... royal!" she said admiringly.

He blushed slightly and he looked down at the outfit.

"Maybe I ought not to wear it, then," he muttered. "It doesn't really suit me too well."

"Nonsense," said Colleen. "I think they're better traveling clothes than what you had on before. See, there's a mirror over there. Go have a look while I do a bit of exploring."

Frederick walked over to the mirror and blew dust off its surface. At first, he looked at the outfit, which fit him remarkably well and was in perfect condition. *I do look rather royal,* he thought to himself, turning around and looking over his shoulder at the cloak.

But then he caught his own eye and turned again, looking harder. His dark hair was unkempt, and his face was dirty. The eyes that stared back at him did not seem royal to him, but were just a fourteen-year-old boy's eyes, not yet lined with too many cares, but filled with uncertainty. He knew that he was anxious, even frightened, not any sort of warrior at all.

I want to be, though, he thought. *I really do want to help Colleen find her mom.*

He stared a moment longer and then said aloud, "I suppose that's at least a start. Maybe if I just wear the armor and sword and cloak and boots, my heart will follow."

"What's that?" called Colleen from across the room.

"Nothing," he said, and turned away from the mirror. "I was just thinking about the centaur's riddle and... and other stuff. Let's go."

He left the room and Colleen followed. They continued down the hall, looking in each open door. Six more rooms were nearly identical to the first with the exception of their size, and the torches that sprang to life on the walls in each one were of different colors. The suits of armor were of various sizes, some quite large, even larger than Colleen's father could wear, and he was the biggest man Frederick had ever seen.

When they came to the smallest of the doorways, Oracle happily walked in through the three-foot high passage and began to bang his stick on the little suits of armor that lined the walls.

"What's he doing now?" said Frederick, poking his head through the door.

"Let us down for a moment," said Mrs. Wigglepox. "I want to see this room more closely."

She and Lily and Rose went in, and Frederick and Colleen followed.

"We'll get a neck ache in here," said Frederick as he crouched down to avoid bumping his head on the low ceiling. "But have a look at that – those suits of armor are just the right size for Oracle. There must have been a load of leprechauns his size once upon a time."

Oracle had now found a small table in the center of the room with low seats. He plopped himself down in one, banged his cane on the table, and shouted, "Order!" Then he snickered and got up and went on rummaging about the room.

Lily and Rose found a row of tiny silken dresses, which appeared to have slits in the backs.

"Those are fairy dresses, children," said Mrs. Wigglepox, "woven long, long ago from the finest silk. They've not been made in the Valley of Fairies for centuries!"

There were also leprechaun clothes, all much too big for the Wigglepoxes, but would just about fit Oracle. He fingered a fine bright green coat, looked at his own rather faded clothes, said "humph!" and walked by.

However, when he came to a shelf that contained four pots that were black as onyx, he paused, caressed them carefully, looked at the Wigglepox family, and smiled a knowing smile. But he left them on the shelf and walked on, hitting chairs and walls and most everything else with his cane as he went.

At last, he seemed to grow bored and left the room, followed by Mrs. Wigglepox, Lily, and Rose, and Frederick and Colleen came silently behind.

The seventh room, while looking much the same, was vastly different in size. The table and chairs were absolutely huge, and the ceiling stretched upward over forty feet to a massive chandelier.

They all stood in silence for several long moments, staring at the mammoth furniture, when Frederick noticed the tapestries.

"Look," he said, pointing to one of them. "Those are *giants* pictured there!"

Indeed, the scene showed a huge figure, and to its right stood a human man, less than a quarter its height, and on the right side of the man was a tinier figure that barely reached his knee.

"Oh my," said Mrs. Wigglepox. "So they are."

"This must have been a room where giants came," said Colleen.

"Yes," said Mrs. Wigglepox. "In fact, I think that these seven rooms we have just seen were meant for each of the other seven races – the elves, dwarves, goblins, trolls, men, giants, and little people."

"But what about a room for the Orogim?" asked Rose.

Oracle seemed to shiver at the mention of the name and drew his cloak close, and Mrs. Wigglepox said, "We rarely speak of them, dear. They were never allowed into the councils of the wise."

"Well, I've heard of little people and elves and dwarves and goblins and trolls, and of course men, but what are the *Orogim*," asked Frederick.

Mrs. Wigglepox gave a little shudder and said in a hushed voice, "A terrible people. Though they were not always so terrible, or so it's said. But they are the most feared of all the races. Pray that we never meet one of *them*!"

"What makes them so terrible?" asked Colleen.

"It is best not to speak of them," she said. "But suffice to say that few who have met them have survived to tell of it. Perhaps in another time and place, I will tell you the tales that I know."

Leaving the giants' room, Frederick poked his head into several more doorways, which proved to be storage closets.

"Look here, Colleen," he said, lifting a green robe and cloak from a hook and handing them to her. "This just might fit you, and here's a decent walking stick as well, and a pair of boots."

"I don't need those things," she said, looking at the clothes.

"Now whose turn is it? You made me put on this fancy stuff. What if we hit a rainstorm or something – you'll be needing a cloak and some decent shoes. Come on now, have a go – see if these things fit. Here, you can use this closet to change."

Colleen began to protest, but Mrs. Wigglepox said, "He's quite right, my dear. Besides, the owner of these things has been dead and gone for a long,

long time. These things were left here for a reason – for someone like you who needs them to come along one day. Go on, then, try them on."

"All right, then," she said, and took the whole lot from Frederick and went into the closet.

A few moments later, she opened the door and emerged. Her golden hair streamed down the back of the dark green cloak. She spun around and smiled. Frederick's jaw dropped open.

"How do I look?" she said.

"Actually, rather, uh, well, pretty good," he said awkwardly, but inside he felt a rather queer knot in his stomach.

"But your nose is dirty," he added hastily, at which Colleen smiled broadly and scrubbed her nose with her old dress, which she then threw into the closet.

"Won't need that old thing," she said, and led Badger down the hall.

"S'pose not," said Frederick,

Now the stone centaur loomed before them, staring fixedly ahead with unblinking eyes.

"You don't mind if we pass, do you?" said Frederick to the centaur.

It said nothing, but remained motionless and silent.

"I think it's gone back to being just stone," whispered Colleen. "Let's get past it while we can."

Behind the statue was a pair of great stone doors nearly twenty feet tall, standing open, and beyond these was a large landing with broad steps leading upward. High white railings lined the upper balconies on either side of them.

Colleen led the way through the doors and Frederick followed with many a glance toward the centaur, hoping that it wouldn't change its mind and come to life again.

Colleen looked up at the high staircase that led upward before them, then patted Badger on the nose and sighed.

"Might as well go up," she said, "but I don't think Badger can make it up those steps, especially with the dwarf."

She tied him to the banister, and said, "Stay here, boy. We'll be back soon."

Badger snorted and stamped a foot, and Colleen rubbed his nose.

"Stay," she said, and started up the stairs.

Frederick followed Colleen up the short stubby steps, past a landing and to the left, where the stair split to either side of the hall, and onto a second landing at the top.

Torches flickered on in succession as they walked along the balcony above the downstairs hall, and they peered into the rooms as they passed them.

These proved to be bedrooms or sitting rooms, all filled with dust and cobwebs. But when they reached the middle of the hall, another hall turned to their right, and this they followed for a short ways when, suddenly, Colleen stopped and put her finger to her lips.

"Look!" she whispered. "Look at the floor!"

They all looked down at their feet.

"I don't know why I didn't notice it before," she said, "but the dust out here is all disturbed, like someone has been using this hallway all along, but has never cleaned it."

Dust lined the hall in front of and behind them, but it was not settled as it had been in the rooms behind the closed doors, but clumped and bunched together against the walls.

"There *is* someone here," hissed Frederick.

"I knew I saw someone!" whispered Lily.

"Best take care," said Mrs. Wigglepox. "Whoever it is knows we're here, and they haven't harmed us yet. It may be that this is Lily's old man after all, and perhaps he's friendly, but our welcome so far has not been a very good one. There may be more tricks in store for us. Frederick, you just keep that sword ready."

Frederick looked surprised, but nervously put his hand on the sword hilt.

Slowly, they walked down the hall, Colleen and Frederick side by side and Oracle following behind, his cane tap-tap-tapping as they went. They reached a corner and Frederick peered around.

"Take a look," he whispered. "The disturbed dust stops at that door down there."

Colleen leaned forward to see.

"He must have gone in there," she whispered.

They all stood motionless for a few moments, and Frederick began to wonder what sort of person would live in a place like this. Was it a goblin? An evil wizard? A madman? Who would have lived here for so long and escaped from the Witch and her spies? Or was he one of her spies?

But it was little Rose who broke the silence and said, "Why don't we just knock on the door?"

"I think that is an excellent idea," said Mrs. Wigglepox. "We're here for the night, and we might as well meet our host. After all, he already knows that we are here."

They slowly made their way down the hall and stood in front of the door.

"Frederick, would you do the honors?" asked Mrs. Wigglepox.

Frederick swallowed hard and then stepped forward and knocked. There was no answer.

"You'll have to do better than that, I think," said Colleen, and she took her staff and rapped on the door. The sound echoed down the empty hall, and she immediately regretted knocking so loudly. But there was no answer from inside.

"Do you think he's in there? Maybe he ran out through a back door or something. Or maybe he's not in there at all," said Frederick.

"Well, let's go in, then," said Mrs. Wigglepox, "Frederick?"

"What? Oh, right, well, then...OPEN!" he said.

His face fell when nothing at all happened.

Frustrated, he pushed hard on the door. It moved slightly and then stopped. "It's locked from the inside," he said, "with a regular lock this time."

Colleen rapped on the door again and said loudly, "Hello? We mean no harm. We only wish to be friends and spend the night here. Please, do come and open the door."

There was no answer for a moment. They were all wondering what they might do next when there came a loud *thunk* on the other side of the door and it opened just a sliver.

They all stepped back and saw an eye peering through the crack at them.

Then an old scraggly voice said, "How did you get in here? Go away!" The door slammed shut.

"Please, sir," said Colleen loudly. "We need to talk with you. Why won't you come out and see us? We have someone with us who needs help."

The door cracked open once again, and the eye peeked out at them.

"Who are you?" the old voice demanded. "Are you with the Witch?"

"Heavens no," said Mrs. Wigglepox. "We are on our way to see the Lady Danu. But we have a long way to go and need shelter for the night. Now come out here and speak to us properly!"

At that, there was a good deal of huffing and grumbling, and the eye looked back and forth at them, and then the door slammed shut again. They could hear a whole series of locks and chains clicking and dragging, until finally, the door was slowly swung open and the head of a very old, very short man of about four feet tall with a long gray beard peered at them from behind the door. He was quite obviously another dwarf and was wearing tattered brown pants with black suspenders.

They all stared at him, not knowing what to say.

"Well..." he said in his old voice. "You had better come in and not stand there in the hall."

He motioned with a bony old hand for them to enter, and they slowly filed in. Frederick came first, carrying Lily, followed by Colleen, who was carrying Mrs. Wigglepox and Rose, and lastly Oracle, who thumped in and gave the door a whack with his cane.

The dwarf quickly shut the door behind them and began locking dozens of locks and bolts and chains. This process took nearly a minute to complete, and he then hefted a large ironclad oaken bar across it.

"There now," he creaked. "The nasties won't get past that! And I hope you shut the front door behind you."

He grinned broadly, and Frederick noticed that quite a few of his teeth were missing.

"But see here," he said, looking at them in a sidelong manner, "you say you youngsters are going to see the Lady? Well, that's no easy task. And how did you get here in the first place? And, blimey! A tall leprechaun like olden times! Bless my soul!"

"First," said Mrs. Wigglepox, "we must have introductions. May we ask who you are?"

The dwarf looked at them for another long moment, considering, and then shrugged his shoulders and said, "A name is not an easy thing to entrust to strangers. But you may call me Doc. Yes, Doc the Dwarf at your service."

He gave a bow so that his long beard brushed the floor.

"I'm Colleen McGunnegal," said Colleen. "And this is my cousin, Frederick

Buttersmouth."

"And I am Edna Wigglepox, and these are my daughters, Lily and Rose," said Mrs. Wigglepox.

Lily and Rose waved from their pockets. Oracle said nothing, but stared at the dwarf with squinted eyes.

"We call him Oracle," said Frederick. "We're not sure what his real name is. He's a bit mad."

Doc looked at each of them thoughtfully, and he said, seemingly to himself, "Leeeprechauuuuns!" His gravelly voice drew out the word. "Well, bless my soul."

Then he said, more to them, "I haven't seen your like around the mansion for... for... well, it's been a long time. And going to see the Lady! And traveling with a young..." He paused for a moment, looking hard at Colleen, then continued. "Say, girl, you're elvish, aren't you? And here we have a boy. A human boy! It's been a mighty long time since I've seen your lot."

"Colleen and Frederick are both humans, and they have come to our land through the Mirror in the Wood," said Mrs. Wigglepox.

"Ooohhhh!" creaked the dwarf. "Through the mirror! Why no one has come through that in ages... not since... since the cursed Pirate, I should think! It was him that stole away our beautiful sleeping princess and brought the Witch back, he did. Stole the gold and treasure too."

Doc grumbled a bit under his breath, then seemed to come to himself and went over to Colleen, eying her up and down and said, "Are you sure you're human?" he asked.

Colleen was not sure what to say at first, but finally replied, "My mother is Ellie McGunnegal, who came here through the mirror from our land accidentally, and who the goblins have captured. My father is Adol McGunnegal, strongest man in all Ireland."

Doc snorted at this and mumbled something about humans and elves and pixies and then stepped over to Frederick, peering into his eyes.

Frederick stared nervously back. The old dwarf's eyes were sunken and gray, and wrinkles covered his aged face. In fact, Frederick could not remember ever seeing so many wrinkles on a face before. It was as if his skin had cracked over and over a hundred times, leaving not the tiniest spot unwrinkled.

"Human he is, at least mostly," the dwarf said at length. "Although there's something else deep in his blood. Something... I would have said 'dwarvish,' but that's not it. Something ... *regal*, though."

Frederick did not know what to say, so he just continued to stare back.

Doc glanced at Lily and Rose and Mrs. Wigglepox. "And it's obvious enough that you three are leprechauns."

Then he went over to Oracle, grunted as he bent low, and looked into his face. He stared for a long moment, and then a strange look came over him, as if he recognized something, and his eyes grew wide and he drew back.

But Oracle took his cane, jabbed the dwarf on his foot, and said, "Swigian!"

"Ouch!" said Doc, and hopped on one foot. "What was that for? He *is* a bit mad, isn't he? For a moment, I thought I recognized him, but I must be mistaken. Well, anyway, my eyesight isn't what it used to be. But I can see well enough that you're not with the Witch's people. They all have *her* look, if you know what I mean," he said.

"Of course we are not with the Witch," said Mrs. Wigglepox. "As we said, we are going to see the Lady. Colleen's mother has been captured by the goblins and so has my own husband. We're going to see what can be done about it."

"Humph!" said the dwarf. "Little enough, it would seem... But look here! Come in and sit. But say, didn't you bring a horse with you? I saw one from the window."

"It was you!" said Lily. "I knew I saw someone looking at us from the window!"

"Yes, that was me. Forgive my earlier rudeness. It's a hard thing to live alone in these woods, what with the Witch's spies about and all. How was I to know that you were *against* her? That's a rare thing nowadays."

He motioned to two chairs for Colleen and Frederick, and pulled up a low footstool for Oracle. Then he excused himself, leaving through a side door, from which they could hear a good deal of rustling and banging, until the dwarf returned a few moments later with a tray bearing cups, bowls, a jug of drink, and a covered dish.

"See here, I haven't forgotten my manners completely." He sat the tray down and poured four cups of something from the jug, handed out the plates to Colleen and Frederick and Oracle, and from the dish scooped out helpings of stuffed mushrooms, which smelled delicious.

He paused for a moment, thinking, and then, realizing that he had nothing to serve the Wigglepoxes, scurried off grumbling to the side room again, where there was additional grumbling and banging, until he once again returned.

"It's the best I can do," he replied, and laid out three thimbles and a small teacup saucer. The thimbles he carefully filled with drink and he placed a single mushroom on the saucer and cut it into tiny pieces with a knife.

"Best give thanks," said the dwarf, and he mumbled a blessing of the dwarvish sort, which managed to stretch on a bit and included something about rocks and earth and mines as well as the food, though Frederick could not quite make it all out, so quiet and gruff was the dwarf's voice.

But when he was finished with his blessing, he grinned expansively and said, "Eat! And tell me your tale! It's been a long time since I've had company. A *long* time."

They ate, and Frederick thought that these were the best mushrooms that he had ever tasted.

"Where did you get these mushrooms, and what are they stuffed with?" he asked with a mouth full as he reached for seconds. "I've never tasted anything like them!"

"Ah!" said the dwarf, taking a long draft from his mug, his drink spilling down his beard.

"I grew them me-self! Down in the mines, you know. I know the old ways, I do, and there are places beneath the ground here where no goblin or witch has ever been. And the secret ingredient? Fish! Fish from the river beneath the mines. Deep and swift are its waters, and pure. The old Witch doesn't know about it, I'll wager, or she would have poisoned it long ago."

He giggled with glee at the thought, and then grew serious.

"And she must never know," he said. "These waters touch the Lady's lake, and feed the springs of the Forest, keeping the Spell at bay."

"I have often wondered," said Mrs. Wigglepox, "why it is that near the springs, the meadows and trees are not so much under her spell? I think now our own spring next to the Wigglepox Tree is the only thing that has kept it awake."

"Aye, could be, could be," said the dwarf. "I knew there were some of the old trees left still green, but I didn't know of any of the little people left in them. I thought they had all gone to the Lady or been captured by the goblins... Whoa, there, little man! Slow down on those mushrooms! Too much of a good thing will make you wish you'd had none at all!" he said as Frederick reached for thirds.

They ate on in silence for a few minutes, savoring the extraordinary flavor of Doc's food, and indeed Frederick began to wish he had not taken thirds, for his stuffed stomach began to feel a bit upset.

He put his hands on his belly, leaned back, and said, "That was really good."

Then a thought struck him.

"Mr. Doc," he began, but the dwarf held up a hand.

"Just Doc, lad!"

"Very well, Doc," Frederick said. "You said that the river runs to the south, to the Lady's Lake. How do you know that? Is there a passageway that follows the river that far?"

"A good question, lad," said the dwarf. "Yes, there is a passage, or there used to be. Long ago, when my people lived here in greater numbers, we made a passageway along the river that ran all the way beneath the Great Hills in the south and came out on the other side. In my younger days, my brothers and I would walk the River Path far to the north and south, opening new passages east and west in search of gems and gold. The little people would trade wishes for such treasure, and both our peoples prospered greatly. But I've not ventured so far as the Lake in many, many years. Last time I tried, the course of the river had changed, and there had been cave-ins."

"But if the passage is still there, could we follow it to the Lady's Lake?" asked Frederick.

"Too dangerous," said the Dwarf. "The old way is too unstable now. You might be able to belly-crawl through the blocked passages, but it would take you three times as long, and that horse would never make it."

"Are there any other ways down to the river between here and the Lake, Doc?" asked Colleen.

"No, lassie," he said. "This is the only place in this wood that I know of, and the only reason there is one here is because of this house."

"What's so special about this house?" asked Colleen.

"The wizards met here," said Doc. "Sages from all the races would meet and discuss their craft, even the Wise Ones of the Dwarves, and here we mined down, down, and we found many, many gems. When we broke through to the river, we found gold enough to buy all the kingdoms of the world!"

Doc's eyes shone in his old face at the memory, but then the light left them and his face grew hard.

"But now they are gone. All gone." He nodded and looked down at his plate.

"What happened to it all?" asked Frederick.

"Stolen! Stolen by the cursed Pirate!" Then he breathed a great sigh and said, "Well, anyway, it wasn't all him. But he took what was left after the War. And even when he returned it all, the goblins came and carried loads of it away."

"Doc," said Mrs. Wigglepox. "You said that the Wise Ones of the dwarves met here with the sages of the other races. Were you... were you one of the Wise Ones?"

Doc looked down again and was quiet for a long moment before he replied, "How long ago it was, I can't remember. The years have rolled by far too long. But yes, there were seven of us once, seven of us from the royal family who were once called the Wise Ones. We were the ones who discovered this hill and directed the building of this house. Now those were the days! There were elves and dwarves and men and giants and little people – the wisest of the wise from all the races. And even the Great Wizard came, and everyone prospered. But that was before the dark days – before the Witch and the goblins."

He was silent for a time and then spoke again, "I think I will trust you all. Yes, I was one of those that met. My full name is Doctor Eitri Sindri. But, as I said, you may call me Doc."

"You are a magician, then?" asked Lily.

Doc laughed a crackling laugh and said, "Ha! After the manner of our folk, you might say so. But our magic, if that's what you want to call it, isn't like elvish or wizard or giant magic. Our wisdom is that of stone and rock, of gems and gold, of building and tunneling, of shaping and carving and gathering and making things. We're children of the stone, and so our *magic* is of the stone too. And I was a Doctor of Stone. I was sent as a representative of my people, to give what help and wisdom we could and to receive in return what I could learn from the others. Aye, my brothers and I made many a magic thing for many folk."

He sighed and then continued. "But all magics fade under this accursed Spell of the Witch. Long it's been since I've mounted a bright gem in a shining ax whose blade will not dull, or carved a pillar of stone that will never break, or shaped a suit of armor that can't be pierced, or mounted a hammerhead that would fly like lightning when thrown. Once I did all these things, but no more."

He then eyed Frederick's armor and said, "But well, now, I do see that you have some fine armor on! May I see it?"

Frederick nodded, removed the cloak, pulled the mail shirt over his head, and handed it to the dwarf.

"Where did you get this, may I ask?" asked Doc.

"Well," said Frederick, looking at the ground, "it was downstairs in one of the rooms. I thought the original owners were long dead by now and wouldn't mind if I borrowed it, you know, seeing that we're going to face the Witch and all that."

"Downstairs!" he creaked. "You got into the rooms downstairs? But how? Those doors have been locked for ages. Even I haven't opened them in many a year."

"I did it, Doc," said Colleen. "I'm sorry... I just asked the doors to open and they did. I didn't mean any harm, honest."

The dwarf looked hard at her, as if trying to decide something. Then he sighed. "Ah, well, strange things are happening these days. Now here's a human child who has power in her voice to loose what's been bound." Then he muttered something under his breath about elves.

"But see here, Frederick. You just keep this armor and wear it well. That's no ordinary suit that you have there, lad," he creaked. "It was made in the Good Days, when there were no evil goblins and no Witch. These suits of armor were made through the combined skill of all the races. Why, I had a part in their making as well!"

"You did?" said Mrs. Wigglepox incredulously. "But I thought you said that armor was made in the Good Days, before there were evil goblins and such? Why, that would make you..."

But Doc cut her off and said, "Well, yes, then. It would make me quite an old dwarf. But such skill was once not beyond me. Now, though, with the Spell and all, and no one to help, I've not fashioned such armor in many, many a year."

Again, he sighed, and then his expression became shrewd and he lowered his voice to a whisper. "But! I still can do a thing or two – as you saw when you tried to come into this house and walk down the hall!"

"You did that?" asked Colleen.

"Aye, I didn't know that you weren't with the Witch. There was that goblin outside and all," he said.

"Yes!" said Colleen. "What ever happened to it?"

"Well, it got more than it bargained for. I sent a load of boulders rolling down the hill at it. It danced a jig like you've never seen, hopping about like a jack rabbit to avoid my rocks. Then when the door shut, it ran off into the woods. Aye, the stone still hears me now and then, especially in great need.

And I've got a workshop far, far underground, down by the river where the Witch's spell is not so strong! There, where the river runs deep, and the power of the Lady still holds sway – there I can still do a thing or two, and there I have a few things that the Pirate missed and that the goblins know nothing of. This may be the very chance I have waited for! You must come with me to my workshop and see what I have kept. It may be that these things will help you on your journey."

The old dwarf's face beamed with excitement, and then he glanced out the window and said, "But see here, it is getting dark outside, and we must be getting into the tunnels. Can't have the Witch's people seeing any lights on in here. She doesn't know that I'm still here, you know. Come, come, and follow me now."

"But what about Badger?" said Colleen.

"Badger?" asked the dwarf.

"Yes, my horse!" said Colleen. "He's tied up at the bottom of the steps. And, oh! How could we have forgotten, we have another dwarf with us. He's sleeping on a litter that we made for him. We found him in a gorge sleeping fast and nearly buried under leaves and sticks."

Chapter 21 – Brother Dvalenn

"My brother, Dvalenn, once so keen,
Lost yourself, where have you been?
Sleeping long beneath the Spell,
What sad tales you could tell.
Once so sharp and keen and bright,
Your eyes now close to heaven's light.
Once you made the tools of gods,
Now your sleepy head just nods.
Even when you seemed to rise,
On useless things you kept your eyes.
You gathered gravel and stones you found,
That only weighed your pockets down.
I hope one day you let them go,
And look for treasures deep below,
Down, down you must descend,
To mine for treasures that will not end."

– The Lament of Sindri for his brother Dvalenn

Doc's eyes opened so wide that Colleen thought they might pop out. He leaped to his feet, spilling his drink and knocking his chair over.

"A dwarf!" he cried. "Take me to him!" And he ran to the door and began unbolting its many locks.

"You go with him," said Mrs. Wigglepox. "We'll be fine right here."

Colleen and Frederick ran after the dwarf, who was already out into the hallway, and Oracle thumped his cane behind them, trying to keep up.

"He's at the bottom of the landing," called Colleen, amazed to see how quickly the old dwarf could run.

Down the stairs they sped, and Doc darted past the horse and fell on his knees beside the sleeping dwarf.

He brushed the long stringy hair back and looked deeply into his face, then began to weep.

"He's my brother, Dvalenn!" he cried, and nearly fell on top of him for joy and sorrow.

Badger whinnied and Colleen soothed him.

After a moment, Colleen said, "I suppose we should take him upstairs if we can."

"How long ago did you find him like this, and where was he?" asked the

146

dwarf, choking and wiping tears from his face.

"It was about an hour or so before we got here, in a deep gorge to the north. He was nearly buried in leaves beside a tree, and we nearly passed him by," said Colleen.

"Bless your sharp eyes, child," said Doc. "Dvalenn disappeared *years* ago. I searched long for him, but never did find him. In the gorge! Why I'd been by there many a time, but never saw him. How strange."

The dwarf looked again at his brother lying on the litter and shook his head.

"I thought the Witch had taken him, just like all the others," he said.

Then his eyes narrowed and he looked deep in thought. "It's been twenty years or more since I've been by that gorge. I'll bet my golden ax that he was captured, and escaped, and made it all the way to the gorge, but was overcome by the Spell and fell into the Black Sleep."

He sighed, then wiped his eyes on his sleeve.

"Speaking of the little folk, you best go and get Mrs. Wigglepox and her lasses. We've got to get Dvalenn down into the mines," he said.

Frederick ran up the stairs and returned shortly carrying the three little people in his pockets, and munching another mushroom. Oracle came sliding down the stairs on his behind, looking rather gleeful. Frederick shook his head as he passed the little man.

"Now, if you would all please step back a pace, I'll open the door," said Doc, and he motioned for them all to move away from the steps.

They all stepped back, and the dwarf turned to face the stair. Then he did what Colleen thought was a very funny jig. And as he danced, he moved back and forth in front of the stairs, and ended in a flourish of floor stamping and one final leap in which he landed with his arms spread wide. He turned, a sheepish grin on his face, and winked at Colleen. Just as she was about to giggle at the sight, a whole section of the stairs opened inward, leaving a large doorway from which a yellow light glowed.

"Amazing!" cried Colleen, and ran forward to give the old dwarf a hug. "Doc, you would do marvelously well in an Irish pub! My people love to dance!"

"Indeed!" said the dwarf, the grin on his face growing even wider.

"But why did you do that?" asked Frederick.

"Ha!" said Doc. "It's a *secret* door, you know. One has to know the password for secret doors. And this one's password is a *dance*. It was one of my other brothers, Avliss, who came up with the idea. Now he was a merry fellow. Loved to dance, he did."

Oracle hitched a ride by climbing up onto Dvalenn's chest and planted himself where the remains of the bird nest were still intertwined in his beard.

Doc led them into a passageway that sloped downward almost immediately, and they had not gone far when the door in the stair swung shut behind them, leaving nothing but a stone wall where it had once been.

"No one knew about that door except the dwarves, I think," said Doc. "We made it as an emergency exit from the building."

"But I thought this place was built during a time of peace, when all the races were friendly toward one another," said Mrs. Wigglepox. "Why would you need secret doors and... and suits of armor?"

"I suppose that's true. But we dwarves are a careful lot when it comes to building things. And we always have a back door that's secret, you know," he said. "And there were the Orogim. We sensed a tension in the very rock – as if something evil were brewing. We prepared for it." He fell silent for a moment, as if remembering some old pain.

"But see here," he said. "It's a long walk ahead of us. Let me tell you a tale or two, and perhaps you might tell me one as well."

He cleared his throat, thought for a moment, and said, "Long, long ago, before the War between the wizards and the Witch, all the peoples of all the lands were good and noble. Why, even the goblins and trolls were once decent folk, and aye, even the Orogim. But none of the races knew of the others, except maybe the fairies – and they kept their secrets, until Anastazi the Great Wizard opened the Gates, and all of them opened into the Timeless Hall, where the peoples freely came and went."

"What is the *Timeless Hall?*" asked Frederick.

"Ah! It's a place *between* the worlds, or so they say. The Great Wizard either found or created it, and there he built the Gates. And as long as you stay there, you never age! In fact, no time passes at all."

"You mean I could go in, sit for a year, and come out and no time would have passed?" asked Frederick, his curiosity growing.

"That's right, my boy! Least ways not for you," said the dwarf. "That's why it's called *timeless!* Oh, time for the *worlds* still passes, but as long as you're in there, you never age, or at least not enough to notice."

Then a sly look crept over his face, and he lowered his voice and said, "The Gate to this world was lost after the Cataclysm, and the Witch doesn't know where it is, or she would surely have tried to open it by now... but there *are* some people who know where it is!"

"And what was the Cataclysm?" interrupted Frederick again.

"That was the terrible destruction that was unleashed at the last battle between the Witch and the wizards that I told you about," said Mrs. Wigglepox.

"Yes!" said the dwarf. "Everything was changed. The sea, the land, the hills, the desert, even the forest above us, and the magic not only destroyed things, but *rearranged* them – that's the best way I can put it. It was like the whole world got *shifted around.* So that's why the Witch could never find the Gate once she came back. And that's why the sacred places of the little people got lost too."

"But I thought that these wizards were really powerful, and all the legends back home of the little people say that they can grant wishes and do all sorts of magic too. If this land was *filled* with little people, how could just one old witch and a few goblins take over?" said Frederick.

"That's the sad part of the tale," said Mrs. Wigglepox. "There was betrayal."

"Betrayal?" asked Colleen, shocked.

Mrs. Wigglepox shook her head sadly. "Yes, one of our own people betrayed us. One of the grandsons of the Elders, Lugh himself. He gave himself over to the Witch and taught her our magic. And it's said that he even surrendered his own pot of gold to her."

"But why would he do such a thing, Mother?" asked Lily.

"Greed for power, my dear. Greed for power," she said. "The Witch promised to give him power over people – to make him a god. Can you imagine that? A little leprechaun pretending to be a god? Why, how absurd it would be, to see the smallest of the peoples sitting on his tiny throne with giants and goblins and men and trolls and elves and all the great spirits bowing to such a little thing? But, Lugh didn't see it that way. The Witch wove such lies in his mind that he began to believe such nonsense, and he gave all his power to her. He spent all of his wishes and wasted all of his magic gold and gems on her, and what did he get in return? He was lost, that's what he got, and he was cast down from his self-proclaimed greatness by one who was truly great."

"Yes," said the dwarf. "'Tis a sad tale. Lugh did have much power in this world, and you might as well say that he traded his pot of gold for a pot of beans – and bad beans at that. Sad, sad. The little people were taken by surprise again and again, because the Witch seemed to know everything about them – where their pots of gold were hidden, where their trees were, how many of them she would face – all because Lugh was feeding her information while pretending to oppose her. By the time Lugh's betrayal was discovered, the Witch had gained much power and the little people had lost just as much. Many people think that Lugh used his Last Wish in the Cataclysm."

"Hush!" said Mrs. Wigglepox sternly to the dwarf. "You mustn't speak of such things!"

"Ah, come now, Mrs. Wigglepox. You know it's true," said the dwarf.

"Yes, but the Last Wish is a sacred thing to the little people. We do not speak of it openly!" she replied, crossing her arms.

"But why? What's a last wish?" asked Frederick.

Mrs. Wigglepox began to speak, but the dwarf put a finger to his lips and said, "Perhaps another time we shall speak of this. Come along, we're almost there."

"Doc," said Colleen, "you said a moment ago that some people know where the Gate of Anastazi the Great is. If the Gate is not at the castle anymore, who can we talk to, to find out where it is?"

The old dwarf positively cackled with glee at Colleen's question, and continued to do so until Frederick whispered in Colleen's ear, "Do you think he's gone a bit mad, like Oracle back there?"

Doc suddenly stopped laughing and turned to face them. "*Mad?*" he said. "*Mad? Well, lad, it may be so! But it was not *madness* that made me laugh, no!*" And again, a fit of cackling took him.

Then he stopped laughing and a mixture of seriousness and wonder and delight all at once filled his aged face.

"I must warn you all," he said. "At your peril, do not stare for more than a moment at what you are about to see!"

Chapter 22 – Fight at the Inn

The next night at the Five Springs Inn, so many people turned out from the town and the surrounding land that there was standing room only when the McGunnegal children took their place in the middle of the dining hall and began to sing.

The cook gave Aonghus a large hat to place on the floor and, as they sang, coins began to fill it. At first, they thought this was a grand thing, but while Bib and Abbe were singing a duet about the sea, their sweet voices carrying across the hall and charming their listeners, Henny tugged on Aonghus' sleeve. He bent down and she whispered in his ear.

"There's a funny-looking man over at that big table," she said. "He keeps staring at me. I think he wants to take me away."

Aonghus looked briefly at the table where Henny indicated and there was indeed a fellow with an untrustworthy look about him. His shifty eyes kept darting between Henny, Abbe, and Bib, and more than once to the hat that was filling with coins. But his eyes kept coming back to stare at Henny.

Aonghus looked into Henny's frightened eyes and said, "Don't you worry, Pumpkin. I'll take care of you."

He lifted her in his great arms and glared at the man. The man met Aonghus' eyes once and then they flitted away to the hat, then back to the girls.

The evening proceeded uneventfully, and their hat was filled to overflowing, not only with copper and silver, but with gold as well.

But during their last song, Aonghus noticed that the shifty-eyed man rose from his seat, nodded to a fellow across the room, and both of them left. The first slipped into the hall that led to the stairs, and the other left through the front door.

As the girls sang a verse on their own, Aonghus whispered to Bran, "There's likely going to be some trouble tonight," he said. "Two shady-looking characters just slipped out of separate doors. I'll bet that hat of coins there's more of them too."

"Do you think they're after the money?" whispered Bran.

"That and the girls, I think, especially Henny. Keep your eyes open," he said.

Just then, the girls finished their verse and Aonghus and Bran joined in the final chorus in perfect harmony and the song ended to a roar of applause and a shower of coins.

The children could not help but notice Mabel sitting at a front-row table, smiling broadly and eying the money.

With a flourish of bows, the evening ended and the children collected the coins that had been thrown about them. They would not all fit in the hat, and so they stuffed their pockets full and headed for the kitchen.

Aonghus came through the door just in time to see a dark figure slip out of sight. He motioned for his brother and sisters to come close and he whispered, "Something's going on here. There are shady folk about, and I just saw one leave through the back door. Stay close, but don't look too suspicious."

But as they made their way to their rooms, nothing further happened.

"Come on, Bran," Aonghus whispered. "Let's help the girls count the coins."

In the girls' room, they emptied the hat and their pockets onto the bed and began to count.

"There's twelve pence to a shilling and twenty shillings to a pound," said Bib.

"Look at this one!" said Bran, holding up a gold coin.

"Let me see that," said Bib, taking it from him.

She inspected it for a moment and then said, "This one's a British India coin. It's got Queen Victoria on it."

"And what's this?" said Henny, holding up another.

"That's a crown. It's worth five shillings," she replied.

"I've never seen so many coins in one place," said Abbe, looking at the pile.

"Well, to figure out how much it is, we've got to remember that a florin is worth two shillings, a crown is five, a half-crown is two and a half, a tuppence is worth two pence, and a thrupence is three pence. If you find a guinea – that's a gold one – it's worth one pound and one shilling."

"That's too confusing," said Bran. "I've not held more than a shilling in my hand before today."

"There's more," said Bib. "A groat is worth four pence, a tanner is six, a ha'penny is worth half a penny, a farthing is a quarter penny, and a mite is worth one eighth of a penny."

Bran shook his head.

"What'll we do with it all?" said Abbe.

"We pay the taxes on the farm, that's what," said Aonghus. "No more worries about that. But see here, let's not get all worked up over this stuff. I wouldn't want greed taking hold of us. Just our daily bread – that's what we need, and enough to pay Caesar his due. I'm thinking the rest of it ought to go to help our neighbors. There's plenty of food here, and almost none back home. I say we buy a shipment of food and send it back home, first thing tomorrow."

"Skibbereen needs it most," said Bib. "The famine is worst there."

"Aye," said Aonghus. "Now let's finish counting."

They divided up the coins by type and Bib did the final count.

"It comes to fifty-eight pounds, six shillings, and three pence," she said.

"Not bad!" said Bran.

Suddenly, there was a knock at the door. Aonghus tossed a blanket over the pile of money and went and opened it to the round form of Ted.

"I've come to wish you good night, but if you care to listen, there's a late night speaker down in the common room. The Five Springs sometimes hosts political figures, or scientists, or adventurers. Tonight, it's a fellow named John Michaels. I hear he's quite passionate about helping Ireland through the famine. Thought you might be interested."

"Thanks, Ted, yes, I'd like to hear what he has to say."

"Well, he'll be starting soon. There aren't any seats left, but you might be able to hear from the stairs. Good night to you all," said the cook, and he turned and left.

"I'd like to hear this," said Bib.

"And me too," said Bran.

"Come on, then," said Aonghus.

They left the room together and Aonghus locked the door, then they sat lined up on the stairway that overlooked the common room. In the middle, where they had sung that night, stood a young man, perhaps in his late twenties, with dark hair and a kind face. The Master of the Inn had just introduced him, and the room grew quiet as he began to speak.

"Friends," he said, "tonight, less than a hundred miles away, children are hungry. They are hungry, not only from lack of available food, but because of ill-conceived policies and greed. I am newly come from the shores of Ireland, and have seen horrors beginning that no human being ought to endure. Disease is taking hold. Decent folk are run from their homes. And landlords plunder the mean hovels of the impoverished and destitute so that they might graze their fat cattle and build bigger barns on the backs of the poor.

"I would call us tonight to consider Ireland as Lazarus, and we as the Rich Man of the parable. Lazarus sits at our door. Dare we sit by day by day and watch the dogs of famine and pestilence lick his wounds? Nay, we must act now, before we are called to account for his inevitable death. And more than one beggar is he, for he is millions.

"This famine in Ireland is no small thing to be trifled with. Our government must be made aware that multitudes of our neighbors, yes, even members of our own empire, will soon have nothing to eat. These poor folk watch as the grand policies of the Market are enacted and they sink beneath the weight of its injustice. Let me read to you hard words that are being spoken by those suffering under this scourge."

Aonghus looked out at the crowd as the young man pulled a piece of paper from his coat pocket. A woman in a satin dress pulled a fan from her bag and began to fan herself with it. Others fidgeted, looking uncomfortable as the speaker went on.

"We are expecting famine day by day. And we attribute it collectively, not to the rule of heaven, but to the greedy and cruel policy of England."

At these words, a murmur went up from the crowd, and their faces grew dark and angry.

"Let me read on," said Michaels more loudly, and, clearing his throat, he continued.

"Our starving children cannot sit down to their scanty meal, but they see the harpy claw of England in their dish. They watch as their food melts in rottenness on the face of the Earth, all the while watching heavy-laden ships, freighted with the yellow corn that their own hands have sown and reaped, spreading all sail for England."

Michaels paused, surveying the crowd. Some met his gaze with dark glares, while others looked away. He went on.

"I do not bring these words to our shores lightly, nor do I wish to accuse. I only wish to inform and plead with the good people of Britain to send aid, and to petition our government to act swiftly, and not send analysts and bureaucrats, but food and medicine to the Irish. Stop the export of food from Ireland and feed it to the people, stop the destruction of homes and give the homeless shelter, stop the burden of heavy taxes and let the people work the land, and give relief to Lazarus before he dies, and the soul of our people is called to account for failing to see him lying at our gate."

Michaels went on for some time, describing the terrible sights that the

McGunnegal children were all too familiar with. An hour passed, and then he closed his speech.

"Friends, I know you are a good and generous people. Will you not help? I watched as you tossed good coin to Irish singers tonight for their magical voices. I tell you, a whole nation like them awaits you now. Will you not send them aid? Not only a few pence or even a few pounds, but your voice and influence as well? Write to the House of Commons and the House of Lords. Visit the Parliament, and speak for the needy. I will be here for another hour if any of you would like to discuss these things further. Thank you for your time and consideration."

The crowd began to rise from their seats and mingle, forming little groups, and more food and drinks were served.

Ted came halfway up the stairs and said to Aonghus, "They'll be going on for quite a while now, discussing the speech. All sorts of politics will get bantered about tonight, I reckon. I'm in for a long one. Well, good night to you all."

"Night," they said, and rose to return to their room.

"I think we ought to sleep on the floor of the girl's room tonight," said Aonghus to Bran.

"Right," he said. "I was thinking the same thing. I haven't forgotten that shifty-eyed fellow."

They all settled in, and Aonghus and Bran made themselves as comfortable as they could on the floor behind a room divider.

"It seems that there are some folk here in Britain who care about Ireland," said Abbe.

"I hope they care enough to listen to that Michaels fellow," said Bran. "I don't think the folk here know how bad it's getting."

"Let's pray they listen and do something. Well, let's get some rest," said Aonghus.

"Night," the others replied, and soon Aonghus could hear their breathing change to the slow, steady rhythm of sleep.

But he could not rest. John Michaels' words kept repeating in his head. Was the British government really that oblivious to their plight? Didn't they see what was happening?

He lay thinking about this for some time, and finally dozed off. The Inn had grown quiet, and all the guests finally retired for the evening or left, when something brought him wide awake. It had been a little sound – just a creaking floorboard in the hall.

Bran opened his eyes and whispered, "What is it?"

"Shh. Listen," he whispered.

Another creak, then a third.

They quickly roused the girls and held fingers to their lips, and Aonghus lifted Henny, who was still asleep, and placed her behind the room divider.

"Watch her," he whispered to the girls, then he and Bran stood on either side of the door and waited.

A few moments later, there was the sound of a key being placed in the lock, then a quiet *click*, and the slow turn of the doorknob. The door swung open ever so slowly, and a black clad figure slipped in through the door and tiptoed toward the now empty beds.

A second, then a third came in, and when they were all slinking forward, Bran closed the door behind them.

All three turned around, and the last thing that the third man who had come in saw that night was Aonghus' fist punching him square in the nose. He fell with a resounding crash and did not stir.

The other two men, barely able to see anything in the dark other than Aonghus' huge shadow, rushed forward together and attempted to grapple with him.

One tripped over something, which turned out to be a broomstick, which Bib had stuck out from behind the divider.

Bran picked up a large spittoon and forced it down over the other man's head. He went whirling this way and that, tripped backward over one of the beds, and lay still on the other side.

The man whom Bib had tripped was on his feet in a moment, but tripped over his unconscious partner and fell flat on his face.

"Get the lights, Abbe," said Aonghus, and a moment later, an oil lamp was lit.

Aonghus strode forward and picked up the tripped man by his black shirt. He wore a black mask, which Aonghus ripped from his face. It was the man with shifty eyes that he had seen earlier that evening.

"Who are you and what do you want with us?" demanded Aonghus.

Before he could answer, there was a scuffling of feet outside the door, a loud yell, and a bang, as if a gong had been struck, and then the door opened and the round face of the cook peered in, his bald head covered in sweat and a large iron frying pan in his meaty hand.

He took in the scene with a glance. "Well, I see you have things well in hand here, Aonghus. There's a third... oh, rather a fourth one out cold in the hall," he said, spying the unconscious figure with the spittoon on his head lying across the girls' bed with his feet in the air.

Aonghus smiled and then turned back to the man whose feet were now dangling off the floor.

"As I asked," he said to the man, who was now struggling to breathe. "Who are you?"

When the man did not answer, the cook said, "I can tell you who he is. His name is Dranshot, Fred Dranshot. He's been in and out of prison half a dozen times that I'm aware of. And that fellow there with the broken nose is Ernie Stripjaw – another bad potato."

Bran walked over to the third man, hefted him over the bed and onto the floor, and with a yank, removed the spittoon, which came off with a pop.

"I might have guessed," said the cook. "Dortus Crumpleshoe – another fly in the stew."

Just then, a voice from the hall called for lights and the voice of the Master of the House could be heard.

"What's going on here!" he said in a hushed voice. "You'll wake all the gue..."

But he went silent when he saw the unconscious black figure in the hallway, peered into the room past the cook's considerable girth, and narrowed his eyes.

"What is this?" he said. "Who are these people?"

The cook moved aside to allow the Master in and said, "Looks like some shady characters tried to do a bit of kidnapping, sir. Lucky that these young lads were watching out tonight. I was up, well, taking care of some business, when I thought I heard someone walking in the hall. I peered out from my room and, sure enough, this fellow in the hall was standing by the door here, keeping guard like. When he heard the ruckus going on inside the room, he turned to open the door. That's when I came right up behind him and knocked him in the head."

"Kidnappers? In my establishment? This is outrageous!" the Master hissed. "If word of this gets out, I'll have no further business! Quickly now, bring that man in the hallway in here."

The cook dragged the unconscious man in.

The man still in Aonghus' powerful grip was struggling frantically now to free himself, and was turning purple in the face.

"Better let him down, Aonghus," said Bran. "I don't think he can talk too well, hanging in the air like that."

Slowly, Aonghus lowered the man to the floor and allowed him to breathe.

"Why were you trying to kidnap my sisters!" he demanded, his face terrible with anger.

The man cowered, trying to pull free, but could do nothing to escape the iron grip that held him in place.

"We... we were paid..." he stammered.

"By who!" demanded the Master of the House.

"I... I... d...don't know!" he whimpered.

Aonghus tightened his grip and looked even more threatening.

"It w...was a m...man in a dark r...red cape! He gave us three pounds each." The man's tongue seemed to loosen the more he talked, and now he spit out the whole story in a rush.

"He was at the dinner last evening, and heard them sing. He promised us seven more pounds once we delivered the girls to him," he said in a rush.

"Where?" said Aonghus simply. "Where were you going to deliver the girls?"

"Around back, by the stables," he pleaded.

"Tie these blokes up, Bran, Ted, if you could please help," said Aonghus.

"Gladly," said the cook and, taking the man from Aonghus, took his great frying pan and soundly knocked him cold. "Let me get some rope," he said, and waddled out the door, returning a few moments later with rope and rags, which he unceremoniously stuffed into their mouths, and tied them up.

As soon as they had been bound, Aonghus slipped from the room and quietly went out the back door. The barn stood a short distance off from the Inn, and he stole silently across the yard, slipping into the shadows and around the side of the barn.

His sharp ears could hear hushed voices coming from the other side of the barn.

"They'll steal a pretty price once we gets them to the proper place," a grizzly voice said.

"Aye, a few hundred gold pounds each, I'd say!" said another.

"Or maybe none at all," said Aonghus as he banged their heads together and they fell senseless.

Going back to the room, he found the four kidnappers tied hand and foot and gagged, with the cook and Master standing discussing what to do with them.

"If you young men wouldn't mind," said the Master, "I'd like to take these worthless... gentlemen to the jail this very hour, rather than make a disturbance for my guests in the morning."

Both Aonghus and Bran frowned, but agreed.

"There are two more out behind the barn," said Aonghus. "They have a cart that should serve nicely."

Aonghus carried one man, Bran another, and the cook and Master huffed and puffed their way down the steps, carrying a third. The girls kept watch over the unconscious fourth one until Aonghus came back and, tossing him over his shoulder, carried him out as well.

When they had all six of the men bound in the back of the cart, they threw a tarp over them. "We'll take care of them from here," said the Master. "You two go back up with your sisters and care for them."

Off they went then, and Aonghus and Bran returned to the girls' room and found that Henny had finally woken. She had slept through the whole thing.

"Well, there, little one!" said Aonghus. "We're all safe and sound now."

"What happened?" she asked, her little girl's eyes wide with wonder and fear.

"Never mind that," said Aonghus. "But we'll be leaving in the morning at any rate. No more staying here for us, no matter what Cousin Mabel says."

"That's for sure," said Bib.

And so they tried to get back to sleep, but only Henny dozed off, and the rest of them talked until morning.

When breakfast time came, there was a knock on the door. Aonghus rose and opened it to find the cook, who bustled in and shut the door behind him.

"Good morning, ladies, gents," he said. "Hope you were able to rest a bit after all the excitement last night."

He looked at their faces and realized that they had not slept at all.

"Well, at any rate, those blokes who broke in last night are in the local prison. The police will want to speak to you today. I expect they'll be here by mid-morning," he said.

"We're planning to leave as soon as possible," said Aonghus.

"Of course," said the cook. "And I don't blame you. Only you'll want to give testimony to the break-in and identify them so that they get what's coming to them."

He paused and then removed a large pouch from his hip.

"And I brought you this," he said, handing Aonghus the pouch. "It's your money from a few nights back. I haven't counted it or anything, but it's a fair amount. Probably not as much as you got last night, though."

Aonghus accepted the pouch and thanked him, extending his hand.

"You've been a good friend to us, Ted. We're in your debt. If you ever need a strong hand, you've got mine."

"Friends, then," said the cook, shaking his hand.

"Friends," said Aonghus, and proceeded to give the large man a bear hug.

"Good Lord, man," said the cook, catching his breath. "In all my days, I've never met a lad like you. You don't know your own strength!"

Aonghus smiled, and the cook bid them all farewell, bidding them come down for breakfast as soon as they were ready.

And so they busied themselves getting ready to depart, and Bib counted the money in the bag.

"Look here, all," she said excitedly. "We have nearly sixty-five pounds now."

"We've got to get that to Father," said Abbe.

"Yeah," said Bran. "But how?"

"Can't we send it to him?" asked Henny.

"Not the way the mail is," said Bib. "You can't send cash. It would sure as anything be stolen. One of us will have to take it back to him."

"I'll do it," said Bran.

They all looked at him.

"It just makes sense," he said. "See here, we can't send one of the girls, not with what happened last night. And you need to watch over them, Aonghus. That leaves me. I can take care of myself."

"No," said Aonghus.

"Now see here..." began Bran, but Aonghus cut him off.

"We'll all go," he said.

"All of us? But we've just gotten here. Father said..." began Abbe.

"Father told us to stick together, Ab," he cut in.

"But we'll need to get on a ship," said Bib.

"That shouldn't be hard. We have the money for passage now," said Abbe.

"But what about Colleen? We should wait until she arrives so she can go back with us," said Bran.

"If we leave now – right now, I mean, we might be able catch a ship back before she even leaves," said Aonghus. "See here, we'll talk to Ted the Cook about the idea. He might know if there are any ships sailing back to our port in Ireland in a day or two."

They went down to breakfast together and found Mabel busily consuming a large plate of eggs, cakes, and sausage.

Ted the Cook spotted them and motioned for them to sit at a table. He served them all the same, along with fruits and milk.

"They sure eat well here in Britain," said Bib.

"You mean you don't eat like this in Ireland?" said Ted.

"No, sir," said Bib. "What with the famine and all, folk are beginning to starve. It's been a hard year for us."

"So what that fellow said last night is true, then?" asked Ted.

"Yes. We only hope that the crop is better this year," said Aonghus. "A good many people are getting sick too, and more can't pay their rent, and so are getting evicted. Who knows where they'll go."

Ted looked shocked. "I'd not heard it, no I hadn't, although folk around these parts are often unkind to your countrymen and don't speak well of them. But I say you're decent men and women, and I'll put an iron pot to the head of anyone who says otherwise. Just 'cause a man's accent is different doesn't make him less of a man."

The cook shook his head. "Well, you all enjoy your breakfast. It's on me today," he said, and bustled off to the kitchen.

After finishing their meal, Aonghus said, "They truly do eat well here. I'm stuffed."

"Aye, at least at this Inn they do," said Bran. "But I'm not so sure I'd want to eat like this all the time. Might end up like Cousin Mabel over there."

He nodded toward Mabel, who had just finished cleaning her third plate with a biscuit and was leaning her great bulk back to make room for her belly, but eying the table for some last sweet to complete her significant meal.

"Bran!" said Abbe, scolding him. "You shouldn't say such things!"

"He's right about one thing," said Aonghus. "Seems to me that too much pleasure turns one jaded."

"What's 'jaded'?" asked Henny.

Aonghus leaned over to her and said, "It's sort of like putting too much honey in your tea," he said. "At first, it's really sweet. If you down it anyway, it makes your stomach upset. If you just keep putting too much honey in your tea, pretty soon that's the only way you can drink it, even though it makes you feel sick after you do. Seems to me that most sorts of pleasures are like that. A little makes life sweet. Too much just makes you bored and restless and not satisfied with much of anything."

Henny nodded with understanding, having, on occasion, put too much honey in her tea.

While they were eating, Aonghus beckoned to the cook and he came over.

"Ted, we've decided that we're going to return to Ireland as soon as possible. We've earned enough money in the past two nights to do it," he said.

The cook looked surprised. "Why, I thought that you lot were off to school or something."

"Well, we were," said Aonghus. "But that's changed now. Can you find out what ships are sailing back in the next few days? It would have to be soon. We need to meet our sister there."

The cook looked at them and said, "Well, that's a good school you were heading to. Shame to miss the chance, I'd say. But," and he sighed, "I'll check for you. Shouldn't take more than an hour or so. I'll send my lad Teddy."

With that, he bustled off, shaking his head.

"Well, we'll have to delay Mabel until we get word," said Bran. "Might as well go and unpack..."

The girls grinned and raced up the steps to their room, where they busied themselves with undoing their morning packing.

Aonghus and Bran began to follow, not wanting to leave the girls, but Mabel called them over to her table.

"Be ready to leave within the hour, boys," she crooned. "Our coach will be wanting to depart soon."

"I suppose we better go pack our things," said Bran.

An hour later, there was a knock on the door and Bran opened it to a shy serving girl. She blushed when she saw him and timidly said, "Your Cousin Mabel bids you come down with your belongings – the coach is ready."

"Thank you... what is your name?" he asked her.

"Lizzy," she said.

"Thanks, Lizzy," he said, and smiled broadly at her.

She blushed and hurried down the hall, glancing back at him once before disappearing around the corner.

"What do we do?" asked Bran. "Teddy doesn't seem to have come back yet."

"Let's take our things down one at a time. I'll do it. You lot stay put," said Aonghus and, with that, he took one bag in his arms and carried it down to the waiting coach.

He fussed with it for several moments, positioning it this way and that on top of the coach until Mabel shouted from inside, "What are you doing up there?"

"Well, we don't want to make the coach imbalanced, cousin," he said. "We wouldn't want to tip over."

"Well, hurry along!" she said irritably.

Aonghus went back to the Inn and found the cook and his boy Teddy in the room with the others.

"Teddy here just arrived," said the cook, "and I'm afraid his news will be disappointing to you."

He was a thin boy, quite unlike his portly father, and a few years younger than Bran. Looking into his large brown eyes, Aonghus could see that he was a fine young man and trustworthy.

"Right," said Teddy. "The dock master says that there won't be any ships leaving for the whole east coast of Ireland for nine days."

"Nine days!" said Abbe. "But that's too late!"

"They say the government is planning things out and making sure shipments get done properly," he replied.

They were all silent for several moments and then Aonghus said, "Thanks, Ted, Teddy. We really appreciate it."

"Not a problem, Aonghus," said the cook. "Sorry it didn't work out for you."

"Well, we'll get along okay," he said. "Could you do one more favor for us?"

"Name it," said Ted.

"Take this money and buy a load of food with it, and send it to the town of Skibbereen in Ireland. It's down south, in County Cork."

"Won't you be needing that?" asked the cook.

"We've saved enough out for the trip back and to pay the taxes," he replied.

They shook hands again, and Aonghus said, "Might as well get your things, everyone. No sense in delaying now."

So they all gathered up their belongings and trudged down to the waiting coach where Mabel scolded them for being so slow.

"We'll miss our train if you don't hurry along!" she called from inside the coach.

"A train!" said Henny. "I've never been on a train before!"

Soon they had their bags stowed in the carriage and away they went, with Aonghus and Bran hanging on the back at times and trotting beside the horses.

It was not long before they rounded a bend, and the deep sound of a steam whistle reached their ears. The horses snorted in response, and the driver whipped the reins for them to gallop.

"Best hurry," he shouted. "That's the warning whistle. They're boarding now."

Chapter 23 – The Gate of Anastazi the Great

Doc led Colleen, Frederick, and the Wigglepox family down to the end of the passageway and stopped at what appeared to be a bare wall.

He placed his hands on this and a door swung silently open. A wide hall opened before them.

As they entered, the dwarf cried out in a loud voice, "Behold the Gate of Anastazi the Great!"

Colleen gazed in wonder at an enormous door that was set in the wall opposite them. Shining like the moon, its silver radiance pierced the darkness like a song. Frederick let out a low whistle, the little people all gasped, and even Badger whinnied and shook his mane. Oracle slid from Dvalenn's beard and came around to gaze at the sight. But Colleen simply stared at its incredible beauty.

Standing at least forty feet tall and twenty feet wide at the base, its double doors rose upward to a peak. A golden frame surrounded the massive gates, carved and inlaid with intricate scroll work and figures of little people, elves, dwarves, men, giants, and others that Colleen guessed were peoples she had never heard of. But there were no evil creatures on these gates – all were bright eyed and happy, and the golden frame of the doors seemed to be some sort of history, telling some tale of long, long ago.

For a long moment, Colleen stood transfixed, her mind filled with visions of antiquity – of heroes and wizards and princes and princesses – of all the legends and fairy tales that she had ever heard and, as she stared, it seemed that they all might be true in some way – that beyond those gates might lie worlds without end, where any dream might become a reality.

She did not hear Doc's voice saying, "Do not stare at it for long!" for once again, something seemed to awaken within her in that moment. It was a bit like the way she felt when she was standing on the Hill back on the farm, singing that night with her family all around. How long ago was that? Was it a day? Or a week? She could not remember. But this feeling was even deeper, as if she were suddenly roused from a deep sleep, awakened from a dream that she had been dreaming her whole life long. The runes and images on the door grew sharp and clear to her eyes and mind, and she *read* them – *understood* what they said, and knew that they were indeed a history, and that somehow she was a part of it.

She stretched out her hand toward the Gate, dropping Badger's reins, and began to walk forward, enthralled by the sight. One step, two, and then she was hurrying forward.

Distantly, she heard everyone shouting warnings to her, but the Gate held her gaze, its power and beauty capturing her mind.

Then suddenly, Frederick's face loomed in front of her, blocking her view of the shining doors, and strong hands gripped her shoulders from behind.

His voice, loud in the echoing chamber, snapped her mind into focus.

"... got to stop, Colleen!" Frederick was saying. "There's a rushing river right in front of you! You've got to..."

She blinked and stared at him.

"What?" she said.

"You're going to ... or, it looked as though you were in some sort of trance or something, Colleen. Colleen? Are you all right?" he asked, worry written on his face. "Colleen? Don't look at the Gate, Colleen, look at the floor!"

She looked down then, and just a few feet behind Frederick was a rushing river, the sound of which now filled her ears. The cavern, Frederick, Doc's old hands on her shoulders, and a worried Lily peering out of Frederick's pocket all came rushing back to her.

She rubbed her eyes and then peered around him at the still shining Gate, then back at Frederick.

"What happened?" she asked. "I feel as if I've just woken from a long sleep."

"Perhaps you have," said the dwarf. "Such is the power of the Gate to those with eyes to see."

"See what?" asked Frederick, looking at the dwarf. "Can we move away from this river's bank? It makes me nervous."

"Yes, please do," said Lily.

They moved back and sat down against the wall behind them, and the dwarf bade them not stare directly at the silver doors that Colleen now realized were on the other side of the wide river. Now she knew that she had very nearly tumbled right into the swift current that cut across the massive hall.

"How... how did the Gate get all the way down here?" asked Colleen after a moment.

"As I said, young lady, things got *shifted*. Whether the Gate moved or the land moved around the Gate, who can say? But here is where I found it, long after that terrible day. Deep beneath the ground right across the river from my tunnel. So, either by chance or by Providence, I became the Keeper of the Gate. And here's what's more – I've been here alive and well ever since that day so many thousands of years ago."

"Thousands? How is that possible?" asked Frederick, disbelief in his voice.

"Well, dwarves are a long-lived people, although not usually this long. Personally, I think the Gate was damaged in the Cataclysm, and is *leaking,*" said Doc.

"Leaking?" asked Colleen. "Leaking what?"

"*Timelessness!*" said the dwarf. "Or *agelessness.* When I'm down here, I just don't seem to age much at all. And even when I'm up in the house, it seems nearly the same. It's as if the magic of the Timeless Hall is leaking out of that Gate and filling this whole area. Now that I think of it, it could be how Dvalenn survived out there all those years."

The thought suddenly struck Colleen that she was in a place that time had forgotten – with a dwarf who was thousands of years old. And now she was no longer aging either – that the power of the Gate of Anastazi the Great was flowing all around her and in her and through her, making her ageless in this strange underground world.

"But wait a second," said Frederick, interrupting her thoughts. "You grow mushrooms down here. *They* certainly must age or they wouldn't grow."

"A very good point, young man," said Mrs. Wigglepox.

"Indeed," said the dwarf. "The magic only seems to affect creatures like you and me, but not fish or plants or insects that I've encountered. I don't know how it might affect your horse, Badger."

Colleen pondered this for a moment and then a dreadful image came to mind.

"Frederick," she whispered. "Outside, the Spell of the Witch is creeping through the forest, putting everyone into a dreadful sleep. This door is leaking timelessness into that same forest. Do you suppose the two magics are mixing together, and the little people out there go on sleeping forever in some dreadful unending life of nightmares? What kind of world is this?"

"I hadn't thought of it that way," he said, frowning. "What an existence that must be! Do you think they even know it? I mean, are they just lying there, dreaming away, and not even aware that they are sleeping on and on, their whole life one big fantasy? Do they even know anymore that there's a real world that they could awaken to?"

Colleen shook her head.

"I don't know, but it's all the more reason for us to try to help them. And now's our chance, Frederick. This is the Gate of Anastazi, right in front of us.

It's time for us to go through it and get home and bring back some real help."

"Lass, it's not going to be that easy," said Doc. "That door has been locked for thousands of years. I've tried a hundred times to open it, and failed every time. I'd have gone home long ago and brought an army of dwarves here if I could have, but Anastazi the Great himself locked it. It would take a magic greater than his to unlock it – unless you had the key."

"I've got to try," said Colleen. "Can you get me over there?"

"Aye, but first things first. Let's get Dvalenn to my workshop," he said.

Colleen looked back longingly at the Gate as Doc led them away. Could she open this door like she had the others up in the house? And if not, what would they do now? Hope and despair mingled in her heart as they turned a corner and the shining light disappeared.

Doc led them on for some distance until they came to another blank wall. Once again, he touched the rock and a door swung silently open. Through this, they entered another tunnel that was illuminated with bright glowing gems that twinkled as they passed. The floor was smooth, but not slick, and was made of great slabs of green and brown agate. The walls were swirls of orange and yellow and red and white that seemed to take in the light of the gems and hold it, making the passage warm and beautiful to behold.

"Did you make this passageway?" asked Colleen.

"Aye. It's taken me many years, and I'm still working on it, but aye, I made it."

"But it's incredible!" said Frederick. "How could one person do it all alone?"

The old dwarf smiled and actually seemed to blush. "We dwarves know a thing or two about stone craft, as I've told you. It's in our blood. Kind of what gives us meaning in life, you know."

"To cut stone gives you meaning in life?" asked Frederick.

"No, no, boy," said the dwarf. "It's more than cutting stone. You see, we believe that when the dwarves were made, we were given a great task – to build great halls and rich tunnels and grand caverns. Not just for our own glory, mind you, but for the Creator who made us, and to share these with everyone else. If we don't try to accomplish the very thing we were made to do, then there wouldn't be much meaning in life. Why, what good would it do, in the long run, just to *exist* without *doing* what you were made to do and *being* what you were made to be, and then sharing it with others? And *that* is another reason that I am quite pleased to see you. At long last, I have someone that I can share all of this with. And wait 'til I show you the Crystal Cavern."

"The Crystal Cavern!" said Rose excitedly. "What's that?"

Doc grinned a toothy grin, winked at her, and continued down the hall.

Chapter 24 – Leprechaun Gold

The passageway twisted and turned as Doc led them on. Frederick watched the eerie light of glowing crystals rise and fall as they passed by, and Badger's hooves echoed *clippity-clop* with every step. The echoes, the lights, and the growing sense of moving steadily deeper and deeper underground was beginning to weigh on him. Minutes ticked by, and Oracle began to hum a tune in time with the horse's footfalls.

"Are we there yet?" Frederick said at last.

"Just around the bend," said Doc, and a moment later they came to a dead end.

"Another secret door?" asked Colleen.

Doc smiled and said, "Step back a bit. That's it – just a bit more."

As they backed up, the dwarf cupped his hands against the wall and whispered something that they could not make out. Without warning, the floor under Doc's feet began to sink.

He lightly stepped aside as a large, perfectly round hole appeared, the white stone sliding silently away, and they could see a green ramp descending into darkness.

"I'm afraid your horse will have to stay here, Colleen," said Doc. "He could go down the ramp, but not beyond the next chamber."

"But what if he wanders back to the river? He might fall in and drown!" she said.

"Now don't you worry about that," he said. "I have just the place we can keep him."

He cupped his hands once again against the wall to their right, whispered something, and this time, the wall itself slid aside, leaving an opening large enough for Badger to walk through.

"Bring him along," said Doc as he entered.

Frederick followed as Colleen led Badger through the open wall. He found himself in a chamber that had a distinct earthy smell, and, looking about, saw a great many mushrooms growing on shelves and in buckets and on decaying logs.

"It's your mushroom garden, isn't it?" said Frederick.

"Yes!" said the dwarf. "And I have just the place for this fine horse. I had a horse a long time ago. A long time ago."

He paused, remembering, then shook his head and led them to the far side of the room, where there was a stone rail and wall that surrounded a stall, of sorts, the floor of which was covered with pine needles.

"There are certain kinds of mushrooms that need a bit of acid in their soil, so I keep a bin of pine needles for just that purpose. It's a bit low right now, and would make a nice soft bed for your horse, and we can tie him to the rail."

"Wonderful!" said Colleen. "But I wouldn't want to leave him for long."

"He'll be fine," said Doc. "I've even got a bit of something that he might like."

He went to an adjacent bin and brought out an armload of brown dried grass.

"You use that to grow mushrooms too?" asked Frederick.

"Of course, and many other things as well. You can flavor your mushrooms by the humus that you create for them to grow in," he said. "But come along now. I want to show you my workshop. Please, help me with my brother."

Frederick and Colleen untied the litter from Badger and gently lowered it to the floor.

Colleen patted Badger and whispered in his ear that she would be back soon, and led him into the stall. The old horse began to munch happily on the grass and seemed content to stay put.

"Come now, help me with Dvalenn," said Doc. "Let's get him down to my workshop."

With Doc on one end and Colleen and Frederick on the other, they picked up the litter and carried it out to the ramp.

"Your brother is heavier than he looks," panted Frederick as they reached the ramp.

"Dwarves are a sturdy folk," said Doc. "Dense bones, you know. Now watch yourself – don't drop him, especially when we get to the bottom."

"Why?" asked Frederick as they descended. "What's at the bot..."

But he did not finish his question, for as they reached the base of the ramp and walked through yet another door, a cascade of colors suddenly met Frederick's eyes and he stopped dead. His mouth dropped open, and he stood speechless, staring. Then they all lowered Dvalenn to the floor and slowly walked forward, and the wall slid silently closed behind them.

A dazzling kaleidoscope of rainbows and shining gold washed over both of them and they stared up in wonder.

"It's gold," whispered Frederick, more to himself than anyone else. "And gems and crystals. There must be a million of them!"

For several long moments, they stood in awe, gawking at the gigantic room they had entered, whose golden walls arched upward to form a great red-gold domed ceiling that was crammed with crystals of every color, some as thin as hair, and others huge and jutting from the ceiling like great spikes. All were shining, radiating brilliant light that filled the cavern with a multitude of rainbows. The floor was gold as well, and every inch of the room was so perfectly polished that it reflected everything around them as if they were surrounded by mirrors, or perhaps were inside a mirror. The effect was to make everything seem to stretch outward forever and ever, the light and gold and rainbows going on and on until it went beyond their vision.

"Behold the Crystal Cavern – the Hall of Sindri!" he cried.

Mrs. Wigglepox let out a gasp and put her hand to her heart, then both hands over her mouth, and stared. Oracle squeaked with delight, and Lily and Rose both said, "Oh!"

"What's wrong, Mrs. Wigglepox?" asked Colleen. "Are you all right?"

For a moment, she did not answer, but then seemed to come to herself and said, "I don't believe it!"

Doc grinned expansively and danced a little jig across the polished gold floor. Reflections of himself jigged around the walls and floor and ceiling, casting the illusion that a dozen other dwarves danced with him.

"I told you I saved a few things from that pirate and the Witch!" He laughed, then danced about again.

"Not in all my years..." began Mrs. Wigglepox, and then she repeated "Not in all my years..."

"Mother," said Lily, "are we inside a pot of gold?"

"Yes!" shouted Doc with glee. "Yes, indeed you are, youngster, and it's the biggest pot of gold in the world, made from leprechaun gold and gems and dwarvish magic!" And once again, he just could not help himself and stamped his feet and danced about.

"But... but how?" asked Colleen. "Where did you get so much gold and so many gems?"

"And leprechaun gold at that!" said Mrs. Wigglepox.

"I can see myself everywhere," said Frederick, turning around and around, and watching hundreds of golden reflections of himself turn with him.

"Yes," said Doc in a serious tone. "You truly *can* see yourself in here. *Every bit* of yourself."

"I suppose so, with so many reflections," said Frederick.

"No, he doesn't mean that," said Colleen, gazing at herself in the nearest wall. I can see..." She paused, tilted her head sideways, and then frowned and looked down.

"What's wrong?" said Frederick.

"That's a side of myself I don't like to look at," she said quietly.

"You look all right to me," said Frederick. "I mean, you don't have any zits or anything."

"No, boy," said Doc. "Look closer in the mirror. Look at any one of your reflections in this room and it will show you a bit about yourself. It reveals one little aspect of who you *really* are."

"I don't get it," said Frederick.

Doc sighed.

"You see how these crystals refract the light, taking in normal white light and breaking it up into all the colors of the rainbow?"

"Sure," said Frederick, looking at the ceiling.

"Well, this room – these walls and floor and ceiling – do that to your image. They refract the image of *you* into all its pieces, and show you each color of your heart and soul and mind and body – the whole *you*. All you have to do is look carefully enough and you'll see."

Frederick paused, looking at the image of himself before him. He stared for a moment, and suddenly it was no longer just a reflection of his body, but a darker image. Its greedy eyes darted back and forth to the gems around it. It smiled malevolently, reaching out to grab one of the glowing stones. Frederick shut his eyes.

"You see?" asked Doc.

"I don't like looking at myself like that. I'd rather not even see that stuff," said Frederick.

"None of us do," replied Doc. "But the real power of the room can only be experienced once you face who you truly are. If one just dares to stand and face himself, then the power becomes available to do something about it. Until then, the room holds no power for that person."

"And what is that power?" said Frederick.

"It's the power of the Wish," said Mrs. Wigglepox. "One of the most potent powers in the universe."

"You mean I could make a wish in here?" asked Frederick.

"You could," said Doc. "But you must not! Not while there are so many of you dancing about the walls. You never know what might come about with so many Fredericks making a wish. It might turn out to proceed from a rather ugly part of you, and the wish would surely turn sour. You first must clean every image within you and, having done that, unify them all into one grand, bright image."

"How does one do that?" asked Colleen, looking at the half dozen images of herself that stared back at her.

"It can be a lifetime of work. You need a guide, and all the good powers of Heaven and Earth helping you. The Hall of Sindri only shows you how far you have to go. It doesn't give you solutions. But, for starters, just being honest enough to stare your ugly self in the mirror goes a long way. Once you've gotten yourself together, you'll look in the mirror and see a single image – your true self – the person you were made to be in the first place. When that person walks into this hall and makes a wish, it will never go astray. Now leprechauns, they're natural wishers, and except for those that got turned into gremlins and such by siding with the witch, they should be able to look at themselves in these mirrored walls and see just who they are."

Oracle hobbled over to one wall and banged his reflection with his cane. A single reflection of himself stared back.

"Put us down, please," said Mrs. Wigglepox.

As soon as they were on the floor, the three little leprechauns joined Oracle and stared at themselves in the walls. Three Mrs. Wigglepoxes stared back from various places around her, and for Lily and Rose, there were only two.

"See!" said the dwarf. "Not as much work to be done with these good folk. They've fought a good fight against the Witch and her spells."

"That's too much to think about," replied Frederick, feeling a bit embarrassed that so many Fredericks stared back at him all around.

"But I can see that if word got out about this place, there might be an all-out war to get it. Can you imagine being in control of a place where you can wish for anything? I mean, I know some people that would do just about anything to have this place. By the way, where did all this gold and these gems come from?"

"Well, to answer the first question, I suppose you can actually *thank* the Pirate for that," said Doc. "It was strange... after stealing so much from the little people, one day he showed up with the *whole lot* of it, and left it right there in front of the house. Just left it there and disappeared and never returned. It took me all day long to get a load of it into the house and many days more to haul it all down here, and *years* to build this room. But before I could get it all hidden, a whole troop of those goblins showed up and took the lion's share of it away. I stowed what I had saved down in these tunnels and, over the years, assembled it all in this – the Crystal Cavern!"

He waved his arms about the room, still grinning, and then continued. "And here's my plan. You see, the Witch probably thinks that *she* has all the leprechaun gold. Sadly, she does have most of it. But, as you can see, she hasn't gotten it all. I figure if we can get enough good little people down here in this room, maybe they can plumb *wish* away the old Witch and all her goblins, or something near to it. But I'm real cautious about it, mind you, what with the Betrayal and all that. You never know which of the little people, begging your pardon, Oracle, Mrs. Wigglepox, Lily, Rose... which of the little people are *safe* to let in on the secret. But the Hall is a revealer of hearts, see. I'll bet if a black leprechaun came in here, the whole room would go dark with the reflections it would give off."

Mrs. Wigglepox looked sad.

"What is it?" asked Frederick, who could see her face sticking out of Colleen's pocket. "What's wrong?"

She sighed and then said, "Well, it's not even as easy as that. You see, a leprechaun can't use just *any* gold. Not even another leprechaun's gold. Each piece must be found and blessed with leprechaun blessings and placed in the pot just so, and buried in a certain way and a rainbow called down on it, and other secret things as well. It could take *years* to make a decent pot of gold that's any good for granting wishes. And even then, wishes are tricky things. You might wish for something that you think is good, and something even worse comes of it. Why, you might wish that the Witch were gone from our land forever, only to find that some evil giant has appeared, smashed the Witch flat, and is now wandering about smashing everything else in sight too. And there are limits to wishes. So, you have to be very careful what you wish for. The safest wishes are for the good of people, not for their hurt. That's why the little people were given the power to grant wishes in the first place – to help others. Wishing for bad things almost always turns into something bad for the wisher."

Now it was Doc's turn to look downcast. "Do you mean," he said quietly, "that all my work here was for naught?"

"Oh, no!" said Mrs. Wigglepox. "I can see that this indeed *is* leprechaun gold, and most of these gems were from leprechaun pots as well. There is a *great* deal of leprechaun magic in this room, Doc, and a great many leprechaun blessings as well. And just look at these rainbows! But I really don't know what would happen if I tried to use it. It is *very* powerful. I have never felt so much magic in one place. But if I made a wish here, with the gold of hundreds and hundreds of leprechauns all mixed together, why, the wish might go astray, or go too far, and do some great harm. I think that the only way to use this room would be for at least *three* experienced leprechauns to focus all their powers together to control the wish. And a new pot of gold is best if it has the blessing of a leprechaun Elder as well – one in direct descent from the First Elder. Alas, the last Elder of our neck of the wood disappeared many years ago."

"Mrs. Wigglepox," said Colleen, "there are *four* leprechauns here. You and your children and Oracle!"

"Alas," she replied, looking sadly at her two daughters. "Lily and Rose have not even made their *first* wishing. There's been no chance even to look for gold since the times have been so hard. If only they could find a bit of gold for themselves, then I could begin to teach them."

Doc, who had begun pulling on his long white beard, suddenly brightened and said, "You all wait here and enjoy these rainbows. I'll be right back."

Then he stood in the middle of the room, did another dance, and the floor beneath him began to lower him down, down in a circle about three feet across, until he and Dvalenn completely disappeared from their sight. When he was gone for several minutes, Mrs. Wigglepox led her children around the room, pointing out various kinds of gems and the pure quality of the gold.

"It really is amazing," she said. "But to think that I have so many tainted reflections of myself. I've got work to do before I start wishing again."

A moment later, Doc rose out of the floor, the stone circle lifting him upward until the floor was as whole and smooth as ever.

"I left Dvalenn in the workshop," he said. "Come now, gather close around me. And hold on to one another. I wouldn't want you falling off before we reach the bottom."

They gathered around him and the little people were carefully placed back in the pockets of Colleen and Frederick, and Doc did his dance. All at once, Frederick felt his stomach lurch inside him as the floor dropped downward. Colleen grabbed his hand and held it tight, and he noticed how rough her hand was, calloused by hard work on their farm, he supposed.

She smiled at him as they descended.

"Don't let me fall, now," she said.

"Ha, I'm the one who's likely to go tumbling off this thing," he said.

She laughed, and he suddenly felt glad that he was here with her. He hoped his hand wasn't sweating. That would be just like him, he thought, to ruin a perfectly good moment of kindness by getting nervous.

Suddenly, he noticed that Oracle was not on the platform with them, but had walked over to the golden wall of the room and had both hands stretched out on it and his head bowed.

He mumbled something that was indecipherable, and just as Frederick dipped below the floor and lost sight of the bent leprechaun, there was a change in the room above, as though the air had suddenly become charged and brighter, and the rainbows grew crisp and clear. Energy seemed to fill the room, and Frederick was wondering what was happening when the face of Oracle appeared, peering down the hole at him.

"Fredersmouth!" he called, and jumped.

"Whoa!" Frederick cried as the leprechaun came falling down at him. He let go of Colleen's hand and barely caught the little fellow and put him on the floor, saying, "Are you out of your mind? What if I had missed catching you?"

But Oracle said nothing and only giggled his coarse laugh.

Colleen grabbed Frederick's hand again and took Oracle's with her other.

They descended in a shaft of golden light for a moment until even it faded away and darkness took hold.

"Nobody move," said Doc. "You wouldn't want to fall now."

Frederick watched as the bright hole in the ceiling became smaller and smaller, until it was a tiny circle – a star in the black void that surrounded them. He was beginning to wonder how far down they would go when the stone slab stopped with a quiet *thump*.

"Keep together," said Doc, "and follow me."

"Where are you?" said Colleen.

"Here," he said from the darkness in front of them. "Step forward."

They did and, a moment later, there was a *SWOOSH* behind them. Frederick looked back, but could see nothing. He looked up, and the tiny circle of light far above winked out.

"Doc?" said Frederick.

"A moment," said the dwarf from some distance away. "I'll get the lights."

Chapter 25 – Doc's Workshop

Colleen stood in the darkness, holding two hands – Frederick's with her right and Oracle's with her left. She was struck by the difference between the two – Frederick's was warm and soft. He'd not done much manual labor, she decided. Oracle's, was small, like a child's, but as calloused and bony as her grandfather's. Somehow, the old leprechaun reminded her of him, and she realized how much she missed the old man. Had he come here too? Or was he off to some other world, finding his *true self,* as he had said that night he disappeared? And what of herself and Frederick? Would they do the same in this strange land? Would she discover why she felt both deeply at home and strangely out of place back in Ireland? Were all her reflections in the Hall of Sindri truly pieces of herself that she needed to reconcile and bring together to find out who she really was? And this strange little man standing next to her had only a single reflection. What could that mean? He seemed almost crazy at times.

She shut her eyes in the darkness and focused on him, trying to read him, understand him, feel what he felt. There was something hidden beneath his old cloak – something more... She reached out with her heart and mind for it. But just as she did, lamps sprang to life all around them, and the little leprechaun let go of her hand and banged his cane on Frederick's foot.

"Ouch!" he said, releasing Colleen's hand and hopping on one foot. "What was that for?"

"Careful!" cried Lily from Frederick's pocket.

"Oh, sorry!" he said. "I forgot you were there."

Oracle only grinned.

Colleen looked around. The room in which they were standing was carved from gray stone that ran in a high shaft far above them into darkness.

"Over here," called Doc, waving to them.

They went to where he stood and, as they did, a stone door swung silently open before them.

"Welcome to my workshop!" he said, and led them all inside.

The room was illumined by large, radiant crystals mounted on the walls, and they could see many stone tables and chairs laid about, and on these tables were various hammers and chisels and saws, and many, many uncut or partially cut stones and gems. Along one wall ran a small shallow stream. Its waters gurgled softly as it slowly ran along the entire length of the room, appearing out of one wall and disappearing through a hole at the other end. In one corner was a cot of sorts with some old blankets and a hay-stuffed mattress and pillow on which Dvalenn lay sleeping.

The walls and floor, though smooth, were plain and gray.

"Why haven't you made your workshop as beautiful as the halls and caverns outside?" asked Frederick.

"What's that?" said the dwarf. "Oh! Well, why would I?"

"My father has all sorts of things in his study back home – rare paintings and statues and tea cups and swords. It's like his own personal treasure chest," said Frederick.

"We dwarves aren't like that, you know. Our workshops are just that – workshops. All the beautiful things are to be shared and enjoyed by all. It's our joy to make them and share them," he said. "One day, I hope that I will be able to open up these tunnels as the grand Road to the Gate of Anastazi."

"All the stories I've heard about dwarves," said Frederick, "are that they love to hoard gold and gems and fight anyone who tries to take it away from them."

Doc looked grave and said, "I've been away from my homeland for a very long time. It would be sad if such a thing has befallen my people. That's not our *natural* way, if you take my meaning. It would be most *unnatural* for a true dwarf to hoard gold and such in his workshop for himself. And besides, it wouldn't mean much in the end, would it?"

"No, I suppose not. In our world, it seems like some folk collect wealth just for the sake of collecting it," said Colleen. "The more they get, the happier and more miserable they seem, all at the same time."

"Yes, and just think about this too," he replied. "If I go and hoard all this leprechaun gold and all these gems and rainbows and such for myself, I'd be no better than the Pirate or the Witch, now would I? She'd like that, you can be sure, if I kept it all to myself."

"She would *like it?*" said Frederick skeptically. "I thought she wanted it all for herself?"

"Of course she would like to have it," Doc replied. "But, more than that, she wants *power* - power over people. If I give my heart over to living like her, then she's truly defeated me. She might one day break in here and steal my life's work away. But if she doesn't steal my heart, then she hasn't won anything more than a pile of rocks in the end."

"But look here," he said, brightening a bit. "I have a job for these little people. How about hopping down and coming over here to my little stream."

Colleen and Frederick put them down and they all went over to the slowly flowing brook.

"I've been meaning to do some panning for gold in this here stream, and, what with all my other labors, I've not had a chance to do it yet. Now how about you all take these," he handed them three tiny pots, "and do some panning for me. And I'll tell you what, you just keep the first load that you find. And, Oracle, here's one for you as well."

Oracle took the pot, turned it over a few times, and then handed it back to Doc, shaking his head.

"Suit yourself," said Doc with a frown.

Mrs. Wigglepox looked at the pot she was holding and turned it over and over in her hands.

"This is a leprechaun pot!" she said.

"Straight from the Pirate's treasure!" he replied. "And there's a load more where that came from."

He strode over to one wall, opened a cabinet door, and waved his hand. Inside the shelves were lined with scores and scores of tiny pots.

Tears filled Mrs. Wigglepox's eyes, but she wiped them and turned to Lily and Rose. "Come, children, let's see what gold we can find."

Oracle followed the Wigglepox family as they walked to the edge of the stream. He seemed most curious to watch what they did.

"And you youngsters, come with me," said Doc, and led them to the other side of the room.

"You're not s'pose to watch or see when or where leprechauns get their gold from," he said. "So how about you make yourselves comfortable for a bit. Here, Colleen, you take this old bed next to Dvalenn. Kick off your shoes and rest. And Frederick, here I have a hammock set up that you can rest in."

"Thank you, Doc," said Colleen. "I am rather tired."

She lay down, and Frederick climbed into the hammock. Within moments, she noticed that Frederick had closed his eyes and seemed to be asleep.

Poor thing, she thought. *Trudging all this way with me. He must be exhausted. He's not such a bad chap, after all.*

Soon she too drifted off to sleep.

* * *

But Frederick's mind would not let him rest. He lay there thinking of all that he had seen and heard that day – of pirate gold and treasure and magic. How much had the Pirate stolen and then returned? And why did he return it? His father had been right – there was a huge treasure to be had, only now it was in the hands of a Witch that everyone seemed to think was terribly evil and powerful.

But this dwarf had a load of treasure too, and probably more in his vast halls. Why, just one of those glowing crystals in that chamber out there would sell for a king's ransom back home. If he could only take one of them back, his father would be so proud of him. *No*, he thought, *they are not mine to take. Maybe if I found one lying about, that would be different.*

His thoughts trailed off and sleep finally took him, and as he slept, he dreamed of finding a great treasure chamber, and stuffing his pockets with gold, returning home to rescue all of Ireland from the famine, and making his family rich beyond their wildest dreams. But through his dreams, the aged voice of Doc kept interrupting and saying something about guarding his heart. Sometime in the night, he woke with a start, looked about him, and saw the old dwarf sitting on a low stool with his chin in his hand and mumbling something he could not hear. So he shut his eyes and dreamed no more until morning.

Chapter 26 - The School

As they neared the train station, Aonghus could see the smoke of a steam engine billowing up over the houses and the distinct clang of a bell ringing.

"Best hurry, Miss Mabel," said the voice of the coach driver. "That would be the boarding call."

He cracked the whip and the horses surged forward. A moment later, the coach rounded a corner and pulled up in front of a large black steam engine with the words "Southern Railway" painted in yellow letters across the side. The driver leaped from the coach and ran to the ticket collector, who was just boarding a passenger car, and spoke to him. The man stepped quickly over to the coach and said, "You just made it, folks. Come quickly now, get your things and get aboard. Follow me, please."

Aonghus and Bran unloaded Mabel's things, including her heavy trunk, and carried them aboard the train car along with their own things. The girls carried their own luggage, as well as Colleen's small bag that she had left on the ship and which they had been toting along with them.

After being shown to Mabel's cabin, where they placed her belongings, they were shown to a second cabin, significantly more cramped, where they would be spending the journey. It would not be a long trip – just a few hours – so no sleeping quarters were provided, except for Mabel.

"I do believe it is time for a bite to eat," she said to the ticket collector as soon as she was settled. "Would you be so kind as to show me to the dining car?"

A moment after she had gone, there was a lurch of movement and a loud whistle, and the train began to roll.

"Now's our chance," said Bib.

"Right," said Aonghus.

He led them to Mabel's cabin, but when they arrived, the door was locked.

"Not a problem," said Bib, and she pulled a hairpin from her mop of red hair and quickly opened the door.

Aonghus led the way in and shut the door behind them, then opened the trunk. He found four large bags of rocks within, pulled them out, and handed them to the others. Then they quietly left the cabin, locking the door behind them.

As they entered their own cabin, Henny said, "Oughtn't we to have asked Cousin Mabel if we could take those rocks?"

"It's not as though we're stealing them," said Bran. "They took them from *our farm*. They stole them from us. You can't steal what's your own."

"Henny, you would be right in any other situation," said Aonghus. "Any time you take something that isn't yours without the owner's permission, it's stealing, no matter how small it is. But in this case, our cousins actually took something from us without *our* permission. Dad told Rufus that he could take a few of these stones, not whole bagful's of them. It's really ours, see, so it's not stealing to take it back."

She nodded, but her face still looked troubled.

"Tell you what, Henny. When we see Dad again, you can ask him. If he thinks we should give these rocks back to the Buttersmouths, we'll do it."

She smiled then, and they proceeded to pick rocks from the bags and look at them. Each one had some emblem or writing engraved on it.

"See there," said Abbe, "these things must be worth money, or Rufus wouldn't have taken them. These sorts of symbols are carved all around the farm. I wonder what they mean?"

"First chance I get, I'm going to do some research. Maybe the school will have a library that will help," said Bib. "Or a teacher who can read this language."

She ran her finger across one of the symbols and looked thoughtful.

"This language must predate even the Celtic Tree Alphabet, and that dates back to around the fifth century A.D.," she said.

"How do you know that?" said Bran.

"Haven't you ever read about the Ogham inscriptions, Bran?" she asked.

"Well..." he replied.

"Come now," she said. "There are hundreds of Ogham stones all around the Irish Sea. They're inscribed with Ogham, or the Celtic Tree Alphabet. But these carvings don't look anything like that. It's a much more complex language, it seems to me."

"We best hide these bags among our own, and once we get to the school, we can investigate them further," said Aonghus.

After hiding the bags, they talked on about the stones, wondering what ancient civilization might have existed thousands of years before their time – who they were, and what they might have been like. But before they knew it, the hours had rolled by. The whistle sounded, a bell clanged, and the train pulled into a station.

"Let's help Mabel with her things," said Aonghus to Bran. "Ladies, can you handle our things? They're a bit heavy."

"No problem," said Abbe, and she went to pick up two bags of rocks. But she quickly put them down again.

"Maybe they are a bit heavy," she said sheepishly.

"All right, then. You all stay here while Bran and I unload Mabel's things, and we'll be right back.

Aonghus and Bran went to Mabel's cabin, took the chest from the train, and then returned for their sisters. When they were all outside, Mabel looked them over and shook her head.

"Well, then, children, here we are," she said in her most drawling voice. "The school is outside of town, down by the seashore. You can see it from here."

They turned and looked where she pointed, and they could see about a half mile from the train station, down a long hill, a series of brick and stone buildings surrounded by green gardens.

"Professor McPherson is the headmaster of the school. He is expecting you. I wired ahead and told him that you five would be arriving shortly."

"Aren't you coming with us, Cousin Mabel?" asked Bib.

She chortled a rather false laugh and then said, "Heavens, no, child. You have to *walk* down there. I shall be going to London on the next train, which, I believe, leaves in twenty minutes. I have some... some business there. You children will walk down to the large stone building in the center of the campus and go in the front door. Tell the receptionist that you are the McGunnegal children, sent by Rufus Buttersmouth, and that Professor McPherson is expecting you."

She looked at them all gravely and then said, "Well, hurry along now. Just follow that path down." She indicated a dirt path that led down the hill toward the school.

"All right, then," said Aonghus. "You take care of yourself, Mabel. Will you be contacting us?"

"Contacting you? Oh, I suppose, now and then. We'll have to see. But off you go then," she said, and waved her hand for them to be on their way. Then she turned and made her way into the train station without a backward glance.

"Would you get a load of that!" said Bib. "Dumps us off in the middle of Wales, with hardly a good day, just like that!"

"Come on," said Bran. "Let's just get down to the school."

Aonghus glanced one more time at Mabel, shrugged, and picked up three bags of the rocks as well as his own bag, and started down the dirt path toward the collection of buildings that Mabel said was the Ismere Boarding School. Bran took the last sack, and they all followed behind.

The path, although dusty, was not at all bad, and soon they were walking past brick buildings that appeared to be apartments of sorts and a large stone building with the word "Ismere" carved into a stone arch above two large, bright red wooden doors.

Aonghus led them up a flight of steps to a wide porch, opened the door, and held it as his brother and sisters filed in. As he followed behind and closed the door, he found himself in a great hall with green marble floors and ornately carved pillars. Red draperies framed the windows, and there was a bronze statue of a man in a robe with a plaque on its marble base that read "Professor Evan Ismere, founder and philanthropist."

Several boys who were standing in the hall stopped in mid-conversation and stared at them. They were dressed in black knickers and white shirts and wore smart-looking red jackets.

"Can I help you?" said one of them after a moment. "We don't accept solicitations here."

They looked the McGunnegals up and down and turned up their noses.

Aonghus started to say something, but Bib elbowed him in the ribs and walked over to the boys.

"We're not here to buy or sell anything," she said, putting on a beautiful smile, showing her perfect white teeth. "We're here to enroll in school. Could you boys help out a lady and show us where to go?"

They blinked, and one of the boys shut his mouth, which had been hanging open. Somehow, Bib had gone from being the brains of the family to an amazingly attractive young lady.

"Yes, of course!" said the older of the two, who appeared to be about sixteen, and who was now speaking a bit too loudly. "My name is John. Follow me, I'll show you to the secretary!"

He turned to lead her to the other end of the hall, but managed to bump into the other boy, who was standing and staring at Bib.

John punched the other boy in the arm. "And that's David," he said, and pushed past him.

Bran turned to Aonghus and whispered, "Did you see that? She's got those boys practically falling over each other. Where'd she learn that?"

"Don't try to understand girls, Bran," said Aonghus as he picked up his bags.

They followed the boys, who were now giving Bib a guided tour of the expansive hall, explaining its ornate architecture and massive pillars. Bib appeared to be listening intently, with wide eyes and many a "you don't say" as they led on. But she turned and winked at her brothers and sisters as they followed.

The boys just shook their heads as they passed through a set of wide doors that had carvings of grape vines around them and entered a somewhat smaller hall. There, a gray-haired woman wearing small spectacles low on her nose sat at a large desk.

She looked over her reading glasses as they entered and said in a very proper English voice, "Ah, you are the McGunnegal children. I am Miss Fenny, the school secretary."

Miss Fenny wore a beehive hairdo and a heavily starched white blouse with a red tie and jacket and checkered skirt. The McGunnegal children had never seen a woman dressed like this before.

She paused, looking at them for a long moment, and then said, "And where is your sister?"

"She'll be coming along on the next ship, ma'am," said Abbe, when no one else spoke.

"And when will that be?" the woman inquired.

"In about two weeks," said Aonghus, stepping forward to the desk.

He towered over the small woman even though she stood from her seat and straightened herself to her full height.

"Well, young man," she said, looking up at him and placing her hands on her hips. "I certainly hope so. The semester begins in just under three weeks. Now let me see..."

She paused, picking up a piece of paper and examining it.

"You must be Aonghus? And Bran, Abbe, Bib, and Henny," she said, pointing to each of them in turn. "That means that Colleen is the one coming later? Fine, then. John! David! You may stop goggling and be excused now. I will ring the bell when I need you."

The two boys seemed to awaken from a trance and shook themselves, then quickly left the room through the doors they had entered.

"You best watch that talent of yours," whispered Bran to Bib. "You'll have all the boys in the school drooling all over their desks if those two fellows are any example of what the lads are like around here."

Bib gave him a quizzical look as if she was not sure what he was saying.

But Miss Fenny was speaking again and he could not respond. "... Segregation of genders, and that means that there are two strictly separate halves of the campus, with this building being the sole place that boys and girls may interact. If we find any young ladies on the boys' side of the campus or any young men on the girls' side, there will be *serious* consequences."

"Do you mean we can't visit our big brothers?" asked Henny.

Miss Fenny seemed thrown off guard for a moment and, looking at Henny's big, innocent eyes, she seemed to soften. "That is correct, child," she said. "However, for someone your age, and seeing that you certainly *should* see your brothers, we can arrange times for you to meet here."

She gave a faint smile, and then returned to her business self.

"Well then, I shall show you around the building," she said, stepping around her desk. "Follow me, please."

Aonghus listened with detached interest, and noticed that the others did not seem to be paying attention much either, except for Bib, who seemed genuinely fascinated as Miss Fenny described the thirty-eight classrooms on two levels, the history of the school, and various "departments," which included History and Archeology, Religion, Classical Literature, Science, Athletics, Mathematics, Agriculture, and "Foundations," which Miss Fenny described as the most important elements of education, and included reading, writing, and arithmetic.

"You shall have some exposure to all of these departments for the first two months of your time here and, after that, you shall choose a main discipline in one department. Choose your discipline well, since it will occupy most of your time here at the school. After you choose a discipline, you will join that department's "house," and you will move to that house's dorms and live with other house members who have also chosen that same main discipline."

On and on she went, describing the various houses and walking about the building, showing them each of the thirty-eight classrooms, fire escapes, bathrooms, and other places, until she came at last to the center of the building where a large oak door stood shut before them.

"This door leads to the Dean's personal studies and offices in the Tower. You are never to walk beyond this door without permission of the Dean, Professor McPherson. He is a private man and does not take kindly to children snooping around his private quarters. You will note that the door is locked," she said, giving it a slight shove.

"Professor McPherson!" whispered Aonghus to Bran. "We've got to see him!"

"Excuse me, ma'am," said Aonghus. "Will we be meeting the Professor today?"

"Oh, no, he is a very busy man and cannot individually meet every new student. You will meet him on the first day of the semester at the General Assembly in the Great Hall. In fact, I was just about to take you there. It is in the basement. Please follow me," she said, and walked briskly down the hall and led them down a long flight of stairs and showed them a large auditorium that looked to seat at least four hundred people.

Finally, their tour ended and Miss Fenny, finding her assistant – an older student named Jane – asked her to show the girls to their rooms. She then picked up a small bell from her desk and rang it.

John and David nearly fell in through the door and came hurrying up to Miss Fenny's desk.

"But where will our sisters be staying?" asked Aonghus.

"Never you mind, young man. It's not for the boys to know where the girls stay," she replied firmly.

Aonghus frowned and said in a kind but firm voice, "Miss Fenny. I promised my father that I would look after my sisters while we were here. I wouldn't take kindly to anything bad happening to them. Please, at least let us know what building they are in so that we can send them a message if we hear from home or there's an emergency."

Miss Fenny looked him up and down, as if considering his massive form, and frowned, a hard look crossing her face.

She began to speak when Henny said in a quiet voice, "Please, Miss Fenny?"

For a moment, she seemed flustered, and her hard look softened. She stood as if dumbfounded, and then said, "Building Three-G."

"And where will Aonghus and Bran be, ma'am?" asked Henny.

She paused again and said, "Four-B. Now, off you go. John, show these boys to their rooms. Jane, you take the girls."

Having said this, she sat down in her chair, picked up a pile of papers, and began to shuffle through them.

"Come on, follow me," said John.

Aonghus paused for a moment, picked up Henny, and gave her a hug.

"Now don't you worry, little one. Bran and I aren't far away, and Bib and Abbe will watch out for you," he said.

Henny waved goodbye and headed off behind Abbe and Bib, looking back with a sad face, and Aonghus and Bran followed after John.

"That little sister of yours could melt a witch's heart, I think," said John after they had left the room and gone some distance, well out of Miss Fenny's hearing. "I've been here for five years and I've *never* seen Old Fenny soften up like she did for her. She actually *told* you what building the girls would be in. That's just unheard of!"

The boys said nothing, but walked on behind John as he led them outside and across the campus grounds. Aonghus, however, determined that he would most definitely be finding out just where Building Three-G was.

Chapter 27 – Four-B

Aonghus followed behind Bran as John led them to an aging stone building with broad battlements around its top. It loomed tall and silent before them, with two large windows on either side of a wide, green door. Aonghus felt as though he were approaching some great crowned head with closed eyes stuck in the ground. The letters "4B" were engraved on an archway over the door.

"Here we are," said John. "You two will be on the fourth floor, and you've got a good room that overlooks the old lake out back."

He pushed open the door and walked in. An image of the great head swallowing John flashed through Aonghus' mind and he smiled to himself. A stone entry hall with dark wooden flooring greeted them as they walked in. The floorboards creaked under their weight as they passed aging oil paintings of stern-looking men and women dressed in rich clothing.

"It feels… *old* in here," said Aonghus. "The very floors have voices. How many years, I wonder, have these old boards spoken to those who walk on them, and what stories might they tell?"

John glanced at him, but said nothing until they reached the bottom of a polished oak staircase.

"You be careful about saying thing like that, Aonghus," said John in a serious whisper.

"Why, what do you mean?" said Aonghus.

"That talk of the floors having voices," he said, lowering his voice even more. "Some of the boys here say that they do – that some nights they creak all on their own, and when you go to look, no one's there."

Aonghus and Bran looked at each other, but John was going on.

"And that lake out back – you watch yourself out there too. They say that years ago, some kid went swimming in there. He came back all crazy in the head, saying he had seen strange things down in some underwater caves, like a dead man lying on a rock and all sorts of weird creatures that guarded the body and wouldn't let him near it."

"Do you think it was true?" asked Bran as they began to climb.

"Maybe just a story to scare us away from swimming there," he replied. "But who knows? It's a weird lake, anyway."

"How so?" asked Aonghus.

"You just look out your window at night when the moon is full and shining down on it and you'll see what I mean," he said. "The shadows in that water are sort of eerie. I mean, they, well, *dance*. That's the best way I can put it."

Four flights of stairs later, with John huffing and puffing, but Aonghus and Bran not even breaking a sweat, they pushed through an oaken door that sported a large brass knocker that looked like the bust of a man with a long beard.

They entered a cozy hall with stone walls covered with tapestries. Aonghus reached up and ran his fingers along one that held a golden lion on one side and a red dragon on the other.

"Beautiful," he said.

"It's the coat of arms of one of the school benefactors. Must not be a recent one, though, to end up here. Anyway, this is the lounge for the fourth floor. It's where you can just hang out with the other Undesignateds, like these blokes here," he said, waving a hand at a few teenage boys who sat about the room.

Aonghus walked over to one of them and held out his hand. The boy rose, spilling several books and a stack of papers to the floor. He was thin and wiry, and only came up to Aonghus' chin.

"I'm Aonghus McGunnegal," he said, "and this is my brother Bran."

"Pleased to meet you, Aonghus, Bran," said the boy, taking his hand. "David's the name. David Rhigy. And this is Afan Ceredig, Aaron Malo, and Govan Bell. Pull up a seat and chat for a spell. We've been debating what discipline we want to take."

"Let me show them their room first," said John. "Then I'll leave them to you. Come on, then, here you go."

"What are 'Undesignateds'?" asked Aonghus as John led them through a door with a number seven on it.

"You're an Undesignated until you decide what your main discipline is going to be."

"Are there many Undesignateds?" asked Bran.

"Sure, plenty," said John. "Probably about thirty right now. They're probably out by the lake or something. You've got a while before you have to decide what main discipline you want."

"What's yours?" asked Bran.

"Athletics," said John. "Say, Aonghus, with your muscles, I'll bet you'd be great at rugby and the pole toss. And Bran, I bet you can run pretty well with those long legs. How about you guys come down to the athletic field tomorrow afternoon after lunch? We're having some tryouts for the school teams and you might enjoy it. Plus, the girls are allowed down there too – that's the other place we can meet with them. I'll bet old Fenny didn't tell you that, did she? She doesn't approve, but McPherson says that it's okay."

Aonghus looked at his brother and they smiled at each other. Neither of them had ever been outdone by any human being of their age, except each other, in any athletic contest in which they had ever competed.

"Take a look out over the lake," said John, leading them across the room to a large window.

Aonghus looked down and, a few hundred yards away, there was a beautiful lake shining in the sun, which covered several acres. Its shores were lined with trees and gardens, and he could see a number of students lounging in the shade.

"Doesn't look eerie at all to me, especially when you've been in the old bog back where we live. This looks like a garden paradise," said Aonghus.

"You just wait until night and a good full moon, then let me know what you think. Anyway, here's where you'll be living for a while," John said, gesturing at the big room.

Two spacious bunks, a bookshelf, oil portraits of British nobility, several cushioned chairs, a washroom, and a bowl of apples sitting on a good-sized table that had four chairs around it met their gaze. There were also various decorations and tapestries along its long walls, including several suits of armor and oil paintings of ships and lighthouses and coasts along the sea.

"This room is for just the two of us?" asked Bran.

"I know it's not much," said John ruefully. "But you'll have to make do until you choose a discipline."

"Not much?" said Bran incredulously.

"Shabby, I know," said John. "But the Undesignateds get the old stuff that the other houses don't want."

Aonghus wondered what the other house living quarters must look like if all of this was just leftover and rejected furniture and decorations.

"This is... fine," said Aonghus, dropping his bags on the floor and sitting in one of the big chairs.

He sank deeply into its ornate cushions and whistled. He had never sat in a chair quite so soft and comfortable.

"I could get used to this," he said.

"And grow fat doing it," said Bran, laughing.

"Well, I'll leave you to your room. Dinner will be served at six in the dining room of the Great Common Hall, just beside the room where you met Old Fenny," he said, pointing to a large grandfather clock that adorned one corner. "Nothing special, mind you, since school hasn't started yet. You've got about an hour to wash up. I'll see you then."

Aonghus and Bran just looked around the room and then at each other.

"Did you ever imagine in your wildest dreams of being in a place like this?" said Bran. "And check out the beds..."

He flopped himself on one of the lower bunks, which was twice as wide as his bed at home. The mattress was stuffed with goose down, and he sunk down deep into it.

"Oh, man, I don't think I could sleep on this," he said after a moment. "I might never wake up. It's too comfortable."

Aonghus lay on his own bed and said, "I'm with you there. I think I might try it tonight, but I might end up on the floor instead."

"Well, might as well get washed up," said Bran.

"Right," said Aonghus, going to the washbasin and splashing himself with water.

As they made their way back into the lounge, Aonghus called to the boy they had spoken with earlier.

"Tell me, David, what are you thinking of for your discipline?"

"Dunno. Maybe Religion. Or Sciences. We all think that Aaron, over there, is going to be a hermit," he said, indicating a boy whose face was hidden behind a large book. "This is just about as social as he gets. We're lucky he's emerged from his room today."

Aaron peered at them over the top of his book and then sank behind it once again. Aonghus could see that it was entitled *Inferno*.

"What's that you're reading, Aaron?" said Bran.

Aaron's eyes appeared again and he mumbled something about Hell, then sunk back behind his book.

"He's always reading stuff like that," said David. "Last week, it was something from Plato – something about a myth. Anyway, we don't know what we want to do, really. Miss Fenny keeps scolding us for having *lack of vision.* But we have a whole year to figure it out."

Aonghus and Bran took seats and talked for some time about the school and the students and teachers, until Aaron silently stood and left the room. A bell rang somewhere in the distance.

"That's the five-minute dinner warning," said David. "Aaron always knows when it's going to ring even without looking at a clock. Best get down to the Great Common Hall."

"Right," said Aonghus as they rose and followed Aaron out the door.

In the Great Common Hall, Aonghus and Bran found their sisters and joined them. Dinner was, by their standards, quite sumptuous, though it was really a simple meal of meat, vegetables, cheese, and bread, with water to drink.

"Aonghus!" said Henny as they ate. "Is your room as big as ours? We have giant soft mattresses and great red curtains and paintings and all sorts of mirrors and decorations. It's like a museum!"

They all smiled, and Aonghus said, "Yes, Henny. I think we'll be seeing a whole different world here at this school, with lots of stuff that we don't have back home. But don't lose yourself in it– it's just *things,* after all."

After dinner, a dark-haired girl with equally dark eyes came up to them and said, "You must be the new lot. My name's Jenny. I'm off to the library. Want to come?"

"We do indeed," said Bib.

"Nice how she speaks for the rest of us," said Aonghus with a wry grin.

"Come on, Aonghus," said Abbe. "You might as well find out where it is. You can't spend all of your time running around on the athletic field, you know."

Jenny looked at Aonghus, went over to him, and touched him lightly on the arm. "Aonghus, is it? And might a lady walk with a gentleman such as yourself?"

"Oh, of course," said Aonghus.

Jenny took his arm, smiled at him, led him out of the dining room, and said, "The library is just down the hall."

"Get a load of that," said Bran to Bib. "First you, now Aonghus."

Bib punched him in the arm, then followed after the pair, and the rest of them came behind.

"The library is quite grand," said Jenny as they passed through a pair of ornately carved wooden doors. "See?"

Aonghus stopped and gawked. They had walked out onto a high balcony that looked down upon a massive room filled with thousands upon thousands of books. Shelves lined the walls and floor and, all around the balcony, which spanned the entire room, a second story of the collection met their eyes.

Bib let out a squeal of delight and grinned. "I'll see you all later," she said, and headed for the stairs that led down to the first level.

"Closing time is nine o'clock," said Jenny after her.

Bib waved and was gone.

"Come on, Henny," said Abbe. "Let's see what books we can find for you."

"And how about you, Aonghus?" said Jenny, still holding his arm. "What will you be studying here at school?"

"Agriculture," he said.

"Truly? So am I," she said. "Let me show you that section."

Aonghus turned and raised an eyebrow at Bran as Jenny led him away.

"How do you like that?" said Bran aloud to himself. "They've all left me. Well, might as well do a bit of exploring. It's the lake and the woods for me."

With that, he turned and left and headed outside.

* * *

The next few days were uneventful, and Aonghus found himself spending more and more time on the athletic field with Bran. The other boys were amazed at his incredible strength and Bran's speed, and the sidelines began to be frequented by more and more girls who came to see the new boys that had come to school and whose reputation was spreading.

One day, as they were on the field practicing rugby, Aonghus noticed a new, rather big fellow, walking onto the field.

Will Green, a friendly blond-haired boy with long lanky legs and arms, nudged Bran and said, "Look out, chaps, here comes trouble."

"Who's he?" asked Bran.

"That would be Ed Choke. He sort of rules the roost here, him and his cronies. And look – there's Fred Hinder right behind him. Watch out for that lot," said Will.

Choke was a tall boy, as tall as Bran, and well-muscled. He strode toward them with an arrogant look on his face. Hinder, on the other hand, was short and stocky, tough looking, and rolled onto the field like a boulder ready to smash anything in his path.

"Great, and here comes Slick and Bigs too," said Will, indicating a greasy-haired boy with shifty eyes and a very short, thin boy with a sour expression, pushing through the crowd. "Their real names are Hank Slips and Billy Sour."

Slick and Bigs jogged up behind Ed and Fred as they approached, and Aonghus saw right off that they wanted trouble.

The rugby game came to a stop. The other players backed up a few steps, leaving Aonghus, Bran, and Will standing alone.

"Hello, Ed," said Will, wiping sweat from his face. "Back for the season, I see."

Ed looked at him condescendingly, and then eyed Aonghus and Bran, sizing them up.

"Bran McGunnegal," said Bran, introducing himself. "And this is my brother, Aonghus."

Bran held out his hand, which Ed looked at, but didn't take.

Bigs stepped forward and said, "I hear that these fellows think they're something special, Ed. I've been keeping an eye on them, see, and on your girl Mary. She's been visiting the field here ever since they showed up. I think she's got eyes for this one."

Ed pushed Bigs aside and came nose to nose with Bran, a sneer on his face. He was just as tall, but broader than Bran, and now the crowd was gathering in a circle, anticipating a fight.

"So, been moving in on my girl, eh?" snarled Ed.

"Now see here, Ed," said Bran. "I have no intentions of moving in on your girl. I don't even know who she is. What's this all about?"

Just then, a pretty raven-haired girl pushed through the crowd and wedged herself between them. She was tall and shapely and had rose-red lips. Her eyes were dark and, in that moment, Bran thought she was the most beautiful girl he had ever seen. He could not help but stare.

"Leave him alone, Ed," she said. "He's not done anything."

"So, Mary, you're taking up for this Irishman?" said Ed with a sneer.

Ed noticed Bran's gaze at her, narrowed his eyes, and pushed Mary away.

She stumbled and fell, her face heading straight for the ground.

Bran moved so quickly that for a moment he seemed to have vanished. But before Mary hit the ground, Bran had caught her around the waist and gently set her back on her feet. They came face to face with Bran's arm around her.

"Are you all right?" he asked gently.

"I'm fine," she said, glaring up at Ed. "Thanks."

Then Bran felt a hand grip his shoulder and spin him around and, an instant later, saw Choke's fist coming for his nose.

He ducked, stepping in under Ed's left arm that gripped his shirt and ended up behind him. He pushed him from behind just as Ed's punch swooshed in the empty air. Ed stumbled and fell face first into the mud.

The crowd laughed and then began to chant, "Fight! Fight!" and the circle tightened around them.

Ed jumped to his feet and dove for Bran. But he simply stepped to the side, and Ed slid in the mud, dirtier than ever.

Suddenly, Bran felt both of his arms gripped from behind, as Slick and Hinder grabbed him and tried to hold him for Choke to pound.

But just as quickly, he was released, as Aonghus hefted one in each hand in the air and said, "None of that, now, chaps. Let the man fight his own battles."

Slick and Hinder thrashed about for a moment in the air, their feet dangling, and then went limp, realizing that this big Irishman was too much for both of them.

"Thanks, Aonghus," said Bran as Ed slid in the mud next to him in another futile attempt at a tackle.

"Goodness, Bran," laughed Aonghus, "this is the second fight you've been in this week. Whatever has gotten into you?"

Ed was getting up again and, this time, his fists were up like a boxer's, and he approached more carefully.

"Now see here, Ed," said Bran. "I've got nothing against you... yet, and I'm not trying to steal away your girl. Why, just now is the first time I've met her, thanks to you. Although I must say, you're a lucky man if she'll have you. Why don't we end this silliness here and now? How about we shake and call it a draw?"

Bran held out his hand to Ed.

"I intend to end it here and now," said Ed, and dropped his fists. Then he grasped Bran's hand. But instead of shaking, he squeezed as hard has he could, making Bran wince with pain, then pulled him close and brought his other fist in hard, driving it toward Bran's ribs.

But Bran saw it coming and once again danced aside, then pushed forward under Ed's right hand that he was clasping, and spun around, bringing Ed's arm up and behind his back.

"Right, then," said Bran. "You're obviously the sneaky sort and don't like to fight fair. I'll bet you've bullied everyone here at one time or another. I think that's about to change, though. I think it's time you became a bit more polite to people."

Ed struggled mightily, but Bran held his arm firmly behind his back. The crowd around them looked on in silence now, seeing Ed, who had indeed been the school bully, so humbled, and his two sidekicks still dangling in the air in the powerful arms of Aonghus.

But suddenly, the crowd parted, and onto the field strode Miss Fenny, followed behind by Bigs.

"You see, Miss Fenny," Bigs was saying, "just like I told you. Those two new kids are starting fights."

Fenny looked at the scene, opened her mouth once, then pursed her lips and narrowed her eyes.

"Mr. McGunnegal!" she said to Aonghus. "Put those boys down this instant!"

Aonghus let them go and Slick and Hinder dropped in a heap at his feet.

"And you, Mr. McGunnegal!" she shot at Bran. "You let Edward go. All five of you, to my office, now!"

She turned and walked away, expecting immediate obedience.

Aonghus and Bran looked at each other and shrugged and followed along.

"This isn't over, McGunnegal," hissed Choke. "Not by a long shot."

Bran ignored him and walked on.

"Guess we're in for it now," whispered Aonghus, and turned to see Choke, Slick, Hinder, and Bigs all following them in a huddle, whispering to each other. Behind them came Mary, a worried and angry look on her face.

When they reached the door of the hall, they were greeted by a tall, thin man with short blond hair who appeared to be middle aged. There was a distinct scar on his left cheek that gave him an embattled look, but his eyes were deep and wise.

"Ah! Professor McPherson!" said Miss Fenny. "These boys were fighting. Fighting! Out on the field! Mr. Sour here says that these McGunnegal boys started the whole thing."

"That's not true," said a voice from behind, and Mary shyly pushed her way forward. "That's not true, sir," she said.

She looked sidelong at Choke, straightened, and then said, "Ed started it, sir. Bran and Aonghus were just playing rugby and Ed stepped onto the field and started trouble... like always."

"That's a lie!" spat Choke. "You're only saying that because you've got eyes for this Irish..."

But Professor McPherson cut him off and said, "It so happens that I was watching from my window, Edward. Would you care to elaborate on exactly what happened?"

Choke looked down and said, "No... sir."

"Then I suggest that it might be useful for you to do a fifteen-page report on the merits of civilized behavior. It will be due in three days. You are dismissed," said the professor.

Choke gave Bran one last menacing look and then stomped away.

"Ms. Fenny, I'm sure these two gentlemen would be more than happy to do some extra cleaning in the hall for a day or two," he said, indicating Slick and Hinder. "And if you would, please send for the McGunnegal sisters. I might as well meet them all."

"Now, Aonghus and Bran are your names, right? Good. Please, do come with me to my office," he said.

As they turned to go, Mary piped up and said, "Professor, they really didn't do anything to start that. And Bran could have really bashed Ed, I think, but he never hit him at all."

"Thank you, Miss Nottingham. You may go now," said the professor.

Then he turned and strode through a door to one side that led up a flight of steps.

Aonghus and Bran followed after him and, just before they turned a corner, Bran looked back and noticed Mary still at the bottom of the steps, looking up after them, concern written on her face.

"Come, gentlemen," said the professor as he entered through a large wooden door on the right. "Have a seat."

Professor McPherson sat down behind a large, ornately carved wooden desk. Behind him on the wall were many strange pictures, carvings, masks, and odd ornaments. Shelves lined the other walls of the office, and these were filled with books of all sizes and shapes. To one side was another door that was marked "Private – Do No Enter."

The professor looked at Aonghus and Bran with his deep, penetrating eyes and said, "Well, while we wait for your sisters to come, how about you tell me about yourselves?"

"Professor," said Bran, "I'm really sorry about the fight."

"Never mind that, Bran," he said. "You handled yourself like a true gentleman. However, I suggest that you watch yourself around Edward. Please, tell me about yourselves."

A thought struck Aonghus and he said, "Professor, may I please run back to my room for a few minutes. I have something that we need to show you."

"Certainly," he said. "Bran and I will chat until you return."

Aonghus thanked him, dashed out the door, and ran all the way back to his room. There he grabbed a bag of the rocks from home and ran back to the professor's room, just in time to meet the girls as they were coming up the steps.

"Now's our chance," he said to them. "We're going to tell Professor McPherson the whole tale."

Chapter 28 – Traveling Plans

Frederick awoke with a start. Someone was shaking his shoulder. For a moment, he was disoriented, and then he realized that the old cracked face of the dwarf was leaning close to his.

"Ho!" Frederick said. "You startled me!"

"Sorry, young'un," creaked Doc. "Them there leprechauns is done with their gold-gatherin'. It's time to be makin' plans, it is."

"How long have I been sleeping?" he groaned, rubbing his eyes.

"All night," said Colleen, who was already awake and sitting at a table, her long hair spilling over the shoulders of her green cape.

"No one should look so nice after waking up," he grumbled, and brushed down his own mat of dark hair, knowing it to be a mess.

He made his way to the table and sat down. Doc offered him a cup of something steaming.

"Drink!" said the dwarf. "It'll give you strength."

Frederick sniffed the cup. It smelled of an odd cross between mushrooms and lemons. He took a sip, and the hot liquid tingled in his mouth and throat. Heat seemed to spread across his face and down his arms.

"Wow!" he said. "What is that?"

"Ha! My own secret recipe," said Doc. "An old family tradition. Nothing bad, mind you. A mug of that will keep you going all day long. In fact, I've got a small keg of it for the journey."

"*The journey*?" asked Colleen. "Do you mean that you'll be going with us?"

"Well, I've been thinking about that," he said. "I'm truly torn. At first, I was inclined to stay put and guard the Gate and all. But now that Dvalenn has showed up, and won't wake up, I feel that I've got to get him to the Lady. If anyone can wake him from this dreadful sleep, it's her. But the Gate... someone has to guard it, you know. If the Witch ever got hold of it, well, it would be mighty bad."

"It would be wonderful if you could come with us, though," said Colleen.

Doc was silent for a long time, staring at his brother. Then, he quietly said, "Would you take him to the Lady for me?"

"But how will we get him there? We can't have Badger drag a litter all that way – we would wear him out," said Colleen.

Well," said Doc. "I've got a cart, of sorts, that I use to haul rock and such through these tunnels. It's just about big enough for Dvalenn to sleep in. We could harness it to your horse."

"I suppose we could try," said Colleen. "But I do wish you would go with us. It's terribly scary, you know, traveling by ourselves."

The old dwarf looked at the two children and nodded his head.

"You're right, it is a frightful thing to go about these woods alone. But, you do have these Wigglepoxes with you, and that Oracle fellow, for what he's worth. Although I wouldn't discount him too much – he's an odd bird, he is, but there's something about him that makes me glad he's with you."

Frederick looked skeptical. He really didn't think the little people would be much help if goblins or the Witch showed up.

"Right then," he said. "So, what's the plan?"

"First, we've got to make sure we have enough food," said Colleen.

"No problem there," said Doc. "I've got dried fish and mushrooms aplenty, and my special recipe." He tapped the side of his mug. "And I've also got a sack of tubers and a bit of nuts and dried fruits. That ought to last you for weeks."

Colleen smiled.

"Thank you, Doc," she said. "At least we won't starve to death or be eating berries the whole way."

Suddenly, there was a noise from the bed where Dvalenn was sleeping. They all turned their heads to look, and the dwarf was yawning widely. He rubbed his eyes once, blinked, then shut them again and began to snore.

Doc ran over to him and shook him.

"Dvalenn!" he shouted, "Dvalenn! Wake up! You've got to come out of this sleep! Dvalenn!"

But the dwarf only smacked his lips, turned over, and snored on, a frown on his face.

Doc turned to the others. "You see, the Spell is not so strong down here. But the trouble is that once you give in to it, it sort of sinks into your bones. I think you carry it with you wherever you go after that. Almost becomes a part of you, it does, and on your own you can't seem to shake it, although you have to be willing to try."

He paused for a moment, staring at his brother.

"Dvalenn!" he whispered, a tear falling from his eye.

"I've got to get my brother to the Lady. I hear that she's broken the Spell from loads of the little people, least ways that's the rumor that I hear in the rocks," he said, almost to himself.

"But then I... I can't..."

He sighed and returned to the table.

"I'm guessin' we'd best be finishing up our plans and then get you on your way," he said.

"That's true," said Mrs. Wigglepox.

"But how will we know where to go?" asked Colleen.

"Ah!" said the old dwarf. "Let me show you something."

He went to a closet and began to rummage around among a load of buckets and brooms and stacks of paper until he found a rolled scroll of sorts. He brought it over to them and carefully unrolled it on the table.

"Now this here is a map of the lands after the Cataclysm, but before the Pirate came and brought the Witch back. My brothers and I made this, and I don't think that the land has changed all that much, although it's been about fifteen hundred years," he said.

"This map is 1500 years old?" asked Frederick.

"No, this here is a copy of one we made back then. We dwarves are masters with maps, and we don't make mistakes with 'em. Now see here," he said, pointing his finger at a lake drawn on the map.

"That's the Lady's Lake. It's about three days away from here, I would say, assuming that you find a decent path and the forest hasn't closed in after all these years. There used to be the Great Road that led from the Seven Houses all the way north to the Gray Sands and the Ices and all the way south to the White Sea. But it's long overgrown now, far as I know, but you can see bits of it now and then still sticking up through the brush and forest floor. That would be the path to follow. It passes by the Lady's Lake, or used to."

"What are the Seven Houses?" asked Colleen.

"This is one of 'em! They're the houses that my brothers and I built and looked after. Each had a watchtower, and each of us watched the lands around our house."

"Watched for what?" asked Lily.

"Why, at first, we watched for friends. From those towers you can see mighty

203

far, farther than with your natural eyes, mind you. It's a special thing when you ascend into the watchtower and take note of all the land. But when the Witch came, we watched for her and her lot as well. And that takes a bit of doing. The goblins are sneaky, you know, and can slink through the forest like a shadow, and it takes a careful eye to pick 'em out and make a defense against 'em," he said.

He sighed then and said, "Ah, but six of our houses are fallen, fallen along with my brothers."

"Was that pile of ruins that we climbed once a house like this?" asked Frederick. "The one that Mrs. Wigglepox showed us – where we found Oracle?"

"Off to the north? Aye, it was. That was Dvalenn's house, poor thing. After he disappeared, his house slowly crumbled and went to ruin. I couldn't maintain both his and mine. Without him there, it got ransacked by the goblins and, over time, just fell to pieces," said Doc. "But I did manage to hide the secret passages under his house. There are more than a few magic things buried there."

He paused, looking sad, glanced at his brother, then looked down at the map and continued, "Now look here – another few days' walk from the Lake brings you to the Great Hills. The road used to run right through them to the Burning Sands, and that," he pointed his finger to a picture of a castle on the map, "that is the old Wizard's Castle. It's in the middle of the desert, about three days walk from the Great Hills, if my memory serves me right. That's where we found *her*, you know."

"Found who?" asked Colleen.

"The sleeping lass. She was a beauty, she was. Found her in a glass room of sorts in a tower, sleepin' like a baby. Sleepin' like Dvalenn over there, though her sleep was a peaceful one. Her hair was golden red – rather like yours, Colleen."

Suddenly, the dwarf stopped and looked hard at Colleen, his old eyes wider than she had seen them yet. He opened his mouth and was about to say something, then shut it and shook his head and looked down.

"What is it, Doc?" Colleen asked.

"Oh, nothing... nothing at all. Just an old dwarf's imagination," he sighed.

"Please, Doc, what's wrong?" she asked.

"It's just... just that ... well, it's been a very long time you know, since I've seen her," he replied slowly. "But you... you remind me of her in a way. Your hair and your eyes... why... why... it's rather uncanny..."

He paused, staring into Colleen's eyes for a moment more, and then added quickly, "But never mind all that. Come now, let's get back to our planning. Now, where was I?"

"You were telling us about the Wizard's Castle," said Frederick.

"Right. Now, there's water there, or there used to be. This river used to run right under it, and there was a well that the wizards sank down to it that supplied the whole castle. My brothers and I used it for years. That's where you'll have to re-fill your water sacks. But, mind you, back then, it was a *wishing well.* The leprechauns helped us make that, they did. Take care what you say around it. If you throw a piece of leprechaun gold in and make a wish, it's as good as a leprechaun granting you that wish!" he said.

"Does anyone live there?" asked Lily, who had walked out onto the map with Rose and had seated herself next to the picture of the castle.

"Who knows these days?" said Doc. "We left there long, long ago. Somethin' strange happens there – the air itself shimmers and shifts and, at times, you have strange visions. We didn't think it was safe any longer after we lost the lass, so we left. But I don't hear any rumors of it, and the news from the rocks is rather sparse from so far away."

"Do you talk to the rocks?" asked Rose.

"You might say so," he said. "I've rather mastered the old dwarvish art of rock listening. No one else to talk to down here, you know, except the fish and the mushrooms, and they don't talk back. But the rocks, they have long memories, and their stories hold long and hard, just like them. A good dwarf can hear those stories if'n he listens careful enough. But it's a real faint whisper that comes from those parts, and it takes a long time to hear it."

"That's amazing," said Frederick. "I always thought rocks were just, well, stupid old things that just sat there and didn't *do* anything at all."

"Shame for you that you never took time to look closer and listen harder to the world around you, boy. Then again, I s'pose you are just human. My recollection of most humans is that they're rather like old Dvalenn over there, sleepin' away, eyes shut to a bigger world that's all around 'em, preferin' their troubled dreams to bein' waked up and really livin' like they could. Shame," he said, shaking his head.

"But maybe there's hope for you lot," he continued. "Here ya are on a trip to meet the Lady! She might do a thing or two for you all as well."

Frederick was not sure what to say, but his interest in meeting this Lady Danu was growing the more he heard about her.

"Now, see here," continued Doc. "After the Sands and the Castle – another two or three days to get out of it – and you come to the Sea."

"It looks like your map ends at the Sea," said Lily, walking to the edge of the parchment.

"Aye, that it does," said Doc. "We aren't much of a sea-faring folk, you know. What lies beyond that, I don't rightly know."

"The Island of the Waking Tree is out there somewhere," said Mrs. Wigglepox.

"So it's said," said Doc. "And also the Witch's fortress. That's where she keeps her prisoners."

"Then that's where we need to go," said Colleen. "That's where my mother will be."

"You're likely to be right," said Doc, "although I don't know how you might expect to get her out. That Witch is powerful, and she's got loads of goblins in her army. I suspect there'll be quite a troop of 'em guarding that place, wherever it is. Them there wizards were *mighty* folk, and they plumb failed to do her in. You'll need plenty of help, I'd say."

"Wait a second, do you mean you don't know where her fortress is?" asked Frederick.

Doc looked a bit embarrassed. "No one knows, except those goblins," he said. "No one's ever escaped from her before."

All at once, the same thought struck them all, and they turned and looked at Dvalenn, who was still sound asleep on his bed.

"Dvalenn did!" said Colleen excitedly. "And he made his way here. That means he must know the way back!"

"For all the good that is," said Frederick. "Just look at him – snoring his life away when the world needs him most."

"All the more reason to get him to the Lady," said Doc. "And you're right. He's the first one I've ever heard of escaping from the Witch's lair. I'll bet he'll have a tale or two to tell."

Frederick turned back to the map and studied it for a moment. "Wait a second," he said. "There's something strange here."

"What?" asked Colleen.

"Well, my father has a map that looks an awful lot like this one," he said.

"Your father? But how could that be?" she said.

"I'm not really sure," he said. "But I've seen it before. It's actually three maps... or four now that he's got a copy of that one over your fireplace, Colleen."

"What four maps?" asked Mrs. Wigglepox.

"That's what my father has been searching for the past twenty years. He found three pieces of a map that someone made a very long time ago. The fourth piece was over the fireplace back in Ireland. It seems to me that when you put them all together, they look quite a bit like this map, except for that fourth part, which I think would be here," he said, pointing his finger at a section of the map where there was a small house.

"Why, that's just about where we are now, you know – that house is the one above us, and see here...." Doc pointed a short distance away. "... that is the Mirror Wall where you two came through."

"So," said Colleen, "that means that the maps back home *were* made by the Pirate – Atsolter the Pirate! And they're not maps of Ireland at all – they're maps of the Land of the Little People!"

"Aye, it may well be," said Doc. "He was here long enough to make such maps."

"But there's just one difference," said Frederick. "On those other maps," he pointed to the eastern side of the map, "the sea had two islands in it. The one in the east had a big tree on it, and the one in the west had a sort of castle on it."

"Then that spells it out for us," said Doc excitedly. "The Island of the Waking Tree is in the eastern part of the Southern Sea, and the Witch's fortress is in the west!"

"So we've got to find a ship or boat or something and head southwest and rescue my mother."

"The Sorrows shall be harrowed!" Oracle said suddenly, and he climbed up on a low stool, peeked over the edge of the table, and stabbed a finger at an empty spot on the map in the middle of the sea.

They were all silent for a moment, once again unsure of how to deal with Oracle's madness.

"Right," said Colleen at last. "We might as well go now. No time to waste."

Chapter 29 – Lily's Wish

Colleen listened as Doc hummed some dwarvish tune as he crammed a huge pack to the brim with all sorts of supplies – pots and pans and containers of mushrooms and dried fish and roots and blankets and clothes and tools and just about everything else he could fit into its nooks and crannies.

"What's all that for?" asked Frederick.

"I know, I know," said the dwarf. "It's a bit small, but I wasn't sure just how much you could carry."

"Small!" said Frederick, amazed. "You expect *me* to carry that thing?"

"It will just have to do," said Doc sadly.

Frederick's mouth dropped open.

"I... I can't carry that!" he objected.

Doc paused, looking confused, but he winked at Colleen.

"I'm just kidding with you, lad. See here, this one is for you."

He produced a smaller pack just large enough to hold two blankets, a pouch of food, a flask of water, and a few odds and ends.

"Shew!" sighed Frederick with relief.

"And one for you, young lady," he said, and produced a slightly smaller one for Colleen.

"Now, Oracle, here's a side satchel for you." He handed the hunchback a small bag with a shoulder strap. Oracle accepted it with a grin, slipped it over his head, and let it dangle down his back.

"Not that way," said Doc, and adjusted it for him.

Oracle grinned again.

"And for the Wigglepoxes," he said, and laid out three small cloths and tiny sticks, and several piles of finely chopped mushrooms and nuts and several extra cloths to serve as blankets.

"You'll have to wrap your own things," he said. "My old hands aren't nimble enough for that anymore."

He left the room and returned a few moments later with a large cart lined with dried grass.

"Now, help me with my brother," said Doc.

Together, they put the sleeping dwarf up in the cart, and Doc took hold of the cart poles and pulled it down the hall, back to the Crystal Cavern.

"Best go fetch Badger, Colleen," he said.

"Right," she replied, and went down the hall and found Badger happily standing in his stall, munching on the pile of grass.

"Come on, old boy," she said. "Time to get on with our adventure."

She led him down to the Crystal Cavern, where the others were gazing up at the rainbows that danced around the golden ceiling.

"Fixed up this cart last night so that your horse can pull Dvalenn along in it," said Doc.

"It's a shame that Badger is so old," said Frederick. "Then he could pull that cart and carry us as well."

Colleen looked at the old horse for a moment. He was a bony old thing, ribs showing, and head sagging.

"It is a shame," she said. "My mom used to say that when he was young, he could pull a plow all day long."

Suddenly, Lily, who had been gazing intently at the old horse, smiled broadly and disappeared into the depths of Frederick's pocket, only to re-emerge a moment later with her tiny pot in her hands. Its contents shone in the light of the Crystal Cavern, and a tiny rainbow descended from the ceiling and settled in the gold that she clutched in her arms.

Everyone stared at the little rainbow, its delicate, mesmerizing beauty.

"Now, dear, what are you doing...," began Mrs. Wigglepox.

But Lily's little voice broke in, "I wish Badger were a mighty stallion with the strength of ten horses, and that he could carry us all forever wherever we needed to go, and the wagon were grand and magical!"

"LILY, NO!" cried Mrs. Wigglepox.

But it was too late. Rainbows began to flash about the room, dancing wildly from floor to ceiling and all of them converging on Lily's little pot of gold. There was a blinding flash. Badger whinnied and reared up, Colleen gasped, Frederick yelled, and Doc cried, "Glory be!" Oracle raised his cane over his head and then was hidden from sight amid the wild spectacle of colors.

Lily collapsed into Frederick's pocket, and Mrs. Wigglepox cried out in fear. And then, as suddenly as it had begun, all was still, and the Crystal Chamber returned to its normal brilliant self, its array of rainbows lazily shining from one crystal to another.

They all turned to look at Frederick's pocket, worry on their faces.

"LILY!" called Frederick, opening his pocket wide. "Are you all right? LILY!"

But there was no response.

"LILY!" cried Mrs. Wigglepox. "My little Lily!"

With great care, Frederick reached into his pocket and pulled the little leprechaun out and laid her on the floor. The tiny figure was limp and still. They all gathered around and knelt beside her, worried looks on their faces. Then, a single rainbow seemed to appear, reaching from Lily's body and upward through the ceiling.

Mrs. Wigglepox leaped from Colleen's pocket to the floor and took her child in her arms.

"Lily!" Mrs. Wigglepox wailed again. "Come back, child!"

But she was still, and the rainbow began to fade.

Frederick knelt over her, and gently, ever so gently, he took Lily from the arms of Mrs. Wigglepox and laid her in his hand.

"Lily!" he whispered, tears in his eyes. "Come back!"

Oracle jumped in the air, waving his cane at the fading rainbow, muttering something indiscernible. For a moment, Lily lay still, then she took a deep, shuddering breath and opened her eyes. She smiled weakly up at Frederick. Then, pointing at Badger, she said, "Look!"

They all turned around, and their jaws dropped and their eyes grew wide.

In place of the old, graying horse stood the most magnificent stallion they had ever seen. Its muscles rippled and its long mane shone brilliantly in the Chamber's light. And he was *big*. In fact, he was the largest horse Colleen had ever seen. But his eyes were Badger's eyes, and he whinnied as Colleen carefully approached his massive head, and he leaned down to her and nuzzled against her cheek, nearly knocking her over with his newfound strength.

"Badger?" she whispered.

The horse whinnied quietly and nuzzled against her again.

"Badger!" she cried, "Look at you! You're ... grand!"

He tossed his mane and snorted.

"And look!" said Doc. "He's got on a new saddle!"

Indeed, on Badger's back was a new shiny saddle with new blankets and saddle bags, and a new harness with golden buckles, and his feet were shod with golden horseshoes.

Frederick whistled and said, "He looks like a war horse! That was some wish, Lily!"

The little leprechaun sat up slowly in his hand.

"Frederick," she said. "I heard you... you... you called my name and I heard you. I was... I was... And there was another voice too..."

"I thought you had left us, Lily," he said. "Somehow, I thought that if I just called your name, maybe you wouldn't... wouldn't..."

But he could not bring himself to say "die."

Mrs. Wigglepox was not staring at the magnificent horse that had suddenly appeared, but only at Frederick, tears of joy and wonder spilling down her cheeks.

"Frederick, forgive me for ever doubting you," she wept. "You saved my little girl."

"Saved her? I didn't do anything at all. I was just so scared that... well, I just didn't know what to do, so I just called her name," he replied, embarrassed. "I didn't do anything, really."

"You don't understand," she said. "I saw her going over the rainbow. You called her back!"

Oracle stared at them from behind, a mischievous smile on his face.

"Please, would you put Lily here with me?" said Mrs. Wigglepox.

Frederick gently put her back on the floor, and Mrs. Wigglepox held her close, tears of joy spilling down her face.

"Well," she said after several moments, "wonder of wonders." A concerned look crossed her face and she said, "Let me see your pot, my dear."

"It's still in Frederick's pocket," she said.

Frederick fished the tiny pot out and handed it to Mrs. Wigglepox. It was empty.

"Oh, dear," said Mrs. Wigglepox.

"What's wrong?" asked Colleen.

"She used up her gold with that wish," she said.

"What's that mean, Mother?" asked Rose.

"Well, I've never heard of it happening before – at least not on a First Wishing. It usually only happens on a leprechaun's Last Wish," she said gravely.

"Can't I just get some more gold from the river?" asked Lily.

"Perhaps," said Mrs. Wigglepox. "But usually after a leprechaun grants the Last Wish, he or she begins to ... to ... well, never you mind. It may be that this room, with all its leprechaun gold and these dwarvish gems and such did something that's never been done before. We'll just have to wait and see."

"Am I going to be all right, Mother?" asked Lily.

"I'm sure you will be just fine, dearest," she replied, although her face betrayed her worry. "Your gold seems to have been all used up, but your heart was pure in making that wish, and that means a whole lot."

She smiled at her daughter then, and gave her a hug.

"Well, you leprechauns are welcome to go and get more gold if you like," said Doc.

"It's not so easy as all that," said Mrs. Wigglepox. "You see, we can usually only receive gold from each place once in our lives, and we have to be offered it. Taking more from one place would be greedy, and that would turn our wishes sour. We'll just have to hope to find gold somewhere else, and see if Lily's pot will accept it."

"All right, then," said Doc, "you best be off. But I must say, I've not seen a wishing like that in many a long year. What a horse! And look at what's become of my old cart!"

In place of the old wooden cart stood a delicately carved wagon large enough for all of them to sit – two or three in the driver's seat and room for all of them and their packs in the back. Its wheels had spokes of brass and rims of gold. It was finer than the finest coach Colleen had ever seen.

"You really did do well, Lily," said Colleen. "Thank you."

They hooked up the wagon, which they found attached perfectly to the fittings on the saddle and bridle, to Badger, and they all climbed into the wagon, with Colleen and Frederick in the driver's seat and Doc and Dvalenn in the back. Colleen took the reins and said, "Let's go, boy!"

Effortlessly, the great horse pulled and the cart silently moved forward. Not a squeak or a grind did the great wheels make as they rolled up the ramp out of the Crystal Cavern.

"Now this is a day that I'll never forget!" said Frederick.

"That's for sure," said Colleen.

"Let's stop at the mushroom farm and get a few more supplies," said Doc. "This wagon can hold a bit more now."

They loaded it up with supplies until Colleen was fearful that even this new Badger would not be able to pull it.

But the horse easily pulled them all along the hall, and soon they came to the Gate of Anastazi.

"Do you still want to try and open it?" asked Doc.

"Yes," said Colleen. "I have to at least try."

"Then follow me. But I'm afraid your horse will have to wait here or swim the river," he said. "There's only a small tunnel through the ceiling, and I don't think he'll fit."

"Take me across then," said Colleen. "I'll come back for him whether the gate opens for me or not."

"I'm coming too," said Frederick.

"I need you to stay here with Badger, Frederick. Let's just see what happens," she said.

"No way," he said. "I saw what that thing did to you. I'm coming."

"We'll stay with Badger," said Mrs. Wigglepox. "Just set me up by his ears so that he can hear me."

"All right then, as long as Badger will let you," said Colleen.

"Of course he will," she replied and, sure enough, the big horse lowered his head, allowing Colleen to place Mrs. Wigglepox right between his ears.

Doc led Colleen and Frederick to a blank piece of wall and, with a wave of his hand, a door opened for them. Up a small flight of steps they went, through a passage and down again, to a second door that opened on the other side of the river.

"Don't stare at the gate," said Frederick. "Remember what happened last time."

"I wasn't ready for it then," she said. "Here we go. If something goes wrong, promise you'll keep going, Frederick."

Frederick swallowed hard.

"I'll do my best," he said.

She walked in front of the gigantic doors and gazed up at them. Their strange radiance threatened to draw her mind into them. But she knew what to expect now, and she fully embraced their power. Placing both hands on the doors, she closed her eyes. A whirlwind of thoughts and images leaped into her mind, and thousands of years of history coursed through her in an instant. Her eyes shot wide open and she gasped. Then the power of the gate seemed to flow into her – the timeless magic that radiated from it like light from the sun. A strange vision of an eternity past and future swept through her. She felt small and insignificant, the miniscule thirteen years of her life less than a drop in the great ocean of time and timelessness. She knew that this gate – the Gate of Anastazi the Great – stood as a portal between those two vast realities and existed simultaneously in both of them. And it was locked – bound by the magic of both realms, shut fast by the twin locks of time and eternity.

But then she saw it – a tiny *bend* in the lock of time, allowing the Gates to open ever so slightly outward, into time. If she could cause that lock to bend just a bit more, the Gates might open wide. She focused all her thought on that bend, willing it to bend more.

"Open," she whispered.

In that moment, the door moved and with it, the very universe around her seemed to, ever so slightly, shift. There was a terrible grinding and bending, and Colleen suddenly had a flashback, as though she were remembering something. Images of the Cataclysm came to her mind – a piece of the vision she had seen when she first touched the door. The fabric of time and space had been rent and torn then. Had that caused this lock to bend? Was she about to do the same?

She was suddenly aware of a trembling in the ground under her feet and the voice of Frederick calling to her. She willed the door back to its place, the pressure on the locks ceased, and everything grew still.

Colleen pulled her hands from the door. Her breathing was ragged and she sank to her knees.

Frederick rushed to her side and put his arm around her.

"Are you all right?" he said.

She looked up at him and nodded. "I think so."

After a moment, her breathing calmed and she said, "I saw it, Frederick. "I saw how he did it."

"Did what?" he said.

"How he made the Gates and how they're locked," she said.

"Say nothing!" said Doc quickly. "Come, first we must go up to the house."

They returned to the other side of the river and Colleen took Mrs. Wigglepox from between Badger's ears.

"What happened, Colleen?" she asked. "For a moment, it looked as though the light of the gates flooded over you and you vanished. Then, a moment later, you were back and Frederick was helping you up."

"Let's get upstairs first," Colleen said.

As they left the Gate of Anastazi, Badger reared his head and gave a great neigh and stamped his gold-shod feet.

"Easy there, boy," said Colleen, and urged him forward.

She glanced back once before the brightness of the doors vanished behind them, giving way to the magical light of Doc's tunnel.

Badger pulled the wagon up the passage until they came to the dead end, then Doc opened the wall beneath the stairs and they went out into the House of Mysteries.

"Now tell us, Colleen, what happened down there at the Gates?" asked Frederick. "It seemed to me that you became part of the door or something. That's the best way I can explain it. I've seen you do that sort of thing before, like with the stone centaur."

"Honestly, I don't know what you mean by that, Frederick," she said. "I tried to unlock the Gates – or break the locks. But something terrible started to happen. I knew that I had to stop."

"The ground and air all started to tremble, Colleen. I'm glad you stopped whatever it was you were doing. What was going on?" he said.

"I'm not sure," she said. "But I experienced something that words can't explain. Something *other* than myself. Something much bigger. It made me feel very small. It was as though I glimpsed the edge of eternity, Frederick. It was another place... no, not a place... a *state?* I don't know how to describe it."

"Maybe it's best left unsaid, lass," said Doc. "Some things are best *tasted* rather than thought about and analyzed."

"Yes, perhaps you're right," she said.

They were all silent for a moment until Doc finally said, "Well, here's where we must part, I fear."

"Won't you *please* come with us, Doc?" begged Colleen. "I would be so much less afraid."

Doc hung his head and said, "I've thought it through, Colleen. My responsibility lies here, guarding this door. The Witch must never get it, and she must never get the Crystal Cavern either. There are other things I've hidden down there that those goblins would love to have. Why, if she and her goblins were to get hold of this house and find out its secrets, it well might be the end of not just this world, but your world and mine as well. That's all I dare say."

He paused, looking about the hall. "One moment, before you go," he said.

Getting down on his hands and knees, he pressed his ear to the floor and shut his eyes and became very still. For several minutes, he stayed like this, until Colleen and Frederick both began to wonder if he had fallen asleep.

But just as Colleen was about to get down herself and rouse him, he stood up and said, "The rocks say that the goblin that was here the other day seems to be gone from the area about the house. In fact, the strange thing is that there's no sign of it for miles around. It either left straight away or is no longer in contact with the ground."

"You mean it could be hiding in a tree or something?" asked Frederick.

"Aye, could be," said Doc. "You'll have to keep your eyes open today and keep watch tonight. Even if it left, it will have gone on southward to warn the Witch of your presence. Never sleep in the open. Find a tree or a cave or some shelter to hide in during the night."

He walked over to the doors and, with a flourish of his hands over the symbols surrounding them, opened them wide.

He stepped out onto the porch and took a deep breath of air.

"Ah, it's been some time since I've been outside and seen the sky and the wood. I think that I shall walk just a short way with you," he said.

"What about the steps?" asked Frederick. "I don't think this wagon can go down those very easily.

Badger shook his head and snorted as if in protest.

"Sounds like Badger disagrees with you, lad," said the dwarf. "We'll just have to take it slow.

Leading the great horse forward, they brought the wagon onto the front porch, which was easily large enough to hold it.

"Let's take it nice and easy, old boy," Colleen said to the horse.

To her surprise, he turned his head, looked her in the eyes, snorted, and began to pull. One step, two, three... down he went until the front wheels of the wagon were right at the edge of the porch, and then, with almost a human look, he turned his head, considered the situation for a moment, and then continued down the steps.

The wagon gave a "THUMP" as its front wheels rolled off the porch and on the top step. But Badger held his ground, and the wagon went no further. Then, he slowly went down the steps, and bump by slow bump the wagon made its way down, until at last they were on the ground.

"Do you see that opening over there?" said Doc, pointing to a wide gap in the trees.

"Yes," said Colleen.

"That's the Old Road. That's the way you should take as long as you're able," he said.

Off they went, with Colleen driving the wagon and Doc walking alongside. Frederick rode in the back with Dvalenn and Oracle and, as always, Mrs. Wigglepox and Rose rode in Colleen's pocket while Lily rode in Frederick's.

Doc looked back at the House of Mysteries and sighed.

"It's been a long time since I've left that house for any length of time. I've been waiting a very long, long time for this day. But I knew it would come eventually. Things would have to change – they generally do, you know. But I'm a right bit surprised at the way the change is coming," he said.

"What do you mean?" asked Colleen.

"I mean, who would have thought that two human children would come to this land so long ruled by the Goblin King and his Court Witch and seek to change the state of the whole world," he said.

"I didn't come to change the world," said Colleen. "I came here quite by accident."

"Accident?" said Doc. "Accident? Well, if there are such things as *accidents*, I don't believe you coming here was one of them."

"But it was," said Frederick. "I fell through the mirror quite by accident, and Colleen just fell in right after me."

"Sometimes, we don't see the purpose in things that happen," said Doc. "But, we just need the patience to wait and see what comes. I'm the last dwarf in this world, or I thought I was before you found my brother. I've been stranded here for a long, long time. But I trust that my time here has been important, and that gives me hope. Never be idle with the time you're given. You don't know how you're shaping the future, or even Eternity, by what you do today. You're here for a good reason, and not by accident."

For a moment, they were all quiet and only the sound of Badger's hoof-falls and the crunching of leaves under the wagon wheels could be heard. Ahead of them, the Old Road stretched into the forest, its broad path still visible through the ancient trees.

Colleen wondered where this adventure would take them, and what a strange adventure it was already in so few days. She glanced back at the sleeping dwarf behind her, at her cousin who was now whispering with Lily, then at Doc walking next to her, at Oracle, who had a foolish grin on his face, and then down at Mrs. Wigglepox and Rose riding in her pocket.

How very strange and wonderful and incredible, to be riding here in a wagon-load of fairy tales. In fact, living in a fairy tale! she thought to herself.

Her thoughts drifted away to all the strange and wild Irish stories that her mother and father had ever told her. She had always thought of them as great fun. But she had never *really* considered that some of them just *might* be true.

After some time, they came to the top of a rise, and there Doc called them to a halt.

"Here's where I stop," he said.

Colleen climbed down from the wagon and gave him a huge hug, at which he blushed.

"I will miss you, Doc," she said.

"Aye, and I'll miss you too, lass. You just stay on this road and it will lead you to the Lady. And remember what I told you. *Watch,*" he said. "Oh! I almost forgot. Take this." He reached into his pocket and pulled out a golden key. "The only lock this key has ever failed to open is that Gate down there. It's magic, see. Take good care of it. It's the last thing I have that my brother Fafnir made. Who knows when you might need it, especially if you ever make it to the dungeons of the Witch."

"Thank you, Doc," she replied, and slipped it into her pocket.

Frederick climbed down and extended his hand. The dwarf took it in his firm old grip, then led Frederick a few paces away.

"You watch after that girl, Frederick. I think your part in this adventure has not yet been seen. But it's important, mind you," he said.

"But what if the goblins come?" whispered Frederick.

Doc looked hard at him and then said, "I remember the valor of men long, long ago. You may be young, Frederick, but you are *human*. Seems to me that humans could dig deep somehow and find courage and loyalty and strength. It's just buried down deep in your heart. Pray that you find such virtues when the time comes for you to need them."

He nodded then and walked back to Colleen.

"Well, Oracle, Wigglepoxes, Colleen, Frederick, fare you well. Tell the Lady about me, and ask her to wake Dvalenn from his sleep," he said.

He then climbed up the side of the wagon and looked long at his brother.

"Farewell, Dvalenn, farewell. Shake the heavy sleep from your eyes, and remember our true home," he said.

Then he turned with a wave and trotted down the hill, whistling a tune. They watched him go and then Colleen sighed and said, "Well, then, let's go find the Lady Danu."

Chapter 30 – Gnomes

The hours rolled by, and the road wound its way around through deep glens and thick stands of huge trees, as though its makers did not wish to disturb the natural lay of the land or the forest.

Occasionally, they stopped at a stream or field to rest, until the sun began to sink in the west, and Mrs. Wigglepox said, "We had better find a place to sleep tonight. It will not do to be out after dark. Help me look for a large tree that is still showing a few leaves."

For another hour, they pushed on until finally, Colleen said, "How about that big old tree over there?" She pointed just to the east.

There a huge tree stood majestically above the others, its massive branches reaching outward and upward and still showing a scattering of green leaves in its high canopy.

"Let's have a look," said Mrs. Wigglepox. "I'll need to have a bit of a conversation with it."

They trotted through the fallen leaves and rode up to the massive trunk. Around the base of the tree, tiny yellow flowers grew in a green patch of grass.

"Ah, this is a Great Oak – one of the Ancients. It's still fighting the Spell. Colleen, put me down by its roots," she said.

Colleen dismounted and carefully put the little lady down at the base of the tree, where a tiny spring issued from the ground, then backed up a few steps while Mrs. Wigglepox walked to the tree trunk, cupped her hands against it, and began to sing.

They could not hear what she was singing, but in a few moments, she stopped and pressed her ear against the tree as if listening for it to say something in reply. Again, she sang to the tree, and listened again. Four or five times she did this, and with each pause in her singing, her face grew more and more excited, until with a creaking and a groan, a small door opened in the base of the tree and out walked three tiny people. All three of them wore what Colleen thought were very silly-looking red and white striped tights, green shorts, yellow shirts, and pointed slippers. They also each wore a pointed hat – one blue, one yellow, and one brown, and all had reddish-brown beards and mustaches.

Oracle, who had climbed into the front seat, chattered to himself in his unintelligible language, a grin on his face.

Mrs. Wigglepox clapped her hands and actually giggled, and walked over to the three little men and spoke with them in whispers, while the three of them looked nervously up at the towering children and the even more enormous horse and wagon. After a brief conversation, Mrs. Wigglepox turned and walked back over to Colleen and beckoned to the others.

"These fine gents are named Zelo, Nemon, and Humble. They are gnomes," she announced.

The three little men removed their hats, revealing bald heads, and bowed low. Colleen curtsied, and Frederick bowed in return. Oracle waved and looked gleeful.

"Hello," said Colleen. "My name is Colleen McGunnegal."

"And I'm Frederick Buttersmouth," said Frederick, bowing again.

"I'm Rose."

"And I'm Lily," said the Wigglepox girls in turn.

"And Frederick," Lily added. "Next time you bow, *please* remember that I'm in your pocket! I nearly fell out!"

Oracle said nothing, but just kept waving at the three little gnomes.

Zelo, Nemon, and Humble bowed again, and Zelo stepped forward and said, "Mrs. Wigglepox says that you are on your way south to free your mother and wake the Waking Tree."

"*That* is the best news we've had in years," said Nemon.

Zelo began to sing and dance about, kicking his knees high, Humble bowed low, and Nemon rubbed his chin, looking bright, but very thoughtful. Then Humble walked up to Colleen and waved for her to come near. She stooped down so that her face was quite near his.

In a rather shy voice, he said, "If you would honor us, please do spend the night under our tree. You do know that we live *under* it, don't you? You're much too big to fit in our little hole, but I think our tree might be able to help us out there. Our home is not much, and our garden is not grand, but we would be quite glad to have you stay."

The other two gnomes looked on for a moment, and Colleen looked over to Frederick, who just shrugged.

"The honor would be ours," said Colleen.

The gnomes threw their hats in the air and began to dance arm in arm in a circle, singing a happy tune. Colleen and Frederick backed up several steps, for as the gnomes whirled about, the great roots of the tree began to shift and move like great arms, and the earth began to open up with a grinding sound like stone against stone. A cloud of dust and debris rose about the tree and, for a moment, Colleen was afraid that something was terribly wrong, or that the tree had come to life and was angry. But a moment later, all grew still, the dust settled, and there before them was a large hole in the ground framed with thick roots, and a dirt ramp that led down into darkness.

"Welcome to our home!" all three said at once, picking up their hats and placing them back on their heads. "Please, come in!"

"Don't go in there!" said a voice suddenly from the west side of the road.

They all turned to see another gnome who wore a faded yellow jacket, red shorts, and a rather tattered blue hat. "It's no good under their tree," he said. "Come and stay with me in my thorn bushes. That's where the real safety is."

The gnome made his way out of a thick patch of thorns and walked over to them. "Rich is my name," he said. "I couldn't help overhear that you need a place for the night. It's much more comfortable in my thorns, and no goblin will get you there."

"No," said Zelo. "Your thorns do nothing but choke out anything good that you plant, and they're just a snare when the goblins come. It's hard to deal with the Witch's people when you're all caught up in a sticker bush."

Just as Colleen was about to speak, another voice sounded. "Don't listen to them," it said. "Come and stay in my rock garden."

They all turned again, and coming down the path was yet another gnome all dressed in gray and black.

"Rock is the safest place to be," he said. "You can't be hurt there."

"But your garden can't take root, Stony," said Nemon.

"Ah, we all get the same seeds, and mine shoot up plenty good. So what if they die off in the sun – who needs a garden anyway?" said the gnome. "Hard rock, that's what you need to be safe these days, not gardens."

"I disagree," said yet another voice.

"That's Path," said Humble. "He lives under the leaves beside the old road. Tries to grow his seeds right on the road, but the goblins keep trampling it."

"It's just too much trouble to worry about planting and tilling. Life is short, and you've got to try to enjoy every moment you can. Gardens are hard work – it's much easier to just toss the seeds along the way and see what comes of them. You can join me under my pile of leaves and be safe and sound," said Path. "You would be right by the road and could be on your way in no time.

Now that huge wagon would have to be parked by the road, but who needs a big old wagon and horse anyway when you can just hide under the leaves whenever you want, then troubles won't find you."

"You'll be snatched away by the goblins one day, Path," said Zelo. "You ought to move in with us. We could teach you how to care for your garden properly."

"I'll keep my thorns any day over that tree and garden of yours," said Rich.

"Thorns, ha! Rocks are the only safe place," said Stony.

Soon they were all debating the merits of planting and living among thorns or rocks or by the roadside, and seemed to have forgotten the visitors.

Humble whispered something to Mrs. Wigglepox and she waved for Colleen to follow them down the ramp and under the tree.

Hesitantly, they all went in, Colleen leading Badger down the sloping ground and into a high tunnel. The wagon barely fit, and Badger snorted and blew nervously as Colleen urged him forward.

The darkness, however, lasted only a moment, for as they passed beneath the great trunk, they found that the entire passage was lined with the tree's roots, and these were covered with glowing green and orange lichens that dimly illuminated the path.

"It's sort of spooky," whispered Frederick. "Do these gnomes really live down here all the time?"

"Well, of course they don't live down here *all* of the time," said Mrs. Wigglepox. "This is their home, though, and you had better be on your best behavior, young man."

Frederick looked nervously about, remembering the Wigglepox Tree.

Soon they passed through the glowing hall of roots and rolled down into a rather large chamber. Colleen looked up and it seemed as though they were directly under the heart of the great tree. The gigantic roots spread outward to form what appeared to be pillars all around them, supporting the vast roof that was the base of the tree. Even brighter green and orange and blue glowing fungus grew in an ornamental fashion above them, and intertwined with the roots were white and green vines from which yellow and pink flowers hung in small bunches.

Frederick whistled. "Now *this* is pretty cool!" he said.

"I regret that we haven't got much in the way of accommodations, you understand. We've never had any of the big people under our tree before," said Humble, removing his brown hat. "Please forgive our poor little garden. Not much grows underground, you know, and what little we can put around our tree we must arrange to look natural so that we do not call attention to ourselves."

"Yes," said Zelo, whose hat was yellow, "but it is quite exciting to have visitors, especially from a distant land."

"Yes, quite curious," said Nemon, taking off his blue hat. "It has been so very long since the big people have come."

"Oh," said Zelo. "We have nowhere for you to sit. A moment, please."

The three gnomes huddled together, linked arms once again, and seemed to hum a low tune. As they did, the roots along one side of the chamber shifted and moved about, shaping themselves into a good likeness of two armchairs.

"Amazing!" said Colleen as she climbed down from the wagon. "May I?"

"Please do, and Frederick as well," said Humble.

Frederick climbed down, and they sat in the chairs. To their surprise, they found them quite comfortable and, as Frederick leaned back, the roots shifted and leaned back with him, and others rose up under his feet, so that he was nearly lying down.

"I like this tree!" he said.

"This is quite comfortable," said Colleen, leaning her head back and closing her eyes. She began to hum an odd tune that seemed to suit the tree.

Frederick looked over at her and was going to say something about the song, but stopped. Where had she gone? In her seat was an odd old stump with four roots and old Spanish moss on top of it. He blinked, then shut his eyes and rubbed them. But when he opened them again, Colleen was rising out of the chair and complimenting the gnomes on their marvelous house.

"That's the third time..." he began, but then shook his head and said, "This is a weird land. But I like your tree."

The gnomes looked terribly pleased, and soon they were all talking about their adventures and the state of the forest, and how Colleen and Frederick had happened into their land. For some time, they spoke to one another, and the three gnomes, who turned out to be brothers, wanted to know everything there was to know about the land of the Big People, as they called it. Did they know of any gnomes there? Were there still fairies in that land? Did they have witches there too? And on and on with a hundred questions, until it was quite dark outside, and Mrs. Wigglepox said, "Do you think we should close the door for the night?"

"Oh my, yes," said Zelo, glancing out through the dark passageway.

The three gnomes clapped their hands and did a dance again, singing a song to the tree and, a moment later, the roots of the tree drew together with a sound of moving and shifting earth.

A nervous thought of being trapped underground struck Frederick, but he pushed it away, reminding himself that he would have some grand tales to tell his brother when he got home.

So their conversations continued, and both Colleen and Frederick told them as many tales as they could remember that had anything to do with leprechauns or fairies or gnomes or sprites or pixies, or any other kind of little people that they could think of. The gnomes and leprechauns, and especially Oracle, listened on and on.

After a time, Frederick asked, "What about those other chaps outside – will they be safe? Why don't they come in and live with you?"

"We've invited them many times," said Humble, "but theirs is mostly a sad tale. Once we gnomes were the Forest Gardeners, you know. We kept the most beautiful flowers and vines and rocks and plants, and arranged for the berries to grow just right and the root harvest to be prosperous. But when the Spell came, all that changed. Now our people are divided into a confused lot. Rather than gardening, many just toss their seeds any which way, just like Rich and Stony and Path. They've lost their way in this world and have forgotten who they are. It's not natural for us to live like that, not caring for the forest and not planting properly. I fear they're on the road to becoming gremlins."

There was an uncomfortable silence for a moment until Mrs. Wigglepox spoke. "Well, we've had a very long day and simply *must* get some sleep. Thank you so much for helping us! I'm sure your garden will grow brighter for your kindness."

"We're forgetting our manners!" said Humble. "Please, rest now, and we will talk more in the morning when the sun is shining."

They said their goodnights, and Colleen and Frederick lay down in the wagon, one on either side of Dvalenn, and the gnomes led the three leprechauns through a small hole beneath a curved root, saying that they had plenty of apartments for visitors now that so few little people came by. Oracle climbed up into one of the root chairs, wrapped his gray cloak around himself, and lay down.

* * *

Once in the night, Frederick woke, hearing a commotion outside. The muffled sound of harsh voices and barks, and what he thought were squeals of terror reached his ears. The tree above him began to creak and groan, and the shouts grew louder. His breathing quickened as he listened, and he was about to wake Colleen, but then the sounds faded and seemed to slip away into the distance. The tree grew still. He lay back down, wondering what had happened, listening for any sound, but only hearing the pounding of his own heart.

How long he lay there, staring into the darkness, hardly daring to breathe, he could only guess. But at last, he closed his eyes against the night and fell back into a fitful sleep.

Chapter 31 – Shadows and Pixies

Someone was whispering. Three someones. Frederick could hear them going on and on, disturbing his sleep.

"It happened in the night," said one.

"And they're gone now?" asked another.

"Taken. All of them," said the third.

"They didn't watch," said the first.

"Never did," said the second.

"Do you think there's any hope for them?" said one.

"There's always hope," said another.

"And what of us? Will they come again?" said the third.

"Yes, now that they've found us," said the second.

"What about the boy? He is of the Old House," said the third.

"Yes, he could protect us," said the second.

"He's only a boy," said the first.

"Shh. He's awake."

Frederick opened one eye. The three gnomes were sitting in a circle a few inches from his nose on a wide root. They all turned and stared at him for a moment, then Humble rose and bowed.

"Forgive us," he said. "We did not mean to wake you."

Frederick yawned and sat up. Shafts of light streamed in through several open knotholes over his head, dimly illuminating the interior of the cavernous room.

"What were you all talking about just now?" he said. "And what was that noise in the night?"

"So you heard it, then?" said Zelo.

"I heard what sounded like distant shouts or something," said Frederick.

Colleen sat up and stretched. Her golden hair spilled down her shoulders as if she had just combed it.

"Good morning," she said, smiling.

"I'm afraid it isn't so good," said Neman.

"Why?" she said. "What's happened?"

The gnomes looked at each other.

"Come, we'll show you," he said.

Humble climbed from the root where he was sitting, walked to the far wall, and spread his arms wide. The great roots began to move with a noise of shifting soil and the smell of tilled earth. A wide tunnel opened before him, and suddenly a dazzling flood of sunlight burst through, hiding the little gnome in its blinding radiance and casting a long shadow behind him.

Frederick shielded his eyes against the light, but Colleen rose and walked into the radiant beam, lifting her face to feel its warmth.

"What's wrong?" she asked. "It looks to be a beautiful day."

"Come," said Humble, and he walked up the dirt ramp.

The other gnomes joined him, and Colleen and Frederick followed. Oracle peered over the wagon's edge, then climbed down and came behind.

When they had reached the top, Frederick stopped and stared. The ground all around the tree had been trampled, and the flower garden lay uprooted and ruined. But worse than this, where Rich's thorn bush had been was a broken jumble of half-burned thorns, and hanging among them was Rich's little cloak, tattered and ripped.

"His own thorns snared him, and he couldn't escape when the goblins came," said Humble.

They were silent for several long moments, until Colleen said, "What about the others – Stony and Path?"

Frederick walked a short distance away to where Stony's rock garden had been. It had been dug up, and its stones scattered. Its former occupant was nowhere to be seen. He walked on, and found that Path's house of leaves was nowhere to be found, and the forest floor was tossed here and there, as though rough hands had been digging and searching through the humus. Path too was gone.

"They not here," called Frederick. "Their houses are a mess too."

"We'll be next," said Neman, bowing his head. "Tonight they will come and take us away too."

"Then there's nothing for it," said Colleen. "You're coming with us."

The three gnomes looked up at her hopefully.

228

"You would take us with you to see the Lady?" asked Humble.

"Of course we will," she replied. "Now you just go quickly and get whatever you can carry. We've no time to lose."

As the gnomes ran back into their tree, Frederick kicked at the strewn rocks of Stony's house. Colleen and Oracle made their way over to him and stared at the ruin.

"It's a wonder they lasted as long as they did," said Colleen. "They had no protection against the goblins out here."

"Yeah," said Frederick. "Did you hear all that commotion last night? I think the tree got downright angry and came to life and drove them off. I'm glad we didn't stay with Rich or Path or Stony. We'd probably have been caught too."

"I didn't hear a thing," she said. "I must have been out cold."

Oracle was silent. His usual grin was gone, replaced by a look of deep sadness. As Frederick and Colleen walked back to the tree, he sat down among the rocks of Stony's former garden and bowed his head.

It was not long before the gnomes were ready, and in fact only carried a small satchel each. Colleen went back into the tree and fetched Badger, leading him out into the sunshine.

"We must say farewell to our tree," said Humble. "Will you give us a few moments alone with it?"

"Of course," said Colleen, and she and Frederick led the great horse some distance away.

After a few moments, there was the familiar sound of earth and stone shifting and moving. The great tree's branches swayed, as if waving farewell, and then it grew still. Humble, Zelo, and Neman came walking slowly to the wagon, their faces sad.

When they were all loaded, with Oracle coming last, and looking sadly at the burned thorns of Rich's house, they finally started out.

"I do hope the old tree will be safe," said Neman.

"It will be," said Zelo. "The goblins want us. If we're gone, they'll leave the tree alone."

Frederick was not so sure of this, but said nothing. He had seen a number of huge trees that seemed twisted and bent, as if something terrible were happening to them – as though they were slowly writhing in some silent agony. He hoped the gnome tree fared better if the goblins returned.

For a good portion of the morning, as they rode along, the gnomes told stories of their part of the forest and how the goblins had often come and taken away the folk that lived there.

"Now, more to the south," said Nemon, "I remember there used to be a Pixie Tree. Who knows if it is still there? It would be eight or ten days' walk for us."

With that, he went off into a song about giants and horses and warriors that he seemed to be making up as he went along.

The afternoon passed, and they saw no sign of goblins, nor of the Pixie Tree that Nemon had spoken of. The sun was sinking in the western sky when Frederick said, "I'm beginning to feel terribly sleepy, and it must not be half past four yet. Something is different about this part of the woods."

"I feel it too," said Humble.

"Perhaps we could just take a nap before it gets too dark," yawned Colleen.

"No!" said Mrs. Wigglepox. "This is the Spell of the Witch. It seems to be getting stronger the farther south we go. We've got to keep moving and find the Pixie Tree. If we rest now, we might well end up like poor old Dvalenn."

"She's right," said Zelo. "Do you see them?"

"See who?" asked Frederick, looking around.

"The Shadows," whispered Zelo.

"The Shadows... what are they?" said Frederick, nervously looking about.

But Mrs. Wigglepox urged them to slap their cheeks and stamp their feet and rub their eyes.

"Zelo, what are these Shadows?" asked Colleen as they moved on. "I don't see anything except a few leaves blowing about."

"They are not easily seen. You must be watchful for them," he said. "But they carry within themselves the Spell of the Witch."

"You mean they're creatures of some sort?" she asked.

"Yes, of a sort," said Humble. "They are creatures of the air that have no home. They do the bidding of the Witch because she promises them dominions of their own when the entire world is under the Spell."

"That's terrible!" said Colleen, yawning, and rubbing her eyes to stay awake.

"Only to the very watchful eye can their movements be seen," said Nemon, "and the listening ear can hear them."

Colleen tilted her head to one side and listened. At first, she heard nothing, but then a very faint sound seemed to come. Yet it was not something she heard with her ears or even with her mind – it came from some other sense – something deeper and beyond them both.

"They are so sad – and angry!" she said. "And they are... cold."

She shivered involuntarily and, as though in a trance, she stared straight ahead and whispered, "I don't want to sing with them."

"Will they harm us?" asked Frederick, looking about.

"No, not directly, as such, or at least not usually," said Neman. "Their job is more subtle than that. They just take the power of the Spell and spread it about to all the living creatures they find. They even try to spread it over the rocks and trees of the forest. That's why we're so sleepy here. There are several of them in this area flitting about and spreading the Spell. That means there must be some of the little people still nearby."

Colleen roused herself and looked about, but she could see nothing except an occasional branch waving in the wind. Still, she felt so extraordinarily tired that she could not help but believe that what the gnomes said was true.

"There are ways to fight the Spell, you know," said Humble. "We've been fighting it for years and have discovered a few things."

At this, Oracle seemed to perk up and listened intently.

"Well, tell us," said Mrs. Wigglepox, yawning and stretching.

"First, you have to realize that you can't fight it on your own," said Humble. "You need to help each other."

"Then," said Zelo, "you have to *want* to fight it. You've got to know what you stand for, and what that old Witch stands for, and you've really got to fight to stay awake. Sometimes, it takes all you've got, and all your friends have got, but you've got to *want* to be awake like a gnome in the desert wants water."

"And you've got to remember," added Nemon. "Remember that the Witch is a *witch* – and that you are not *hers*. You've got to remember how your mam and pap taught you to live. You've got to remember what's right. You've got to remember that there's a better life than the tortured *sleep* that the old Witch wants to put on you. You've got to remember that you weren't made to sleep your life away, or consume your whole life with procrastination, but to be and become something more."

"And I might add," said Mrs. Wigglepox, "that you've got to be always on the watch, just like old Doc said. The Witch is sneaky at times, and will try to get you in all sorts of ways. Might be a goblin or a shadow today, and it might be someone who you think is a friend tomorrow. Always keep watch for her tricks, and always watch your thoughts. See, once the Spell starts to *stick* in you, then those shadows and the Witch herself can start to whisper things in your mind. That's sort of the nature of it, you know – once the dark magic starts sinking in, it's like a channel for her power to work on you. You can actually start thinking that what she's doing is good for the land and its people, when really her goal is to enslave the whole world."

"How could anyone who is a slave think that it's good?" asked Colleen.

"Because the Spell makes you forget yourself," said Nemon. "You start to think that there's no other life to live. First, you drift off to sleep, then those goblins come and take you to the pits, and there you stay, slaving away digging treasure for her or making shoes for the goblins. And after a while, you just give in to it and start to forget that there was ever anything else."

"That sounds awful," said Colleen.

"Aye," said Nemon. "Aye."

As the hours passed, and the sleepiness seemed to gather about them like a dense fog, they helped each other ward it off. They told stories, sang songs, and now and then even gave one another a little shake.

Through it all, Dvalenn snored loudly, and Oracle simply sat, occasionally interjecting a bizarre word.

Soon the sun was sinking below the horizon, and they were all blinking heavily with sleep when Zelo cried out, "There it is! See the lights?"

Frederick peered ahead and, sure enough, a large tree lay just ahead, and among the branches were several glimmers of light.

"Pixies!" cried Rose happily. "See how they shine!"

Indeed, as they rode up to the tree, Colleen could see several little winged pixies flitting here and there among the tree's branches, their bodies and gossamer wings shining in the failing light of evening.

"Hey there, ho there!" called Humble. "Pixie friends and goblin foes, we have come to visit your tree!"

The pixies, seeing the gnomes and leprechauns among the big people and their horse, danced and flitted about all the more, and called down from the tree branches in high singing voices, "Ho, gnomes and leprechauns! What a strange sight you are, riding with the big people to the south! What brings you to our tree in this sleepy wood?"

"We need a place to spend the night," said Mrs. Wigglepox. "Would you allow us to stay with you for the evening?"

Two pixies then swooped down out of the tree and flitted about them, just out of reach.

"How do we know you are not spies of the Goblin King?" said one of them.

"Because we are his enemies," she said. "He has taken my husband and this human girl's mother captive, and we are on a journey to rescue them. But first we are going to see the Lady Danu for advice and help."

"Three little leprechauns, one *big* leprechaun, three gnomes, two human children, and a dwarf who has fallen asleep, are going to rescue them from the goblin dungeons? Surely you jest!" said one of the pixies, its high voice somehow a mixture of mirth and sadness.

"We have no other choice," said Colleen. "We can't just sit back and do nothing."

The pixies stopped their flitting about and hung in the air before them, looking hard and long at all their faces.

"Some say there is no Goblin King," said one of the pixies.

"That'd be me!" called a voice from above them.

They all looked up to see a rather dim-looking fairy sitting on a branch. Her shine was nearly gone, and they could see no wings on her back.

"And there's no such thing as the Witch either," she continued. "All that sort of talk is nonsense."

"Hello," said Colleen. "What do you mean, no Witch?"

"Just that," said the pixie. "There's no such thing. Have you ever seen one?"

"Oh, shut up, Intelli," yelled one of the other pixies. "Don't you mind her. She's gone all drab, she has, poor thing."

"My name is Apetti. This is my sister Irassi," said the pixie, indicating the fairy flying next to her.

"And that one up there," she said, pointing to the wingless fairy on the tree branch, "is our sister Intelli."

"I've not gone all drab," yelled Intelli. "You're the nutter, what with you flitting here and there and talking to imaginary *shadows* and all that. There's no such thing as shadows either!"

"Is too!" shouted Apetti. "Mam said so!"

"*Mam said so!*" mocked Intelli. "*Mam said so!*"

"Shut up, both of you!" shouted the third pixie. "I want to hear what these people have to say."

Apetti stuck her tongue out at Intelli and then looked glum, and Intelli turned her back on them all and mumbled, "Who knows, they might not exist either. They might just be a dream or a bit of bad acorn or..." and off she went, mumbling about not believing in things.

"My apologies," said Irassi. "My sisters are constantly fighting and arguing and bickering about something. I do wish they would make amends."

"It's your fault," mumbled Apetti. "You're the one who always wants to go find the Waking Tree or chase away shadows or go on some other fool adventure. Why can't we just stay here and enjoy the sun and the tree. It's so much easier!"

"If you weren't so bothered with your silly *pleasures* all the time," retorted Irassi, "then maybe we'd get somewhere."

Apetti and Irassi began to argue about this and that, and then Irassi threatened to leave, and Apetti pulled her hair. They began to fight, buzzing about like angry bees until Intelli shouted, "Will you two stop that bickering! I'm trying to think of important things!"

"You must forgive my less intelligent sisters," said Intelli to no one in particular. "Irassi always wants to do something grand. Apetti just wants to have fun staying here at the tree, and the two of them just can't cooperate any more. If they would only listen to me..."

Then as quickly as they had started, Apetti and Irassi stopped fighting, and Apetti said, "Oh come on, this is no fun. We're being rude. Let's play a game with our new friends here. Forget about that old Goblin King and all that and let's play!"

Intelli rolled her eyes, and Irassi said, "Games! Games! That's all you ever want, Apetti. I say we go with them. I want to go and help them out. Now you two shape up, we're going!"

All three of them began to quarrel again, and Mrs. Wigglepox sighed heavily.

"This is what happens to fairies under the Spell," she said sadly. "They've lost all their powers because they're not unified like they used to be."

"They've lost their powers?" asked Frederick.

"Well," said Mrs. Wigglepox. "Fairies, and pixies in particular, work as a team. Together, they have the gift of not just wind walking, but *world* walking, and of world *seeing*."

"What's world walking and world seeing?" asked Colleen.

"It's both seeing into and traveling between the worlds. I have a mind to think that that's how that mirror in the wood was made – fairies helped make it – a whole lot of them, I would guess. You see, when they act and think and live as *one*, then their powers all come together and they can *see* and *shift*, as it were, between the worlds."

"Do you mean that maybe the reason we have stories of fairies in our world is that, well, we really *did* have fairies there?" asked Frederick.

"No doubt," said Mrs. Wigglepox. "See, of all the little people, it was the fairies that were given this great gift of world seeing and walking. And if three of them were one, it was as though they were one soul, and together they could even see and travel into the Blessed Realm, and the stories that they told... why you would be amazed! It's said that it was the fairies that first met the Great Wizard, Anastazi the Great. Perhaps it was they who helped him find or make the Timeless Hall, but..."

Mrs. Wigglepox was going to say more, but Intelli cut her off.

"Blessed Realm? There is no such thing! I've never been there and I'm a pixie!"

"I want to go there!" shouted Irassi, "But these two won't let me. Apetti just wants to lie around and play games, and Intelli doesn't even want to try because she doesn't believe in anything and is always lost in thought. But I say we go!" Once again, they went off into a heated debate.

"The Spell, the Spell," said Oracle in a moment of clarity, then slipped back to his ramblings and said, "It dakesmonwull."

"Nutter!" cried Intelli.

"This is getting us nowhere," said Mrs. Wigglepox. "We've got to get going and find somewhere else to spend the night."

Sadly, Colleen flicked the reins, and they rolled away. But it was only a short time before they came to a good-sized cave in a cliff face that could be seen a short distance from the road. Its dark mouth opened wide, as if in some great yawn in response to the sleep that hung heavy about them.

"How about that?" asked Frederick. "Looks like as good a place as any."

Colleen turned Badger off the road and through the trees toward the gaping mouth and stopped in front of it.

Stalactites of wet green moss hung from its upper rim, creating the illusion of great jagged teeth.

"This place is scary," said Rose after a moment. "I don't like it."

"Well, it's the best we can do for the night," said Mrs. Wigglepox. "Best get inside. But do be careful, Colleen."

They slowly went in, passing the dangling moss and entering into the dim light of the cavern.

"Maybe I was wrong," said Frederick. "I have a bad feeling about this place."

Even as he said it, there was a grinding sound, and the light of the cave began to fade. Lily and Rose shrieked in fear, and they all turned about and watched in terror as the mouth of the cave began to close, clenching its moss teeth together. In the next moment, they found themselves in absolute darkness.

The hair on the back of Frederick's neck prickled, and his blood ran cold as a cackling laughter came echoing from deep within the blackness before them. A sickening feeling rose in the pit of his stomach. They were trapped.

Chapter 32 – Chasing the Goblin

Adol McGunnegal sat in his room on the farm, staring out the window. He desperately missed his children, and felt terrible at having sent them all to Wales, now four days ago. But what could he do? He had to provide for them somehow, and he felt as though this opportunity was Providence lending him aid.

Yet he still could not shake a strange feeling that something was not quite right. There was an uneasiness about the farm. Even the wild birds and animals were more skittish than normal. Was it just his imagination, or just the stress of having lost his wife those months ago, his father-in-law just days before, and now having sent his children away, getting the better of him? And to make matters worse, Badger had wandered off, or been stolen, and he had not found any trace of him, nor had any neighbors seen him.

For the past few nights, he had not slept well, and his meetings with Rufus had also been uneasy. He asked too many questions, and Adol began to believe that his children had been onto something – something important. Was there something here on the farm that was valuable beyond imagination? He and Rufus had signed a contract, giving Rufus and Mabel legal ownership of the farm if he failed to pay back the taxes within three years. There had also been a good deal of legal language that he did not understand, but that Rufus assured him were just minor points, and not to be concerned.

He sat for a long time, pondering these things, searching his heart and mind for some answers to the tension that he felt. He was about to get up and lock the house when something outside the window caught his eye. The sun was just dipping low in the west, casting long shadows across the farm, and he was sure that he had spotted someone, or something, dash away in the direction of Grandpa McLochlan's hut.

Adol stood and lifted the lid of the trunk on which he had been sitting. He rooted around in it for a few seconds and then produced a large club. It was an old thing, passed down through his family, from when, he didn't know. Probably used for tenderizing meat, he thought, but it was the closest thing to a weapon that he had.

Quickly, he slipped down the stairs and out the kitchen door, dashing silently, almost too silently for such a big man, across the field and toward the McLochlan hut.

When he arrived, he found the cellar doors open. In the shadows that filled the basement, he could barely make out another shadow – something cloaked in black crouching by one wall. It was holding something in its gray, bony hand – something round and made of glass. Adol surged into the basement with a tremendous bellow, his club swinging over his head.

The creature sprung to its feet and spun around, hissing. The black hood covering its head hid most of its features, but Adol could make out two yellow eyes and a distorted gray-green face. It stood, poised, only for a moment, and then turned and *leaped*. For a moment, Adol thought that it would collide headlong with the back wall of the cellar, but instead, it dove *through* something and *vanished*.

Adol dashed forward, his club held ready, expecting to see the black figure hiding in a hole or something. But instead, there before him was a framed doorway of sorts, with a brown forest beyond, and the black creature rising from having tumbled into the leaves. The thing hissed at him again and the scene before him began to swirl.

"No!" he bellowed, and dove headlong at the swirling mist.

But he was too late, and he crashed hard into his own reflection. He stared at himself for a fraction of a second, threw down his club, grabbed and lifted the huge frame as easily as another man might lift a hat from a rack. He expected the black creature to be behind it, but only a stone wall was there, with a triple spiral carved on it. He put the mirror down, looked about the room again, and picked up his club.

Where had this mirror come from? Had Grandpa McLochlan hidden it down here all these years? Had Ellie known about it? A moment ago, it had been – a doorway? He ran his hands along the edge of the mirror, feeling the intricately shaped brass branches and leaves that made up its frame, searching for some secret to open it again. But the mirror held only his own image and that of the basement. And what of the crystal that the creature had been holding? What had that been? He stared at his reflection for a long time, waiting to see if the window would open again. But the night grew black outside, and soon all was dark. Slowly, he turned and left the basement, looked back once, then walked back to the house, pondering what all this could mean. Strange things were happening around the farm, and he intended to find out why. There were plans to be made.

* * *

The goblin lay sprawled in the leaves for several minutes, staring at the mirror and its own reflection. It had dropped the crystal ball when it dove through. Realizing this, it began to frantically search through the leaves. At last, it found the perfect sphere and stuffed it into a pocket in its black robe. It sat for a long, long time, breathing heavily and staring, waiting.

At last, it rose, went to the mirror, and took the crystal into its gray hand. The mirror changed. Darkness filled the scene beyond the portal.

Cautiously, it looked around to be sure no one had seen, and then it slipped back through the mirror. It then went to the door and peered out. There was the man, walking in the moonlight back toward his house. It waited until the man was far away, and then slipped into the night.

With glee, it cackled as it ran. "I have it! I have it!" Then it reached the wall, climbed over, and sped toward the center of the bog.

Chapter 33 – The Hag and the Hermit

Colleen pushed down the feeling of hysteria that was rising up within her, but she could not help but feel as though they had just been eaten alive. The mouth of the cave had closed down like some great maw and shrouded them in absolute darkness. And what had been that laugh? Who lived here in this dank place of fear?

"Look!" hissed Frederick. "What's that?"

There before them, a bobbing orange light appeared. It appeared to be floating in the air and was coming toward them. It stopped some distance away, and they could see a thin figure with long, stringy, white hair dimly outlined by the light. A moment later, an old woman's voice called to them from the darkness.

"Follow me," it said, and the figure turned and walked back the way it had come.

Hesitantly, they followed, inching forward through the darkness until they rounded a bend. There, the dim light of a small fire sent shadows dancing across the walls of a chamber. Hunched beside the flames was what appeared to be woman with wild, unkempt hair, bare feet, and wearing a ragged brown dress that hung in tatters down to her thin, boney knees.

She turned her head in their direction, and gave them a nearly toothless grin.

"Ah, a fine, fine catch," she whispered, then cackled madly.

Her tongue darted out of her mouth, licking her lips, and shot back in again, almost snake-like. Then she clenched her gnarled hands into fists, shook them victoriously over the fire, and laughed again. "A fine catch, indeed!"

She rose and took a step toward them. Her hollow, sunken eyes were wide with a look of covetous delight.

"I have just the perfect place for you, my young lovelies," she said.

Then her expression changed to almost a look of pity and she said, "Ah, poor things. You must be tired after a long day's journey. Come in and rest by the fire. Here, let me help you. Do you have any good gingerbread cookie recipes?"

Something about this old woman deeply disturbed Colleen. First, she was as big as they were, and she looked to be human. No one they had met had mentioned anything about another human living here in this land. Then there was all that talk about *catching* them.

But she seemed harmless enough, and the fire did look welcoming after their long journey.

"Please, ma'am," said Colleen, "who are you?"

"Just a little closer, dearie," she crooned. "That's right, come up to the fire and warm yourselves. Just a little closer… *HA!*"

"Look out!" cried Mrs. Wigglepox, as something came swooping down from the darkness above them. Colleen was snatched into the air and carried upward. She screamed as she felt herself gripped by unseen hands and thrust roughly into a cage that hung suspended from the ceiling. The door of the cage slammed shut of its own accord, and she grabbed its iron bars and shook them. The cage swung back and forth and she could see that it was suspended by a chain from the ceiling.

Frederick cried out, "Hey, hey!" and then flew past her and into an adjacent cage. She could barely make out his face in the dim light.

"What's going on!" he shouted.

Badger whinnied and stamped, then began to neigh wildly. They both looked down and could see the old woman waving a thin stick in her hand, as though she were conducting an orchestra, and saying something that they could not quite make out. The horse quieted, hung his head, and appeared to fall asleep.

The woman walked past him and up to the cart, then in a louder voice said, "And what have we here? A family of leprechauns! Maybe I'll keep you for myself as pets!"

"You just keep away from us!" shouted Mrs. Wigglepox, and pushed Lily and Rose behind her.

The old woman reached out a hand to grab them and they ran to the far side of the cart.

"What fun!" she crowed, and climbed into the cart after them.

"You leave them alone!" shouted Colleen.

The hag looked up at her and grinned.

"Patience, love. Momma's going to make us a nice pie." She laughed madly and grabbed all three of the leprechauns.

"And look here!" she cackled in delight. "Three gnomes!"

Then she proceeded to scoop up Humble, Neman, and Zelo.

Lily and Rose screamed, and Mrs. Wigglepox beat on the bony fingers that gripped them. The old woman climbed down from the cart and began to hum a tune. She walked over to one wall and produced what looked to be a

241

birdcage and, into this, she placed the Wigglepoxes and the gnomes.

"Frederick, we've got to do something!" said Colleen. "She's going to eat them!"

Frederick shook his cage, kicked at the door, and even tried throwing his body against the bars. But he only succeeded in making it swing wildly, banging into Colleen's.

The old woman was humming a tune and boiling water in a pot now, and began cutting up roots and putting them into the water.

"Oracle!" shouted Colleen. "Do something!"

A moment later, Oracle's head peeked over the back of the wagon. He looked as though he had just awakened from a nap. He yawned and stretched, then stood up and banged his cane on the wood of the seat.

From the direction they had come into the cave, the sound of stone grinding on stone could be heard, and a voice yelling, "Mal? Are you home, Mal?"

The hag stopped what she was doing and called out, "Who's there? Come so soon?" Then, in a regretful voice, she said, "And I've not even had time to cook the pie."

She sighed heavily and walked past the wagon, seeming not to see Oracle, and continued out to the front of the cave.

Colleen strained to hear what was being said, for a conversation between the hag and someone else seemed to be going on. Soon the voices grew closer and they could clearly hear someone saying, "No, no, it's no trouble at all, Mal. I shan't stay for long."

"I'm in the middle of making dinner, Cian. Come back tomorrow and we can talk," said the hag.

But apparently, the visitor was insistent and bustled right on into the cave, the hag trailing behind, wringing her hands. To Colleen's and Frederick's great surprise, the visitor turned out to be a little man nearly as tall as Oracle, and quite obviously a leprechaun. As soon as he came into the circle of firelight, he stopped, looked about, looked up into the shadows of the ceiling, and frowned.

"Now, Mal, how many times have I told you not to trap people for the goblins. And what is this – a family of leprechauns in a cage, and three gnomes? And a boy and girl, no less! For shame!"

The hag looked down at her hands and dug her shoe in the dirt. "But, it's just a few of them, and the goblins only take them to see *her*. It's no harm done.

And they trade with me for such catches, you know. What else can a poor old hag do for a living in these dark times?"

"*Trade* with you, Mal? You mean they give you their putrid ooze in exchange for prisoners. These are *people*, Mal. You can't trade in people. I've told you this before. I'm afraid this is the last time. I'm really going to have to send you away," said the leprechaun.

The hag stopped suddenly and cocked her head as if listening. "Hmm," she said. "Seems as though I might have an extra catch today!" she said. With that, she leaped to one side and waved a hand. Out of the darkness from above, a shadow swooped down upon the leprechaun. But just as it did, a stick came flying out of the wagon and struck the shadow.

Colleen and Frederick were not quite sure what they had seen, but it seemed to them that Oracle had thrown his cane, and that when it struck the shadow, the darkness of it seemed to crack into pieces and shatter. Something that looked like gray ash floated down on top of the leprechaun, which he brushed from his shoulders.

"You really should keep your place a bit tidier, Mal," he said.

The hag's face grew hard and full of anger. She waved her hands again and muttered an incantation. There was a sound like a gong that made everyone in the room, except the hag, hold their ears. Then the hag screamed and ran for the cave entrance. Her last words before she disappeared were, "I'll have a catch yet!"

The leprechaun looked about the room once again, went over to the cage that held the Wigglepox family and gnomes, and broke it open.

"Thank you, kind sir," said Mrs. Wigglepox as he placed them on the ground. "Can you get our friends down as well?"

"Let's see what can be done," he said. He walked over to the far wall and found two ropes tied to fixtures on the wall. These ropes went up to the ceiling where they were strung through pulleys and then were tied to the chains that held the cages.

"I'm a bit short," he said, as he tried to reach the knot that tied the ropes.

After several times jumping, he managed to hang onto the end of the rope, pull himself up further, and began to untie the knots.

"I'm not sure if it's a good idea to untie…" began Frederick as he watched.

But before he could finish what he was saying, the knot gave way and both cages began to fall to the ground. Both Frederick and Colleen braced themselves for the inevitable crash.

243

But the crash never came. Just before hitting the ground the cages both stopped abruptly – the ropes had knots in them that had jammed in the pulleys.

"Well, friends," said the little man. "You had best get out of those cages and come over to the fire."

"The doors are locked," said Frederick.

"I dare say you could open them," he said.

Colleen suddenly felt very foolish. Of course, she could open them. She found the key that Doc had given her and slipped it into the lock on the door.

"Why didn't I think of that a few minutes ago?" Colleen said.

The leprechaun shrugged and walked over to the fire. "Please, come and sit for a time and we will talk."

Hesitantly, Colleen took a few steps forward.

"If I may ask, who are you?" she said.

"Ah, there will be time for introductions soon enough," said the leprechaun. "Come, now, sit with me by the fire and we shall talk."

Colleen glanced at Mrs. Wigglepox, who nodded her head. They all walked over to the fire and sat down across from the little man.

"I'm Colleen McGunnegal, and this is Frederick, Humble, Neman, Zelo, Edna, Lily, and Rose. May we ask your name, sir?" asked Colleen.

The little man smiled. "I am only a poor recluse living as best I can in these troubled times."

"Who was that old woman? Was that the Witch?" asked Frederick after a moment.

"No, no," he said. "Her name is Mal. I have been trying to help her for years. She came here long, long ago, though, and has been capturing little people and giving them to the goblins in exchange for ooze. Still, I hold out hope for her. She and the goblins built this place as a trap of sorts for passersby. But her luck has not been so good recently. She and I have an odd relationship."

"I'd have almost thought you were friends with her by the way you talked," said Frederick.

"Friends? For my part, yes, I try to be a friend to her. But she doesn't care much for me, although she is afraid of me."

"Afraid of you?" said Frederick. "But you... you're too *tall* to be one of the little people, like Oracle over there, and too short to be a dwarf... what *are* you? Why would she be afraid?"

The little man laughed a clear, hearty laugh that echoed in the chamber.

"But I *am* one of the little people," he said. "Mrs. Wigglepox could tell you that."

They all turned to her and she looked down, a bit embarrassed.

"I don't understand," said Colleen. "Then why are you so... so *big?*"

"I am not *big*," explained the little man. "It's just that these others are rather *small*."

"It's true," said Mrs. Wigglepox. "We are small. But, good sir, please, won't you tell us who you are?"

He looked hard at Mrs. Wigglepox for a moment, nodded his head, and said, "My name is Cian."

"I heard the old woman call you that, but surely, you are not *the* Cian?" she said.

"What's wrong, Mrs. Wigglepox?" asked Frederick, and he stood, looking suspiciously at him.

But the little man continued to stare at Mrs. Wigglepox, an odd twinkle in his deep brown eyes.

"But you couldn't be... *him*," she gasped.

He laughed again and said, "But I am. You know it in your heart."

"What's going on?" asked Colleen. "Mrs. Wigglepox, what *is* the matter?"

But Mrs. Wigglepox only stared and said nothing.

"Right then," said Frederick. "Let's have it plain. So, your name is Cian. A funny name, but I've heard worse. See here now, how about telling us who you really are and what your business is?"

The little man smiled up at Frederick and said, "Please, Frederick, sit and be at ease. Give Mrs. Wigglepox and me a moment."

Frederick slowly sat down and Cian and Mrs. Wigglepox stared at each other, as if they were searching each other's faces for some deep secret.

At last, Mrs. Wigglepox spoke. "I believe you. But it's *really* hard to believe! How did you escape *her?*"

"Ah, Mrs. Wigglepox, that is a tale. But I think our guests here deserve some explanation," he said.

He looked at Colleen, at Frederick, and at all the little people, who all were mesmerized by this little man.

"I am Cian," he said, "last of the Sons of the Elders of the Little People."

They all stared at him.

"You mean that you are a son of one of the Seven that woke up on the First Morning inside the Waking Tree?" asked Rose.

Cian smiled broadly at her and said, "Yes, daughter! And you are of my tribe!"

"That makes you my great, great, great... Grandfather!" said Rose, and she ran forward, jumped up into his lap, and hugged the button on his brown coat.

His smile broadened even more and his face turned a bit red.

"Indeed I am," he replied, gently picking her up and hugging her, then placing her back on the ground.

"But, Grandfather, you are rather big, as big as Oracle," she said to him sheepishly.

They glanced back at the wagon, but Oracle seemed to have disappeared.

"And who is this Oracle?" asked Cian.

"Why, he's a leprechaun, as big as you, although he looks much older," said Colleen. "But he seems to have vanished. He is a bit disturbed, you know."

"I should like to meet this big leprechaun," said Cian curiously. "But perhaps he does not wish to meet me, or perhaps later. I heard rumor of your coming and thought you might pass this way. I hoped that you would not meet Mal, the old hag of these parts. She can be troublesome."

"Troublesome!" said Mrs. Wigglepox. "She was going to make a pie out of us!"

"It was providential for you that I came along, then," said Cian. "But come, perhaps we can make use of her fire and make something better than a leprechaun pie."

He smiled and winked at Lily and Rose, then began to dig through a pouch that hung at his side, adding spices to Mal's stew that she had begun to cook.

They all settled down, watching him for several minutes, and then Frederick spoke up, wanting to break the silence.

"You know, it's the fault of those crazy pixies just back a-ways," said Frederick. "We couldn't convince them to let us stay with them for the night, so we moved on. What a bunch that is! But at least Intelli seemed to try to think about things and not just buzz about. She seemed to be the most reasonable of the three."

"Ah, Intelli!" said Cian as he stirred the pot. "Yes, she is often lost in thought. But for her that has become simply sitting on a dead branch and listening to a constant babble of thoughts, while there is a whole universe of mysteries just waiting for her to experience. She was made to wander between the worlds! But she just sits there, becoming more and more skeptical that anything at all is true or real."

He sighed and then continued. "But all of that is a side effect of the Spell. The pixies live deeply wounded under its influence. They have become rather scatterbrained. It shows the evil craft of the Witch, for the pixies were once one of her greatest foes. Now she has divided, and so conquered them. They are no longer a threat to her."

"Sounds too deep for me," said Frederick.

"Deep calls to deep," said Cian.

"People keep telling me that!" said Frederick. "What's that supposed to mean?"

"I think you will know soon enough," Cian replied, looking thoughtfully at Frederick. "As for these little folk, and Mal, it will take a lifetime of work to heal them of the wounds they have taken, unless the Spell can be broken. But that is one reason I come here on occasion – to help them along their way and to keep them from falling to the final end of the Spell, and to teach them to find what is truly deep."

"What is the *final end* of the Spell?" asked Colleen.

She wondered what could be the end of a life lived under this terrible black magic.

"It is different for different people;" he said. "Some, as you know, fall into the sleep and may never waken. They will just go on and on into endless and deepening nightmares. But for the pixies, it is different. If they cannot find a way to be reunited to each other and live in unity, and so fight the Spell, they will eventually *fade*. Their wings will wither and disappear, even as Intelli's have already begun to. Their brightness will become a dull gray. They will abandon each other in the end, and wander aimlessly about looking for something to bring them happiness, but never finding it, for their *real* life can only be found with each other."

"That's so sad!" said Colleen. "Can you help them?"

"Yes," said Cian. "But they must want the help first. On occasion, I stop by and remind them of this, and give them a word or two of encouragement. If they are ever to be healed of the Spell's influence, then they must wholly turn away from their troubled way of life and return to their natural state."

Colleen thought about this for a moment and then asked, "What does it mean for a pixie to be in its natural state?"

Cian smiled a sad smile, then said, "The fairy folk are naturally creatures of light. But the source of their illumination is not within themselves. The Spell has tricked them into trading who and what they really are for a cheap copy.

"You see, Intelli must turn away from her one-dimensional reasoning. She has begun to think that she can be illumined simply by thinking about things. She has forgotten that she must seek contemplation of the other worlds and the light that fills them.

"Irassi believes that self-determination is the path to finding light. She wants everything her own way. She is fond of saying, 'If you can't trust yourself, who can you trust?' But she must turn from her self-will, and away from her personal ambitions, toward selfless love of her sisters and all others, and learn that real light is gained through humility and service.

"Then there is Apetti. Poor thing, she seeks fulfillment in distractions and pleasures. If she would only gaze into the Blessed Realm at the Uncreated Light that ever dwells there and everywhere, then all her passions would be transformed and she would never seek the cheats that the Spell offers her again. She would truly live."

He sighed, and then said, "If they would do these things, then they will be given wings that would carry them as one across the boundaries of the worlds, and free them to live as they were intended, and they would truly be filled with a light that would never fade."

Cian looked thoughtful for a moment, and then said, "Then there's poor old Mal. She wasn't always a hag, you know. Once she was like a princess, so sweet and beautiful. But she gave herself over to the Witch in exchange for power. Do you think that what she got was a fair trade?"

"Sounds like she got the short end of the stick," said Frederick.

"Indeed," said Cian. "Everyone who deals with the Witch is cheated in the end. I suppose they actually cheat themselves."

"What about our people?" asked Mrs. Wigglepox. "I know the Spell keeps us from wishing, but what can we do about it?"

"Ah, much! But first, you must be aware of how you are wishing. You know there are four levels of wishing," said Cian. "The first is the *wish of words*. That is just *saying* 'I wish for this' or 'I wish for that', but nothing deeper in you is moved or engaged. Little magic is stirred by such wishes.

"The second is the *wish of the mind*. That's when you wholly concentrate on your wish and your mind doesn't go beyond the words of your wish. That's better, but still doesn't stir the deep magic.

"Then there is real wishing, when your mind descends into your *heart*. That's where the real magic lives, and where the leprechaun finds her true self – her *wishing self*. That is where the real work of wishing can be done."

Everyone was quiet for a moment, and then Rose spoke up. "Please, sir, you said that there were four kinds of wishing. What is the fourth?"

"Ah!" said Cian, a satisfied smile on his face. "Now *that* is where the deepest magic of all is found. It is the *silent wish*. No words can express it. It goes beyond words, beyond the mind, beyond the imagination, perhaps even beyond the heart. It is the wishing that touches the *beyond*, and takes the leprechaun into magical realms that are free of all spells and witches and words and images and every sensible thing, to the very *uncreated source* of all wishes. Some call it the *wish of contemplation*. It is the place where the fairies go when they too find their true selves. It is the place that all creation is intended to go and find its fulfillment."

Silence filled the room. No one spoke. Frederick stared at the flickering fire before him. The embers glowed red, the flame filling their charcoal bodies with mysterious light. What kind of beings were fairies and leprechauns that could be like these coals – filled with fiery light, and yet not be turned to ash? And what about him? He felt empty somehow, as though he were just a black burned twig, outside of the fire, apart from these strange beings that surrounded him. They could literally slip into other worlds. Still, hadn't he done the same? He had come through the mirror. Was there a doorway that he might step through, even into this Blessed Realm of which they all spoke?

A sudden feeling of longing stirred deep inside him, a yearning to run madly down every trail and path of all the worlds – to go and explore and experience and see everything. To find himself amid the vast ocean of creation. To find his place in it all. For a moment, he felt as though he would burst with excitement and expectation. Had he begun that journey already? He tried to think this through, and his brain began to hurt. He shook his head, and the feeling quietly slipped away, like water through his fingers. He suddenly felt a great loss, as though for a fleeting moment, he had been on the verge of experiencing something remarkable, but rather than embracing it, he had tried to analyze it, and so lost it completely.

He looked over at Colleen. She was sitting cross-legged, staring into the flames. The Wigglepoxes and gnomes seemed deeply thoughtful.

Cian seemed to sense his feelings and smiled at him.

"Well, come, I think it is time for a tale," said the leprechaun. "Perhaps Oracle will join us to hear it. Come close and I will tell you the tale of the Waking Tree and of the Seven Elders, and of the coming of the Witch."

Mrs. Wigglepox, Lily, Rose, and the three gnomes all quickly gathered around Cian. Frederick and Colleen looked at each other and then drew in closer as well.

Cian looked serious for a few moments, as if remembering, and then began to chant in a clear voice that filled the chamber.

"In days of old the Wondrous Three
Shown down their single Light.
And pierced the void of nothingness,
Filling its dark night.

With a word the Triune spoke
And worlds did come to be
And on one grand isle,
They made the Waking Tree.

Grand it was, so tall and fair,
Its branches pierced the Sky.
And in its depths the Three in One
Made seven brothers and their wives to lie.

Each they gifted with strong gifts
To share among their kin.
That should some evil come their way
Together they might win.

To one was given understanding,
And love for all that's good.
To the second, fortitude,
To live just as he should.

To the third 'twas temperance
To guide him 'long the way.
And to the fourth 'twas justice
To make the night like day.

To the fifth was faith,
Great obstacles to move.
And to the sixth, charity,
To help and heal and soothe.

And to the last 'twas given hope,
That sadness might not stay,
But be dispelled by his clear voice
And find a brighter day.

To each was also given power
With which to live and be,
And plant the seeds of the future
Beyond the Waking Tree.

To wish, to see,
To walk, to grow,
To dig, to find,
To believe, to know.

To meditate and contemplate
To spread the forest fair,
That from the Waking Tree
Might come a world so rare.

And for long years all was well,
And peace and grace did reign.
Until the Door was opened,
And Anastazi came.

Tall he was, his robes of blue,
His hair of silver-gold.
His wisdom found no match
In those days of old.

And others came soon after
Through the Silver Door.
And Little People ventured forth
Other lands to explore.

Lugh of Cian, Elder's son,
Did find a world so fair,
And found that Men revered him,
And feared his power there.

A darkness crept into his heart,
A lust for power grew.
And Lugh did grant men wishes
In exchange for what they knew.

Much evil in the world of Men
His wicked hands did sow.
His evil wishes dragons brought,
And sorrow men did know.

And when at last he did return
To the land of Little Folk,
He lusted more for power
O'er Leprechaun and Oak.

And 'tis said that he himself
Did cause the Witch to be,
And when she came he saw his chance
To seize the Waking Tree.

What dark councils they did have!
What plots and evils planned!
For soon the Goblins came
And joined their evil band.

Then after years of dark toil,
Their dreadful trap they sprang.
And from the sea a dark tide swept,
And an evil song they sang.

All would have died, both Folk and Tree,
Except that on that day,
Anastazi the Great they met,
Along their burning way.

His eyes of lavender did flash,
As he stood upon a hill,
And looked down on Goblin hosts,
Their voices cruel and shrill.

Like a shining star
Amid a sea of black,
Anastazi's voice rang out,

And halted their attack.

But the Witch strode forth, robed in gloom,
And in that fateful hour,
She wove her spells of darkness,
To fight the Elf's bright power.

But brave he was, and none could match
The Elven Lord's great strength.
And around him Little Folk
Gathered and fought back.

The battle raged throughout the day,
A clash of dark and light,
Until the Elven Lord and Witch
Came face to face to fight.

Her weapon was enchanted fire,
Her tongue was filled with lies.
With promises of power she sought
To draw him to her side.

But he cursed such vain gifts
And drew near to strike the blow
That would put an end
To Goblin, Witch and foe.

Her fire roared, his lightning flashed,
He seized her in that place.
And drew the blackened hood
Off of her hidden face.

But when he looked into her eyes,
Anastazi shrunk away,
And did not slay the Witch,
But left her there that day.

And so she fled the way she came,
Sailing south into the sea.
And Anastazi left as well,
Fading into memory.

But great harm there was done,
And greater treachery,

For Lugh's betrayal cast a curse
Upon all the Tuathi.

And all who had involved themselves
In his wretched blame,
Began to shrink in size and heart,
And small, indeed, became."

His chanting voice faded and all was silent for some time until Colleen spoke.

"Cian, what happened to Anastazi the Great? Why didn't he kill the Witch?" she asked.

"No one knows," he said. "But it is said that he left that field of battle greatly distressed, as if his heart had been broken."

"Has anyone seen him or the Witch since then?" asked Frederick.

"The Witch – yes, we have seen her, though rarely," he said. "She relies on her goblins to do her bidding. But Anastazi – there have only been rumors about him. No one that I know of has seen him since that day thousands of years ago."

They were quiet for a moment and then a thought struck Frederick, and he asked, "Sir, why is she called the *Court* Witch?"

"Ah," said Cian, "it is because she pretends to be the court witch of the Goblin King."

"Pretends?" asked Frederick.

"Aye, pretends. She is the real power behind the goblin throne in the land of the Little People. It is said that no one has ever seen the goblin king himself for hundreds of years, except in his royal chamber, and that is deep in the pits of his dark fortress somewhere in the sea. She uses him, I think, to control the goblins."

He paused and then his eyes brightened.

"But see here, we have other friends visiting us this night!" he said, pointing to the cave entrance.

They all turned to look, and indeed, just at the ends of the fire light, a number of gnomes had gathered and several fairies.

"Come, come, friends!" said Cian, and they all scurried in, seven in all, eying the big people cautiously as they came.

"They know that when I come, Mal runs off to find the goblins and will be gone for quite some time. We will be safe for a while," Cian said. "Deep down inside there is a piece of her that isn't a hag, you know. That is true of anyone who serves the Witch. There is always hope."

"The mice of the wood told us you were coming," said one gnome. "We saw Mal go running through the woods all in a fluster."

"Well, here we all are, and there are tales to be told!" Cian said.

Introductions were made, and Cian explained that these few little people lived nearby under the roots of an old tree. They had eluded both Mal and the goblins, always setting a watch for them, and they would come and listen to Cian when he came by.

There was a great deal of chatter among them all for several minutes as Cian tried to explain why the big people had come and what they were doing, and that they were not with the Witch, and that they needed help and guidance.

Through all of this, Oracle remained hidden in the wagon.

Cian raised a hand and called for quiet, and when they were still, he said, "Dear friends, you have all been introduced to our big people friends here, but in the wagon, there is a sleeping dwarf. He has fallen under the Spell and cannot wake himself. And there is a shy little person too, I think."

Some of the little people ran to the wagon and climbed up the wheels to peer in at Dvalenn, while others went and stroked the legs of Badger, who was awake now, and didn't seem to mind at all. Oracle had buried himself beneath the hay, and no one seemed to notice him.

It took some moments for Cian to call them all back to order again, but when he had, he continued.

"This is Colleen, a *girl* from the Land of Men who comes with gifts to our aid. And this is Frederick, a *boy* from the same land, of noble blood, who will do great deeds and be tested sorely before the end. And I believe that some of you may know Mrs. Wigglepox and her children and these fine gnomes who are traveling with them," he said.

They all bowed, and the little people bowed in return.

Cian went on to tell of their journey, but Frederick was not listening. He was thinking about what Cian had just said. *I will do great deeds and be tested sorely before the end. Just what is that supposed to mean?* he thought to himself. *And just what is "the end"?* He was determined, before this night was through, to ask Cian those questions.

* * *

Colleen also was thinking similar thoughts. Just what *gifts* did she have to give these little people? She was just a thirteen-year-old girl, after all.

But Cian seemed to know their thoughts, and he called to them and said, "Listen to me, my friends. Tonight, you must stay in this cave. Stay within the ring of light that the fire casts. Your presence in the forest is known now, and the Witch's people will be looking for you."

"But won't they come here first?" asked Colleen.

"Yes, they will come," Cian replied. "Mal has alerted them."

"Then we should leave and find another place to spend the night!" said Frederick.

"No," said Cian. "You must stay here tonight. But you will come to no harm, and the goblins that come will not find you as long as you stay within the fire's light."

"But won't they see us if we are in the light?" asked Frederick. "Wouldn't it be better to go deeper into the darkness of the cave and hide there?"

"Ah, Frederick, running into the dark will not hide you from goblin eyes. But they hate the light and fear the fire. As long as you remain in the light, the goblins will not come near you."

"But they will see us, won't they?" asked Colleen. "Surely, even if they don't like the light, they will just wait outside the cave until we starve to death."

"No," he said. "Do not be afraid. You will see. Already they are coming."

Chapter 34 – Bite of the Goblin

There was a harsh sound outside, coming faintly into the cave.

"Goblins!" whispered Mrs. Wigglepox, her voice fearful.

There was a rush of whispers and nervous looks among the little people, but Cian seemed unconcerned, and slowly rose from his place by the fire and said, "Remember, no matter what you see or hear, stay in the ring of light. Do you understand? Stay in the light!"

Then he casually strode past them all and toward the cave entrance.

"Cian!" whispered Mrs. Wigglepox, but he did not seem to hear her, and disappeared around the corner.

"Oughtn't we to go after him or something?" said Frederick to no one in particular.

"No," said Mrs. Wigglepox. "He said to stay here. I suspect he knows what he's doing."

"But won't he be captured by the goblins?" asked Frederick.

Then, a rather large leprechaun, if seven inches tall could be considered large, went up to Frederick and said, "Good sir, would you come with me to the edge of the light and listen?"

Frederick looked down at him, then looked at Colleen, nodded, and followed the little man to the very edge of the fire light.

Colleen cautiously followed them, staying close behind Frederick, and then the whole group tiptoed forward.

"Now listen!" whispered the big leprechaun.

Frederick strained his ears, but could only hear muffled voices outside, some of them high and harsh, and others gruffer.

There were loud exclamations and shouting, and the haggardly voice of Mal yelling above the din.

"There it is!" she squealed.

"Catch it, quick, before it goes back in the cave!" yelled another voice.

There was a good deal of running about in the sticks and leaves, with four or five harsh voices all yelling things like *"there it goes!"* or *"where did it go?"* and *"there it is, you ninny!"* and similar things, until all the voices were confused.

This went on for several minutes, until the clear voice of Cian rang out, seemingly from some distance away and said, "Hear me, brother goblins!"

There was a sound of a "*Huh?*" and a "*Duh!*" and something like a "*Hoo!*" and then a "*There it is, up on the top of the cave!*" followed by a great deal of scrambling around again.

But Cian's voice continued, "Brother goblins! I have a word for you!"

The running about stopped, and one of the goblin voices said, "*What does it mean?*"

By the sound of it, Frederick imagined to be a rather slow-minded goblin.

"*It means it wants to talk, you idiot! But never mind that, let's get it and take it to the Witch!*" said another harsh voice.

"*And then make pies with what's left in the cave!*" said Mal.

"*To the Witch!*" cried another.

"Ah, the Witch!" said Cian loudly. "Do you know what the Witch has done with your king?"

"*What does it mean, 'done with the king'?*" said the slow-sounding goblin.

"I will tell you what she has done with him!" exclaimed Cian. "She has used him, and is even now using him. When did you last see your king outside of his royal throne room?"

There was some muttering among the goblins that Frederick could not make out, but Cian continued on.

"Yes, do you know why he does not leave the throne room?" asked Cian.

"*It's because he's the king!*" shouted one of the goblins. "*Now come down here, and we'll take you to see him!*"

"No," said Cian. "He does not leave his royal throne room because he cannot! He has been bewitched by the Witch herself, and she desires to rule over you. In fact, she *does* rule over you."

"*What does it mean, she rules over us?*" asked the dull-sounding goblin.

"*Shut up, Nous. Don't listen to it. The Witch warned us not to listen to these little brutes. They've got poison tongues,*" said another.

"*What ya mean, it's got a poison tongue, Haram?*" asked Nous.

"*Never you mind, just climb up there and bring it down,*" said Haram.

"*You climb up and bring it down,*" said Nous. "*If it's got a poison tongue, I'm not going up there. It might bite me. And besides, what did it mean about the Witch, anyway?"*

"*I'm in charge here,*" said Haram, "*and I says you're going to climb up there and grab it and bring it down. Now here's a sack - go and get it!*"

There was a *whack*, and Frederick imagined the hand of Haram slapping Nous hard.

"*You'll be sorry for that!*" yelled Nous, and returned the *whack*.

There was a great deal of yelling and tussling as Haram and Nous began to roll about and fight and the other goblins cheered on one or the other.

"Farewell, friends!" came the voice of Cian through the din. "Remember my words! You are all slaves to the Witch, as is your king! I counsel you to go and see this for yourselves! When did you last speak to your king, and when did he last answer you? I tell you, he cannot answer for himself, but only as the Witch moves him. Go to him and see!"

"*There it goes!*" yelled another goblin. "*It's getting away!*"

The fighting stopped, and Haram yelled, "*After it!*"

"*You go after it,*" said another goblin. "*Just what if it's right? I haven't seen the king for years. Have any of you?*"

"*We haven't been to the fortress for years, you idiot!*" yelled Haram.

"*Well, I say it's time we go back,*" said another.

"*Right,*" said Nous. "*I've had enough of this running around chasing these little beasts, what with their poison tongues and all. I'm going back to the Island on the next ship.*"

Without another word, he turned and trudged away through the forest.

There was some murmuring among the other goblins, and then Haram screamed, "*Get back here, Nous, or you'll be mighty sorry!*"

There was a pause, then a *twang* that sounded like a bowstring. Faintly, Frederick thought he heard a yell.

"*Anyone else want to desert the troop?*" asked Haram.

There was silence, and then Haram said, "*That's what I thought. Now follow me and we'll pick up the trail of that little beastie.*"

"*What about Nous?*" said a goblin.

"*You want to join him?*" said Haram.

Then they could hear the sound of footsteps trailing away through the leaves, and a moment later, Cian walked into the circle of light from the cave entrance.

"The goblins and Mal will follow my trail far from here and then lose it," he said. "They will not return tonight, I think. But they have wounded one of their own, and he lies dying in the wood."

"Can we help him?" asked Colleen.

"You have a good heart, Colleen," said Cian. "Yes, we can help him if we bring him here to the fire."

"Come on, then," she said to Frederick. "Let's bring him in."

"You want to bring a goblin in here?" said Frederick.

"We can't just let him die out there," she said.

"You know," said Mrs. Wigglepox, "that goblin out there would leave you to die, or worse, if he found you wounded in the forest."

"Well, I'm not a goblin," she replied, "and it wouldn't be right to just leave him."

Frederick looked doubtful.

"Are you coming or not?" asked Colleen.

"All right, then," he replied, and the two of them headed for the cave entrance.

Cian and all of the little people followed after them.

They found the body of the goblin fallen in the leaves, an arrow protruding from its back.

Dark blood stained the forest floor, but it was still alive, its breath coming in labored gasps.

It wore an entirely black robe and on its feet were hard black boots. Its head was covered by a black hood, and at its side hung a wicked-looking blade. Dirty yellow claw-like fingernails made its gray, gnarled hands look rather like birds' feet.

Frederick reached to pull the arrow out, but Colleen stopped him.

"He might bleed to death if we pull it out," she said. "Let's get him by the fire. I remember Badger was accidentally shot by our neighbor with an arrow. He missed a target he was aiming for and the arrow went wild and hit poor Badger right in the shoulder. Dad took a hot knife and sealed the wound with it after he pulled out the arrow."

"Let me handle it, Colleen," said Frederick. First, he drew the goblin's blade and threw it into the woods, then with a grunt and with Colleen's help, managed to get the goblin over his shoulder.

The goblin gurgled a groan, but lay limp as Frederick slowly carried him into the cave and laid him down by the fire where Cian had cleared a spot.

"You know," said Frederick, "I thought these goblins were bigger, but this one is no taller than I am. But oh, man, it stinks!"

"Do not underestimate them," said Cian. "Although they may be your size, or even smaller, they are strong and of evil temper. And they sometimes possess dark powers that make them even more dangerous."

"Well, bad or not, we still need to help him," said Colleen, and she pulled the knife at her side from its sheath and began to heat the blade in the fire.

Soon the tip was quite hot, and she said, "Frederick, pull out the arrow."

Frederick looked worried, but gripped the shaft of the arrow, and with a tremendous yank, pulled the arrow from the goblin's back.

The creature groaned, and then lay still. A sticky wet stain quickly formed on its black robe.

"Quick, Frederick, you've got to tear away that robe it's wearing. I didn't think of that."

Frederick grimaced, but bent down and tried to tear the robe away from the little hole that the arrow had made. Soon his hands were covered in the creature's dark blood.

"I can't do this," he said with disgust.

Then Cian, who had been standing watching, stepped forward and said, "Please friends, allow me."

Frederick and Colleen stepped back and Cian bent down over the goblin. He carefully rolled it over and pulled the dark hood from its face.

Colleen gasped and stepped back, and Frederick's eyes went wide.

It was a hideous creature, with gray-green mottled skin, an overly large bulbous nose, and large, hairy, pointed ears. Its black tongue lolled out of a wide mouth full of crooked, sharp, and yellowing teeth. Its grayish-purple hair was thin and unwashed and hung in limp, wet strands across its wrinkled forehead. Its breath stank, making them want to gag and its eyes were shut tightly in a grimace of pain.

But Cian looked at the creature with sad eyes and carefully stroked the dirty hair from its face, caressing the beast with pity, even care.

"He is near death," he said.

"Oughtn't we to seal the wound?" asked Colleen.

"He will not live through such an ordeal," said Cian.

Colleen and Frederick looked at one another for a moment, and then Colleen said, "Frederick, we've got to try. Here, help me roll him over."

They bent over him and were about the roll him over on his stomach when a voice came from the darkness and said, "Leave the hobgoble."

They turned to see a little figure hobbling forward from the direction of the wagon. Several of the little people gave a gasp.

"Now see here, Oracle," began Colleen, "maybe it is a goblin, and an ugly one at that, but still, it doesn't seem right to just let it *die* without at least trying to help. I mean, I know it's your enemy and all that, but my dad always says that you're supposed to help any anyone who's in need, even your enemies."

Oracle walked from the darkness. His hood covered his face and, in one hand, he held a small, round pot by its handle and, as he approached, the children could see that something shiny was inside it.

Frederick's eyes went wide as he peered inside, this time at the sight of two pure gold nuggets that sat in the bottom of the pot. They shone like the gold in Doc's cavern, and even more so, for as Oracle reached in the pot and pulled out one of the nuggets, it reflected the light of the fire so that it seemed to be on fire itself.

The little people in the cave gave an audible "*ooohhhh!*" as Oracle placed the pot next to the goblin, knelt down next to him, and stroked his face.

Cian stared, a look of shock and astonishment and wonder on his face. He was about to speak, but Oracle held up a hand and silenced him.

Then Oracle slowly pulled back his hood and their eyes met. A look of recognition washed over Cian's face. He opened his mouth to speak, but Oracle said, "Shhh! Wisssshhhh!"

Cian stood and took a step back, then hesitantly, he stepped forward and knelt down beside Oracle.

Shutting his eyes, Oracle held the gold in his left palm and placed his right hand on the goblin's head and muttered something. Cian placed his hand on the gold nugget, his face filled with surprise and joy.

Colleen watched as a rainbow descended from the ceiling – or rather through the ceiling from somewhere *beyond* the cave, and enveloped the kneeling forms of Oracle, Cian, and the unconscious goblin.

The gold in Oracle's hand blazed with light for a moment, shining through both of the leprechaun's hands, and then seemed to move, blending itself with the rainbow and enveloping the goblin. Then, both rainbow and gold faded away until only the light of the fire remained.

Oracle bowed his head slightly, then he touched the goblin's bony hand, and it opened its eyes and blinked twice.

"I had a funny dream," it said in a voice that was gruff and thick.

Seeing Oracle and Cian, it jumped in surprise. Then its eyes darted to Frederick and Colleen and the other little people, and it backed away on all fours until it hit its head on the cave wall with an audible "*humph!*"

"Do not be afraid, Nous," said Cian. "You are safe with us."

"You're the one with the poison tongue, ain't you?" said Nous, his voice fearful, shrill, hissing, and slurring all at the same time.

Cian laughed, then said, "I see you are fully recovered, friend. No, I do not have a poison tongue. I only speak the truth. And see, we have removed the arrow that Haram shot you with."

Cian bent down and picked up the black arrow and held it up for Nous to see.

Nous paused, and then reached behind his back to feel for his wound.

"Well, he must have missed or something," said Nous. "And I... I must have tripped over a root and been knocked cold. Yeah, that's it."

He seemed to be speaking to himself now, not looking at the others.

"No, Nous," said Colleen. "That other goblin shot you and you almost died. See your blood on the arrow? I think Oracle and Cian made you well. I think they made a wish for you."

Nous narrowed his eyes and looked at the leprechauns.

"Leprechauns, make a wish for a goblin? Ha! That would be the day!" he spat.

But he reached around his back again and felt his torn robe. It was wet, and he looked in wonder at the blood on his hand.

"But..." he began, and he screwed up his face as if some deep thought was struggling to get to the surface.

"But, leprechauns..." he began again, but then screwed up his face even further.

Then he began what seemed to be an argument with himself. He got up and began to pace back and forth, seemingly having forgotten the presence of the others.

"Now let's get it straight," he said. "The Witch says they're evil, that they want all the goblin gold and would sneak into our own world and rob everyone blind. That's right."

Nous nodded to himself and then began again. "That's why she's put the sleep on 'em – to keep 'em out. Best they work in the mines and dig gems and gold for us rather than sneakin' about and getting it all for themselves and wishin' harm on us. Bad enough we're stuck in this world."

His face seemed to grow angry then, and he said, "They did it! They're the ones who locked the door! Curse them! And she promises to pay them back for it!"

Then Nous caught sight of Oracle and Cian, eyed them suspiciously, looked confused, and continued his monologue.

"But then... then... why would *it*," and he pointed at the leprechauns, "... why would *it* make a wish to... to make me better?"

He paced on, back and forth, mumbling now to himself and looking at the blood that still stained his hand. Colleen and Frederick and all the little people watched with growing interest.

"I think it's having an argument with itself," whispered Frederick to Colleen.

"Yes," she whispered back. "He seems quite confused."

Just then, the goblin voice grew louder and they heard it say, "Ah, but *it* doesn't know, does it? *It* doesn't know how many of those little things I've snatched up and taken to the *ship*, does it? Ha! Hundreds, I'd reckon. Lost count years ago. 'Course now they're getting a bit scarce since we've loaded must of 'em up. And what about that *big* one last year? Now *that* was a catch."

The goblin laughed in glee, and then grew serious again and said, "Too bad about old Pwca. That big one was a witch in her own right, she was. Made him vanish right into thin air, poor thing."

Then the goblin slowly turned and stared at Colleen. Its yellow eyes turned into slits, and it showed its equally yellow teeth in a snarl.

"Waits one second. That one!" It pointed its bony hand at Colleen and began to breathe heavily. "That one looks a good bit like that other big one we put on the ship that made Pwca disappear!"

Suddenly, it leaped forward, springing with a speed and agility that surprised them all.

Somehow, though, both Frederick and Colleen saw it coming. Colleen jumped to the side just as Frederick jumped in front of the goblin. At the same time, Oracle stuck his cane out, tripping the goblin and sending it sprawling into Frederick.

The two of them tumbled to the ground and rolled over and over, both yelling and kicking and punching. The goblin managed to end up on top and began to batter poor Frederick mercilessly.

"Hoblestop! Frederstop!" cried Oracle, and danced about, waving his cane in the air.

Frederick spun his body to one side and wrapped one leg over the goblin's neck, grabbed one of its flailing arms, and straightened his legs, pushing with all his might.

The goblin was slammed to the ground and began to thrash about violently, but Frederick held onto its arm for dear life, holding the arm between his legs while trying to keep the twisting body away at the same time.

Soon, all the little people were running to and fro, trying to avoid the fight.

"Enough!" shouted Cian.

"Hoblestop!" yelled Oracle.

"Stop!" shouted Colleen.

"I'm trying!" shouted Frederick. "Ouch!"

Then they began to tumble about again, but somehow Frederick got behind the goblin and put his arm around its throat in a chokehold and wrapped his legs around its body. Putting his other arm behind its head, he squeezed the sides of its neck. It thrashed madly for several long seconds and then went limp.

Frederick jumped away from it and stood up. His left eye was red and swollen, and he had many scrapes on his arms and face.

"Frederick, you killed it!" cried Colleen.

Frederick looked down at the goblin and said, "No, just knocked it out. See, it's still breathing."

They all looked and indeed, the goblin's chest rose and fell. A line of drool was running from its mouth.

"Where did you learn to do that?" asked Colleen.

"I get picked on a lot in school," he replied, smiling shyly. "A friend of mine taught me a trick or two."

"Are you all right, Frederick?" asked Cian. "Did the goblin bite you?"

"What? I'm all right. And I don't think it..." he began, but then noticed his left arm.

Indeed, there was a bite on his arm – two puncture wounds where the goblin had broken the skin with its yellow fangs.

"Frederick, I must tell you something," said Cian. "The bite of a goblin is never a good thing. Strange things happen to one bitten by their kind."

Colleen looked worried and said, "What's wrong? What's going to happen?"

"It depends on the person. Those who are strong may ward off the Phage. Others who do not resist..." Cian paused.

"Say it," said Frederick.

"... they become goblins," he said, and looked down.

Frederick looked in horror at the wound on his arm and then at the hideous goblin lying on the ground.

Oracle hobbled over and looked at Frederick's wounded arm.

"You should have let it die, Oracle," said Frederick. "Why did you let it live if you knew it could do such a thing? Why should any of them be allowed to live?"

Oracle only bowed his head, looking sad.

Frederick looked desperately around the room and his eyes fell on the fire and the hot knife still sitting beside it. He hesitated only a moment and dashed over and grabbed the blade.

"What are you doing?" cried Colleen.

There was a mad look in Frederick's eyes as he walked back to the goblin with the knife in his hand, its tip red-hot.

"Frederick, don't...," whispered Colleen.

He lifted the knife, gazing at its glowing tip, and then looked at the goblin.

"Don't...," pleaded Colleen.

All the little people were silent, watching.

The goblin opened its eyes and saw Frederick standing over it with the knife.

Frederick stood for a long moment, staring down at the creature, his own breath labored. The creature stank and it sickened him. How many others had it killed or taken away? How much damage had it done in this world of suffering? How many others had it infected with this foul Goblin Phage? It deserved to die!

He looked again at the knife in his hand, then at the goblin that cringed at his feet. He swallowed hard and his breathing became ragged. The bite marks on his arm throbbed, and thoughts of hatred toward this vile creature spun in his mind.

"*Kill it!*" whispered something in his ear. "*Pay it back for all that it has done!*"

Tears rolled down his face as the pain in his arm grew intense. Then, suddenly, he saw Lily and Rose staring up at him, their faces filled with fear and pleading.

"Don't do it," whispered Lily.

The red-hot knife, the cringing goblin, his bleeding arm, and the faces of the little people swirled in a haze before him. Doubt, fear, pain, and uncertainty clamored in his mind.

"Please…," she whispered again, her voice pleading.

He stared at her for a moment and something in his heart gave way. With a cry, he turned and ran into the darkness.

Sobbing, he stared at the knife in his trembling hand, then at his wounded arm. "*Maybe if I…,*" he thought, and in a moment of decision, brought down its hot tip on one of the oozing wounds. He cried out in pain, pulled the knife back, and then did the same to the second bite mark. Then he dropped the knife, sank down against the cave wall, and wept.

The goblin looked after him, amazed.

"The boy… the boy did not… did not kill," it croaked, rubbing its throat. "Why?"

"Because he is not a murderer, Nous," said Cian. "Nor are any of us. We are not like the Witch. You are free to go if you wish. Or you may stay and eat with us if you would prefer."

"It did not kill…," mumbled Nous, looking at the darkness where they could still hear Frederick quietly sniffing.

"And that one made a wish..." grunted Nous, looking at Oracle. "And that one helped it," he whispered, looking at Cian.

"And that one," he grunted, turning to look at Colleen, "is sister to the Pwca-killer, but it did not kill either."

The look of deep confusion flooded the goblin's features again as it tried to grasp these things.

"It's called 'mercy'," said Cian gently to Nous, and he walked over to him and placed his hand on the goblin's arm.

Nous flinched from the touch, as if it were hot.

"Do not be afraid, Nous," said Cian. "No one here will harm you."

Nous looked around the room and shook his head in amazement.

Slowly, he got to his feet, looked once toward Frederick, and slowly backed away toward the cavern entrance.

Then he moved faster, then turned and fled from the cave.

Cian gave a deep sigh and said, "Frederick, please, may I see your arm?"

Frederick slowly came back into the circle of light. His dirty face was streaked with tears, and he held his arm close to his body.

"Can you... can you heal this too?" he asked Cian, a look of hope in his eyes. "Oracle... Oracle... can you...?"

Cian looked closely at his arm, and then looked at Oracle, who stood next to him, gazing at the punctures. The bite marks on Frederick's arm were oozing blood and something gray. Tiny black spidery veins ran in all directions from the bite marks.

"Hobgoble bite infectonates. Problemicky," said Oracle.

"It may be that we could help," said Cian after a moment. "But there is dark magic at work in the goblins, Frederick. Leprechaun magic is strong, to be sure – a gift to our people. But the Goblin Phage comes from a strong magic as well – from the Great Worm that rules their world."

"The Great Worm?" asked Colleen.

"Never mind that," said Frederick. "Could you at least try?"

Cian looked at Oracle, who walked to where his pot sat, picked it up, and sadly shook his head.

"We have no more gold, Frederick," said Cian. "I am sorry."

"Hobgoble bite dreadible, atrociable," babbled Oracle.

"But there's one more piece of gold in that pot!" said Frederick.

"You cannot ask Oracle to do that, Frederick," said Cian.

"But why not?" he cried.

"It would be his last wish," said Cian.

"Well, Lily did the same thing, and nothing has happened to her," he pleaded.

"Has it not?" he said.

Colleen was not sure if it was a question or a statement.

They all turned and looked at Lily, who had been standing quietly watching, tiny tears rolling down her face.

Then little Rose strode forward, and in her hand was her own little pot. She placed it on the ground, and with her two tiny hands, she drew out one lump of gold that filled the whole thing.

"I will give my last nugget for Frederick," she said. "I'm not afraid."

Mrs. Wigglepox rushed to her side and said, "No, Rose. If anyone is to grant their last wish for Frederick, it will be me. He saved Lily back in the Crystal Cavern. I owe him that much."

She too drew out her little pot, and in it, they saw a single nugget.

"But can't you do something without it?" he asked, his eyes pleading.

"Under this Spell of the Witch, our strength fails us. The goblins have taken our treasure," said Mrs. Wigglepox.

Frederick looked from one leprechaun to another, and then he said, "What will happen to a leprechaun who makes their last wish?"

There was a moment of silence, and then Cian spoke. "We become mortal."

Frederick opened his mouth to speak, and then shut it again. He looked at the Wigglepox family, who now had their arms around each other and were looking up at him.

Oracle drew out his last piece of gold, held it out to Frederick and said, "Touch and wish."

Frederick knelt down on the ground beside them, his shoulders sagging, and his head drooping. He looked at the bite marks on his arm, and the black tendrils creeping outward from it. The flesh around the bite was now gray.

Then he took an unsteady breath and said, "No."

"Frederick? Come on, you need to wish it away," said Lily.

"No. I can't let any of you sacrifice yourself for me. Besides, it might not be that bad. I'll be all right, you'll see," he said. But his voice was thick with emotion as he said it.

"Brave Fredersmouth," said Oracle, coming up to him. "Deep, deep is the snaple bite of the hoblegoble."

"What does that mean?" asked Colleen.

"It means that you must be careful, Frederick," said Cian. "This Goblin Phage is not only a physical thing. It is something that affects you more deeply than that. You must be careful that you do not become a goblin in a boy's body, or a boy in a goblin's body."

"Be careful? How do I... I mean... is there something I should or shouldn't do?" asked Frederick desperately.

"From now on, Frederick, the choice of how goblin-like you become is in your hands."

"I don't understand, Cian," he said. "What, exactly, am I supposed to do?"

"Become truly human, my boy," he said. "It seems to me that somehow you humans can be full of light if you want. It is light that drives back the Phage. That is why the goblins hate it and move about in the darkness and avoid the sun as much as possible."

Frederick looked confused, and felt even more so.

Cian looked at him seriously and said, "Don't be afraid. You will understand in time. I also think that the Lady Danu will be able to help you, if you are willing when you see her. Just remember that light and only light will drive back the Phage. The Phage breeds in the darkness."

He paused, looked carefully at Frederick, and then leaned in closer toward him. He furrowed his brow, and spoke in a serious, low voice. "One thing more, Frederick- you may begin to ... remember things."

"Remember things?" he said in a quavering voice.

"Yes, boy, remember things – things that you did not remember before. Places, voices, sights that you have never seen before. Dark places filled with dark shadows," he said.

The glow of the fire made Cian's face strange and frightening as he continued on.

"You may dream of unholy places - of pits and darkness and dangers. It is part of what the Phage does. It opens the mind of those contaminated with it to the influence of the Great Worm and its minions. I have never heard of a human contracting the Phage before, so I do not know how it will affect you. Strange that this should happen now, but there is a reason, Frederick, though we do not yet see it. But come now, you must rest. Do you have blankets? Come, lie by the fire."

Frederick did not understand all that Cian had said, and he fingered the wounds on his arm. They burned and itched and throbbed all at once, and he feared what might come of them.

But he lay down by the fire and curled into a ball and eventually drifted off to sleep, and each one in the cave did the same. It had been a terrible day.

Once in the night, Frederick dreamed that he was walking deep underground into a dark chamber. Before him was a black throne with a huge hunched goblin on it, and behind the throne stood another figure cloaked in a black robe and leaning on a staff.

He awoke covered in sweat, and Colleen was leaning over him with a concerned look on her face.

"I'm all right," he mumbled, and rolled over, falling into a fitful sleep.

* * *

Colleen lay awake for a long time, thinking about all that had happened to them. *Where had Oracle gotten that pot of gold?* she wondered. Who was he anyway? And who was this Cian fellow? She thought that Cian had recognized Oracle when he first saw him. Oracle was obviously a nutty old leprechaun. Or was he?

She was scared for herself and even more for Frederick. And she didn't know just what to think or do. She hoped that they would reach this Lady Danu the next day and not have to spend another night in this wood so full of nightmares. Would they make it in time, or would Frederick become a goblin as the leprechauns feared?

At last, Colleen began to doze off to the sound of Oracle snoring and Frederick muttering something about worms. They had been catapulted into a terrifying and wondrous land, but tomorrow they would discover just what this strange new world had done to them.

She shivered once and fell into a troubled sleep.

Chapter 1 – Journey to the Lake

Frederick Buttersmouth twitched and mumbled in his sleep. His hooded face was hidden, but his gray arm lay uncovered at his side. Black spidery veins radiated outward from the goblin bite he had received the night before.

Suddenly he cried out, "Stop! Stop!"

His eyes shot open and he jumped to his feet, shaking himself and looking around. The nightmare scene of his dream faded, and the dim interior of a cave formed into waking reality.

Now he remembered where he was – in a strange land that he and his cousin, Colleen McGunnegal, had blundered into by accident through a mysterious passageway in her grandfather's basement. She was here, along with a collection of little people that they had somehow picked up along the way.

Colleen reached out and touched him. "Frederick, are you all right?"

He wiped the sweat from his face and nodded.

"I'll be okay," he said. "It was just a nightmare - a terrible nightmare."

"Want to talk about it?" she asked.

He shook his head, and then remembered the fight with the goblin. His wounds still throbbed.

"How's it doing this morning?" asked Colleen. "Any better?"

"Why isn't your hair ever a mess in the morning?" he asked grumpily, avoiding the subject.

She smiled at him and shrugged, then took a good look at his arm again.

"We better get going soon," she said gravely.

They ate a breakfast of nuts and berries and a stew of roots that Cian the leprechaun cooked up for them. Everyone else ate it with relish, but Frederick thought that it tasted a bit woody.

Cian sat cross-legged before them, his two-foot tall body hunched over his bowl of stew.

"For us wee folk, the Lady's Lake is at least a ten-day march," he said. "It's said that she is gathering the remnants of the little people who still fight on against the Spell and the goblins."

"What is she like, Cian – this Lady Danu? We have old legends back home about someone with such a name. They say she once gave a great sword to a king," said Colleen.

"She is a beautiful and terrible sight to behold," said Cian. "I have known her for many a year, although we have rarely spoken in these later days."

"Is she dangerous?" asked Frederick.

"Dangerous?" mused Cian. "Yes, dangerous to those who hate what is good and right and full of light, and dangerous to the goblins and to the Witch and all her minions. The Lady does not answer to any of us, although she watches over us, and, I think, many other places as well."

"Is she human?" asked Frederick. "Or one of these... *spirits* that seem to inhabit this world?"

"Not human, I think," replied Cian. "Nor wholly an immaterial spirit either. She seems to be something else, and she appeared in our world before the Witch came. I remember long, long ago, when the world was young, and life was simple, I first saw her at that very lake. So bright and beautiful and big! She was the first of the big people that I ever saw, if it is right to call her that. But she did not stay here then. She only greeted me with a smile and disappeared beneath the waves of the lake. It was only after the goblins came that she remained for any length of time. Her power is very great, although now she contends against a great tide of darkness. There are times when I fear even for her."

He sighed and shook his head.

"At any rate, you should get on your way. Mal will return soon after her long night of trying to find me, and she may lead others back here as well."

Humble, Nemon, and Zelo, the three gnomes they had met along the way, inched their way forward, heads bowed.

"Begging your pardon, Mr. Cian, sir," said Humble. "We would love to stay with you and hear the tales of when the world was young and all that, but we would also like to go with Colleen and Frederick to see the Lady."

Cian laughed and said, "Of course, friends, you should travel with them. They may need you along the way. Who can say what they may face, and you should see the Lady too."

So they packed up their things, and the three gnomes decided to ride in the back of the cart with Dvalenn, the sleeping dwarf whom they had found in the forest, while the Wigglepoxes sat on the seat between the children. Oracle just went about banging on things with his stick and occasionally giggling.

Frederick wondered for the hundredth time about the odd leprechaun. He seemed crazy at times, doing or saying ridiculous things, and yet at other times, mysterious things happened when he was around. In any event, he seemed not to be touched by the Spell, unless it was the cause of his strange behavior.

"Farewell for now, my young friends," said Cian.

Oracle gave a snort, at which Cian smiled and said, "Perhaps we shall meet again in better times."

The two big leprechauns looked each other in the eye, and Frederick thought he saw Oracle wink.

"Until then," said Cian.

They said their goodbyes and started out once again, a strange band of two children, four leprechauns, three gnomes, and a sleeping dwarf, all riding behind Badger, the shabby old farm horse turned magnificent warhorse by a leprechaun's wish.

Colleen, in her green cloak, and Frederick in his blue, looked like young nobles riding off to an important engagement, and Oracle, a little midget of a man, grinned a goofy grin at the little people and Cian as they pulled away. Waving goodbye, they pulled out of the strange cave, leaving behind the little hermit they had found in this sleepy wood. But, in their hearts, they were fearful at leaving their newfound friend, and they wondered what the new day would bring.

The sun began to rise in the morning sky, and as it did so, a beam of its rays shone down on their little band. Immediately, Frederick let out a cry of pain and grabbed at his arm.

"What's wrong?" said Colleen.

"The sun is so bright! It hurts my arm," he said, and pulled his cloak over his wounds.

Colleen said nothing, but Frederick could see the obvious concern on her face.

He lifted the cloak, being careful to keep his arm shielded from the sun. His arm looked terrible, and the grayness and black spidery veins seemed to be creeping steadily outward, toward his hand and elbow. He shut his eyes and took a deep breath, trying to calm himself and not think about what was happening to him. Cian had said that those bitten by goblins became goblins. He hoped they would find help before that terrible fate took him.

As the day passed, they rode on deeper and deeper into the forest, following the remnants of the old road that led south. Often it was overgrown, and Badger valiantly heaved his way through tangled underbrush. Frederick wondered at the great horse's power and endurance, marveling that it had been so transformed from a bony old thing to a fabulous warhorse by Lily Wigglepox's wish back in the Hall of Sindri. Great trees, many of which had a sickly look about them, lined the road. Twisted trunks and sagging branches surrounded them, and the bare canopy of the forest was a knotted tangle that cast weird shadows across their path.

"This place is spooky," said Frederick after a time, looking up at a great black tree with huge knots on its trunk that gave the illusion of a frowning face with closed eyes.

"Yes," said Humble, one of the gnomes. "But more sad than spooky. Sad that where there was once so much life, now there is only the long Sleep filled with nightmares, and if that doesn't snare you, the goblins probably will."

"It's hard," said Nemon. "You've got to always remember that they are there, maybe just around the next tree. They don't forget about you, you know."

"That's right," said Zelo. "Most of them don't seem to tire of trying to hunt you down and cart you off to their black pits, so you've got to be ever vigilant and watch out for them."

"And even if you've escaped their nets and traps for a hundred years, never think that you can just relax and that they'll never get you. Don't get all proud and think too highly of yourself, like you're somehow special and won't get caught," added Humble.

"Right," said Nemon. "That happened to poor old Bumble a few years ago. He had managed to keep himself from the goblins for decades. But one day, he said that he was tired of worrying about them and just wanted to take a walk in the woods. After all, we hadn't seen any in months. So off he went, all alone, and, wouldn't you know it, that just happened to be the day that the goblins were setting traps. Bumble walked headlong into one, and they scooped him up and took him away. Poor Bumble, he should have been more watchful."

As they chatted on, telling stories of other little people whom they had known and who had been snatched away by the goblins, Frederick thought that his eyes were beginning to play tricks on him. The shadows in the forest seemed to shift and flit about, as though they were dashing from tree to tree.

When he was sure that he *had* seen something dart behind a big old oak, he nudged Colleen. But she was already looking into the woods.

"Over there, Frederick," she whispered. "Watch the shadows between the trees. But don't stare! Just pretend you're talking to me, but watch."

"What is that?" he said.

"Just watch!" she said.

Mrs. Wigglepox overheard, and stopped telling a tale of her great cousin Eldred and gazed into the woods as well.

"Cluricauns!" she said in an urgent, hushed voice.

The gnomes all stopped talking and climbed to the rim of the cart to have a look.

"What are cluricauns?" asked Colleen nervously.

"More spies of the Witch!" said Mrs. Wigglepox. "They are little people who have given themselves over to her, and she has granted them powers like the Shadows to spread the Spell."

"Will they try to harm us?" asked Frederick.

"Not as long as we stay together," replied Mrs. Wigglepox. "But they will try to summon the Spell with renewed strength and have us all fall under it. They may try to separate us from each other. Once they do that, then they have great power."

"Well, let's stop them," said Frederick, trying to sound brave.

"Easier said than done," said Zelo. "They're like fleeting shadows and can hide most anywhere."

"Well, I'm going to try," said Frederick, and he jumped down from the wagon and drew his sword.

"Frederick!" said Colleen. "Just what do you think you're going to do with that thing?"

"Scare them off, of course. After all, they're just little things," he replied, and he let the wagon pass and ran into the woods, brandishing his sword.

"Wait!" cried Mrs. Wigglepox. "We must stay together!"

But Frederick did not heed her warning, and as soon as he stepped off the road, the shadows converged around him, pressing in from the surrounding trees. The view of the wagon rolling away was swallowed up by the night, and the air grew thick and oppressive.

Within the sudden darkness, Frederick could see tiny faces – scores of them, peering out from roots, in the branches, on the trunks of the trees, and in the air, and all of them looked at him with scorn and hatred, as though he were some loathsome thing.

Fear swept through his mind, and he could hear them putting thoughts in his head. "*You are nothing. We will take you away. Drop your useless weapon and surrender to us. We will take you to the Witch, and you will serve her. You know that you wish to be a goblin – you are already becoming one!*"

He sank to his knees and only just managed to hold onto his sword. His injured arm began to feel strange, as though a will other than his own were moving it. He struggled against it, and his mind whirled with a sea of thoughts and images that seemed to come from the faces in the darkness all around him. He did not know how long the voices howled, only that he fought them, resisting the temptation to drop the sword.

Just as he was about to let go, the sound of thunderous hooves and a great neighing burst through the tumult of noise in his head. Through the circle of darkness burst Badger, with Colleen riding on him, her golden-red hair and green cape whipping in the wind behind her as the great horse galloped into the oppressive night. Badger reared on his hind legs, neighing wildly and kicking at the darkness in defiance.

For a moment, the faces wavered and looked doubtful, and their clamor was broken. The voice of Colleen parted the tumult like a mighty ship plowing through a storm.

"Take my hand!" she shouted, and she bent low and stretched it out to him.

278

Numbly he stood, and then reached up with his pained left arm. She grasped his wrist, and with strength he did not think she possessed, she hefted him up on the saddle behind her.

But the darkness recovered from its momentary distraction, and began to close in again.

"Light, Frederick," came Colleen's voice from somewhere. "We need light!"

With all the strength he could muster, Frederick lifted his sword in the air and shouted something that he could not even hear himself say.

There was a brilliant flash from somewhere above him. Badger reared, throwing him backward. His head struck the ground hard, and the last thing he saw was Colleen leaping from her saddle, sweeping his fallen sword into the air, and then her whole visage seemed to burst into flaming light. But the darkness took him, and he knew no more.

When he finally awoke, he was lying beside Dvalenn in the wagon as it once again bumped along through the woods. The three gnomes sat on the dwarf's chest, their worried faces staring at him.

"What happened?" he asked, pushing himself up. His head pounded, and he groaned.

"Just lie down, Frederick Brendan, and I'll tell you," scolded Colleen.

"You acted like a foolish boy, that's what!" said Mrs. Wigglepox.

"Braviculous Fredersmouth!" said Oracle, and whacked him on the top of his head with his cane.

"Ouch!" said Frederick.

"Frederick, you ran into the woods and vanished into the shadows. It grew dark all around you, and you started to move away, deeper into the woods," said Colleen.

"Yes," he replied, "and there were terrible faces in there!"

"As soon as that happened, we couldn't see you. We called and called, but you didn't seem to hear us. So, I jumped down, unhooked Badger, and went riding after you. Badger is marvelous to ride! He charged right into the darkness as if he wanted to fight it himself. But then I saw the faces too, and they were shrieking. I pulled you onto the saddle, but Badger went wild at their sound. You lifted that sword, and then it happened."

"Then what happened?" he asked.

"The sword – it started to shine with a brilliant white light!" she replied. "The faces all shrieked louder than ever. Then you were thrown from the saddle, and dropped your sword. I jumped down after you and grabbed the sword, and suddenly they all fled. It was the strangest thing. I thought they had left, but in a moment, they started to return. Their rage was terrible, Frederick. I was really afraid, but Oracle came strolling in among them, singing some silly song and started chasing them with his cane. They ran away and didn't come back. And, I might add, I had to drag you all the way back to the cart and get you in by myself. You're rather heavy, you know."

Frederick felt at his side and found the sword was missing.

"Don't worry, its right here," said Colleen, and she handed it to him.

Frederick took it. The blade was bright silver and engraved with symbols and runes, and the handle was inlaid with smooth green and blue gemstones.

"I think there's something special about that sword, Frederick," said Colleen.

"I'd say," said Zelo. "A blade that drives cluricauns away and shines like that is more than special. You just hang onto that, Frederick. We may need it again."

Frederick looked at the sword again. Had it heard his cry for help? Was it a magical weapon? And who had forged it? Elves? Dwarves? Someone else? Then he remembered that Doc the dwarf had said that he had a hand in its making, along with all other armor and weapons in the House of Mysteries. Who was that old dwarf anyway? More than he seemed, that was for sure.

He lay back in the wagon and rubbed his head, and then realized that he felt in control of himself again. But he looked at his arm, and the grayness and spidery black tendrils had spread even more. He sat up and looked into the woods. Strange shadows flitted this way and that.

"They're still there, aren't they – the Shadows, I mean?" he asked.

"Yes," said Colleen, "although they've been keeping their distance."

"Don't underestimate them," said Mrs. Wigglepox. "You can be sure they won't forget what you did back there, Frederick, and I think they'll be looking to get at Oracle too. We need to be sure we stay together from now on."

Frederick climbed out of the back of the cart and sat down next to Colleen. Oracle sat perched on Dvalenn's beard, singing a nonsensical song, and the little people sat in the hay, listening to him.

"Are you okay?" Colleen asked him.

"I'll live," he said. "Thanks."

He glanced back at the little people who were riding behind them and said, "I suppose I should thank Oracle too. That's twice he's done me good. But he's a weird chap, isn't he? I mean, he seems like a total loon at times, and then strange things seem to happen when he's around. Where did he get that pot of gold from back in that cave? And back in Doc's Crystal Cavern, I saw him put his hands on the wall and lights started flashing. Then he chased those cluricauns away with his cane. Now he's just acting odd again."

Colleen looked at the old leprechaun, who seemed to have suddenly fallen asleep. She shook her head, then shrugged, unsure what to think.

"You scared me back there, Frederick. Still, I think what you did was very brave," she said.

He blushed and turned away.

"Thanks," he mumbled.

They rode on down the ancient road for some time, but as the sun climbed high and then began to sink, the sleepiness in the forest around them began to grow once again, and they could see the shadows in the wood deepening.

"There's a heaviness about this place," said Colleen, rubbing her eyes.

Frederick was slouching in the seat beside her, Badger's great head began to sag, and Mrs. Wigglepox yawned.

"Cluricauns!" she said sleepily. "As the sun gets lower in the sky, their power gets stronger. We've got to keep moving!"

Onward, they slowly went, and it seemed that the further they trudged on, the sleepier they got, until before Colleen realized it, they had stopped altogether. Badger was asleep on his feet, the Wigglepoxes were out cold, and Frederick was sitting hunched over, his chin on his chest. But Oracle was awake again, and was once again singing an odd song.

Colleen rubbed her eyes and shook her head, and felt her eyelids closing. She forced herself awake, but the drowsiness was overcoming her.

"You're going to fall out of the seat and squash Mrs. Wigglepox and Rose," she said to herself. *"Now wake up, you silly girl!"*

With a tremendous effort, she tried to open her eyes, but they would not obey her, and she felt herself slipping to one side.

"Do something!" that inner voice urged, *"Do anything! ... Sing, Colleen, sing!"*

With her last bit of conscious will, she forced her lips open and began to whisper.

"When the singer and the tree
Meet in a place that none can tell.
And there she whispers words that free
The sleeping forest from its spell..."

She did not know where the words came from, but they seemed to go along with Oracle's tune. As she sang them, her eyes fluttered open, and she rubbed them again, and, taking a deep breath, she sang louder.

"Oh singer come, oh come this hour,
Your voice can break the evil power
Of curses, spells, and darkest gloom.
Oh sing, oh sing and free us from our doom."

Badger snorted, tossed his head, and began to pull. Frederick, Mrs. Wigglepox, and Rose began to stir, and Lily yawned hugely in his pocket and opened her eyes. Colleen sang on, louder now, and stronger.

"Come singer over mount and sands,
And cross the wide sea 'tween our lands.
Come singer from a distant shore.
Come sing and free our people 'yor."

As she sang, the trees around them began to sway, their bare branches scraping and scratching one another, as if a wind were blowing, but no wind blew. Now another sound rose – a growling and whining rising from the shadows, and dark, angry faces appeared, glaring at them as they rode by.

Colleen stopped singing and, in a few moments, the trees grew still and rustled no more.

Mrs. Wigglepox looked up at Colleen with amazement.

"My dear child," she said in awe, "you have just wakened the forest with your song. For a moment, the spell of the Court Witch wavered!"

"I what?" asked Colleen.

"Please, child, sing more. I feel the sleep coming ag..."

But Mrs. Wigglepox did not continue. She was asleep again, and Colleen also felt her eyelids getting heavy. She sang on, trying to hear what Oracle was singing and letting his scratchy voice fill her mind.

The others woke once again. In fact, they found that as long as she sang, they felt almost fully awake, and as Badger carried them along, the trees all around them stirred, the shadows dispersed, and it seemed to Frederick's ears that along with Colleen's song, the trees were whispering – a strange sound like wind in the leaves.

"What are they saying?" Frederick asked.

"It is very sad," said Lily. "They are asking us to stay and sing to them. *We have slept too long! 'Ere long we will not wake again, unless you stay and sing to us!'*"

"Frederick," said Lily, "I don't like this part of the woods. Something is very bad here. We shouldn't be so tired."

"Lily is right, Mother," said Rose, who had been listening in. "I don't feel so sleepy in our tree back home."

"Yes," said Mrs. Wigglepox. "You are both quite right. There is something terribly wrong here. The Witch's spell is so strong! It's as if she's put more effort into this place, and the cluricauns are whispering."

Frederick slowly, with great effort, pulled his cloak away from his injured arm and looked down at it. The grayness had spread all the way to his fingertips and up to his shoulder, and now a sickly green was blending with the gray. His fingernails were turning a dirty yellow, and his knuckles were growing knobby.

In despair, he let his cloak fall, and his chin dropped to his chest. He could not fight any longer, and he so wanted to let the Sleep take him. But something kept buzzing in his ear.

What is that? he thought to himself. *If it would just go away, I could get some sleep.*

Colleen sang song after song, sometimes seeming to follow along with Oracle, and sometimes he followed her, until she ran out of songs to sing and started over with the first one. One hour went by, then two, and her voice grew tired. When at last Colleen was only whispering her song, the heaviness of sleep began to overtake them once again.

"We all must sing!" said Mrs. Wigglepox with a yawn. "We must all sing and help Colleen!"

* * *

And so they all sang, and for a while, this helped. But when nearly four hours had passed, Lily and Rose were nearly asleep again and Frederick sat listlessly in the seat next to Colleen. Was he snoring, or was he croaking out some song that she could not make out? She could not be sure. But periodically, he would wave his injured hand as if shooing away a mosquito from his ear.

Badger was trudging slowly along, his head again drooping to the ground. Only Mrs. Wigglepox and Colleen and Oracle continued the songs, although Colleen's throat ached and was parched. She could barely speak, and the struggle to keep singing weighed her down like a stone. Again and again, she nearly gave up, but shook herself and kept on whispering her song, fighting with all her might against the heavy spell that the Court Witch had laid on the land and that the cluricauns made stronger with their evil whispers.

When she finally felt as though she could not utter another word, and it seemed as though even Mrs. Wigglepox had grown silent, and Oracle's words were just gibberish, they broke through the trees and walked out onto a grassy meadow that was covered with white and purple flowers, which led down to the edge of a brilliant shining blue lake.

Chapter 2 – Professor McPherson

All five of the McGunnegal children crowded into Professor McPherson's office.

He smiled as they all entered, and said, "Well, at last I meet the McGunnegal family... except I hear that Colleen has not yet arrived. I am so very pleased to make your acquaintance. Now, let's see. As you know, I am Professor McPherson, and let me guess your names.

"Aonghus, your reputation precedes you! The children are chattering like chipmunks about how strong you are. And Bran, fastest player on the rugby field. Pretty good in a fight, I might add."

Bran started to reply, but the professor cut him off. "But never mind that for the moment. Let's see... hmm... Abbe. You are the oldest of the girls, correct? And you have a great interest in our lake, I hear. Perhaps you and I could walk around it later, and I will show you the various flora and fauna that live in and around it."

"I would love that, Professor," Abbe replied.

"And Bib," he continued. "You've been spending lots of time in the library. Good, good. And, I have my own special collection of books here in my office and in my tower office that you are welcome to investigate. Just make an appointment."

Bib grinned and said, "Thank you, Professor!"

"And, of course, dear Henny," he said. "Henny who can melt the heart of even old Miss Fenny. And what would you like to learn about at our school?"

"I would like to learn about fairies and mermaids," she replied innocently.

"Fairies and mermaids!" replied the professor with great enthusiasm. "Indeed you shall! But what makes you think we could teach you about them?"

"They live here, don't they?" asked Henny, her eyes inquisitive.

The professor grew serious and thoughtful and glanced out his window, which overlooked the field and the nearby lake. Then he came around his desk, bent down, and looked Henny in the eyes.

"My dear Henny, there are many things that are mysterious in this world – fairies and mermaids among them. Our lake and the grounds hold many surprises. Keep your eyes open. Who knows what you may see?" he replied.

He stood then and said, "Now then, as to the matter of the fight. Bran, please tell me what happened."

Bib glared up at her brother and said, "You were in a fight already?"

"It wasn't my fault!" he said defensively. "We were just playing rugby on the field when this Ed fellow came up and accused me of stealing his girl, Mary. I'd never met her before then, but he tried to slug me."

Bib now had her hands on her hips in a motherly way and poked her tall brother squarely in the chest.

"A likely story!" she scolded.

Professor McPherson cleared his throat and interrupted. "Perhaps you could allow me to ask the questions, Bib."

"Oh! Sorry," she said ruefully.

The professor continued. "That's what I thought I saw, Bran. Aonghus, is that your story too?"

"Yes, sir, and they tried to gang up on Bran. I held two of them back. Dad always said that if you have to fight, fight fair," replied Aonghus.

"Thank you," replied the professor. "I think that will be enough for now. I do believe your story, Bran, and thank you for not hurting Edward – something you seem to be more than capable of doing."

"Dad taught us to fight really well. There's not a man in Ireland that can top him. But he said you don't hurt people just because you can. You only try to get them to calm down and keep your own cool while you're at it," replied Bran.

"A wise man, your father. I would like to meet him one day. Strength is not always found in the powerful, but often in the meek and lowly things of life, or in a patient man who bears with the rudeness of others without taking offense," he replied.

"Professor," said Aonghus after a moment. "Before we go, may we show you something?"

"Certainly," he replied. "I was wondering what was in the bag."

Aonghus reached into the bag and pulled out one of the white stones that had the markings carved into it and handed it to the professor.

He took it and examined it closely for a moment, and then said, "Aonghus, please close the door."

Aonghus did so, and the professor said, "Where did you get this? Are there more like it in that bag?"

Aonghus handed the bag to him, and the professor took them out one at a time and examined each of them briefly.

"We got them from our farm, sir," said Abbe. "There are thousands of them piled in a big wall."

"And there are more really big stones in our basement that have those carvings on them," said Bran.

"We think they're the reason why Rufus Buttersmouth is paying our way here – to get us out of the way so that he can get to them, and maybe take our farm as well," said Bib.

Professor McPherson was silent for a few moments as he examined some of the stones closer. He looked very thoughtful and finally said, "Children, this is of very great importance. You are to talk to no one else about this. Do you have more of these stones?"

"Yes, sir," said Aonghus. "Four more bags. Mabel was trying to steal them, and we took them from her trunk."

"I see," said the professor. "And are they in your room at the moment?"

"Yes, sir," he replied.

"May I see them as well?" he asked.

"Of course. I can get them now if you would like," said Aonghus.

"No, that will not be necessary. But I would like you to bring them to me after the evening meal. This will be your *punishment* for fighting on the field today – you boys are to come to my office with cleaning supplies – and those bags of stones – and tidy things up in here for a few days. You girls shall volunteer to help as well," he replied.

Aonghus grinned and said, "Right!"

"May I keep this bag of stones here and study them further?" asked the professor.

They trusted him instinctively, such was his noble bearing, and so they immediately agreed.

"I have also decided that I am granting all of you – and your sister Colleen – scholarships to my school. Rufus Buttersmouth will not be paying an English penny for your tuition or room and board," he added. "I shall also see to it that your travel expenses here and on the way home are taken care of."

"Professor, are you serious?" asked Aonghus.

"Entirely serious, son," he replied. "You do not realize yet what this means, and perhaps I do not either. But we must make plans to go to Ireland immediately, just as soon as your sister and Frederick arrive."

"But why?" asked Abbe. "We just got here!"

"Let me show you something," he said, and he walked over to the wall behind him, removed a brick of white stone from a shelf, and placed it on his desk next to the pile of stones that he had taken from the bag.

"Look closely," he said to them, and they gathered around.

The carvings were nearly identical.

"Where did you get that from?" asked Bib. "Did that come from our farm?"

"No," he replied.

"But those runes look almost exactly the same as the ones on our stones," she said.

"Yes," replied the professor. "It has been handed down through many generations in my family."

"But where did it come from?" asked Abbe.

"You would not believe me if I told you," he replied.

He paused, considering, and then continued. "But let me say this – these stones may well represent the most important archaeological discovery made on this planet in a thousand years."

Chapter 3 – The Lady Danu

Colleen rubbed her eyes for the hundredth time and urged Badger forward. Slowly, he walked toward the lake edge, but before they reached it, a new sound reached her ears. Someone *else* was singing too.

It was a sweet voice. *No, more than sweet*, thought Colleen. Words escaped her to describe its beauty, even to herself. It was a voice beyond a voice. Powerful as a raging river, subtle as a falling feather, deep as an ocean, high as the sky, rooted as a mountain, but also sweet as honey and gentle as a breeze.

As soon as they heard the song, they were all instantly awake, and no trace of drowsiness remained, and as they listened, their minds grew sharp, and their bodies felt rested.

In that moment, Colleen felt as though she had been awakened from some long winter's night and would never need to sleep again.

The voice sang in a language that she did not understand with her ears, but in her heart and mind, it became clear as crystal. When she would later try to recall it and put words to it, she would shake her head and be silent – such was the power of its memory.

Colleen and Frederick jumped down from the wagon and led Badger to the lake's edge. It was a crystal blue, bluer than the sky, and into its pure depths they gazed. Its center ran deep – too deep to see any bottom at all, and it fell away into a blue infinity that stretched beyond their vision.

Frederick pulled his cloak around himself as they neared the water, and he grabbed his arm as if a sudden pain shot through it.

The grass all around the lakeside was a brilliant green with many wildflowers merrily swaying in the breeze. Flocks of birds danced in the sky above, playfully soaring about, and their dance seemed to be to the song that spread itself out over the lake.

Then, all at once, they saw her. Sitting gracefully by the lake on a large rock was a lady dressed all in white, and she was singing.

She sat there on the horizon of the world where the land met the sky, but she seemed to be of neither land nor sky. She was, like her song, totally *other* than both, yet of them both.

She saw them, and without pausing in her song, reached down and cupped water in her hands. It trickled playfully between her fingers, sparkling in the bright sun, as it touched the surface of the water again. Its sound added to her music, and together they seemed like some mystical orchestra that had played for all eternity.

Then the lady paused in her song, although it seemed to still echo across and around and through the lake. She scooped water in her hands and drank, then smiled a deep, satisfied smile. Dipping in her hands again, she made a gesture of welcome that seemed to embrace not only the little group of travelers, but the whole land around them. To the grass and flowers and trees, and to all that would heed her invitation, she offered a drink.

Again, she sang, and in the depths of that song, they heard words of beckoning, *"Come, taste and see..."*

The words that followed struck some chord in their hearts, raising them to the song's eternal heights and fathomless depths. All fear, and even memory of fear of goblins and witches and the sleeping forest and its shadows, was washed from their minds as they went forward to the water. It seemed as though the very grass and flowers around the lake were singing as well, inviting the visitors to come.

Then they noticed that little by little, curious faces were emerging from behind the trees of the sleeping forest and were shyly creeping down to the water's edge to heed the singer's invitation.

Colleen and Frederick carefully put the little people down, and Oracle climbed over the side and slid down the wagon's wheel, tumbling head over heels in the bright grass and lay there.

All but Oracle and Frederick went to the water's edge, knelt, and lifted a handful of water to their lips. Even Badger bent his head and drank deeply. All around the lake now, the animals of the wood were gathered - foxes and rabbits and squirrels, birds and mice, and none feared the other, none pursued the other. All seemed to be joining in the song and drinking from the lake.

As Colleen drank, the water's cool sweetness flowed within her, and she knew that she would never be the same again. No earthly water would ever satisfy her, she knew, for she had tasted something that seemed heavenly, and she felt as though she could stay there by that lake forever. Deeply she drank from the waters until she was refreshed beyond her mind's and body's ability to comprehend. She looked at the little people, and their faces seemed aglow with joy and peace.

Gnomes danced, leprechauns twirled, and pixies flew high in the air, then low over the lake and back to shore again, and the light of their bodies seemed intensified to a piercing brightness. It was as if they were all sharing a dream, but it was realer than anything she had ever experienced.

"Colligal shines!" said Oracle with a gleeful grin, peeking over the grass.

"Frederick, you've got to taste this water!" she called.

He was watching them all, seeing the delight on their faces, and wondering if he ought to try it.

"I don't know..." he replied. "It's terribly bright, and, well, my arm is aching in this light. And the lady, she is ..."

But he fell silent and shaded his eyes, for now she approached them, and her flowing dress was radiant in the sun. She was tall and stately, and her graceful stride spoke of royalty. Her white limbs were perfect, her back so straight, her form lovely beyond measure, her hair golden beyond gold, her lips redder than the reddest rose. She seemed neither young nor old, but simply ageless. There was wisdom and restfulness in her eyes, and yet, beyond all of this, it seemed to Colleen that she bore a hidden power that also made her seem, almost, *worshipful.*

"*No, not that,*" said a thought that seemed to come from the lady herself.

"*Then, venerable,*" Colleen said to herself.

When the lady reached them, she paused in her song and spoke. "Welcome, friends," she said. "I am the Lady Danu. I see that you have traveled far and through many dangers. Stay for a time and you will find rest. No dangers from the sleepy wood can touch you here, and no goblin dares approach these waters."

Frederick stared at the Lady, his mouth wide open, and she smiled at him. He realized that he must look foolish, so he closed his mouth, blinked several times, and then said, "Who *are* you?"

She laughed a joyous laugh, and it seemed as though all the lake sparkled with a million shafts of light at its pure sound. "Why, dear Frederick," she said. "I have told you, I am the Lady Danu. I have other names as well, although I would tire you in the telling of them all. This is my home, and you are welcome to share it with me for a time. "

"How... how do you... know my name?" he stammered.

"Why, you are as clear to me as the waters of the lake are clear, although there is a shadow on you," she replied. "Won't you come? Taste and see that it is good! Do you not see how Colleen shines?"

Frederick looked at Colleen and, to his amazement, she did indeed seem to be *radiant* somehow, like the Lady, yet far less so. In fact, all around them, the land and the little creatures seemed to possess that same radiance.

Frederick slipped his arm from beneath his cloak for a moment and looked at it. Immediately, it burned as though he had gotten too near to a bonfire. He flinched and hid it again.

The Lady saw this and said, "Ah, and I see that you bear a wound, young one. We shall speak of it later. But I ask again, will you not drink?"

"I... I don't feel... I mean, just the light of it hurts my arm. I'm afraid to touch it," he admitted, ashamed.

"Ah, that is the way of it, child. These waters can either burn or brighten, blind or illumine, bring distress or comfort, hurt or heal. One could say that they show you just what you already are, deep down inside. That is their magic. But if you would chance this fire, it may burn away this hurt you have taken. Did you not try your own fire to staunch this wound, and it did not avail you?"

Frederick remembered the red-hot knife he had used to cauterize the wounds. He stared at the shining lake. But to him, it was like staring at a full moon on a clear night. It was too much, and it hurt his eyes. A part of him wanted to run forward and leap into its magical blue depths. But the more he thought of it, the more the ache in his arm throbbed and spread. It seemed to be moving upward now, toward his neck. He was about to say something more when a little voice broke the silence.

"My Lady," said Colleen, "how is it that everything is so *alive* here, when the forest is so dead?"

Again, she laughed and said, "Ah, the old Court Witch has no power here. Her spells of gloom and sleepiness cannot overcome my song, nor the light of the waters. She has tried many times, but the magic here is far deeper than hers, and is beyond the knowledge of those that use her."

She paused, smiling at them, and said, "Come with me, dear ones, let me show you something. But first, untie your horse and let him graze."

Colleen unhooked Badger from the wagon, and he contentedly began to munch on the sweet grass by the lake.

It was then that Oracle popped his head out of the grass and shyly grinned at the Lady. She noticed him then, and a look of surprise and joy swept over her face. She curtsied to him, and some unheard communication passed between them as their eyes met again, for she nodded and said, "Welcome, good sir, to the Lake. Please, grace my home by drinking of these waters and refreshing yourself."

Oracle rose from the grass, picked up his cane, hobbled over to the shore, and took a long draught of the shining waters. He smiled broadly and said, "Ahhhh!" very loudly, then danced a little jig.

"He's a bit like that, you know," said Frederick to the Lady.

"Yes," she replied, "but do not judge by mere appearances."

She stared at Oracle for a few moments and then spoke again.

"But, come, follow me. And the invitation stands, Frederick. Taste and see..."

Frederick picked up the Wigglepox family with his good hand and put them in his pocket. The Lady turned and led them up a hill that looked over the lake. Its top reached just above the highest trees, so that they could see the vast brown expanse of the forest stretching out before them.

"Look around us," said the Lady as they reached the summit. "It would seem that the whole world is under the spell of the Court Witch. See, the forest sleeps, and many of its creatures have become her spies. Your coming to the Lake is known to them, so they strengthened the Spell against you. It may be that if you, Colleen, had not sung and the power within you had not fought against her, you would now be in her hands, captured by her dark servants."

"So that's why we were so sleepy," said Frederick.

"Yes," the Lady replied. "You were in grave danger."

"But how could I, just singing, make any difference?" Colleen asked. "And besides, the others sang too, even Oracle."

The Lady Danu gazed at her intently for a moment, and her eyes seemed to see right into Colleen's mind and soul, even beyond them to see in a moment's time her entire life.

"I see that you have not yet learned of your destiny, nor of your history, Colleen. The future is always dim to we who are created, but history, and the present – that can be looked into, at least a bit. I can tell you that your coming here was no accident, and you have great deeds to accomplish before your journey ends," replied the Lady. "You have many songs yet to sing. Is it not true that you can sing the songs of all things that you are near?"

"I'm not sure what you mean, Lady Danu," she said.

The Lady extended her arm and, with a sweeping motion, indicated the brown forest. To the north, east, and west, the trees stretched to the horizon, brown and dead, and to the south, it spread out for many miles until it reached long, high hills.

"All this lies under the Witch's spell, my friends. Yet each of you possesses power to fight that spell. Not the whole thing, of course, not yet, at least. But for yourselves and those around you, a song of hope will wake the sleeper. But come, let us sit and eat together. I see that you are hungry, although the waters of the lake have refreshed you."

The Lady Danu waved a hand, and they looked in the direction in which she pointed. There, a short distance away, were a number of large stones that were set deeply into the hill so that only their surface showed, and in the middle of these was a large circular stone, also set deeply in the ground, so that the entire arrangement appeared to be a round stone pavement surrounded by a dozen round stepping stones.

The Lady seated herself on one of the smaller stones and invited the others to do the same, and when they were all seated, with the Wigglepoxes all sitting together, she began another song.

It was a song of thanksgiving, and its sweetness filled their minds with a profound sense of gratitude for all that was.

As the song ended, Lily gave a squeal of delight, for up the hill, on all sides, were coming scores of little people. There were gnomes and leprechauns and sprites and fairies, and folk of every sort, many the size of little Rose, but some at least a foot tall, and some as tiny as dandelion seeds when they fly in the breeze. Most dressed in green or brown or red, but some of the fairies were dressed in gossamer of gold or silver or white.

Colleen and Frederick gaped wide-eyed at the sight. Up and over the hilltop they came, hundreds of them, gathering around the table and darting here and there in the air.

Soon the whole hilltop was filled, and when everyone was quiet, the Lady Danu spoke.

"I see that we are all here," she said, and then she looked at Colleen and Frederick.

"These are the remnants of the little people who have fled the Sleeping Wood and come to me for protection. So few, so few!" she sighed.

"My songs and the waters of the Lake keep them safe and hidden here where the eyes of the Court Witch and the Goblin King cannot yet see. But look! All around us, the great Sleep has taken hold. Here alone, and in a few hardy trees where the little people yet dwell, is there yet wakefulness," she said.

"Do you mean that these are the only people left in the whole world who are free from the power of the Witch, besides those few with Cian?" asked Colleen.

"Cian!" she said with surprise. "So, you have met him? That is good. I have not spoken with him for some time, although I hear that he is well. But, no, these are not *all*. As I said, there are a few others, like Mrs. Wigglepox and her daughters, who fight on," replied the Lady.

"Is the Witch that powerful?" asked Frederick. "Isn't there anyone who can fight her?"

The Lady smiled at him and said, "Oh, yes, Frederick. Everyone can fight her. But her greatest power, unless you should meet her yourself, is this Sleep that she has cast across the land. It is not only a drowsiness of the body, but of the heart as well. Once, the spirits of the trees here were lively and strong and true, but she has lulled them into forgetfulness and inactivity, and they have nearly all truly fallen asleep. Intertwined within the Spell, she spreads the fear of the Gray Man, and this gives it strength. She can be fought, though. We all here fight against her spells. We sing, and our song is something that she has no power over, nor can she overcome the light in the Lake, and she fears it, lest it one day overflow its banks, flow into the forest, and awaken it. She knows then that the spirits that dwell there would awaken, and their wrath would be great!"

"*Spirits?*" asked Colleen. "Are there actually ghosts or something living in the woods?"

"I will tell you the *Tale of Beginnings,*" said the Lady, "But first, we must eat together."

She waved her hand over the round stone pavement before them and, with a flash, there appeared dozens of dishes spread out before them. Some were tiny, just the right size for the little people and others were large enough for the children. All were filled with fruits and vegetables and breads and muffins of all sorts. Glasses and pitchers of many colors and shapes were there as well, and delicious smells rose from steaming pots and bowls. A cheer went up from the little people, and they all came forward, helping each other load their tiny plates with every sort of good thing.

"Help yourselves, my young friends," said the Lady, and Colleen and Frederick gladly took plates and filled them with every sort of dainty that was there.

"*Today we feast in the midst of a sleeping world*," sang the Lady, "*and tonight we rest with the restfulness of the Waters of Light. But, tomorrow we begin a new thing.*"

Colleen had never tasted such delicious food before, nor drunk such sumptuous drinks. There was nothing that tasted bad, even in the slightest, although all was different. She ate her fill and felt completely satisfied, although not stuffed, as did all the little people that had come for the feast.

But she noticed that Frederick only nibbled at his food.

"What's wrong, Frederick?" she asked. "Don't you like the food?"

He paused and said, "Well, it's not *bad*, exactly. It's just that my throat kind of hurts when I swallow it."

He turned to look at her, and she noticed that the gray color and black spider veins were now creeping across his neck.

"Are you all right?" she asked.

He nodded, pulling his cloak closer about him. But Colleen felt a growing concern for him. His mood was all wrong for this happy place, and while everyone else danced about or lay in the sunshine, Frederick kept his hood pulled over his face, and kept glancing toward the shadows of the trees.

Mrs. Wigglepox talked happily to the other little people, and Lily and Rose ran here and there on the hill with the many little children who had come. Pure delight was in their eyes to find so many of their own people alive and living so well in the care of the Lady Danu.

Colleen and Frederick talked with many of the little people, who were quite curious about them, for most of them had never seen a human before, and they were amazed at their size. Many of the children of the little people came up to them shyly and asked permission to touch them, just to be sure they were real.

And when Colleen offered to lift some of them in the air, they were delighted, and laughed as she gently lifted them up and held them high.

Then a shining pixie flew to Colleen and introduced herself.

"My name is Alephria," she said.

"Pleased to meet you," she replied.

The pixie curtsied in the air, sparkled, twirled about laughing, and then vanished.

Colleen looked about, wondering where she had gone, but the Lady turned around and gazed out over the lake. The others followed her gaze, and there, right in the lake's center, a bright pink twinkle appeared, and Alephria's high laugh rang out over the waters. Again, she vanished and reappeared right on top of Frederick's head.

For a moment, he was startled, but then managed a laugh that sounded more like a snort.

"You can disappear!" he said.

"It is because the Witch has no power here," she said with glee. "See!"

She vanished again, then reappeared, and all of the other pixies began to flit about the shores of the lake.

"I am Meadow," said a green one and, all around Frederick's feet, flowers burst into bloom. She called to the trees around the lake, and they answered her by shaking and twirling their branches until she quieted them.

"And I'm Leleuma," said another, who shone a bright blue.

She swept across the lake, raising a high wave that took the shape of a powerful stallion that galloped across the surface of the waters, and then sent it splashing down again, sending ripples across the surface. On the lake's shore, Badger neighed and kicked at the air with his front hooves.

Then all three of the pixies flew high above their heads, and fairy dust rained down upon them like fine gold. As it landed on them, it seemed not to settle *on* them, but *into* them.

"Strange things can happen to people who are sprinkled with fairy dust," said the Lady Danu. "And few have had the blessing of three so notable fairies at once. Beware, my friends, for you may find yourselves awakening to your true selves after today!"

Then, a fat gnome strode forward and bowed to Colleen and Frederick and all around him. "I am Earwin," he said. "I can hear the stories of the earth."

And Earwin put his ear down to the ground and just listened, a look of deep satisfaction filling his face. "The land speaks to me here," he said. "It says that no goblin's feet have soiled this place."

He then took a handful of the earth and tossed it in the air at the feet of Colleen and Frederick.

"May the blessing of the earth be upon you," he said. "Now quiet your heart and listen – what do you hear?"

Both of the children got down on the ground and pressed their ears to the ground. At first, they heard nothing, but then a quiet murmur came to them. It was a sound of flowing water, of stretching roots, and the odd sounds of shifting rock far below.

Frederick shut his eyes and listened deeper, further.

"I hear..." He paused, listening, and then it was as if something gripped his mind, and he heard himself saying, "I hear far, far away, the sounds of hammers and shovels and picks ringing beneath the ground in vast tunnels that stretch to untold depths and there is much sighing and many tears amid deep pits."

He shivered and looked around, embarrassed.

They all stared at him and, after a moment, Earwin said, "Few can hear so far, Frederick. You have heard the echoes of the pits of the Goblin King far, far to the South in the midst of the sea."

For the first time since they had arrived, Colleen's heart grew heavy as she remembered her mother. She bowed her head and a tear trickled down her cheek.

The Lady knelt next to her and put her hand on her shoulder. Frederick watched with amazement as the light of the Lady seemed to flow into Colleen through that touch until she shone with the same radiance.

"There is yet hope, Colleen," she said. "There is hope for her and for all who are bound in the Witch's dungeons and pits. As long as you are here and are free, there is hope that you will rescue them."

"But what can I do?" she said. "Couldn't you free them? You seem to have power that the Court Witch can't overcome. Won't you come with us and help us?"

The Lady looked sad and said, "Alas, child, I cannot. Here there are unspoiled waters that hold hope for this world. If I should leave them, the Witch may indeed find a way to darken them, and through them to spoil other lands. I guard not only this place – this last refuge from her dominion. I guard other lands as well from all who would spoil what is good and right. I cannot leave that charge."

She paused then, looking intently at the two children. After a moment, Frederick spoke.

"Lady," he said. "It seems as though everyone here has some gift – some power within them to use against this Witch. But I have nothing. I'm just a boy. I can't sing like Colleen and I can't do anything like these marvelous pixies and such. What use am I? Especially with this..."

He threw back his cloak, and a murmur of shock and amazement ran through all the little people as they saw his arm and hand and neck, now a mottled gray-green. A searing pain shot through him, and he quickly pulled his cloak back, hiding his infected flesh from the light of the Lake.

"You too are here for a reason, Frederick. There is some great part that you must play before the end," she said. "I cannot see all ends, but I foresee that some great struggle lies before you, and in you, but beyond that, I cannot see."

Frederick looked down, feeling small and sad. And then a thought struck him.

"What about Dvalenn?" he said.

"Yes!" said Colleen. "I almost forgot about him. He's still sleeping in the cart!"

"Dvalenn sleeps hard under the Witch's spell, children. It will be no easy task to awake him. I shall take him tonight to a place where he may choose to fully wake. But for now, we shall hear the tale I spoke of!"

Excitedly the little people all gathered around the Lady and grew silent, and Colleen and Frederick seated themselves to listen as well. Oracle sat down at her feet and looked up into her lovely face.

Then the Lady began the tale. It was not a song, so much as a chant, of sorts, and its words Colleen would never forget, for they seemed to be carved into her memory by the powerful voice of the chanter.

"In times of old, 'ere worlds were born,
'Ere stars did shine, before first morn,
Songs did rise in heaven's halls,
And waters flowed from hallowed falls.
The sacred sea did rise and shine
With Wind and Light of kind divine.
The Wind did blow, the Light did blaze,
And from that Sea leapt many Waves.
With voice and praise they leaped and then
Returned into the Sea again.
But some did venture from that Sea,
Lifted by the Wind to be
Eternal voices fair and strong,
To sing forever heaven's song.
And in those halls, before that Sea,
What ages passed, what came to be,
Only rumor now can tell,
Whispers of those who know so well.
But for a cause the gates spread wide,
And the Sea gushed forth, a thunderous tide.
A River of Fire flowed from the throne
And rushed in mighty currents of foam.
Into the Deep, like brilliant falls,
Spilled forth the waters from heaven's halls.
And falling into that Chasm far,
Dispersed and spread, a mist of stars.
Yet still within that sea remained
Those who had fallen back again.
With the stars they were swept along,
And in that dew 'twas heard heaven song.
For they once again were given voice,
To sing and praise fair heaven's choice.
But those who were outside the Sea,
Watched, and the River of Fire did see.
And they were told to guide each star,
Lest they disperse into the Deep too far;
To bring them back into their course
Where the River of Fire flowed from its Source.
But one who came was strange and bold,
One who had leaped from the Sea of old.

Not back again to the River of Fire,
But to himself was his desire -
To sway the stars not to their Source,
But to a place that was his course.
And so he wove the storied lie
That all the stars, and themselves, would die
If they 'ere should ever flow
Back to the River's fiery glow.
"Not back to heaven's placid Sea!
Into the Deep, come follow me!"
And with such speech, he swayed a third
Of the hosts with his convincing word.
And so the Kingdom rent and tore,
And evil came to Time's fair shore.
But soon not only stars did shine,
For new worlds the Maker did design.
And so He made the Spheres, and then
Those spirits of fire entered in.
And finding mount or meadow or tree
Took them as their house to be.
Dwelling there and clothed therewith,
Became the stuff of legend and myth.
And other folk He then did make
And gave them power their worlds to shape.
Yet 'ere did the Dark One go
And seek to spread his dread and woe.
Yet to each world the Light gave Light
To shine however dark the Night.
And to give them hope when shadows fell
He gave the Lady of the Lake to dwell
In every world of trial and test,
To bring the Waters that give them rest.
To stay the Night that comes too soon,
And tell them of the Light Triune.

The song ended and all those that heard it sat in silence and awe, its memory echoing, as it were, in their minds and hearts, bringing strange thoughts of ages long past.

At length, the Lady spoke again. "So, do you see, children, where the spirits of the Forest come from? They are ancient – more ancient than this land – and, they came to it long, long ago 'ere even the little people were born under the Waking Tree. They are mostly sleeping now, lulled to slumber by the Court Witch."

"She must be terribly powerful," said Frederick.

"Yes, she is," said the Lady, "but her power is not all her own. She is but the vessel of one darker than herself, and it is that one's power that she wields, although she believes it not. For long ago, she gave herself over to the Great Darkness, and it entered into her. She is but its channel.

"You must be wary of her, my friends. Her magic is great, and she can do you great harm. But her tongue is her fiercest weapon, and she will seek to sway you to join her before she seeks to destroy you. She seeks to pervert all good folk, just as she has done to many of the little people."

"I simply do not understand how any of the little people could follow her," said Mrs. Wigglepox.

"You have never met her, good lady," she replied. "Although I foresee that that day will come all too soon, and you will be tried. But yes, there are those even of the little people whose hearts have been darkened through her deceits, and they walk among your people, seeming to be free, but are her secret servants."

At this, a murmur went among the little people, and they glanced around, doubt sweeping across them like a troubled wind.

"Do not fear!" said the Lady. "There are none here who have tasted of the Waters of the Lake who are under her spell, for these are the Waters of Light, filled with a virtue that breaks all spells of darkness. None who taste of them can be forced to do her bidding, although they still may *choose* to do so."

"I wonder," whispered Frederick to Colleen, "if there are any here who have *not* drunk from the Lake, or might really be on her side anyway. *They* might be here as spies."

Even as his said it, Frederick saw Oracle turn his head and look to the wood, and there he thought he saw a small group of little people slip down the hill and into the trees. He stood up and peered down the hill where they had gone, but they were nowhere to be seen.

"What is it, Frederick?" asked Mrs. Wigglepox.

"I thought I saw... well, maybe it was nothing," he replied.

But the Lady Danu was also gazing into the forest where they had gone and looked sad. "Beware, young people. Not all hearts are pure, and even your own will be tested," she said.

For some time, the gathering of people talked with the Lady Danu and with each other until the sun began to set low in the west and the assembly began to disperse. At last, only Colleen and Frederick and the Wigglepox family were left alone with the Lady. Even Oracle had wandered off, following a group of leprechauns that had gone off toward a large tree.

"Now," said the Lady, "we must try to wake Dvalenn."

She rose, and they followed her down the hill and to the wagon. She gazed down at the dwarf, who snored contentedly beneath the dusk sky.

"That's the most peaceful I've seen him," said Frederick.

"I must take him into the Lake," she said. "There, he must make a choice regarding his fate."

She lifted him from the wagon and held him effortlessly like a child, then walked back into the lake until the water was up to her waist.

Looking down at the sleeping dwarf, she said, "Hear me, Dvalenn. Your long night is ending. I give you a choice. You may choose to stay forever in your troubled sleep, or awake to the light, and come to the end of your days."

Dvalenn's eyes remained closed, but in a weak voice he croaked, "Waken me, my Lady. I cannot bear this dark night of my senses any longer. Waken me, oh Lady! Waken me!"

"Then first, you must wash away the Spell in these waters, for their light will drive away the dark night of sleepiness," she replied.

"Dwarves don't care much for water, Lady. I might die beneath these waters," he said.

"Yes, so you shall. Still, you must if you wish to fully awake," she replied.

He was silent for a moment and then said, "Then take me."

She nodded to him and carried him into the deep water. The waves of the Lake began to rise, and as they went in deeper, three times the waves swept over their heads, and on the last wave they heard the Lady say, "Rest friends. I shall see you again soon." Then the water completely covered them, and they were lost from view.

When Dvalenn and the Lady did not return that night, Colleen and the Wigglepox family slept by the shores of the Lake. Frederick, however, climbed into the wagon and curled up in the hay.

"I wonder where they went," said Colleen to Mrs. Wigglepox.

"Well, she said that this is not the only land that she cares for," she replied. "I think that the goblins are her great enemy, and wherever they seek to spread their dark domain, she is there to oppose them. Perhaps she took Dvalenn to a different land. I wonder if we will ever see him again."

That night, the sky was brilliantly clear, with so many stars that Colleen lay on her back in the sweet smelling grass, just gazing upward for long hours. The lake glowed with a white-blue light that often drew her eyes into its depths, and both lake and sky somehow seemed equally deep and compelling, each filled with mystery and wonder, and holding secrets that she could only imagine.

* * *

But Frederick lay wrapped in his cloak, and muttered to himself, "The stars are strange here. I don't see any of the constellations."

He gazed into the unfamiliar sky for some hours, thinking of all that had happened to him. Not so long ago, he would have called anyone who believed in goblins and dwarves and little people foolish – something his father had passed along to him. To believe in superstitions was beneath the educated person, his father had said.

Frederick snorted. *How ironic*, he thought. *Now I'm becoming a superstition.*

Would his family know him when he got home? Would they still accept him as their son with this Goblin Phage coursing through his veins, changing him into something unrecognizable – something inhuman?

He held his infected hand up to the stars. His knuckles were bulging, and his fingernails were growing long and pointed. He made a fist, then spread his fingers wide. There was an odd sensation of physical strength in that hand that he had never felt before. Something about it had a whispering appeal – a subtle temptation seemed to be rising within him to embrace this thing that was changing him. But it also felt *alien*, not entirely his own – as if some part of him were slowly coming into contact with, or was becoming, something totally foreign to his own humanness.

After some time, he fell asleep and dreamed that he was in a great battle. Goblins surrounded him, biting him again and again, and as hard as he tried, he could not run away, for his feet had turned into goblin feet. He wallowed in some sticky muck that threatened to pull him down into its reeking depths. But just beyond the muck was a shining lake, and a voice kept calling to him to try harder and run to the lake, to dive in and escape from the goblins.

He woke once, covered in sweat, and found that the left side of his face felt hot and burned. He pulled his hood up to cover it, and it immediately felt cooler. Then he drifted off into a fitful slumber. But in the early hours of the morning, one more dream came to him, clear and full of purpose.

* * *

On the shore of the Lake, Colleen and the little people slept peacefully through the night, also dreaming of many things.

Chapter 4 – The Dismal Bog

For several days, Adol had found signs that someone, or something, was coming and going from Grandpa McLochlan's house, and the trail always led south, toward the Dismal Bog.

He had tried setting animal traps, but none of these were ever sprung, so on the third day, he decided it was time to do some tracking.

Taking a knife, his club, and a pack of supplies, he headed out of the house and across the farm, following the signs left by the visitor – a broken stick here, matted grass there, and occasionally some sort of dark, oily film that stank.

He reached the wall of white and gray stones that bordered the bog, sighed, and climbed up to the top and sat down. Immediately, the smell of rotted vegetation hit him, and the great field of misshapen trees and vines, hanging moss, and wisps of fog lay before him. For nearly a mile, this tangle spilled southward, and from there, a dank leech-filled stream flowed, along whose banks angry insects buzzed, and strange worms dug in the fouled banks. He wondered why this place was even called a bog – it was more of a swamp.

He had been in here on numerous occasions, but always a feeling of uneasiness accompanied such ventures. It was as though there was a *presence* here – a spirit of malice that strove against all that was free and living. It bent its will against them, but drew kindred evil to itself. Over the years, there had been many tales of thieves and robbers and lawless people hiding out in this place. Adol had twice led the authorities through its strange depths to root out escaped criminals. He turned his head to his farm and breathed deeply once, and then climbed down the wall into the bog below.

There was no clear trail apparent, but still, signs of something passing were there. What was worse, as he slowly made his way toward the center of the bog, there were small pools of a black oily skim that covered patches of the already dark waters.

For an hour, he moved silently through the twisted shadows, trudging through thick muck and only occasionally finding solid ground on which to stand. His boots were heavy with mud and rotting weeds, and his nostrils were full of the dank smell that never left the fetid air. At last, he came to the place he was seeking – a place he had been only once before – the place his son Bran had mentioned when they were on the Hill. It was here that he suspected the black creature came – a place fitting for such a thing.

Up a small incline he trudged, thankful for at least some solid ground under his feet. And yes, there were the signs of the thing's passage. In fact, there were so many obvious footprints and trampled grasses that there was no doubt – this seemed to be where it had made its lair.

Adol circled a pile of broken rock that he thought must have at one time been a wall. The huge stones were stained with ages of lichen and moss and vine growth, but there was one place in particular for which he was searching. He knew it was here somewhere, for he had seen it once before when he was a youth.

Then he found it – three blocks as tall as himself, cut as perfect cubes and inscribed with many runes, and beneath them was a hole that led down into darkness.

The memory of this place came rushing back. He had slipped down into this dark pit those many years ago. He had been hunting in the wood east of the bog, and it had been growing dark, when a deer leaped across the trail in front of him. It had been covered with sweat, its mouth was lathered with foam, and the coppery smell of fear filled the air. It was gone in an instant, but behind it, bounded a huge dog. It had to have been a dog – wolves in Ireland had supposedly disappeared half a century before. But it was close on the heels of the deer.

He had followed the chase into the bog, and the deer fell. It had been too dark for him to see clearly, but he knew the dog had killed it and dragged it away – to this very place – to this very hole in the ground.

He had lit a torch and gone into the pit, and found it to be more than a pit. A broken staircase led downward, and the most intense sense of dread that he had ever experienced flooded his soul. Yet, down he had gone until he came to a dark hall, and from there to a closed and locked stone double door. A bottom portion of one of the doors had been broken, leaving a hole large enough for the dog to drag the deer through, but too small for him to enter.

He had shoved the torch into the hole and looked in, but could see nothing but something huge and shiny – like a wall of black tiles, but nothing more.

It was beyond those doors that lay the source of that dread that was growing in his mind and soul by the second. It was not the dog – he had no fear of that. There was something else here, something beyond his experience or imagination, something that desired nothing but to *consume.* And it was famished. He could put no other words to that feeling.

He had backed away, and when he had climbed out of that pit, he had run. He had run through the bog and climbed the wall and tumbled down into the farm, breathing deeply and basking in the freedom from the oppressiveness that had pursued him out of that place.

But here he was again, over twenty years later, and he did not want to go down there again. Something terrible was down there – something, he believed, that was the cause of the bog's very existence. Something that lay trapped and hidden from long, long ago, which must never be released. And, he thought, this black-robed thing had been living down there. It had been drawn to this place, and here would be his best chance of catching it. He did not know if the creature was in its lair or not, so he moved from the hill to a grove of twisted trees where he could watch the entrance but be out of sight, and there he sat down and waited.

He did not have to wait long, for very soon, a black-cloaked figure slunk up the hill. It paused briefly at the entrance to the pit, pulled a small shiny crystal ball from its cloak, held it up to the setting sun, cackled madly, and then slunk down into the pit.

Adol was tempted to go after it then and there, or to move a great boulder over the hole and trap it, but he was not sure what lay beyond the broken door where he had been those years ago. He would bide his time. Now he knew for sure that the creature was here. Rising from his hiding place, he silently slipped away, back toward the farm.

As soon as he was well away from the hill, he picked up his pace. Back over the wall he went, breathed the good air of the farm, and then ran to Grandpa's hut. He hooked his club to his belt and went to the cellar.

There, next to one wall, was a huge, ornate mirror. Days before, he had discovered it, although how it had come to be in this cellar he could not say. He knew that it was more than simply a mirror, though, for the black creature had somehow opened a doorway *through* it to somewhere else, and had escaped capture. He would not allow that to happen again.

"Can't leave this here," he said to himself. *"At least now that thing won't be going anywhere that I can't follow."*

Picking up the mirror, he carried it across the fields and back to the farmhouse. He took it down the basement, threw several old blankets over it, and then proceeded to pile things in front of it, hiding it from view.

Then back upstairs he went, and locked the cellar door, putting the key in his pocket.

"Tomorrow the hunt begins," he said aloud, and went to the kitchen to make a pot of tea and think through his plans.

Hours later, in the dead of the night, Adol heard a distant scream outside, coming from the direction of Grandpa's hut. It made his skin crawl, but he smiled anyway, turned over, and fell asleep until morning.

Chapter 5 – Parting

Colleen awoke to the warm sun on her face. She sat up and looked around. Frederick was sitting in the shade under the wagon. His hood was pulled over his head. He looked up, saw her staring, and he waved his right hand at her.

"Have you been awake long?" she asked him.

"About an hour," he mumbled.

She stood and walked over to the lake and took a deep drink. It satisfied her right down to her bones and, when she was done, she cinched up her robe and put her feet in. The water was perfect, and soothed her feet like nothing she had ever felt. It seemed to sink into her somehow, satisfying and relaxing her, quieting her whole being. It was as though everything in her grew still and at ease.

"Come and join me, Frederick. Put your feet in the water," she called over her shoulder.

He considered the invitation for a moment, then shook his head.

"Colleen," said Frederick. "I had a dream last night."

Colleen left the water and walked over to him.

"I have to go, Colleen," he said sadly. "In my dream, the Lady told me so. She said that it was really important."

Colleen looked at him. She could not see his face, covered as it was with the hood.

"Look at me, Frederick," she said, but he did not raise his face.

"Frederick, are you all right?" she said.

Very slowly, he lifted his face, and with his right hand, he slid his hood back. She involuntarily gasped and stepped back, for his entire face was changed. It was gray and misshapen, his nose and ears had grown, and his hair was a mop of dark purple, almost black tangles. Quickly, he pulled the hood back and bent his head to his chest.

"She told me that my only hope was to plunge into the Lake, Colleen," he said. "She said it would burn away the Phage. But that I would have to go down deep into it if I wanted to be really healed – to dive all the way through – that I couldn't just splash around the edges and then leap out again. Only then would I come out healed. I'm scared, Colleen, really scared."

She sat down beside him and touched him on the shoulder.

"But you would be healed, right?" asked Colleen. "Why not do it? Don't you want to be healed?"

At first, he wanted to say yes, but then hesitated, and unconsciously scratched at his wounded arm. A strange reluctance came over him, as if a part of him wrestled with the idea of actually being free. Something nagged at his mind – a whisper that said he would lose out on something if he let this thing go. Why not let the Phage take its course? What *would* he become? Would he become a dark wizard with mysterious powers? The goblins supposedly possessed magic – would the Phage grant him that as well? Perhaps he would become a goblin leader. Fantasies of greatness and power whirled in his mind.

"Frederick?" said Colleen when he did not respond.

He blinked and shook his head, suddenly coming to himself. What had he been thinking? Where had those thoughts come from?

"Well, of course. Who wouldn't want to be rid of it?" he said.

He took a deep breath and continued. "But there's more. The lady said I won't be able to get back this way if I do this."

"Why not?" she said.

"I have to pass through the waters completely – all the way through the deepest and brightest part of it – only then will the Phage completely die. Only then will I be rid of it and it won't come back again, unless I allow it to. And Colleen – if I make it, I'll pass through to the other side," he replied.

"And what is on the other side?" she asked.

"Home, Colleen. Back to our world," he said.

"Home!" she whispered.

He nodded. "The Lady told me in my dream that she could send me back, and there, I was to find help."

Frederick expected Colleen to yell or cry or do something emotional, but instead, she only nodded her head and sighed.

"I'm scared too, Frederick," she said. "I don't want to go on alone, but I had a dream too. The Lady said you had to go, but that you could, perhaps, come back as soon as you did something really important."

"But maybe you could just stay here at the Lake until I get back, Colleen. It's safe here," he suggested.

"No, I can't. My mother is in danger – somehow, I know it. I've got to keep going. The Lady said I could go with you if I wanted. But I can't, Frederick, I just can't!"

She started to cry then, her tears streaming down her cheeks.

"Oh, Colleen, now don't do that." His own eyes blurred, and he hastily wiped them on his sleeve. "I'll be back, I promise, just as soon as I can. And I'll bring help if I can."

"But how? That goblin has the crystal ball, so you can't come through the mirror," said Colleen.

Just then, the Lady Danu appeared, rising out of the middle of the Lake and walking toward them. Her steps made neither splash nor ripple on its crystal blue surface, and she was carrying something long and wrapped in a golden cloth.

"Good morning, my young friends," she said, smiling. "Did you rest well?"

"Yes, Lady Danu," said Colleen, wiping her eyes.

"Perhaps you know what you must do next?" she asked.

"Yes, Lady," said Frederick. "Although I don't know how to do it."

"There is a way, dear Frederick," she said. "We will sit and talk while we eat breakfast."

She led them back up the hill to the stone slab where they had eaten the day before, and there, waiting for them, was a sumptuous meal all prepared. Many of the little people, including all of the Wigglepoxes and the gnomes, were already eating or were finishing their morning meal.

"Ah, the sleepyheads are awake at last," teased Mrs. Wigglepox when she saw them coming to the top of the rise. "We were all wondering if you were going to sleep forever. I've heard of such things, you know."

"Aye," said Humble the Gnome. "That's what happened to old Dvalenn."

"Yes," said Nemon. "And then there was that other tale of the young maiden who slept in the Wizard's castle for hundreds of years."

"I thought it was a thousand years. And what about..." began Zelo, but he was cut off when the Lady Danu laughed.

"Please, please, dear friends!" she said, smiling. "If we tell these good folk all the tales of the land, we shall be here for the rest of the year and into the next! Come now, let them eat in peace. Go and enjoy the sun and the lake for a time while I speak with them. There is little time before they depart, and some of you will be going with them."

"A grand idea!" said Rose, and they all danced away down the hill toward the lake.

The Lady watched after them until they were out of earshot, and then turned to face the children.

"Did Frederick tell you what he must do, Colleen, and why?" she asked.

Colleen looked at the ground and said sadly, "He said he has to go back home. He said that it's the only way he will be healed, and that he has something to do."

"Indeed he does," she replied. "I foresee that many dangers and adventures lie before him."

She held out what she had been carrying, and Frederick took it from her and unwrapped the golden cloth. Inside was an ornate sheath for a sword and a gold and silver belt that was light as a feather. Frederick turned the sheath over and over, marveling at its intricately carved body, which was laced with gold and tiny gems.

"It's marvelous!" he said.

"But where is the sword that goes in it?" asked Colleen.

Frederick unbuckled the sword that hung at his side and handed it to Colleen. "I think you might need this," he said, then buckled the empty sheath in its place.

Colleen took the sword without a word and fastened it around her own waist.

"But why an empty sword sheath?" asked Colleen.

The Lady held a finger to her lips and did not answer, but held out something else to Colleen. It was a white pouch with a silver drawstring that fit in the palm of her hand. Colleen took and opened it and removed its contents. Inside was a small crystal container in the shape of a pitcher, with a small, ornate lid. Even in the sunlight, they could see that it glowed with the same blue radiance of the Lake, only the glow seemed deeper somehow.

"In this container is water from the very source of the Lake, Colleen. It will cure many ills caused by the goblins and disperse every evil spell. Use it wisely and sparingly, and only at the greatest need. You will know when the time comes. Remember that it has the power to break every spell cast by the Witch and her minions, and to heal and give life."

She looked at her for a moment longer, as if considering something.

"Colleen, do you remember how the pixies, while here at the Lake, are able to call to the world around them? How Leleuma raised a stallion from the waves, and how Meadow caused the flowers to bloom? And all that the others did?" asked the Lady.

"Yes," she replied. "It was quite amazing!"

"I would like you to do something for me, Colleen. Look around. What do you see?" she asked.

"I see the sun shining on the lake. It's like a thousand pieces of light dancing in the wind," Colleen replied.

"Yes," she said. "The wind on the water is like a symphony. Every dancing ripple in the sunlight sings to me. It so reminds me of the First Day. Do you think you can sing with it?"

"Sing with it?" Colleen asked. "How would I do that?"

"Look and listen to the music all around you, child. A symphony surrounds us of all there is to see. The orchestra of nature plays unendingly. The whisper of the wind, the roar of the sea, the silence of a meadow, the songbird's harmony – yet so often, people fail to see its beauty and the truth it so clearly declares. It reflects the Maker himself, in a way. But also, in this land, there are many ancient spirits – in the trees, in the lake, in the rocks, in the mountains and meadows. As the tale that I sang to you tells, they came long, long ago when this world was young, and they are still here, although so many now slumber beneath the Spell. But you, Colleen, may be able to awaken them," she replied.

"Do you mean that I could make the water stir like Leleuma did?" she asked, amazed.

The Lady smiled. "There is more to you than you know," she said. "Was it not your song that got you here through the sleeping forest, even though the Spell is so terribly strong around this place? Come, now, listen to the music of the Lake and sing with it. Open your heart to what it says."

Colleen gazed out over the shining waters and tried hard to listen. Gradually, her mind grew quiet, and it seemed as though some great peace filled her. There were no thoughts at all in her mind, only the peace. In that moment, it seemed that all was at peace around the lake, although it was like an island in some great storm.

She sensed that all about the lake, the Spell of the Court Witch was at work, pressing its terrible weight upon the forest, causing the last vestiges of its strength to slip away into a fitful sleepiness, and a great weariness lay from horizon to horizon. But the lake stood free of it, a refuge and a fortress untouched by that weight, although the Spell strove against the lake like a raging sea against a lighthouse on a granite cliff.

Then it was as though she saw something more. It was only a glimpse, but just for a moment, she saw *deeper* than her eyes alone could see. Beyond the water, beyond the shoreline, beyond the trees, she saw... saw... But no, she could not describe it. No thought seemed fitting for it. It was something that she perceived, not with her physical senses, but with another sense, that, for a moment, awoke within her.

It was not the scores of little people that she glimpsed who lay sleeping amid fitful dreams beneath root and trunk in the dreadful night of the Spell. Nor was it the hidden spirits that dwelt in many of these things that now transfixed her, although she saw these too – those creatures of another time and place that had come to dwell within these things and made them their homes so long, long ago. No, this was even deeper than them, for it encompassed those spirits as well. It was like a song, although it was not with her ears that she was now hearing it. The forest sang it as well, and its part was deep and sad, and had sunken to a whisper, as though it longed to be released from its deepening slumber.

Now, she saw her own place in that song – the part that *she* was to sing in it. If she could just stay within that part, and seek nothing beyond it, desire no more than her given portion, and yet let none of her responsibility within it to slip, all would be well. She could see how the Spell strove against the Song and sought to dominate and control it. It was like a noise that rose to drown out the sweetness of the music so that none could hear it and would grow weary under its constant clatter.

Colleen tuned her heart to the music and began to sing. And as she sang, she saw those ancient powers stir and turn, as it were, toward her. The waves stirred on the Lake, and within them water sprites danced. The trees around the edge of the forest murmured and shook their branches, and she could see the dryads within them smiling. In the breeze, a voice whispered, blowing in mighty gusts through the grass and trees. It was a joyous wind, not a raging gale, and nothing was harmed by it.

Then she was aware of the Lady speaking to her, although her voice seemed almost distant. "Once, long ago, there were the Great Ones who were granted this gift. I believe that gift lives in you now. Yet there is even more to you than that... something..."

The Lady looked closely at Colleen, her face amazed. "There has only been one other..." she said, almost to herself. Then she continued, "Beware, Colleen, there are those who have corrupted their gifts into a desire for power and now use such gifts for their own ends."

Suddenly, the vision was gone, the wind subsided, the waves splashed back into the Lake, and all was calm. Colleen sat transfixed, keenly aware that she had just participated in something so incredibly *beyond* her, yet of which she was also a part.

After a few moments she said, "Is that what the wizards were - people with gifts that others do not have?"

"In a way," replied the Lady. "At first, they were all good and used their strengths for the bettering of the worlds and their peoples, but many were corrupted. The Court Witch is one such person. Something dreadful happened to her, and she has lost her place in the Great Song. It is a sad thing, for she was once a great singer."

She looked sorrowful for a moment and then said, "Remember, Colleen, use your gifts for good, and do not overstep your bounds. And your bounds appear to be quite large for one so young. I wonder what you will become when you are grown?"

The Lady looked curiously at her again, as if pondering some deep thing.

"But I still don't understand, Lady," replied Colleen. "Just what *is* my gift, and why do *I* have it?"

The Lady looked even more thoughtful for a moment before continuing.

"I cannot teach you all that you will need to know in one day. And you and I are not of the same kind. There are things about you that I do not know, nor ever will know. Only one of your own kind can truly teach you. All I can tell you is to keep your heart true wherever you go and whatever happens to you. That is the first step in becoming what you were made to be. Remember, child, others have been turned by the Witch and her spells, and much evil has come upon the world because of it. However, I can tell you this – to you has been granted to taste of the nature of other beings. What they sing, you can sing. You need only be near them to hear their song and learn it. Take care how you sing – you may find that strange things happen when you do. I believe this gift is awakening within you."

The Lady looked intently at both of the children for a long moment and then said, "It is time. Frederick. Are you ready?"

He gazed out across the lake and shivered. Then he looked at Colleen, remembering their plight.

"I suppose so," he replied reluctantly. "But I really don't want to leave Colleen by herself."

"She is *not* by herself, you silly goose," said a small voice behind him.

They turned to see Lily standing with her hands on her hips, gazing up at him from the grass. Mrs. Wigglepox and Rose stood beside her, and behind them, Oracle grinned.

"We will be going with her," she said.

"Well, now," said the Lady. "Are you sure that you all wish to go with Colleen? It will be a dangerous journey, filled with hardship and loss. There is more for you to face, I think, even than the goblins and the Spell of the Witch."

"That's why we're all going," said Mrs. Wigglepox. "She's going to need us!"

"There will be one other who will go along as well, at least for a time, but I will speak of that later," said the Lady.

Frederick smiled under his hood and said, "Well, I do feel much better knowing that you will have such good companions. But I promise, as soon as I am done what I have to do, I'll come back somehow if I can."

"Come friends, gaze into my lake!" said the Lady. "Tell me what you see." She waved her hand out over the lake, and it grew still. It was as though it went from a dancing lake surface to a perfect piece of glass.

Frederick turned to the lake and shielded his eyes with his good hand.

"Look!" he said. "There's something... something like a picture moving on the waters!"

Frederick and the Lady Danu leaned forward, as did Colleen, and the little people gathered at the edge of the lake, staring out onto its reflective surface.

"It seems to be changing," said Colleen. "Like it's shifting scenes or something."

Oracle stepped forward and began to chant, and for once, his voice and words were not garbled, but distinct and clear.

"Water of Light and fairy dust,
Into a crystal ball was thrust,
Suffused with magic from 'tween the lands,
Shaped of old by Dwarven hands.
Blessed by Elven magic bold,
Wished upon by Leople's gold.
Passed to Humans long ago,
And where it went, we do not know."

He ended his chant and stared at the mirrored lake and its shifting scenes with his big brown eyes. He looked, for the first time, deeply thoughtful rather than silly.

"Is that how it was made, Oracle?" asked Colleen. "The crystal ball, I mean?"

He turned and looked at her and said, "Colligal had it?"

"Yes, Oracle, I had it, but I did not know what it was. Now a goblin has it."

Oracle looked dismayed and turned back to stare at the waters.

The scene in the water shifted from a shining lake high in a mountain range, to an ornately carved stone pool filled with water. It shifted again, and there was a woodland lake near some large college or mansion, which somehow seemed familiar to Frederick. Again, it changed, and a shining pool shrouded in some heavy darkness in a dank cavern was pictured. Colleen shivered at the scene, and just before it changed again, she thought she had seen a pair of eyes staring out at her hungrily.

The next scene was that of a gigantic lake with an immense bridge over it. It seemed to stretch for many miles, but the bridge was crumbling and in disrepair. Again, the scene changed, and a lovely forest and wildflowers around a lake edge were pictured, and Colleen realized that it was the very place that they were sitting.

"Many doors open from this place," said the Lady. "The Witch would dearly love to seize it for herself. Frederick, you must choose one of these doors, and before the scene changes, you must step in. Are you ready to accept this task? You must find help and bring it back here."

Frederick took a deep breath and leaned closer. Again, the scene changed, and each time, there was a lake or some other body of water. Together, they watched as strange and wondrous and even frightening scenes shifted before them until there was a still lake reflecting a blue sky with white clouds. Maple and oak trees sat on the banks, their gnarled roots hanging low as if drinking from its cool waters.

Once again, the scene changed, and there was again an underground scene with a shining lake.

"That's the one," he said, and glancing once at Colleen, then at the Lady, who nodded to him.

He hesitated a moment, trembling. Then he threw back his hood and whipped the cloak over his back. His face was gray and distorted, with green blotches spreading over his cheeks and bulbous nose. He cried out in pain, and his very skin writhed as the light of the lake shone upon it. His heart pounded, and a great struggle seized his mind and body, as though his mind and passions violently fought against this mad action that he was about to undertake.

Then, something in his heart rose above his rebelling reason and burning flesh, and with one great cry, he ran toward the lake and, with all his might, dove in head first, swallowing mouthfuls as he plunged downward into the blue depths.

Colleen reached out for him for an instant, and then withdrew her hand as the vision in the lake swirled into three interlaced spirals. It seemed to her eyes that he was falling into the midst of them, down into a great depth. Then the image vanished, and only the infinite blue remained.

Frederick was gone.

Chapter 6 – The Sword in the Tree

Frederick dove into the water with one thought on his mind. "Wash it away! Wash it away and take me home!"

He fully expected the lake to burn him like fire – to sear his wounded flesh like the hot knife had done in Cian's cave. But to his utter astonishment, nothing of the kind happened. As he swallowed the cool water and felt it touch his infected skin, he felt not a fire, but both a warmth and a coolness at once sinking deep down, driving away the poison in his veins.

His face seemed to stretch and pull, as though something was peeling away from him. He looked over his shoulder, and for a moment, he saw a deformed and twisted shadow of a goblin writhing in the brightness. It reached out for him with one ghostly hand as he left it behind, then it seemed fade, vanishing into nothingness as he plunged onward into the mystical blue depths.

As he left the Goblin Phage behind, he thought he heard the Lady say – or perhaps it was an echo from his dream – *You will be free, unless you allow the goblins to bite you again – and then the Phage will return, and with a vengeance. Remember.*

Then he was falling swiftly and, in an instant, the world was a dazzling blue, and then began to shift around him. He heard the distant voice of the Lady calling after him, saying, "Take care, young Frederick, and seek the king in the sea!"

Down and down he tumbled, falling, ever falling, and then he knew that he was through, and found himself underwater – normal water, and he knew he had to get to the surface.

A vague light above him told him which way was up, but a faint glow below him spoke of light as well. He hesitated a few seconds, holding his failing breath, but fascinated by the orange whisper of light that seemed to be coming from ... what was it? A cavern? Yes, it must be. But his air was gone now, and he was sinking fast – the chain mail coat he was wearing was weighing him down. He kicked hard toward the surface again and again, gaining inches with each kick. Just when he thought his lungs would explode and he could hold his breath no more, he reached the surface and gasped, drinking in stale air that now surrounded him. He blinked and looked around. Everyone had vanished. He was alone, treading water in the middle of ... of what? A cavern?

Frederick looked about in the faint light as his eyes began to adjust. There, some distance away, there appeared to be a torch burning. He swam toward it, and found that it was not very far – perhaps only fifty feet. Still, it was a hard swim with all he was wearing, and he was quite exhausted as his feet touched bottom and he began to wade neck deep toward the shore.

Suddenly, something bumped into him. It was large, as big as himself, he thought, and it hit him, pushing him back toward the deep water, and then swam by. He hurried on toward the land, and again the thing swam around him and pushed him back. Then again, and again. He pushed forward, scared now, and desperate. Then there were two of them, bumping and jostling him, always away from shore, and he thought he felt slippery hands grabbing at his ankles, slowing his progress. He reached down to his side to draw his sword, and then remembered that he had given it to Colleen. Only the empty sheath was there. He struck at them with his fists and kicked furiously. They darted away from him, and he desperately pushed himself toward the shoreline.

Again, they came at him, this time from behind, grasping at him, pulling him, drawing him back toward the deeper water. Again and again, he kicked at them as he pushed himself through the water. But he was nearing the shore now and, with one last desperate effort, he kicked and then found he was in shallow water. He struggled to the shore and collapsed there, exhausted.

He looked out at the dark water before him and shivered. What had that been in there? He sat for several moments, breathing heavily, trying to get hold of his fear.

Then he remembered himself and he felt his face and ears. The bulging nose he'd had a few minutes before was gone, and the formerly drooping, pointed ears seemed to be his own again.

He smiled and looked at his left arm. It was his own. The black spidery veins and gray-green skin were gone, replaced by his own human flesh, and the bite marks were only faint scars.

"Well, that's to be expected, I suppose," he said aloud. "I suppose I'll always have the memory of it as well as the scars."

But he felt free, and taking a deep breath, he looked about. Not far away was what appeared to be an ancient fountain, although no water flowed in it now, and beside this was a large gnarled tree with dead branches spreading out and upward to a stone archway. It was as though the ancient tree were gripping the damp stone, forbidding it to fall. A torch was fixed to the tree in a metal bracket, its flickering light casting eerie shadows over the scene.

Over one branch was hung an old cloth that appeared to have once been red and white. He walked over and took it, shook it once, and wiped his face dry, then stuck it in his pocket without further thought.

As he walked around the strange tree, a stone bench came into view, and on this was stretched out a prone figure.

"Hello?" Frederick called.

He saw now that it was a very old man. Long white hair fell from his head, and a long white beard and mustache lay on his chest. Bushy eyebrows nearly hid his closed eyes.

"Hello?" he called. "Are you all right?"

The man did not answer.

Frederick paused for a moment. The old man's face was grim and absolutely ancient. Was he sick? Did he need help? Was he... dead?

"Hello, my good man!" Frederick called. "I say, are you all right?"

But the man still did not stir. He lay still as death. Frederick walked up to the prone form and looked down at him. He wore a tattered robe that looked as old as he was, and by his left side was a twisted walking staff.

"Sir?" said Frederick. But the man did not move.

Frederick reached out to give him a little shake, but when he did so, his hand passed through some sort of an invisible barrier and it went icy cold, or perhaps *cold* was not the word for it. It was as though his hand simply *stopped* before reaching the man's body. Stopped moving, stopped working, stopped *being*. He jerked his hand away with a cry and stepped back. Slowly, the weird feeling faded, and his hand returned to normal.

He picked up a small round pebble and tossed it at the man's chest. As soon as it got within a foot of the prone figure, it simply stopped in midair, and seemed to *float*. Then he noticed that there was a collection of things floating above the man – droplets of water, a fine mist, and dust. It was like a thin film surrounding him. But all were suspended with perfect stillness in the air about the figure, immobile and silent.

Frederick studied this for several moments, and then leaned against the tree to think. As he did so, his shoulder touched something, and he turned to see what it was. There, stuck into the tree, nearly all the way to the hilt, was a brilliant, beautiful sword. What showed of its blade was ornate and covered in runes, and its hilt was studded with gems and gold and silver. It was truly magnificent, like no sword he had ever seen. It did not appear that the sword had *pierced* the tree, but rather that the tree was, somehow, *holding* the sword.

322

Hesitantly, he reached out and put his hands around the handle. It was not cold to the touch as he expected, but was warm, even welcoming. He pulled. It cleanly and effortlessly slid from the tree with a singing ring of steel. It flashed with a brilliant green-white light in the darkness, momentarily blinding him. The tree seemed to shudder from deep within, and its branches, for a moment, trembled, and the fold that had held it closed.

The weapon felt perfect in his hand, balanced and true, much like the dwarf-made sword that he had given Colleen. This one was longer, however, more than three feet long, he thought, and he wondered how so large a sword felt so good in his hand. He slashed it through the air a few times, and marveled at the ease with which it obeyed him. Effortlessly he swung it around his head and the air *swooshed* with its passing. Then he remembered a portion of the dream he had the night before. It had been dark, like this. And yes, there had been a sword.

He looked at the steel in his hand, then at the sheath at his side. He slid it in, and it fit perfectly.

"Like it was made for it," he said aloud to himself. "She sent me here to get this sword. But what about this old man? He wasn't in my dream."

He turned to look at the old fellow. He still lay on the stone, surrounded by the weird dusty cocoon suspended about him. Frederick pulled the sword from its sheath again and looked at it.

"I wonder..." he said to himself, and he leveled the point at the pebble that he had thrown and jabbed at it.

As soon as the sword tip pierced the layer of floating dust, there was an audible *swishing* sound as all of the bits of dust and water fell onto the old man or on the stone on which he lay. The pebble went *plink* as it dropped to the man's chest and rolled to the ground, and the creatures in the water began to leap and splash.

But what startled Frederick the most was that the man drew a great shuddering gasp of air, his eyes flew wide open, and his chest began to heave up and down as though he had been running a great race and was catching his breath. He looked about the ceiling of the cavern, moving only his eyes at first, but then, after a moment, slowly turned his head and, seeing a figure holding a sword above him, moved with a speed that Frederick did not think possible for so old a man. Off the stone table he rolled, seizing the staff that had lain beside him, and crouched in a pose like a trained warrior, his staff held before him like a weapon. An eerie light burst from the tip of the staff, and the old man seemed to grow ominous and threatening, possessing a hidden power that seemed about to burst forth in a raging fury.

Frederick backed away, still holding the sword before him.

"Wait! I...I didn't mean to disturb you. I've come to..." stammered Frederick.

The old man relaxed slightly and then, slowly, he looked about the cavern again, yet still watching Frederick with suspicious eyes. The fellow's beard hung down to his waist, and his hair halfway down his back. Dark eyes looked out at Frederick from beneath thick, bushy white eyebrows. Then the man said something in a language that Frederick could not understand. His voice was strong, stronger than it should have been for so old a man, although Frederick thought he sounded extraordinarily tired.

"Sorry," said Frederick, still keeping his distance and holding the sword. "I'm not sure I understand."

The man seemed to relax slightly, but still hesitated, looking at the sword. They stood staring at one another across the stone table for a moment, and then slowly, the old man stood upright and leaned on his staff. The hidden power that had been present a moment ago faded and the imposing presence that had filled the room was replaced by an ancient wizened figure who seemed old beyond reckoning. Frederick slowly lowered his sword.

"The Lady… I mean, someone sent me," he said. "I'm... on a mission."

There was a sudden stirring in the water again, and Frederick glanced around. In the dim light of the torch, he could now see many faces watching them. Their hair was long and green or brown, like seaweed, and there were both men and women.

The old man saw them too and said something in his strange language. Frederick hesitated again, not knowing what to say. But the man seemed to grow weary and his face flushed. His legs gave way beneath him, and he began to fall. Frederick rushed forward and caught him, helping him to sit on the stone slab. The man said something again, leaned heavily on his staff, and hung his head down.

After a moment, he looked at Frederick, reached out and touched him on the head with his staff, shut his eyes, and murmured something.

A strange sensation shot through Frederick's mind, as if in an instant of time the old man had read his thoughts and knew all that he knew. He scrambled off the rock shelf and backed against the tree, which quivered at his touch.

But the old man only smiled weakly at him and said, "Do not be afraid, Frederick."

Chapter 7 – The Wizard

Frederick stared at the old man for a moment and then said, "What did you do to me? I can... I can understand you now."

"And I you," he replied. "Don't be afraid. I have not harmed you, nor will I. It was a simple thing to learn your language. But now, see here, I thank you. I seem to have been... been... I do not know. Nor do I know where we are now. But somehow, I think that I have been under an enchantment. And this place – where is it? It is underground, is it not?"

Then Frederick remembered why he was here, and he did not answer the old man at first. There must be a passage out of here somewhere, he thought, and knew he had to find it. He went to the tree, took the torch from its bracket, and walked around the bit of land on which he was standing. It was a small island, surrounded by water on all sides. But he could see no passages beyond the boundary of the lake, only rock walls that reached upward to a stalactite-covered ceiling.

"Yes, we are underground," said Frederick. "I am on an errand for... for a friend. I can't stay here for long."

"Please," said the old man. "Sit with me for a moment. I am weary, but there is a great deal I must know."

Frederick looked out into the water and once again could vaguely make out a dim glow coming from the underwater passageway. The faces of the lake people watched him intently.

"Are they friendly?" asked the man.

"I don't think so," replied Frederick. "They gave me a fit when I arrived."

"Please, grant an old man a moment," he said.

Frederick looked at the lake and then at the old man. He sighed and went to sit next to him.

Then, an impossible thought struck him. He knew it was impossible and absurd, but he had already seen so many impossible and absurd things in the past few days that he could not help but ask.

"Sir," he said. "Are you a wizard?"

The old man looked sidelong at him and said, "A wizard? What makes you ask such a question?"

"Well, you look the part, you know. What with that robe and beard and bushy eyebrows and staff and how you *were* a few moments ago. And besides, I've heard quite a few stories lately about wizards. Why, the Lady Danu..."

He stopped himself, for the old man looked at him curiously at the mention of the Lady.

"You know the Lady Danu?" asked the man softly.

"Er, well... all right, then, yes. I've only met her just the other day. We spent the night at her Lake."

"We?" said the old man.

"Well, yes, my cousin and I and ..."

The old man raised his eyebrows questioningly. Frederick somehow felt that he could trust him. He *needed* to trust him – needed someone to help him. He took a deep breath and sheathed the sword.

"Fine then," he said. "I've been in the Land of the Little People with my cousin and we found the Lady, and I've come back to get help to fight a witch that's taken over the land. There it is, then."

The old man sighed.

"She has taken over the whole land, then?" he asked quietly.

"Well, that's what they say, at least," replied Frederick.

The old man looked about again and fell silent for several long moments.

"The reason I ask," said Frederick, "is that I think a wizard would be, you know, *useful* if you're going to be fighting a witch. I'm supposed to be finding help. Maybe you're the one I'm supposed to take back with me."

The old man looked deeply thoughtful at this and, at length, seemed to come to some conclusion.

"Well, to answer your question, yes, I am a wizard. But last I remember, I too was fighting a witch in the Land of the Little People. We were in a fierce battle. There was a collision of powers such as the world had never known. It seemed to me that the sky itself ripped in two, and there was a terrible

327

explosion. The last thing I remember was falling on a stone bench, then waking up here."

"Were you in the Council of Wizards?" asked Frederick, amazed.

"You seem to know quite a bit, lad," he replied.

"Well, I've learned a thing or two lately," he said. "But please, you know my name – what is yours?"

"It is no small thing to give one's true name, especially to a stranger," said the wizard. "And I am still uncertain of all this. This arch, and this tree, for instance – they are familiar and yet... *aged.* How long, I wonder, have I been here, lying on this slab of stone? And who put me here? Was it the Lady?"

"I don't know," said Frederick. "The Lady didn't mention you when she sent me. I've come to find help, though, and would welcome yours if you can give it."

The man looked about him in wonder once again, then at Frederick. He considered him for a long time and then said, "Very well. I shall tell you one of my names, and this name you may tell to others. I am Gwydion, member of the Council of Wizards."

For some reason the name sounded familiar to Frederick, although he could not recall how.

"Come now, Frederick, you must tell me more. You say that the Lady sent you and that you fight against the Witch?" said Gwydion.

"It's all really quite by accident that we got there – into the Land of the Little People, that is," he replied. "We came through the mirror in the wood."

"Mirror in the wood?" asked Gwydion. "Was it a large mirror with many shapes and runes about it?"

"Well, yes, as far as I remember. We didn't have a lot of time, and I... I lost that crystal ball, so we couldn't get back. That goblin got it. But we made it to the Lady's Lake, and she sent me back," he replied.

"All of this is very strange news to me. Is this cavern somehow connected to the Dwarven mines? Is that how she sent you here?" asked Gwydion.

"We're not in the Land of the Little People anymore," replied Frederick. "We're back in the World of Men. As to how I arrived, I leaped into the Lake and *fell* here, you might say. Or went through that lake to this one. But see that light down in the water? That must be the way out. I've got to go for it."

"I am weary," said Gwydion. "I do not know if I could swim down to that light and then back out again. Surely there is another way?"

"Not that I know of," answered Frederick. "But, I am sorry. I've got to try to make it through. I'll tell someone that you're here, if you like, and they might make it back to help."

The old man looked at the light that twinkled dimly beneath the water, then at the faces that continued to stare at them from the lake.

"I wonder if they will even let us try," he said. "But perhaps we might convince them. You have a sword, I see. Can you use it?"

Frederick slid it halfway out of its sheath. It glittered in the light of the torch that he was still holding. As he did so, the old man's eyes went wide again with amazement.

"Where did you get that sword, lad?" he asked.

Frederick glanced at the tree. "It was stuck in that tree. I pulled it out. But the Lady Danu gave me the sheath."

"May I see it?" asked Gwydion.

Slowly, Frederick pulled the sword out and hesitantly handed it to the wizard.

The wizard turned it over in his aged hands several times and said, "This grows stranger by the moment. I am almost certain that I have seen this sword before, although not in the hands of a boy. But it has come to you now. Bear it well. Again, I ask, can you use it?"

"I... I don't know," replied Frederick.

"Well, lad, let us find out. Together, we shall see if these lake people are friendly, and can face an old man with a staff and a boy with a great sword," replied Gwydion, handing it back to him. "Come, my new young friend, we will brave these waters together."

Frederick placed the torch back in its bracket, then went and stood next to Gwydion on the shore. The old man leaned on his staff.

"Let us try speaking with them," he said to Frederick, and then, in a loud voice, said, "Friends of the lake, will you let us pass? We must leave this place, and we bear you no malice."

A single figure approached them in the water and came near to the shore. She was beautiful, Frederick thought, although strange. Her hair was green as seaweed and her eyes were as dark as amber, and although he could not see it well, the lower half of her body was silvery and sleek, and he thought that he could make out a tail. When she spoke, her voice was high pitched, and sounded like running water.

"We are the guardians of the Sword, the Wizard, and the Tree," she said.

"Are you... a mermaid?" asked Frederick.

When she did not answer, he said, "I've been sent by the Lady Danu. Please, she sent me to find help for the Land of the Little People. Please, let us pass."

"You have taken the Sword that cannot be taken, and have awoken him who cannot be woken. You must wait for the fruit of the tree as well, and restore it to the sun," she said.

"What? I don't know what you're talking about. I just need to go and get help and get back as quickly as possible," he said.

Then she began to chant, and the music of her voice was spellbinding.

"When the sword within the tree
Shall once again be taken,
Then wizards once again shall rise,
And kings of old shall waken.
One of royal lineage shall come,
As prophecies once told.
And do great deeds upon the earth,
As 'twas in days of old.
The wounded tree that withered,
Its fruit shall give once more.
And what was burned shall live again,
As 'twas in days of yore."

"Right," said Frederick. "I don't know about any of that. But I can't wait for some dead tree to bear fruit underground. I'm coming through and going for help for my cousin and Mrs. Wigglepox and Lily and Rose and the all the rest of them."

"But you must wait for the tree to bear its fruit," said the strange lady.

Frederick looked back at the tree. The torch bathed it in orange light, and its withered branches still gripped the stone arch. But to his surprise, he saw a single blossom on one branch – a small yellow flower, bright and beautiful.

"Now I am sure that I know this tree!" said Gwydion. "It is nothing less than the tree from the courtyard of the castle in the Land of the Little People. Ever it blossomed with bright yellow blossoms such as this, and its fruit gave life and strength to all who ate it, and those who lingered under its fair branches found all weariness of life leave them and their youth renewed. But the fruits were ever seedless, and the tree was the only one of its kind. The little people named it the First Child of the Waking Tree, and planted it there as a token of friendship to the big people, as they called us. It held a special place in their prophecies. But I greatly fear now that some dread thing has happened in that land. For I am certain now that both this stone arch and this tree once were there. Yet how is it that they have come here? Come, Frederick, we must not go yet. Let us sit and watch."

Together, they returned to the stone slab and sat. To Frederick's amazement, the blossom brightened, then folded in upon itself, and a small green fruit formed and slowly grew. Soon it was larger, and bright yellow, and hung heavily upon the old branch.

"It is ripe," said Gwydion. "And I think that it is your place to pick it."

Frederick walked slowly to the fruit that now hung low before him. The old tree seemed to have shrunken further, as though it had poured the last vestiges of its life into this one fruit. It was shaped rather like a pear, although rounder, and it gave off a sweet fragrance that made his mouth water. He reached up and carefully pulled. The fruit popped from the branch. The tree shivered and seemed to sigh, and then was very still. Frederick wondered if it had died. He cupped the beautiful fruit in his hand and took it to Gwydion.

"What shall I do with it?" he asked.

"Keep it safe for now. I do not know what role this fruit shall play in days to come. But know this, Frederick, that it is not by mere chance that you have come to this cave in this hour, pulled the sword from the tree, breaking what enchantments I cannot say, and now this tree, in its final hour, has given its last fruit to you."

Frederick looked at the fruit in wonder. It fit easily in the palm of his hand and was warm to the touch, and firm. He took a handkerchief from his pocket and carefully wrapped the fruit in it and placed it in an inner pocket of the blue cloak that he still wore.

"I hope that I don't smash it," he said to Gwydion.

"Yes, take care that you do not. Nor eat it! It is given for some purpose that I cannot see," he replied.

They both looked at the ancient tree. It seemed shrunken now, and brittle, as though it were withering before their eyes.

Frederick gazed at it for a few moments, and then said, "I think we ought to go now. Look – the torch is going out."

Indeed, the light of the torch seemed to be fading with the tree, and as it did, Frederick noticed something dimly shining at the tree's base.

He walked over to it, stooped down, and began to clear away the dirt.

There, buried just below the surface, was a shining vial of clear, bright liquid.

He pulled it from the ground and held it up.

"How did this get here?" he said aloud. "This looks exactly like the one that the Lady just gave to Colleen."

He wiped the dirt from it and stuffed it into an inner pocket of his robe, wondering what would become of it.

"Come!" said the mer-lady. "We shall escort you to the surface."

Hesitantly, Frederick and Gwydion stepped into the water. Frederick sheathed his sword, and Gwydion gripped his staff as they waded deeper and deeper, until they took one last breath, and dove beneath the waters toward the dim light below.

Suddenly, Frederick felt strong hands grasp his wrists, and he was pulled downward. Although his vision was blurred, he could make out two mer-men swimming swiftly, pulling him down, down toward the light. Gwydion also had two pulling him, and soon they passed through a cavern entrance. But already his air was running out, and he struggled not to breathe in water.

Out of the cavern entrance, he pushed into a dim light, and under the water, he could hear the voices of the mer-people singing to them as they rose upward toward the surface.

Frederick's lungs were burning now, and his limbs did not want to move. The weight of his clothing and the sword at his side tugged at him, but the strong hands of the mer-men did not let him slip.

When he could take it no more, and his body and mind howled in agony, he burst through the surface and, choking, gasped in great gulps of air.

Then Gwydion was beside him, clinging to his staff.

The mer-men held them for only a moment, and then, in the moonlit night, said, "Farewell, sleeping wizard. At the Lady's bidding, we have guarded you for long ages. Now our task is done, and we shall return to our home in the sea. Farewell!"

Slowly, they slipped beneath the waters of the lake and disappeared into its depths.

Frederick, however, found that his strength was gone, and he began to sink again. He tried to tread water, but his clothes were soaked and weighed him down.

"Come!" said Gwydion. "We must make for the shore. See, it is not far."

But he slipped downward, and kicked frantically, struggling to regain the surface. His head rose up, and he gasped for air. He splashed, raised a hand toward the sky, and sank.

"Frederick!" yelled Gwydion, and stretched out a hand to him.

Frederick vainly tried to reach Gwydion's hand, but he was too far away. He tried to yell, but water filled his lungs, and as he sank, he saw the old man trying to swim down after him. As he lost consciousness, his last memory was of powerful hands gripping his own and a rushing sensation of being pulled upward.

Chapter 8 – The Return of Frederick

The hour was late and the moon was full. Aonghus and Bran sat by the great window of the common room in their hall, gazing out across the lake.

"Where do you suppose that stone of McPherson's really came from?" said Bran.

"Who knows? He said it been passed down in his family for longer than anyone could remember. His ancestors must have come from Ireland long ago – maybe from the area of our farm," said Aonghus. "They must have taken that rock with them when they left."

"Could be. Anyway, it's really good of him to go to Ireland with us to see the farm himself and meet Father," said Bran. "Now we just have to wait until Colleen and Frederick get here."

He gazed out over the lake, watching the full moon's light dance on the rippling waters. Strange shadows danced beneath the waves, giving the illusion of things swimming beneath the surface. Suddenly, he leaned forward and stared hard into the night.

"Aonghus... what... there's someone thrashing about in the lake... come on!"

Bran dashed from the room. Aonghus glanced out the window, then followed his brother, speeding down the stairs after him. Together, they ran out the door and sprinted like deer to the lake's edge and peered out on the water. Moonbeams fell on the rippling surface, revealing a struggling figure. For a moment, a face shone pale in the dim light, then was gone. A hand reached up, and then sank beneath the waves, but did not return. Then, a second figure broke the surface and looked around desperately.

Bran and Aonghus both moved, running into the shallows and then diving in, swimming hard to the place where the remaining figure was now treading water. He appeared to be an old man with a long white beard and hair.

"Help him!" gasped the man.

They dove down together and, twenty feet below, they saw someone sinking – a boy. Down they swam and, far below, Aonghus thought he could see something very strange – shapes – almost human shapes – swimming down, down, and entering a cavern. He looked up and saw that Bran was swimming with the boy to the surface, so he lingered a moment longer.

One of the shapes below turned and looked upward at him. He thought that surely the shadows were playing tricks on him, for there was the face of a woman – a beautiful woman – with long green hair floating all about her fair face and body – but the lower half of her body bore a silvery sheen. She paused before entering the underwater cave with her companions, waved at him, and with a flip of what appeared to be a tail, she vanished.

He blinked and looked again, but she was gone. He looked upward to the surface. Bran was already there and almost to the shore. He swam hard, upward, and saw that the old man was slowly making his way there as well.

"Are you all right, sir?" said Aonghus.

"I will be fine. Help the boy," he said.

Bran was already dragging him onto the grass as Aonghus' feet touched bottom and he hurried to his brother's side.

"He's not breathing," gasped Bran.

Aonghus turned the boy on his side and began to push his legs, bending them up against his chest and then straightening them again and again. Water poured out of his lungs. For a full minute, the boy did not respond, but then began to cough violently. Bran brushed his wet hair out of his face and looked at him and gasped.

"Aonghus, look! It's Frederick Buttersmouth!" he said, astonished.

"What in the world is he doing here – and in the lake?" said Aonghus. "And what were those..."

He looked back at the water, but only ripples now danced in the moonlight.

"Something was in there," said Aonghus. "Something..."

"And what's this?" said Bran, seeing the sword at his side. He unsheathed it and held it up in the moonlight.

Frederick coughed and choked, but managed to sputter out, "... my... sw...ord... found... it.... Aonghus... Colleen... needs... help."

"What do you mean, boy? Spit it out! Where is Colleen? What's wrong?" demanded Aonghus. "Is she in that lake?"

"No... not... there... a moment..." he said, and coughed violently.

"Give him a moment," said Bran.

The old man had now reached the shore, and Aonghus went to him and helped him climb up the bank. He leaned wearily on a wooden staff, breathing heavily.

"Are you all right?" asked Aonghus.

The man waved a hand and nodded, but said nothing.

Frederick continued with his coughing spasm for several minutes, and then finally said, "We think we know where she is, Aonghus! Bran – we think we found your mother!"

Aonghus seized him by the shoulders and his face grew dark and threatening, like none Frederick had ever seen before.

"If this is some sort of cruel joke, so help me..." he began.

"No!" said Frederick. "She is, or we think she is... is... in a different place. I cannot explain it. But I left Colleen there, and she is going after her."

"I thought you said you had found our mother, Frederick. Now where is she and where is Colleen?" said Bran, impatiently.

Suddenly, these two brothers that Frederick had thought of as rather big, jolly oafs looked tall and terrible, their faces livid with expressions of anger and expectancy. In that moment, he had a sense that something *primal,* some uncontrollable power was rising up within them that would burst upon the world and lay it waste to rescue their mother and sister.

"Please, give me a moment to explain. You're going to find it all hard to believe!" he said.

"Try us," said Aonghus through gritted teeth.

But then, Bran's face softened somewhat, and he said, "Aonghus, let's get him inside and into some dry things. He can tell us the whole thing in our room."

Aonghus exhaled and nodded.

"Wait, Gwydion should come too," said Frederick through another coughing fit. "I'll explain."

The four of them made their way back to the brothers' room and, as they went, Gwydion looked all about, observing everything he saw with great wonder. When they finally arrived, Frederick and Gwydion began to dry off.

"Where did you get those clothes?" asked Bran as he saw the blue robe and cloak, and the chain mail shirt and sword at his side, and saw that the old man was wearing an odd robe and carrying a staff.

"And this sword – it's marvelous!" said Aonghus, swinging the blade in the air so that it sang.

"Never mind all that. Tell us your tale now," said Bran. "And you can introduce your friend as well. Please forgive us, sir, but we are most anxious to hear of our mother."

"I am just as anxious to hear his tale," said Gwydion. "Mine can come later."

Frederick paused, looking at the expectant faces of the two huge brothers, and at the old wizard who had taken a seat nearby and was wringing water from his beard and hair.

"It was a mirror in your grandfather's cellar," he said. "It's magic, or maybe some marvelous invention. It turns into a doorway of sorts."

"A doorway to what?" said Bran. "What are you talking about?"

"It's like a doorway to another place – a land or world or something. And there are little..." He was going to say "little people," but realized that this would sound too incredible, so he said, "There are people there. Bad people. And they have captured your mother. Somehow, she went through the mirror to this place, and they took her. And Colleen and I fell through it too and ended up there. We found out your mother was there and we've been looking for her. We think we know where she is, but we need help. I left Colleen there with some decent folk that we met, but she's going on without me. We've got to get back to her and help."

"What's all this about?" demanded Aonghus. "That's rather hard to believe. Why can't you Buttersmouths be straight about things? Now let's have it. Where is Colleen, really?"

His face was stormy, and Frederick was not a little afraid of what might happen next, so he said, "Aonghus, I know I've not been very trustworthy in the past, and you have a right to think I'm lying. But I swear to you that I'm telling the truth. We went through that mirror and ended up in that strange place. You've got to believe me!"

The brothers looked hard into the face of Frederick, and, after considering him, Bran said, "I think he's telling the truth, Aonghus. I don't see any lies in his eyes."

"Neither do I," said Aonghus, softening. "But how could it be?"

"Aonghus, would you have believed what we've been speaking about all evening, even a day ago? Suppose this mirror also came from... from the same lost culture we've been talking about?"

Aonghus thought for a moment and then nodded.

"All right then, Frederick, let's say what you're saying is true. How did you and this fellow get into that lake? And what's all this you're wearing, and what about this sword? And how did you get back here from... there?" asked Aonghus.

"One thing at a time, please," said Frederick.

There was a knock at the door and in came Professor McPherson.

"Aonghus... Bran... and who is this? I saw you dashing down to the lake. Is everything... *Frederick?*"

Professor McPherson's face lit up with surprise and delight at seeing Frederick, but he immediately composed himself and said, "Frederick Buttersmouth, you are soaking wet... and how did you get here so soon? And who is your guest, who is also soaking wet?"

Frederick looked at Aonghus and Bran, and Aonghus said, "It's all right, Frederick. Tell him everything."

Chapter 9 – The Waking of Dvalenn

Colleen stood on the shore, gazing down into the depths of the lake. Frederick had disappeared, and she felt terribly alone. He had been her only connection with her own world, and the thought struck her that she was the only human being in this entire land.

Except for Mother! she thought. *Or perhaps that old hag, Mal.*

That gave her a little courage.

"Colleen," said the Lady. "Frederick has arrived back in your world. Do not be afraid. You will not be alone. Come and walk with me. I would like to show you something."

Colleen walked beside her and marked how tall and beautiful she was. Then she noticed that the Lady Danu cast no shadow, but rather illumined all that was around her. She was like no earthly woman she had ever met, and she seemed to radiate both goodness and a sort of holy fear, as if one might become *undone* by being in the presence of such a power. It was a strange mixture of awe and peace and dread to walk beside her.

When they had reached the rock where Colleen had first seen her, the Lady said, "I would like to show you something of this world, Colleen. Please, stand here on this stone and look into the Lake."

Colleen climbed onto the rock and gazed into the infinite shining blue depths. All at once, a scene appeared, and she could see what she knew was the forest – but it was green and growing, and all sorts of little people danced and played and worked among the trees. There were leprechauns, gnomes, pixies, fairies, sprites, and many others that she did not recognize. Some were knee-high to her, and others so tiny that they were like cherry blossoms floating on the wind. All were happy and productive, and they spread the Forest across their world seed by seed, planting and harvesting and grooming it into one majestic whole where they lived in peace.

"This was the Land of the Little People before the coming of the Witch," Lady Danu said.

FLASH! The scene changed, and a shining silver double door appeared in the wall of a cavern, and out stepped a blue robed elven lord with a golden crown on his head. He greeted the little people that gathered to see this strange sight, and he became their friend. The scene changed again, and there was a great castle being built in the midst of the forest, and seven great gathering houses were raised. Big people came and went, and for a brief time, all was well.

FLASH! The scene changed again, and a terrible battle was taking place. A great giant rained down blows on armies at his feet, lightning struck at the giant, whirlwinds howled, and fiery flames raged. A tall figure on a tower raised a white staff. There was a brilliant flash of blue and red, and it seemed as though the sky itself tore open, swallowing the giant. Then, as the wounded heavens seemed to close and heal, something huge came hurtling through, ripping it open once again, and crashed upon the tower where the man had been.

FLASH! Great heat and flames and lightning crashed together. The forest was blown down for miles and miles in all directions. A great section of the castle was hurled through the air, flung far away, and there was a strange collision of lights and shadows, as if the very fabric of existence were ripping apart. A great earthquake struck, sending a great piece of land hurtling into the sea. A terrible wave followed the concussion, the fallen trees were swept away, and the land was gouged down to bare rock.

FLASH! The Cataclysm passed, and a ruined castle sat in the midst of a broken and flooded land. Nothing stirred.

FLASH! Years sped before Colleen's eyes, and she watched as a desert formed. The castle of the wizards and the Witch herself were nearly forgotten, fading into legend.

FLASH! Dwarves braved the desert, and found the castle, and there settled for many a year in tunnels beneath its broken towers. There, they found a thing of great beauty – a maiden of golden-red hair fallen on the floor of a glass room and sleeping there. But they could not wake her.

FLASH! An island appeared in the sea and, with it, a ship, and on that ship was a pirate. He explored the land, crossed the desert, and found the castle, and there found the bones of the last wizard under a cairn built by the dwarves.

He took an amulet from the wizard's skeletal hand and put it around his own neck. Then, in the castle, he found the beautiful sleeping woman. He kissed her, and the amulet swung from his neck and touched her on the chin. She awoke, but she did not know her own name. But the dwarves were in their tunnels when he came, and when they returned, their sleeping lady was gone, and they searched long for her, but did not find her. At length, they left the castle in despair and returned to their houses in the forest.

FLASH! The pirate and the lady sailed the seas, finding great treasures from ancient times, and plundering the Land of the Little People of many of its gifts. But the maid was lost to the pirate and, in that time, the Witch returned. The pirate fled, leaving the world to the Witch, and lamenting his lost love. In his grief, he returned all but a few of the riches he had looted, and was not seen again.

FLASH! Goblins came, and the Great Sleep crept over the forest. Year by year, fewer and fewer trees blossomed, but fell under the dread spell, as did the little people. They and their children grew smaller and smaller through the years, and their powers diminished as well until they were small indeed.

FLASH! The lake scene changed one last time to a barren and deserted forest. No little people danced under the dead trees. Thick black waters sputtered from polluted springs, and in the midst of it, a lake of black ooze gurgled up hideous fumes that hung like smog over the whole land.

Then suddenly, Colleen found herself staring into the bright blue depths of the clear Lake again.

A tear rolled down Colleen's cheek and fell into the Lake, sending tiny ripples across its surface.

"The final vision that I saw, Lady - is that fated to happen? Will this shining Lake become a stinking black blight on this land?" she asked.

"Few things are fated, Colleen," replied the Lady, "and this is not one of them. All that we do with the time we are given shapes the future of all things. Even the single tear that you have shed and which has fallen into this Lake, Colleen, has become a part of the Waters of Light, and will ever shape them as they flow to all the worlds.

"But if the Darkness has its way, it will not be tears of pity and mercy that are shed and shape the worlds, but tears of fear and grief and woe and bitterness that blacken hearts and minds – a black ocean of impenetrable night that hates the Light. The same darkness that inhabits the world of the goblins will make its way here in full measure, and into all the worlds, unless it is stopped."

"But what can I do?" asked Colleen. "I'm just a little girl."

"You can finish the task you have been given," she replied. "Carry on to the very end. Never stop part way. And don't give in to fear or despondency. Pity the goblins and even the Witch that live in the darkness. They do not know what they are doing, and are only puppets to a greater evil. Keep your mind in her dark pits, and do not despair."

Colleen stared a moment longer into the infinite blue, and then the Lady said to her, "Today, you will rest your body, soul, and mind by my Lake, Colleen, for today it is still free and full of light, and in that, you will find strength and peace."

So she did, talking to scores of little people, listening to their stories, and telling them of the World of Men, and of the legends of their races that were told there. Then night came, and the sky over the lake was brilliant and clear. Colleen found a soft patch of moss and lay down on it, and there, to the song of tiny fairies, she fell into the most restful sleep she had ever known.

The next day, she woke with daisies woven into her hair, and to the voice of the Lady Danu calling her.

"Come, come!" she called. "Someone is here that you will want to meet."

The clear blue of the Lake began to change, and rising from those depths came a bearded figure, striding as if he were climbing some great height. Upward he came until he broke the surface of the water and stepped onto the shore, and yet he was completely dry. He gazed about him, a look of bewilderment and wonder on his face.

"Dvalenn!" cried Colleen, and ran to him and gave him a hug.

Even deeper surprise flooded the dwarf's face, and he held Colleen at arm's length, gazed into her face, and said, "Do I know you? I was dreaming..."

"Oh, I forgot! You've been sleeping all this time. My name is Colleen McGunnegal. Frederick and I and some of the little people brought you here from your brother Doc's house," she replied.

"My brother Doc's house?" asked Dvalenn, looking all about him.

"Yes. Doc... Sindri... He decided to stay and guard the..." Colleen began to say the "Gate of Anastazi," but decided against it.

"... the house," she finished. "He also said he was too old for such a journey. But it seems the Lady has wakened you from your long sleep!"

"Sleep?" said Dvalenn slowly. "Yes, I was asleep, wasn't I? But how long? I had such terrible dreams."

"We're not sure, although Doc thought it was at least twenty years," she replied.

"Twenty years!" said Dvalenn. "But how could that be? What dark magic..."

Then he paused, looking about him again and, for the first time, seemed to see the Lady.

"Lady Danu!" he said, and bowed. "Forgive my lack of greeting! The pits of the Witch make one calloused, and I have endured them for many years. I have forgotten my manners. But how did I... the last thing I remember is lying down by a tree. I was so very tired."

"The Spell overtook you, Dvalenn," said the Lady. "You gave in to its power and fell under the dread Sleep. You might have gone on in its nightmares until you were carried to the Eternal Sleep, had not Colleen and Frederick brought you here. But now, you are free!"

"Free. Am I?" He spoke the word as though it were something alien to him. "Yes, I do feel free! And I hope that I shall never sleep again!"

The dwarf danced a little jig on the shore of the shining Lake, and Colleen laughed with glee to see him so happy.

The Lady laughed as well, and her voice spread like music across the Lake.

"You are free indeed, Dvalenn. But beware, you may still fall under the Spell if you are not careful. You must be ever vigilant and watchful, for those who have been touched once by the Spell may easily be swayed by it again."

"Thank you, Lady," he said, and bowed low. As he did, he spotted a shiny pebble on the shore and picked it up. He gazed at it for a moment and then dropped it again.

"Take care, dear dwarf. You have slept long under the Spell, and your time of departure is near. When that moment comes, you must choose your path – to go to the house of your fathers within the stone, or dwell alone in the dark and lonely places beneath the earth," she said.

For some time, they spoke, with Dvalenn asking many questions about the world and what state it was in, about Colleen and how she had come to the land, and about his brothers, especially Sindri. He listened with particular interest when Colleen told him about the Crystal Cavern that his brother had made, and in which Lily had made a wish by which Badger had become a mighty war horse.

"I wish I could go see this hall of Sindri," said Dvalenn. "What a place it must be!"

They talked on, until at last the Lady Danu sighed and said, "Well, you must prepare to leave us now. I have seen to it that your wagon is well supplied with more than you will need for your journey, although I found that others have supplied you well already. And you may find other help along the way. There are still some who oppose the Witch."

"Must we go so soon, Lady?" asked Dvalenn. "I would stay here and live in the light of this Lake forever by your side."

"Ah, Dvalenn," she said, "time is so short. Colleen and these others have a great task to do, and your path lies with them for a brief time. But whenever you sit by a spring, or see the ocean, or swim in a lake, or walk among the *fountains*," and she emphasized the word *fountains*, "then remember me and the Waters of Light that have awakened you from the dread Sleep. Remember this day, Dvalenn, when the Witch's Spell would try to bring the darkness to you again. And watch over Colleen and the Wigglepox family for as long as you can."

"Yes, Lady, I will remember," he said.

"And to you, Colleen, I give these words – remember the gifts that have been given to you. An ancient bloodline runs pure in you. Be true to what you know is right and do not listen when the goblins and Witch try to persuade you to follow them."

She paused then, looking intently at Colleen and said, "I cannot see your future, Colleen – it is hidden from me. But I think that perhaps your destiny lies among many worlds."

She stooped down to look Colleen in the eyes and placed her hands on her shoulders. Colleen gazed back into the most beautiful face she had ever seen – a face radiant with goodness and peace.

"Do not be afraid, Colleen. Only be true," she said.

"I will try, Lady Danu," she replied, and a tear rolled down her cheek.

Then the Lady led Colleen a little ways away from the others and said in a low voice, "Colleen, Dvalenn's time of departure is near."

"But I thought he was going with us," she said.

The Lady looked sad, bowed her head, and said, "Dvalenn is dying."

"Dying!" whispered Colleen. "But you have just awakened him! And I thought that..." She lowered her voice and continued, "I thought that the Gate was leaking timelessness into this land. How could he be dying?"

"The Spell takes its toll on even the hardiest of folk – even on dwarves," she replied. "He would have fallen into the final sleep out in those woods had you and Frederick not rescued him. Oh, his body may have gone on and on in this never, yet ever-dying world, but even timelessness does not truly preserve a person. Something much deeper must happen for *that* to take place. Now Dvalenn has a chance to make his final choices. It is true that he can choose to stay in this place and go on and on, never wholly healed of the effects of the Spell, but that would not be living as life was intended for him."

"How long does he have, Lady?" asked Colleen, feeling very sad.

"That is not for me to know. I can only see a shadow falling upon him. But I do not know when it will overtake him completely," she replied.

"Does he know?" asked Colleen.

"He feels it within himself, but he fights against it. He is not yet ready to depart. There will be a struggle before his time here with us is over," said the Lady. "But come now, wipe your eyes and let us go back to the others."

Together, they walked back, and the Lady Danu said, "I foresee that we will meet again, friends. Fare you well! Stay to the course you have set and you will reach your destination."

Colleen, Oracle, Dvalenn, and the Wigglepox family walked to the wagon, and Colleen hitched up Badger. She then climbed into the driver's seat and took the reins.

Hundreds of little people gathered to see them off, all of them looking somber. They waved and followed the wagon to the forest's edge and, as they entered the sleepy wood again, Colleen looked back and saw the Lady standing on the waters, her hand raised in farewell.

Chapter 10 – The Southbound Road

Soon they were on the southbound road, and once again, the weight of the Spell was upon them. Colleen felt it at once as they left the protective power of the Lady Danu behind, and Dvalenn seemed to hunch his shoulders under its oppressive presence.

"I had forgotten this weight that I bore," said Dvalenn, "and I am loath to feel it again. I wish we could go back to the Lady."

Colleen did not say anything, but instead began to sing quietly. Immediately, their spirits all lifted, and the heaviness around them lessened. She urged Badger on faster, knowing that the Spell was strongest around the lake, and the sooner they put some distance between them and it, the safer they would be. She sang as they rode on, and Oracle hummed happily along.

When she finally felt it was safe, she stopped singing, looked over at Dvalenn, and said, "Dvalenn, tell me about yourself. Your brother, Doc, said that you had disappeared many years ago. What happened?"

"Ah, that is a long tale. Too long, I think. But I'll tell you what. If you tell me your tale, I'll tell you mine," he replied. "And I'd like to hear the tale of these Wigglepoxes as well, and of this Oracle fellow who says so little."

"Fair enough," said Colleen, and she began to recount the tale of how she and Frederick had accidentally come to the Land of the Little People, and of all that had transpired since then. On she talked for a good hour as they continued down the old south road until finally, she had finished and said, "So here we are, traveling together to free our families from the Witch."

"An amazing tale!" said Dvalenn. "Truly amazing! I wish I could have met this Frederick. He seems a brave lad. But here now, I will begin my tale with telling you why I am even going with you on this journey.

"Of course it was because of the Lady. She took me to a strange place, Colleen. It was a place where I awoke from my long sleep, and she made me face myself."

"That seems to happen a lot here," said Colleen.

"She made me look into my own heart and mind and soul and face exactly what I had become, and then she had me choose. Choose to serve the Witch, or myself, or to return to who I really am – the person I was made to be. She then said that it would be a choice that I would face every day. She said that I needed to go with you because she saw that my time was short, and that with what time I had left, I needed to help you."

He looked down at the ground for a moment, and then continued. "Did Doc tell you about the seven of us? We were all Doctors of Stone, you know, and each of us had a house that we governed here. It was our assignment from the High King of the Dwarves. We were to come here and build and manage these great meeting houses for the other races."

"Yes, Doc mentioned something about that," replied Colleen.

"Well, we did that for a time, until the Witch came. Then there were rumors of trouble in other worlds too – the Lands of the Goblins and Trolls and Giants and Orogim all had strange reports coming from them. Then a terrible thing happened. We heard news that the trolls had invaded the world of the dwarves by surprise and had stolen the Great Stone – the heart of our world, and had taken it through the Gate of Anastazi to their own land. We seven brothers began to prepare armor and weapons in our houses as a defense should the trolls come here. The War of the Trolls was a dreadful one, and many lives were lost.

"But then the war with the Witch and the goblins came, and the Black Orogim were revealed. There was chaos everywhere in all the worlds. Giants turned evil, and there was a civil war among them. Wizards rose and fell, as did and many great heroes.

"In the end, Anastazi the Great shut the gates and was never heard from again. I suppose there were folk from all the races that were trapped in the various worlds, just as we were trapped here. And somehow, the Witch got trapped here too."

He paused for a moment and then continued. "Did Doc tell you about the beautiful sleeping maiden that we found in the castle?"

"Yes, he did mention her, and a pirate," she replied. "And I saw the maiden in the Lake. The Lady showed her to me, although I could not see her face. Our path takes us to that castle, you know."

"Yes. If we make it that far, I will show you where we found her. But at any rate, when the Witch returned (she had been gone for a long time after the War of the Wizards), that's when the Sleep began to creep across the forest.

"Now comes a part of the story that I do not relish telling, but I think you should know. I was out alone one day – a foolish thing to do when there are witches about. But I had begun to grow confident that the Witch would never catch me and that her creeping spell did not affect me, for I was young and strong and was a Doctor of Stone, and wielded power over rock and earth.

"It was then that I met her. Or I suppose it was her in a guise – as the beautiful maiden that we had rescued and who had disappeared with the pirate. I thought our maiden had returned, and I rejoiced and wanted to go and call my brothers. But she forestalled me, and bid me listen to her tale.

"We sat in the cool of the day and she told me of many travels she had made, and said she had met this so-called witch, and that she was not a witch at all, and undeserving of the attacks upon her. In fact, it had been the little people who had begun the war against her, beginning with Lugh himself, and he had wished a terrible plague upon the good goblin peoples that horribly disfigured them. And nearly the whole of the leprechauns had followed after him, and through their evil wishes, were destroying whole worlds. They were even involved in the civil war among the giants.

"She said that the witch was actually a good sorceress from the World of Men, who was trying to stop the madness of the little people, and especially the leprechauns, and the only way she found to do so was to put them all to sleep temporarily – a harmless spell that would stop their evil and not harm them.

"She also said that she had discovered great caverns of gems, and veins of gold that were untouched by the greedy leprechauns, who would have it all for their pots of evil wishing. These would be given to us if we would help her.

"Through her arts, she showed me a vision of these things, and I longed to see such marvelous places with my own eyes, and mine their gems of power. Slowly, I began to believe her lies.

"She bid me not tell my brothers, for she wished to tell them herself, and she gave me a map to follow to where these great mines could be had. This I followed, and indeed, I found the caverns as she had said. And there I met the Witch again. She was cloaked in black, and bid me take all I wanted – for these gems were gems of great power, and would give me power over the wicked little people who strove to corrupt the worlds.

"I took the gems and hoarded them, although this was unlawful. We were forbidden from taking anything from any world without the permission of the king of that land. But the Witch said that there was no king in this land, for the Elders of the Little People had corrupted themselves and abdicated their authority.

"The more I mined, the more I felt my power grow, but in truth, the more I was deceived. Soon, I was living only for the gems, and when I had mined all of them, I sought for others. Long I dug and gained more and more for myself, always encouraged on by the Witch.

"When the gems and gold and silver were gone from those mines, I took to gathering lesser stones, for my hunger for these things was never satisfied.

"When even the lesser stones were all hoarded, I hoarded yet more. Every stone I desired, and I fell to the place where I even gathered worthless pebbles if nothing more could be had.

"At long last, I fell into the black dust of my mines and, seeing the emptiness around me, I wept, for I hungered for yet more, but there was no more. My mines were played out, and I was left with nothing. I returned to my vast treasuries, and lo, they were empty, for the Witch and her goblins had stolen away my long years of labor.

"Then the goblins came and took me to the pits, and there I slaved in their mines for many years. I went mad there, and even considered consuming their filthy ooze, so great was my desire for… for anything! When finally I came to my senses, I said to myself, 'My brothers live in good houses, and here I sit in the dust. I will escape and go home.'

"So, on a moonless night, I used the last vestige of my rock craft and slipped away. I hid among the cargo of a ship, and eluded the goblins in the terrible crossing of the sea, then slipped ashore at night. I crossed the desert – how, I cannot remember – then came through the Great Hills and returned to the forest that I had left so long ago.

"But I found the Spell had grown strong, for the Witch had used all the gems of power that I had dug and made her own power stronger with them.

"I grew weary, but pressed on, but when I came to my old house, it lay in ruins. I ran blindly through the forest, seeking my brothers, but every house was destitute. Only Doc's house was left to return to, but I was too weary, and the Spell pressed upon me. I lay down in a ravine against a tree and fell into the dreadful Sleep. I will not speak of what I dreamed."

"That's where we found you, Dvalenn!" said Colleen.

"And for that I am ever in your debt. I would still be in that torment if it were not for you," he replied. "And in repayment to you and the debt I owe this whole land, I will go with you as far as I may."

The wagon bumped, and they came to a place on the old road where the stones were raised up above the ground and no grass or weeds grew on them.

"Ah! See here!" said Dvalenn, "Would you stop for a moment?"

Colleen stopped Badger, and Dvalenn climbed down from the cart and examined the stones. He ran his fingers over them as if caressing their smooth surface and then said, "Fine, fine stone! Dwarven carved, you know. See how they are neither chipped nor worn even after all these years? These were made from good hard rock and given special blessings. I think we have come to the Northern Spoke – a seventy-mile stretch that leads straight to the castle."

Dvalenn caressed the stones once more and mumbled something about revenge, and then climbed back into the cart.

"Seventy miles!" said Colleen. "That will take days and days!"

Badger snorted, tossed his head, and danced his front hooves on the stones of the road.

"Your horse doesn't think so," said Dvalenn.

Colleen laughed and said, "Yes, I think Badger would run a hundred miles if we let him. But we would bounce right out of this cart, I think. And we need to stop and rest and eat and such. But perhaps we could give him a little rein. This road seems smooth enough, and the way seems straight through the trees."

Colleen slackened the reins and said, "Hold on, everyone. Let's go, boy!"

Badger neighed and shot forward like a bolt. The Wigglepoxes and Oracle, who were sitting in the back of the wagon, went tumbling into the hay. The leprechaun girls laughed, and Mrs. Wigglepox gave a little shriek. Dvalenn held on to the seat, and Colleen's hair flew in the wind like a golden flame.

She had never felt such power in a horse before as Badger ran faster and faster, his great head poised as if he were in a great race.

"Whoa, boy! Slow down!" she called, laughing, and the great horse reluctantly slowed to a trot.

"I wonder how your horse might do in a race?" said Dvalenn. "Seems to me, my brother, Sindri, had a horse like him once. Big thing, if I remember right, and the same color. But that was years ago, and I can't recall his name now."

They moved southward, speaking now and then about the World of Men and Dwarves and of the Little People, and Colleen was amazed at how alike and yet how different they all were.

It was not long before they came to a region where the land began to rise and fall, and the road had been cut through the hills. Dvalenn remarked on the skill with which the Dwarves had carved this region and had mined the hills as they built the road and given the riches they found to the little people in the area.

They steadily climbed upward until ahead they could see that they were coming to a great hill, and the road passed directly through a tunnel that had been carved in its side.

"This is the Tunnel of Agap the Gnome," said Dvalenn. "He was in charge of its construction. It runs for a half mile through this hill – the Great Hill of the Great Hills! We dwarves aided in its construction. You will love the masterful work that was done on it! And the stone through this region was rare indeed!"

But as they approached, they could see that they would not be able to pass through, for the entrance, although at least twenty feet high, was completely blocked by huge boulders that had been rolled in front of it.

"Goblin work!" spat Dvalenn. "They hated Agap, you know, because he thwarted them so many times. He had a power over the Spell when it came. I wonder whatever happened to him, poor thing. I do hope he escaped the Witch somehow."

They rode up to the great boulders and stopped. Dvalenn got out of the cart and walked over to them, examining them carefully.

"We might go around, through the woods," commented Colleen.

"No, I think if we can go through here, we should," he replied, and began touching the boulders, which were twice his own height.

"Ah, not bad stone," he said. "I could carve these into good building blocks."

Then he began looking about and said, "And this hill – ah, the Great Hill! Good solid stone too! See, even the pebbles by the roadside shine. Good quartz!" He stooped down, picked up a handful, examined them, and slipped them into his pocket.

"Dvalenn," said Colleen. "Oughtn't we to be doing something about his blockade if we are going to go through this tunnel?"

"What's that? Oh! Yes. Well, let me see," he replied.

Once again, he put his hands on the boulders and mumbled, "Good stone. Did you happen to bring a hammer and chisel?"

"Whatever for, Dvalenn?" asked Colleen.

"Well, just to try this stone a bit. It might be worth saving – for later, of course," he replied.

"Dvalenn!" said Colleen, a bit exasperated. "We need to move on."

Oracle had climbed into the front and was watching the dwarf carefully. He squinted his eyes and said, "Creepicouns."

Then Colleen saw them – dark little faces peeping out from the shadows around the boulders, staring at Dvalenn as he caressed the rock.

"Dvalenn! Get away from there! Come here to the wagon!" she cried, and began to back the wagon away from the tunnel entrance.

She glanced to the right and left to see which way she could take them, and decided that the right seemed more open.

Mrs. Wigglepox, who was peeping over the seat and looking at the tunnel, said, "They're cluricauns! I think they're trying to cast the Spell on Dvalenn again! The more they distract him toward what he loves the most in this world, the more it will take hold!"

Dvalenn was now trying to wedge himself through the boulders to get into the tunnel.

"Dvalenn! No! You've got to snap out of it!" shouted Colleen.

Oracle peeked over the wagon's edge, waved his cane in the air, and ducked down again. All at once, there was a trembling in the ground. Badger reared, and the boulders began to shake and move. The little faces in the dark shadows vanished with a screech and Dvalenn seemed to come to himself. But the ground continued to shake, and the boulders began to roll toward the cart and down the slope. Dvalenn dodged out of the way and barely escaped being crushed.

Colleen pulled on the right rein and yelled, "Move, Badger, move!"

The horse pulled hard, dragging the wagon off the road. The boulders bounded by, just barely missing them.

Then Colleen saw it. It was a gigantic thing – a spirit that was somehow *in* the hill – or was it the hill itself? How she saw it, she did not know, but it was there, and was waking, stretching as it were, and shaking the ground as it rose from its slumber.

It looked out of the hill at her for a moment, seemed to smile, then gazed about. A frown crossed its earthy face, and a deep moan echoed from within the tunnel, like a deep pipe organ playing its lowest note. The sound resonated deep in the ground, and spread out, echoing through the forest. For a moment, the trees around them stirred, but as the sound died, they slipped back into their slumber.

But four black-clad cluricauns that had been hiding among the boulders flew frantically about for a moment, hating the light of the sun that now shone upon them. Filled with dread, they sped away into the shadows of the woods. The tunnel seemed to sigh, and it seemed to Colleen that the guardian lay back down again and then vanished.

The rumbling ground grew still, and Colleen exclaimed, "Did you see that?"

"See what, dear?" asked Mrs. Wigglepox.

"I thought I saw something, or someone – the spirit of the hill, I suppose. I think it woke up for a moment, and then went back to sleep."

Dvalenn came walking back to the cart, his head down. "Forgive me, Colleen. I did not know what I was doing. I... I got distracted."

Colleen could see that the pockets of his trousers were quite stuffed with rocks and pebbles.

"And I had forgotten about the Guardian of the Tunnel of Agap. It once watched over all travelers who came this way. But it seems mostly asleep now. Even it seems to have fallen under the Spell," he said.

"But it woke for a moment," said Colleen. "This world is full of all sorts of creatures that one can't see outright, isn't it? That's what I saw back at the Lake – trees and rocks and streams and hills, all the homes of beings just beyond our sight."

"Oh, yes," said Dvalenn. "Isn't it that way in your world?"

"I don't know about that," she replied. "I suppose some people might think so. At least I've heard stories like that. But if they are there, I've never seen them."

"Well, at any rate, I think the tunnel is safe now. It looks as though the cluricauns have fled. Shall we give it a try?" asked Dvalenn.

"All right," said Colleen, "but it looks very dark."

"Ah, it is true that from the outside, the Tunnel of Agap can seem dark and fearful. But once you enter into it fully, it is quite bright and cheery. You'll see," he replied.

"Dvalenn," said Colleen, "shouldn't you empty your pockets of all those stones?"

Dvalenn looked down and blushed. "Oh, well, one never knows when a good stone will be needed. Might as well hang onto them for now."

Colleen looked at him doubtfully, but said nothing. Oracle shook his head sadly and returned to the back of the wagon with the Wigglepox family.

She maneuvered the wagon back on the road and they set off, passing into the wide mouth of the dark tunnel. For a moment, they were shrouded in darkness, as though the light from outside could not penetrate into this place. But an instant later, they could see a steady glow growing before them. It was warm and inviting, and with every step that they took, it grew in both warmth and intensity.

The interior of the tunnel was perfectly round, and ornately carved with many pictures of all the races, all of them happy and joyful – friends sitting under trees, lovers walking hand in hand, families dining together, fathers holding their children, and many other scenes of love and friendship. Here again was a place where Colleen felt the power of the Spell lifting the further in they went.

"Prepare yourself, Colleen," said Dvalenn. "This tunnel has a special power about it that makes you see yourself as you really are."

Indeed, as they slowly made their way along, to Colleen's mind came many memories of her still young life – her mother and father, her brothers and sisters, and friends. Mostly fond memories, but also tinged with sad memories of how she had hurt someone's feelings or spoken or thought badly of someone. These memories, good and bad, seemed to rise sharply in her mind, and she decided that should she see the people she had hurt in any way again, she would make it right. But the feelings and thoughts of deep fondness and love for her family and the people of her community swept in like a wave, and she thought to herself, *That's how one ought to feel and think about everyone.*

She looked over at the Wigglepox family and saw that each of them was deep in thought, and that a tiny tear trickled down Mrs. Wigglepox's cheek.

Dvalenn also was deep in thought, a pained expression on his bearded face. He too was remembering his past, and somehow deeply examining himself.

What memories, she thought, *would a dwarf who had lived for thousands of years have to face going through this magical tunnel?*

His hand slipped into his pocket, and he seemed to be grasping the stones stuffed in there.

"This is beautiful," Colleen said after some minutes. "Did you and your brothers carve the whole thing – every scene, I mean?"

Dvalenn seemed to shake himself and said, "What's that? Oh! Yes. Well, Agap directed the whole thing and considered this tunnel one of his grandest achievements. It was the work of many, many years. He wished to make it a reminder to everyone who passed this way just what was most important in life."

"And what is that?" asked Colleen.

"I suppose each of us has to decide that," replied Dvalenn as he fingered the stones in his pocket.

They rode on in silence, although Colleen wondered why the dwarf seemed so glum in such a beautiful place.

They emerged on the other side to see that the land and the road steadily fell toward a great valley below, and far, far to the south at the horizon was a thin line of tan.

"Behold, the southernmost stretch of the Sleepy Wood. Beyond the edge of these hills lie the Burning Sands," said Dvalenn.

"Why don't we rest here and have a bite to eat," suggested Colleen.

"A grand idea," said Mrs. Wigglepox.

They untied Badger and let him wander a bit, then looked in the wagon to see what they could make a meal of.

"Mushrooms!" declared Dvalenn with glee. "I've not eaten mushrooms in... in... I can't even remember how long it's been!"

"From your brother Doc's own stores," said Colleen.

Dvalenn picked one from the sack and popped it in his mouth, savoring its exquisite flavor.

"And we shall have some of Cian's roots," said Mrs. Wigglepox.

After she had laid these out for them, she saw another sack that the Lady Danu must have given them. It was a dark red sack, and when she opened it, she found three sacks, each filled with water, and a bag of assorted nuts. There was also a note written on a roll of pure white parchment in a delicate hand that read, *"This water is from my own spring, and has my blessing. Even a little will quench great thirst."*

So they sat together at the mouth of the Tunnel of Agap and ate a small meal and sipped some of Doc's draft, having decided to save the water from the Lady for the trip through the desert.

As they were preparing to leave, Badger, who had been grazing in a small patch of grass, whinnied and bolted directly toward Colleen, charging full speed.

"Badger? Badger, stop!" she yelled, but the horse charged forward, the whites of his eyes showing, his golden hooves pounding the ground furiously.

"Badger, what's wrong?" she yelled again.

Colleen and Dvalenn and the Wigglepox family ducked down as the great horse thundered right up to them, and then, with a great leap, jumped right over their heads and landed behind them.

They spun around just in time to see Badger slam into a goblin that had been sneaking up behind Colleen. It had a club in its hand, and it now screamed and went rolling backward into Agap's Tunnel.

It vanished behind the veil of darkness that cloaked the tunnel's interior, but inside they heard the goblin gasp, hiss, and then begin to shout, "No... no! It's not my fault! He did it, not me! No, *NO!*"

Its screams faded into silence as it ran blindly into the depths of the tunnel.

"What happened?" asked Colleen, shaken.

"Goblins don't like the Tunnel of Agap. They call it the Tunnel of Judgment. It makes them see just what they really are," replied Dvalenn. "Good thing Badger was keeping watch."

"Yes!" said Colleen, and she got up and soothed Badger, who was pacing back and forth in front of the tunnel, snorting and blowing.

"Good boy," she said to him, and hugged his neck.

"We had better post a watch from now on," said Dvalenn. "It's too easy to forget that this land is controlled by the goblins and their Witch. I suspect that the great bellow that the hill spirit gave attracted this goblin's attention. There might be more on their way, so we'd best be off, and quick."

While the others packed up, Colleen hitched up Badger, and they started down the slope toward the valley. But they were on their way for only a moment when Rose screamed.

Colleen turned, only to see dark shadows leaping through the woods on either side of the road and drawing closer.

"He-ya!" yelled Colleen and whipped the reins. "Run, Badger!"

Badger ran, but even as he did, a black shape leaped from the trees and grabbed hold of the rear of the wagon. Its feet flew off the ground as Badger ran faster and faster, and it held on for dear life.

Its hood flew back, revealing a hideous gray-green face with a long pointed nose. Yellow and brown jagged teeth filled its mouth, and it pulled itself forward and came face to face with little Rose, bearing its teeth in wicked grin.

Colleen glanced over her shoulder just in time to see Mrs. Wigglepox jump in the air, allowing the wind to carry her to the back of the wagon. She jumped again and landed square on the nose of the goblin, and with courage that amazed Colleen, she kicked the creature right in its great yellow eye with her pointed green shoe.

The goblin let go of the cart and grabbed its pained eye, and both it and Mrs. Wigglepox went tumbling backward off the wagon.

"Mother!" screamed Rose.

Colleen knew instantly what she had to do. She reined in Badger and brought them to a halt, just in time to see Mrs. Wigglepox run from the road and into the woods. The little woman dodged left, then right, but the enraged goblin was right on her heels, and now several of the other goblins had caught up and surrounded her. Both Lily and Rose screamed and began to cry.

Colleen grabbed her walking stick and leaped down from the wagon. She hit the pins that held Badger to the cart, releasing him, jumped up into the saddle, wheeled him around, and charged back at the pack of goblins, yelling like a banshee.

The goblins spun about to face her, and Mrs. Wigglepox dashed behind a tree and vanished beneath the leaves.

Colleen drove through the goblins, howling and swinging her staff, sending them running. But there were seven of them now, and although Badger was frightening as he neighed and stamped and reared, the goblins were sly, and circled around her and behind trees where the great horse could not kick them. Soon they were all around her, laughing their hideous laughs, and began to tighten their circle. Badger pranced in place, ready to fight, but Colleen was growing increasingly scared. She knew that they would take her eventually, but she had to give the others time to escape.

"Dvalenn!" she shouted. "Get the others and run for it!"

Dvalenn did not answer, but instead came leaping from behind a tree, and with a sound *crack*, knocked one of the goblins in the head with a hefty stick. Down the goblin went, but instantly two of them were on top of him. One of them got it in the ribs, but the other tackled him and the two went sprawling.

One of the other goblins took advantage of the distraction and, jumping onto Badger's back, grabbed Colleen, and sent her tumbling to the ground.

She screamed and kicked and managed to get to her feet. She swung her staff about her madly and called "Badger!"

But three of the goblins had seized his reins and were tying him to a tree. He neighed and kicked and pulled and thrashed his great head, but the bridle held fast.

Now four goblins circled about her, and she glanced to one side and saw Dvalenn lying unconscious on the ground, although three goblins lay there groaning as well.

Then she remembered the words of the Lady Danu. Reaching out with something beyond mere thought, she sensed the slumbering beings all around her – in the trees, and the giant in the hill. She reached out to them and felt their latent power – felt it begin to flow into her.

There was a sudden whipping of wind in the trees, and the deep moan of the tunnel, but in that moment, the goblins jumped. She was hit from behind, and the last thing she saw as she fell was the little form of Mrs. Wigglepox tugging desperately on the tied reins of Badger.

Chapter 11 – The Professor, the Wizard and the Sword

Frederick took a deep breath to steady himself. Would anyone believe him? *Could* anyone in their right mind believe what he was about to say? The eyes of Professor McPherson, Aonghus, and Bran were fixed on him as he began to tell his tale.

"First, let me introduce my... friend here," he said. "This is Gwydion. He is... well, I suppose he comes into my tale last of all."

Gwydion smiled and said, "Indeed, only in the last hour. But please, tell your tale from the beginning."

"Well, it all started when Colleen and I snuck away from the ship just before it sailed," he began.

Professor McPherson held up a hand and said, "Wait, Frederick. The other McGunnegals should hear this too if it involves Colleen. Is she here or still back in Ireland?"

Frederick swallowed hard and said, "Neither."

The professor raised an eyebrow and said, "Then where is she?"

He gulped again and said, "She's ... in a different land."

McPherson looked hard at him and said, "Do you mean she boarded the wrong ship and sailed, perhaps, to France or Spain?"

"No, sir," replied Frederick. "We didn't board a ship at all." He looked about uncomfortably and said, "We fell through a mirror into a different land... a whole different world."

The professor looked questioningly at Aonghus and Bran and then said, "Frederick..."

But then he paused and saw the sword that was propped against the wall. He walked quickly over to it, picked it up, and examined its blade and hilt.

"Frederick, where did you get this?" he said.

"It was in a cave under the lake out there. It was guarded by..." he began, but was cut off by Professor McPherson.

"Hush!" he said, and went to the door, opened it a crack, and peered out.

He then looked at Gwydion for a moment, hesitating.

"I trust him," said Frederick. "He was there when I found the sword."

McPherson raised his eyebrows in surprise.

"Under the lake?" he said.

Frederick nodded.

"It is true," said Gwydion.

Professor McPherson paused, thinking, then took the sword, wrapped it in a blanket from the bed, and said, "All of you, come with me, quietly."

The five of them silently left the room, and Professor McPherson led them through the Common Room, down the stairs, and back across the yard to his office. He shut the door behind them and locked it.

He then shut his windows and pulled the curtains shut. Only the light of one lamp illuminated the room, giving it a rather eerie appearance with all the strange objects that lined the wall, and the many books.

Gwydion looked about the room with great interest. But the professor then sat down at his desk, unrolled the sword, and laid it out before him. "Please sit down," he said, indicating two seats in front of his desk and several to one side. "Now, Frederick, begin again. Where did you get this sword? No, actually, begin at the beginning, from the time you left the ship. Do not leave out any details," he said.

Frederick told the whole tale, beginning with their leaving the ship, falling through the mirror, of the Little People, the goblins, of finding Dvalenn, and meeting Doc, and seeing the Gate of Anastazi the Great, of the pixies, of Mal and Cian, and fighting the goblin in Mal's cave. He told them that he had nearly become a goblin, but had been healed, and showed them the two scars on his arm. Then he told of the cluricauns, and then of the Lady Danu and how incredible she was, and how she was the one who had sent him back to bring help.

They all listened with great interest, at times looking at one another with questioning eyes, and now and then they stopped him, asking questions or having him repeat what he had said, so extraordinary was his tale.

"And then I was in that cave, and *that* is where I found Gwydion lying on a slab of stone, and there was this sword and those mer-people, and I was nearly drowned, and would have been if it hadn't been for Aonghus and Bran here. And oh, there was the strangest tree..."

Suddenly, he remembered the fruit in his cloak pocket, and he carefully pulled it out, unwrapped it, and examined it.

"It blossomed and grew this fruit," he said.

It was unharmed by the whole experience, and he placed it carefully on the professor's desk, allowing them all to see its bright form and smell its fragrance.

"Then the tree seemed to die. We left the cave, helped by the mer-people, and that's when Aonghus and Bran found us floundering about in the lake," he said.

The whole story had lasted for nearly two hours. All the while, the professor had listened intently, occasionally fingering the sword. Then he stared at Frederick for a long time.

"It's all true, Professor," said Frederick flatly. "Whether you believe it or not, it's all true."

He was silent again for a long time, staring at the sword and thinking.

At last, he hesitantly spoke and said, "That is an incredible story, Frederick. No one in their right mind would ever believe you."

A look of distress washed across Frederick's face, and he began to protest, but the professor held up a hand.

"But perhaps I am not in my right mind," he said.

"You believe me then?" asked Frederick, looking hopeful.

The professor smiled a half smile and then continued. "I have something to tell you. It is a secret I would only share with my own son."

He glanced at the others, and noticed that Gwydion was watching him, his deep eyes intent under his bushy eyebrows.

"Something important is happening here, my friends. This meeting tonight is no mere chance, I think," said McPherson.

He paused, then continued, "And here is Gwydion – I know the name! It is an ancient name. But if it is true, how is it that you came to be in this cavern under the lake?"

"My own tale is long," replied Gwydion, "and I do not yet know many things. As to how I came to be in the cave, or how long I was there, I do not know. The mer-people hinted that it had been long ages, although how that could be, I cannot say. What is the year?"

"It is the year of our Lord, 1846," replied the professor.

"More mysteries," said Gwydion. "I do not understand what that year means. My last recollection was that it was the nine hundred and eighty second year after the opening of the Gates."

"The opening of what gates?" asked Aonghus.

"The Gates of Anastazi the Great, of course," said Gwydion.

They stared at him blankly, and he realized that they did not know what he was speaking of. Then Frederick spoke.

"That's the gate that I told you about, under Sindri the Dwarf's house," he said.

"Yes, and it was not there when I was last in that land," replied the wizard.

"Wait, wait," said the professor. "There are too many stories to tell here."

He smiled at them then and said, "Let me show you just one thing – something that will likely keep you awake and thinking."

He then placed the white brick that he had shown them before on the table and one of their own stones that they had left with him beside it, and then laid the sword beside these two.

There, on all three, were the same strange letters and runes and symbols of the language.

"What does it mean, Professor?" asked Bran.

"Obviously, all three come from the same culture. The same people who built on your farm are the same people who made this sword, and some time, long ago, my ancestors knew those people and passed this stone down through the generations. The family stories that surround it are quite incredible as well."

Frederick was staring down at the sword, a look of wonder on his face.

"What's wrong, Frederick?" asked the professor.

"Gwydion, was there a wizard's castle in the World of Men?" asked Frederick.

"Why, yes, there was. But it was destroyed not long ago... Or was it very long ago?" said Gwydion thoughtfully.

Frederick's mind whirled. Could it be that the wizard's castle in the World of Men had been built... on the McGunnegal farm?

But before he could express the thought, Gwydion spoke.

"Professor, tell me, where did this white brick come from? What do your family stories say?"

Professor McPherson looked at each of them for a long moment and then said, "It came on the last ship... the last ship from Atlantis."

Chapter 12 – Captured!

Colleen woke with a headache. She was lying in the wagon next to Dvalenn, and she found that her hands and feet were tied, and she had a gag tied over her mouth. Dvalenn was likewise bound, and he was staring at her with a concerned look. Oracle was nowhere to be seen, nor were the Wigglepoxes.

The wagon was bumping along at a slow pace, and Colleen could hear harsh goblin voices arguing.

"It's your turn to pull it, Grip. I'm tired," said one voice.

"Shut up and do the deed, Bof," said another, who must have been Grip.

"Don't tell me to shut up!" yelled Bof.

"Both of you shut up, or I'll have your tongues. Now all four of you pull!" said another.

Colleen surmised that there were four goblins pulling the wagon, and she wondered what had happened to Badger. Had Mrs. Wigglepox freed him in time? She hoped that they had not harmed him!

And what about Lily and Rose and Oracle? She lifted her head and glanced about the wagon but could not see much. At least the two leprechaun children were nowhere in sight.

The goblins went on arguing with one another, but the wagon slowly rolled on.

All at once, there was a tiny whisper into her ear. It was Lily. "Colleen!" she said. "I'm hiding under the straw by your head, so don't roll over. I think Mother got Badger loose. She climbed up his harness and sat between his ears and... Oh, what a sight! Oracle said to hide, so we did, but not before we saw Badger kick two or three of the goblins real good. They didn't get back up after that, but then the others pulled out swords, and Mother made Badger run into the Tunnel of Agap, where they wouldn't follow. You can bet she went for help, or is following from a distance. We're not sure what happened to Oracle. I don't think we should untie you just yet. Wait until tonight and then we'll get you loose. Don't nod, just remember that we'll get you loose first chance we get."

They rolled on and on, and the goblins grumbled on and on as well, occasionally having yelling matches. Once a fight broke out over who was going to walk in the shade, and Grip, the head goblin, had to break it up.

"Next time there's any of that, I'll rip your cloak off and tie you up in the sun!" he said, and after that, the arguments settled down a bit.

The sun began to set and the stars came out, and the goblins quickened their pace. Long into the night, they rolled on until the goblins began to grumble again about needing a break, and after a few more minutes, Grip reluctantly agreed.

"We stop here for four hours rest, no more!" he growled. "Make a camp!"

Colleen was desperately thirsty now, and as the wagon came to a stop, she tried to peer around to see if their packs had been discarded. Fortunately, they had not, but she did not dare to ask for anything.

But as if in response to her thoughts, Grip looked over the edge of the wagon and snarled.

"Make sure the prisoners are still tied securely," he yelled. "And give 'em a drink. They'll need it in the desert."

The goblins all laughed their hideous laughs.

"What shall we give 'em? Maybe some gribic?" asked another.

Again, they all roared with laughter, and Grip said, "They couldn't take it. Just give 'em a mouthful of whatever they brought."

One of the goblins began to rummage through their packs and found the water sacks that the Lady Danu had given to them. He squeezed one of them once and jumped into the wagon. He then went to Dvalenn, yanked the gag from his mouth, and splashed it on his face. Dvalenn sputtered, and the goblin laughed, then poured more of it into his mouth.

Dvalenn swallowed the water and sighed. The goblin then kicked him hard and turned to Colleen. She stared up at the creature with scared eyes, thinking that it would also deal her a blow. A tear rolled down her cheek.

To her utmost surprise, the goblin knelt down, gently removed her gag, lifted her head, and gave her a drink. She drank long, and the goblin allowed her to drink her fill. It then loosened her gag and replaced it, and likewise checked her bound hands and feet, made them more comfortable for her, and turned to go. It paused for a moment as if thinking, then pulled back its dark hood and looked at her.

"Nous!" she muttered through her gag, which was really no gag at all, now that the goblin had loosened it.

The goblin glanced up to be sure the others were not watching, put a finger to its lips, turned to Dvalenn, kicked him again, and jammed his gag back in place. It then put the water sack back, hissed at Dvalenn, looked at Colleen, then leaped from the wagon and went back to setting up camp with the other goblins.

Colleen shut her eyes and breathed a sigh of relief, hardly daring to believe what had just happened. Then she lifted her head and looked around, but could not see or hear any goblins close by. Turning slightly, she looked at Dvalenn. His right eye was swollen shut, and there was dried blood on his forehead.

"Are you all right?" she whispered through her gag.

The dwarf grunted and nodded.

"Dvalenn, don't worry. We still have a chance. Lily and Rose are with us and are free, and Mrs. Wigglepox has Badger. I'm sure she went for help. But I am worried about Oracle. I don't see him in the wagon," she whispered. "But did you see what that goblin did?"

Dvalenn rolled his one visible eye and grunted again.

Colleen lay back just in time, for she heard the voice of Nous say, "What ya wanna do with these ones for the night? I'm not gonna watch 'em."

Grip hissed, then barked, "You'll do what you're told, especially after deserting your own troop! You'll be in for it with the Witch when we get back, unless you shut up and follow orders."

"I told ya I never left 'em," lied Nous. "They lefted me. Musta thought I was dead."

"Well, you can just guard the prisoners now and be happy about it," said Grip.

Nous hissed, but Grip said, "And give me any trouble and *we* just might leave you for dead too, if you get my drift."

The other goblins laughed at this and Nous slunk back to the wagon, climbed up, and sat hunched on the seat and began to talk to himself.

"They left me for dead," he hissed under his breath, "but this one didn't." And he looked down at Colleen. "But *that* one," he said, raising a bony finger and pointing it at Dvalenn, "*that* one gave me a whack in the side. Haaa, now it's my turn to pay it back!"

He made a threatening gesture toward Dvalenn, then turned his back on him and went on mumbling something that Colleen could not make out.

"Now, this big leprechaun!" And he hissed more loudly. "That one will fetch a pretty price!"

Nous grew silent for a time, and Colleen could make out bits of the conversations that the other goblins were having.

"What about this rebellion down in the pits?" asked one of them.

"No such thing," said another. "The King and the Witch wouldn't allow it."

"I hear that there's big trouble," said a third. "They say there's a Sorceress that's risen up and fights against the Witch."

"Bosh!" said another that Colleen recognized as Grip. "No one's ever contended against the Witch and survived. Even those evil Wizards way back. They're all dead, and she's still here."

"But there have been losses, they say," said another. "Escapes."

"Where would they escape to?" said another voice. "They're all in the middle of the sea."

"Nobody knows," said the other. "But they've been disappearing all the same."

The conversation went on, shifting from news of this rebellion to stories of finding and capturing little people.

After some time, the noise of the goblins grew silent, and Nous climbed down from the bench, quietly rummaged around in the food sack, and pulled out some of Doc's mushrooms and a sack of water.

He then went to Colleen, bent low next to her ear, and said, "The not-Pwca-killer must promise not to speak or try to escape."

Nous' body and breath stank and nearly made her retch, but Colleen nodded her head. He then pulled down her gag and untied her hands. He then pulled back his hood, sniffed the mushrooms, wrinkled his nose, and handed them to her, along with the water. She gratefully took the food and water, took a bite, and then pointed to Dvalenn.

Nous hissed and whispered, "Not that one!"

Colleen leaned closer to the goblin and whispered, "Please, Nous, he was only trying to protect me. Please let me give him something."

Nous thought about this for a moment, a strange expression on his face as if he were trying to figure something out.

"*Quick!*" he hissed at her, then climbed back to the seat and turned his back, watching the camp.

"Thank you, Nous," she whispered, then scooted over to Dvalenn and untied his gag.

He was already awake and had been watching, but she held a finger to her lips, fed him a few mushrooms, and gave him more water. She then ate one more herself and took a drink.

Then re-tying Dvalenn's gag much looser than it had been, she shifted back to her own place. She remembered the crystal jar of water that the Lady had given her. She checked all of her pockets. It was missing.

"Oh no," she whispered.

She knew there was nothing she could do at the moment, so she tugged on Nous' black cloak. He hissed and turned. "Thank you, Nous," she whispered. "You are a friend."

A confused expression crossed his face for a moment, replaced by the harsh one that was generally there.

"Nous, what about the big leprechaun?" she said quietly. "Where is he?"

Nous grinned wickedly and nodded toward the front of the wagon. Colleen peeked over the edge and saw, to her horror, that Oracle was tied, hands and feet, to one of the wagon poles. He hung there limply, like some animal caught in a hunt, being carried home like a trophy.

"Nous!" she said, "You've got to let him loose! Put him back here with us. What if he dies, hanging there like that? I don't guess the Witch would be happy about that, would she?"

Nous pursed his gray lips and spat over the edge of the wagon. "Let it die," he said. "It's lost its mind anyway."

He climbed down into the wagon, retied Colleen's hands, although not too tightly, and put her gag loosely back in place. He then climbed back up on the wagon seat, curled up, and seemed to fall asleep.

Colleen shut her eyes, worrying about Oracle, worrying about where they were being taken, but also wondering about the goblins. Nous had actually been *kind* to her, in a way, although not to the others. What did that mean?

She woke some hours later to noisy shouts of goblin voices as they broke camp, and Grip stalked about, making sure all was in order.

"Check their bindings, Nous," he croaked.

Nous crawled down into the wagon and tugged on their ropes. Seeming satisfied, he glanced once at Colleen, hissed at Dvalenn, and climbed down from the wagon. There was a thud and a groan, then a good deal of laughter from the goblin band and Colleen could only imagine that they had done something cruel to Oracle.

It was still dark as they headed off again, with Grip once again sitting on the driver's seat and the four goblins pulling the wagon.

They slowly bumped along for several hours before the goblins began complaining again, and one of them yelled at Grip.

"Why can't those prisoners pull this thing? There they are lying in a soft bed of hay while we work and sweat down here. I say we let them pull it, and we ride up there," it said.

Grip grinned a wicked grin and shouted, "Halt the wagon! Let's see just what these prisoners can do."

The wagon stopped, and Nous was the first one into the wagon. He quickly untied Colleen, and removed her gag, then proceeded to do the same with Dvalenn.

"Out with you two!" he barked and gave Dvalenn a kick.

The dwarf groaned and slowly sat up, rubbing his wrists and feet where his bindings had given him rope burn. With Colleen's help, he slowly stood, wobbled, and then fell back in the hay.

"Up, I said!" shouted Nous, and would have slapped him, but Colleen looked hard at him, and instead, he grabbed Dvalenn by the shirt and hefted him up and over the side of the wagon, dropping him to the ground. The dwarf fell and rolled, and all the goblins laughed. Colleen jumped down after him and helped him to his feet.

"He can't pull the wagon in this condition!" she said to the goblins. "He can hardly stand up!"

They barked and hooted their harsh laughs, and Grip said, "Then perhaps you, little one, would like to pull the wagon yourself?"

Dvalenn struggled to his feet and said, "Never you mind, Colleen. I'm all right."

Then he slowly walked around the wagon and took hold of one of the poles.

Colleen followed him. Now they could clearly see the plight of poor Oracle. He was indeed tied like a pig to a spit, and his eyes were squinted shut as if in pain.

"Please let him go," said Colleen turning to whom she thought must be Grip. "He could help us pull, after all."

The goblins howled and leered again, and all jumped into the wagon.

"Why not?" said Grip. "Go on, then, untie him yourself."

Colleen went over to the leprechaun and began to struggle with the bindings. They were terribly tight, and she could not get the knots undone.

Dvalenn dropped his pole and helped her, and together they managed to free Oracle and lower him to the ground.

He lay there for a moment, breathing heavily, then opened his old eyes.

"We have to pull the wagon, Oracle," whispered Colleen. "Can you walk?"

Oracle slowly sat up, rubbing his legs and arms.

He looked up at Grip seated in the driver's seat and grinned. But there was no mischief or malice in the smile. It was simply a grin.

"He's insane!" cackled Grip. "Now get him up and have at it. Tie a rope around him. He'll be out in front."

One of the goblins tied the ends of a rope to rings on either pole, then threw the middle of the rope at Oracle.

"Pull, slaves!" yelled Grip.

"I'll bet you ten to one they can't even get it started," jeered one goblin.

"Maybe we should beat them with the whip. They'd pull then!" hissed another.

"Pull!" yelled Grip. "Pull like your life depends on it – because it does!"

Colleen and Dvalenn pulled on the wagon poles, but the wagon only rocked a little, and did not move. Oracle, weak as he was, added nothing to their effort, and without his cane, he even had trouble walking.

"Pull, I said!" screamed Grip.

Colleen looked over at Dvalenn, and he looked back at her with his one visible eye.

"I'm not a dwarf for nothing," he whispered through the laughter of the goblins. "And dwarves made this road. Let's see what we can do with it."

He began to sing a dwarvish song – a song of rock and labor and pulling and pushing of stone. It was a simple tune, and Colleen began to hum along, her sweet voice adding to his old dwarvish one.

Oracle looked back at the dwarf and nodded his approval and strained forward against his ropes.

Dvalenn sang, Colleen hummed, and they all pulled, and somehow the wagon slowly began to move. Oracle reached into his cloak for a moment, shut his eyes, and Colleen thought that for a moment there was a flash, like the briefest rainbow had come and gone. A moment later, a breeze began to blow. Leaves swirled in the air in front of them, and the forest debris was blown from their path.

The goblins took no notice of this and laughed loudly, hooting and slapping their thighs as the wagon rolled along.

The more they sang, the easier their burden seemed to be, and once they got going, although it was a heavy load, they found that they could do it. It was, after all, a wagon created by a leprechaun wish in a most extraordinary place.

But after some time of this, the goblins realized that something was not quite right, and one of them said, "Wait a minute. How is it that little thing and those old grumpers there can pull this big old wagon? And I don't like that singin' that they're doin'. And how is it that there's a wind up ahead and, we never feels it? Tell 'em to shut it up, Grip."

"You want to pull with 'em, Hapless? Go on, you can join 'em if you want," said Grip.

Hapless started to reply when another of the goblins riding in the cart said "Hey... hey! I smell somethin' funny here. It smells like... like... like little people!"

He began to dig about in the hay as though some frantic fit had taken hold of him.

This got the attention of all of the goblins, and they all began sniffing about. Colleen knew that Lily and Rose were still hiding under the seat and beneath the hay, and that she had to do something right then and there to distract them.

"Dvalenn, Oracle, we've got to run for it, now!" she whispered.

"I'm no good at it!" replied Dvalenn.

"Well, do something!" she yelled, and dropped her pole and took off at a sprint.

Dvalenn grabbed Oracle and dove under the wagon and out of sight, and found that there was a storage cubbyhole that they had not seen before, which he quickly opened, unceremoniously shoved Oracle in, then crawled in after him, shutting the door behind them. Colleen saw him do this, and sped away as fast as she could.

All five of the goblins leaped from the wagon and Grip cried, "After them!" and took off after Colleen, not seeing Dvalenn or Oracle anywhere.

But Colleen was fast, and as she raced down the road, she began to outdistance the goblins. This actually worried her, because she realized that she was running away from the wagon where all of their supplies were, and she wanted to lead the goblins far enough away so that Lily and Rose would have time to get out and escape. So she slowed down and pretended to tire, allowing the goblins to gain on her a bit.

At this, they shouted and howled, and called out, "Come back here, you little beast, and we'll show you what we do with escaped prisoners!"

"You'll never catch me!" she yelled, and ran on down the road.

Back at the wagon, Dvalenn cracked open the baggage compartment, saw and heard nothing, and slipped out, looking about the dark wood.

"Now you just stay put, Oracle," he said, shutting the door and leaving him in the compartment.

Suddenly, in the trees, a great dark shape moved. Dvalenn froze, knowing that it was much too big to be a goblin. He knew that there were other creatures in these woods at night, and as the great black shape drew near, he steeled himself and prepared for the worst. He knew he had to face it to give the little people children time to escape.

"Lily! Rose! Get ready to run!" he yelled.

The leprechaun girls climbed to the edge of the wagon, their faces tense with fear as it drew nearer and nearer. Then a huge shape emerged, and out of the woods trotted Badger, his great black mane waving in the breeze and Mrs. Wigglepox riding between his ears.

"Bless my soul," said Dvalenn. "I nearly died of fright. But my, I'm mighty glad to see you."

"We've been following you all night long," said Mrs. Wigglepox. "And when we saw the wagon stop again and heard the commotion, we snuck up a little closer. Then we saw Colleen run and the goblins go chasing after her."

"We've got to get Badger hooked up to this wagon and go after them," said Dvalenn. "Good thing I grabbed these pins."

He reached into an inside pocket and pulled out the pins that held Badger's saddle to the cart poles. Mrs. Wigglepox maneuvered Badger into place and Dvalenn hooked him up.

"I've gotten pretty good at horse-ear riding," said Mrs. Wigglepox. "And Badger is a real joy to ride. Quite a gentleman, but fierce in a fight. Where is Oracle?"

"Oh!" said Dvalenn, and quickly opened the compartment and helped him out.

"You best ride in the back," said Dvalenn. "I bet you could use a rest and a stretch."

He helped Oracle in and the old leprechaun lay down in the hay and shut his eyes.

Off they went down the road as fast as they dared in the dark, with all four of them sitting on the seat. It was a harrowing ride, but soon they began to wonder why they had not caught up to Colleen and the goblins yet. Surely they could not outrun Badger, so great a horse, and tireless.

They rode on, but saw nothing, and finally Dvalenn brought the wagon to a halt and said, "Begging your pardon, Wigglepoxes, but I think we must have passed them by, or the goblins have gotten Colleen and taken her away through the woods to one of their hideouts. Surely we would have caught them by now."

"I've been thinking the same thing, Dvalenn," said Mrs. Wigglepox. "But I'm not sure what to do about it. We can't just sit here, and we can't go back. We've just got to go on. The forest isn't safe at night."

"I suppose you're right, miss," replied Dvalenn. "Still, I wish we could see better in this dark. It's a good thing this old road is still around. At least it knows the way."

Dvalenn's eyes widened and he straightened in his seat.

"Why didn't I think of it before?" he said, and climbed down out of the wagon.

The little people watched as he brushed the leaves away from the stones of the road, laid his ear against them, and shut his eyes.

"Mother," said Rose, "is Dvalenn listening to the stones the way Doc did?"

"I believe so, dearie," she replied. "But let's be quiet now and see what happens."

Dvalenn lay on the ground for a long time, and then slowly rose and said, "They've been this way, all right, and they're not that far ahead of us. But the stones go silent just ahead of where they are. Let's get going."

He climbed back into the wagon and off they went, once again flying down the road as quickly as they dared.

Colleen raced on. She had been running for at least half an hour now, and she could tell that the goblins were tiring, for she had slowed considerably since they had first begun this race. She thought about Dvalenn and Oracle and Rose and Lily back at the wagon, and she glanced back to be sure that all five goblins were still after her. They were. She only hoped and prayed that Mrs. Wigglepox would come with help before the goblins tired of their chase and returned to the cart.

She slowed down again, making sure the goblins were staying with her. She was not tired yet, although she felt the oppressive weight of the Spell still bearing down upon her and upon the whole forest. Still, she was sure that if she just kept a song in her heart and often on her lips, its weight would be bearable and she could run on, even with a pack of goblins on her heels.

A moment later, one of the goblins, through labored breath, yelled, "I say we shoot it, Grip, before it gets away!"

"And I say you're an idiot, Bof," panted Grip. "You know the order – no big people get shot – they get taken to the ship and to the Witch herself."

"Bosh with orders!" heaved Bof. "This one's too fast. We could just wound it and knock it senseless, then take it to her."

"And what if we do kill it?" said Grip. "Word gets back to her and then we're all done for."

"Who's to know, Grip? Just one arrow and if we kill it, who's to know?" said another goblin.

Suddenly, there was a twang of a bowstring. Colleen heard it and dodged aside just in time to hear an arrow *zing* past her ear.

"You foul idiot!" screamed Grip. "Put that thing away. You're a lousy shot anyway, Bof."

"I've had just about enough of you, Grip," yelled Bof.

Cries of anger and sounds fighting from the goblins reached Colleen's ears, but began to fade as she ran on. She turned to see the shadows of two goblins rolling about on the road and the other three dancing about them and shouting for one or the other.

Then a club was in the hand of one of them and the other took a hard blow on the head, then another, and it lay still in the road. Colleen stopped and dashed behind a tree to see what would happen. She was glad for the rest, but fearful of what might come.

"So much for the mighty Grip!" said the victor, which was obviously Bof. "I'm in charge now! Throw him in the trees over there and cover him up with leaves."

Two of the others grabbed the limp body of Grip and unceremoniously tossed him in the trees and piled leaves over him.

"What we do now?" said the third goblin, and Colleen recognized the voice as that of Nous.

"We go back to that wagon, that's what," said Bof.

"What about the girl?" asked Nous.

"Forget her. The stalkers will do her in anyway," said Bof.

Nous stood very still for a moment and then said, "How abouts one of us goes after the girl and the others go for the cart? Then we meets up tomorrow night at the big tree down by the desert?"

"The big tree?" said Bof.

Colleen thought that Nous was speaking much too loudly now, and the thought struck her that he was letting her in on their plans.

Good old Nous, she thought. *I think he's actually trying to help me.*

"Yea, Bof," said Nous. "You know, the one at the desert's edge about a half day's march from here. It's hidden just a ways off to the side of the road. Use to be some old nutter there 'til he moved closer to that evil lake."

"Shut up, Nous. Now listen to me. We're going to need all four of us now to pull that cart. So you just come right along with us, hear?" said Bof.

"What about Grip?" said Nous. "Is he dead?"

"Never you mind him. If he's not dead, he will be when the stalkers find him," sneered Bof.

Nous stared at the mound that was Grip for a moment, trying to think of something that just wouldn't quite rise to the surface of his mind. He seemed to wrestle with something within himself, wagging his body back and forth.

"Nous!" shouted Bof, who had already begun walking up the road with the other two goblins.

Nous looked after them, then back at the mound again, and then down the road where Colleen had disappeared. He scratched his head, then turned and walked slowly behind the other goblins. Bof seemed satisfied with this and quickened his pace back to the cart. But Nous stopped again, glanced over his shoulder, and then dashed into the trees and disappeared into the shadows.

The sound of the three goblins faded into the night until Colleen could no longer see or hear them. She listened a moment more, then slipped from her hiding place, wondering about Grip. What were these *stalkers* that they had been speaking of? If Grip was alive, she just couldn't leave him to be eaten by... by who knew what.

Staying in the shadows at the edge of the forest, she silently made her way to the mound that was Grip, knelt down beside him, and brushed the leaves away. In the dim light, she could see that something dark and shiny stained his ugly face. But she could also see that his chest was slowly rising and falling. He was still alive. She pushed back the black hood and propped up his head. A long gash spilled the dark blood from his forehead. He was hideous, with a long pointy nose, which appeared to be broken, and large bat-like ears. His black tongue lolled from his filthy mouth, and his body stank.

She swallowed hard, found some moss at the base of a tree, and began to staunch the flow of blood from the wound.

"Why?"

The voice behind her made her jump. She spun around, startled and scared, and out from behind a tree came the shape of a goblin.

"Why?" it said again.

"Nous!" said Colleen. "Nous, you scared me!"

"Why does the Colleen help us?" Nous asked.

"You called me by my name, Nous. Thank you for not calling me *it*," she replied. "And I help because you're supposed to do to other people what you want them to do for you."

Nous drew closer and crouched down beside her, looking into her face, then down at Grip, and then at Colleen again. His face was just as ugly as Grip's, and he stank just as bad. But somehow, in his eyes, Colleen could see a question rising, or something that was confusing this goblin so deeply that he was forgetting that he was in the service of the Witch, forgetting his wicked upbringing, and forgetting that he could easily pounce and overpower her.

"We need to get Grip some help, Nous," said Colleen. "And what are these *stalkers*?"

But before he could answer, there was the sound of a *CRACK* behind them as if something had broken. They both spun around, and there, coming through the trees, was a set of red eyes.

Nous whipped a club from his belt and hissed.

"Run!" he said. "The Colleen must run!"

The creature bolted forward out of the shadows, and Nous and Colleen both dove to one side as its great bulk leaped into the moonlight, landing on all fours in front of Grip's fallen body. It was gray and hairy, and its head appeared to be a mixture of wolf and bat, but it was the size of a huge bear. It lifted its head to the sky and bellowed a howl that was like nothing Colleen had heard on earth, and it was answered in the distance by another. The creature sniffed the body of Grip, licked dark fangs with its tongue, lifted its head, and howled again. As more answering calls came, it turned to face Colleen and Nous, lines of saliva running from its gaping mouth.

Then Colleen heard another sound – the sound of hooves and a wagon, approaching fast. She then did something that totally surprised the creature. With speed that made Nous goggle, she sprinted forward and yelled, "Nous, grab Grip and drag him to the side of the road! Do it now!"

Then she was leaping through the air and landed on the back of the unprepared beast. She dug her fists hard into the creature's fur as it reared up and shook, trying to throw her off. It howled and growled and screamed its unholy cries, and now the answering calls were closer. Too close.

Nous grabbed Grip by a foot and pulled him roughly from the woods and to the side of the road. The sound of the approaching horse grew louder, and as the beast ran itself backward toward a large tree in an attempt to crush her, she jumped from its back, rolled, and dashed after Nous. Running into the road, she could see Badger galloping toward her with Dvalenn at the reins.

"Dvalenn! Badger! Here!" she yelled frantically.

Dvalenn pulled the wagon to a stop.

"Best get in," he said urgently.

The stalker, momentarily dazed by having slammed itself into the tree, was angry now, and seeing them, it charged.

"Into the wagon, Nous, but Grip first," she commanded.

Nous obeyed, and together they heaved Grip over the side and jumped in just as the creature charged out of the woods and came face to face with Badger. The great horse reared, threatening to upset the wagon, but then he came down hard with his mighty hooves on the head of the creature. It bellowed furiously and crashed to the side of the road. Colleen climbed to the front seat, grabbed the reins from Dvalenn, and said, "Run, Badger, run!"

He neighed and took off, just as two more stalkers came bounding from the woods.

"Run, boy, like you've never run before!" she cried.

Dvalenn went tumbling backward into the wagon, and Colleen nearly joined him, such was the strength and speed with which he surged forward.

"What's this!" cried Dvalenn, as he rolled right over top of Grip and into Nous.

The goblin hissed at the dwarf, and Dvalenn seized Colleen's walking stick, which lay within arm's reach. Nous raised his club, which he still had, and the two would have come to blows had Colleen not yelled, "Dvalenn! Nous! Stop! Now you just climb back up here, Dvalenn, and leave Nous back there with Grip!"

Nous hissed again and kept his club raised, but Dvalenn pulled himself back to the front of the wagon, still holding her walking stick, and climbed into the seat. He eyed the goblin suspiciously.

"Are you telling me that you have befriended goblins?" asked Dvalenn.

"Just hold on and I'll explain later!" she said.

He looked back again at the goblins, and at the stalkers that were now in pursuit.

"Well, those beasts are still behind us, and we nearly ran down three goblins on the road a ways back, and ... *look out!*" he shouted.

There in front of them in the road, another beast had appeared. It was smaller than the two that were chasing them, but it blocked their way.

Colleen could see no way around. Great trees hemmed them in on both sides, and there was no way to stop.

"Jump, Badger!" she yelled and, with a mighty leap, Badger jumped, flying over the head of the creature and pulling the wagon's front wheels off the ground.

As the wagon came down, it did so right on top of the beast, and it howled and went tumbling, just barely missing the spinning wheels, but taking a hard whack on the head and back. The two stalkers in pursuit jumped over its rolling form and continued their chase, and were managing to gain ground now.

"They are coming! Perhaps if we feed them?" hissed Nous, and he pointed at Grip.

"No, Nous, we're not feeding Grip to the stalkers. Just hold on tight. It's going to be a wild ride!"

"Hee-yaaa!" cried Colleen, flicking the reins. "Faster, boy!"

Now sweat poured from the great stallion's body and he gleamed jet black in the moonlight as he thundered on, his shining horseshoes like streaking whirls of gold in the night.

"They still come," came Nous' hiss. "They are creatures of the Witch, and they run with her whip at their back!"

"Dvalenn, what can we do?" she asked desperately.

Then the voice of Oracle came from the back of the wagon.

"Night hates Light," he said.

"Then I hope Badger can run until morning," said Dvalenn.

But Oracle was rummaging about in the back of the wagon, digging in the hay. At first, he found his cane, and said, "Ah ha!" with great glee. Then he found Frederick's sword and set it aside. He found the vial of water that the Lady Danu had given to Colleen. This he stuffed inside his cloak and kept rummaging. Finally, he found what he was looking for - a water sack with the water from the Lady. He dragged the sack to the back of the wagon, grinning at Nous as the astonished goblin watched. But the sack was nearly as large as he was, and Colleen, looking over her shoulder, could see that he could not handle it alone.

"Take the reins, Dvalenn," she said, and climbed back to help Oracle.

"What are you doing?" yelled Dvalenn.

"Just drive!" she shouted.

The stalkers were gaining ground. She helped Oracle open the sack of water. The beasts drew nearer... nearer. Then Oracle jumped on the sack, and a spray of water droplets rained on the first creature. It howled in protest and dropped to the ground, pawing at its face where the blessed water had splashed it. The second one, with a sudden surge of speed, leaped forward and grabbed hold of the rear of the cart, its great black claws clinging as they raced on. It opened its fetid maw and lunged forward, but Colleen pushed Oracle off the sack, picked it up, and dumped it down the creature's huge throat. The stalker swallowed, and its eyes bulged huge. A weird whimper escaped its throat, and it fell backward from the cart and went into spasms.

She stared as it disappeared in the distance behind them, then she sat down heavily and sighed, shaking.

"I think we're safe now, Dvalenn," she said. "But let's keep going, just in case."

Nous was staring at Colleen, almost with a look of admiration on his face.

"The Colleen and the Leprechaun saved us again," he said.

"Well, I'm sure you would have done the same for me. But let's have a look at Grip and see how he's doing," she replied.

She took a piece of cloth and, wetting it with water from another sack, reached over to clean the wound on Grip's head.

Nous hissed, and she froze.

"Whatever is wrong, Nous?" she asked.

"Does the Colleen wish to kill him?" he asked.

"Of course not!" she replied. "His wound needs to be cleaned."

"Not with that!" growled Nous. "Did the Colleen see what it did to the stalkers?"

"Goblins are not stalkers," she replied.

"But still Witch's people," he replied. "Water from the evil Lady kills all the Witch's people. She said so."

"You can't believe what a witch says," said Colleen. "I don't think that those blessed waters would kill anyone."

Nous snorted. "Goblins hate the Lady and her waters. Too bright! And it burns us, it does. It burns all the Witch's people."

"Well, maybe it would burn the bad right out of you if you soaked in it long enough," she replied.

"Deep fried goblin, that's what I'd be," he said.

Colleen laughed, and she realized that the goblin had actually made a joke. Was he actually befriending her? She was more convinced than ever that there was a spark of good somewhere inside them, and an idea was beginning to form in her mind.

"Please, Nous, we need to clean the wound. Let me try just a little," she said.

First, she wiped away the dark blood from his face with a dry end of the cloth, and then with the damp end, began to dab at the wound. Grip groaned hoarsely, and Nous watched with wide eyes as Colleen carefully cleaned the gash. It was a dreadful wound – deep and long, extending from the top of his forehead down to his eye, and it was still bleeding quite badly. To their astonishment, as Colleen cleaned it, the bleeding began to stop, and all along the cut, Grip's skin had turned from the rough, mottled gray-green to smooth, lavender-purple.

"Scarred!" said Nous. "See, it burns! Only baby goblins have such ugly scars, but we fix them."

"Your babies have lavender-colored skin?" asked Colleen.

"Yesss! Poor things. Cursed! But as soon as they're born, we dip 'em in the Ooze, and that fixes them right up, it does," he replied.

Then he glanced at Colleen and said, "In fact, they look a bit like you. I could fix you up a bit with the Ooze, and you wouldn't be so ugly."

Colleen almost wanted to laugh, but instead, she asked, "You dip your babies in an ooze? Whatever for?"

"To get rid of the scars, yes," said Nous. "Grip will want to bathe in the Ooze too, to get rid of that scar."

Colleen was not sure what to make of this, but the wound on Grip's head had stopped bleeding now, and she felt that at least he would not bleed to death.

"Would you watch him for me, Nous? I'd like to talk to Dvalenn for a bit," said Colleen.

Nous lay down in the hay next to Grip and Oracle planted himself on the other side of the wounded goblin, watching him intently.

Colleen climbed back into the seat and took the reins. Mrs. Wigglepox, who had been holding on to the seat for dear life, sat more easily now next to her.

"Mrs. Wigglepox, I have an idea... what do you know about the Waters of Light and this goblin Ooze?"

"The Waters of Light?" replied Mrs. Wigglepox. "Well, it's said that they flow from the Source – from the Fountain of Heaven, it's called. No one's really sure where it is – except maybe the Lady – and that the Light that's in them is that same Light that shone when all things were first made. I think that's why the Witch's folk can't stand it. They've turned away from that Light to follow the Darkness."

"What is the Darkness?" she asked.

Dvalenn glanced back at the goblins and leaned close to whisper to Colleen.

"It's said that the goblins worship it. There was a time when even the goblins were good. But something happened to them – something terrible that changed them from creatures of great beauty and talent to what they are today. The Witch might have been involved in it somehow, or maybe Mor-Fae, Anastazi the Great's daughter - although no one seems to know exactly how. But the goblins were the Keepers of the Fountain. It was from their world that the Lady first came and began to spread the Waters of Light to all the worlds after the Gates of Anastazi were opened. It was a glorious time!"

"Yes," said Mrs. Wigglepox. "But when the Darkness came, there was a terrible struggle. The Lady was involved in it, and she strove against that Darkness. But there was betrayal among the goblins, and the Source was cut off, or lost, and the Ooze took its place in their world, or so it's said."

"But what is this Ooze?" asked Colleen.

"No one knows for sure," she replied. "Some say it is the filth of the Darkness that entered the world of the goblins. Some say it is something from the goblins themselves, and some say both are true. But whatever it is, the goblins seem to delight in it."

"Nous said they bathe their children in it after they are born," replied Colleen. "He said that they are scarred when they are born, and look rather human and that the Ooze heals them."

"That I didn't know," said Dvalenn.

"But when I washed Grip's wound with the water that the Lady gave us, it looked like it changed his skin, and Nous said it was a scar like their babies bore. I wonder if maybe it's the other way around," said Colleen.

"What do you mean?" asked Dvalenn.

"I mean, what if it's this Ooze that scars them? What would happen if they stayed away from it and bathed their babies in the Waters of Light?" she said.

"One can only guess," said Mrs. Wigglepox. "But they say that the Light in the Lake is torture and fire to them."

"But it isn't," said Colleen. "It's wonderful and beautiful and refreshes you."

"Yes," replied Mrs. Wigglepox. "Being immersed in those Waters makes one feel clean and warm through and through. I don't understand why the goblins and the Witch would hate it so, but they both hate and fear it. It is the Light within that they loathe."

Colleen felt a tap on her back. It was Oracle, and in his hand was the vial of water.

"Thank you, Oracle!" she said, taking it from him.

She gazed at it for a few moments, wondering what this pure water would do – water from the very source of the Lake, the Lady had said. She put it back into her cloak pocket, and on they rode through the Great Hills, quietly pondering these things that seemed so strange.

Chapter 13 – Sailing Plans

The next morning, word came to all of the McGunnegals that they were to meet with Professor McPherson in his office right after breakfast. As they sat eating, Aonghus looked about the room for Frederick, but didn't see him anywhere.

"What's it all about, Aong?" asked Abbe. "I heard a rumor that you and Bran and someone else were in Professor McPherson's office late last night."

Aonghus leaned forward across the table and whispered, "It's big news, Ab. But I can't say anything just yet. You'll see when we get there."

They finished their breakfast as quick as they could and then headed out the door. There were whispers among the other students as they passed, but their sharp ears could hear many of them.

"They're going to be expelled before they get started," said one blonde-haired girl to another.

"That's right," she replied. "The biggest one, Aonghus, tried to drown a boy in the lake last night, I hear. And the police have been called."

"No, no," said another girl. "He didn't try to drown him – they were all swimming and the fool boy got himself in trouble and Bran saved him from drowning."

"I hear that an old man drowned in there last night," whispered another.

"That's right," said another, "and that Bran fellow was the one that drowned him!"

How could it be, thought Aonghus, *that so many rumors had begun already?* No wonder his parents had always told them not to believe everything people said, and that idle chatter led to trouble.

They made their way to the professor's office and Aonghus knocked on the door.

"Come!" said a voice.

Frederick was seated in front of the professor's desk and was looking at a map. He was wearing the same blue robe that he'd had on the prior night when they pulled him from the lake.

"Frederick!" said Bib in surprise. "How... where is Colleen? And why are you dressed in such ridiculous clothes?"

"A moment, please, ladies," said the professor. "Now all of you, take a seat."

Then they noticed an old man in the room with them. He was examining various artifacts sitting on the shelves about the room. The boys noted that he was no longer dressed in his old robe, but was wearing an outfit that a school professor would wear.

"Good morning, Gwydion," said Aonghus. "You're dressed... differently today."

"The good professor's idea," he replied, smiling. He looked much more rested than he had the night before.

The professor had arranged chairs around his desk, and each of the children took a seat.

"Is Colleen all right?" asked Abbe as she sat down. She looked back and forth between the professor and Frederick, her eyes questioning.

"When I left her, she was fine," answered Frederick.

"You mean you got an early ship, and you left without her? How is she going to get over here now? Why, of all the irresponsible..." began Bib, but Aonghus cut in.

"Easy, Bib. It's not like that. Just listen," he said.

"First, ladies, let me introduce someone to you. This is Gwydion. He has just arrived with Frederick," said the professor.

"Pleased to make your acquaintance," said Gwydion.

"And you, sir," they replied.

"Now let me begin with this," said the professor, and he lifted the sword that Frederick had retrieved from the cave and placed it on the desk on top of the map.

Its golden-silver blade shimmered in the sunlight that fell through the window, and its gem-studded hilt sparkled. They stared at it for a moment, while the professor took their broken rocks from the bag and placed them one by one next to the sword.

"This sword must have been made by the same people who lived on our land!" said Abbe. "But what does that have to do with Colleen?"

"Ladies," said Aonghus, "there was something down in Grandpa McLochlan's basement – a mirror."

He paused, not quite sure how to express what he was about to say, then blurted it out.

"Colleen fell through it," he said.

"Oh my!" said Bib. "Did she cut herself? Is she all right? Did Dad take her to the hospital?"

"No, you don't understand," said Frederick. "The mirror is a doorway to... to other places. She and I both fell through it – it's like a portal or something. We ended up in a different land somewhere. It's a magic mirror!"

Bib stared at him and then replied sarcastically, "And I'm the queen of England. Now tell the truth, you, or I'll... I'll..."

"He's telling you the truth, Bib," cut in the professor.

Bib's mouth worked, but no words came out.

"It's true, Sis," said Bran. "We believe him. But she's in trouble, and we've got to get to her."

"Or maybe Frederick left her behind and made up this whole story as a big joke. Sounds like something a Buttersmouth would do, you know," she replied.

"Listen," said Aonghus. "We pulled Frederick and Gwydion here out of the lake last night. There was something in there – something... a lot of somethings... alive... they were... I think they were mer-people! And he had this sword, and he was dressed like he is now."

Bib crossed her arms and sat back, looking doubtful. But Henny slid off her chair, walked over to Frederick, and stared up into his face.

She looked at him for a long moment and said, "Frederick, tell me where Colleen is. Tell me the truth."

Frederick looked down at her and said, "She is in the Land of the Little People, Henny. When I left her, she was with the Lady Danu. I promised her I would come back and bring help if I could. I know it's terribly hard to believe. I

387

wouldn't believe it myself. But I made a promise to her, and I intend to keep it."

Henny continued to stare up at him for a time, and then said, "I believe you. But why did you go there?"

"It was an accident. We both fell through the mirror. That little crystal ball is the key to making the mirror work, and we lost it. A goblin has it now, back in Ireland. She's trapped there unless we find another doorway to that world. And we've got to get that crystal ball back from that goblin." He blurted it all out with a feeling of desperation.

Henny went back to her seat, crawled up, and sat down.

Aonghus turned to his brother and sisters and said, "That fixes it for me. Henny has that funny way of seeing things. She can tell when people are lying, and they just can't seem to lie when talking to her."

"That's true, Bib," said Abbe. "Maybe there's something to this whole thing."

"Still..." said Bib, not wanting to believe this incredible story.

"But you were in the *lake?* And with this old chap?" asked Abbe. "What's that all about?"

"Well, Frederick," said McPherson. "I think it is time for you to tell your tale one more time."

Frederick looked at the girls. Bib still wore an unsure expression on her face, but they all leaned forward, ready to listen. So, once again, he told the tale, beginning with their slipping away from the ship and ending with the events of the night before. When he was done, they simply stared at him and at Gwydion in wonder, until Professor McPherson said, "So, it would seem that we need to either catch that goblin or find another doorway to this Land of the Little People."

"Begging your pardon, professor," said Bib, "but magical doorways are in short supply, or at least they are in Ireland. I say we sail back home and see what's really happening there. And what's all this about a goblin?"

"Bib, remember that black-robed man – or thing – that was seen the night that Mom disappeared?" asked Aonghus.

"Yes," she replied.

"We think it came through that mirror. And maybe... maybe Mom went through the other way... maybe she fell through the same way that Colleen and Frederick did," he replied.

"But I thought that crystal ball was supposed to activate it?" she said.

"Oh no," said Henny.

"What's wrong, Sprite?" asked Aonghus.

"I was at Grandpa's that day with Mom," she said. "He was sitting in his chair like always when Mom went down the cellar. But there was something round and smooth in his hand. I asked him what it was, and he told me it was a secret. He handed it to me, and I looked real hard at it. 'Don't tell anyone about it!' he said. Then he took it back and told me to run along home, so I did."

She looked scared, and her eyes began to tear up.

"I did it, didn't I? I opened the door by accident somehow. It's my fault that Mom disappeared. I must have turned it on, and she fell in, and that bad goblin came out. What if there are more goblins in there with her, Aonghus?"

"Now don't you go blaming yourself, little one. Even if you did turn on that mirror and Mom got in there somehow, you didn't do anything wrong. We don't know how it all happened, or why, but there's a reason for things, you'll see."

Henny sniffed, wiped her eyes on her sleeve, and then brightened. "So Mom and Colleen are in the same place? Maybe we could rescue them both!"

"Brilliant!" said Bran. "What's the plan, Professor? Do we sail back to Ireland and tell Dad, and get on the trail of that goblin thing?"

They all looked expectantly at the professor, and he looked back at each of them.

"That would be one option," he said. "But there is another possibility."

"And that is?" said Bib.

He sat down behind his desk, glanced at Frederick, and then said, "Let me tell you a story. Many years ago, I was a sailor and explorer. I have, since my youth, been fascinated with ancient cultures and relics and such, and I have taken every opportunity possible to go to exotic places around the world where there has been even a rumor of some lost civilization.

"I did this because, as you know, there had been certain artifacts handed down through my family line, along with family stories and legends, which spoke of a time when the world was quite different from today, and of great civilizations that arose, thrived, and were destroyed.

"It was my passion to uncover these mysteries and to find out all that I could about these ancient peoples and where they had gone.

"Why, I ask myself, are there so many legends and stories of giants and ogres and elves and heroes in the ancient past? Are they just fanciful stories made up by mothers to keep their children from disobeying them? Or was there something really there long ago?

"Once I was sailing in the area known as the Bermuda Triangle. Perhaps you have heard of it?"

The McGunnegals passed a knowing look among themselves.

"Yes, sir," said Aonghus. "Captain Truehart spoke of it on the trip over here."

"Truehart!" said McPherson, "So, just what did that old rascal have to say?"

"Well…" replied Aonghus, "he said that he rescued you down there a long time ago. That you had a stone chest…"

The professor held up a hand and put a finger to his lips. Then he whispered, "Do you see this map?" And he cleared the desk so that they could see the map better.

"This is a copy of one of the maps that was in that stone chest, children. Do you see what it shows?" he asked.

"Well," said Bib, rising from her chair and leaning over the map. "This looks like Africa, and this is South America, and this is Europe, and North America. But this large island between them all must be a magnified view of some island out in the Atlantic Ocean. Nothing that big exists out there."

"Ah! Quite right, Bib," he replied. "I see you have studied your geography. I have also pondered that very thing. Is this some small island out there somewhere? But if so, what are these cities and fortresses marked on it? The scale seems all wrong. And do you see the writing? It is the same language that is engraved on this sword, and these stones. I believe that this, my friends, is a map of Atlantis!"

"But where did you get it? Was it on that island that Truehart mentioned?" asked Bran.

McPherson leaned across the desk and whispered to them again, his eyes wide with wonder and excitement.

"I believe that I have been to this very island, children, or a tiny remnant of it. I believe that I have set foot upon the lost island of Atlantis, and I believe that *there* is where we will find our doorway to the land where your mother and sister are."

They all looked at the professor and at one another.

"But, Professor, oughtn't we go home to Ireland first and see if we can catch this goblin? Wouldn't that be quicker?" asked Abbe.

He sat down in his chair and looked at them, then asked, "Are any of you good at tracking and hunting and such?"

"Bran is the best huntsman in all Ireland," piped up Henny.

"All right. Now, Bran – forgive me – but I know you searched for your mother after her disappearance... yes, Rufus Buttersmouth told me the story. And there was this small man – or creature – that we now believe was a goblin – that was in your grandfather's house the night of her disappearance. You tried to track this thing, didn't you?"

"Of course," replied Bran. "Dad and Aonghus and I searched for months and months. We went all over. We saw strange signs and footprints, but whatever that thing was, it was more elusive than any animal we ever encountered. It was smart – real smart."

"And do you think that if we sailed back to Ireland now and went tracking it again that we would have any better luck this time around?" asked the professor.

"Maybe," said Bran. "The trail would be fresh again."

"The trail may be weeks old by the time we get there," he replied. "And we could spend months searching, and may never find a trace of the goblin or the crystal ball. I don't think we should leave Colleen alone for that long in a strange land with unfriendly creatures all about."

"But suppose this island you spoke of can be found. What makes you think that there's a doorway there to this land where Colleen is?" asked Aonghus.

"Because I have seen it!" the professor replied, and there was a strange look in his eye – a look of wonder and joy and madness all at once.

"Did you go through it?" asked Bib.

"Alas, no!" he replied, and his face returned to its normal wise look. "No. I did not go through the door. I fled from that place for fear and wonder."

"But why?" asked Henny.

The strange look returned, and he spoke in a low voice. "Because of the one who still sits on the throne in that dreadful place! When I was shipwrecked those many years ago, my ship was dashed on uncharted rocks somewhere in the middle of the Triangle. My crew was lost to the sea, and I nearly so, but Providence spared me and I clung to a broken piece of the ship and was washed through the jagged spears that surrounded that island and swept onto a broken and rocky shore.

"There, I stumbled inland, moving through that dark night and seeing only glimpses of the land around me through the flashes of lightning. At last, I came to what I thought was a cave, and crawled in to wait out the storm. All my strength was gone, and I could see nothing. I collapsed on a rough and broken floor and did not awake until the next day with the rising of the sun.

"Now, my memory of what happened next is vague, for that place is beyond all remembering. But I remember bones – many bones. And the door! The shining door that gripped my soul! That, at least, is blazoned on my mind, and I shall never forget that silver portal that shone like the moon! But something happened to me. I... I touched something, and a terrifying vision gripped me. It drove me to madness, and I fled from that place. I found the piece of the ship that I had been saved by, and pushed it out, away from that island, past the jagged teeth that surrounded it, and into the open sea.

"I remember watching as that pinnacle of rock faded in a strange fog and vanished, and as it did, I felt within my grip a stone chest. Somehow, I had picked it up in the cave, but how or why, I do not know.

"For many days, I floated, clutching that chest, until I was rescued by a ship – the very one that our good Captain Truehart was a deckhand on."

Professor McPherson shut his eyes and sighed a great sigh.

"Professor," said Frederick, "please, may I ask you a question?"

He opened his eyes, and he was himself again. "Certainly, son," he said.

"Well, I was just wondering – that door – was it really big – like twenty or more feet high? And was it a double door? And was the light a shining silvery light that kind of took hold of you when you saw it – like you just had to go to it and touch it or something?" he asked.

"Yes, Frederick, it was. It was very much like what you described in the Land of the Little People. And *that*, my friends, is why I believe it will take us there. I believe that perhaps those two doors are one and the same," he replied.

"But all the stories that we heard said that there was someone named Anastazi the Great who made those doors, and that he had disappeared long ago and had locked them," said Frederick.

"Ah, friends," said Gwydion quietly. "This is a strange tale. I know... or knew... Anastazi the Great. He did indeed create the Gates. But the Gate to the World of Men was not on this Island of Atlantis, last I knew. But the palace of the son of Anastazi was there. And there was a rumor that he had built something – perhaps a door or portal of some sort – but a terror came to his land after he had built it, and his kingdom was destroyed. The whole island vanished from this world, and we could not find it again. But if that door *has* been found again, it may be that it does indeed lead to the place we seek."

"But where *was* the Gate to the World of Men that Anastazi made?" asked Frederick.

"Ah, it still seems strange to me, all this talk of *was*, when to me it seems like just yesterday that all this happened. How long have I been bewitched, I wonder? But where *was* it, you ask? Why, it was on the Emerald Isle. It was within a great hill, inside the walls of the Wizard's Castle. But who can say where that now is. If Anastazi locked the gates, then none can open them. He alone bore their key, and he never revealed their secret to anyone, save perhaps his son and daughter, and they are lost long ago, it would seem."

"Gwydion," said Abbe excitedly, "there *is* a big hill on our farm back home. It's a strange place. It does seem magical at times, and it's inside the wall of rock that surrounds our farm. Do you think that it could be... could it be where this Gate of Anastazi is?"

Gwydion looked thoughtful and said, "I would have to see it to be sure. But if the gate is locked, then without the key, it would do us no good."

"But aren't you supposed to be a wizard?" she replied. "Could you do some spell or something to open it up?"

He smiled at her and said, "You do not understand. I am or was a wizard in my own right. But Anastazi was, or perhaps is, an Elven Lord extraordinaire. There has never been his equal. None could stand before him in either contest or battle, and what he shaped, none could undo or destroy. And what he locked, none could open."

"Doc said the Gate in the Land of the Little People was *leaking.* He thought it had been damaged in the Cataclysm," said Frederick.

"The Cataclysm?" said Gwydion.

"It's a long story," replied Frederick. "But it apparently blew things up and down and inside-out in that land."

Suddenly, a thought struck him.

"Gwydion... maybe it blew you right out of that world and back into the World of Men, along with that arch and that tree down under the lake. Wouldn't *that* be something?"

"It would indeed," replied Gwydion. "This tale grows stranger every moment. I would dearly love to go to your farm and see all that has befallen the land there. It was said that the portal, or whatever it was that Atlantis built on his island, had a secret to opening it that only he knew. If only we could find him, or his tomb, then we might be able to discover that secret."

After a long pause, Aonghus spoke. "We seem to have three choices, then," he said. "First, we can return to Ireland and hunt for the goblin in hopes of getting the crystal ball back. Second, we can return to Ireland and start digging up hills, looking for a long lost door. Or third, we can sail for Bermuda in search of some long lost island that the good professor here accidentally found decades ago. None seem good to me."

"Ireland," said Bib. "It only makes sense. There, we can do two things at once."

"But the Lady Danu told me to seek the king in the sea!" urged Frederick. "Surely this is what she meant – we're to set sail and find this island!"

"I say we vote on it," said Bran.

"Right," said Abbe.

"Yes," said Gwydion. "We must all agree. My heart is too troubled by all these things to see clearly which path is best, although I think the Emerald Isle – *Ireland,* did you call it? That seems best to me, at least at first. Is it far from here?"

"Only a day away, or two at the most," said McPherson.

"I want to go home and see Dad," said Henny.

"Where Colleen is concerned, we should talk to Dad," said Aonghus.

"Well, then, it is decided," said the professor. "We sail to Ireland first, but as soon as we see what may be there, I counsel that at least some of us go on to search for the lost Island in the Triangle."

"To Ireland, then," said Bran. "And I will hunt the goblin."

Frederick looked glum. "To Ireland, then," he said, but in his heart, he knew that he must set sail soon and find this island – and hopefully there find the king in the sea that the Lady had spoken of.

Chapter 14 - The Desert's Edge

The dawn broke in the east without further incident. Badger had pulled them through the remainder of the night, and seemed tireless even as they rode over the last low hill, broke from the forest, and gazed upon an incredible sight. A vast desert stretched out before them, a sea of brown sand that ran from horizon to horizon. The road ran straight into hot sands and disappeared.

"There's a place to hide here," said Nous.

"Yes," said Colleen. "I heard you saying that to Bof back there."

"No, not there," he said. "Goblins don't go there. It's a cursed place. No, there's a place of the *Ooze* nearby. That's where we can rest and be refreshed."

"Nous, what is a place of the Ooze?" asked Colleen, a hint of concern in her voice.

"Nous will show you!" he said.

He climbed from the wagon and began to walk quickly along the desert's edge. They followed him for a short way and came to a black pool.

An oily looking skim covered its dark surface and, from time to time, acrid bubbles burst, releasing rotten-smelling gases. There was one absolutely gigantic tree beside it, but it was twisted and black and dead. It looked as though it had died a long, agonizing death in the presence of the dark pool. For some distance from the Ooze, the smaller trees were similarly bent as if writhing in silent agony and longing to be set free.

Oracle stared over the edge of the wagon at the great black tree and tears filled his eyes. He grasped his cane, climbed over the edge, and slid down the wheel to the ground. He slowly made his way around the dank pool to the twisted tree.

Setting his cane down, he placed both hands on its enormous roots and shut his eyes. His head and shoulders sagged as if some great weight of grief bore down upon him, and they could see him shaking, silently weeping for the dead tree.

"Do you see this pool and that tree?" said Mrs. Wigglepox angrily to everyone. "That was once a Sentinel Tree – one of the Great Trees planted by the Fairy Folk. Do you see? This is what the Witch has in mind for my world. She would turn every spring and pool into a source of death for everything that lives."

Then she turned to Lily and Rose and said, "Look hard, children, and see the work of the Witch. If she is not defeated, *that* will be the fate of the whole forest, even our Wigglepox Tree."

They stared in horror at the grotesque sight for a moment before Dvalenn broke the silence.

"Now you know where the goblins get their smell from," he said aloud, and he turned his head away in disgust.

But Nous threw off his black robe, revealing a skinny, gray-mottled body with a tattered cloth around his waist. He splashed gleefully into the pool and submerged in it up to his neck.

He called to them and said, "Come, come, join me in the Ooze! It will take away your ugliness! See! It makes us feel alive!"

He seemed rather giddy as he splashed about for several minutes, and then he crawled up out of the slimy pool, bent down, and, to their horror, took a long drink from it. It looked to Colleen as if small black worms or leeches clung to his body. But Nous did not seem to notice, and slipped his ragged black robe back on.

"Ahhh! Now we are refreshed!" he hissed. "Nous thinks the dwarf should take a dip, and the Colleen too, and the little people! Ahhh! You would feel much better, especially with the evil sun rising. And Grip will want to drink of it!"

He grinned a wicked grin and then flipped his hood up to cover his face.

"No thank you, Nous. And I think that Grip will have to do with just plain water," replied Colleen. "But I would like to see this other place that you mentioned to Bof. Some sort of hideout or something?"

"Hhhhhhh!" hissed Nous. "It is here! But not so nice as the Ooze. It is a bad place. Very evil."

Nous led them around the pool of Ooze, and Oracle slowly followed, glancing back more than once at the dead Sentinel tree.

Badger hurried past the sickly pool and, not far away, they came to another great tree, bigger than any they had seen before and, at the base, a clear spring of water flowed and made its way into the forest.

Mrs. Wigglepox exclaimed, "It is the mate to the dead Sentinel Tree back there! They always grow in pairs not far from each other. Let me speak to it!"

Colleen carefully put her on the ground, and she walked to the base of the mammoth tree.

Mrs. Wigglepox cupped her hands against it and said something that they could not hear, and immediately, the tree responded. There was a groaning and creaking that sounded not a little angry, and Mrs. Wigglepox backed away.

She glanced back at the others and said, "The tree will not allow the goblins near. It says they murdered its mate, and it will crush them if they approach."

"See! See!" exclaimed Nous. "It is an evil thing!"

Colleen said, "Please, Mrs. Wigglepox, tell the tree that I will vouch for these goblins. If they do any harm, the tree may do to me whatever it wishes. We need to rest before we enter the desert, and there are dangers in the forest right behind us."

Mrs. Wigglepox again cupped her hands against the tree, and again, it creaked and groaned, and this time, shook its branches threateningly.

"I will not go in that tree anyway," said Nous. "Trees swallow goblins and eat them. I've seen it myself. That's why we spread the Ooze on them – to tame them and make it safe for us."

"Please, Nous, we must rest, and we must stay together," pleaded Colleen.

But he was emphatic and would not go near the Sentinel Tree.

"Grip and I will stay by the Ooze today in the shadows of the black tree," he said, and he proceeded to roughly pick up Grip, throw him over one shoulder, and climb out of the wagon.

He then walked back toward the dark pool.

"And what if the other goblins come?" shouted Colleen.

Nous ignored her and kept walking.

"Should we stop him?" asked Colleen.

"Let him go," said Dvalenn. "You see, the goblins are corrupt deep inside and prefer their dark pools to anything that is good and wholesome, even if it would truly help them. And you can see that the forest itself fights against them."

Colleen felt pity for the goblins. She wondered how they had gotten to this wretched state in the first place.

But when Nous and Grip disappeared from sight behind the trees, Mrs. Wigglepox again spoke to the tree. It groaned further, a sorrowful moaning sound this time, but did not open.

"It says it is tired – so tired. It has fought so long. It longs for release. And it does not want to be a host for goblin friends," said Mrs. Wigglepox.

Colleen walked up to the tree, and it seemed to shudder.

"Please," she said, "we need your help. We will try to help you too if you will let us."

Then Oracle walked over to the tree and seated himself on one of its roots. He patted the root and sighed heavily, then looked up into its great branches that spread outward toward the sky. The tree stood silent for a time, and then a door creaked open for them. In they all went, and Badger easily pulled the whole wagon inside. Just as slowly as it had opened, the tree began to close, but openings appeared above, allowing rays of light to shine down on them far from above.

"Mrs. Wigglepox," said Colleen. "How is it that this tree is not sleeping like the others in the forest? There don't seem to be any little people to keep it awake."

"Sentinel Trees have great hearts," she replied, "and this one fights on even without its fairies. But I fear for it. Look at the base of the tree."

They all looked down, and there they could see that a bit of rot had set in.

"What's happening to it?" asked Colleen.

"I would guess that it has grown bitter at the loss of its mate," she replied. "Bitterness is like that, you know. It sinks into your roots and turns you rotten. Did you see how reluctant this tree was to let us in? I fear that this Sentinel will pass the remainder of its days lashing out at goblins and eventually even at others who would befriend it, then die alone, allowing no one to enter its heart and heal it."

"How sad," said Colleen. "Can you help it while you're here?"

"I will try," she said. "And Lily and Rose can help as well."

She beckoned for Colleen to bend low and then whispered, "And I am beginning to wonder more and more about our friend Oracle, here."

Oracle was walking about the base of the tree, examining the rot that had set in and shaking his head, touching the tree here and there and mumbling something they could not make out.

"So am I," whispered Colleen.

"He is rather extraordinary," said Mrs. Wigglepox, "and keeps on doing things that I've not seen a leprechaun do in many an age. But he acts so silly most of the time. I don't understand him."

She considered him a moment longer and then said, "Well, it's been a long day and we must try to help this poor tree."

Colleen put the children down, and they and Mrs. Wigglepox walked over to a hole in the wall and entered. Oracle also paused before a larger door, looked back at Colleen and Dvalenn, and then disappeared inside the tree. The tree moaned once and then was silent.

It had been another exhausting day in every way. As Colleen lay still, thinking of all that had happened and wondering what other strange things they might encounter, she glanced over at the old dwarf. She was about to ask him a question, but saw that he had already fallen asleep and had begun to snore.

"Tomorrow, we brave the Burning Sands," she said to herself, and drifted off to sleep.

Chapter 15 – The Announcement

The next day, during breakfast at the Ismere School, Professor McPherson rose from his usual table and called the students to attention.

"Good morning, students!" he began cheerfully. "I hope you are all enjoying your last few free days before classes begin. This year, we are going to be doing some things a bit differently."

There were glances around the room, and the students grew extra quiet.

"This year," he continued, "there will be a series of extended field trips as part of your studies. As usual, each of you will be visiting a neighboring country, but this time, some of these trips will last for several weeks rather than the usual three or four days."

At this, there were a number of expressions such as "Oh!" and "Yes!" and "No!"

"Some of you will be traveling to France, Ireland, Norway, Denmark, Germany, and to some select islands. During these trips, you will be studying your particular Focus in light of a different culture, under the guidance of a sponsor."

This remark brought nothing but groans.

"Indeed, the very first group of students will be leaving tomorrow, and I shall be their sponsor. You and your parents will each be notified of the time of your trip. Best wishes to you all in the coming semester."

As soon as he had finished speaking, he left the room. Immediately, the room broke out with scores of discussions about where they might be going and what they might study while there.

The McGunnegals and Frederick, who were all seated together, leaned in close.

"So that's how he's going to do it. We couldn't just head off somewhere across the ocean without some good reason," said Bran.

"Do you think he'll really make us study along the way?" asked Abbe.

"Let's hope so," said Bib. "I don't want to get behind on my studies."

"You would say that," said Aonghus.

"But won't it be grand?" said Frederick. "I mean, sailing! Real sailing! Don't you just love the sea, with its vastness and mystery?"

"I suppose so," said Aonghus, "although I'd never thought of being a sailor."

"I have," said Frederick.

"Well, I guess we'd better get things packed then. And I think you'll be needing some different clothes," said Aonghus.

"The professor has already taken care of that. I've got a whole new wardrobe. But I will be taking those things I found in the Land of ... well, you know where." Frederick said the last in a whisper, not wishing to draw attention.

"Where did you put the sword?" whispered Bran.

"The professor has it," replied Frederick. "After all, it would look rather odd for a student to carry a sword around the campus."

"Right," said Aonghus.

"Is the professor going to tell Dad that we're going on a field trip?" asked Henny.

"Oh, that's taken care of too," said Frederick. "He mentioned to me that my mother has been notified that I arrived early and am fine and that I will be immediately leaving for Bermuda and neighboring islands, with a short stop in Ireland. A letter is also being sent to your father. Of course, we will be seeing him anyway.

"There are field trips mentioned in the school agreement that he was given, of course, and it does mention that some may be cultural field trips to neighboring countries. And this will just be a rather extended field trip. Don't worry, the professor will make sure everything is in order."

They spent the remainder of the morning getting their things ready to go, and saying farewell to their new friends. When afternoon came, they gathered together on the shore of the lake and gazed down into its clear depths.

"Do you see that dark rock wall, way down there?" said Frederick, pointing to a dark patch toward the middle of the lake.

They all gazed down into the water, but it was quite difficult to see anything since a breeze was blowing and the surface of the lake was shimmering in the sunlight.

"I don't see anything," said Abbe.

"Well, it's there," said Frederick. "I'm sure that's the spot. If you swim down about thirty feet, you go under a ledge, and there's an underwater passage. Follow that in for about ten feet and it rises up and into the cave where I found... it. And that tree is down there too, and so are *they*."

"This is so hard to believe," said Bib.

"But I saw them too, Bib," said Aonghus. "They were... beautiful, but otherworldly, you might say. And they had *green hair!*"

"If it came from anyone else, big brother, I'd say they were a bit loony," she replied.

But before he could respond, there was a voice from behind.

"So, the Irish are off on a little field trip, eh?"

They turned to see Ed Choke, Slick, Bigs, and Fred, along with six very sour-looking characters behind them, who obviously were not students at the school.

"Hello, Ed," said Aonghus. "No hard feelings, I hope."

"Better tell your little sisters to beat it, boy. And you too, Buttersmouth," said Ed.

Aonghus' face grew stormy as he looked at the ten boys who had wicked grins on their faces.

"Go ahead, Abbe, Bib, Henny – and you too, Frederick. Go on back to the commons. We'll be there shortly," he said.

"Aonghus..." began Bib, but he silenced her with an upraised hand.

The girls slipped away, but Frederick remained.

"Frederick?" said Bran. "Are you sure you want to be a part of this?"

Frederick did not answer, but looked stonily at Ed.

"Right then," said Bran, grinning broadly. "Frederick, how many of them do you want to put in the lake?"

"I say we let him have 'em all," said Aonghus with a sudden laugh, seeing the look on Frederick's face. "He looks mad enough to take them by himself!"

Before any punches could be thrown, there was a strange sound coming from the nearby woods. They all turned, and out of the trees came a herd of deer – about a dozen of them, headed by a huge buck with an impressive rack of antlers. They came charging directly at the group of boys and, as they came, the great buck lowered his head and sped forward.

"Look out!" yelled one of the boys, and the group scattered, some running this way and some that. Ed Choke ran directly into the lake and dove in as the buck followed him into chest-deep water.

Aonghus and Bran stood totally still, and Aonghus' strong grip on Frederick's shoulder kept him frozen in place.

The herd thundered around and past them, chasing the group of boys as they scattered, until they had all run from the lake shore. In the end, only Ed Choke remained, treading water as the great stag pranced back and forth in the shallows, daring him to approach.

Casually, Abbe walked from the woods, with Bib and Henny behind her, then down to the shore where the stag was. It snorted once at Ed, then trotted over to Abbe.

She wrapped her arms around its neck in a hug and said, "Thank you, good stag."

It tossed its great head once, then trotted away, calling to its herd, which returned to him, and they all returned to the woods.

"You're a bunch of freaks!" yelled Ed from the lake. "Devils! That's what you are!"

"Come on, Ed, get out of the water. There are things in there worse than deer," called Bran.

Ed looked hesitantly down at the water and quickly began to swim ashore. Aonghus waded out to meet him, and offered his hand to help. But Ed refused it. Aonghus only shook his head sadly as they both waded ashore.

Ed looked at the six of them, and as he turned and ran from the shore, he shouted, "There's something mighty weird about you all, and I aim to find out what it is."

"Ah, well," said Aonghus. "Some people are just nasty, I suppose."

"Say, ladies, that was some trick," said Bran. "How did you get those deer to do that?"

"Henny spotted them in the wood where we went to hide and watch," said Bib, "and Abbe just ran over to that big stag, gave it a hug, and pointed out Ed Choke to it. We could see that those boys were ready to start something bad. Then the whole herd went running from the wood and right at them. It was amazing! Henny and I just stayed out of the way."

"I knew you were good with animals, Abbe," said Aonghus, "but that's pretty amazing!"

Abbe blushed and said, "Thanks. I'm not sure just how it happened. It just did, that's all."

"Come on, let's get back to the Commons. I'm sure Choke and his buddies are spreading rumors already."

They headed back, washed, and went to dinner, then retired early, having everything packed and ready to go. Frederick stayed with Aonghus and Bran, but they could not sleep, and the three of them talked long into the night, wondering what the next day might bring.

Chapter 16 – The Field Trip

Morning came, and the McGunnegals and Frederick were up with the sun. They met in the Commons, where they found the professor. Gwydion was nowhere to be seen.

"All packed and ready to go?" said Professor McPherson.

"All set, sir," replied Aonghus.

"Good, the ship is at the docks downtown not far from here. Gwydion is waiting for us. He and I took a carriage there early this morning. I've arranged for all of the supplies for our voyage," he replied.

After a good breakfast, they all gathered their belongings and followed the professor outside. There, they found two cars waiting for them.

"Marvelous!" said Bib excitedly. "Are we to ride in these steam cars to the docks?"

"Yes," said the professor. "This one is mine," he said, indicating a fancy black car that puffed gray steam, "which I've just had serviced this morning, and this one belongs to my friend, Rodger Wilcocks."

A tall thin man with graying hair, wearing a red cap and brown trousers, tipped his hat to them.

"Pleased to make your acquaintance," he said.

Rodger's car also puffed steam, but was larger than the professor's vehicle, able to seat six with a cargo area in the rear.

"Load up your bags onto Rodger's car, and you boys ride with him. Ladies, I believe there is just enough room for the three of you in my vehicle. Come now, let's be off," said the professor.

In a few moments, they were ready, and with a toot of horns and clouds of steam, they rolled away toward the docks.

"Sir, how did you acquire a steam-powered car? I've only seen them a few times, but I've heard all sorts of rumors about them back home," said Bib.

"Ah, I have a friend who is an inventor. This one was an older model of his. He has created a much better one, so to help finance his projects, I purchased this one from him. Rodger is his partner. They hope to start a business selling them one day," he replied. "We shall be taking this car along with us on our journey. Who can say where we may need to travel?"

"Wonderful!" she replied. "Do you think I might have a go at driving it? I mean, if we find a good open space where I wouldn't hit anything?" she asked.

Professor McPherson laughed and said, "Of course, my dear. You shall all give it a try as soon as we are able, although that may not be for some time."

For the rest of the journey, Bib and Professor McPherson chatted on about autos and ships and building things, and where the world might be going with all the new inventions that were coming about.

The professor was amazed at Bib's insights into so many fields of science that he said, "Bib, I do believe that you are destined to be an inventor one day. How about making your Focus *Science and the Exploration of the Natural World* when we return to school?"

"Well, I really do like making things and tinkering and just plain thinking. I don't have the weird talents that my brothers and sisters have," she replied.

"What do you mean by *weird talents*, Bib?" he asked.

"Well, I mean, take Abbe here, for example. You might as well say that she can talk to animals," said Bib.

"No, it's not like that," piped up Abbe. "They just seem to know what I want them to do, and they know I won't harm them, and they do it."

"And then there's Henny," continued Bib. "She can see and hear things that nobody else can. It's like she's got eagle eyes or something. And she's got this *really* strange ability to play hide and seek, and *nobody* has *ever* been able to find her. She also has a way of keeping people honest. You just can't lie to her or fool her. She has a way of seeing right through you."

Henny's cheeks blushed with embarrassment.

"And what about your brothers?" asked the professor, growing more curious all the time.

"Oh, Aonghus is just about busting with muscles. I've never seen anything or anybody as strong as him, except maybe Dad. And Bran – he can shoot an arrow through a bull's-eye from a mile away or catch an arrow right out of the air. And those two can run like horses."

"And what of your sister Colleen?" he asked.

"Well, she inherited Mom's voice. It's... I know it sounds funny... but it's *magical*. Stuff just seemed to happen when Mom sang. And Colleen seems to have that same talent. Dad used to say that Mom could sing the stars right out of the sky if she tried," replied Bib. "But me, I just think a lot."

"Don't let Bib fool you, Professor," said Abbe. "There's never been a puzzle that she hasn't been able to solve. She says she can see the solution to things in her mind like it's a picture in front of her. Plus, she makes the boys practically swoon with that smile of hers."

"Oh, hush!" said Bib.

"Don't sell yourself short, Bib," said the professor. "Each person has hidden talents that they only discover when they are needed. They may lie hidden for years and years. And besides that, having a keen mind is a rare gift."

They rode on in silence for some time, and the girls' thoughts turned to their mother. Could it be that Colleen and Frederick had actually found out where she was?

But soon the trip drew to an end, and the docks came into sight. The two cars puffed up alongside the wharf where a rather beleaguered-looking small ship was docked. It had old tarps hanging over its rails and bow, giving it an almost haunted appearance. Two tall masts jutted skyward from which yellowing sails hung limply. The group of them got out of the cars and stared at the old ship.

"Is this the ship we're sailing in?" asked Frederick.

"Yes," replied Professor McPherson. "She's seen many voyages."

"But where is the crew?" asked Bib.

"The crew? Oh, didn't I tell you? *You* are going to be the crew of this ship," he replied.

"We are?" said Aonghus.

"Yes! Well, you and a few others. I could only find three lads on such short notice, but we are only sailing to Ireland, at least for the moment, but our ship is small and needs only a few experienced crewmen and a half dozen others who are willing to listen and learn. I shall be your captain," he said. "Now, let's get your things aboard."

They all wondered if the professor was playing a joke on them, but as they gathered up their belongings and walked across the gangplank, they could only see three sailors going about the ship, getting her ready to sail. Professor McPherson carried a heavy bag and something wrapped in a blanket as they walked aboard.

"I think he's actually serious," whispered Bran to Aonghus. "This is madness!"

"Oh, don't worry, Bran," said the professor, overhearing. "You will all do just fine. It will be a short trip."

"What's your ship's name, Professor?" asked Henny.

"She's called the *Unknown*, my dear. I named her that because so many times we have sailed there together, off into the unknown," he replied. "She was built as a prototype of the bigger clipper ships we see today, and she's just as fast."

He led them across the deck, which was littered with old barrels and ropes and tarps and various other items, leaving only a small path for them to walk.

Frederick looked about at all of the junk and aged appearance of everything and secretly wondered if the old ship would even make such a short voyage. But the professor beamed with pride as he led them down through a hatch into the hull of the ship.

They descended a flight of stairs through a passage whose walls were draped with what appeared to be old blankets and quilts and curtains.

"Wait here one moment while I put these things in my cabin," he said.

He went through a door at the end of the hall, and re-emerged empty handed, trailed by Gwydion.

The old man was dressed in modern clothes rather than his old robe that they had seen him in before, and he sported a maroon coat with tails over a white shirt, and light brown britches with black shoes. In place of his tall staff, he leaned on a gentleman's cane, and his long beard and hair were both tied in ponytails.

"Hello, children," he said with a grin, revealing full set of white teeth.

"Hello, Mr. Gwydion," said Henny. "You look different today."

"And you look just the same as I remember from yesterday," he replied, and patted her on the head.

"Come along then," said the professor and he opened a door on the right. "Here are your quarters."

"This cabin is for the ladies," he said.

They all went in to find a fair-sized room with two sets of bunks against the walls and a small table with four chairs around it. An oil lamp hung from a gold chain that was attached to the ceiling, shedding a warm light about the room, and the walls were adorned with old tapestries of lighthouses and sea cliffs and other seaside landscapes.

"It's actually quite cozy," said Abbe. "I think we'll be quite comfortable."

They each picked a bunk – Abbe and Bib taking the lower ones and Henny climbing up into an upper one and grinning broadly.

"And now for the gentleman's quarters," said the professor.

He led them across the hall to a similar room that had somewhat larger bunks, which Aonghus and Bran were glad of.

"I might actually fit in this one," said Aonghus, stretching out on one of the lower beds.

Frederick selected an upper bunk and put his bag up on it.

"Now the galley is the next door on the right, and the mess hall is directly across from it on the left. You'll have plenty of time to see those rooms later. Gwydion will be staying with me in my cabin on the spare bunk, and the rest of the crew will be in the large crew quarters through that last door.

"But we must be off very soon. I have a good deal of teaching to do for you all, and there's no time to waste," said the professor. "Come along now, to the upper deck for your first lesson."

They marched up on the deck to see Rodger carefully driving the professor's car across two wide planks onto the ship.

"In all my days!" said Gwydion in surprise. "What wizardry is this? A horseless carriage?"

"Oh, it's not wizardry," said Bib to the old man. "It's technology."

"Technology! I have not heard of that. Is it akin to alchemy?" he asked.

"Yes, you could say that, although today, we would call that *chemistry,*" she replied.

"Well, Bib, you and I must have a discussion regarding this *technology* and *chemistry,* and we shall compare them to wizardry and alchemy. Truly the world has changed!"

Rodger had now maneuvered the car onto the ship, and they walked over to it to steady it while the planks were removed.

Gwydion walked about it with a look of amazement. "*Technology,*" he whispered. "It is a *device*, is it not? I sense heat and steam coming from its belly."

"Indeed," said the professor. "It is a *machine*. The knowledge of mankind is advancing quickly, and we build more and more complex machines as our understanding of the world grows. This machine is run with steam power. A fire heats water and produces steam, and that steam is used to turn an engine inside, which turns the wheels and *voila!* You have a horseless carriage."

"Indeed, I have awakened into a strange and wondrous world," whispered Gwydion.

The old man examined the car, and Professor McPherson explained some of its parts further.

"Where's he been, off on an island somewhere?" whispered Rodger to Bran with a smirk.

Bran breathed a little laugh and shrugged.

"You might say that. You know how old folks are with technology," he whispered back.

Rodger smiled and nodded.

"Well, very good, then," said the professor, concluding his explanation to Gwydion. "Let's get the car secured in the lower hold. Over here there's a large hatch for stowing the cargo."

He led them over to a brass ring that was set in a raised section of the floor of the deck, and, moving aside a bundle of old rope and a few barrels, they could see a large doorframe about ten feet square with brass hinges opposite the ring.

He unbolted two large sliding bolts that locked the door down, and untied a rope and hook from one of the masts that was attached to a pulley up above. He attached the hook to the brass ring and then pulled the rope tight.

"It generally takes two or three of us to lift this door, but Bib says that Aonghus is quite a strapping fellow. How about taking care of it for us, and tie it off once you have the door open. Bran, you stand ready to give your brother a hand. Bib and Rodger and I will maneuver the car into place. Gwydion would you like to sit in the passenger's seat? Everyone else, please clear a path for us."

Gwydion carefully climbed into the seat that McPherson indicated and looked at the dashboard, pedals, and knobs.

"Amazing!" he said, listening to the steam engine sputtering.

"Everything in the hold must be secured and tied down, or when we hit rough seas, it will shift or fall and break open. That goes for your personal belongings in your cabins as well, and everything in the galley and mess hall, and on deck. That is why you see so many ropes lying about. We shall need them to lash down our cargo, our belongings, and perhaps, even ourselves at times," said Professor McPherson.

Aonghus took the rope that was now hooked to the ring in the deck from the professor and pulled. The huge trap door in the deck lifted open silently, revealing a wooden ramp that extended down into the bowels of the ship. Aonghus tied off the rope to the mast and watched as Bib, now behind the wheel of the car, was listening intently to Professor McPherson's instructions on the use of the accelerator, brake, and steering. Gwydion listened carefully, taking note of everything. In a few minutes, a path had been cleared, and Bib maneuvered the car in front of the ramp, and then the professor showed her how to turn it off.

"Give us a little push, would you, Aonghus? Not too hard now," said the professor.

Aonghus got behind the car, and pushed the car forward so that its front wheels were on the ramp.

"Now ease off the brake just slightly, Bib, and let her roll on down to the bottom of the cargo hold," said Professor McPherson.

Bib did so, and slowly the car rolled down the ramp into the hold.

Aonghus walked behind, his hand still on the bar that ran around the rear of the car.

Suddenly, the brake on the car slipped, and it began to roll without restraint down the ramp. Gwydion's eyes went wide, and he gripped the dashboard in front of him.

But Aonghus pulled hard, slowing the car, and brought it to a stop at the bottom of the ramp.

"Well!" said the professor. "I shall have a look at that brake before we use the car again! Thank you, Aonghus."

"Yes, thank you, Aonghus!" said Gwydion.

"Bravo, Bib!" said Bran. "I didn't know you could drive a car."

"Neither did I," she said, smiling.

Gwydion said nothing, but looked in wonder again at the horseless carriage. At length, they climbed back up the ramp and onto the deck of the ship.

"Now, Rodger, would you take care of securing the car for me, please, and oversee the loading of the rest of our supplies?" asked Professor McPherson. "I would like to take our young students to the Green Tree Inn for a brief lunch, and then we shall set sail."

"Certainly, sir," replied Rodger, and he went down into the cargo hold and began to secure the car with ropes to rings mounted in the walls.

"Come now, students, we shall have an early lunch and then be on our way," said the professor. "Gwydion, would you care to join us as well?"

"Indeed," he replied.

McPherson led them off the ship and down the wharf past a number of tall sailing ships to a friendly looking inn that had a large green sign hanging above the door that said, "*The Green Tree Inn – Welcome.*"

The professor opened the door, and the girls filed in first, and the others were about to follow when a voice from down the wharf called out, "Frederick Buttersmouth, is that you?"

Frederick stopped and looked, and walking toward them was the large form of Baroness Helga Von Faust. She had dark circles under her eyes, and she looked tired.

"What a surprise," she said in her thick German accent, "and oh, I see that the McGunnegal children are with you as well. And Professor McPherson! We have just arrived, and your father is unloading his things. But what are you doing here at the Green Tree?"

"Uh..." began Frederick, but Professor McPherson interrupted.

"Ah, Baroness, how nice to see you again," he said cordially. "As you can see, I am treating these students to lunch at the Inn. Would you and Rufus like to join us?"

"No, no," she replied wearily. "I did not sleep a wink on the trip back. I hate sailing, and always get sick. How could anyone be a sailor? I feel as though I will fall asleep on my feet. But what is this? You rode all the way from the school to bring these children to the Green Tree Inn for lunch?" she asked, a hint of suspicion in her voice.

"Well, here we are," replied the professor, "and we are also doing some educational work as well. Today, I shall be teaching each of them a bit about sailing. I have my ship docked just up the wharf there, and we shall be casting off just as soon as we have eaten our lunch."

He pointed to where the ship was, and they could see Rodger and a few other men loading barrels and crates aboard.

"Ah, your... *ship*... yes, I remember seeing it when we first met. Still floating, is it? Well, do not take it too far," she laughed, "or you might be giving these children swimming lessons!"

She laughed with her deep harsh laugh and turned to go, but then spotted Gwydion and stopped.

"And who might this be?" she asked.

"Ah," said McPherson. "This is my friend Gwydion. He is visiting and will be setting sail with us."

Helga looked the old man up and down and sniffed.

"Well, have fun, Frederick. Stay within sight of land, just in case! I shall tell your father that you are here in town, although I doubt he will have time to see you. He is going to the train station to take some sto.... well... *items* for inspection at the museum."

"I have notified Mabel," said Professor McPherson, "that we will be going on an extended field trip today. A letter is waiting for Rufus at their home as well. Please extend my greeting to him when you see him again. Good day."

* * *

Helga watched them as they turned and went into the inn. She rubbed her chin, thinking. Strange that even before the school semester had begun, they were heading off somewhere.

"What are those McGunnegals up to, I wonder," she muttered under her breath.

Then an idea struck her. She wandered up toward the professor's ship and watched as the men finished loading the last few crates of supplies down into the cargo hold. She looked at the seagulls for a moment, then turned and pretended to be strolling away, but was actually listening carefully to their conversation.

"There's one more big one at the butcher's shop," said Rodger to one of the men. "We'll take my car and load it in, then bring it back."

The three men piled into Rodger's car, and he started it up. It *poofed* out a head of steam as they rolled away toward the butcher.

Helga casually strolled up the gangplank.

"Just a quick look around," she said to herself.

She wrinkled her nose at the litter of debris about the deck, then slipped down the stairs below deck.

Poking her head into each of the rooms, she saw the crew quarters, the galley, and the mess hall, and then went to the end of the hall and opened that last door. It was the Captain's cabin. She slipped in and shut the door, peering about the lamp-lit room at the same drab tapestries that had decorated the other rooms. But then something caught her eye. There was a bulging bag of something next to a desk in the middle of the room. She opened it, and there inside were the stones that she and Rufus had given Mabel to take with her back to Wales.

"Those McGunnegal rats have stolen the stones and given them to McPherson!" she hissed.

Grabbing the heavy bag, she made her way back down the hall and up the stairs to the upper deck and was going to leave when she saw Rodger and the other men drive up the wharf and park the car next to the ship. She was near the open cargo hold, so she quickly slid down the ramp, nearly tumbling head over heels. The sight of the car in the cargo hold surprised her, making her even more curious about their journey, but she could hear the men walking up the plank and talking, and knew that she must not be seen, especially with the bag of stones.

"This one go in the cargo hold too, Rodger?" asked one of the men.

"Yep, just set it down there behind the car and lash it down. That will be the last of it," he replied.

Helga looked about frantically, and then squeezed behind a stack of crates, peering through a crack between them. The two men brought down a large box, placed it behind the car, and proceeded to tie it down with ropes. Then they walked back up the ramp, and Helga heard Rodger say, "That's it, men. Thanks for the help. Oh! One last thing, give me a hand with this."

She thought that they were going to bring one more thing down, so she stayed in her hiding place, waiting. All of a sudden, the sunlight shining down into the cargo hold grew dimmer and dimmer, and with an audible *WHUMP*, the heavy trap door fell shut, and she found herself in absolute darkness. The dull slide and click of two bolts being thrown quickly followed. Shock and surprise flooded over her, and she squeezed out of her hiding place, and tried to make her way back to the ramp.

"Wait, you idiots!" she yelled. But in the darkness, she tripped over one of the ropes that tied down a crate, gave her head a good knock, and was out cold.

* * *

Back in the Green Tree Inn, the McGunnegals, Frederick, Gwydion, and Professor McPherson finished their lunch and headed out the door and back toward the ship. The three sailors, having had their own lunch, joined them.

Rodger was sitting in his car waiting for them, and as they approached he said, "She's fully stocked, Professor. The kitchen is loaded with at least a week's worth of supplies, so you shouldn't have to dip into the stores in the cargo hold for quite a while."

"Thank you so much, Rodger," replied Professor McPherson. "I am in your debt once again."

"No, no," he replied. "Glad to help. You kids enjoy your trip. Gwydion, nice to make your acquaintance."

They all said farewell, and then walked across the gangplank, where the professor began to give some instructions while the three sailors looked on, amused smirks on their faces.

"Well, now, since you're all new to sailing, let's go over some basic rules," he said.

He went over basic safety rules of the ship, often stopping and asking them to repeat these back to him.

"Now, the first day or so, we may stay in sight of land, just so you all can get your sea legs on and learn your part as the crew. Now, who's best with heights and has the best eyes?" he asked.

Henny raised her hand. "I love to climb trees and look about, Professor," she said.

"Well, lass, do you see that crow's nest way up on the top of the main mast?"

He pointed, and they all looked up to see a platform with rails around it.

"No way, Henny," said Aonghus. "You are *not* going to climb up there."

"But I can do it!" said Henny.

"I'm sure you can, little one," he replied. "But it's too high. If you fell..."

"Oh, she would not fall, Aonghus." interrupted the professor. "There is a special place there to tie in. Even on your way up, there is a rope to secure you."

"I would have to see that for myself," he replied.

"Fair enough. You're a good brother, Aonghus. Now, the next job is to keep the decks clean."

They all looked about the deck at the mess, and several of the sailors laughed.

"Aye, you Irish swabbies will have your hands full cleaning this beaut!" called one of them, and they laughed louder.

"Professor," said Abbe, "one can hardly *see* the deck, much less keep it clean."

He laughed and said, "Ah, you shall see what I mean soon enough."

"Then, there is the pilot. The pilot must know how to follow the sun and the moon and the stars, and be familiar with the currents and landmarks along the shoreline. There are many maps to study and become familiar with. This is a job for someone who can learn and remember things quickly."

"That would be Bib," said Bran.

"We also need some stout lads to secure the rigging, let down and hoist up the sails, do a good bit of climbing on the masts, and know how to tie the right knots for each rope."

"Sounds like a job for the boys," said Bib.

"And we also need a captain – that would be me, of course – and a first mate and a cook."

"Ah, I know a thing or two about cooking," said Gwydion.

"Excellent," said the professor.

"However, I would like each of you to try out each job, and learn how to do it well. As we sail, I shall be holding lectures on various subjects so that your schooling truly goes on for the next two days until we reach Ireland."

"I thought we were sailing to Ireland to rescue Colleen and Mother," said Abbe.

"Ah, true, true," replied the professor. "But even when you are on your way to do important things, you mustn't neglect other aspects of your life. We have a day or two before we arrive. We might as well redeem the time and do something useful."

"Now," he continued. "Knot tying..."

Soon the professor had them all practicing various knots with lengths of rope, tying lines to masts, posts, anchors, and securing two lines together. Gwydion demonstrated a few knots that even the professor didn't know, and they watched as he tied a complex triple slip knot that he said his kin had used on their ships.

The professor was soon satisfied that they had mastered these, and quite impressed that they did so very quickly.

"Well, then, let's be off! Our next lesson will be with the sails," he said.

He described to them how to let down the sails just enough to move them slowly from the docks and out into the channel, and Aonghus and Bran were the first to climb the masts, followed by one of the crewmen named Jake.

When they reached the top, Jake said, "By the looks of it, you Irishmen haven't done much sailing. See here, what's this here professor doing with you lot? Three crewmen and a split dozen of kids to sail the seas? Not that you two are kids, mind you, but it seems odd enough. And who are you, anyway?"

"We're students at the professor's school. He's taking us on a field trip of sorts and we're learning how to sail while we go," replied Aonghus.

"Well, the old man says that Ireland may not be our last stop. He pays well enough, mind you, but if he wants to venture out into the Atlantic, he best find more than the ten of us to man his ship, I can tell you that," said Jake.

Aonghus and Bran said nothing, but watched below as the girls and Frederick untethered the ship from the wharf and pulled in the gangplank. Then, with Jake giving instructions, they loosened the sail ties, allowing them to drop halfway, then climbed down again.

The ship slowly began to move, and Professor McPherson and Henny took the ship's wheel and guided it into the deeper water, while Gwydion stood on the upper deck and watched with great interest.

"Let down the sails," called the professor after a time. "Be sure you tie them securely! We don't need our sails to be footloose!"

Aonghus started to climb the rope ladder up the mast again, but found that Frederick had beaten him to it and was already ten feet above him. Frederick grinned down at him and climbed on. Aonghus glanced over at the professor, who was also grinning, looking positively proud at the sight of Frederick.

"Are you sure you know the ropes, Frederick?" he called.

"Yes, sir!" he called back. "I never forget something once I hear it!"

Indeed, Frederick easily climbed out onto the mast, let down the sails, and secured them.

* * *

The sails caught the wind and billowed out, and the little ship shot forward. But Frederick was expecting this, and was holding tightly to the mast. With the wind in his hair and the smell of the sea all about him, he felt as if he had been set free. He smiled broadly, and looked about as they sailed swiftly away from Wales. Then he climbed up into the crow's nest, found the anchor rope, tied himself in, and sat down on a low stool that was part of the whole setup. Seagulls danced about him as the land rushed away and the open sea greeted them. He felt free – freer than he had ever felt before. And there was another feeling as well. It was as if the sea *called* to him – as though he *needed* to sail out into the great blue waters. Some destiny lay out there, but what it was, he did not know. He was only glad to be sailing toward it at last.

Then all of the adventures of the last few days rushed back to his mind. The Lady Danu had said that a great task lay before him, and that he was to seek the king in the sea. He wished that they were now sailing toward Bermuda. Would he ever get there now? He hoped so. But as the smell of the sea grew and the wind whipped his raven-colored hair about, he leaned forward on the rail and gazed outward, letting his mind wander out across the great expanse of blue that lay before him.

Chapter 17 – The Tomb

Adol McGunnegal sat very still in his hiding place amid the tall reeds in the bog. Three days had passed since he had seen the black creature, but there had been signs that it was moving about, doing what, he did not know.

Its trails crisscrossed the length and breadth of the vast bog, and he had a growing sense that something very bad was happening in this place. For one thing, strange sounds had risen up from its heart last night, and he had seen odd lights that would wink on and off, then disappear entirely. He had also learned from a neighbor, old man Gernie, that there was a rumor among the nearby farms that odd things had begun to happen. Shadows had been seen dancing in the fields under the moon, and dark shapes in the sky. A general feeling of uneasiness was settling over the area.

Some town folk were blaming the McGunnegals. They said that they had seen queer things running across their farm at night, and Gernie claimed that he had seen a ghost in the old McGunnegal graveyard while he was out walking his dog. Mothers had started to close the shutters at sundown, and good folk locked their doors until the morning's rays shone in the east. Children crawled into bed with their parents as bad dreams woke them, and there was word that the potato blight was spreading far and wide. There was something ill at work in all this, or so Adol surmised. This black creature was at the heart of it, he knew, but catching it was proving to be tricky, and it seemed to be able to vanish into the mists at will.

He suspected that it knew that he was tracking it, and it was being careful. The more time he spent in the bog, the more he felt that he too was being watched and stalked. The nameless *presence* that he felt here weighed upon him continuously, and he had a sense that smaller, although still malevolent, eyes watched from the twisted roots and boughs of ancient trees and stumps and holes in the rocks. He did not dare to go into the bog at night. Even now, the day was drawing to a close, so he rose from his place and stealthily stole down the now familiar path back to the farm.

Behind him, a black hooded shape rose from the deepening shadows and began to slink along, tree to tree, watching him depart. But Adol was an extraordinary tracker and woodsman, and it was not long before he sensed that something was indeed following him, keeping its distance, and biding its time.

When he reached the wall and climbed over and into greener pastures, it paused, waiting, and then it too climbed slowly upward and peered over the edge. When it did not see Adol, it slowly, slyly, inched its way upward, trying to get a better look, and stayed in the shadows that the trees cast on the top of the wall.

All at once, Adol's huge form sprang upward, right in the face of the creature. The big man lunged at it, but it leaped upward in the air like a startled cat, screaming a hideous cry of surprise and fear and rage, and Adol missed it by an inch. Off the wall it sprang, back into the bog, and Adol was over and after it in a flash, his big club in his massive fist. Down trail after trail, he pursued it, and as the minutes passed, the sun began to set behind the western horizon, and the shadows grew long and ominous. Onward he chased it, running through thick tangles of trees and across wet ground. Although the black creature was smaller and quicker than Adol, a rage now pounded in Adol's heart, and nothing would stop his pursuit.

Suddenly, a great boulder loomed before him, and the creature dove into a small cave beneath it. It was an old animal den, he knew, but he bellowed a great cry and, with a tremendous *heave*, he rolled the rock away. The black creature lay huddled on the barren earth, and hissed at him in fear. He leaped forward, but again it dove away, and ran down a side trail, heading for the center of the bog.

Now a mist had begun to rise, and Adol could just see the black shape as it weaved and bobbed in its mad flight. A light twinkled to his left, distracting him for a moment, and in that instant, the creature vanished beneath the haze.

He ran to where he had last seen it, but only swirls in the gathering fog showed any sign that it had been there. Adol furrowed his eyebrows, set his jaw, and walked forward. The darkness was deepening now, and as he made his way in what he thought to be the right direction, he thought that he heard a sound like little padded feet following along beside him, now on his left, and now on his right. Something shapeless flitted through the air by his ear, and he waved it away – a bat. He sighed with relief.

Mustn't let my mind play tricks on me, he thought.

Gathering his wits, he looked at the last light of the fading sky in the west, turned north, and hurried onward.

"*Nearly caught it!*" he whispered aloud to himself in frustration.

Through the old trees he went, and their branches seemed to hang low and grab at his clothes and scratch his face. He had lost all trails now, for the mist was as thick as pea soup about him, and only his keen sense of direction kept him from turning about and wandering aimlessly. Rustles and scratching and weird sounds like something pulling out of the mud could be heard from time to time, and once he thought he saw a black shape rise before him and then vanish away as he lifted his club against it.

Such a queer place – an evil place! he thought as he made his way onward.

Although his heart was bold, and the shadows and sounds in the mist did not make him afraid, still he wished his sons were with him. Best to deal with such dank places in the light of day and with good company.

All at once, the Wall rose before him. He was far to the west of the normal place he would have crossed it, but he climbed up and to the top, and looked out over the old graveyard of his ancestors. Behind him, the bog spread outward, a great white, shrouded sea with many twisted branches of dark treetops poking through like so many reaching fingers. Strange sounds began to echo in the mists – croaks and chirps and something that sounded like a high-pitched laugh. Only a slight mist curled its way among the graves on the other side of the wall. After glancing one last time southward, he dropped down and into the lighter air of his farm.

The great mounds that were the graves of the McGunnegals-past now surrounded him, and he felt no animosity from them, but something was different on this night. Was it his imagination – or did he sense a *restlessness* in the air, a sense that something was amiss?

As he passed by the largest of the mounds – the grave of Geer, son of Laar McGunnegal, he paused. The earth had been disturbed. He bent low in the dim light and looked. There, dug into the hill, was a tunnel of sorts. Adol ground his teeth and snarled. That black creature dared even to defile the graves of his ancestors! Anger rose up in him. He could not let this go until morning.

From a small pouch at his side, he pulled out an oiled cloth, wrapped it about a branch that he found nearby, and with his tinderbox, lit it as a torch. Placing his club in his belt, he held the torch in the entrance of the tunnel and looked within. It was a thin passage, barely wide enough for him to squeeze through if he lay flat, but beyond this low entry way, it appeared to broaden considerably, and he could dimly see a wall of sorts some ways in. At this wall, the floor of the passage seemed to change from brown earth to gray stone.

Now curiosity began to replace his anger, and despite some misgivings and a moment's hesitation, he pushed the torch into the hole, lay on his belly, and wriggled into the passageway.

It was a tight fit, and dusty, and the close air and loose earth threatened to choke him. Nevertheless, he pushed forward and, in a few moments, lay at the entrance to a square room about ten feet wide, on the floor of which was a single slab of gray stone about six feet wide and four inches thick, and on this was engraved a great rising sun over a plain. The slab lay shifted, revealing a crack or hole about an inch wide, with a dark hollow space beneath it.

Is this the tomb of Geer? he wondered.

The black creature had obviously tried to move the slab, but the room was too small to slide it to the side completely, and the slab was heavy.

Good, then it has not defiled my ancestor's grave, he thought.

Adol tried to maneuver it back in its place, to cover the gap, but here, with only his shoulders in the room, and the rest of his body still in the tunnel, he could find no leverage. Pulling himself fully into the chamber and sitting on the slab, he looked about. The masonry on the wall that he had entered through was broken. The creature had no doubt managed to find a loose stone, and once it pushed that one inward, the others easily moved as well, although they were good-sized blocks, at least a foot square. He knew he had to act quickly, for the room was filling with smoke from his torch.

Moving to the other side of the room, he put his back to the wall and his feet against the slab and gave a slight push to maneuver it back into place. However, the heavy stone did not yield. He pushed harder, then harder, and all at once, with a *bang,* it slid sideways and hit the opposite wall. Adol growled in frustration. Sometimes, he did not know his own strength. Now a gap of at least two feet lay exposed, but he was more curious than ever. With great care, he held the torch above the opening and peered down, thinking that he would see the bones of Geer.

But there were no bones to be seen. Rather, a white stairway led downward, how far, he could not tell. He lifted his torch, thinking. These grave mounds had been a matter of family legend and bedtime stories for generations and generations, and here he was inside one of them. He could not resist the urge to explore this further, so he squeezed through the opening and slid down to the steps into the darkness below.

Chapter 18 – The Hammer of Geer

Adol followed a long marble staircase that led downward for a long way to a white tunnel whose ceiling towered far above his head. Many, many years must have passed since this crypt's construction, for the marble was calcified, and stalactites hung in places from the ceiling, and their mated stalagmites rose from the floor to meet them.

The hall ended at a tall door made of a single slab of stone that nearly reached the ceiling. Inscribed on this was the same symbol of a rising sun over a plain that he had seen on the covering to the staircase, and around its stone frame were carved many strange runes.

There was also a large handprint carved in the door – much too large to fit a human hand – easily eight inches across and twice that in height – and within that hand, a smaller one, although still large, as though one were overlaid upon the other – a hand within a hand. Adol placed his palm in the smaller of the two carved prints and, to his complete surprise, there was a hiss of stale air and the door swung out. The smell of a chamber shut up for long ages met him.

He stepped back, not for fear, but in wonder, for the flicker of his torch caught a bright glint of something within. For a moment, he considered shutting the door and leaving the grave of his ancestor in peace, but he had come too far now and curiosity gripped him. Slowly, reverently, he stepped through the door and held his torch high. The sight inside made his eyes grow wide and his mouth drop open, for shelves of vessels and goblets and chests lined a large stone room, and in the center, on a raised dais of three large steps, sat a great white sarcophagus.

Adol looked in amazement at the adornments all about him. Never in all his wildest dreams did he imagine that such a thing lay beneath his farm, buried with Geer McGunnegal for untold generations past. To an archaeologist, this would be invaluable. It would tell stories of ancient Ireland never before told. Yet, even as he saw it, he knew that he would not take any of it, not unless others threatened to rob this place. He would save these graves from the plundering of modern men. At least for now, the mysteries here would remain at rest, and the treasure house of Geer, son of Laar, the first McGunnegal, would remain a family secret.

With these thoughts, he ascended the large stone steps to the dais where the sarcophagus lay. It was huge – twelve feet long and six feet wide, and easily four feet tall. It was polished and smooth, except for a bright yellow golden sun rising over a field of green stones that were inlaid in its surface.

What surprised him even more, however, was that sitting atop this marvelous and gigantic coffin, was an amazing hammer. It had two heads wrought of a strange bright metal. There was no dent or flaw in the perfect mallet, its head was a foot wide from end to end, and each head was at least three inches broad. Its ornate shaft was deepest black, and its handle wrapped with a scarlet red material dimpled with golden studs. A large and equally ornate belt lay circled about it, trimmed with silver and gold and the same black material. Adol reached out a hand to touch it, so beautiful and compelling was its workmanship, but he withdrew it quickly.

How many centuries, he wondered, had this hammer and belt laid here on this grave? Had it been a parting gift from the son of Geer? Surely, it had been Geer's own hammer – a mighty war hammer by the looks of it, or perhaps a symbol of power, or of some office.

Suddenly, a sound to his right, a soft *hiss*, interrupted his thoughts. He turned quickly, and there was the black hooded creature peering up at him. Adol roared in anger. How *dare* that filthy thing enter this sacred burial chamber?

With speed and reflexes that surprised even him, Adol snatched up the hammer and threw it at the beast. It flew through the air, humming as it tumbled swiftly toward the place where the black shape had been. However, the creature had been quicker, and it was gone before the weapon left his hand. Nevertheless, the hammer flew, striking the stone pavement outside the door and splitting it in two. To Adol's absolute and total astonishment, it flew back to his hand, and he caught it effortlessly.

He stared at the weapon for only a moment, considering, and then scooped up the belt and ran after the black creature. When he squeezed out of the stairway, and back into the upper chamber, however, it was gone, and he knew he could not catch it now, nor would it return here soon. Frustrated and angry, he returned to the grave of Geer, carrying the belt and hammer.

It was strange, he thought, how *right* it felt in his big hand. It was heavy, to be sure, but not too heavy for his great strength. How had it *returned* to him?

He sat the hammer carefully on the step and examined the belt in the light of his torch. It was of marvelous artistry, flawless, and had a hook of sorts on the side where he realized the hammer attached by its handle.

Suddenly, he realized that his torch was burning low, so he made a decision. He would keep the hammer and belt, at least until morning. He picked up the hammer once again, left the burial chamber of Geer, pulled the great door shut, climbed the stairs, squeezed through the opening, and this time positioned the stone slab over the stairway evenly so that not even a crack showed.

His torch burned out, so slowly he felt his way to the dirt tunnel and squeezed through it, pushing his prizes carefully before him, trying not to soil them. In a few moments, he was through and breathed deeply of the clean air.

Holding up the hammer to the rising moon, he said, "I shall call you Geer, after your last owner. May you serve me well in the days ahead, and may I bear you well."

Then holding up the belt in his other hand, he said, "And you I shall call Laar, who once held his son Geer."

Removing his old belt, he fastened Laar about his waist. It fit him well, although how, he did not know, for it appeared to be very large when he first picked it up in the tomb. Then he found how the hammer clipped onto it, and, fastening it in its place, he headed back to the farmhouse.

* * *

Beyond the wall, a pair of greedy eyes watched as the big man walked slowly away. They blinked, and then disappeared into the mist.

Chapter 19 – Mirror Mirror

Adol was tired from his chase of the black creature, and the night was getting on now. Still, he took his time, walking slowly in the cool night air, thinking of the strange things that were happening. He was glad to be under a clear starry sky, and his spirit lifted somewhat as he drew near his home. But as he gained sight of the farm, he knew that something was amiss. Everything was too still. Even the crickets were silent. Then he noticed it – the back door of the house was sitting ajar.

He quickly ran the length of the field to the house and silently slipped into the kitchen. The cellar door had been forced open, and he could hear a good deal of scuffling and shifting. Something was down there.

Then he remembered. The mirror – it was after the mirror. Somehow, it had found out where he had hidden it.

Quickly, he lit an oil lamp and held it in his left hand, then took Geer in his right. He slipped through the cellar door and quietly closed it behind him, hoping that the creature would not be able to hear him through all the noise it was making. Then he rushed down the stairs and to the back of the basement.

He was very nearly too late, for there was the creature standing before the mirror. Its hood was thrown back, and for the first time Adol beheld its grotesque head and face as it stared at its own reflection. It looked like a deformed little man with over-sized ears and a bulbous nose. Its skin was a blotchy gray-green, and what remained of its hair hung in long dark strands down its bony face. Large yellow eyes stared at him through its reflection for only an instant, and then it swiftly held up the crystal ball.

The image in the mirror swirled into mist and then changed to a dark forest. The creature grinned wickedly, revealing brown and yellow teeth and fangs, and leaped, passing right through the mirror and into the forest beyond, and then ran. This time, however, Adol moved just as quickly, and with a great cry he dove headlong at the mirror, and just before the scene began to swirl, he was passing through it, and he found himself tumbling into a bed of leaves. He jumped to his feet, seeing the creature dashing away through the wood, and instantly he was after it.

To his surprise, it turned and ran around a huge tree. Adol pursued, and the creature, with amazing speed, sped back to the mirror, holding up the crystal ball as it ran.

"No!" he bellowed, as the black thing dove back through and into his basement.

The scene in the portal swirled, and as Adol reached it, only his own reflection greeted him. For a moment, he had the urge to strike the mirror with Geer, but, realizing that it was his only way home, he stopped, hung his head, and sank to his knees.

"What have I done?" he said aloud, realizing his mistake.

The creature was wily and full of tricks. He should have been more careful. Even as he reproached himself, he heard a snapping of sticks and a low snarl behind him, and he turned.

Coming through the trees, he saw a horror that he had never encountered before, and he knew why the black little creature had turned and run the other way. Adol gripped the hammer and braced himself as a huge shaggy beast the size of a great bear, but looking more like an unearthly wolf, growled, bent its head low, and showed its massive teeth. He readied himself for its lunge, but even as he did, two more of the creatures came leaping from the darkness and began to circle around him.

Before the first one could attack, Adol remembered what Geer had done in the tomb. With a sudden movement, he hurled the hammer at the foremost beast, striking it straight between the eyes. It howled and dropped to the ground and lay motionless. The weapon flew back to him, and he caught it, just as the other two creatures leaped forward, throats growling and jaws snapping.

He met the first one with a blow to the chest and grimaced as he felt its bones crush and snap beneath the power of the hammer. However, the third creature bowled him over, knocking Geer from his hand. He grappled with it, rolling over and over. Terrible teeth snapped inches from his face, and long claws sought to tear at him.

In that moment, something seemed to awaken deep within him – something that had nearly lain dormant throughout his life, but had always been there, and only seemed to show itself in moments of great need. A surge of tremendous strength washed over him, and with a mighty heave, he threw the monster from him and it went rolling across the forest floor, slamming into a great tree. It stumbled to its feet, lifted its head, and howled a deafening howl. Distant calls answered it, and it howled again.

Adol snatched up the hammer and let it fly with all his strength. It struck the creature, knocking it senseless, then flew on, and with a sickening *crack,* collided with the tree behind it. There was a snapping and grating sound as the massive tree shattered. It cracked straight down the middle, and then broke in two. Down it came, and Adol ran from its path as its dry branches swept downward with the moaning sound of an anguished wind, struck the earth, shuddered, and then lay still. The hammer of Geer circled back through the air and returned to his hand.

Adol looked about, listening. A huge full moon was rising now, cresting the horizon above the forest. The barren trees were cast like black skeletons against its great white face, and as he gazed at it in awe and wonder, for a moment, he forgot the creatures, forgot that he had stepped through the mirror, and simply stood in the silence, bathed in a shaft of soft light that shone through a gap in the trees. A strange sensation swept through him, a sudden sense of participating in a primordial event that had occurred for untold ages – of being in an ancient place that whispered secret tales of long forgotten years. He hardly dared to breathe, every part of him unwilling to step away from that profound moment.

But then a thought broke through the spellbinding experience and the strange world around him rushed back in. Dark shadows lay still as death all around, and a feeling of heaviness hung in the air, almost like that of the Dismal Bog back home, but more profound. A sense that this place was *alien* took hold. Where was the familiar face on the moon and why was it so big? It was bright and strange – different from any moon he had ever seen, and it illuminated the whole world with a soft light. Where was he?

He looked about, peering through the trees, and saw something hanging on a low branch. He went to it, pulled it from its place, and held it up to the moon. He recognized it immediately – it was Colleen's sash.

His mind whirled. How could she be here? The thought of his little girl lost in these woods with such horrible creatures all about nearly burst his heart. Yet, he had seen her get on the ship. She was in Wales now, at school. Surely, this sash could not be hers. He examined it again, and there was no mistake. Had Colleen come here before, and lost it then? She would have told someone of this place – this dead wood that was haunted by evil beasts. He clutched the sash close to him, and then stuffed it into his shirt. He had to know if his daughter was here, and he had to know now.

The raw power and strength he had felt moments ago still coursed through his veins, and he felt as though he would burst if he did not somehow expend it. Howls in the night drew near, and he had a sudden urge to burst through the wood and pursue them, to hunt them down and chase them to their foul dens in search of Colleen. But he steadied himself, and began to look for signs of a trail, anything to indicate that she had been here and walked away of her own accord.

Within a few moments, he saw something else that made his eyes go wide. For very clearly, on a patch of soft ground where the bright moonlight spilled through the trees, there was a hoof print, and the mark of a young boy's shoe. Badger? That would explain his disappearance. Someone else was here as well. A young boy. Henry? Frederick? No, not Henry - the shoe print was too large to be his. Frederick then, or perhaps one of the neighbor boys?

Adol urgently stooped low and looked about. There was another hoof print a little ways off. In fact, the leaves were clearly disturbed in that direction, although the trail was many days old.

With the howls of night-creatures drawing closer, Adol McGunnegal sped off into the night of a strange land in search of his beloved daughter, not knowing that he had stumbled into the Land of the Little People.

Chapter 20 – Grip

Colleen awoke to the sound of Dvalenn snoring loudly. The Wigglepox family and Oracle were nowhere to be seen.

Perhaps they're still in some cubbyhole in the tree, she thought.

Through the knothole high above, she could see the fading light of dusk. Then she remembered Nous, and wondered if he was all right. And what about Grip?

She rose and stretched, then shook Dvalenn to wake him. The old dwarf opened his eyes, smacked his lips, and sat up, looking around the tree.

"Oh! I dreamed I was still sleeping next to that tree in the gorge. Dreadful, just dreadful!"

"Well, the sun looks like its setting. I think we should be going, but we need to find the Wigglepoxes and check on the goblins," she replied.

Dvalenn wrinkled his nose and said, "If you ask me, Colleen, those goblins will only do us harm. There's no sense in taking them with us. They'll only betray us to the Witch. I hope they left while we slept."

"Dvalenn, I think that Nous is actually grateful that we saved his life. He hasn't quite figured that out yet, but I think he will," she replied.

Just then, Mrs. Wigglepox, Lily, and Rose came out of a small hole.

"You know, Colleen," she said, "Dvalenn is probably right. The goblins may very well betray us. In fact, they most certainly will. We have never, in all our history, known of a good goblin."

"But Nous seems different, Mrs. Wigglepox," argued Colleen. "I just wonder if something is *shifting* deep down inside him. Maybe he can't leave the service of the Witch on his own, but maybe we can help him. In the meantime, he can help us. He knows all about the Witch's operations."

"So do I, in a way," said Dvalenn. "I say we leave them here. Let them fend for themselves. That's what they're best at."

"No, Dvalenn. At least Nous is coming with us," she said firmly. "And we can't just leave Grip by himself if he's not well."

"I certainly hope you're right, Colleen," said Dvalenn. "As for me, I'll be keeping my eyes on them, and a good staff in my hand."

It was just then that Oracle came tumbling out of a hole in the tree with a queer giggle, as though he had come down some great sliding board and was having a bit of fun. He grinned as he picked himself up and brushed leaves from his gray cloak.

Dvalenn shook his head in bewilderment at the old leprechaun. Then he looked up at the fading light coming through the knothole and said, "Best be off as soon as possible, ladies, so how about a bite to eat?"

They ate a hasty supper from their supplies, packed up, climbed into the wagon, and then Mrs. Wigglepox spoke to the tree, and it slowly groaned open with a great sad wail, as though it was mourning for the cruelty of life and the loss of its mate.

Colleen flicked the reins, and Badger pulled the wagon out. No sooner had they left, the great tree slammed shut with such force that it sounded as though it had snapped in two. Badger surged forward, and Colleen had to rein him in.

They rolled back toward the pool of Ooze and the dead Sentinel Tree. There they saw Nous crouched beside the pool and Grip submerged to his neck in it, staring at them with a look of malice.

Nous stood as they approached, and Colleen reined the wagon to a halt. Grip only scowled, but was still as a stone. Dvalenn gripped his staff as Colleen climbed down from the wagon and walked over to Nous.

She touched him gently on the arm and smiled. "I'm glad you are all right, Nous. I was worried about you."

She turned to Grip, whose head seemed to be floating on the surface of the black pool. Colleen could not help but begin to giggle, and then laugh.

"Grip, you look positively hilarious in that pool! It looks as though you've become a disembodied head just floating there!"

Dvalenn snickered, and then began to laugh as well, and a moment later, the Wigglepoxes joined in. Nous looked from one of them to the other, and then looked down at Grip's head.

"Grip, you do look like a floating head," said Nous.

He spurted out a laugh that came awkwardly at first, and then more easily, until all six of them were truly laughing together at Grip's ridiculous frowning face bobbing on the surface of the stinking pool.

In that moment, it was as though a tension that had been building for days snapped, and all of the stress, fear, and foreboding that had weighed upon Colleen vanished away as she, the dwarf, the goblin, and the three little people giggled at the funny sight. Oracle peered over the edge of the wagon, a wry smile on his wrinkled face.

Grip, however, sneered at them all and growled, "Go ahead and laugh now. Soon enough, you won't be laughing. The Witch knows of your presence here by now, and she will be hunting for you. We will track you and hound you and capture you and take you to the black pits, where you will spend the rest of your days slaving for our king."

The reality of their situation rushed back in on them, and only Nous continued to giggle a bit, and then even he stopped.

"Ah, Grip, they ain't done us no harm. Fact is, this Colleen here saved our lives. I think she might be a goblin friend, I do. Not like those others who do us harm," said Nous.

"So, Nous, you are a *friend* of these foreigners? I'm sure the King and the Witch will be very interested to hear that," replied Grip, and he pulled himself from the pool of Ooze.

His body was much like Nous', skinny and mottled gray-green, and now covered by the same black leeches that had fastened themselves to Nous.

"Nous, you come with me," said Grip. "You know our orders."

Nous looked from Grip to Colleen. He gazed down at the bubbling pool, then back at Colleen again.

"Orders, Nous!" growled Grip. "You go with them and it's over for you!"

Nous now looked curiously at Grip's body and at the black slugs that hung limply on him.

"What'd we ever get by following *her* orders?" said Nous, half to himself and half to Grip. "Seems to me all we ever got was this Ooze. Look at it – full of worms. And it stinks."

"You speak of the *Ooze* like that!" shouted Grip. "Have you forgotten that it is the *gift* of the *Great Worm* to the Goblin people? What else could give us such freedom, such power, such intoxication, such delight – and how else could we *live*? Don't be an idiot, Nous. You can see just as well as I can what the Ooze does for us, and what it does to our enemies. It killed this evil tree, but gives us strength and life!"

Grip, animated in his defense of the Ooze, positioned himself between the others and the pool, as if to defend it. Colleen was amazed that the goblin would be so passionate about this stinking pool of death.

She climbed back up in the wagon and said, "We're leaving, Nous. Please, will you come with us? Grip... you could come too. I think that if we could just break the Spell of the Witch somehow, and if you stopped bathing yourself in that awful stuff, you would find out that you haven't been living at all, but withering away. Look at yourselves – you goblins are nothing but skin and bones and covered by... by *worms,* of all things! I'll bet every one of those things is leeching the life right out of you. There has to be a better way for you. Won't you come with us and help us find it?"

All this time, Oracle had been peeping over the side of the wagon watching the whole exchange. His eyes were fixed on Nous.

Colleen held out a hand to the goblins, but they only stared at her, as if considering what she had said.

Suddenly, Grip spat toward Colleen in disgust and sneered.

Nous looked at him, then back at Colleen, at the Ooze, at Grip, and then at Colleen again. Then he took a sideways step toward her.

"Nous, get back here!" shouted Grip.

He stopped and looked back, hesitating, thinking, debating with himself. Then he turned his back on the pool of Ooze, ran forward, and leaped into the wagon.

Colleen flicked the reins, and Badger began to pull.

"You'll be sorry, Nous!" shouted Grip. "When the burning sun dries up your flesh like cracked leather, and you have no Ooze to run to, then you'll remember my words!"

As they rode away into the Burning Sands and the sunset filled the western sky, Colleen looked back one last time at Grip. As the day ended, and night took the world, Grip slid his skinny body back into the pool. The black worms that covered him seemed to shake with delight as he sank down into the stinking slime, until once again, only his head remained floating on the surface. This time, Colleen did not laugh, nor did any of the others. They only rode on in sad silence.

She looked back once more and saw Grip shut his eyes and slide completely beneath the black muck. There was a frantic commotion of worms in the pool, and a bubble rose from where Grip had disappeared. It burst its stink on the surface, and then the pool was still.

Chapter 21 – The Burning Sands

The evening sky was a fiery red as Badger pulled the wagon south and a warm wind blew from the desert as they came to the top of the first sand dune. Colleen reined him to a halt for a moment as they looked out over the vast desert. They could see nothing but dunes before them, and the road was completely lost from sight, buried long ago beneath the blowing sands.

"We'll keep the sunset to our right as long as we can," said Dvalenn, "and then we'll have to rely on the stars to guide us southward."

Colleen nodded, flicked the reins again, and Badger pulled them down the dune. The sand was difficult even for the great horse to pull through, and the going was slow. However, Badger showed no sign of tiring, although he strained mightily up and down the dunes. The Spell still hung in the air, although it seemed to come in waves as if it were rushing past them on its way to the forest. The night grew cold as the moon rose, and each of them wrapped themselves as best as they could in their cloaks.

Hour after hour, they rode on, speaking few words until Colleen began to grow sleepy. When she felt she could fight it no longer, she handed Dvalenn the reins and said, "Would you mind driving for a bit? I just need to lie down for a few hours."

Dvalenn glanced back. Oracle lay in the hay at the front of the wagon, sleeping, and Nous was sitting in the far back corner, his arms wrapped around his knees.

"Just watch that one," he whispered. "I don't trust him."

Colleen climbed into the back of the wagon and sat down next to the goblin. They sat in silence for a few moments, and then Colleen said to him, "Nous, why did you choose to come with us?"

Nous did not answer at first, but gazed up at the brilliant stars that shone overhead. Then he shrugged and said, "Nous wonders."

"About what?" she asked.

"The Colleen," he replied.

"Me?" she asked.

"The Colleen is very strange," he said.

Colleen realized that the goblin was actually having a conversation with her.

"Why do you say that, Nous?" she replied.

He thought for a moment and said, "The Colleen has been... been..." and then he could not seem to find the right words to say.

"I care about you, Nous," she said. "I care what happens to you."

"Yes, very strange," he replied.

"I would like to think that you care about me too," she said.

He looked at her sidelong, and then turned away.

"Nous is tired," he said, and curled up in a ball in the hay.

Colleen watched him for a moment and then curled up next to him and was soon asleep.

She awoke some hours later to Nous shaking her.

"The Colleen must wake up! Wake up!" he whispered sharply.

She rubbed her eyes and looked around. They had stopped, and Dvalenn was not in the driver's seat. After a moment, she saw him. He was on the ground digging in the sand and looking very excited.

"Dvalenn, what is it? What have you found?" she called.

He seemed startled by her voice, and jumped up, holding his hands behind his back.

"Oh ... oh, nothing," he said. "Just... giving Badger a rest, that's all."

"What have you got behind your back, Dvalenn?" she asked.

Dvalenn shuffled his feet and looked down and said, "Nothing, nothing, guess we better be going."

"Dvalenn!" scolded Colleen. "Let me see your hands."

He slipped both hands into his pockets, which Colleen noticed were bulging even more than before, then brought them out empty, and smiled. Then he quickly climbed back up into the wagon and flicked the reins.

Colleen noticed that the Wigglepoxes were all sound asleep on the bench, and Oracle snoozed in the hay. Dvalenn looked back at her, grinned, and then kept right on driving as if nothing had happened.

She was not sure what to make of all this, so she whispered to Nous, "Nous, what was Dvalenn doing?"

"Stones," he replied. "The dwarf was picking up shiny stones."

"Whatever for?" she asked.

"His kind likes shiny stones, it's said," replied the goblin.

"For what?" asked Colleen.

"It's said they just carry them about and shine them and collect them and hide them away in their caves. Then they grow fat by sitting and counting them. And when they've grown fat enough, we goblins come and take it all away from them!" Nous cackled.

Dvalenn turned his head and eyed Nous suspiciously, then turned back and drove on.

"Do you think that might be what happened to Dvalenn's brother, Fafnir?" asked Colleen.

"Maybe. Might have been before my time," he replied. "Anyway, we just take such things and give them to the Witch or throw them into the Ooze. Orders, you know."

"You throw precious stones into the Ooze?" asked Colleen incredulously. "But why?"

"Orders. It makes the Ooze better," he said.

"Nous, where does this Ooze come from?" asked Colleen.

Nous grinned wickedly and said in a low voice as if he were sharing a great secret, "From *us!*"

He cackled, then said, "It drips from us, we scrape it from ourselves and, bit by bit, fill the Ooze pits. Sometimes, it sinks into what we touch, and especially if we *bite* it! *Then* the Ooze takes root in what we bit. It starts to become like us."

He had showed his yellow fangs at the word *bite,* and Colleen shuddered.

"But surely your people weren't always like this, were they?" asked Colleen.

Nous looked serious then, and said in a low voice, "There are stories that say the goblins did not always have the Ooze. But when the Great Worm came, it gave us the Ooze, and we ever after possessed it."

"And what is the Great Worm?" asked Colleen.

"Nous does not know," said Nous. "Nous has never seen it."

"But wouldn't you like to be rid of this horrible stuff?" she asked.

Nous' expression changed from shock to suspicion, then to anger, and then serious. Emotions flowed across his face like a tide, and for a moment, Colleen was afraid that he might leap at her or fly into a rage. However, he seemed to settle down after a moment, hissed, and said, "It is the Ooze that lets us *live*! Without it, we would dry up and die. Nous has seen it once."

"One of your people *dried up?*" asked Colleen.

"That's what we call it. Stay too long away from the Ooze and at first you grow ugly. Scars, like poor Grip had from the evil water, start to form. That poor gloat that dried up - his ears and nose rightly fell off his head. His whole body was one big scar. He came to the pits talking like a mad goblin. Said he had been out in the desert for forty years, and had met a hermit and lived with him. He had bathed in the Evil Lake, and said the Ooze had died in him. Said he came back to take anyone who wanted to follow him out into the desert to get rid of the Ooze. Said there was some sort of oasis out here where it could happen. Poor thing." Nous shook his hooded head.

"Did anyone go with him?" asked Colleen.

"Noooo. Who would want to? Besides, we threw him into an Ooze pit. When we pulled him out three days later, nothing had happened to him. Fact is, all the worms in the pit died. Ruined a perfectly good Ooze pit. The boss was rightly angry with him and had him killed then and there. Said he would pollute the whole pit if we let him live," replied Nous.

Colleen, shaken by the cruelty of the goblins, wondered what had actually happened to the goblin that had been freed of the Ooze.

"Nous, you said there was an oasis that the... the mad goblin had been to. Do you think we could find it? Did he mention where it was?" asked Colleen.

"Don't know," replied the goblin. "North of the Wizard's Castle, I think. Goblins do not go that way."

"Then we just might come across it!" she said.

Nous seemed to shudder and drew his cloak tighter around him, but said no more.

She watched him for a moment and then climbed back to the front of the wagon and told Dvalenn that she would drive for a while. He nodded, handed her the reins, and climbed to the back, staying as far away from Nous as possible. He then gathered his own cloak about himself and fumbled in his pockets. Oracle awoke and climbed to the front with Colleen, being careful not to disturb the Wigglepoxes.

The night grew steadily colder, and the chill crept beneath their cloaks and into their bones until Colleen was shivering and praying for the dawn as the hours passed by. Oracle sat silently by her, wrapped in his own cloak, staring at the distant horizon as they traveled on.

Suddenly, there was the sound of Badger's golden horseshoes on stone, and the wheels of the wagon clattering. The Wigglepoxes awoke, and Colleen reined the horse to a stop. The sand had given way to a stone pavement, and all about them were broken and jagged walls, giving the impression of decaying teeth jutting upward from the land.

Colleen urged Badger on, and as they slowly moved through the ruins, a great arch loomed before them, black against the night sky. Colleen pulled up to it and gazed at its spectacular height. Unlike the rubble around them, the arch was still intact, seemingly untouched by time or the scouring winds of the desert.

"Dvalenn, Nous, look at this!" she said, waking the dwarf and goblin, who had both been asleep.

They all stared at the strange sight, but Dvalenn leaped from the wagon and ran forward to the arch. He touched it, caressing its smooth surface, then turned back to the others and said, "It is the Arch of Regin, my brother. This place was his house."

"Dvalenn, we have to keep moving. We can't stop here and explore," said Colleen.

"Oh, but it will be dawn soon. We need shelter, and here we might find it, or at least some shade under the arch," said Dvalenn.

Colleen looked at the sky. Indeed, there was a glow in the east, the first hint of the coming dawn.

"Well, I suppose you may be right. Who knows when we might find shade again today," she replied reluctantly.

"Good!" said the dwarf, and began to examine the structure.

Colleen pulled the wagon under the arch, then climbed down and unhooked Badger. There was no grass for him to graze on, so she took some of the hay from the wagon and gave it to him to eat.

"Colleen," said Mrs. Wigglepox, "would you mind carrying us about in your pockets for a bit?"

"Of course," she replied and, one by one, carefully put them in the pocket of her green cape.

Mrs. Wigglepox then whispered to her and said, "I'm still not so trustful of Nous, you know. He is a goblin, after all, even if he's like no other I've ever heard of."

They watched as Nous climbed out of the wagon and crawled under it, curling into a ball, his robe wrapped tightly around him.

"We must hide from the burning sun," he mumbled into his robe.

Colleen was about to reply when there came a "Whooohoo!" from behind them. Even Nous uncurled himself and looked. It was Dvalenn, and he was dancing about under the arch, looking very excited.

"Whatever is the matter?" asked Colleen.

"I have found it! The secret ..." Then he stopped, seeing Nous staring at him. "Oh, er, nothing," he said, and walked away from the arch, kicking at stones and picking up a few and cramming them in his already stuffed pockets.

"The dwarf is mad," growled Nous, and curled back up under the wagon.

As soon as he was sure Nous was not watching, Dvalenn tiptoed back to the arch and frantically waved for Colleen to come and have a look at what he had found.

"Look! It's the secret door that my brother made in the arch, still here and hidden," he whispered.

He pointed to some engraved dwarven runes in the side of the Arch. Colleen looked at the runes and then at the dwarf. His old face was full of excitement.

"What was this thing for, Dvalenn?" she asked.

Dvalenn looked over at Nous and then said, "It is magic. See all around? Alas, the House of Regin has fallen, but the arch has not! The magic he wove into this stone still holds fast, and this – this is the secret door that leads down into his tunnels and chambers. Once they led down to the river, and from there..."

Dvalenn paused again, looked in Nous' direction, and whispered even lower. "And from there, the tunnels ran all the way to the Wizard's castle."

"Are you saying that we could follow Regin's tunnels under the desert?" asked Colleen.

"Yes!" he whispered, almost squeaking with excitement.

"And who knows what magic things wait in his workshops," said the dwarf. "We might find things of great power with which to fight the goblins and the Witch."

For a moment, Colleen was quite intrigued by the idea, but then Mrs. Wigglepox spoke up.

"But is this door big enough to take Badger and the wagon through? And are the tunnels still intact after all these years?" she asked.

"No," said Dvalenn. "The door is not big enough."

He looked sad for a moment, and then a glimmer shone in his eyes again.

"Badger might fit without the wagon, though," he said.

He paused, looked over at Nous again, and frowned.

"But I will not allow the wicked goblin to enter the last vestiges of my brother's house!" he hissed. "He and his kin and their witch are the cause of this!" He spread his arms wide at the ruinous scene all around them.

Colleen looked about her at the broken remains of the House of Regin. The silence and emptiness of the place was only broken by wisps of wind that kicked up little dust devils amid the crumbling walls. She looked in his pained eyes and felt pity for him.

"I'm sorry for your terrible loss, Dvalenn," she said. "But we must go on together. Something good is happening to Nous. We have to give him a chance. And besides, he knows the Witch's lair and how to get in there. He is our one hope of rescuing my mother!"

Dvalenn's face grew hard.

"No. He has only been half-friendly to you because you saved his life. But he has done nothing good for me at all, nor will he ever wish to. He is a goblin, Colleen. You don't know their kind. You've never been in their pits of gloom, nor labored under their whips. I have been there, and I will never trust them. Once a goblin, always a goblin," he said.

"Please, Dvalenn, Nous is changing, I can see it!" she said. "We need to give him a chance. Yes, he is a goblin. But that's the only life he has ever known. Don't you think that maybe, just maybe, if we show him a better way, and show him that we're willing to live that way ourselves, he might actually leave behind his goblinish ways?"

Dvalenn sneered. "It will take more than a good example to change their kind. You'd have to do a whole heart transplant on them to change what they are. They're wicked to the bone."

Colleen was silent for a moment, then said, "Mrs. Wigglepox, what do you think?"

She looked thoughtful for a moment and then said, "I have never heard of a goblin turning good, Colleen. They have terrorized my people for hundreds and hundreds of years. They serve the Witch and themselves and no one else."

"But Nous himself said that there was once a goblin who did just that! I know it seems impossible, but I believe in him," she said.

"Colleen," said Dvalenn, "we are here to rescue our families from these goblins. Can we really risk taking a goblin with us? You've seen how he treats me. If I were to find one of my brothers in their black pits, do you think that Nous would help me bring him out? No, he would betray us all in a moment."

Colleen looked at the goblin, who was still curled up under the wagon.

"Doesn't anyone care what happens to him?" asked Colleen sadly.

"I care," said a little voice from her pocket.

"And me too," said another.

It was Rose and Lily. They had been listening quietly to the whole exchange.

"I don't want to act like a goblin, Mother," said Rose. "They would leave us behind, or worse, if they were in our shoes. I think we ought to act like leprechauns, and help out poor old Nous if we can."

"That's right, Mother," said Lily. "Aren't we supposed to wish good for others? And what good would be our wishing if we didn't *do* something too?"

Mrs. Wigglepox was silent for a moment, then took her daughters in her arms and hugged them.

"Forgive me, children. You are right. What good would it be to be a leprechaun if we didn't wish what is good and right for people, even our enemies," she said. "I say Nous comes with us."

"Leoples!" said Oracle, grinning at the Wigglepoxes.

"Well, what of it, Dvalenn?" asked Colleen.

The dwarf looked hard at the goblin once again. He seemed to struggle within himself for a long time.

But then he set his jaw firm and said, "No. I have decided. The goblin will not enter the House of Regin."

"Dvalenn, please," said Colleen.

But Dvalenn turned to the wall of the arch, and gestured over the runes that covered it. A door silently slid aside, revealing a dark green staircase that descended down into the darkness.

Oracle stepped forward and in a serious voice began a little rhyme.

"Weighed, weighed, the giponderous stones,
From pocket to heart their burdensome goes.
Hear them call? Let them fall! Their greedousness dropped!
Only then, then, Dvalenn's way won't be stopped."

"Dvalenn..." said Colleen, pleading.

The dwarf glanced at Oracle and frowned, and then looked at Colleen, turned, and walked into the darkness, his pockets sagging under the weight of the many stones that he had stuffed into them. The door slid silently shut behind him. Colleen stared at it for a moment and then sighed a heavy sigh. "I hope he comes back by evening," she said.

The sun was rising now in the east, and she felt very tired, so in the shade of the great Arch of Regin, they settled in to try to sleep through the heat of their first day out in the Burning Sands.

Chapter 22– Dvalenn's Decision

Dvalenn's pockets sagged heavily as he made his way down the stairs. The walls of Regin's tunnels glowed with an eerie green light that somehow emanated from deep within them. He had walked for over an hour, ever descending down, down into the depths of the earth. He was very tired, and the weight of the stones in his pockets was wearing on him.

"Got to keep going," he said to himself. "Too late to go back now."

He trudged on for some time, and then said, "But what about Colleen and the little people, you old fool. You've left them with a goblin!"

Downward he went, and then said, "They were fine without you before, they'll be fine without you now. And no goblin will set foot in these hallowed halls. Might be the last place in all the land that their foul feet have not polluted."

On he went.

"But she's just a little girl!" he said to himself.

Downward...

"More than that, any fool can see - there's a power in that one. And if we find Regin's Workshop, we can help her out better."

Downward...

"Right, then."

Onward he padded, until after a long while, he came to the last of a thousand stairs, and a wide chamber of many, many doors opened before him. There were so many doorways in the immense room that he could not count them all. Dvalenn sat down on the steps and looked about the glowing room.

Which would it be? he wondered. *Might as well try them all.*

One by one, Dvalenn opened the doors, counting them as he went. The first led to complete darkness. No glowing hall lay beyond. The next was a stair, also leading down into darkness. And the third likewise opened into complete blackness. On and on he went – ten doors, then twenty, then fifty – all leading into impenetrable night that his eyes could not pierce.

"Where did you hide it, Regin?" he shouted into the darkness as he opened door after door.

Sixty doors, seventy... ninety. Dvalenn was panting now, leaning heavily on the glowing green wall.

"Where is it?" he whispered through his labored breath.

At last, he came to the final door, next to the stair that he had descended in the first place. He gripped the handle and pulled. It was locked. He examined the frame, the handle, the door, the floor, the walls, anything for a clue to open the door. But he could find no keyhole.

Suddenly, Dvalenn felt very tired. And so old! How old was he? He could not remember. But a great weariness seemed to be coming upon him.

"Where is the key, Regin? Where did you hide the key?" he said, trying to shake off the heaviness.

And then he saw it. A tiny, tiny inscription on the doorknob, which read:

"To find true gold, you must dig deep."

"This must be the door!" he whispered.

But for the weariness that he felt, and the burden of the stones in his pockets, he would have leaped into the air.

Hardly containing his excitement, Dvalenn recalled the ancient dwarven magic that so very long ago he and his brothers had used to shape things of beauty and might, for locking and opening, for finding and hiding. He hastily breathed the words of opening, and the lock on the door silently opened before him. Beyond it was a roughly cut room barely ten feet wide and long with no doors leading from it. In one corner were propped a pick and shovel and a bucket.

"What is this?" said Dvalenn indignantly. "Where is the gold and treasure of Regin?"

He waddled over to the tools and noticed that in the bottom of the bucket was a rolled up scroll.

Carefully, he picked up the old parchment and began to unroll it. He licked his lips as the first words appeared in the dim green glow of the chamber. It read, *The Dwarven Way – The Sayings of Regin.*

"Ah!" he said aloud. "This must be Regin's treasure map!"

He turned the bucket over and sat on it, hunching his shoulders, and allowing his gray beard to drag on the ground.

Eagerly, but with care, he unrolled it further. The page was inscribed with golden ink, and read:

True Gold

Gold, gold, scattered like sand,
Deep beneath the troubled land.
Dig, dig, toil and mine,
Only then will you see it shine.
Wash, wash with water so clean,
Then burn it 'til no dross is seen.
Give, give, to the craftsman to fix,
To fashion vessels, censers and candlesticks.
Find, find that which you seek,
For not of earthly gold do I speak.

Dvalenn looked puzzled, and then brightened.

"Ah, Regin was a clever fellow. Spoke in riddles to hide the location of his treasure!" he said to himself.

He unrolled the scroll further. A second inscription appeared and read:

Greed

Dark is the Dwarf who falls to greed,
Who bears within, that bitter seed.
An all-consuming fire it grows,
Until a dragon's heart he knows.

Dvalenn hurriedly unrolled another bit of the scroll. There was yet another saying, then another, and another, one entitled *"Desire,"* another *"Gems,"* another *"The Pit,"* and all sayings that Dvalenn could not comprehend the meaning of.

Surely these must tie together somehow – these riddles and sayings must lead to the treasure that Regin had found, and surely hoarded in these chambers somewhere, he thought to himself.

He unrolled the whole scroll to the very bottom and read it. It was not a rhyme or saying as the others had been, but a note that read the following:

"To my brothers:

Our brother, Fafnir, has discovered the final end of all earthly desires. I tried to dissuade him, but he has plundered my house and his. Here in this bucket I leave all that is left to me, and I find this more valuable that all my lost treasures.

I am delving deep now. Deeper than I have ever dug, to find the secret treasures that lie beyond the reach of pick and shovel.

Follow in my footprints, if you dare. You can bring only yourself. Nothing else can pass this way. It will cost you all to find what is most precious."

Dvalenn looked down at the floor and, for the first time, he noticed footprints that seemed to be etched into the floor. They led from the door and directly to the wall, and there stopped. He went to the door and put one foot in the first footstep, then in the next, then the next, until he was standing in the last set of footprints in front of the wall. He reached out his hand, and to his complete surprise, it passed into the rock. He moved forward an inch, and his outstretched arm passed further into the stone before him. Slowly, he moved forward, his eyes wide in amazement. He stretched out his other arm, reaching, and began to enter into the solid stone of the wall.

Ah, Regin what magic you possessed! he thought.

But suddenly, he found that he could go no further. Something was blocking his way. He pushed, but felt as though something was pushing him back – by his pockets. He looked down and saw that his bulging pockets would not pass into the stone. He pushed harder, and harder, but try as he may, he could not move any further into the wall.

Dvalenn leaned forward, pressing his face into the stone, and as he did, a strange vision came to his eyes. There, just within the rock, was a white stone path that led away through a beautiful, shining pillared hallway that grew wider and wider as it went, until far in the distance, he could see a marvelous white city that shone with a brilliant radiance. Again, he pressed forward, trying to force his way through the wall of rock, but again, his stuffed pockets prevented him.

He pulled away from the wall and looked at it. Why did he feel so tired? He sat down on the bucket again and stared at the rough wall. Gathering his strength, he stood uncertainly and stumbled forward, arms outstretched. But once again, his stuffed pockets prevented him from going on completely.

Realizing what was happening, he reached into one of his pockets and pulled out a handful of stones. He looked down at them and, for the first time, noticed that they were nothing but worthless gravel. No gold, no silver, no precious gems.

He hesitated, staring at the common stones. Why had he picked them up? He couldn't remember. But there had been a reason. And why did he feel so tired again? He put the stones back in his pocket and paced slowly about.

Regin had found it... he had found what every dwarf had heard of from the time their mothers told them bedtime stories. He had found the White City of Dwarves – the place where all dwarves could go if they could just find the way. But it was said that one only found it at the end... at the end of their life.

That final thought struck him like a hammer blow. He had come to the end. He had a choice to make now. The Lady Danu had hinted at this. He could go to the White City, and live there forever, or walk away and roam these dark tunnels in search of treasures of his own making. And Oracle – that stupid little leprechaun and his ridiculous riddles – he had said something about stones and letting go.

But couldn't I just take these few things with me? he thought.

He pulled the gravel from his pocket again and picked through it. Surely there was something of real value here. He knew there was. There had to be. He had borne the burden of it all these miles. But for some reason, he couldn't think of why it had been so important when he picked it up.

Then a thought struck him. He got up, turned the bucket over, and began to empty his pockets into it. Soon it was filled to overflowing, and it was *heavy.*

Dvalenn trudged over to the wall, carrying the bucket. But it would not pass through the wall. He turned around and tried to back in, and indeed, without all of the stones barring his way, he was able to slip easily through the wall and into the radiant white hall that lay just beyond. But when he tried to pull the bucket through, it would not budge.

Exhausted, he sat down in the white hall, one hand feebly gripping the bucket of gravel on the other side, and stared at the distant White City. It shone like a radiant sun, its brilliant walls beckoning to him, and sparkling fountains glittered in its courtyards. Then he saw them – dwarves – hundreds of them, all dressed in festive colors as they walked among the fountains and statues and other structures that were becoming clearer to his eyes the longer he gazed toward it. A great desire to join them rose in his heart, and he felt as though he might burst if he didn't.

"Just let go of that old bucket of worthless stones!" said a voice inside his head.

Slowly, he slackened his grip and, one by one, his fingers slipped from the handle until just the tip of his index finger still touched the handle. But just as the bucket was about to fall, Dvalenn seized the handle, gripped it all the more, and stepped back into the darkness.

Regin's scroll lay unrolled on the floor at his feet. He stared at it and read the last words of his brother again.

"...It will cost you all to find what is most precious."

For a moment longer, he stared at the words, then at the gravel.

Then, in a moment of decision, he looked up at the ceiling, gazing upward through the rock and earth, and said, "Forgive me, Colleen! My time has come."

Then he heaved the bucket of stones at the far wall and ran for the secret doorway. He did not stop as he passed through the wall, but with a flood of relief and joy, ran on and on to the White City of Dwarves.

Chapter 23 – Farewell to Dvalenn

Dvalenn did not return that day, and as the blazing sun beat down on the ruins around them, Colleen barely slept. The heat was unbearable, even in the shade, and more than once she got up and drank some of Doc's draft or the Lady's water.

Nous lay in the darkest corner of the Arch of Regin, and kept moving to stay in the shadows as the sun rose high and then sank in the western sky.

The Wigglepox family did their best to rest under the driver's seat of the wagon, where Lily's wagon had yielded up yet another surprise. There they found a hidden compartment that had tiny beds within it, and these they gladly crawled into and slept quite comfortably, with Mrs. Wigglepox saying again and again, "That was some wish, daughter, some wish."

Oracle also rested in the shade of the Arch, his old head lying upon a stone, and Badger stood above him, his head hanging low.

But when she could no longer lay in the heat, Colleen rose one last time and began to prepare something for them to eat.

"Nous, are you awake?" she said.

Nous stirred from his shady spot and uncurled himself.

He glanced at the sky and said, "The evil sun still shines."

"I know," she said, wiping sweat from her forehead. "But I thought you might be hungry. Dvalenn hasn't come back yet."

Nous crept over to the wagon and looked at the things that Colleen was unpacking. The aroma of Doc's mushrooms and the Lady's provisions wafted up from the sack.

"Stinks," said Nous.

"Well, it's all we have," said Colleen, "plus these roots and nuts. You should eat something wholesome, you know. Look, it's really good."

She took one of the stuffed mushrooms and popped it in her mouth, savoring the flavor.

"Yum," she said, and picked up another and offered it to Nous.

Nous carefully took it and rolled it over and over in his hand. Colleen noticed that his hands were filthy and that dirt was caked under his yellow fingernails.

He sniffed it, wrinkling his bulbous nose, and screwed up his face.

"Oh, try it, Nous. You just might find that it's good," said Colleen.

Nous squinted his eyes shut and popped the mushroom in his mouth. He stood motionless for a moment, grimacing, but then his expression seemed to soften, and he began to chew.

He slowly opened his eyes, and they grew wide, and a look of wonder crept over his face.

"Haven't you ever had mushrooms before, Nous?" asked Colleen.

The goblin shook his head and continued to chew slowly, then swallowed. A rare look of delight crossed his face, and he reached into the sack and pulled out another mushroom, and ate it.

"Mushrooms, yes, but not like this!" he said.

Colleen laughed and said, "What do goblins usually eat, Nous?"

Nous stopped chewing for a moment, and looked at her.

"The Colleen does not want to know," he said.

"Well, what about something to drink, then? We have the water from the Lady, and..." began Colleen.

"No! Nous will not drink the evil water!" he said firmly.

Colleen took a drink from the water sack. It was warm, but delicious and refreshed her completely.

"It's wonderful, Nous. I think if you tried it, you might find that you like it, just like the mushrooms," she said.

Nous hissed and turned away.

"Well, how about some dwarven brew then?" she offered.

Nous sniffed at the brew and then took a drink, then another.

"See, you like dwarven mushrooms and dwarven drinks," said Colleen. "They're really not such bad folk, now are they?"

Nous snorted and put the sack down.

"We have stories about the dwarves – evil stories. They have been enemies of the goblins since we had stories to tell. They do nasty things to goblins, just like the little people do," he replied.

Colleen thought about this for a moment and then said, "Nous, do your people have any stories about the world of Men, where I come from?"

Nous looked sidelong at Colleen for a moment and then said, "Goblins in the land of the Little People have not met many humans. Nous has only seen four."

"Four?" asked Colleen.

"Four. The Colleen, the boy, the hag, and the Pwca-killer," he replied.

"Nous, you've mentioned the Pwca-killer before. What is a Pwca?" she asked.

"Pwca was our goblin Captain," he replied. "The Pwca-killer was an evil Witch that made him vanish."

"You mean there was more than one witch in this world?" asked Colleen.

"The Pwca-killer witch appeared and attacked us. But we captured it and took it to the Goblin King," replied Nous.

Colleen thought for a moment and then said, "Nous, what did the Pwca-killer look like?"

"Ugly," he grunted.

Then he looked at her sidelong again and then, almost seemingly embarrassed, mumbled, "Looked almost just like you, just bigger."

Then he looked at the ground and kicked a stone.

Colleen smiled, and then a thought occurred to her.

"Nous, you said that the Pwca-killer looked like me. How so?" she asked.

"Same hair. Same face. But bigger," he replied. "Same as all humans. Ugly."

"Where did you catch her, and where did you take her, Nous? Was she all right?" asked Colleen.

She was sure that Nous had been one of the goblins to capture her mother.

"We caught the Pwca-killer by the mirror in the woods. Took it to the black ship. It escaped twice, but we hunted it down. Fast, that one was. Had to call on another goblin band to help catch it. But we found it. Nasty thing. Fought hard," he said.

"Was she all right when you captured her, Nous?" asked Colleen again. She was beginning to worry.

"Knocked it cold!" declared Nous triumphantly. Then he narrowed his eyes and hissed.

"We'd have done worse, but the Witch's orders were not to hurt any big people too bad and to bring 'em to her straight away," he said.

"Nous, I can't believe my mo... that the Pwca-killer... would actually kill anyone. Are you sure that's what happened?" she asked.

"Pwca jumped onto the Pwca-killer when it appeared in the woods, and it threw him into the mirror. Poor Pwca – vanished! Threw him into the Abyss, I say," growled Nous.

"Nous, Pwca isn't dead. Pwca is back in the World of Men! He's been sneaking around our farm for months now – we just didn't know what he was.

"He went through the same mirror that Frederick and I came through, just the opposite way! In fact, I'm quite sure that Frederick and I saw him. He almost came back through with us," said Colleen.

Nous screwed up his face, trying to comprehend.

"The Colleen came through the mirror from the world of Men?" he asked. "And Pwca is there now?"

"Yes, Nous, we accidentally fell through. I think my ... I think my *mother* came through the same way. I'm sure she didn't mean to throw Pwca through the mirror. She was probably just surprised, and he managed to fall through to the other side before the mirror shut down," she said.

Nous thought for a moment and then, to Colleen's surprise, began to chant a strange chant. His voice was raspy and cold as he sang, and a weird look was in his eyes – something wild and primal.

"When opens once again
A portal to the World of Men,
Then let all goblins sing!
And battle horns, let them ring!
For at long last the door
So long hidden 'neath forest floor
Shall open for them then,
And ancient kings shall rise again.
Goblin armies shall be free
To claim new lands amidst the sea."

He stopped his chant and looked solemn.

Colleen stared at the goblin for a moment and then said, "Nous, where did you learn that from?"

"Olden times," he replied. "Handed down from olden times. Don't know who spoke it first."

Colleen glanced at the sky and decided to change the subject. The idea of armies of goblins running freely through the Gate of Anastazi down in old Doc's caverns was, to say the least, scary. What if they did invade the world of Men? She decided that there were some things she would keep to herself and not discuss with the goblin.

"Nous, back when we were tied up in the wagon, I remember the other goblins talking about some sort of rebellion in the pits, and that a sorceress had risen up and was fighting against the Witch. What do you know about that?" she asked.

"Not much," he replied. "Lies started by the little people. I've not been there for a long time."

"But what do the other goblins say about it all?" she prodded.

Nous glanced around and then lowered his voice to a harsh whisper.

"They say it all started half a year ago or so. Nobody knows where she came from. Just appeared in the pits. Then prisoners started disappearing. The Witch herself got involved, and there was some sort of fight. Huk, the Captain of the Pits got killed, they say, from a blast of fire from the Witch's staff that was aimed at the Sorceress."

Nous looked about again and lowered his voice further. "Then, they say, the Sorceress made the pits come to life. Like some giant rock creature, they say, and the Witch... the Witch had to flee."

Colleen wondered what this could mean. If the Witch was so powerful, and had defeated so many of her enemies, who was this Sorceress?

"Nous," she said, "we've got to find out more about the Sorceress somehow. She could be an ally."

He narrowed his eyes at her and, for a moment, she was afraid he was going to grow angry. But the look passed, and he said, "The Witch has served the Goblin King for long years. Her power is in fire. Nothing she sets her fire to can survive, not even this Sorceress."

They both fell silent for some time, and then Colleen looked at the sky.

"We better get going soon," she said. "It's getting dark. I do hope Dvalenn comes back soon. I don't like the thought of leaving without him. I suppose we ought to wait a while yet."

They waited, and time slipped away, but still Dvalenn did not return.

"Do you think we should leave yet?" Colleen asked Mrs. Wigglepox.

She looked thoughtful and then replied, "Yes. I think that Dvalenn has decided not to return to us. But I feel that he has somehow found himself. It's not a bad thing, Colleen. Something good has happened to him, I think."

"What about it, Oracle?" asked Colleen.

Oracle then did a very strange thing – he took Colleen by the hand and drew her down next to him. He then stooped down with his face to the ground, shut one eye, opened the other as wide as he could, and, with his nose in the sand, stared downward, as though he were trying to see deep underground.

Colleen giggled at the funny sight, thinking that he was simply performing one of his antics. But then she thought better of it and followed his lead. Still holding his rough, leathery hand, she closed her eyes and focused. Immediately, she found herself seeing a vision of deep tunnels and long stairways. Down, down her mind descended, and she felt as though Oracle was leading her, his gentle presence simple and without guile, and for the first time he seemed untouched by the Spell.

Suddenly, she saw Dvalenn. He was struggling with something that looked like – yes, it was a bucket of stones. She could also see the White City, and knew that the dwarf was at his final decision point in life – that he could choose to hold on to his earthly treasures, or release them and finally go to the halls of his fathers.

The moment came, and Dvalenn made his choice. She watched, and a smile beamed on her face. Oracle giddily laughed, and Colleen could not help but laugh with him.

"He made it!" she said. "He made it home!"

After a moment, the vision faded, and Colleen sighed heavily.

"Time for us to go as well," she said, and, rising from the ground, went to pack the rest of their things.

The sun was setting as they set out southward. Colleen looked back at the dark shape of the Arch of Regin and wondered if they would ever pass this way again.

She felt a twinge of loneliness without Dvalenn, and a little apprehensive at the thought of traveling with just the Wigglepox family, a mysterious old leprechaun, and a goblin. But she was more determined than ever, now that there was more news of her mother. So southward they rolled, the mighty Badger pulling their magnificent wagon through the Burning Sands.

Chapter 24 - Pwca

Pwca the goblin sat for some minutes in the basement of the house, breathing heavily. His bat-like ears moved up and down in time with his chest, and his scraggly black strands of hair hung limply over his gray-green face.

"The big one got itself a magic hammer, it does," it said to itself. "But it won't survive the *stalkers.*"

He grinned at the prospect.

"But Pwca needs more friends. Allies. Yes, Pwca must go back and bring more – more than just the evil little ones."

He stood and paced about the basement, thinking. Now that the man was out of the way, he was free to do as he wished. A thought struck him and he stopped pacing.

"Magic hammer..." he said aloud, and slowly a toothy grin spread across his deformed face. "Magic hammer to break the chains..."

He lifted the crystal ball before the mirror. The dark wood opened before him, and he quickly slipped through and put the crystal back in his cloak. As the mirror swirled, Pwca dashed behind the wall and peered out, looking into the darkness. To his amazement, several stalkers lay dead in the leaves, and a great tree lay split in two, fallen in the forest, with a third stalker lying dead at its base. Pwca frowned. They had been nursing that tree with bits of Ooze. Now they would have to start over with another one.

Looking about, he slunk from behind the wall and examined the ground, then the dead beasts.

So, the man survived, thought Pwca.

The goblin was surprised, but now he was even more interested in the hammer that the human bore.

More howls sounded in the distance. Yes, the stalkers would be tracking this man. And Pwca would follow them. Off through the woods he flew, dashing from tree to tree, pausing to listen, and then running on, sometimes on all fours, and sometimes upright. All the while the howls drew nearer, and soon he came to what he knew was the main trail through the forest that led to the goblin encampment. The Troll Bridge was up ahead, so he slowed his pace and drew up behind a tree, peering out at the two bridges.

There, standing on the farther wooden bridge, was the man. Four stalkers had him trapped on the bridge, two on either side, and Pwca knew that more would be coming, likely the entire pack, which in these parts numbered at least twenty. Pwca watched, transfixed, as the huge beasts howled in delight and slowly moved forward for the kill.

With a movement so fast that the goblin could hardly believe his eyes, the great hammer flew from the man's hand, striking one beast on the far side of the bridge, knocking it completely off the bridge with a yowl of pain, and sending it crashing into the river below. The hammer flew on and circled back, striking the second stalker in its path. The creature crumpled and lay still, and the hammer returned to the man's hand.

He turned and, with a great bellow, swung upward as one of the two remaining beasts leaped upon him. He caught it under its chin and sent it spinning backward into its companion, and both of them went careening over the railing of the bridge. There was a splash as they struck the water below.

The man looked about, but saw no more opponents. His jaw was set, and his face was grim and resolute as he crossed the bridge and continued on up the road into the dark night.

Pwca slunk from the trees and went to the edge of the bridge, then peered down into the darkness of the gully. The river gurgled in its course, but amid its babbles came another sound – the sound of heavy, rasping breathing. He strained his eyes, and there by the stream bank he could dimly make out the shape of the two stalkers that had fallen. One of them was stirring now, wagging its head as if trying to get its bearings. It lifted its head as if to howl, then its voice was cut off, and Pwca saw a great shape towering above the beast. There was a whimper, the stalker went limp, and the giant shadow dragged its victim away toward the Troll Bridge.

"The old troll!" hissed Pwca. *"He'll dine well tonight!"*

Pwca started to cross the wooden bridge in pursuit of the man, but then another thought struck him. He stared up the river at the Troll Bridge. The troll had already disappeared into the shadows beneath it. Silently, he slipped back the way he had come and crept up next to the Troll Bridge, listening intently. There were muffled sounds of chewing, and the occasional *snap* as something was broken beneath the bridge. Pwca waited until the sounds died away, and then slowly, carefully, he inched his way down the steep bank beside the bridge.

When he was sure he was in a place where he could easily run, he called out, "Troll! I have a proposition for you!"

There was no sound.

"Troll!" called Pwca louder. "I wish to speak with you! In the name of the Witch, I ask for a parley!"

Still, no sound was heard. Pwca wondered if the old thing had fallen asleep after its meal, and was just preparing to slip further down the bank when, with no warning, the gigantic face of the troll rose before him, and two great arms lunged at him. The green monster bellowed a dreadful cry as it came at him, mouth still fouled with its last victim's remains. Pwca leaped into the air just in time, barely saving himself, and scrambled up the bank. To his surprise, the troll did not follow, but stared up at him, gasping as if catching its breath.

Then it spoke.

"What … is it … the goblin … wants," it said through gasping breaths.

Pwca stared down at the creature. It was massive and green and bore a chipped and broken skin of scales. Its claws were long and ragged, and its bulbous bald head looked rather like a misshapen blob sitting upon a thick neck. Its pinched eyes seemed too small for its large face as they stared back at him.

"I wish to free you from this land of the Little People," he said.

"Free … me..." said the troll flatly.

"Yes, free you. Take you from this dreadful place. Take you to a place where you can have meats other than fish and worms and stalkers and goblins."

"You … lie …" it said. "Come … down … and I will … have you … for dessert."

"You know of the mirror in the wood?" asked Pwca, now fingering the crystal ball in his pocket.

"Mirror …" breathed the troll.

"Yes, the one some ways down the trail – the one that's been there for ages and ages now. But perhaps you have forgotten. Perhaps you are too old and feeble of mind to remember it," said Pwca.

The troll growled and spat, and foul things flew from its mouth.

"What … of it?" it said.

"I have obtained the key to open it!" he declared, and pulled the crystal from his pocket, holding it up to the night sky.

The moon shone down upon him, striking the crystal ball and seemingly illuminating it so that it glowed with a blue-silver light.

"Where … did a … goblin … get … that?" it wheezed.

"Ah! Does it matter? Come with me and I will show you what it can do! We shall go together to the world of Men, and there you will be free to hunt!" declared Pwca.

The troll was silent for a moment and breathed heavily.

"And what … does the … goblin … want from me?" asked the troll.

"Just your strength," said Pwca. "There is a little thing that I need moved. A mirror on the other side – a heavy mirror, too big for one poor little goblin to carry. Help me and I will give you more than you can dream of. Come now, a new age is about to be born in the world of Men, when old things shall awaken and walk the earth once more! Creatures of the night are gathering, gathering around a great and terrible Presence. Come with me, and you will feel it! You will worship it!"

Pwca was growing exuberant, but the troll just stared at him for a moment, then looked back beneath its bridge.

"Long … years … I have … lived … beneath this … bridge," said the Troll. "I … built it … so long ago … It is mine!"

"Ah, and you may keep it if you wish. Once we have the mirror, all the bridges in all the worlds will be yours! Only come with me and see," answered Pwca.

The old troll hesitated and then said, "I will … come and … see. And if … you lie... I *will* … eat you … for … dessert."

The green creature, at least ten feet tall, slowly climbed the bank and then stood towering over the goblin. It was thick and broad, with legs like tree trunks, and a broad barrel of a chest that hung with aging fat and muscle.

"This way," said Pwca, and led the way down the trail.

The ancient troll followed, breathing heavily, and after a long while, they came to the mirror in the wood.

The troll looked at the dead stalkers and sniffed.

"The man – he killed them with his magic hammer. We must stay away from him, yes, until *we* can get the hammer. Come and watch!" said Pwca.

He pulled the crystal ball from his pocket again and held it up. Instantly, the mirror before them swirled, and there was the basement of the McGunnegal house, dark and still.

Pwca stepped through.

A look of surprise crossed the troll's fat face.

"Come!" said Pwca.

The troll bent low and passed its hand through the mirror, then with great effort, squeezed through, its chest and back scraping the mirror's sides as it entered the basement. It looked from side to side, then, seeing a dim light filtering down from an open door up a stairway, pushed through completely.

Pwca put the crystal ball away.

"Now for our little agreement," he said to the troll. "You see this mirror? We shall have it for our own. Just pick it up and carry it up these stairs, across a field, over a wall, and into a bog where the Presence is. Then! Yes, then we shall bring the creatures of the night to the Presence, and the new age shall begin!"

The troll stood breathing heavily for a moment, considering. Then it gripped the heavy mirror with its powerful arms, lifted it, and followed the goblin up the stairs. The wooden steps groaned and cracked under its weight, and when it reached the top, it would not fit through the doorway with the mirror. The troll breathed heavily for a moment, then with one mighty blow, it smashed the doorframe, sending splinters flying into the kitchen. Up it came, a thing of horror and might that had not stalked the green earth for many an age.

The goblin cackled with glee as it led the troll to the back door, which it also smashed open with its massive fists, and, wheezing as it went, followed the goblin step by step. Together, they disappeared over the wall and into the Dismal Bog.

Chapter 25 – Trouble in Ireland

All day, the McGunnegals, Frederick, Gwydion, and Professor McPherson sailed northwest toward Ireland. An extraordinarily strong and steady breeze had been with them, and the *Unknown* skipped lightly over the sea northwestward after they had rounded the bend of Wales. They spent considerable time talking and learning and cleaning, with a noontime break during which Gwydion had produced the most amazing meal of soup and bread and cheese that they had ever tasted. Gwydion and Bib spent hours working together and talking about the advancing technology of the present age and about magical things of ages past.

"From what you say, Bib, magic seems to have faded from the world to a thing of legend and myth – the stuff of bedtime stories and fireside tales. I wonder what happened?" said Gwydion.

"Do you mean that it wasn't that way in your day?" asked Bib.

"Oh, there have always been legends and myths," he replied, "but when the Gates were open, the gifts and powers of the races were a thing of everyday life, at least for the folk that we met. But there were few of the race of Men who had such abilities. It was only after the mingling of the races that some were born with the gifts."

"Do you mean that after this Anastazi the Great opened the Gates, and the various peoples walked in each other's lands that some folk of the race of Men started to *become* magical?" she asked.

"No, no, I didn't mean that, though I have heard such rumors. What I meant was that the races *mingled*. Anastazi himself took a human wife. Their children bore the traits of both human and elven peoples," replied Gwydion.

"Do you mean that *you* have *elvish* blood in you? Are you related to this Anastazi the Great?" asked Bib, amazed.

"To answer your second question, no, I am not related to Anastazi the Great, unless it might be through an ancient bloodline of the elven folk. But my father's father's father was a great elven lord. Njord was his name. He loved the sea, it is said, and left the Emerald Isle to find lands of his own. My grandfather, Freyr, took most of our folk – all except my father and mother, that is, and went in search of free lands. It has been many years since I saw him last," replied Gwydion.

He paused, and then said, quieter, "Many years."

Bib was about to ask him another question when the voice of Frederick called from high above. He was in the crow's nest and had been watching out over the sea.

"I can see land ahead!" he called.

"Already?" said Professor McPherson from the ship's wheel. "Truly, we are sailing fast!"

Indeed, as they gazed out over the bow of the ship, they could see the coast of Ireland steadily drawing nearer. Soon it loomed large before them, and the professor called them to make ready for docking. Frederick climbed down as the ship glided into the same harbor that Captain Truehart had sailed from some ten days before. They raised their sails, and two rowboats met them. After securing ropes to the ship, they slowly made their way to the docks.

As they went ashore, Frederick was reminded that the Irish people were starving, undergoing one of the worst famines in their history. The men standing around the docks were thin, and some appeared to be sick. Emaciated children stared with hollow eyes, looking on as the little group made their way down the docks. He silently wondered how long they could endure such hardship.

They soon found the dock master, and the professor spoke to him about the ship and how long they would be docked there. They then found a farmer with a large wagon who was heading their way and hitched a ride, with the professor and Gwydion sitting in the front and the rest of them in the back. Gwydion sat watching the landscape roll by as they made their way toward the farm, but the children talked in whispers among themselves.

"It will be wonderful to see Father again," said Henny.

"Yes," said Bib, "and the farm. There's so much to talk about, and I'm sure the professor and Gwydion and Father will know what to do once all the plans are made. We'll catch that goblin and make things right in the land."

Soon they came to a crossroads, and the farmer said, "I'll let you out here. Tell your dad that Emmit says hello and that I hope he's well. These are hard times. Hard times."

He shook his head sadly.

"This will be fine, sir," said Aonghus. "It's only a few minutes more. Many thanks."

They piled out of the wagon and waved good-by. The farmer turned to go, but paused, then said, "You all watch yourselves. Some folk about here are blaming your family for the blight. Strange things have been seen on your farm – strange things. Not that I believe all the stories, but I'm just a-warnin' ya." He turned and headed down the lane to the right.

"What's that supposed to mean?" said Bib.

"I'm not sure," said Abbe. "Let's just get home."

As they walked along and neared the house, Henny tugged on Aonghus' sleeve and said, "Aonghus, can you carry me? I'm scared."

Aonghus picked her up and said, "What's wrong, Sprite?"

"Something's bad," she said. "The farm doesn't look right."

But the farmhouse was still some distance away, and it looked the same as always. The old brown wooden house and its dark thatched roof stood next to an old oak tree, a pile of firewood still lay stacked to one side.

Yet as they drew near, something did feel wrong. They hurried on down the road and passed through the gate. All was quiet. Too quiet. A wind blew across the yard, licking up a whirlwind of dust before passing on over the fields.

"Dad?" called Abbe as she ran to the front door.

They all followed behind. The door was ajar, and when they entered, a frightening sight met their eyes. The house was wrecked. Furniture was overturned, a chair was smashed, and as they went into the kitchen, they found the cellar door ripped from its hinges and broken into splinters.

"Dad?" called Aonghus.

Immediately, they began to run through the house, calling for their father, almost panicking with fear, but suddenly, Gwydion called out loudly, "Stop!"

They all stopped, shocked at the commanding voice that the old man had used.

"Quickly, come here," he said.

They returned to the kitchen where he stood, and looked where he pointed. There on the floor by the remains of the cellar door were huge muddy footprints leading away from the cellar and toward the back door. The prints were at least two feet long, and where toes would have been there were scrapes and marks on the wooden floor, as though claws had rent the old planks under some tremendous weight.

"What is it?" asked Bran, leaning close. "This mud looks to be maybe a day or two old."

Gwydion leaned down next to him and examined the marks.

"Come, all of you. Stay close. Do you have any weapons here?" he said.

Aonghus ran upstairs and returned a moment later with a staff and Bran's hunting bow.

"The upstairs is a mess too," he said grimly.

Gwydion looked at the staff and bow doubtfully and said, "Follow me."

The back of the house was no better off. It looked as though something huge, too big to fit easily through the door, had made the doorway bigger by simply smashing through the wall. A terrible thought struck Frederick.

"Oh no," he said aloud.

They all stopped and looked at him.

"Frederick?" said the professor.

"The mirror!" he said, a look of horror on his face. "What if the goblin opened a doorway into some other world and brought something terrible through, and got into the house?"

"Then we need to go and see this mirror," replied McPherson.

They hurried across the fields and to Grandpa's house. Lighting a lamp, they went down the cellar, and Frederick led them to the place where the mirror had stood.

"It's gone!" he said.

They looked at him skeptically.

"It was here, I swear!" he said. "I'm not lying!"

Gwydion looked grim. "If it was the mirror of Mor-Fae of which you speak, one goblin could not move it. It would take many. But I fear that Frederick may be right. Something else may have come through. Something far stronger. We must stay together."

They left Grandpa's and went back to the farmhouse and gathered in the broken kitchen.

"Where's Dad?" asked Henny, pulling on Aonghus' sleeve.

"We're not sure, lass," he said. "But you know Dad. He can take care of himself better than any man alive. I'm sure he's out looking for this goblin thing."

"But the house..." she said, a frightened look on her face.

"Never mind that," he replied. "I know it looks bad, but you can bet all this happened while Dad was away doing something. He might come back any minute, or maybe..."

"Or maybe he ended up there too," cut in Frederick.

"End up there?" said Professor McPherson.

"I mean maybe that goblin *did* open the door to the Land of the Little People. Maybe it brought back something... like a troll. We met one there. I remember it. It was *huge*. And I remember seeing its footprints in the mud. They were about the size of those marks on the floor. Maybe Mr. McGunnegal followed the goblin into that land, and maybe he got trapped there," said Frederick.

"Then all the more reason we hunt down that thing and get both the mirror and the crystal ball back," said Bran.

"Perhaps," said Professor McPherson. "Or perhaps we should split up. Frederick, you said that this Lady Danu told you that you were to find a king in the sea?"

"Yes," he said. "I'm sure that I am supposed to sail out there and find him."

"No," said Aonghus. "I think we should stay together. If that goblin is going about bringing other evils into our world, we've got to stop it."

"And how shall we do that?" asked Gwydion. "It has the crystal ball – the key to the mirror – and with that, it can travel to any world, and bring many things here that have not walked in the world of Men before. I have seemingly slept long, and I do not know what has befallen the other worlds. But I do know that three of the eight worlds fell into darkness in my time, and a shadow had fallen over four others."

"The eight worlds?" asked Bib. "What are they?"

Gwydion was about to answer when Frederick cut in.

"Under the hill lay eight doors.
Some lead to sun, and some to moors."

"What did you say, Frederick?" asked Gwydion.

"It's the rhyme," he replied.

"Tell me of this rhyme," said Gwydion.

Frederick cleared his throat and began.

"Under the hill lay eight doors.
Some lead to sun, and some to moors.

In one, you find the Little Folk,
With treasures hidden under oak.
There I found the lady sleeping fast,
And broke the spell that had been cast.

But, no princess prize was she,
Indeed, a witch turned out to be.
Oh, what treachery was this,
That I should wake her with a kiss?

Door two finds Trolls, their cruel hearts long
To rob and steal and do folk wrong.
Once architects and builders tall,
Now under bridges they do crawl.

A third finds gold and gems and ale,
And treasuries and spear and mail.
Magic ax and armor bright,
And carven halls of dwarven might.

Four is where the Giant roams,
Beware him lest he crush your bones
Into his bread and nasty meal
To feed his lusty gullet's zeal.

470

The fifth you must not pass, be sure!
For demons wait beyond that door.
Your soul they seek! From them I fled!
Do not open! This I have said!

The sixth leads home, remember it when,
You wish to return to the world of Men.
And there find rest and peace at last,
When you return from the looking-glass.

The seventh finds Elf and tree and song,
Spells, and laughter all day long.
Bright never-dying folk and friend,
And maids so fair your heart will rend.

Open eight and find sure gloom,
An ancient plague, the goblin's doom.
And there the Worm that brought the blight,
Calling all into its pits of night.

Behind these doors such perils lie,
And lo, no keys to these have I!
Yet to these worlds I yet have passed,
Through a simple looking-glass.

The portal to a perilous maze
Into which I have dared to gaze.
No simple trek around a wall,
But beyond it I have placed it all -

A king's ransom, oh, and so much more!
Things of might and magic stored.
Things too great for mortal men,
Things so great that I, a brigand, send

Them far away from mortal lands
Into, I hope, far wiser hands.
Yet three things I dare not leave
Lest too, our world, become bereaved.

The first, this map to mark the place
That leads beyond our time and space.
The next an orb so small, yet rare!

With it you travel, but oh, take care!

And last, a looking-glass to see
Wherever the traveler may be.
And at special places you may pass
And step through the looking-glass.

What secret powers these things possess,
None have fathomed, none have guessed.
Yet with simple folk who have no cares,
I leave these things from wizards' lairs."

They all looked at him and were silent.

"It's on the map above the fireplace," he said.

"Those are the Eight Worlds, aren't they?"

"There is a map?" asked Gwydion.

Aonghus led them into the living room, but to their further dismay, they found the map was gone.

"It took the map too!" said Abbe.

"It would seem that our goblin is gathering many things to itself. But to answer your question, yes, those are the Eight Worlds – of Little People, Trolls, Dwarves, Giants, Orogim – I believe the rhyme called them *demons,* although they are not – Men, Elves, and Goblins. They are the eight that Anastazi the Great opened doors to, although perhaps not the only eight that exist. Who can say? But where did this riddle come from? What is this map of which you speak?" asked the wizard.

"It's an old thing," said Bib, "passed down from generation to generation in our family."

"It was drawn by Atsolter the Pirate," said Frederick. "He got the crystal ball somehow and went to those worlds, I suppose. He's the one who wrote the rhyme."

"Was that all that the rhyme said?" asked Gwydion. "Please, tell us this riddle once again."

Frederick recited the whole thing to them again, and they listened carefully. When he was done, they were all silent for a long moment.

"I say we find this goblin here and now," said Aonghus, "before it causes more trouble."

"And what of Colleen?" asked Professor McPherson.

"We take one day. One day to track down this thing and make it give us the crystal. If we can't find it in one day, then we set sail and return no later than four weeks. But if we find its lair, we seal it up, and make sure it can't get out," he replied.

"Aong, we tracked that thing for weeks and weeks, and never found it," said Bran.

"We have a bigger trail to follow now," he replied. "And we didn't have a wizard with us then."

They all looked at Gwydion. His dark eyes returned their expectant gazes, but he was silent.

"Very well, then, but there is something you need to know about this place, if indeed this is the same place where once I dwelt. There is something that we, that is, the wizards, buried here long, long ago. It may lay still beneath the earth," he replied.

"What is that?" asked Bran.

"It was an ancient evil. We... chained it," he slowly replied.

A sudden wind whistled through the broken kitchen door, and a shiver ran down their spines.

"What was it?" asked Henny, her eyes wide.

"A black thing," he whispered. "A terror that fell upon the world of men and ravaged it. We warred against it for long years, and at last, we captured it, and would have slain it. But one among us forbade its destruction. So, deep beneath the earth we chained it, and there kept it far from the lives of simple men. And there it may yet dwell, haunting the world with its nightmares and nameless fears, but impotent to do ought else."

"Gwydion," said Aonghus, a thought coming to him, "there's a bog just south of here. It's an evil place. There's something about it that makes your blood run cold and fills your heart with fear. The farther you go in, the more you feel it."

"I've been there too," said Bran. "Right in the middle of the bog there's a broken place, and a cave of sorts that descends down into blackness. I'm sure that's the source of it all."

Gwydion took a deep breath.

"Then that is where the goblin will be," he replied. "This terror that I speak of will draw all such creatures to itself. Let us hope that it, itself, has not been wakened."

"I don't like the bog," said Henny. "Dad said not to go there."

Aonghus knelt down next to her and looked into her blue-lavender eyes. Her golden hair hung down across her rosy cheeks, making her look cute and lovable, but her face bore a worried expression.

"Don't you worry, Sprite," he said with a smile. "I think Dad would approve. What we're doing now is really important, okay?" He tousled her hair and said, "We'll be fine."

"I think that we should not waste any time," said Professor McPherson. "But I do not think we should send the girls into the bog. Nor do I think it safe for any of us to go there. If there is a goblin and a troll, and this nameless terror that you speak of, and now who knows what other creatures, could we face them alone? How do we plan to get the mirror and the crystal ball back from them? Will we fight them? And if so, then with what?"

They were quiet for a few moments, and then Aonghus spoke.

"Bran and I will. We know this bog pretty well, and we know exactly where to look for this goblin. And we know some hiding places where we can spy things out. The professor is right – we shouldn't take a whole troop of us blundering into the heart of the bog, just to be spotted by these creatures and ambushed," he said.

"Now hold on, Aonghus," said Abbe. "I want to go too. Believe it or not, I've been in there myself a time or two."

"You... when did you go wandering in there?" he asked.

"Never you mind," she replied. "But I know a thing or two about it as well."

"No, Abbe. I need you to stay here and watch over the others. If there's trouble, you'll know what to do," he replied.

She started to protest, but then stopped, seeing both a stubborn and pleading look on his face.

"All right then," she said grudgingly. "I suppose we can try to fix up the house a bit."

"Frederick and I will stay with the girls and lend a hand with the house," said the professor. "No, Frederick, no protests. Perhaps you and I can talk a bit while we work."

"I think that I shall accompany you to the bog," said Gwydion. "But we should return well before dark. That should give us four or five hours yet. And we may wish to consider staying on the ship this evening. It may be difficult to secure the house in its present condition."

So the girls, Frederick, and Professor McPherson set about cleaning up the house while Gwydion, Aonghus, and Bran headed across the farm toward the bog.

"Everything has changed here," said Gwydion. "Once there was a great white castle with marvelously tall towers. Every one of its stones was enchanted and carved with runes of great power against the evils that stalked the world in my day. The Council of Wizards met there, and peoples of many worlds came and went, and the McGunnegals were..."

He stopped and looked at the boys.

"I don't know why I never thought of it before, but there were McGunnegals who lived on the outskirts of the castle. They were … big men. Do you know your family history?" he asked.

"Some of it seems a bit vague when you go back more than six or seven generations," said Bran, who had studied the history of both the McGunnegals and the McLochlans. "There are weird stories on both sides, though. Family stories of strange things happening, I mean. But the oldest stories say that the first McGunnegals were *really* big, and came to Ireland thousands of years ago. We have a graveyard, but only the McGunnegals are buried there, no McLochlans."

"Indeed? I would like to see it, perhaps tomorrow. I wonder if you are related to the McGunnegals that I once knew?" replied Gwydion.

"Well, it's a pretty common name," said Aonghus. "Could be no relation at all."

"Perhaps," said the wizard, and they walked on in silence.

When they came to the wall, Aonghus said, "Well, here we are. The bog is on the other side."

Gwydion examined the stones piled up to form the wall and shook his head.

"There is no doubt," he said. "These are the broken stones of the Wizard's Castle."

"Well, whatever it was, it happened a long time ago," said Aonghus. "This wall has been here as long as anyone can remember."

"And is there a way through?" asked Gwydion.

"No, we just climb over," said Bran, and he nimbly mounted the wall and sat on top with a smile on his face.

But when he looked out over the bog, his expression changed, and a look of shock replaced his smile. The others followed him up, and when they looked south, their eyes grew wide, and a feeling of dread crept over them. There, like a vast sea, stood a dense gray fog, with only the very tops of barren trees reaching their twisted branches beyond the dank roof. And it stank.

"What has happened?" whispered Bran. "It was always a bit misty, and always smelled of decay, but never like this!"

"Some devilry of that goblin, I'll wager," said Aonghus. "Just like the black rot that's killed our crops."

"There has been a plague?" asked Gwydion.

"Oh yes, started last year when our mom disappeared, and that thing first came," replied Aonghus.

"Devilry indeed," said the wizard. "We must be cautious. Can you lead us through this fog?"

"I never get lost," said Bran. "I'll lead us."

Down they went, descending into a cloud of mist that swirled about and clung to them as they walked. With the mists, there was also a feeling of uneasiness all about them. A feeling that they were being watched and that something else was here as well – the dark brooding presence that they had so often felt before when they dared to walk the bog's paths.

"It will take a bit to get to the center," whispered Bran. "I say we move carefully and quietly. I never did like the feel of this place, but even less now."

The others nodded and followed him, with Aonghus behind Bran, and Gwydion bringing up the rear.

The fog was as thick as pea soup, and even Bran paused every twenty paces or so to get his bearings. An acrid smell permeated the dank air, sinking into their clothes and hair until they were wet and stank.

As they slowly moved toward the bog's center, they began to see what they thought was movement – small dark creatures that peered at them from the rotting weeds, but which vanished in a swirl of mist when they paused to look closer. And as they went on, the sense of uneasiness began to weigh heavily on their minds, like a black dread that was growing as thick and heavy as the fog.

Suddenly, all three of them stopped, although they did not know why. But whether it was by some instinct or a sense that the air around them had quite noticeably changed, they immediately gripped their weapons and turned back to back. Bran notched an arrow to his bow and held it ready, and both Aonghus and Gwydion gripped their staffs.

Then they heard it – an eerie cry in the distance, coming through the mists like some great dying beast's final wail. It rose and then died away with a haunting echo through the dead trees. Both Aonghus and Bran felt their blood run cold at the sound. They looked at each other and then at Gwydion, but the wizard was staring into the fog, his eyes wide, and his face grim.

"What was that?" whispered Bran. "I've never heard that in the bog before."

"Hush!" hissed the old man.

He appeared to be listening intently. Then, with a suddenness that startled them, he moved.

"Into the trees, quickly!" he rasped and ran into a thicket of gnarled willows and tangled brambles.

They followed him, and all three of them crouched down and peered from behind the twisted trunks. A moment later, there was the sound of something coming toward them. It made no secret of its presence, for it was stomping heavily through the muck, making its own path by breaking branches and trampling the underbrush. There was another sound as well – a sound of *flapping*, like the beating of many, many wings.

Then they saw it. It came through the fog like a lumbering giant, at least ten feet tall, and its breath came in great wheezing gasps. Although it was man-shaped, it was no man, for it had a thick green hide and a massive head, with a great deformed nose and ears and beady yellow eyes. Its legs were thick and squat, and its feet clawed with sharp yellow nails. It was clad only in a ragged brown waist wrapping, and in its great fist, it bore a tree trunk at least eight inches thick and six feet long.

All around it flew bats. Hundreds and hundreds of them fluttering about, forming a great swarming shadow that blotted out what little light of the sun filtered through the fog. And beneath this canopy of darkness, all about it on the ground, small black creatures scurried, although they could not make out what they were. It was like a scene from some dark nightmare, but Aonghus and Bran knew that it was all too real.

On it came, directly toward them, and through the gloom that surrounded the creature, they could see that it was looking this way and that, as if it were searching for something. A broken yellow fang protruded from its bottom lip, and a line of thick drool ran down its wrinkled chin. When it reached the place where they had left the trail, it suddenly stopped, looking at the ground. The bats whirled in a wild frenzy all about it, and the black creatures on the ground scurried about, somehow following the mad dance of the bats.

Then the creature lifted up its head and gave a great cry. Whether it was a battle roar or howl of defiance, they were not sure, but in that moment, it turned in their direction, roared again, and charged. Instantly, the bats flew into an even greater frenzy, spreading outward and above them like a black roof. With three great bounds, the creature was upon them, swinging its massive club as it came.

Even as it took its first step, an arrow from Bran's bow whistled through the air and struck it clean between the eyes. To his astonishment, the arrow bounced off. Seeing this, Aonghus leaped from behind the tree. The beast turned on him and swung its club down in a killing blow. But Aonghus sidestepped and brought his own staff up under the beast's chin with a tremendous *whack*. His staff broke, and the creature stumbled backward with a howl. Instantly, it recovered with a roar, baring its huge broken fangs at him.

Aonghus suddenly found himself surrounded by a swarm of black bats. They whirled round and round him, scratching at him with their hooked claws, trying to tear at his face and arms. He instinctively swatted the creatures away and, in that moment of distraction, the creature was upon him. It picked him up with its two massive hands by the shoulders and brought him close to its great bulbous head that was nearly as big as his chest. It stared him in the eyes for an instant as if pondering how it might eat him, and then opened its great maw wide. Aonghus retched as its fetid breath came in great wheezing gasps and, for a moment, he wondered if this would be the last thing he saw – the gross gullet of an unearthly monster.

But the thing did not eat him. There was a sudden bright flash, and the creature stood still, gripping him in its stony hands, its face frozen. Then he realized that something had changed. He looked about and could *see*. The bats were gone, and in their place was a great swarm of flies buzzing about.

Bran stood poised behind the creature, his knife drawn and raised above his head, ready to strike it in the back, a look of fear and astonishment and surprise all at once on his face. He hesitated for an instant, then, leaping upon the thing's back, he brought the knife down, hard. The blade struck and threw sparks, breaking its tip, but the creature still did not move. Gwydion casually walked over to the beast and placed a hand on the outstretched arm that still gripped Aonghus.

"What..." began Aonghus.

"Trolls do not like the sun," he said, rapping on its head with his staff.

"Trolls!" said Bran, coming to his senses. "This is a troll?"

He slid off its back and cautiously walked about it, watching its face. It looked just as gruesome as it had a few moments ago, but was as still as a statue.

"It is indeed," said the wizard, "and as I said, they do not like the sun. It makes them rather... stiff."

"More like turned to stone," said Aonghus, struggling now in the huge hands of the troll, and still staring down its wide-open mouth.

His feet were dangling above the ground, and his arms were pinned to his sides.

"Well, big brother," said Bran, now beginning to laugh. "Let's see you muscle your way out of this one!"

Aonghus furrowed his eyebrows and gave Bran a stern look.

"Now see here," he said. "I was nearly eaten by this thing a moment ago and you stand there laughing. And would you *please* get these flies off my face!"

Now Bran did laugh, and Gwydion could not help but chuckle.

"Here, Aonghus," said the wizard. "Let me help you a bit. We better get you out of there before the sun goes down and the troll revives."

"This thing is going to come back to life?" asked Bran.

"Oh, it may indeed. And I would suggest that we be far from here when it does," replied Gwydion. "In this fog, I do not know if the troll has turned permanently to stone or not."

The wizard looked about and found a broad leaf, picked it, and brought it back to the troll.

"Any shade may turn this stone to flesh again. If it does, break free as quickly as you can, Aonghus," he said.

He nodded and Gwydion held up the leaf, casting a dim shadow on the gripping hand of the troll. Almost immediately, the fingers began to stretch and flex. Aonghus pushed hard, dislodged his trapped shoulder, and dropped to the ground. A swarm of flies buzzed away into the bog and scores of black beetles dashed away from where he landed. Gwydion pulled away the leaf and the hand froze once again in the dim light. Aonghus rubbed his upper arms and shoulders.

"That thing was *really* strong," he said. "I've never felt anything like it."

"Trolls are not easily dealt with. Let us be thankful that we met it in the daytime," said Gwydion.

"But the bats..." said Bran. "What happened to the bats? They were there one moment, and then next they were gone, and just a bunch of flies were left in their place."

"And those black things on the ground... you turned them into beetles, didn't you?" said Aonghus.

Gwydion only frowned. He was looking at the flies that were now congregating on the troll's head and shoulders, and the beetles that were now crowding about its huge clawed feet. The troll began to twitch.

"We must go back," said the wizard.

"But we've got to find that mirror, and that goblin thing," protested Bran.

"Yes," he replied. "But don't you see what has happened here? The goblin has already traveled to another world and brought back this troll. We do not know what other things it has brought back. This may be the only one, or there may be scores of such creatures waiting for us ahead in the fog. And believe me, there are worse things than trolls among the worlds."

"Are you saying that there could be a whole *army* of these things multiplying in this bog?" asked Aonghus.

"I have no idea," he replied. "But we three will not wish to find out by ourselves, especially as the light begins to fade."

"But what are we to do?" asked Bran. "What of the mirror?"

"What if we fail in this? What if we go deeper into this swamp and fight what awaits us there and fail?" said Aonghus quietly, "What will become of the girls, and Frederick, and the professor... and of Ireland?"

"And what if we wait too long, Aong?" replied Bran. "I say now is the time to strike, before they can grow their numbers. We've got a wizard with us, don't we?"

"You have," said Gwydion. "But I am still only one, and I dare say that this goblin is capable of a bit of dark magic as well. You saw the bats."

They were silent for a long moment and then Gwydion said, "This is your farm and your homeland, and it is your battle. I will help in any way that I can. But here is my counsel. Warn the countryside and villages that an evil has entered the bog. They must band together and even call the authorities in the land. Tell them to use this *technology* that this age possesses to arm themselves.

"But we cannot risk a prolonged battle with dark forces swarming out of a magical gateway from other worlds. I think that this goblin is cunning, but also greedy. It *has* brought creatures from other lands, such as those black things you saw at the feet of the troll. They are creatures of darkness that we would not want to meet when the sun goes down – gremlins of great mischief.

"This troll, however, was not an ordinary one. Did you hear how it gasped for breath? It was either ill or very old. This goblin is bringing creatures here that it can control. I would say that it desires power – power for itself. It would be unwise to force its hand into bringing something larger and more dangerous. I think that it will be some time before its plans are fully laid. But I also suspect that its lair will be well protected. We may well encounter greater perils than this troll if we continue on."

"Then what shall we do?" asked Bran.

"Warn the farms and then sail for Bermuda. Your sister still needs rescuing. And there may be help unlooked-for there. Perhaps we can open a door of our own," he replied.

Aonghus and Bran looked at the huge troll. It was now beginning to move its beetle-covered feet.

"If only Father were here," said Bran. "He would know what to do."

"Yes," said Aonghus, "he would. But he's not, so here's what I say we do. We check with the neighbors and see if they've seen him. If he's off somewhere, he would have left word with someone. But if he's somehow gotten into some other land, then all the better we find a way there quick as may be.

"Let's wait one day, and if Dad doesn't show up, we warn the neighbors that some bad folk have taken up in the bog, and they best arm themselves, then we sail for Bermuda."

Bran thought for a moment and looked toward the middle of the bog through thickening fog, as if considering their options. Then he nodded.

"All right, then," he said. "Let's get out of this place."

As quick as they could, they made their way back to the farm, and none too soon, for even as they left the troll, the flies and beetles returned in force and began to cover its entire body. Bit by bit, its fat and muscle began to quiver and move.

By the time they reached the wall, the sun was moving down toward the horizon. They climbed up and over, and felt immediately safer as they dropped down into the farm. Soon they were back at the damaged house, where they told their tale to the others, leaving out the part about Aonghus nearly being eaten. The girls listened intently, their faces full of worry.

As the sun set and the shadows lengthened, they heard off in the distance a howling roar. Aonghus and Bran looked at one another knowingly. The troll, no doubt, stalked the bog once again.

That night, they set a watch, Gwydion and Professor McPherson first, and then the boys. But none of them slept well, for strange sounds came echoing across the farm from the south. Dark things were on the prowl.

Morning came, and they fixed a meager breakfast, after which Aonghus and Bran took off, running to the neighboring farms and inquiring about their father. Soon they returned with bad news.

"No one has seen Dad for some days," said Bran, "and he left no word with anyone. We've warned all the farms of trouble brewing, and that a band of ruffians is laid up in the bog. They'll be arming themselves, and they're calling the authorities as well."

"Then I think if we are not to be delayed with many inquiries and questions about it all, we ought to be going very soon," said Professor McPherson.

"Yes, indeed you should, as quickly as you can," said Gwydion.

"You said *you* should," said Frederick. "Aren't you coming with us?"

Gwydion was silent for a few moments, and all eyes turned to him.

"No," he finally said. "I think it best that someone stays here and makes sure things do not get out of hand. As well-meaning as your neighbors and authorities might be, I think that there may be some work for a wizard to do, and there is a great deal that I need to learn. So much has changed since I was... away."

"But we may need you, Gwydion," said Frederick. "What, with this Witch and all that – oughtn't we to have someone like you to set things right?"

"Maybe," he replied slowly, "but something tells me that I may be needed here even more. Someone *should* hunt for this goblin. I will do what I can."

When they began to protest further, Professor McPherson spoke.

"I think Gwydion is right," he said. "Someone should also look over your home for you. We can tell the neighbors that you have lent out your house to a friend while your father is away for a time, to keep an eye on things until the authorities can take care of the situation in the bog."

"Indeed," replied Gwydion, "and I shall do more than look after things – I shall do my best to fix them. I have some skill in carpentry and stonework. I will see what I can do to fix your house up as good as new, and with your permission, I will add a few, shall we say, improvements."

They were all sad about Gwydion's decision to stay behind, for they had become very fond of the old man even in the few short days that they had spent together. It was as though they shared some kinship that they could not explain. But they gathered together what few things they needed, and by noon were ready.

They said one last goodbye to the farmhouse, hating to leave it in such a wretched condition. But they shut the gate behind them and headed down the dirt road back toward the village and the ship.

Gwydion waved to them from the door and watched as they disappeared around a bend. He stood gazing after them for a time, thinking. Who were these amazing children? Could they be related to the McGunnegal family that he once knew? There was a resemblance, but also a resemblance to another family – a family that had vanished from the face of the earth – or so he had thought. After some time, he turned and walked back into the house and surveyed the damage.

"*They* will be coming," he said to himself, "and this old place is no defense. It ought to be torn down."

He sighed, looking at the broken and dilapidated walls. "But, let's see what can be done."

He held aloft his staff, and a soft white glow began to shine from its carven top...

Chapter 26 – The Storm

Frederick stood on the bow of the ship, watching dolphins leap beside them as they sailed southwest toward Bermuda. They had delayed as long as possible, but could find only six more crewmen, all Englishmen, to join them on this journey, and so had set sail, trusting that their nine crewmen and the able-bodied McGunnegals and Frederick would be enough.

"After all, there is hope for fair seas this time of the year," said the professor, "and the *Unknown* is a small ship, in any case. She doesn't need a large crew."

They had been sailing for a full day now, with good strong winds and favorable weather, and the old ship slicing smoothly through the waves. Professor McPherson said that if this wind kept up their whole journey, they would make it to Bermuda in less than ten days, but he thought it unlikely that their luck would hold, and the winds would not shift or even die.

"Strange things happen in the open sea," he had said. "We'll just have to hope that Providence is with us, and we make good time."

The McGunnegals and Frederick had occupied themselves with their chores about the ship, straightening things up, winding ropes, scrubbing the decks, and generally getting the ship in order, all the while listening to stories of the sea that the crewmen told.

"You're an amazing lot, you are," said Professor McPherson as he watched them all work.

Frederick had done his part, but his eyes were ever drawn to the sea. Something about it called to him – its vastness and depth. It held secrets that no man had ever beheld, and the legends surrounding it inspired him like nothing else could.

Each day, the professor gave them lessons about navigation by compass, by the stars, by the sun and moon, about knot tying, fishing, gathering water, sea life, and many other things as the hours rolled by. They all amazed him with how quickly they learned and remembered everything that he said to them. By the end of the second day, they knew every aspect of the ship – how it was made, the type of wood that was best for such ships, how the prow and rudder and masts and shape of the hull all contributed to the Clipper ship's great speed.

They had sailed for many hundreds of miles now, but no land was in sight. The sky was a brilliant blue, and the noon sun was warm and friendly.

Frederick found that what he loved most was gazing out at the water. His thoughts often drifted to Colleen and the little people, and he wondered where they were and hoped that they were all right.

"We're coming, Colleen. I promise," he whispered.

Suddenly, something caught his eye, and his attention came into sharp focus. Off in the distance, there seemed to be a gray line at the horizon. He stared at it for several moments and saw that it seemed to be growing. An odd sense of dread began to grow in the pit of his stomach, and he backed away, then turned and ran to the tallest mast and began to climb the rope ladder to the crow's nest. Up he went, climbing as if he had done it all his life, and then jumped into the nest and gazed southwest where the darkness seemed to be gathering. Wind licked at his dark hair – not the steady breeze that they had been sailing with, but a wild gust.

"Professor!" he called down to McPherson, who was standing behind the wheel and chatting with Aonghus.

He looked up from the deck and waved at Frederick.

"Professor!" he called again. "There's a storm ahead!"

Everyone stopped what they were doing and turned to look up at him, and then where he pointed. Professor McPherson and several of the crewmen quickly went to the bow of the ship and looked out. The dark clouds were very visible now – an angry wall of forbidding blackness that seemed to be rushing toward them.

One of the crewmen turned to another and said, "It's the bad luck of the Irish, I say. If I hadn't needed the cash, I would never have come."

"Enough of that!" said the professor. "This is no time for such bigotry!" He paused only a moment longer and then shouted, "All of you come here! Frederick, come down quickly!"

They gathered around him, a foreboding in their hearts.

"Forgive me, my friends. This storm will not be a kind one. We are not in the season for hurricanes, but I fear that we are quickly approaching one. We must tie down everything quickly. Don't worry about the cargo hold – that was secured before we left. But everything in your quarters and everything on deck must be tied. We will try to go around the storm, but we must prepare for the worst. Put on your life vests now, and let's get to work."

The crew looked at one another with dark expressions, but quickly hurried to make the ship as secure as might be. Each of the McGunnegals and Frederick had been assigned a place on the deck that was their responsibility, and each of them had a partner – Aonghus and Henny, Bran and Bib, Abbe and Frederick – and so they quickly tied down everything that was movable or took it below deck.

The sails were flapping in the wind when they finished, and a dreadful wall of black clouds loomed nearer. Professor McPherson had turned the ship east in hopes of sailing around the huge storm and perhaps gaining sight of the coast of France or Portugal, but the darkness seemed to pursue them. Soon the first sheets of rain could be seen, great gray washes falling from the forbidding clouds, and whitecaps began to break against the prow of the ship.

Professor McPherson gathered the children around him and said, "Don't be afraid – we will ride out the storm. We have a good old ship that's weathered many a gale and an experienced crew, and we have a lifeboat if things should turn bad. Remember all I have taught you.

"But now, time is short. We must tie up the sails and let the ship be driven by the storm. We will need to watch for land – for any lighthouse. I will need two sets of eyes to help me with that, and one set of hands to keep things tied down. Ladies, I will need you all below deck to keep all the hatches secure and watch for leaks. Bran, Frederick – you will be my eyes. Aonghus – you will be the rope man. I want you to stretch a rope between each mast so that you can move between them freely. Now, men – you will tie yourself to a rope and tie that rope to the rope between the masts. Off you go now."

They all nodded and hurried to their places, while the professor gave further orders to the crewmen. Abbe led Bib and Henny below, and there they busied themselves making sure all was secure in the cabins and in the galley. No sooner had they huddled together in their cabin, holding tight to the main post that supported the ceiling, when a great wave lifted the ship and dropped it back down upon the sea.

On deck, Frederick and the others watched as Professor McPherson angled the ship to meet the wall of dark rain. It slammed into them like a great hammer blow that nearly knocked them from their feet. They pierced the wall of the hurricane and were immediately drenched and blinded by the torrents that rained upon them.

"Hold your positions!" shouted McPherson above the howling wind. "And watch the sea!"

Great waves bore them up and down in the maelstrom, and more than once, Frederick could see Aonghus, his red hair plastered to his face, gripping the ship's rail with one hand while tying down some stray rope or line with the other. The crew labored manfully against the storm, but there was dread in their eyes as it grew worse.

Suddenly, a sail tore loose and began to flap in the wild gusts. Three crewman, which, he could not tell, untied themselves from their safety lines, climbed the mast through the raging wind, and secured the sail. Together, they descended, watching one another, ready to grab hold should their crewmate slip. But as their feet touched the deck and they reached for the safety line, a tremendous wave washed over the ship. All three men were there one moment and gone the next.

"Man overboard!" Frederick screamed. "Man overboard!" But his voice was lost in the storm.

Aonghus had seen what had happened as well, and rushed to where the men had been. Frantically, he looked into the sea, but they were nowhere to be found. Grabbing a life preserver with a line tied to it, he threw it blindly out into the waves, hoping beyond hope that perhaps they might see it and grab hold.

"Grab the line!" he shouted into the wind. "Man overboard!"

Another crewman rushed to his side, and now Frederick had made his way there as well.

"A wave just took them!" shouted Aonghus. "They're… gone!"

Aonghus began to untie himself, but the crewman stopped him.

"You can't save them, lad!" he shouted. "They're… Look out!"

Without warning, a gigantic wave lifted the ship high into the air, and then sent it careening downward at breakneck speed into a deep troth. Mountains of water surrounded them for a moment, and cries of fear from the crewmen rose above the din of the storm.

Again, they were borne upward by a behemoth wave, and again, they dropped. Every one of them gripped the nearest piece of the ship for dear life as the maddening roller coaster of the ocean threw its worst at them. Then, as quickly as they had come, the towering waves were behind them, carrying away any hope of rescuing the lost men. The stinging spray of the sea swept away the tears that might have flowed as both Aonghus and Frederick stared with empty hearts into the gray of the storm.

The wind howled, the waves crashed, the ship creaked and groaned as though it were in the throes of death. Yet somehow, they sailed on, and still, the storm did not abate. Hour after hour, it raged, carrying its insignificant prey, where, they did not know. All sense of direction was lost to them, yet still Professor McPherson manned the wheel with tireless determination, a grim but defiant look upon his face.

Day turned into night, and, exhausted, they clung to the ship. Frederick's mind began to play tricks on him, and more than once he thought he saw a glimmer of light through the driving rain. But when he looked again, it was gone. He could hear nothing now except the hiss of rain and wind and waves, blending together in a cacophony of wild noise that dulled his senses. Yet he stayed at his post, weary, cold, and wet, his body's strength long gone, but his eyes riveted to the raging sea, searching for some horizon and light that was beyond his vision in this storm.

Then there was a hand on his shoulder, and he turned to see Aonghus standing behind him, holding his safety lines.

"Come!" he shouted.

Weakly, he released the rail and tried to follow Aonghus as he turned to go, but he was immediately swept from his feet. Aonghus grabbed him as he slid by, lifting him to his feet. Together, they held onto the ropes until they reached the first mast. He could see Bran now standing by the door that led below deck, waiting for them, and Professor McPherson still on the upper deck gripping the wheel, his jaw set and his face dark. He and two crewmen appeared to be having an argument, although they could not hear their words above the storm.

"The professor wants us to get below and rest if we can! We rest now, and then relieve some of the crew in a few hours!" shouted Aonghus.

He opened the door, and they hurried in. In the hall, they quickly untied themselves and shut the door.

The storm was silenced to a dull roar, and now the terrible groaning of the anguished ship could be heard, a twisting sound that came up through its belly and ribs like the magnified creaking of a hundred trees blown about in a gale. They hurried to the girls' cabin, but did not find them there.

Bran called out, "Abbe! Bib! Henny! Where are you?"

"In here – in the galley!" called Abbe.

Down the hall they went to the galley, where a fearful sight greeted them. Water two inches deep covered the floor, and they could see it running through a crack in the ship's hull.

"We heard a terrible snap, Aonghus," said Bib. "We ran in here and found this!"

"We've got to patch it somehow!" he said urgently.

"Screws and pitch!" said Bib. "These ships carry them, I'm sure!"

"What..." began Abbe, but Bib cut her off.

"There should be some sort of wooden beams that have screws on top – they're meant to support the hull and decking in times like this. And there ought to be some oakum – rope soaked in pitch, a hammer, and tools that look like chisels, and a barrel of pitch that we can seal the leak with. Check in the supply area," she said urgently.

"Shouldn't we go aloft and get a crewman?" asked Abbe.

A crewman, however, appeared in the doorway and looked in. He was soaked and weary, but when he saw the crack in the hull, his eyes went wide.

"She won't last in this storm with that rip in her belly. If you want my advice, you best grab some line, a sack of grub and water, and make for the lifeboats. This lady is going down!" he said.

He then grabbed a crate of food and ran from the room.

"No time! Hurry!" said Bib. "Find those tools and beams!"

Indeed, the water was pouring in now. Frederick, who was closest to the door, ran out into the hall to the supply room and Bran followed him. They looked about, and sure enough, lying against one wall were four long beams that had iron screws protruding from the top. Together, they picked one up. Frederick found its weight almost unbearable, exhausted as he was, but somehow they maneuvered it through the hall and to the galley. Aonghus then went to the same room and retrieved a large barrel of black pitch and a mop, along with a length of oakum and a box of tools.

"We'll need a T-board for the top," said Bib. "Something we can put the screw-end on. Go find it while we pack the crack with oakum."

Frederick stumbled back down the hall as the ship lurched sideways, and found several small boards, which he grabbed and took back to the galley. Bib seemed to be in complete control of the situation as she directed Abbe and Henny to saturate the top of the T-board with pitch, while the boys hammered the oakum into the crack.

"This stuff is supposed to go in hot, or at least warm," said Bib as Aonghus drove the last of the sticky rope into the leaking seam, "but this will have to do."

At her direction, Bran and Aonghus took hold of the beam and positioned the screw end against the crack, then the other end of the board against the opposite wall.

"Now turn the screw until it's tight!" she ordered, and Aonghus began to turn the big screw while the others held it in place.

Soon it was secured, and the crack stopped gushing water and only trickled a bit.

"Now seal all around it with the pitch," said Bib, and Abbe and Henny took mopfuls of the black tar and jammed it all around the beam.

The leak stopped, and they cheered.

"I think we won't need that lifeboat just yet! But, better check the rest of the hull where we can," said Bib.

Two other leaks were found, and two more screws and the black pitch were used to secure them.

When at last they felt as though they could breathe a little easier, Abbe said, "You boys need some rest. You look exhausted! Go on then, we girls will keep watch over the hull. Get some sleep if you can."

Grateful, the boys went to their cabin, put on dry clothes, and lay down on their beds. But the rocking and creaking of the ship did not help them to rest. Had the beds not been made with railing all about, they would have rolled right out and onto the floor. But so great was their weariness that they somehow fell into a fitful sleep.

The girls, having completed their survey of the ship, and being satisfied that there were no other leaks for the moment, peeked in the boys' cabin and, seeing them asleep, quietly shut their door.

"Poor things," said Henny. "They worked hard up on the deck."

"Up on the deck!" exclaimed Abbe. "Professor McPherson is still up there!"

It had been over an hour since the boys had come down, and now they were fearful for the professor.

"I'll go and check on him," said Abbe.

"No, Ab," said Bib. "Let me go. You know I'm a bit more sure-footed and a better swimmer, if it comes to it."

"No matter, Bib. I'm the oldest, and it's only right that I go. Stay here with Henny," she replied.

Bib was not happy but, with a frown, agreed with her older sister.

"Tie in, then Ab, and do be careful," she said.

Abbe tied one of the ropes around her waist and looked at her two sisters.

"Wish me luck!" she said, and opened the door.

Immediately, the howling rage of the storm hit them, and Abbe rushed out, slamming the door behind her. Bib breathed a prayer after her and she and Henny waited.

Out on the lower deck, Abbe was awestruck by the fury and raw power of the storm that raged all about them. It was pitch black now, and only the continual flashes of lightning illuminated the rocking world about her and allowed her to make her way to the ladder that led to the upper deck. Slowly, carefully, she climbed, clinging to the wet rungs of the ladder until she felt the top and pulled herself up. A flash of lightning illuminated the deck, and in that moment, she saw the brazen image of Professor McPherson gripping the wheel of the ship. An oil lamp was secured to a post by his side, casting an eerie glow over his face in the darkness.

She moved across the deck, trying desperately not to slip, but with every wave, she slid about, unable to gain any sort of footing. Finally, she managed to half crawl, half stumble her way over to the professor and gripped the railing that surrounded the platform on which the wheel was set. In the dim light of the lamp and through the lightning flashes, she could see that he had tied himself to the railing on either side of the wheel.

"What are you doing up here, Abbe?" he yelled through the wind when he saw her.

"Checking on you, Professor. We were worried. Can you come below and rest?" she yelled.

"No, I must stay at the wheel and guide the ship!" he called back.

"Guide it to where?" she asked.

He pointed at the railing in front of them, and there, set in the wood, was what appeared to be a compass of sorts, although it was intricate and beautiful and had a strange design.

But Abbe had no time to admire it, and she said, "What is it, Professor?"

"It will guide us out of this storm!" he said. "But I must stay at the wheel and follow its direction."

"Guide us out... Professor, a compass just ... Oh, Professor, please do come below, you must rest!" she called.

"No, Abbe! Get below. I will be fine! I will get you to safety! I promise!" he said.

Lightning lit up his face. He was stern and full of determination. He looked in her eyes for a moment, then said, "I will not fail you. Now go and rest while you can. If I need you, I will rap three times on the deck."

Abbe looked at him once again in the dim glow of the lamp and then nodded.

"We repaired several leaks in the hull, sir," she said.

He looked alarmed for a moment, and then smiled and said, "So, I brought the right crew, after all!"

Abbe looked about the ship as lightning suddenly lit its decks and masts.

"Where is the crew?" she yelled. "Professor, I don't see the crew anywhere!"

Then she noticed that one of the lifeboats was missing.

"They have abandoned ship," he said, a look of resignation on his face. "Fools! Our best hope was to stay together with the ship. But their fears overcame their reason. We must not allow the same to happen to us. We must stay the course and hold together!"

Abbe's heart sank. How would they sail the ship without the crew? She turned to go, not knowing what to say, and she made her way back to the ladder and then down to the door. Bib and Henny were waiting for her when she opened it.

"Oh, Abbe, you're drenched!" said Henny.

"What about the professor?" asked Bib.

"He's still at the wheel and he won't come below. He says his compass is guiding us out of the storm. I do hope he's all right. But he looks dreadfully tired. But there's worse news. The crew has abandoned ship!" she said.

"What!" said Bib. "Why? We fixed the crack!"

"I don't know!" she said.

"Do you think we ought to wake the boys and have them go back out there?" asked Bib.

Abbe took a deep breath and steadied herself. "Not yet. Let them rest for a bit if they can. What can they do anyway? But we need to keep watch for any further leaks. We'll take turns. I'll take the first watch, then you, and then Henny and me again," said Abbe.

Bib and Henny nodded and went to their cabin, curled up together in one bed, and tried to rest.

Abbe stalked the corridors and other cabins with an oil lamp, watching for any sign of more water. Outside, the storm raged on, and the ship pitched and turned, creaking and groaning like a thing in pain. The hours rolled by, and Abbe felt as though she could not keep her eyes open any longer. She went to their cabin and found Bib and Henny hugging each other, fast asleep on Bib's bed. She did not have the heart to wake them, and so decided just to rest her eyes for a bit.

"But only for a few moments," she said to herself and stretched out on her own bed.

But the weariness and stress of the day took hold and soon she was fast asleep.

Chapter 27 – The Eye

"Frederick! Frederick!" someone was calling. He opened his eyes and remembered where he was. Aonghus stood over him. All was quiet.

He rubbed his eyes and said, "How long?"

"Not sure, lad. But we'd best get back up on deck and check on old McPherson," he replied.

"Right," said Frederick, and steadied himself as he stood up. Then he realized that the ship was no longer bobbing like a cork, but seemed still as death.

"What's going on? Is the storm over?" he asked.

Aonghus said nothing, but beckoned for him to follow.

Bran was up as well, and together, they left their cabin and went out into the hall.

Aonghus knocked on the girls' cabin door, and when no one answered, he peeked in and called, "Abbe?" There was a sudden gasp as Abbe jumped out of bed.

"Oh my!" she said. "What's the time?"

Bib and Henny woke as well, and sensing the storm was over, they sat up and looked about.

"What's going on?" asked Bib. "Is it our shift to keep watch?"

"I think we've all been sleeping too long," said Aonghus. "We're going up and checking on things. It seems terribly still."

"We'd best come as well," said Abbe.

Together, they went down the hall and opened the door that led to the deck. To their surprise, bright sunlight streamed in. They hurried out, and the sight that greeted them stopped them in their tracks.

The deck of the ship was a mess, with torn tarps and frayed ropes strewn about. Both sails hung limp and ripped, their tie ropes broken and dangling. But the dark clouds were some distance from them, and blue sky shown above.

Slowly, they walked onto the littered deck, and then Henny cried out, "Professor!"

They could see him on the upper deck. He lay limply upon his wheel, his knees buckled under him, and the ropes that he had tied about himself holding him up. They rushed up the ladder and to his side. Aonghus untied the ropes that held him and carefully laid him down on the deck.

"Professor!" he called. "Professor!"

For a moment, he did not respond, but then his eyes fluttered open and focused. He squinted at the sky, then at all of their faces. He smiled slightly, and then in a hoarse voice said, "Help me sit up, please."

"I think we rode the storm out through the night, Professor," said Frederick.

Professor McPherson touched his sides where the ropes had rubbed his skin raw, and he winced.

"Help me stand," he said.

Aonghus and Bran carefully lifted him to his feet. Unsteadily, he braced himself against the wheel. Then he looked out at the sea, and the distant clouds. Slowly, he turned his head left and right, and then turned and stared behind him. They followed his gaze. There were clouds all about them – walls of clouds.

Professor McPherson's face grew dark again, and he leaned heavily upon the rail. His chin dropped to his chest and he shut his eyes. Then he took a deep breath and looked at the children.

"Whatever is the matter, Professor?" asked Abbe. "We've come through, just as you promised, haven't we?"

He sighed heavily and then, with great weariness, said, "We are in the eye of the hurricane."

"What's the eye of the hurricane?" asked Henny.

"It's the middle of it, Henny," he said. "We've only come halfway through."

Chapter 28 – The Ghost of Lugh

Colleen, Nous, Oracle, and the Wigglepox family rode steadily southward as the night wore on. A brilliant full moon, and a sky of a million stars shone above them, shedding cool blue light down upon the brown desert floor. Nous rode in the wagon as usual, lying on his back and gazing at the stars, his black hood thrown back, and his bulging yellow eyes seeming to glow in the pale light. Mrs. Wigglepox was telling Colleen a story of the desert – of a mouse that ventured into the Burning Sands and returned with strange stories.

"The mouse said that there are spirits in the desert," she said, "and that they are not all kindly. Still, the desert can do wonders for those who seek to find themselves, so long as they have a guide."

"Why would we need a guide?" asked Colleen. "Couldn't we just keep heading south?"

"Well, the mouse said that the desert has a way of scouring away the Spell. But it also said that it holds rough places and pitfalls and quicksand and monsters, and that hunger and thirst are everywhere. A guide would be an invaluable asset. It also said that the magic of old is out there. The Wizard's Castle still stands, and there is a wishing well that the Spell has not stopped up."

Colleen pondered this for a long moment, wondering what it might mean, and then a thought struck her and she said, "Mrs. Wigglepox, this mouse – could it talk? I mean, can you speak to animals?"

"Well, of course, dear," she replied. "All little people can speak to the animals. Can't the big folk?"

"Not really," said Colleen. "Although, I suppose if anyone can, it would be my sister, Abbe."

"Oh!" exclaimed Mrs. Wigglepox. "You have a sister that can speak to the animals?"

"Well, she can't really *speak* to them as such. But somehow, they know what she wants. It's something less than speech and more than feeling, or so she says."

"Yes," said Mrs. Wigglepox, "that's the way of it. She must be an extraordinary person. I would so like to meet her one day."

"Oh, all of my brothers and sisters are rather special. They can all do the strangest of things," replied Colleen.

Mrs. Wigglepox looked up at Colleen from the seat where she was sitting with Lily and Rose and said, "Colleen, tell me, are there any odd stories about your family, perhaps other relatives, or ancestors?"

"Oh yes," replied Colleen, "all sorts of stories."

"Tell me one," she said.

Colleen thought for a moment and then said, "Well, my mom's cousin, Richard, who lives up north of us, is in his nineties, and claims to have heard voices in his well."

"In his well?" asked Mrs. Wigglepox.

"Yes. The neighbors all think he's getting a bit dimwitted, if you know what I mean. But a few years back, we went to visit him and he told us this story. He said he fell down that well when he was a boy, and there were weird symbols carved all over the inside of it. He was down there all night, and he said he heard voices – singing, in fact, coming from somewhere beyond the walls," said Colleen.

She paused for a moment and then said, "Truth be told, Mrs. Wigglepox, I snuck out that night and went to that well. I got in the bucket and lowered myself down inside. You might not believe it, but I heard singing down there too. I hauled myself right back up and ran back to the house quick."

"That is strange," replied Mrs. Wigglepox. "I've heard tales like that before myself – tales that say there are *thin* places where the echoes of other worlds can be heard. Maybe that old well is just such a place."

Colleen was fascinated by the thought. She resolved that if she ever got back home, she would go and visit her cousin Richard and make another visit to that well.

"Strange things are said to happen out here too," said Mrs. Wigglepox. "It's said that so much magic was unleashed in this place during the Cataclysm that it still lingers and swirls about at times. We must be careful."

They rolled on for some time in silence when suddenly, the wagon bumped, as if it had rolled over something. Then it bumped again, and then again. Nous sat up and looked about nervously. Badger was pulling them up a large dune, but they seemed to be hitting something round, like big logs, that were buried just beneath the sand.

Just as they reached the peak of the dune, a strange red mist swirled in the breeze all around them, and the sand began to tremble and shift, as if the whole hill were moving. Colleen stopped Badger, and they gazed about. In the silvery light of the moon, they could see a number of small dunes that lay to either side, and as they looked, they began to rise up, as though they were coming to life.

"Nous does not like this place!" said Nous. "He thinks the Colleen should get us away from here!"

"Right!" said Colleen. "Go, Badger!"

Badger pulled, and they began to roll down the shifting hill. Just as they reached the bottom, the sand dune moved violently, jolting the wagon and nearly upsetting it. Lily and Rose screamed and barely managed to hold onto the seat pad, and Oracle, who was sitting up front too, just caught Mrs. Wigglepox as she tumbled forward.

Badger neighed and pulled faster, and just in time, for as they rode away, the entire sand dune lifted into the air, along with half a dozen others, and the gigantic form of a man, seemingly made completely of sand, rose up and stood towering above them.

The giant monstrosity moaned a bellowing sound that spread across the desert like a great bass horn. It shook itself, raining down sand, moaned again, and then seemed to see them as they fled.

"Run, Badger!" shouted Colleen, and the horse shot forward.

Badger was fast, but the sands bogged down the wheels and slowed his pace. The giant came for them in great halting steps, sand flying all around it as it came. They could see now what they had rolled over, for the creature was actually a huge skeleton covered and filled with sand, and the dune they had climbed had been its massive rib cage. But Colleen could see something else now – something *within* the apparition's hideous bowels.

"Mrs. Wigglepox, there's something inside that thing. I can see it!" she cried.

The little lady stared wide-eyed at the towering monster, but said nothing. The creature bellowed again, and with a great leap, flew through the air and landed in front of them. Badger reared and kicked, neighing in defiance.

It laughed a booming laugh that echoed across the vast desert, and then it stooped down, its gigantic head drawing close to them, peering at them with blank eye sockets. Then it opened its great maw and bellowed, and a putrid wind blew from its gullet.

Badger backed away, and the little people climbed into Colleen's cape pocket. Nous curled into a ball in the back of the wagon, and Colleen stared into the face of a horror she had never encountered before. Her heart raced, and fear gripped her. She looked to the right and left in desperation, seeking a way of escape, but the giant skeleton planted a foot on each side and laughed again.

Then, to her surprise, it spoke. Its voice was deep and booming, but hollow, and they all covered their ears at the explosion of sound that thundered upon them.

"Who *dares* enter *my* realm!" it cried, anger and indignation in its voice. "These Burning Sands belong to *Lugh!*"

Mrs. Wigglepox poked her head out of Colleen's pocket, a look of astonishment on her face. Oracle, however, stood up on the seat, reached up to the giant with his cane, and poked it in the nose.

"Shame!" said the leprechaun to the giant, and it suddenly stood upright, surprised, it seemed, by the brashness of the little fellow.

Mrs. Wigglepox cried, "Colleen, run! We must run for it!"

Colleen saw a small chance, and she flicked the reins hard. Right between the giant's legs they flew, Badger straining with all his might.

"Fly, Badger, fly!" she cried, and the great horse stretched out his neck.

The race was on. Oracle tumbled into the back of the wagon and into Nous.

The sand man roared, a bellow of surprise coming from its lipless mouth, then turned about.

"You cannot escape Lugh!" it trumpeted, and lumbered after them.

"What is that thing?" cried Colleen, her hair and cape whipping wildly as Badger ran faster and faster.

"I think it is the ghost of Lugh!" said Mrs. Wigglepox frantically. "If it is, then his spirit never went over the Rainbow, and he has become a spirit of malice that haunts the place of his fall! We must run!"

"A ghost!" cried Colleen "How can we deal with a ghost!"

The skeletal army began to march slowly forward all around them. Bone against bone, the scraping and clattering sound of their coming was weird and terrifying. But Colleen gathered her wits and again raised her hands. "Your army shall follow you, Lugh, down to the place of the dead where you belong!"

As if in response to her words, the sands began to move, but leaving the wagon on a still island amid a swirling storm. They watched bones and shields and armor and spears and swords clatter against one another as the sands swept them down, down, swallowing them into its depths. Lugh raged in frantic bellows as he too sank deeper. Then suddenly, with titanic, unworldly strength, the giant surged forward, wading through the whirlpool, fighting against its dragging force. They all watched in amazed horror as it began to draw near to them again. Then it laughed.

Nous' eyes were wide with fear, but then he narrowed them, and he snarled. Leaping from the wagon, he ran right to the edge of the swirling whirlpool of sand.

Colleen watched as he pulled up his right sleeve, and taking his index finger, he dipped it in the stirring dust. For a moment, nothing happened, but then a black streak formed in the current where his finger was, and spread itself outward, as if some dark dye had been poured into a whirling tub of water.

Round and round them, it stretched, and it began to grow, like black streaks in a brown mixing bowl.

Nous withdrew his finger, then pulled his sleeve up further and found one of the worms that dangled limply to his arm. He considered it for a moment, and then plucked it from its place. He held it up, staring at it in the dim light. Lugh was nearly upon them when the ghost's skeletal hips touched the outermost black streak. It stopped in its struggle, a look of surprise on its face, and glared down. Nous looked at the giant, at the worm, then at Oracle, and threw the tiny worm with all his might at the ghost. He turned and ran back to the cart and climbed in.

"The Colleen must make us a bridge, and we must fly!" cried Nous.

Colleen paused for a moment, mesmerized at what was happening to the giant. The black stain was wrapping itself about the great skeleton now, clinging to it, like some thick tar, and it seemed as though the little worm that Nous had thrown at it was growing larger and larger, swimming about the monster amid the black streaks like some shark circling its prey.

"What did you do?" said Colleen.

"No time! Run!" cried Nous.

"Through that?" said Colleen.

"Run!" said Nous, urgently.

Colleen whipped the reins, and Badger obediently surged forward into the trembling sands. Away they rode through a sea of goblin bones that reached out at them, grasping for the wheels of the wagon and trying to trip Badger as he ran. But the golden shod stallion thundered through the skeletal army, smashing them into the dust, crushing them beneath his mighty pounding hooves.

Suddenly, a skeleton gained the wagon. Oracle poked it in the eye with his cane and its head popped off, spinning on the end of the stick like a top, and its jaws snapping wildly. Its body staggered blindly across the wagon before falling off the other side. The old leprechaun flung the skull from his cane, knocking another skeleton from the rear of the wagon as it tried to climb aboard.

Then another was in, and Nous grappled with it. Its old bones broke at the joints as he wrestled it down, and soon he was tossing arm and leg bones out of the wagon at the clamoring skeletal masses as they surged around them.

But a moment later, they were clear of the valley of bones, and Colleen turned to look as Lugh howled one last time, his cry of frustration and anguish following hard after them. He had turned completely black now, a thick coat of darkness dripping from his half-submerged form. She watched as the worm, which had now grown enormous, leaped upon him, and as the ghost grappled with it, they both sank downward, hordes of goblin skeletons following after them.

Lugh's bellowing face was the last bit of him to sink beneath a swirling black sea until his cries were silenced beneath the Burning Sands, and the clatter of bones grew still.

Colleen ran Badger on for some time before bringing him to a walk again. She trembled as she did so, then stopped the horse completely and fought back tears of relief and fear.

After a moment, she took a deep shuddering breath and said, "Nous, what did you do back there?"

Nous grinned a devilish grin and then cackled, "Added a little Ooze to the mixing bowl, and a spawn of the Worm!"

Mrs. Wigglepox, Lily, and Rose re-emerged from Colleen's pocket. The leprechauns looked scared and worried. Mrs. Wigglepox looked particularly grave.

"Are you all right, Mrs. Wigglepox?" asked Colleen.

"I'm okay, and so are the girls," she replied. "But I fear that what was done back there may come back to haunt us."

"You mean the ghost might come back?" asked Colleen.

"Oh, I didn't quite mean it that way," she replied. "I meant that Nous put the Ooze into that whirlpool of yours, and one of those sickening worm creatures. It might have stopped Lugh, but fighting evil with evil never works. I hope nothing bad comes of it."

Nous screwed up his face and looked hurt. "See," he said, "these little people care nothing for goblin help."

"Oh, Nous," said Colleen. "I'm grateful for your help. I'm sure we'll be all right. See, we've gotten away from that thing back there, Mrs. Wigglepox."

"I do hope you're right, Colleen," she replied. "And, Nous, we do care. And I thank you for your efforts. But please, do not use the Ooze again. Only ill can come from that. Find some other power within yourself to help us along our journey. Deep down, I think the real, untarnished Nous dwells, the way the Old Goblins used to be."

Nous said "Hmph!" and turned his back, curling up in a ball in the back of the wagon.

Colleen took another deep breath and flicked the reins. She mused upon the strange things that had just happened to them, had happened to *her.*

Something inside her was changing, though she did not understand what it was. This land of magic and woe had awakened something within her, and it was growing stronger.

What *was* she becoming?

Badger trotted on through the moonlit night, and they rode on, each absorbed in their own thoughts, and Oracle humming a silly tune.

Chapter 29 - Up from the Deep

Professor McPherson leaned heavily on the wheel of his ship. He was exhausted. Aonghus immediately took charge.

"Professor, you are too spent to face another day and night of this thing. Show me what to do. I'll pilot this ship."

The professor looked at Aonghus with admiration and said, "You are right, son. I need you. I need you all."

He straightened himself, willing away his utter weariness and said, "All of you, look here. Do you see this compass? It is no ordinary compass. It ... it knows where to lead us. There is something strange about it. It is the very compass that I found long ago in a stone chest on... on the island where we are going."

"Shouldn't we make for Portugal, Professor, or Africa?" asked Bib. "The ship is a mess. We've already fixed one pretty bad leak, and who knows how well we'll fare when we hit that wall of rain and wind again."

"The storm drove us far out into the ocean, dear children. It shifted our course, and we're far southwest of where we were yesterday. It has, by some providence, actually blown us along the very course that we intended, although how, I do not know. I have never in all my days felt this ship move with such speed. I feared many times that the waves and wind would smash her to pieces. But I suppose your work below shored up the old girl. Destiny has driven us."

He managed a weak smile and then said, "But we must keep heading southwest. We ought to gain sight of Bermuda if we keep our course steady."

"But if we are this far west, perhaps we should try for the Americas," said Bib.

"I fear that for now, we are at the mercy of the storm, dear ones," he replied. "For now, we sail in the eye of the storm. Aonghus, Bran, Frederick – there are spare sails below, but only a few. Hoist them while you can, and sail as the compass guides. Ladies – after these men take down the torn sails, mend the ripped ones if you can – they may be of use too. See now, let me rest while I may. Wake me when the storm draws near again."

He dragged himself below deck, paused for a moment to inspect their repair work, nodded, and then went into his cabin, where he lay down and immediately was fast asleep.

On the deck, Aonghus gave orders. "Frederick, go below and find those spare sails. Bran, Abbe, take the rear mast. Bib, you and I will take the main one. Henny, wait here and gather up the sails as we drop them down."

Up the rope ladders they climbed to where the ripped sails hung limply in the strange air of the eye of the hurricane. They untied the lines that held them and allowed them to drop down to Henny, who bundled them up and dragged them to a clear spot on the deck where they might be mended.

Frederick appeared, carrying a bundle. "I found two sails, or at least I think they are sails," he said.

Aonghus looked at the circle of dark clouds around them.

"Let's wait to put them up, and see if we can repair the old ones first. When we get through, I suspect we'll need the new ones," he said.

He took the wheel and looked down at the beautiful compass. Its golden needle pointed off to their right slightly, so he turned the wheel in that direction a little. As the ship turned, the arrow straightened, and he held their course.

As the others labored to repair the damaged sails, the wall of dark clouds before them drew steadily nearer and nearer.

"We've got one fixed, Aonghus!" called Bib.

Bran folded the repaired sail and climbed the main mast with Bib following close behind. Together, they secured it in its place once again, and none too soon, for the wind was blowing stronger now and filled the sail to its fullest. A moment later and the last sail was repaired, and they secured it firmly to the mast and watched it too fill with wind. The ship was leaping through the waves now. About an hour and a half had passed since they had entered the eye of the hurricane.

"Double check all the rigging, quickly, and all lines on the deck," said Aonghus.

"Shall we wake the professor?" asked Henny.

"Not yet," he replied. "All of you get below. I'll stand at the wheel."

"Not unless you tie yourself in like the professor did," said Abbe.

Aonghus smiled and said, "Right. Give me a hand here."

Then he assured them that he would be fine, and said, "Bran, come up in a few hours and we'll swap off. No sense in getting exhausted like McPherson did. We'll take turns at keeping the ship on course. Pray that the sails hold and speed us through this storm!"

The boys shook hands, and the girls gave Aonghus a hug. As the first drops of rain fell on the deck, they went below and checked the hull once again before going to their cabins to wait.

On the deck, Aonghus gripped the wheel. He gritted his teeth as the sky grew black and rain suddenly lashed down upon him like a whip. The sails beat in the wind again and again, and soon the ship was rising and falling over waves that could easily capsize them. But providence seemed to be with them, for the waves came head on and did not generally broadside the ship, and for this, Aonghus was thankful.

As they sailed deeper into the storm, the winds increased, and soon Aonghus knew what the professor had meant when he had spoken of the ship sailing at incredible speeds. The sails were strained to the breaking point, and within a half hour, the rear sail that they had sewn split apart once again and flapped uselessly in the torrent. But still, they sailed on.

Nearly another hour had passed when suddenly, there was a great lurch of the ship. Aonghus pitched forward against the wheel, and only his safety lines kept him from flying forward and falling to the deck below. It was as though the ship had struck something and come to a sudden stop.

Everyone below deck went tumbling from their beds, picked themselves up, and ran from their quarters and into the hall, and Professor McPherson flung open the door of his chamber.

"What has happened!" he called.

"We're not sure, sir," said Bran. "It felt as if we struck something."

"Tie in together, all of you," he ordered as he made his way to the door leading upward, then dashed out onto the lower deck.

The others quickly tied the rope that lay in the hall around each other's waists and ventured out onto the still rocking ship. They looked about in the gray light, but could see nothing out of the ordinary, other than the great waves smashing against the hull of the ship, the torn rear sail, and Aonghus still at the wheel, looking about just as they were.

Then, without warning, a huge red tentacle at least two feet thick and sixty feet long whipped up out of the water and over the side of the ship, its dinner-plate-sized suction cups gripping the slick wood. A second tentacle of even greater size shot upward on the other side and wrapped itself about the main mast. There was a sickening sound of splintering wood as the thick trunk of the mast split in half and broke, leaving a sharp jagged pole where the mast had been. The tentacle released the broken shaft and down it fell, directly toward the McGunnegals and Frederick.

"No!" cried Aonghus, and with a *snap*, broke the ropes that held him fast and leaped from the upper deck, catching the falling mast in his muscled arms. It barely missed them, but fell with all its weight on top of Aonghus.

The girls screamed his name, but could not reach his prone form, for at that very moment, a mass of tentacles swarmed up onto the deck, thrashing wildly, and a great bulbous head rose up from the raging waves. It was red and brown, easily fifteen feet tall and wide, and a black eye gazed down upon them with cold alien hunger.

Henny screamed and tried to run, but the rigging of the mast had fallen about them, trapping and holding them fast to their own safety line. Professor McPherson was at their side immediately, pulled a knife from his boot, and began to cut them free from the tangle.

"Get below!" he cried as he cut through their ropes, freeing them one by one.

Frederick was the first one free, and he hesitated.

"Go, I say!" commanded the professor, and Frederick turned and ran below, followed by Henny.

Suddenly a great tentacle whipped through the air and gave the professor such a blow that he dropped the knife and was thrown nearly overboard. He only barely managed to grab the railing and hung precariously over the side of the ship.

Bib grabbed the fallen knife and cut herself free, then handed the knife to Abbe. But just as she turned to run below, a waving tentacle seized her, wrapped itself about her waist, and heaved her into the air. She screamed as the creature dangled her high above the deck of the ship, and with snake-like constriction, it began to squeeze.

Bran grabbed the knife from Abbe, cut himself loose, and charged at the creature's massive head. Without regard to his own safety, he flung himself at it and drove the knife to the hilt into its rubbery flesh. A gross shrieking gurgle came from the beast as it hauled itself upward and revealed a great hooked beak at least four feet high and three feet wide, snapping like some loathsome deformed parrot. Tentacles waved about the ship. The second mast snapped at the top, and the rigging fell to the upper deck.

Bran pulled the knife free and stabbed again, but this time, the creature seized him with one of its tentacles and threw him clean off the ship.

Abbe screamed as she saw her brother fly through the air and into the driving rain and raging sea, then disappear. She got to her knees, dazed, and then her eyes met the one eye of the sea monster.

Something clicked in her mind, and she could see – or feel – the raw animal instinct of this beast. It bore no malice – that was not an emotion it could feel. But she felt its primordial need to *feed* – and she knew that *they* were its prey.

But the creature also sensed something about *her*. And for a moment, it froze – its tentacles dangling weirdly in the air, as though somehow its simple mind had been put on hold in those brief seconds.

But then a faint cry tore her gaze from its great eye. Bib hung limply in the crushing grip of the monster. Anger at the creature and fear for her sister filled her mind, and with those raw emotions, she lashed out at it with her thoughts, or perhaps something beyond thought.

To her surprise, it recoiled in fear, and a great jet of dark ink sprayed the deck of the ship. Abbe stood, and advanced on the monster, her mind pummeling it, how she did not know. Opening its massive beak, it shrieked again and once again began frantically waving its tentacles.

Abbe's mind was bound to the beast's, and she would not release it. It struggled to escape, to flee from this unknown threat, back to the depths of the sea, but something bound it to this *presence* now gripping its mind.

Suddenly, someone ran past Abbe toward the great gelatinous head. It was Frederick, come from below deck with a shining sword in his hand. Right up to the creature he ran, and with a cry, he swung the sword. The tentacle that gripped Bib was severed cleanly off the monster's body. Bib plummeted to the deck of the ship, and only just in the nick of time, Aonghus regained his senses, saw what was happening, threw off the heavy mast that lay atop him, and caught his sister as she fell from the creature's grip.

Abbe's control broke, and the great black eye focused on this new attacker before it. The mouth opened, snapping with rage and pain, and half a dozen other tentacles whipped around, grappling with everything in their path on their way to Frederick.

SLASH, went the sword, and another severed limb fell writhing to the deck. SLASH, and there was a piece of another.

Then it had him, and Frederick felt the crushing grip of pure muscle as one of the thing's arms seized him and spun him around. Swiftly, it drew him in toward the snapping razors. Frederick's life flashed before his eyes as he drew nearer to a sure death. He knew that he would do one last great deed, and he held the sword ready as he was drawn toward the gaping gullet.

The great beak opened wide, and Frederick could see row upon row of spiked horns extending down its yawning orifice. Seconds later, he was inside the thing's mouth, kicking frantically as he felt himself being pulled downward into the sickening throat.

With all of his might, and with all the courage he could muster, he stabbed upward, toward what he thought must be the thing's brain. To his amazement, the sword burst into a hot green flame as it sunk deep into the monster's flesh, piercing clean through and out the back of its head.

Just as his sword sank deep, and it seemed sure the horrid beak would slice him in two as it snapped wildly open and shut, he heard a great cry – a war cry, like a man gone mad in the midst of fierce battle. He turned and saw, as the beak flew open for just an instant, Aonghus running toward him, the entire broken shaft of the main mast in his arms like some great spear, and his face ablaze with a ferocious anger. With a mighty *heave*, he drove the sharp end of the shaft directly into the eye of the beast.

As the black eye was pierced and the sword cleaved its tiny brain, the snapping beak froze open in a horrid, silent scream. Then it slowly closed in death, and Frederick was shrouded in thick gooey darkness. A weird silence fell over him as the outside world was shut out. The entire body of the sea monster shuddered, and thrashed one last time, and for a moment, he thought he would be sucked down the thing's throat and impaled on its sharp toothy spikes. Then all was still except for the unending rising and falling sensation of the ship on the waves.

On the deck of the ship, Abbe cried out in fear and rushed forward, "Frederick! Frederick!"

The huge body of the beast quivered grossly, its black eye pierced by the shaft of the mast. She watched as the last light of its primitive mind sparked once and then went out. She felt its death, and knew that something very ancient had just passed from the earth.

But what of Frederick? Aonghus seized the beak with two hands and ripped it apart.

Frederick rolled out of the thing's mouth, blood and goo from the monster covering him, and the sword still in his grip. A wave broke over the bow of the ship, bathing him in seawater, and washing away the filth of the monster. Slowly he stood, shaking, and smiled. Aonghus gave a sigh of relief and Abbe rushed forward to hug him.

"For a moment I thought..." she began.

"I'm all right," he replied.

Their relief at seeing Frederick whole, however, lasted only a moment, for now they looked about the ship and the full gravity of their situation dawned upon them. Two tentacles lay severed, still slightly quivering, and the great bulk of the creature lay upon the bow, its remaining arms limp, some dangling over the ship's edge. The masts were both shattered, and most of the lower deck lay in ruins. Somehow, the wheel had survived untouched.

But Aonghus took all of this in with a glance. Where was Bran? Henny? Professor McPherson? Was Bib injured?

He rushed to Bib's side, brushed the hair from her eyes, and said, "Bib? Are you all right? Please be all right."

She did not answer, so he gently lifted her in his arms and quickly took her below deck, Abbe following behind. He was relieved to find Henny in the girl's cabin, and he carefully laid his sister on one of the beds. She was still breathing.

"Watch over her. See if she has any broken bones," said Aonghus, then he hurried back out.

Back on the deck, he found Frederick trying to haul Professor McPherson up and over the ship's railing. Reaching down with one hand, he pulled the professor onto the deck where he immediately collapsed.

"It was all I could do to hold on, Aonghus. I tried – I tried so hard to pull myself up to help, but the waves..." he began, a pained look in his eyes.

"I know, Professor. Where is my brother?" he said.

They looked about, but Bran was nowhere to be seen.

Then Abbe appeared behind them and said, "Bib is going to be all right, Aonghus. But… but Bran... that thing grabbed him and... it threw him into the sea!"

She began to cry, and buried her face in his great chest, sobbing uncontrollably. Professor McPherson stood unsteadily and, holding onto the rail, made his way along the side of the ship, gazing intently out into the dark waves as the ship was tossed uncontrollably about.

"Get below, Abbe," said Aonghus gently but firmly. "We'll find him. Be strong now and watch out for our sisters."

Suddenly, Professor McPherson cried out, for there, swimming atop the crest of a wave, was Bran. He powered through the waves toward the ship, and the knife he had held was now clenched in his teeth. He reached the front of the ship where the sea monster's arms dangled, took the knife from his mouth, and stabbed it into the dead flesh. He climbed, using the knife to pull himself upward until he reached the outstretched arms of Aonghus and Professor McPherson. Over the railing he came, looked at the dead creature with its split head and the mast sticking out of its eye, then looked about the smashed and broken ship and said, "Well, who slew the beast?"

Frederick and Aonghus both grinned and pointed to each other.

"I'm glad you're all right, Bran," said Frederick.

"It's lucky I found the ship!" he replied. "I was swimming and swimming, and with these waves and rain, couldn't see anything. Then I saw a flash of green light – and lo and behold, there was the ship right in front of me! Good thing that big tentacle was dangling in the water!"

Then they slapped each other on the back and shook hands and laughed for a moment. But then they looked about, and their smiles faded.

"Professor, what was that thing?" asked Frederick.

He looked at it for a moment, and then at them all, and said, "These are strange waters, and strange beasts live here. If I had not seen this with my own eyes, I would not have believed it. But I believe that you and Aonghus have just slain a kraken, if the description in old tales can be believed."

"A kraken!" said Frederick. "But that's just a mythical..."

He stopped and stared at the huge creature that lay dead before them. It looked like a weird cross between an octopus and a squid, but huge. Its great brown beak lay open, revealing its spiked gullet, and its massive tentacles hung limply about the ship.

"It was very old," said Abbe. "Older than... than.... Its mind was so primitive, so..."

But she could not find any further words, and she walked forward to the hulk of the slain beast and touched its bloated head. Its great black eye, still pierced by the shaft of the mast, stared blankly at nothing.

Suddenly, a wave swept over the bow of the ship, drenching them and the huge body with spray. The kraken slowly, limply, together with its severed tentacles, slid from the deck of the ship and into the sea. There it lingered for a moment, its great arms splayed outward until another wave broke over its form and it vanished into the depths. They stared silently at the place it had been, the events of the last few minutes now emblazoned in their minds forever.

When Frederick finally tore his eyes away from the raging sea and looked again at the place where the kraken had died, he saw something. It was long and white, and he knew exactly what it was – one of the toothy spikes that he had seen in the thing's throat. He walked over to it and picked it up. It was over a foot long and two inches wide at the base. Its serrated edges and tip were sharp as razors, but it had a handle of sorts where it had been pulled out by the root from the beast's flesh.

"I will keep this as a token of my battle with the kraken," he declared and held it up to the sky.

The others stared at him, and wondered at how manly this boy had become – a long sword in his right hand and a jagged white token of victorious battle in the other. A wave broke against the ship, sending spray high into the air, casting his form as a dark silhouette against a backdrop of white foam and gray rain.

Broken and smashed, the ship rose and fell with the storm. Somehow, Frederick knew that they had to make it. Something was calling to him from out there – something that was going to teach him who he really was, and would shape his destiny forever.

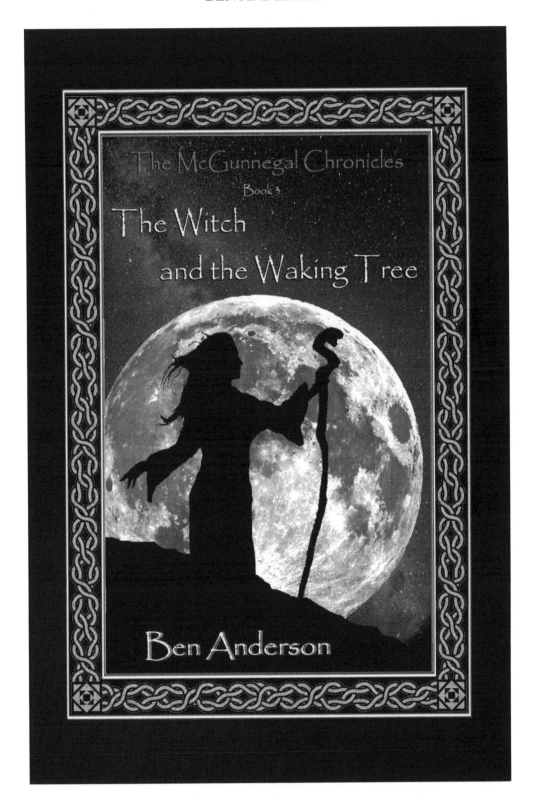

Chapter 1 – The Oasis

Dawn broke over the Burning Sands with a brilliant red and orange sky. Colleen McGunnegal and her strange band had traveled on all night, the memory of the ghostly attack of the prior day sending shivers down her spine. On more than one occasion, she had glanced behind them, thinking that she had heard a far distant wail come drifting across the sands.

Wisps of cold wind had stirred up dust devils throughout the night that seemed to race toward them, spraying sand in their eyes and then dashing away again, causing them to turn their heads and pull their cloaks tight. Within those whirlwinds, Colleen could sometimes see ethereal forms - spirits of mischief that leaped at the chance to play their dark tricks upon these rare passers-by. But the morning sun seemed to dispel not only the desert cold, but the dust devils as well, and they rode southward through a strange calm.

"What a world this is," she thought. *"Here I am, traveling with a goblin, a big crazy leprechaun, and a family of tiny leprechauns. I've lost my only human friend and left behind everyone else I've met and come to care for."*

She sighed heavily and glanced back at Nous. The goblin was hunched in the back of the wagon with his gray-green arms wrapped around his knees. He looked at her, scowled, and flipped up his black hood.

"Evil sun," he muttered, and dug down into the hay to hide himself from it.

Next to him stood Oracle, facing east and watching the rising sun. Colleen wondered once again about this strange little fellow. He had not been frightened at all when the gigantic skeletal ghost of Lugh had nearly killed them, and too many odd coincidences happened when he was around. Now he seemed contemplative and serene, not at all the senile old leprechaun of days past.

"Oasis," he said as he stared at the rising ball of orange fire in the sky.

Indeed, at that very moment, Colleen saw a wavering patch of green ahead of them as they climbed a low sloping dune. As they neared, its mirage-like form solidified, and she could see clearly that it was indeed an oasis of trees and grasses and that a bubbling spring flowed up from the ground and watered the surrounding area.

Colleen breathed a sigh of relief as they rode first through scrub brush, and then into a lush green lawn of grass and low bushes. Ahead, she could see what appeared to be a small gray stone hut that looked rather like a bee hive surrounded by fruit and nut trees. A low wooden door faced them, from which a worn path wandered down to the spring and off to the right through the trees.

As they approached, they could hear someone singing inside. It was obviously a woman's voice, and it was clear and rich, and strangely reminded Colleen of chimes in the wind or birds singing in the branches on a warm summer day.

They trotted past the spring and up to the hut and, just as they did, the door opened, and out stepped a small feminine figure that was no bigger than Nous. Her hair was a deep purple, almost black, and fell straight down her back to her slender waist. Dark eyes and delicately pointed ears accented her fair face, and her skin was a pale lavender, except for her feet, which were gray. She spread her arms wide in welcome, and her sky-blue robe rustled in the warm, fragrant breeze.

"Greetings, friends," she said. "What brings you through this desert to my humble dwelling?"

Oracle turned to meet her gaze and, at once, a look of recognition lit the maiden's face.

"Bless my soul!" she cried, and ran to the wagon, snatching the old leprechaun into the air and twirling him about in her outstretched arms.

Oracle squealed and grunted and said, "Down, ground, hush and shush!"

She sat him down gently, and then noticed Nous in the back of the wagon, and the little Wigglepox family sitting on the front seat.

"Ah, rare guests, indeed. A goblin, a girl, three of the small leprechauns, and … well, a big leprechaun. What wonders do visit me this day?" she said.

"Hush!" said Oracle again, a bit more sternly, and the woman, looking inquisitive, cocked her head to one side so that her long dark hair fell sideways.

Then a look of understanding stole across her face, and she smiled.

"But, here I am, being rude. Please, all of you come into my home and have some tea. I shall introduce myself, and you may all tell me your names and what brings you here."

Colleen helped the little people to the ground and beckoned to Nous for him to follow, but he seemed reluctant.

"What's wrong, Nous?" asked Colleen.

"Nous is … afraid," he said.

"Nous, come on, she's not going to bite you. Come in and meet her with us," said Colleen.

But Nous shook his head and refused to leave the wagon. The maiden, standing in the doorway of the house, saw his reluctance and walked back. She climbed right up on the wagon, sat down next to the goblin, and put her fair hand on his dirty shoulder.

"Nous – is that your name? Well, Nous, my name is Evchi. I would be most honored if you would come into my hut and sit for a time and rest," she said.

Nous looked at her from under his hood, which he had pulled up over his face when she approached. He shrank away from her hand and shook his head.

"Nous is... Nous is..." he began, but she gently shushed him.

"Never mind that, Nous. Let me help you from the wagon," she said.

She climbed out and extended her hand to him. He looked at it and appeared to shiver, but slowly he extended his gnarled and filthy hand toward her. She took it, and he flinched, but he slowly climbed from the wagon.

He was taller than she was by several inches, but he stooped as though hunched, and shuffled along beside her like a scared dog as she led him to the door where Oracle waited and watched. Colleen followed behind, wondering at this strange scene. What could Nous be afraid of?

They all went into the hut, which was brightly lit by the morning sun shining through three windows. On one side of the room was a fireplace in which burned a low, smokeless fire and a bed of coals, and on this was a kettle of steaming brew, which filled the one-room hut with fragrance. All about the walls and ceiling were painted many scenes that appeared to tell tales. Goblins and men and little people and larger green creatures, a giant, and a great black dragon filled one scene. There were also carvings of wood and stone about the room, some life-sized and some tiny, all delicate and perfect in their shapes and forms.

"Please, sit," said the maiden, and she produced a small block of wood that she placed on the table, and gently lifted the Wigglepox family up to be seated.

Nous looked suspiciously about the room, then slid onto the bench next to Colleen. Oracle climbed onto a low stool and sat watching as the lavender maid busied herself with preparing cups and thimbles of tea for all and little nut cakes from her cupboard.

"I haven't much to offer such fine folk as you," she said. "Only these dry cakes, I'm afraid."

"Oh, I'm sure this will be fine," said Colleen. "My name is Colleen McGunnegal. I heard you say to Nous that your name is Evchi?"

"Yes, that is who I am. I have already met Nous. Now who are these little folk?" replied Evchi.

"My name is Edna Wigglepox, and these are my daughters, Lily and Rose," said Mrs. Wigglepox.

Evchi turned to Oracle and, with a wry smile, said, "And what shall I call you, good sir?"

Oracle only grunted.

"We call him Oracle," said Colleen. "My cousin, Frederick, gave him that name. We don't know his real name."

Oracle grunted again.

"He doesn't say much," said Colleen. "And half the time, when he does talk, we don't understand what he's said. Sometimes, it's just so much nonsense. And then sometimes, he's rather mysterious. I'm still not sure what to make of him. But you seem to know him, don't you?"

"Well, so I thought," she replied. "But perhaps I was mistaken."

But she smiled knowingly.

"Well," said Colleen, "we are certainly grateful for your hospitality. It is dreadfully hot out in the desert during the day, and we are surely glad to be indoors. And we are tired. But who are you, and how do you come to be in this place? I've not seen anyone like you in all the days that I have been in the land of the Little People, and although I've seen sprites and pixies and fairies and leprechauns and gnomes and dwarves and goblins, and many strange spirits and even a troll, none has looked as fair as you, except the Lady Danu."

Evchi blushed, and her cheeks grew a deeper violet.

"You are kind, Colleen McGunnegal, but I am not nearly so fair as many in this land. It is in the heart where true beauty lies, not in skin that is lavender or tan or gray, be it smooth as silk or rough as desert sand. I live here in solitude and peace, day by day, and do my little work. But many labor hard in the pits of the Witch and yet retain their courage and hope. They bear true beauty that outlasts all else. But you asked who I am and how I came to be in this place..."

She paused, considering for a moment, and then said, "Once my name was Plani. I lived and labored in the service of the Witch."

"Evchi, were you a goblin once?" asked Rose, all of a sudden.

Evchi smiled.

"*Was* I a goblin? Why, my dearest Rose, I *am* a goblin."

Chapter 2 – The Finding of Helga

Frederick stood on the deck of the wrecked ship, looking at its splintered remains. He was amazed that they were still afloat. All night, the hurricane had driven them wildly, huge waves smashing over their bow and flooding the lower decks, threatening to drown the ship and everyone in it. He and the McGunnegals and Professor McPherson had worked frantically at the hand pumps, and even bucket by bucket to bail out the ship as it steadily filled with water, and none of them had slept since the attack of the terrible sea creature. Both masts were broken, and one of them lost to the sea. Twice, they had repaired cracks in the ship's hull, using the last of the screws and pitch to seal it as best as could be. But still, they were taking on water from somewhere. Worst of all, they had lost their crew. They had all mourned their loss terribly, and the crew's absence was keenly felt.

Now the sun was rising high in the late morning sky, and the storm had abated. They had ridden out the worst it could give them, and they now watched as it swept away on the northern horizon, an angry gray sea of clouds. Still, the seas were not calm, and they had much work to do, although they desperately needed to rest.

"Time to open the cargo bay," said Professor McPherson wearily. "We may have some repair work to do, and I'm sure plenty of re-stacking of the supplies." They cleared the hatch of debris, and, because the mast was broken, they could not hook up a pulley. Aonghus took hold of the brass ring and, with a great *heave*, lifted the door, and then with Bran and Professor McPherson, lifted it further and laid it on its back.

As they descended the ramp, they could see various crates floating about in a good six inches of water. However, the steam car that they had stowed was still tied down and appeared unharmed.

But they all came to a sudden stop when, to their absolute amazement and surprise, a soaking wet and bedraggled form, whose limp brown hair hung in tangled strands down its face, popped up from the back seat of the car.

"What is this?" cried Professor McPherson.

The person slid down so that only the eyes peered over the seat, squinting and blinking against the sun. Suddenly, the figure cried out, and they knew that it was a woman. She stumbled out of the car and fell into the water, then began to crawl upward toward them on the ramp. Professor McPherson, Aonghus, and Bran ran down, helped her onto the deck, and sat her on a crate. The others followed behind and gathered around.

Although she was a large woman, nearly six feet tall, she was weak and trembling, and her head hung down so that her short hair hid her face.

"Ma'am, are you all right?" asked Abbe, brushing back her hair from her pale face. The woman looked up pitifully, and a look of recognition washed over Abbe's face.

"Helga?" said Aonghus, shocked. "How... what were you... are you all right?"

She didn't answer, and looked to be in a stupor.

"Let's get her below," said Professor McPherson. "There'll be time for explanations later."

Aonghus and Bran carefully put her arms over their shoulders, and with great care led her down to the girls' room.

"She's soaking wet," said Bib. "We need to get her out of those clothes and into something dry."

"I'm afraid it will have to be one of the boys' outfits," said Abbe. "Ours will never fit her."

Bran left the room and, a moment later, returned with a dry shirt and trousers.

"All right, boys, out with you all," said Abbe.

"Right," said Professor McPherson. "Come, lads, let's go check on things while these ladies take care of Helga."

They left the girls to tend her and returned to the cargo bay.

Amazingly, the car had remained tied down, but numerous crates and bins had fallen.

"Look," said Bran, "she must have been surviving on the food down here. Several of the food crates are open, and there's an oil lamp, still lit. But how did she get down here in the first place? And why didn't she at least knock, or do something to get out?"

"Stowaways don't want to be found," said Professor McPherson. "As to why she is here, who can say? But I have a mind to question her about it, once she's recovered a bit, and we figure out what we're going to do next."

"Speaking of that," said Aonghus, "what *are* we going to do? The masts are broken, and one is lost. I suppose we might be able to do something with the one whose pieces we have. But oughtn't we try to make for the nearest land?"

"Well, we will speak of that later," said Professor McPherson. "I'm terribly sorry to have gotten you all into this mess, but, well, here we are. Let's inspect the hull and see if there's any damage down here."

They went along the whole inside of the cargo bay and found, to their surprise, only a small leak, and that only at the water line.

But a good number of the crates and barrels that had sat on the floor were wet, and some ruined, and they ended up throwing a good bit overboard, and stacking most of what was dry or at least usable on the upper deck.

"It's a shame to have to throw all that away," said Aonghus after they were done cleaning it up. "Still, it could be worse. I suppose we have at least a few months of food and water."

"Let's get this sea water out with a hand pump," said McPherson, "then secure everything."

Frederick went and fetched the pump and, checking on the girls, found all of them fast asleep, including Helga, who was now dressed in Bran's dry clothes.

"The ladies are all snoring away," he said as he brought the pump down to the cargo bay.

"Let them rest," said McPherson. "But I'm afraid we won't have such luck, at least not for a few hours. Come now, gents, let's get this water out of here."

They took turns cranking the hand pump and moving the suction end of the pipe about the room, flushing the water out and back into the sea.

Two hours later, the cargo bay was fairly dry, but the crack in the hull still leaked when a wave splashed against the ship or it dipped below the water line.

"Too bad we're out of pitch," said Aonghus. "I hope that the crack doesn't get worse."

"So do I," said McPherson. "But at least for now, we're safe. I think we must rest for a while, or we shall fall asleep on our legs. Come, let's get below."

Leaving the hatch open in hopes that it would dry further, they made their way down to their rooms and changed into dry clothes. No sooner had Frederick's head touched his pillow, he was fast asleep, and did not wake again until the sun was sinking downward into the western sky.

Frederick was the first to rise and go up on the shattered deck. Tangled ropes and scattered debris still lay about, and he decided that he would make a start at organizing it all. He had worked at it for some time, when he heard a sound behind him and turned to see Helga coming up from below. Her hair was still a tangled mess, but she looked more rested.

"Good afternoon," Frederick called to her.

"What is good about it?" she replied harshly. "Where are we and what has happened to the ship?"

"Well," replied Frederick. "I suppose it's good that we are all alive and that the ship is still floating."

"Don't sass me, child!" she snapped. "We are out in the middle of the ocean, and it looks as if we have been in some terrible battle. Look at this mess! And, oh! The masts are broken!"

"We've had a little trouble," said Frederick calmly.

"What do you mean, 'a little trouble'?" she demanded.

Feeling a bit irritated at the big woman, he said, "Well... if you'd really like to know, we were nearly shipwrecked by a hurricane, we lost part of our crew in the ocean, and the rest of them abandoned us. We were attacked by a giant kraken. Bran got thrown into the ocean and was almost lost, Bib was nearly crushed by the kraken's tentacles, Aonghus was almost smashed flat by a falling mast, the professor went over the rail and was barely brought back aboard, and I was nearly eaten alive. Other than that, it's been a dull voyage."

He could not help but smile, but Helga did not find it funny.

"So, you think this is a big joke, boy? Wait until your father hears about this fiasco. It will be the last day you spend at this absurd professor's school!" she grated.

Frederick frowned. "I'm sorry, Helga. I didn't mean to make light of the situation, but it seems to me that we might as well make the best of it all. Say, how did you get into that cargo bay, anyway?"

"I was looking out for you," she lied. "I felt as though this Professor

McPherson was not trustworthy and so I snuck aboard and decided to keep an eye on things."

"From the cargo bay?" said Frederick, not believing a word of what she was saying.

"Well, I knew that the professor would not allow me to come along, but I felt compelled to protect you. So I took my chances and hoped that a few days into the trip that the cargo hatch would be opened, and I would pop out and make sure no funny business was going on," she proclaimed.

Just then, Aonghus and Professor McPherson appeared, followed by the others.

As soon as they had all gathered on deck, the professor went to the ship's wheel and studied the compass for a moment. He did a reading with his chronometer, and then double-checked his readings. They all watched him in silence, wondering what their next course of action would be.

He returned to the lower deck and said, "Well, here we are. We have survived a harrowing night, and now we have much to do to repair our ship and get to safety. I have thought much about our next course of action, and I believe we must try to reset our mast and set a course due southwest. I'm quite sure that our original destination is the closest land we can make for. Our other option is to turn due west and sail for the American mainland, or at least the islands about it, or turn northeast and make for the Azores. But I deem that we are closest to Bermuda."

"And how would you know that?" asked Helga. "Frederick here says that we were caught in a hurricane! We could be anywhere."

The professor was silent for a moment, and then said, "My readings show that the storm drove us southwest during the night. Bermuda is the closest island to us. Let's get to work and repair what we can."

Helga muttered something and went below, but the others began to work to straighten up the deck of the ship.

At length, Bran and Bib, in spite of her sore ribs, had organized a pile of splintered wood of varying lengths, and Aonghus and Frederick and Abbe had freed the broken mast from the many ropes that had managed to entangle it.

"Professor," said Bib, "I think we can fix the remaining mast by securing these larger broken pieces around it and tying it with loops of rope. The mast will be much shorter, but it will be better than nothing."

"Yes, I believe you're right, Bib," he replied. "Let's give it a try."

"Before we try to lift the mast," said Bib, "we should secure the sails and rig ropes to hang all the way to the deck so that we can unfurl them without having to climb. And let's just have a single rope ladder. Oh, and perhaps a few ropes at the top to tie to the ship below to steady it further."

Professor McPherson nodded his approval and smiled.

After they had done as Bib suggested, Aonghus and Bran lifted the fallen mast and held it up against the splintered shaft that remained. Frederick, McPherson, and Abbe then tied the broken pieces of wood like a great splint around a broken bone, setting it back in its proper place. They wound it as tightly as they could, and soon the mast was standing by itself.

"I'm afraid that won't hold in a strong wind," said McPherson.

"Of course it won't," said Helga, who had managed to appear after the work had been done. "One good wind and it will come crashing down on our heads."

"Well," replied Aonghus, "have you got any better ideas?"

Helga harrumphed and went back below.

"I suppose we could build a fire with the rest of the splintered wood and send up puffs of smoke," said Bib. "I read once that smoke signals have been used for centuries to communicate over long distances."

"An excellent idea," said McPherson. "But we must be cautious if we take that route. We wouldn't want to burn down the ship. We should keep that in mind if we can't sail any further."

"In the meantime, I think I might secure that mast a bit more," said Aonghus, and he gathered up another long length of thick rope and began to wind it round and round the repaired section of the mast. The rope creaked and stretched as he pulled hard, wrapping it tightly.

When he was done and had tied it off, he pushed on the top part of the mast. It held fast, with no sign of swaying.

"There, then," he said. "It would take another hurricane to bring that down."

"All the same," said McPherson, looking at the repair job, "I don't think you or Bran should climb up there if any work on the sails is needed. You're too heavy. We need someone lighter."

Aonghus and Bran glanced at Frederick. He grinned and said, "Right!"

"But first," said Bib, "let's try to unfurl the sails from below."

They grabbed the two dangling ropes that they had fashioned with slipknots to the sails and tugged. The ropes slipped free, and the one remaining sail that was still in relatively good shape unfurled. The breeze filled it, expanding it outward like a heavy sheet hung out to dry on a windy day. The mast creaked, but held, and slowly the ship moved forward.

"I suppose that will hold in a light wind," said McPherson. "But let's hope that we hit no more storms."

* * *

The remainder of the day passed without event, and the ship slowly sailed southwest on calm seas.

Evening came, and the sun set in brilliant flaming red in the west. It was a moonless night, but the stars shone with such intensity that the whole ship was bathed in soft light. Frederick lay on the bow of the ship where the kraken had been killed, staring up at the incredible sky above. He had never seen so many stars in all his days, and his mind drifted out among them.

I wonder what is out in the vast ocean of space? he thought to himself. Were there ships out there that sailed between the stars, or giant monsters that lurked in the deep places beyond the sky, attacking space sailors at unawares? His mind reached outward, and a great longing came over him to go out there. It was a tantalizing wish, almost an ache and a thirst to go and to explore and know the secrets that the great black well of heaven held.

If I had a wish from one of the leprechauns, he thought, *it would be to have a ship that could sail not only the seas, but between the worlds as well.*

A great green meteor streaked across the sky overhead and disappeared beyond the horizon.

"My mom always said those are wishing stars," said a small voice that drew Frederick's thoughts back to earth.

Frederick sat up. It was Henny, and her golden-red hair glimmered in the starlight.

"Funny thing," said Frederick, smiling at her. "I was just making a wish."

"That means it just might come true," she replied. "If you wish on a star without knowing it, that's the best way to wish, since it might be less greedy that way."

"Well," said Frederick, "that was some shooting star, wasn't it? It was all green and bright. I've not seen one like that before. And it seemed to go right above us, right in the direction that we're sailing."

"Maybe that means we're heading in the right direction," she replied. "Maybe it was a guiding star."

"Let's hope so. This field trip has certainly had its turns for the worst. I wonder why it's been so difficult to get along to our destination?" he said.

Henny shrugged. "Dad says that life is just hard sometimes, but if you keep pushing on, you get stronger."

Frederick thought about that for a moment and all that he had been through recently, and then thought about Colleen. He hoped that she was growing stronger through all the troubles she was facing.

He nodded, stood up, and looked out at the ocean. He had not noticed before, but the wind had died down, and the water was now very calm, a sea of glass. It was so still, and the stars were so clear and bright, even to the very horizon, that he could not tell where the sky ended and where its reflection in the sea began. It was as though he were floating on nothing, suspended in the great empty void of space.

In that incredible moment of deep stillness, surrounded by the majestic glory of heaven and earth, he felt as though his wish had come true. Together, he and Henny stood in silent contemplation of the mystery all around them and said no more for a very long time.

Chapter 3 – The Good Goblin

"You are a *goblin*?" said Mrs. Wigglepox, staring at the beautiful creature standing before her. "But how could that be? You look nothing like them. You are, well... you don't seem like a goblin at all. You are absolutely lovely!"

"Ah," replied Evchi, "but you do not know me, Mrs. Wigglepox. I still bear the stains of the Ooze, like all goblins. Just look at my feet."

She held up one of her delicate feet for them to see. It was gray, unlike the rest of her fair violet skin.

"You see, I am not wholly free of it. There are times that it pains me. But living here in the bright sun, with no Ooze about except that which I carry within me, it is slowly dying, and I with it," she said with a smile.

Nous crept forward like a shy pup, eyed her feet curiously, and then looked at her smooth violet skin. He backed away, as though fearful of something.

Evchi looked at him for a moment, considering, and then, with a smile, said, "Well, tell me, friends, what brings you here to my humble home in the desert?"

Colleen instinctively trusted this strange lady, and they spent the better part of the next few hours telling Evchi of their adventures. She listened with great interest to their tales, asking questions now and then about something to do with the goblins or the Ooze or the state of the Spell.

"Now we are going to find the Wizard's Castle," said Colleen, "and from there we go to the coast and hope to find a way to the Witch's Island and rescue our families."

But all the while that Colleen and the Wigglepoxes were telling their tale, Nous had been huddled in a corner, staring at Evchi from under his hood and occasionally wringing his hands. After a time, he crawled forward and sniffed at Evchi's feet.

He wrinkled his nose and said, "Yes, it is the Ooze. But it is withered and dry. You need worms. Nous could give you worms, and you would feel much better. Come, Evchi, let Nous give you some of his Ooze worms."

He seemed genuinely interested in doing this, and rolled up his right sleeve to reveal several of the black leech-like things hanging from him. He plucked one off and held it up for Evchi to take.

She stood suddenly, her chair falling over behind her, and she backed away.

"Do not give it to me, Nous!" she cried. "Cast it away! Throw it out into the sun on the desert sands, where it will dry up and perish!"

"But the Ooze worms give us strength!" replied Nous, looking hurt. "They will give you back your old beauty, and take away the nasty scars."

Nous looked at the worm, which had begun to wiggle between his fingers.

"Throw it away, Nous!" said Evchi. "Throw it into the heat of the sun and it will be one less that you must deal with. Be free of it!"

Lily and Rose had been watching this exchange with great interest, and Rose turned to her mother and said, "Mother, have any of the little people gotten into the Ooze?"

Mrs. Wigglepox sighed and looked down at her feet.

"I am afraid so, my dear," she said quietly.

Nous gave them a sidelong look and then said to Rose, "Momma hasn't told you, has she?"

A sly grin formed on his ugly face, revealing his yellow and brown teeth.

Rose was quite startled, for it was the first time that any goblin had actually spoken to her. She turned to him and began to speak, but Mrs. Wigglepox spoke first.

"Just what do you mean by that?" she demanded.

Nous' grin broadened, and he said, "The missus does not know either?"

"Know what?" said Mrs. Wigglepox again.

Nous began to snicker.

"What is so funny, Nous?" she demanded.

By now, everyone was paying close attention, and Nous was about to say something when Oracle spoke.

"The leoples wished it," he said, and he bowed his head.

"What?" said Mrs. Wigglepox.

"I think he said the little people wished it," said Colleen.

"That's absurd," said Mrs. Wigglepox. "Why would any of the little people wish for such a thing? It is ruining our whole world."

Nous grinned. "The gremlins and cluricauns – they made the first pools," he said.

"I've never heard that before," said Mrs. Wigglepox indignantly.

Oracle sadly nodded his head.

"But..." she began again, and noticed a tear trickling down Oracle's face.

Evchi said sadly, "It is said among the goblins that they were first brought into this world by the Witch. But there were no Ooze pools then – only what they brought with them. But the Black Leprechauns that had joined her wished to have the black magic of the goblins, and the Witch told them that only by connecting this world to the Great Worm that ruled the world of the goblins could they have such power. They made a great wicked wish, and in the depths of her pits, they called into being the Evil Pool, and from that pool, they began to spread all the others. Those little people that partook of the Evil Pool were changed into gremlins and cluricauns and other wicked little people."

Mrs. Wigglepox stood in silence as Nous grinned, and Evchi looked sad.

Then Colleen asked, "Do you think there's any hope for the gremlins and cluricauns? I mean, could they be free like you, Evchi?"

"There is always hope," she replied.

Evchi moved around the room, opened the door of her hut, and went outside, motioning Nous to come with her, and the others followed.

She led him out beyond the oasis, into the sands that were baking in the sweltering heat.

Nous still held the worm, which was now writhing madly as the sun beat down upon it. He pulled his own robe closer, hating the light that touched his gray and green skin.

"Do you wish to be free of this thing, Nous?" she asked him. "Do you wish to be free of the insatiable hunger and thirst it causes you to have every day? Do you wish to be free of its poison, which distorts your heart and mind and body? Do you wish to be free of this worm that feeds on your very body, leeching the life from your veins?"

Nous looked at it, then at Evchi.

"Would I become... like you?" he croaked.

"Perhaps not all at once," she replied. "You still have many worms hanging onto you, Nous. They must all, one by one, be plucked off and cast away. But, bit by bit, as the worms die, or perhaps if they are all burned away, you will begin to heal, and truly live."

"But... you are so scarred," he said.

"No, Nous. *Think*. I am becoming what we goblins should naturally be. It is the Ooze and worms that distort us and change us and make us what we ought *not* to be," she replied. "Throw it away, Nous. Be free of it."

The goblin stood staring at the worm, his arm outstretched and holding the wiggling thing before him. Then, all at once, he opened his fingers, and it fell down to the burning sands. It writhed for a moment, and then began to crawl back toward him, inch by inch.

He watched it come, then suddenly kicked it violently, sending it flying. A gust of wind picked it up and carried it away, far from their sight. Nous stared after it for a moment and then turned away.

Evchi placed a hand on his arm and looked into his hooded face.

"I know how difficult it is," she said. "The worms drive you mad with desire for the Ooze. Everywhere you go, you look for it, even just a little puddle to step in. In all your other pursuits, the yearning for the Ooze is with you, stirred up by the worms that cling to your flesh. They inject you with their poison and, when they do, in those moments you feel somehow alive. But then, you find yourself still hungry for more and more, for within you is an insatiable famine. Your only recourse is to be rid of *it* and *them* entirely and to replace them with something far better. Even a little – even one worm – will drive you mad, and in the end, when you descend through the final pool of Ooze to which you commit yourself, you will pass through to the Great Worm, having become a worm yourself, and there be consumed by it."

Nous stared at her from beneath his hood. Evchi looked on him with pity as a single tear rolled down his cheek, leaving a bright lavender trail in its wake. Then he turned away and went and sat beneath a tree, gazing out into the desert.

"Let him alone for a time," said Evchi. "He needs to work this out in his own heart and mind. But he will need all the help we can give him."

"But what can I do?" asked Colleen.

"You have already done much," she replied. "It is you who set him on his course to this place, simply by showing him care and concern with no desire for anything in return. That is something that goblins rarely experience. It has touched him deeply. But remember, Colleen, he is still a goblin. Care for him, but take care around him, especially for the little people who are in your charge. The goblins are promised pools of Ooze of their own in exchange for prisoners brought to the Witch. If Nous travels with you, the temptation to betray you to her will be great."

They talked on for some time, speaking of what they hoped to accomplish and what they might face as they went on. But suddenly, Evchi looked up as if she were listening. She rose quickly, went to the door, and looked about.

"Nous?" she called.

There was no answer. She shaded her eyes against the rising sun and looked out on the horizon. Colleen followed her gaze, and there, silhouetted against the blue sky was a tiny black figure.

"Nous!" she whispered.

"What's he doing out there?" asked Colleen.

"Has he gone out into the desert by himself?" asked Mrs. Wigglepox. "Whatever for? Is he leaving us after all this time?"

"Mrs. Wigglepox, would you please wait here with your daughters? Colleen and I will go after him," said Evchi.

"Of course," she replied. "But do be careful!"

"Come on," said Colleen. "We'll ride Badger."

She whistled, and the great horse trotted over to her, a bright look in his eyes.

They climbed onto the saddle and galloped off into the desert, toward the black dot on the horizon.

When they reached the spot, they saw that it was Nous. He had thrown off his black robe, leaving only a cloth about his waist, and he lay face down in the sand. On his back, arms, and legs, scores of black worms writhed in the sun, and they seemed to be trying to burrow into his skin to escape its bright rays.

"Nous!" cried Evchi, leaping from the saddle and running to his side.

Being careful not to touch the worms, she turned him over and looked into his face. Lavender streaks marked his gray skin, but now his eyes were closed and his teeth clenched in a grimace of anguish.

"Nous, Nous. This was a brave deed, but you cannot be rid of the Phage on your own. You need someone to guide you. Too much too soon may only drive the worms deeper, and although you may *appear* to be well, they will consume you from within. I would not wish to see you beautiful and washed on the outside while deep within you are filled with the maggots of the Worm! Come back to the Oasis now, and we will speak of these things."

Slowly, Nous squinted open his eyes and looked at her.

"Nous wants to be free of them, free if *it*," he whispered through his teeth.

"Desiring to be free is the first step. Come with me," replied Evchi. "Although we may have little time together, I will teach you what I can. But I think there will be others who will teach you as well."

She then picked up his black robe and handed it to him.

He hesitated, but she said, "One day, you will be free, even of this."

He took it and reluctantly put it on, and together they walked back toward Evchi's oasis, with Colleen riding slowly behind.

Colleen watched as the two goblins walked side by side – Evchi a delicate and lovely form, upright and majestic in her every movement, and Nous, a slouching, hunched figure shuffling along through the sand.

The morning passed, and Evchi and Nous walked outside together, talking for some hours while the others rested in the hut.

Colleen fell into a deep sleep on a small cot that Evchi provided for her. The noon hour passed and the sun began to sink into the West when she finally woke again. She stretched and sat up, feeling well rested. Outside, she could hear a *tink, tink* sound, as though someone was tapping on a rock with a hammer.

Going outside, she found everyone gathered around Evchi, who was tapping on a rather large upright stone with a hammer and chisel.

The stone appeared to be rather shapeless, but as Colleen walked around to the other side where the others were gathered, her eyes went wide and her mouth dropped open.

There before her was the most amazing carving she had ever seen. It seemed to her that the forms were *emerging* from the rock, as though they were living things, and immediately, she recognized them as herself, Nous, and the Wigglepox family.

Each carving was perfect – an exact likeness, and so life-like that, had they been painted, Colleen would have almost thought that she was seeing herself in a mirror. Her expression was brave and defiant, her hair flowing back as though blown in a great wind, and on her uplifted hand, she wore a ring. At her feet were carved the Wigglepox family, sitting back-to-back, along with a fourth leprechaun whom she did not recognize.

But the most striking figure was that of Nous. But it was only half the Nous that she knew. His lower half was still hidden within the un-carved rock, and he pushed mightily against it, as though he were trapped within its stony grip. His left half seemed to be sinking, but his right side pushed him up and out of the stone's grip. The left half of his face was the familiar face of the goblin – a great bulbous nose and ear, and distorted flaps of skin and warts. It wore a grimace and looked as though it were struggling and in pain. But the right side was smooth and clear, with angled cheekbones and a perfect, pointed ear, and bore a look of determination and strength.

The right arm and hand were perfectly formed and muscled, with no trace of distortion, while the left was the gnarled arm and hand that Nous now bore. On the left half of the upper torso was a tattered and torn cloak, while the right half was muscled and powerful.

"I'm calling this 'The Two Faces of Nous,'" said Evchi as she finished with a last tap. "We have been talking about it all afternoon as I worked. Nous is quite a good student. He even made suggestions about his portrait."

"You carved this whole thing in one afternoon?" asked Colleen incredulously.

"I know it's not the best quality. Rushing such a thing rarely is. But we have so little time, and I wanted to give Nous something to think about on his journey with you."

Evchi stepped back, looked over the statue, and sighed.

"There is so much more that could be said in this," she said. "But at least it will help me to remember you and your struggle." She sighed again and said, "But come, it is time for a meal."

They went into Evchi's hut and sat down while she busied herself with preparing something for them.

"Evchi," said Colleen, "did you paint and carve all of these paintings and statues around the room?"

"What's that? Oh, forgive my poor work. I know it is not much to look at. Still, I do what I can to learn the old ways of my people," she said, glancing at Oracle.

"But they're beautiful," said Mrs. Wigglepox. "They remind me of the tapestries in Doc's House of Mysteries."

"I have never been there," said Evchi. "But I would love to see it one day. It is said that the goblins once were the greatest of craftsmen when it came to tapestries, painting, sculpture, and such. Their gift was to beautify all that was shaped with mind and hands. Alas for my people! Now they pollute and destroy with the Ooze, allowing the spawn of the Worm to leach them of their natural beauty and powers. I was once with them in the pits of gloom, brooding over the slime that was consuming me."

"You've been in the pits of the Witch?" asked Lily, her eyes wide.

Evchi bent down and smiled at Lily. "Yes. I once labored there, digging and forcing others to dig for treasure that we rarely found and never kept."

"But how did you escape?" asked Rose.

"I had help," she replied, and Colleen thought her glance strayed to Oracle. "But that is a long tale. Come, we must discuss your own journey. Where will you go from here?"

"Well," said Colleen, "we hoped to find the Wizard's Castle and from there go to the sea, and then, somehow, get to her fortress."

"In this, I can help you somewhat," said Evchi. "A day's walk south of here lies the Wizard's Castle. I have been there once. You must be wary of it, though."

"What do you mean?" asked Colleen.

"It is hard to explain," replied Evchi. "It is as though the very... how shall I say it... the very *fabric* of the whole place is, well, unstable. I think that echoes of the Cataclysm still reverberate there. Things *shift*, you might say."

Nous had been sitting on the floor by Evchi's chair, listening, and now raised his head and said, "Goblins do not go there."

They all turned and looked at him, and Colleen said, "Why not, Nous?"

He looked at her and said, "Once, long ago, the king sent goblins there. They never came back. He sent more, and they didn't come back either. Never sent any more after that."

"Maybe we shouldn't go there, then," said Colleen.

"The only way around that area is far to the east, at least three days walk, and then follow the goblin road from there to the coast. There is no shade or shelter anywhere that I know of between here and the road. The Castle is the only chance you might have of finding shelter and water for the next two days before you reach the sea," said Evchi.

"There's a goblin road across the desert? Nous, why didn't you tell us?" asked Colleen.

Nous did not answer, but after a moment, Evchi said, "Goblins are not permitted to speak of it. It is the only passageway through the desert between the wood and the sea where the spirits that haunt this desert do not roam. At its end is the port where the black ships of the goblins travel to and from the Witch's fortress."

"Does that mean that we need to go east through the desert for three more days?" asked Colleen.

"If you wish to meet the goblin road, then yes," said Evchi.

"Do not go there," said Nous. "The Colleen will be captured there."

"But what other way can we go?" she asked.

"There are rumors that some little people still live by the sea," said Evchi. "They used to sail the coasts in small ships and boats. If you could find one that still is seaworthy, perhaps you could make use of it."

They were quiet for a moment, and then Mrs. Wigglepox said, "Well, it seems to me that tramping for days and days through a haunted desert, in the wrong direction, into the hands of goblins is certainly the wrong way to go. If we can find the Wizard's Castle, and then get to the sea, just maybe we'll find help there. And if not, at least we can walk east along the coastline rather than through the Burning Sands."

"That sounds good to me," said Colleen. "What do the rest of you think?"

"I think Mrs. Wigglepox is right," said Evchi. "I can guide you part of the way to the Wizard's Castle, but I still have much work to do here in my oasis. My time to leave has not yet come. However, I counsel that great care must be taken at the Castle. This much I will say – the Witch has been there. Who can say what evils she has planted?"

"Evchi," said Mrs. Wigglepox. "If you have been to the dungeons of the Witch, then you know where her fortress is. Can you tell us how we might get in without being captured ourselves?"

She paused, thinking, and then said, "If you come to the Goblin King's fortress by the road from the harbor, you will surely be seen. It is a narrow path with steep, broken cliffs on either side that winds its way upward from a dark surrounding valley – up, up to the terrible gates that are endlessly watched and ever shut, except when goblin patrols come and go.

"*But*, there was a secret way - a tunnel through which ran a water course that was blocked by an iron grating. It was on the west side of the fortress mountain, and all of the filth from the dungeons flowed out of it in a dank waterfall that spilled into a deep chasm. From there, a polluted stream ran all the way to the sea."

She paused again and then continued. "A great warrior would likely fail to enter the dungeons that way, for he would first have to navigate the chasm, in which some nameless horror lurks, then climb those fetid falls, and then somehow break the thick iron bars that form the grate. If he could do all of that, he would have to crawl on his hands and knees through that wretched flow, then come at last through yet another iron grate to the dungeons."

They were silent for a moment until Oracle grunted.

A sinking feeling came over Colleen as she heard a description of the Witch's fortress for the first time. "I suppose that way is impossible, then," she said sadly. "Isn't there any other way?"

But Evchi continued, "I said that a *great warrior* would likely fail in such an attempt. But you are not a great warrior, nor am I."

"Do you mean that you have been that way?" asked Colleen.

Evchi glanced at Oracle, who was staring up at her, and said, "Yes. I and one other escaped the dungeons that way. In each of the iron grates, there is a slight bend, and I and my companion were able to squeeze through them both. I believe that you, small and thin as you are, might barely do the same."

"But what about getting out again with your mother?" said Mrs. Wigglepox. "She is surely bigger than Colleen. How would she get through?"

"That I do not know," Evchi answered. "But that is all I can offer you."

They were all silent for a time, and then Nous spoke again. "Nous would like the Evchi to tell him what happened to her. Why is she so scarred?"

Evchi smiled at him and said, "Perhaps you know, Nous, that, in the Pits of the Witch, there are many, many little people. They toil night and day, digging, mining, making shoes for the goblins, and living in despair. For many of them, their hope is gone. They have lived in the darkness for so long that they have forgotten what the light looks like. Some of them have joined the service of the Witch, and spy for her, hoping to gain some relief of their terrible labors.

"I was once a task master in the Pits for the Goblin King and the Witch. It was my job to watch over the leprechauns, and to be sure that no gold that they found was used for any wishing, although, of course, they had no pots to put it in.

"But there was a certain little person who had marched right up to the gates of the fortress. How he got there, none of us knew. And he was a big leprechaun, not like the general small variety, begging your pardon, Mrs. Wigglepox, Lily, and Rose. But he strode right up to the fortress, and the guards were so surprised that at first, they thought he might be a goblin himself since he was dressed in a ragged cloak.

"Then he spoke, and said he wished to be with his people, and threw back his hood, and lo, it was a leprechaun! The guards seized him and took him to the Goblin King, and he was questioned for a long time by the Witch. Since I was the warden of the leprechauns, I was called to the proceedings.

"I had never seen anything like it. This leprechaun said absolutely nothing to the king or the Witch, and that made them all the more furious. They had him beaten and then handed over to me to put in the lowest of the pits, which I did.

"But, as I was taking him, all in my black mail, and bearing a black spear, he spoke to me, and I shall never forget his words."

"What did he say to you, Evchi?" asked Rose.

"He asked me if I wanted to leave the service of the Witch and be free of the Ooze maggots that were consuming me. He said he had come for me – for me! Imagine that – a leprechaun, braving all the perils of the goblins and the Witch's island, simply surrendered himself to the Witch just to talk to me and offer me freedom from the Ooze and the burden of working in the Pits.

"I thought he was insane, but as we marched down into the Pits, he told me stories – stories of long, long ago when the goblins were a beautiful people, and there was no Ooze or worms or pits or a Witch. I mocked him, but something deep inside made me want to listen. He held a vision before my mind of a bright and beautiful world that the goblins had once shaped. Then he showed me that same world as a dark place, its rivers running with black Ooze, and its people distorted and misshapen.

"As the days and weeks went by, I would secretly visit the lowest Pit to hear his tales. Then, one day, he asked me if I would like to be like the old goblins in those stories – bright and beautiful and free of the Ooze – and if I would like to return to the Land of the Goblins and help them start over again.

"It was there, in that lowest pit, that I said yes. Together, we planned our escape, but he promised his own people, who were still in those pits, that he would come back again one day with help.

"Our journey was terrible, and many times I did not think we would survive, but we managed to escape, board a goblin slave ship at night, and hide deep in the cargo bay. When we reached the shores and stole ashore, we made our way west along the coast, then north past the Wizard's Castle, and finally here. And here I have been ever since."

"How long ago was that?" asked Colleen.

"Now let me see... I believe it will be forty-seven years now," she replied.

"Forty-seven years!" said Colleen. "But surely you are not that old!"

Evchi laughed joyfully.

"You see, Colleen, the more I am free from the Ooze and the worms, the more like myself I become!" she said.

"I'm not sure I understand," replied Colleen.

"Goblins do not naturally die, Colleen. It is the lie that the Great Worm told us long ago - that our race was coming to a final end, and promised that it would make us great and continue on forever if we would only partake of its Ooze. We believed it, and now the goblin race ever grows more and more worm-like, leaching life from everything around them. We have forgotten what it is like to truly live – to truly be who we are. Instead, we think that we find value in possessing more and more worms, and pools of Ooze of our very own. We do not know the meaning of freedom, for we are chained to the maggots that we possess, and which possess us. So you see, Nous, I am not scarred. In fact, all of my scars are healing."

"How sad for your people!" said Colleen. "If they could only see you, they might understand that they could be healed of this Goblin Phage."

"The time is coming, I think, when I will be revealed to them," she said. "But what will then become of them or me, I don't know."

She looked thoughtful for a moment, then said, "Well, look at the hour - it's getting late, and you have a journey to continue. You should rest a bit more before you go."

Evchi rose, and they thanked her many times. She insisted that Colleen take her cot again, and she would rest outside by the spring. Nous and Oracle chose to follow her to a grassy mound where they all sat down and watched the westering sun.

Colleen looked from the door of the little beehive hut and watched as the three of them sat in the shade.

She wondered if Nous would ever become like Evchi – so fair and joyful and noble. She hoped so.

She checked on Badger, making sure he was safe and content, then returned to the hut.

Going back in and sitting by the fire, she said, "Mrs. Wigglepox, it all sounds so hopeless. Do you think we have any chance of rescuing Mr. Wigglepox and my mother?"

"Help comes in unlikely places and unexpected ways, child," she replied. "Think of how far we have come already. Think of Doc and Dvalenn and Cian and the Lady Danu, and now Evchi, and even Nous. All we can do is keep up our courage. Somehow or other, I believe we will make it if we just don't give up."

For a while, Colleen sat by the dying fire, watching the embers slowly fade, and thinking about the days that had passed. Then she rose and looked outside once again, and there she could see Evchi, Nous, and Oracle standing on the mound, watching the sky turn to brilliant orange and red.

She turned back to the cot and lay down. Almost at once, she fell into a dreamless sleep and did not wake until the sun had set, and the early evening stars began to twinkle in the eastern sky.

Chapter 4 – The Wizard's Castle

The moon had begun to rise, and the world seemed quiet. Colleen got up, stirred up the fire, and looked about the room. But finding no one there, she went out among the trees of the oasis and walked along the little spring that ran by the green banks of grass and flowers.

The air was cool and fragrant, and reminded her of summer nights back home, sitting on the hill and watching the stars.

A pang of loneliness ran over her as she thought about her sisters and brothers, wondering what they must be doing now.

Probably worried to death about me, she thought.

Then she wondered – how long had she been here? Was it days or weeks? So much had happened that she had lost count. And how long would it be before she got home again?

Home. She pushed the thought away as tears threatened to spill down her cheeks, and forced herself to think of rescuing her mother. She walked on.

Soon she found Nous sitting alone with his feet in a little pool and staring down at his reflection in the moonlight.

She went and sat next to him and followed his gaze.

What a strange sight, she thought. *A human girl with golden-red hair sitting close beside a gray-green monster – hideous to look at, but somehow changing – somehow different from the goblin that had attacked them and bitten Frederick not so many days ago.*

"How are you, Nous?" she asked quietly.

"Nous is ugly," he replied in a glum voice.

"Oh, Nous," she said, "why do you say that about yourself?"

"Nous is... Nous is not... Nous cannot..." But words failed him, and he only shook his head.

"Whatever do you mean?" asked Colleen.

"She is... the Evchi is... Nous cannot say it," he replied.

"Beautiful?" she replied.

543

"No, no. Something else," he said, hesitating again, as if pondering some deep thing, but not knowing how to express it.

"Then, perhaps *clean,*" offered Colleen.

"*Clean.*" He said the word slowly, as if he were saying it for the very first time. "Yes. She is *clean.* Inside."

"Clean on the inside?" asked Colleen.

"The Ooze – it is not inside her. It only... stains her feet. She is... yes... *clean* on the inside," he said.

"Why do you suppose her feet are still gray?" asked Colleen.

"Nous asked her," he replied. "But Nous did not understand. The Evchi said it was the part of her that still touched the world. That is why her feet were still stained. Does the Colleen understand what the Evchi meant?"

He turned toward her, and she looked in his face. His big gnarled nose had streaks of lavender running across it.

Colleen thought for a moment and then said, "Well, my dad always said that if you keep walking through nettles, you're sure to get stung. Maybe it's like that in this land. Maybe the goblins have been here so long that even the dust has traces of the Ooze in it, and you can't help but get stained by it. I don't know."

Nous stared at her for a long moment and then looked back at his reflection in the water. Suddenly, they both gasped as there was a *splash,* and their reflections vanished as the water flew upward and drenched them.

A mad cackle came from behind a bunch of tall grass, and Colleen could see the head of Oracle bobbing away as he attempted to run from his prank. He had thrown a stick into the water.

"Oracle!" said Colleen, getting up and wiping her face on her sleeves. "Whatever has gotten into you?"

Nous only stared after him, a confused look on his face.

Colleen was about to say something more, when Evchi came down the path. She was singing, and her sweet, melodious voice seemed to blend with the breeze and the trickling spring.

When she saw Colleen and Nous, she laughed merrily and said, "Been

refreshing yourselves, my friends?"

Oracle poked his head through the grass and cackled with glee.

Evchi glanced at him and smiled wryly, then said, "You have a long night ahead of you. Come back to my house for some supper."

She led them back to the hut where she had set out some dried fruits and water.

"I haven't much to offer you," she said. "But it is good simple food to begin a journey with."

The Wigglepox family was already at the table and waiting, and when they were all seated, Evchi turned to the eastern window where the sun was now rising, stood silent for a moment as the moonbeams washed over her, and then motioned for them to sit and begin.

As they ate, Evchi described all that she knew of the Wizard's Castle and the land leading up to it, as well as all that she could remember of the Witch's fortress.

"Just remember," she said, "the castle is a place where the magic of the Cataclysm still lingers. Take care that you do not walk through doors that may lead to places you may not wish to go. They may take you there! Only stay on the straight road."

As they were climbing into the wagon, Evchi walked over to where Nous had settled himself in the back and put her slender hand on his shoulder.

"Take care, my friend," she said. "Find a way to be free of the Phage. I know in my heart we shall meet again."

Nous said nothing, but looked at her under his hood for a long moment, then bowed his head.

Evchi backed away and, with a wave and many goodbyes, they were off once again and heading south.

At first, their journey was uneventful, even peaceful, but as the hours went by, from time to time, Colleen felt a wave of sleepiness roll over her, and then it was gone as soon as it came. The moon set, and still they rolled on through the sand, and the night grew cold under the cloudless desert sky.

"It's spooky," Colleen said to Mrs. Wigglepox as another wave of the Spell rolled past them. "It's like someone is dropping stones in a pond – a ripple spreads out from the source and then passes by, but all the waves pile up on the distant shore of the forest. Do you suppose that's what happening?"

"I don't know, dearie," she replied. "But we may find out soon – look."

Colleen looked up, and before them, far on the horizon, she could see a dark shape jutting upward from the sand, a black shadow against the brilliant stars.

"I think we have found the Wizard's Castle," said Mrs. Wigglepox.

But even as she said it, the air in the distance shimmered a dark, almost black-red, and the image vanished, replaced by stars.

"What was that?" whispered Colleen.

"Ripples," said a voice from behind them.

They turned to see Oracle peering over the back of the wagon.

"Ripples?" asked Colleen.

But Oracle said nothing more and only stared.

Colleen looked forward, and the atmosphere again seemed to shimmer. The dark shadow against the sky was back.

"This is what Evchi was talking about, isn't it?" asked Colleen. "Things *shifting*."

They rode on for several minutes in silence and watched as the shadow against the sky came and then vanished, came and then vanished again. Suddenly, Badger stopped and whinnied, then tossed his head and began to back up, slowly at first, and then frantically.

"What's wrong, boy?" said Colleen.

Suddenly, the air began to quiver and glow with a dull red light, and it seemed as though a great wall of shimmering air was speeding toward them.

Before anyone could say or do anything, the world around them changed. The desert vanished, and they found themselves rolling out of thick forest and down a smooth stone road that led to a white castle that had tall towers and bright banners flying in the wind.

Oracle whistled, and Badger whinnied again and trotted forward.

But then the air shimmered again, and the road became rough and unpaved.

"Look out there, lass!" came a voice from behind.

They turned and looked, and for an instant, Colleen was sure that she was seeing Doc the Dwarf driving a wagon full of white stone blocks drawn by a great black horse, but he seemed younger than she remembered. She opened her mouth to speak, but the air shimmered around them again and she heard the dwarf yell something, and then, he vanished.

A great explosion ripped the air, making Colleen's heart skip a beat. Nous shrieked and pointed in front of them.

Spinning about once again, Colleen saw a great host of goblins all about them, and a company of brightly armored men fighting them with long swords. Fallen goblins and men lay everywhere, and smoke rose from the great castle, which was closer now.

Suddenly from behind the castle, a huge grinning head loomed up and bellowed a great war cry as it lifted a huge hammer and brought it down with terrible force on the castle wall. The explosive sound of rock shattering thundered across the battlefield.

Colleen saw a small figure with long golden hair and robed in green standing on the parapet of one of the towers. He raised a staff in the air and cried out in a piercing voice that reached above the din of battle all around him. A bolt of bright blue light shot from his staff at the giant, but the huge creature swung its hammer and, at the same moment, a red ball of fire rocketed skyward from the battlefield.

The three powers collided with a deafening concussion, and the sky seemed to split in two, a ragged wound opening in the fabric of existence.

The giant howled in rage as it was sucked into the crack in the sky, and just as the great rent snapped shut, it let fly its great hammer.

The gigantic maul ripped through the closing breach in the universe, struck the tower on which the green-clad figure stood, and Colleen watched in horror as its upper half crumbled to the ground, replaced by a sudden pillar of dust and smoke.

The hammer flew on, striking the top of the foremost wall and sent great blocks of stone falling down upon men and goblins alike, then landed with a great *thud* beside the shattered gates of the castle.

The air shimmered around Colleen again, and now they were standing before the castle gates. They were broken down, and all was silent except for the whisper of the wind in the sand at their feet. Beside them, on their left, a huge stone the size of both Badger and the cart lay half buried in the sand and a great black shaft protruded from it.

"The hammer," hissed Nous.

"Quickly, Colleen, get us into the castle!" said Mrs. Wigglepox urgently.

Colleen flicked the reins, and Badger pulled them through the broken gates just as the air outside shimmered once again.

But the world around them remained the same this time.

"What just happened out there?" asked Colleen.

Lily and Rose poked their heads out of her pocket and rubbed their eyes. They had slept through the whole thing.

"I think that is what Evchi meant when she said that things *shift* here. I believe we have just witnessed different events in the castle's history," said Mrs. Wigglepox.

"Do you mean... that we traveled through time?" asked Colleen, amazed.

"Who knows? Maybe we were just seeing into the past, as through a window," she replied.

"Do you think that the battle started the Cataclysm? It looked as though the whole world would rip in two," said Colleen.

"Maybe, but let's just get away from this gate," she replied.

It was just then that Oracle, who had fallen asleep in the back of the wagon, woke up, stretched, smacked his lips, rubbed his eyes, and looked about. Then he chanted a little rhyme.

"Dips and slips the rifts of time,
From historpast comes buckles and slime.
Ripple and dipple it comes and goes.
And where it stops, no one knows."

"I wonder what that was all about," whispered Colleen with a sigh, and flicked the reins.

They now saw that they were in a courtyard of sorts, and that many fallen and broken stones of great size were scattered about and partially buried in the sand all around them. It was difficult to find a clear path through the debris, and their way was quite rough as Badger hauled them forward.

Across the courtyard and before them, they could see another smashed and broken doorway that obviously led into the castle itself. As they drew near, the debris grew less, but an odd crunching sound came from beneath the wagon wheels.

Colleen looked down at the ground in front of them and, to her horror, she could see, protruding from the thinning sand, many bones and skeletons, some small and misshapen, and some large and still wearing sand-scoured armor. She put the back of her hand to her mouth, gasped, and looked away. Lily and Rose ducked down into her pocket, and Mrs. Wigglepox, Nous, and Oracle stared in silence as they rattled over the dead.

"There must have been a terrible fight at the doors of the castle," whispered Colleen.

"Nous wonders who won," said Nous.

"No one, I think," said Mrs. Wigglepox. "This place is nothing but a tomb for goblins, wizards, and men. And I wonder how many little people lie here as well."

They slowly went through the huge, open doorway, and the sand gave way to a dark green marble floor that was littered with many, many skeletons. Armor and shields and weapons lay everywhere, some rusted with age, and some still bright, untouched by the long years. Some of the dead still lay gripping one another in a silent struggle.

Colleen hated just to roll over them, but could think of nothing else to do. Ahead, she could see by the light that came in through cracks in the ceiling that fewer skeletons lay ahead, so she urged Badger to pull them onward.

Soon, they came to the end of the hall, and from there it opened up into a round room from which eight doors of various sizes led. Starting at the left, the doors circled the room, beginning with the largest, which stood at least forty feet tall, down to the smallest, which was about three feet tall. All were broken open and lay smashed or hanging limply from ancient hinges.

"Eight doors," said Colleen. "Do you suppose that *these* are the eight doors that the riddle on the map spoke of? I mean, might the castle back home have been built like this, and had eight doors at the end of its entrance hall?"

"Who can say, dearie?" said Mrs. Wigglepox. "But unless we take that big door, we shall have to leave the wagon and Badger here, or at least the wagon."

"Perhaps we should look down each one and see where it leads," said Colleen. "But I'm so tired. Perhaps we could find someplace to rest for a few hours, and then go exploring. We wouldn't want to miss something important because we're exhausted. Let's take the big passage and see where it leads."

It was massive, towering at least fifty feet over their heads, with a great black arched ceiling that was inlaid with white and blue gems that shone like stars. The walls were smooth, and their color and brightness seemed to be lighter near the floor, and gradually grew darker as it neared the ceiling.

"Why, this hall looks like a sunrise!" exclaimed Mrs. Wigglepox.

"It's beautiful," said Colleen. "I wonder if it changes as the sun rises and sets."

They rolled on down the hall, which sloped steeply downward until it widened to three great doorways. Each of the doors lay broken on the floor, their shattered remains strewn about the rooms, as though they had been blown down by some great explosion from the outside.

"Whatever knocked in those doors must have been terribly powerful," said Colleen.

"Maybe it was the big hammer," said Nous. "Or the Witch."

"Wouldn't it be something to be able to see the rest of the battle that happened here?" said Colleen.

"No," said Mrs. Wigglepox. "I wouldn't want to have been here then. Everything was destroyed. Everyone died."

They stared at the broken entryways for a moment longer, and then Colleen flicked the reins, guiding Badger through the center doorway.

The wagon's wheels bumped over debris, and as they passed the threshold, they found themselves staring at a scene of utter destruction.

A great stone table in the center of the room was smashed in two. What were once gigantic tapestries hung half burned and faded from many, many years of abandonment. What appeared to be a huge bed at least forty feet long and ten feet high had one of its great legs shattered to rubble, and various other pieces of massive furniture stood broken or overturned.

Then Colleen gasped and put her hand to her mouth. To her horror, she realized what she was seeing, and what she had missed because of the sheer size of the place. Lying in the great bed was a giant. Its face was hidden by a great helmet, but one huge arm hung off the bed, its withered brown hand lying limply on the floor. Colleen instinctively backed the wagon away, but then stopped, both horrified and fascinated by the sight.

Swallowing hard, she climbed down from the wagon.

"Where are you going?" whispered Mrs. Wigglepox.

Colleen only put a finger to her lips, and with wide eyes tiptoed over to the great, mummified hand. Its fingers were at least three feet long, but were shrunken to the bone.

"I wonder what happened to it?" whispered Colleen. "What could kill a giant?"

"Maybe another giant," said Nous, coming up behind her. "Maybe it was that giant skeleton we met."

Oracle now joined them and looked sadly at the great hand. He wiped his eyes and turned away.

"Oracle, are you crying?" asked Colleen.

But the leprechaun waddled back to the wagon and said nothing.

"Let's not stay here," said Colleen. "It's spooky – and sad."

Silently, they left and went to the next room. It too was destroyed, its furniture overturned and burned, but there were no dead giants there. The third room was also wrecked, but was not so badly burned as the others, and less debris littered its white and red tiled floor.

"We might as well get some rest here," said Colleen. "I've had enough adventures for one day. Let's just sleep in the wagon."

Nous, however, climbed up on the great bed that was in the room and found it comfortable enough, although the blankets were nothing but rags and dust. But the goblin did not seem to mind, and soon was snoring away.

Colleen, Oracle, and the Wigglepox family lay down in the hay of the wagon and were also soon fast asleep. Colleen woke once, hearing her mother call her name. She sat up with a start, rubbed her eyes, and looked about. But it had only been a dream, and she lay back down and fell asleep again, dreaming of a tall white castle that was surrounded by a sea of black goblins and a terrible giant that bore a great hammer with which he struck blow after blow on the besieged walls.

Chapter 5 – The Source of the Spell?

When they finally awoke, Colleen was stiff and her back hurt. She stretched and looked about. The room was still bright, illuminated by some magic that seemed to match the time of day.

Oracle was already up and poking about the room with his cane, and Nous was sitting on the edge of the bed with his gray legs dangling down. Thin worms hung limply from them like wet noodles. The Wigglepox family stirred in the hay, yawned, and sat up. Colleen climbed out of the wagon and walked over to Badger, whom they had unharnessed from the wagon and tethered to a fallen chair.

"I suppose we ought to go exploring," said Colleen, "but Badger better wait in the main room that we found. I don't think he'll be able to get down those small halls."

Badger whinnied and shook his mane in protest.

Colleen stroked his great cheek and said, "Sorry, boy. No sense in you getting yourself stuck in a hallway or breaking a leg on a staircase. You'll be fine, and I'll make sure you have food and water."

The thought of water reminded her that they had precious little left.

"We'd best eat something ourselves," said Mrs. Wigglepox from the wagon. "Who knows when we'll have a chance to stop and take a break?"

They had a small meal, and even Nous nibbled at their food and water. He seemed to be finding ordinary food less objectionable, and mumbled less often about wanting the Ooze.

When they had finished, Colleen led the way back down the hall, with the Wigglepoxes riding in her pockets, and soon they were back in the hall chamber that joined the various passages. She peered through each of the doorways that ringed the room, and found that, except for their size, all of them were identical, with a large landing that led to a staircase leading upward to the left and downward to the right.

"Which do we take first?" said Colleen.

Nous was nosing about the doors, sniffing at the air, and said, "Stinks. They all stink."

"I can't smell anything," said Colleen, taking a deep breath. "Except stale air.

Well, let's take this middle one first – number three. We'll go up and see if we can get a view of the desert."

They climbed, and the stairs spiraled upward for a long way. They could feel a cool breeze blowing, and they emerged through a shattered hole onto what appeared to be the remains of a tower, now half fallen into ruin. But they could not see outward to the desert, for the standing walls of the castle were taller than the remains of the tower. However, they could see a good deal of the castle itself, and the sight that met their eyes was a terrible one.

The wall opposite the gates through which they had come was completely breached, as though it had been battered down. Great piles of rubble lay everywhere. Sand and chunks of stone covered the outer courtyard, and here and there, great fissures and cracks ran up the height of the remaining walls that stood.

Only one tall tower seemed untouched by the devastation that lay all about it.

"That's where we need to go," said Colleen. "Let's get down and find a way up there."

The very next door in the round hall led them upward many hundreds of stairs until they came to a single closed door. Colleen gripped the handle and pulled, then pushed. But the door was locked and it would not move.

"Remember the House of Mysteries, Colleen," said Mrs. Wigglepox.

Colleen nodded, took a breath, and said, "Open."

Nothing happened.

"Open!" she said, louder. Still nothing moved, and the door remained locked.

"Looks like this door needs a real key," she said.

Then she remembered the key that Doc the Dwarf had given to her. She fished about in the deepest pocket she had and found the key. She was amazed that she had not lost it or that the goblins who had captured her had not taken it. Tiny runes were carved along the length of its small, golden shaft. She slipped it into the keyhole of the door and turned. There was a loud *click*, and the door swung silently inward.

Colleen slowly went through and peered about. Glowing white crystals in the ceiling lit the room, and tapestries lined the walls, depicting scenes of mountains and forests and rivers. One of these depicted a tall blond man with pointed ears, and beside him stood a beautiful woman with long raven-colored hair. They were both dressed in blue and silver and wore thin circlets of gold on their heads.

"I wonder if he was an elf?" said Colleen. "He's so handsome, and the woman is so beautiful! But she must be human, and she looks..."

She was about to say *familiar*, but could not quite place where she had seen her before. There was something in her face and hair that reminded her of someone she knew. She gazed at the perfect image on the tapestry for some moments and then shook her head.

"Must be my imagination," she muttered.

Three more doors led from the room, and Doc's key neatly opened the first. Behind it was a study or library of sorts with dozens of old books and scrolls lining the walls. On a desk sat a small book whose open pages displayed neat handwriting in a language that she did not recognize. She blew dust from the ancient book and carefully picked it up. She fully expected it to feel dry and brittle, and perhaps fall to pieces at her touch, but to her surprise, it was quite solid, and the pages were not yellowed at all. Beside it lay a pen, and beside that a magnifying glass.

Colleen picked up the glass and looked at it. It was of amazing workmanship, and as she held it over the words on the page, she nearly dropped both the book and glass, for beneath the lens were perfectly formed English words. She took the glass away from the book and peered at the page. The strange alien script was all that she could see. Again, she peered through the lens at the words on the page, and again found that she could read them.

"It's a magic magnifying glass!" she declared. "I can read this book with it!"

"Let us see!" said Lily and Rose together, so Colleen carefully put all three of the little people on the desk, sat the little book back down, and held the magnifying glass over it. Nous and Oracle also gathered around, and Oracle climbed up on a chair that was pushed in beneath the desk. Indeed, they could all see the text of the book in their own language. It was truly a magic magnifying glass.

Colleen read aloud from the top of the page. "It is the sixth of September. Our scouts have reported that a great host of goblins is nearing the castle, and with them a great giant, and behind them a black caravan of creatures in the Witch's service. We have sent for help, but I fear it may not come in time. How the Witch hid so great an army for so long, I do not know, but I fear she has breached the barrier between the worlds and has brought them here. They will be upon us soon. I, Anastazi, will make my last stand here. If only we can lure the Witch into the trap we have laid, we shall be free of her. I only hope we can complete the glass chamber in time."

Colleen carefully turned the page, but it was blank.

"That's all there is. This sounds like a diary," she said. "This must be the last entry before the battle started. It sounds like they had plans to trap the Witch somehow, but they must have failed."

"So it would seem," said Mrs. Wigglepox.

"I'm going to take this with us and read it," said Colleen. "It might be important." She slipped the book and pen into a pocket inside her robe and went on to explore the room.

Using the magnifying glass to read the spines and bindings of the books and scrolls that lined the walls, she found many that said strange things such as *Trolls and their Bridges, Goblin Artistic Theory and Practice, Giant Bread-Making Recipes, Dryads and their Voices, Hill Spirits,* and many other strange titles.

As she read one after another, she came upon a very small and thin one whose title leaped out at her. *The History of the Elvish Folk from the Time of the Opening of the Gates to the Building of the Emerald Castle,* by Anastazi. It was the same size as the diary that she had found, and when she opened it up, it appeared to be written in the same small spidery script.

"Now this is one I've got to read," she said, and slipped it into another pocket.

Then she noticed that there were quite a few of these small books, and each one she inspected was written by the same hand.

"This is amazing," she said, calling to the others, who were now wandering about the room. "There's a whole collection of books written by Anastazi the Great himself. I think he recorded a whole history here. We've got to take this stuff with us and get it home if we can. It's priceless just for what it contains. Can you imagine – the complete lost history of the races? My sister Bib would go nuts here."

Colleen looked about for a few more minutes, then took one more book entitled *Languages of the Great Trees,* stuffed it into a pocket, and then said, "We better go check out the other rooms before I weigh myself down with books the way Dvalenn did with stones. But we've got to get all of these books and put them in the wagon. Somehow, I think it's really important to save them."

She slipped the magnifying glass into her last free pocket inside, picked up the little people, and went back out into the main room.

Colleen opened the next door, and there, in the middle of the floor, was a pile of rocks with what appeared to be a headstone with an inscription. And on the far wall was a crystal clear wall of glass with a glass door, behind which a gray fog swirled. A broken window faced north and looked out across the desert.

Colleen walked into the room and went over to the pile of stones. Pulling the magnifying glass out, she sat down on the floor to read the inscription.

"Here lies the last wizard. We found him here by our sleeping princess. Here let him lie forever, her eternal guard," she read.

"This must be the place that Doc told us about," said Colleen. "And that crystal room must be..."

But she had no chance to say more, for without warning, the gray mist inside the glass chamber seemed to form itself into the vague shape of a man. The door swung open of its own accord, and a wave of fear and sleep so powerful swept out that Colleen was knocked backward and was immediately asleep, and all the Wigglepoxes with her. Nous saw Colleen sway, and rushed to her side, catching her and lowering her carefully to the floor. Oracle followed behind him and pushed the glass door shut.

Oracle then went to Colleen and laid a hand on her head. Immediately, she stirred and looked up at their faces.

"What happened?" she asked.

"You fell asleep," said Nous.

Colleen looked about the room and then at the glass chamber. A gray fog had begun to creep about its floor once again.

Then a thought struck her, and she whispered, "Did we just find the source of the Spell?"

Chapter 6 – The Wave

Frederick woke with a start and sat up. He had fallen asleep on the deck of the ship, and now it was deep night. The world around him was still and silent. The sea stretched out in all directions like a sheet of glass as far as he could see. But something had changed – something had roused him from peaceful dreams. There was a tenseness in the air – almost as if electricity charged the atmosphere around the ship. He stood, looking about, and then the door leading to the crew quarters creaked open and, one by one, the McGunnegals filed out, gazing out at the brilliant sky and reflective ocean.

"What's happening?" asked Bib. "We all woke up a few minutes ago – all of us at once."

"I don't know," replied Frederick. "But I felt it too. Something isn't right."

"My skin is all tingly," said Henny.

Professor McPherson came up from below deck and looked about.

"So you feel it too?" he asked.

"Yes," said Aonghus. "What do you suppose it is?"

"It feels like a storm is brewing, except there are no clouds in the sky," said Bran.

They all looked up and, at that moment, something amazing began to happen. There, high in the sky, toward the stern of the ship, shooting stars were raining down and vanishing before reaching the horizon. At first, it was just a few, but as they watched, they became more numerous, and soon they began to fall in pairs, then three or four at once.

"I wish that we would get to the island soon!" whispered Henny in an awed voice.

"It's beautiful!" breathed Abbe.

"Yes," said Aonghus. "But the hair on my arms is all standing on end, and those shooting stars look like they're getting closer."

Indeed, as they stood watching, a large meteor shot downward, its brilliant green tail trailing majestically behind it, until it vanished into the ocean. Minutes passed as the meteor shower continued to grow in splendor, when the ship, which had been quite still, began to rock gently. Low, broad waves advanced and passed them by, coming from the direction where the meteor had plunged into the sea. Then they passed, and with them, the sky grew black once again, and no more meteors came.

"That was amazing." whispered Bib. "That big one must have hit not too far away."

But Frederick was not listening. His eyes were still riveted to the heavens, for far, far away, he could see a green pinpoint of light growing in intensity. At first, he thought it was an oddly colored star, but as it brightened, he knew it couldn't be. But he could see no tail on it if it were another meteor.

"Uh..." he began, and the others turned and followed his gaze.

Once again, their hair began to stand on end as the point of light grew brighter.

"Professor..." began Bib.

"Everyone get below and hold onto something!" he shouted suddenly. "No, never mind, hold onto something NOW!"

Aonghus swept Henny into one arm and wrapped his other arm around the mast.

"Here!" he called. "All of us together!"

The McGunnegals all linked arms around the mast, and the professor ran to the wheel of the ship, gripping it with both hands.

Frederick seized the ship's rail and watched in amazement and horror as the light in the sky became a blazing ball of green fire hurtling down directly toward them.

There was an eerie silence as the huge burning mountain hurtled earthward.

"Hold fast!" cried the professor as the light of the fireball cast weird shadows about the ship.

The sea became a blazing green mirror, and suddenly, the whole world around them lit up and ignited with crackling lightning and explosions and booms that went on and on, until with a final clap of thunder, the great meteor plunged into the ocean, not a quarter mile behind them.

A massive concussion of air pressure detonated about them, first this way and then that, causing the sails to billow back and forth, and sending the ship reeling.

A huge wave leaped from the sea, and almost instantly, it was upon them, carrying the ship upward with a mighty heave that sent them all sprawling to the deck, still clinging to one another.

"Don't let go!" shouted Aonghus.

The ship sped upward on the wave, its nose pointing suddenly downward as though it were riding backward up a great hill. It nearly reached its peak before being caught in the onrushing tide, and then was swept forward in a mad rush, groaning as if in agony from being wrenched so suddenly from the stillness of a few moments before.

The girls all screamed as their speed increased, and the spray of the wild wind and sea blinded them and beat upon their faces. Perhaps even the iron grip of Aonghus would have failed had the ship not been at such an angle that they were pressed downward against the deck. Suddenly, the mast cracked above their heads where they had secured it, and it slammed into the deck right beside the professor, who still clung desperately to the wheel, then it careened wildly into the ocean and vanished.

Still they sped on, faster and faster, and Frederick surely would have tumbled from the deck had not he wrapped both legs and arms around the posts of the ship's rail. Now he was drenched with seawater, and the force of the accelerating ship and the terrible wind had him locked in place. It was all he could do to grit his teeth and not cry out in fear and pain as his limbs were pressed tighter and tighter against the railing.

Without warning, there was a *SNAP* as the posts that held him splintered and broke. He slid up the tilted deck and slammed into the door that led below, breaking it clean off its hinges. Onto the steps he rolled, smacking his head hard. Stars swam before his eyes, but he fought to stay conscious.

He could hear the ship groaning, and wood snapping and splintering as their speed increased. An oil lamp still somehow hung burning in the dark hall, and he could see the extra life vests that hung on hooks along the wall. In the sheer terror of the moment, he thought how bright the little flame was, and how it illumined all the darkness around him.

Then a muffled cry came from somewhere, bringing his thoughts back to the reality of their situation.

"Helga!" he called

"In here!" came her muffled shriek. "The water is coming in!"

Frederick struggled against the acceleration of the ship, and foot by foot crawled up the steeply tilted hall toward her voice. In a few seconds, he was at the door, gripped its handle, and pressed its latch to open it. The door flew open, slammed against the wall, and nearly threw him down the hall with it. Gripping the edge of the doorframe, he looked in, only to see Helga gripping a post in the middle of the room. But his gaze fell past her to the far wall, where water steadily poured in through the ship's planks.

"We've got to get out of here and get the extra life vests!" yelled Frederick. "We can tie them together and make a safety line for everyone to hold onto!"

But Helga did not answer. Her eyes were wide in terror, and she seemed rooted in place.

"Helga!" he shouted. "I need your help! We've got to get the life vests and take them back out on deck! Everyone is out there, and they're in terrible danger! The ship has been hit by a huge wave, and we're being carried along by it! I don't think the ship is going to survive!"

"Forget them!" she sputtered. "Where are the life vests?"

"They're hanging in the hall! Come on! We've got to get them!" he shouted again.

Helga looked madly around the room, gripped the post for another second, and then, in a sudden burst, scrambled and fell and crawled toward the door. A frenzied look was in her eyes, and she pushed Frederick aside, stumbled out the door, and seized a life vest, although she already wore one.

"Helga!" he called. "The others need our help! They're out there!"

But she ignored him and went tumbling down the hall, and then crawled along the steps to the open door.

As she looked out, the wind struck her so hard that she went sailing backward, as if she had been hit in the face. Her head hit the planks, and she did not move again.

"Helga!" cried Frederick.

He crawled to where she lay. He frantically checked to see if she was breathing, and sighed with relief when he found that she was.

He knew that he had to get to the others, although how, he did not know. If the wind had done that to Helga, what would it do to him? She was far bigger than he was. Doubt and fear filled his mind. He was only fourteen years old, after all. He should just find a post to hang onto and hope for the best. But as dark thoughts began to plague him, suddenly the memory of the Lady Danu broke through.

"She said I had something really important to do," he whispered to himself. "Maybe this is part of it."

He steeled himself, stood amid the groaning and splintering sounds of the ship, and took all of the life vests from the wall. Then he took a length of rope that had been hanging beside them and, as quickly as he could, tied them all together in a row. Lastly, he picked up the one Helga had taken and tied it as well. Then he made his way back to the door, and slowly, carefully, bracing himself, pushed himself out. The rush of wind smote him like a battering ram, pushing him against the wall that separated the lower and upper decks. In the bright starlight, through the streaming spray, he could see the McGunnegals still holding fast to one another.

"Aonghus!" he called. "Aonghus! The ship is breaking up! You've got tie into these life vests!"

Aonghus opened his eyes and looked at him. His jaw was set, and a fierce look of defiance was on his face. He looked from one of his siblings to the other, and then nodded.

"If you come over here, the wind presses you against the wall. I think it would be safer for you!" Frederick shouted. "Where is the professor?"

Aonghus looked up to the upper deck.

Amazingly, Professor McPherson still clung to the wheel. He had somehow managed to tie himself in again, and was keeping the ship straight, maneuvering it directly down the wave's front.

"Bran!" shouted Aonghus. "Take Abbe and Bib to where Frederick is! Tie into those vests! Then go to the hall below deck out of this wind! I'll bring Henny!"

Bran looked behind him at Frederick and nodded.

"Quickly!" called Frederick. "But the wind... stay low to the deck!"

Slowly, they let go of the others and the three of them, crawling and still holding onto each other, made it to where Frederick waited, tied themselves to the line that Frederick had made, and dragged themselves into the open hall.

Aonghus followed, shielding Henny from the wind as best as he could. They were all in the hall and could hear the death throes of the ship as it began to crack and heave in earnest now.

"We've got to get the professor down here!" said Aonghus, and he pulled himself outside again, disappearing into the spray of the sea.

"What happened to Helga?" asked Bib.

"She hit her head," said Frederick. "But she's alive."

At that moment, both Aonghus and the professor stumbled in through the door.

The professor was holding something in his hand – it was the compass from in front of the wheel. He hastily put it in his pocket and said, "Children, again, I ask your forgiveness. But do not give up hope! We are all still alive!"

Then he too saw Helga, and a questioning look flooded his face.

"She is too," said Frederick.

"Thank God," he replied. "Quickly, go to your rooms before they flood and take anything you deem precious! We have only minutes!"

"We have nothing," said Abbe. "Nothing but each other."

But Frederick did remember something, and stumbled away, as did the professor. Both returned a few moments later. Frederick had a sword strapped about his waist and the white tooth of the kraken stuck in his belt. The professor clutched a stone chest under one arm and a length of rope in the other.

"Each of you, tie in. We must not get separated when the ship goes down," he said. "Bran, tie Helga to the line. Aonghus, tie this chest to my back – loop the rope through the handles and make sure the latch is secure."

"I'm afraid, Professor," said Henny.

"I am too," he said. "But we will make it through this together."

Helga groaned and opened her eyes. "What a dream," she said, and then moaned again.

"This is no dream," said McPherson. "Now get yourself up. We are all tied together, but I think it unwise for us to stay below if the ship breaks up. Come, we will stand together against the wall on the lower deck."

None too soon, they made it out onto the lower deck, for just as Bran, who was last in line, emerged into the dim light, there was a terrible snapping and breaking noise from below, and they heard a great rushing of water.

Then there was a tremendous *CRASH*, and all seven of them were flung from the deck into the air. But their cries were muffled a moment later as they plunged into the ocean.

Frederick went down, down, and felt the mad rush of the wave carrying him forward, straining against the rope that bound him to Bib on one side and Abbe on the other.

Then they all bobbed to the surface like corks, and their last sight of the ship was that of it rushing swiftly away down the great hill of water, half submerged as it dwindled into the darkness. Then, they too were rushing, tumbling, and falling down that same hill toward, it seemed, their final doom.

Chapter 7 – A Crack in Time

Colleen stood and stared at the glass chamber before her.

"You think *this* is the source of the Spell?" asked Mrs. Wigglepox.

"It could be," she replied. "It somewhat makes sense if you think about it. Remember in the rhyme on the map, the writer said he woke the sleeping lady with a kiss, and she turned out to be a witch? I bet this is the very place that he found her. And Doc said that they found a sleeping princess and that he and his brothers had looked after her until the pirate came and woke her up, and shortly after that, the Witch came back. And here we find Anastazi the Great's own diary, and he said that they were laying a trap for the Witch. I'll bet this room was the trap. They intended to lure her in there somehow, and it was supposed to put her to sleep. They got her in there, but something went wrong. Now it's leaking or something, and spreading the Sleep Spell all over this world. It must build up inside and then, when the pressure of the Spell gets too great, that door flies open, and it all goes rushing out. That's why we were feeling it come in waves!"

"You just might be right," said Mrs. Wigglepox. "And if this chamber is the source of the Spell, then we've got to find a way to destroy it."

Colleen looked about the room.

"Maybe we could break the glass with a hammer or a rock or something. There are plenty of broken rocks lying about the castle," she said.

"Look over there," said Mrs. Wigglepox. "That suit of armor. There's a big iron mace."

Indeed, standing by one wall was a suit of armor, now covered with dust, with a large iron mace sitting propped at its feet. Colleen went over to it and tried to pick up the mace. She could barely move it.

"Nous, could you help me with this?" she asked.

The goblin had been watching and listening to all of this with great interest, and now he said, "Does the Colleen mean that this glass room holds the Sleeping Spell and the power of the gray man? If the Colleen breaks it, will that break the Spell too?"

"Yes, Nous, we think so," she replied.

"Nous does not think it can be broken," he said.

"Why not?" asked Colleen.

"There is a story about this place. The Witch – she came here to destroy it and she could not. So she changed it and sent the Spell. That's what the stories say."

"Is there anything else that the stories say, Nous?" asked Colleen.

Nous hunched down, almost into a ball, looked about, and whispered, "The goblins that have been in the deepest Pits say that there is a power there. It appears as an old gray man."

"Does this gray man have a name?" whispered Colleen.

"None. But this chamber … it *echoes* the Spell. Nous feels it. It smelled of the Gray Man when it opened. That is what gives the Spell its power – what makes it more than just sleepiness."

"It smelled … what smell is that?" asked Colleen.

"Fear," he hissed. "Fear of death. All the weapons in the world cannot conquer that." Then he looked away and said no more.

Colleen stared at the glass walls for a moment and then said, "But we've got to at least try. If there's any chance that this has anything to do with spreading the Spell, then we've got to destroy it."

Nous took the mace in two hands and carried it to the glass door. Then, with all his strength, he swung it. There was a sound like a dull gong, and the mace rattled and fell from his hands.

"See," he said.

Colleen looked down, disappointed.

"Colleen," said Rose from her pocket, "why don't you sing it shut? You can open doors with your voice. Can't you shut them for good too? Or maybe use Doc's key?"

"I would use the key, but there's no keyhole. It's just a glass door that swings on glass hinges and shuts against a glass frame. There's not even a handle. And the door is already shut. I think we need to smash it somehow. But it would take a mighty big and powerful hammer…"

They all looked at one another, and Colleen said, "There *is* a mighty big and powerful hammer – just outside."

"We would need someone mighty big to wield that thing – someone like a giant," said Mrs. Wigglepox.

Colleen sighed. "Well, we're rather short on giants at the moment," she said. "We might as well go and explore the castle further. Maybe something will turn up and give us some ideas. At least we know where it is now."

Down the long staircase, they went, and at the bottom, they found Badger sleeping on his feet. Colleen caressed him and whispered to him. He snorted once and shook his head.

"Might as well try the next passage," said Mrs. Wigglepox. "It's as good as any."

"Shall we go up or down? Looks like all these doors have one up and one down passage," said Colleen.

"Let's try down," chimed in Rose.

Down they went, following the passage just to the right of the one they had come through. This hall had a smooth white floor and sky-blue walls that arched upward about ten feet and were covered in delicate carvings of strange animals and people with slender bodies and long hair. They sat by a river that seemed to radiate light somewhat brighter than the rest of the stone, and the lovely people bathed their feet and swam and waded in the shining river. There were houses of stone, and forests, and animals, each figure perfectly carved and shaped.

"This is beautiful," remarked Colleen. "It reminds me of Evchi's work."

On they walked in silence, looking at scene after scene, always with the shining river flowing through all the scenes carved in the stone. They had not gone for more than a few minutes before a strange shimmering red light could be seen not far up the passage. It flickered, then went out, then appeared again, flickered dimmer, then brighter, then disappeared. And this continued as they slowly, cautiously approached.

Then they saw what it was. They had come to a place where a great crack opened up across their path, about three feet wide, and it split the hall from top to bottom, running upward and out of sight, and downward into blackness. The air itself about the fissure seemed to be twisting and shifting, a red haze forming and disappearing, forming again, then vanishing. And each time the haze appeared, they could see something inside it – people of different sizes and shapes, then a rocky wall, then open air, then the hall on the other side. The misty scenes changed each time they came and went.

"What do you suppose it is?" whispered Lily, who was peering out of Colleen's pocket with wide eyes.

"I'm not sure," said Colleen. "But it sure looks a lot like what we saw outside on our way in. I bet it's another place where reality is shifting. What do you suppose would happen if we jumped through it?"

"I dare say we should *not* try," said Mrs. Wigglepox. "We might end up in some other place or time even more unpleasant than this."

"Do you think we could see the future if we watched long enough?" asked Lily inquisitively.

"Maybe," replied Mrs. Wigglepox, "but I suspect we wouldn't be able to tell the past from the future or even *where* we were looking, much less *when*."

They gazed into the red haze as it appeared again, this time lingering on for a moment. Suddenly, they saw two figures approaching them – one about two feet tall and one standing at about four and a half feet. The smaller fellow had brown hair, a short brown beard, and he was wearing a green top hat, a red shirt, and green shorts with green suspenders. His shoes were black and had curved pointy toes. The second figure was slender, but had well defined muscles and wore a white robe with a sky-blue sash and carried a walking stick that was ornately carved. His skin was lavender and his hair long and the deepest purple, almost black. They seemed to be deep in conversation, but when they reached the fissure, they stopped in their tracks, looked up, and fell silent. They stared directly at Colleen, Nous, and Oracle. The taller figure opened his mouth to speak, but the red haze faded, replaced by another scene.

"That's the second time that's happened," said Colleen. "I'm sure they saw us and we saw them. Whatever is happening here, it's opening up doorways to other times or places. I'm sure we could go there if we wanted to. And I wonder if they could come here?"

Then an idea struck Colleen. "Come with me," she said, and hurried away from the crack and back to where Badger patiently waited.

"What does the Colleen think?" asked Nous. "What does it plan to do?"

"Think about it, Nous. This place may be literally shifting in time. Or time may be shifting around it. At least there seem to be places where these fissures or gates or whatever they are open up, and we can see into other times, and the people there can see back. On the way here, I'm sure we passed through one of those cracks in time and ended up back when this castle was just being built – and when it was being destroyed. Lucky for us that crack shifted back to our own time again, or we might be stuck back then.

"But here's my idea. Suppose we *did* travel back in time – on purpose. We could warn the people of what's coming. Maybe we could even go back far enough and stop the Witch from ever getting here. We could change the course of time, and we wouldn't even *need* to rescue my mother or Mr. Wigglepox, or find the Waking Tree or any of it. We could set it all right!" she said excitedly.

Oracle said, "Hmph!" and sat down on the floor.

Nous was trying to work all this out in his head, and Lily and Rose had a look of wonder on their faces.

But Mrs. Wigglepox looked grave and concerned. "It sounds terribly dangerous, Colleen. These *cracks in time,* as you call them, don't seem predictable or stable. What if we jumped through one of them and ended up a thousand years too early in history, or a million years into the future? And what if we got stuck there and couldn't get back again? We might never see our loved ones again."

"And what if we changed the past and something went even worse?" asked Lily. "I wouldn't want that."

Colleen thought for a moment. She had not considered that they might actually be in their own past or even the future. Indeed, how *could* they know? This desert might look exactly the same for thousands and thousands of years. The thought worried her.

"Maybe you're right," she said glumly.

But then she brightened and said, "But what... what if we could bring someone *here* to help us? Suppose we could get one of the original wizards from the past to step through into their future – into our present? What if we could bring Anastazi the Great himself?"

Oracle looked up and raised one eyebrow, as if considering the idea. Then, with wide eyes and in a sing-song voice, he chanted,

"Colligal can sing the song
To make the shivers stand so long.
Then with mighty voice to call
The ancients to the broken hall.

Stand in tower above the crack
And watch for Anastazi's back!
But battle he shall do that day,
And from that task he must not sway,
Though darkness shall come rushing in,
Cataclysm shall victory win."

They all stared at the leprechaun.

"There you go talking normally again," said Colleen. "Or at least it made some sense."

But Oracle seemed to have lost interest and leaned close to the floor, scratching at the dirt with his fingernails and muttering something to himself.

"Come on," said Colleen. "Let's go up the steps."

The stairs circled the tower, leading steeply upward, but they had not gone halfway around when they came to a crack that seemed to split the tower in two. Here it was not so wide – only about a foot, but the same red shifting air hovered before them in the fissure like a thin fog.

Colleen carefully climbed the steps right to the edge of the crack and tried to peer up and down. But the scene shifted before them, and they could hear shouts and the clash of swords.

"It's shifted to the battle again!" said Colleen.

Then all was still, and they could see long tapestries lining the stairs. The scene shifted again, and they were atop a partially finished tower. The sound of hammers and chisels filled the air, and the sky was clear and blue. Then it all vanished, and they were back in the broken tower. But the red haze had lifted, leaving only a dimly lit crack where distant sunlight slipped in.

"Now!" said Colleen. "Jump across!"

She jumped, and Oracle followed by planting his walking stick on one side and pole vaulting across with a gleeful giggle. Nous leaped across with them, and they continued on. Halfway around the tower again they came to the fissure. This time, they waited until the red shimmering air passed into nothing, and they all leaped through together, although Nous looked back and hesitated as the clear, blue sky of the unfinished tower appeared again. But he caught up with the others, and three times more they passed through the crack without incident.

Finally, the stair ended abruptly, and they walked out onto a landing, which gave them a view of the devastated castle and surrounding desert. A deep fissure ran through the entire structure, splitting the tower in two, and traveled left and right in a deep abyss that stretched outward as far as they could see, until it was swallowed up by the Burning Sands.

The castle walls were breached on either side, and here and there, the air shifted and shimmered with red hues, then winked out, only to flicker again somewhere else.

"This was the tower that the giant destroyed," said Colleen. "It must be. Do you think Anastazi survived?"

"Well," replied Mrs. Wigglepox, "the stories seem to say that he left the battlefield after coming face to face with the Witch. He could have destroyed her, but didn't. So he must have survived."

"Let's watch and see what happens," said Colleen. "Oracle, will you hold the Wigglepoxes for me?"

Oracle put the three little people in his top pocket, and they waited. But they did not have to wait long. Stretching out before them, from east to west, a vast red wall flickered into existence. It rose high into the sky and down into the earth all along the length of the crack. Suddenly, before them was the winding staircase. They were seeing inside the tower before it fell. A bellowing roar reached their ears. The giant had reached the castle wall.

A concussion of power ripped the fabric of time and space. The scene wavered before their eyes, and the terrible sound of stone being crushed and falling filled their ears, and dust and debris completely clouded the scene.

The dust settled, and from the wreck slowly, unsteadily, rose a figure clothed in tattered and filthy green robes. His dirty golden hair hung tousled about his shoulders. His face and hands were cut and bleeding, but he still gripped an intricately carved white staff that bore a clear gem at its tip set in golden bands.

He leaned heavily on a broken chunk of wall and coughed.

For a moment, Colleen and the others dared not breathe.

But then the man faltered and fell to one knee. The scene trembled and began to fade.

"No!" Colleen cried out, and instantly the image snapped back into sharp focus.

The man fell to the ground, and Colleen instinctively rushed forward to help him.

"Wait!" cried Mrs. Wigglepox.

But it was too late. She stepped through the wavering crack in time and instantly choked on the thick dust that filled the air.

Realizing what she had done, she turned to run back. For a moment, she saw Nous, Oracle, and Mrs. Wigglepox, who had her arms outstretched, and Lily and Rose with shocked looks on their faces. In the next instant, they grew hazy and vanished.

"Stop!" she cried, waving frantically at the air. But to no avail. The window had closed.

"Daughter?" said a voice from behind her.

She turned. The man was lying on the broken floor of the tower, breathing heavily. Blood ran down his face from a terrible gash in his forehead.

Colleen ran to his side.

"Anastazi?" she said.

"What magic is this?" gasped the man. "It cannot be!"

Colleen had no idea what he was talking about, but he looked terrible.

"Come on," she said. "I'll help you get down the stairs and out of this dust."

The man struggled to his feet, leaning heavily on Colleen. They descended the gaping hole in the tower floor that led downward, past the great crevasse that now split the tower in two.

"Stay away from the crack," gasped Colleen, struggling under the man's weight. "It's not just a crack in the tower."

Halfway around the tower, the man sagged and Colleen was forced to sit him down heavily on the steps. He was unconscious now, and his breathing was ragged. Then she saw the blood on his shirt.

"Oh my," she whispered.

Carefully, she removed his green cloak and unbuttoned his white tunic. The wound was deep and bleeding profusely. She knew that he would bleed to death if she did not do something now.

She needed something to apply pressure to the gash, and looked about desperately. Then a thought struck her – the Lady's vial of water. She reached into her cloak pocket and pulled it out. It shone in the dull light like a radiant blue star. Quickly, she unscrewed the lid and dipped her finger in the water. She gasped, for a wild sensation of power and healing flowed from her fingertip and through her whole body, mind, and soul. But she gathered her wits and opened the man's mouth enough to allow a single drop of the precious liquid slip between his lips. Instantly, he gasped, and his eyes shot wide open. Colleen quickly closed the jar and slipped it back into her cloak. She watched as the wound on his head stopped bleeding, knitted itself together, and then vanished. His face went from pale to full of color and radiant, and Colleen could see strength flow into his whole being.

The man blinked for several moments, a look of wonder and delight and fear on his face. Then he seemed to come to himself and looked directly at Colleen.

"You?" he said, and then shut his eyes and shook his head.

After a moment, he opened them again and looked at her with a hard, piercing gaze.

"You are... come here, child," he said in a stronger voice.

Colleen stood her ground. She was not quite ready to trust this man, even if he was, as she supposed, Anastazi the Great himself.

"Are you Anastazi?" she inquired hesitantly.

The man stood. He was very tall and stately, and extraordinarily handsome, even covered with dirt. He seemed to absolutely *exude* power and authority.

"And how would you know me?" he asked. "And may I ask your name?"

"There's no time," said Colleen. "I've come here from the future. You opened a crack in time, and I accidentally stepped through it. Something terrible is about to happen – a Cataclysm that will wipe out this whole region and make it a desert. You've got to get everyone out of here!"

But the man stood still, staring at her with his deep lavender eyes.

"You saved my life, child. Thank you," he said. "But the battle still rages. The Giant is banished, but the Witch must be dealt with. Quickly, follow me."

He turned to go down the stairs.

"I have to go back," said Colleen. "I was hoping that you would come with me. The future needs you. I need your help."

He paused and turned to look at her. Somehow, she felt as though he knew more than he was saying, for there was an odd twinkle in his eye.

"The future? Yes, it waits for all of us. You and I shall be there one way or another. But quickly, tell me of this."

As quickly as she could, Colleen told the stories that she had been told, how the whole land had been devastated, and a good portion of it had sunk, and a great wave had swept in, and the Waking Tree had been lost, and how the world was bound by the Spell, and the Witch still held power, and then about the cracks in time.

The man stared at her for a long moment, and then said, "I am Anastazi, Elven Lord and head of the Council of Wizards. Please, tell me your name."

"I'm Colleen McGunnegal, daughter of Adol and Ellie McGunnegal, and my brothers and sisters are Aonghus, Bran, Abbe, Bib, and Henny. We live in Ireland – the Emerald Isle. I came to the Land of the Little People accidentally through a magic mirror that we found in my grandfather's basement."

"There is much to this tale!" he said in amazement. "But no time to hear it now. Come with me, quickly. This tower is not safe."

"But I have to go back to my own time!" said Colleen. "My friends are waiting for me. The crack through this tower – if you step through it when the vision inside changes, you travel through time. It seems to shift between three or four different periods, perhaps more."

"Then you have all the time that you need," he replied. "But I need you now. If the Waking Tree is to be lost, then there is something that we must do. Please, come with me, and then I will bring you back here, and you may return home."

She nodded, and down the stairs they ran as quickly as they could. Out into the courtyard they went, and there goblins and men littered the ground. There was fighting everywhere, and the stench of death hung thick in the air. Colleen froze, and felt as if she would retch at the nauseating scene.

But Anastazi lifted his staff high in the air and, with a commanding voice, he cried out, "Away with you, creatures of the night! Be gone from this fair place!"

He brought his staff down on the marble pavement and, with a blinding flash, the entire courtyard ignited in brilliant white light that spread outward from that spot. Goblins screamed in agony as the light seared their tortured flesh. They began to run about wildly, momentarily blinded, leaving behind panting men shielding their eyes from the terrible brightness.

"Follow me!" said Anastazi, and like a deer he ran across the courtyard to a fountain at its center. She followed, running as though her life depended on it. There, beside the fountain, a tree grew. Its branches reached upward to twine about a white stone archway, and a stone bench sat beside the fountain in its shade. In the midst of the terrible sights, sounds, and smells of the battle, and the agony all round her, for a brief moment, she noticed how beautiful the tree was, covered with bright yellow flowers and bearing sumptuous fruits.

"Behold, the First Child of the Waking Tree," he said to Colleen. "We must save it. The future of the little people lies with its fruit."

But at that moment, the ground beneath them began to shake and crack, and the sky beyond the castle walls split in two. The shredded edges of the ripping heavens were lined with black and red fire, widening like a greedy mouth desiring to swallow the world into an empty void. The tear began to spread downward with a sickening ripping sound, as though gigantic trees were snapping in a torrent of wind. Peals of thunder mounted to a deafening roar, but never ended or rolled away. Both men and goblins looked in terror at the breaking sky. Some fell to the earth and covered their faces, some fled, and others stood dumbfounded as their doom swept upon them. Downward the rent came like a twisting and crooked crack in the wall of the universe, and bent its spreading fingers toward the very place where Colleen and Anastazi stood.

Anastazi lifted his staff in one hand, and grabbed Colleen's hand with his other, and cried out in a language that she did not understand. A rushing of energy burst through her as she stood there gripping Anastazi's hand, and she somehow knew that he was drawing strength from her, and she – she was drawing strength from everyone around her. He looked at her in renewed amazement, and in that instant, their minds touched. She knew that he needed her – that his power alone was insufficient to stop this Cataclysm, or even slow its deadly advance. Their eyes met, and she silently nodded to him.

Blue and gold lightning stabbed skyward from his staff at the descending tear, striking the rip with a tremendous explosion of power. For a moment, the rending paused as healing power struggled against devastation. Colleen bent all of her will against the descending river of death, and the abominable weight of that struggle nearly broke her mind as she comprehended that this tearing of time and space would not only cause the Cataclysm, but would utterly destroy this world - perhaps spread to all worlds. She felt herself trembling, felt Anastazi's grip on her hand tighten, and he too trembled as he exerted all of his power to stem the tide of destruction.

Neither Anastazi nor Colleen, however, noticed a great goblin chieftain stumble to its feet behind them. It shook its burned and bleeding head, and, seeing them, picked up its huge mace. It raised the weapon and brought it down with a great swing. But the blow never made its mark, for a green stab of light came from the castle, sending the creature flying to the ground. It did not move again. A wizard in bright green robes stood at the gates, and now came running to their aid. Colleen felt his presence and power, felt his strength flow into her, and through her to Anastazi, and his magic joined theirs in this unimaginable struggle against the descending rip in the fabric of existence.

Yet other goblins were recovering now as well, and a terrible shout went up from among them, for into the courtyard, through the shattered outer gates, strode a huge dark figure. A black fog of darkness surrounded it, from which no light seemed to penetrate, and where it walked, the light that Anastazi had ignited faded. Had Colleen known their danger, she might have quailed, for this was the Goblin King, endowed with dark powers by the Witch. The huge goblin gripped a black sword in its hand that left a trail of dark smoke in its wake as its wielder swung it about.

The wizard in green ran forward, and with a speed and agility that belied his aged appearance, he engaged the great goblin. Sword and staff clashed. Black smoke and green fire seared the air, until it seemed as though the two combatants struggled amid a black fog in which green will-o'-the-wisps flashed and danced. The wizard blocked a savage slice of the goblin's sword, raised a hand, and a green burst of power sent the creature flying backward to the ground. Immediately, the wizard sent blast after blast of energy at his foe. But the goblin leaped to its feet and charged again, slicing the air with great arcs, forming a shield of darkness that deflected the wizard's attacks.

Now the remaining men in the courtyard were also coming to their senses, and they rallied and pressed the other goblins, keeping them from aiding their dark leader. Seconds ticked by, and then Colleen felt a change in the descending rift in the cosmos. The tide was turning. If they could only continue, they could stop this thing – stop the Cataclysm completely. The rending sound that thundered from the sky began to lessen. The wound began to close and heal. But their strength too was fading. She could feel her whole body trembling, and felt as though she might fail and collapse.

"Do you have something from your world, child? Anything, quickly!" cried Anastazi.

Colleen fished about in her pockets, found her mother's scarf, and handed it to him.

"It was my mom's," she meant to say, but no sound came from her lips, and she slipped to her knees.

Anastazi quickly hung the scarf over a branch of the tree and, with a word of command, the blue lightning from his staff changed to white, covered the tree and surrounding area with a bright shield, and then he shouted, "Now RUN! All good men, RUN!"

Anastazi helped Colleen to her feet, but she stumbled and fell, and the vial of water that the Lady had given her slipped from her pocket and rolled to the base of the tree.

"The vial!" she cried, but Anastazi pulled her away, and with the last of their strength, they stumbled back toward the castle entrance.

Colleen glanced over her shoulder as the growing rent in the sky fell like lightning to the earth, engulfing the white light, the tree, the archway, and the fountain.

In that very moment, the battling wizard and goblin each raised a hand and unleashed their power at one another. Green and black smote the air with a concussion that sounded like a cannon. The goblin was thrown back, but the wizard was also blasted backward, falling into the light around the tree and onto the stone bench. Anastazi spun about, pointed his staff and cried out strange words, then turned and ran on. A moment later, they all vanished – the tree, the archway, the fountain, and the wizard. The light in the courtyard blinked and went out.

The earth where the tree had stood trembled and cracked open. One of the castle towers rocked and went crashing down into the courtyard, and a terrific explosion shook the castle. It was as if the entire courtyard had blown up, and pieces of debris went flying high into the air and far, far away. Colleen thought that she saw, in one brief instant, a reflected flash of light on one big section of wall – perhaps a mirror? But it flew northward and vanished from sight.

Anastazi led Colleen back up the broken tower at a run. A red haze blocked their way as they came to the crack in the stair.

"I know my way back now," said Colleen. "Go, stop the Witch! Put an end to her now so that the future won't fall under her Spell! But if you should fail – if I go back and the Spell is still there – how do I break the glass chamber? The Spell seems to be coming from it and has put the forest to sleep!"

Anastazi looked at her in amazement. "You are destined for greatness, Colleen McGunnegal. Only use your gifts for good, and do not let them be turned to the passions of evil. Beware the guile of the Witch! Listen to me – I think this Spell does not find its ultimate source in this glass chamber that you speak of, but in something – or someone else."

He paused, smiling at her. Dirt and grime and sweat covered them both, but she thought how noble he looked. In the distance, they could hear the bellowing of Lugh. Anastazi looked up as the skeletal head of the giant bobbed over the wall momentarily.

"Still, this chamber may be a conduit for the Spell, perhaps even enhances it, and it may be partly what the Witch uses to spread it so powerfully over the forest. Only a great power can break that chamber. The hammer of Lugh is such a power. I do not know where it has fallen. But go now! We have not wholly healed the rift, and it may yet tear apart and cause this Cataclysm. I sense the gathering storm, and I shall run into it! Although you do not know it, you shall meet me again, but I shall not remember you. The past and future await us both."

Colleen gave him a confused look, but he put his hand on her shoulder, smiled at her fondly, and said, "Do not be afraid. Only live well and fulfill the task before you."

He turned and ran down the stairs. Colleen looked after him for only a moment, but seeing the red haze fade, she dashed on up the stairs, running faster than she had ever run before. Around the tower she sped, pausing, waiting for what seemed an eternity as the shifting scenes of time came and went, and still she ran on, until she finally reached the top. She gazed out across the landscape, and there she saw a field of goblins – thousands of them, advancing on the castle. Behind her, the broken sky groaned and tore a widening rift, a gaping wound in creation itself.

To her left, Colleen could see the skeletal ghost of Lugh shambling about, beating upon the stones of the castle, stomping on goblins and men alike, lifting its white bony fists to the heavens, and raging in its contempt and hatred of all living things. It stumbled northward through the desert, still bellowing, crushing all in its path. Colleen wondered at this – had *they* sent this apparition into the past from the future? That would mean that they had caused their own encounter of this thing back in the desert. *Time* seemed to be something not so fixed, but just as the past influenced the future, so it seemed that the future could influence the past. Her mind swam with the strange possibilities.

Then her sharp eyes saw something that brought her back to the present – a tall figure shining like a blazing torch amid a sea of black – Anastazi the Great bearing his white staff. Behind him, the last remnant of the castle's army marched – both men and little people. Before them, the goblins fled, for the mere presence of the Elven Lord struck fear into all of his foes. In front of them was a high hill, and there they ascended and made their stand.

But suddenly, a deep bellowing horn sounded, and the goblins halted in their frenzied rout. For out of their midst a dark robed figure strode, bearing a black staff that flamed red at its tip. Beside it came a huge goblin, carrying a great horn and red banner that bore the image of a hideous black dragon. The goblins rallied behind this pair and grew silent. The Maiden of the Night had come.

Colleen held her breath, her eyes riveted on the terrible scene. Anastazi, with a dozen men and a few hundred little people, stood on the crown of the hill. The goblin army surged silently around the hill, waiting as the Witch stood staring up at its crest.

It seemed to Colleen that Anastazi and his little band could not survive, engulfed in the sea of darkness that now surrounded them.

White and blue light shot down from the shining staff of Anastazi, and as it did, a roaring red fire swept from the staff of the Witch. The powers collided. A shock wave burst through the air, sending goblins rolling like rag dolls in a hurricane. Colleen was knocked to the floor by the wave of power. She rose, dazed, and tried to clear her head. The castle was trembling, and she lost her footing again.

Suddenly, a hand seized her, and she felt herself being pulled backward. There was a snapping sound, the world grew silent, and the face of Nous filled her eyes. She was back.

Chapter 8 – Down the Wishing Well

"I know what we have to do to break the chamber!" gasped Colleen.

"What happened to you, child?" said Mrs. Wigglepox. "You're filthy!"

Colleen looked down at herself. She was covered with dirt from head to toe, and could only imagine what her face and hair must look like.

"Now the Colleen looks better," said Nous with a toothy grin.

"You're too kind," replied Colleen with a smile. "Nous, I have a question for you. Can you bring back the ghost of Lugh?"

"Bring back the ghost...!" cried Mrs. Wigglepox. "Colleen, why on earth would you suggest such a thing?"

"I'll explain in a moment," she replied, and gave Nous a questioning look.

Nous grinned. "Yeessss!" he hissed. "Does the Colleen want to *own* the giant?"

"Own the giant?" said Colleen questioningly. "Whatever do you mean?"

"Ah!" said Nous. "Nous can bring it back, but it will be very angry. Someone will need to own it to control it. Nous owns the giant now. But he will give it to Colleen if she wants it."

"But how could I own the ghost?" said Colleen.

Nous looked at her for a moment and said, "It is dark magic."

"Dark magic?" she replied. "Do you mean *goblin* magic?"

"Yes, goblin magic. Once someone has gone down into the Ooze, the one who calls him back owns him. If he wishes to stay, and not go to the Worm forever, he must obey his caller," said Nous darkly. "Nous can teach the Colleen how to call them out of the Ooze."

"I'm not sure I understand," replied Colleen.

"Don't you have anything to do with that goblin dark magic!" said Mrs. Wigglepox. "It will lead to no good. Once you start down that path, it will be mighty hard to turn back. I've seen more than one leprechaun tempted by such power, and every time he gave in, he was changed forever, and for the worse. They all ended up on the side of the Witch. That's what happened to

Lugh himself! Don't do it, Colleen!"

"But we have to use Lugh's hammer, Mrs. Wigglepox," she replied. "We need someone big enough to pick it up and smash the glass chamber – it's the only way to destroy it."

"What good would it do to use dark powers to save the whole world if you lost your own self, Colleen?" said Mrs. Wigglepox sternly. "I'll not have it. Suppose you did call back Lugh, and he became your ghostly slave. Suppose you did command him to smash the tower and that glass chamber, and suppose that did break the Spell. Then what? Would you be drawn away by that dark power and become yet another Witch to plague our world? No, I'll not have you do it!"

"You're probably right," replied Colleen glumly. "I suppose it wouldn't be right for Nous to do it either."

"No, dear, it wouldn't," she replied. "We'll just have to find another way. If we just had a good giant around..."

Suddenly, Oracle rapped his stick on the floor and motioned for them to follow him. Colleen stood and began to dust herself off as she followed him down the stairs. They hurried past the cracks in the tower, waiting as the strange scenes came and went.

"Where are we going, Oracle?" asked Colleen.

The leprechaun said nothing, and led them on, back to the chamber where Badger still stood.

He then led them down the smallest of the passages, downward and to the right.

"I wonder if this hall was for the little people once upon a time?" said Rose from Oracle's pocket.

Oracle only danced a little jig and led the way. Colleen had to sit and scoot herself down the winding stairs for quite some way before they came to a landing and a hall that was just tall enough for her to stand without bumping her head. This passage turned slowly to the right, and went on for some way, with several small doors that opened onto deserted, low rooms with broken furniture, and that looked just right for someone the size of Oracle. But the hall ended at a locked door. Colleen pulled out Doc's key and put it in the keyhole, and it opened with a click.

When they stepped through the doorway, they found themselves in a huge chamber with eight doors. A great round table with a hole in the center stood in the middle of the room.

Nous scrambled up on the table, crawled to the hole, and peered down.

"Deep," he said.

Oracle, grunting with the effort, also climbed up and walked across the table, thumping it with his staff, and then peered down into the hole.

Then with a serious look, in a singsong voice he chanted, "Ware, ware, Colligal, the welling wish is dangerful."

Then he thumped back across the table and sat on its edge, swinging his legs in the air beneath his gray tattered robe.

"The welling wish? The wishing well? This is the wishing well?" Colleen asked him.

But Oracle seemed oblivious now and was humming some tune, interrupting himself now and then with some unintelligible mumble.

"If this is the wishing well, then that means we can throw in a piece of gold and make a wish!" said Colleen.

Rose looked up at her from her pocket and said, "I have a piece of gold, Colleen. My little leprechaun pot seems to have made more. I'll give it to you and you can make a wish. Maybe you could wish that we could find the Waking Tree and set all the little people free and rescue your mom and my dad!"

"Let me see that," said Mrs. Wigglepox.

Indeed, Rose's pot now had two tiny lumps of gold in it.

"Well, would you look at that," said Mrs. Wigglepox. "You have a good heart, Rose, for your gold to multiply so quickly. That's how it works, you know. A pure heart brings pure gold, and that's what lets you do the real wishing. But wishing is tricky business. Both the leprechaun and her gold need refining and training. We've had precious little time for either."

"But Colleen would be making this wish, mother. Couldn't we try?" asked Rose. "She could wish for a good giant!"

"Ech!" said Nous. "Not leprechaun magic! Use goblin magic. Much stronger!"

"So," said Colleen thoughtfully. "We have a few choices before us. First, we can use the dark magic of the goblins to summon the ghost of Lugh. I can see how handy it would be to have a giant skeleton under one's control, especially when dealing with an army of goblins and a witch. Second, we could throw a piece of leprechaun gold into the wishing well and wish for a good giant to come along and do the job for us. Or third, we could do nothing, and miss our one big chance to break this terrible Spell that has bound your world for hundreds and hundreds of years."

"It's too risky either way!" said Mrs. Wigglepox.

Colleen looked at Nous, and then looked at Rose, who now held her tiny pot in her hands. A glint of gold sparkled in the magical light of the room.

Her mind raced. Which way should she go? She certainly didn't want to deal with Lugh again, but was this a chance to control a powerful weapon? What could she do with a fifty-foot skeleton-ghost who was bearing a magical hammer that could smash castles at her command? She could bring down the Witch's fortress with such a power and put an end to the goblin armies forever.

Such thoughts whirled through her mind, and she wrestled with herself for a moment. But then her good sense came back to her, and she shook her head.

"Mom and Dad always said that you can't make right by doing wrong," she said. "I'll try the wishing well. It's our only real chance."

Mrs. Wigglepox sighed and said, "Very well, Colleen. But remember, a wish will go astray if you have any poor intentions. One wayward thought while making your wish could bring disaster on us all. Are you sure you want to do this?"

Colleen swallowed hard and said, "Yes."

Rose smiled with glee, reached into her pot, and pulled out one of the tiny nuggets. It was just a tiny pebble to Colleen. As she held out her hand, Rose placed the bright metal in her palm.

Colleen climbed up onto the table, walked over to the hole, and gazed in.

Down, down it went, far out of sight, but it seemed that in those depths, just at the edge of vision before it fell away into blackness, a white mist swirled.

Colleen held her hand out over the Wishing Well, shut her eyes, paused for a moment, then said in a loud voice, "I wish that we had a giant with us who would smash the glass chamber!"

She turned her hand over, and the little nugget fell down into the well. Even as she did, she wondered what sort of giant might come. Would he be like the dead giant in the upper chamber? Or would he be like Lugh?

The dark depths of the Wishing Well suddenly flared with golden light, which shot upward and enveloped Colleen. Mrs. Wigglepox gasped. Oracle thumped his stick. Nous hissed. Lily and Rose dove down into Oracle's pocket. The castle suddenly trembled, and a low *BOOM* rumbled through the rock.

"The giant is here already!" cried Colleen, leaping out of the golden light, off the table, and down the hall, a smile on her face.

"Wait!" called Mrs. Wigglepox, but Colleen sped away.

Nous dashed after her, and Oracle thumped after them both, mumbling something indistinct under his breath. Colleen ran down the hall and stopped, seeing Badger nervously stamping his feet at the sound of another *BOOM*.

"Don't worry, boy, it's okay. Come on, I'll show you – it's a giant!" she said to the horse.

Untying him, she hopped on his back and together they trotted down the hall to the gate, where she dismounted and led him outside to the courtyard, expecting to see the great giant she had summoned smash the tower and the crystal chamber into rubble. But her expectancy turned to horror as a bellowing howl filled the air, followed by a smashing *BOOM* and the sound of shattering and falling rock. There in the courtyard by the tower was indeed a giant – the ghost of Lugh. The great leech that had attached itself to him was gone, but he was stained by brown and gray and black patches.

Badger neighed and reared, kicking his feet in the air at the huge skeleton. Lugh heard him and turned, and seeing them, screamed out his ear-splitting howl. In his bony fist, he held the great hammer that had sat by the gate. In his rage, he bellowed again and swung the hammer with tremendous force at the tower next to him. The hammer smashed through the white stone like toy building blocks, and as it did, it struck the crystal chamber. There was a terrific concussion as the chamber exploded, sending rock and glass and debris flying everywhere. Lugh himself went hurtling through the air directly toward Colleen and Badger. The horse reared again, tore the reins from Colleen's hands, and bolted out of the gate.

To Colleen's dismay, she watched as the sky shifted to a hazy red wall that reached down to the ground. Badger ran right through it and vanished, with Lugh flying right behind him, bellowing as he vanished. The sounds of battle suddenly filled the air. Horrified, she realized what had just happened. Lugh had gone back in time – right into the midst of the battle between Anastazi the Great and the Witch. That's what she had seen when she had stood on the parapet herself. And now Badger had also run right into the midst of it all.

"No!" screamed Colleen, and she ran after her horse.

"Colleen!" came a voice from behind, and someone roughly tackled her, sending them both tumbling off to one side, just as a huge block of stone fell smashing right where she had been. They rolled over and over, and then stopped, and Colleen realized it was Nous. He had saved her life.

"Nous, let me go! Badger has gone back in time and I have to go after him!" she cried.

"The Colleen must look!" hissed Nous, pointing at the castle.

She looked. The castle was crumbling. The explosion of the crystal chamber had been too much for the ancient structure, and now it was falling as they watched.

"The Colleen must go back! The others... the little people are still in there!" said Nous through clenched teeth.

Colleen looked once at the shifting red haze. It winked and went out.

"Badger!" she cried, tears streaming down her face.

But she knew what she had to do. She jumped to her feet and ran back into the crumbling castle and down the hall, with Nous right on her heels. Behind them came a terrible crashing sound as the wall in front of the gate collapsed, completely blocking their way out. They ran on, and soon met Oracle hobbling along in their direction. She picked him up, carrying him as she ran on.

Colleen paused only a moment at the wagon, putting Oracle down and leaping up into it and grabbing a sack of supplies, her staff, and Frederick's sword.

Then she said, "We've got to get down below – back to the wishing well chamber – it's the only safe place. Nous, can you carry Oracle?"

"On my back," he snarled, and Oracle climbed on, a gleeful look on his face.

Down they ran, with the terrible sounds of the falling castle above and around them. Within a few moments, they were there, and they came to a halt, panting.

"We should be safe down here," said Colleen.

But as soon as she said it, a huge crack began to spread across the ceiling and down the wall. Rock began to rain down around them, and the tunnels filled with debris and choking dust.

Colleen looked around frantically and then spotted the table. Could they hide under it... or...

"Into the well!" shouted Colleen. "It's our only hope!"

They climbed frantically up onto the table, helping Oracle, and being careful not to let the Wigglepox family fall from his pocket.

A huge block of stone suddenly dislodged from the ceiling, and Colleen shouted, "Jump!"

Down they plunged, falling into a white haze and down toward the sound of rushing water. The table above them was smashed into rubble as the ceiling collapsed upon it. As they fell, the voice of Mrs. Wigglepox rose to a shout.

"To the island of the Witch, to her very dungeons and to our families take us – this is my last wish!"

A golden light sprang up all around them, enveloping them as they fell down, down into the well.

Chapter 9 – The Pits

Colleen expected to plunge at any moment into the churning water that they could hear but not see, but in the instant that Mrs. Wigglepox made her wish, the world around them changed, and they found themselves standing in a dark, damp chamber of broken and piled stone. Beside them swirled a pool of dark slime, in which thick bubbles slowly burst, releasing a putrid stench that made them gag. It was the utter sense of despair, however, that crashed upon their hearts and struck them like a hammer blow. The atmosphere was thick with it.

All around, scores of ragged and weary-looking little people stood with tiny picks and shovels in their hands, toiling aimlessly against the wet and stinking earth. The *clink, clink* of their tools on the ground stopped as they all turned to look in wide-eyed amazement at the newcomers. The sight of Nous, however, sent them back to their work, their faces fallen and fearful.

Then, out of one dark corner, a large shadow moved. Nous moved in front of Colleen and crouched, ready to leap. She realized that he was defending her. As the shadow moved into the light of the lone torch that was fastened to the wall, Colleen's own fear and horror turned to absolute and utter joy, and she rushed past Nous with a shout.

"Mother!" she cried, bursting into tears and running forward to embrace her mother, whom she had not seen for nearly a year.

Colleen gripped her tightly and for a moment buried her face in her ragged brown dress before looking up into her face.

For a moment, Ellie McGunnegal looked down at her daughter with shock and disbelief in her face, and then pushed her away, backing against the far wall.

"Who are you?" said Ellie. Her voice was tired and strained. "Why have you come here to torment me?"

"It's me, Mom – it's Colleen! I've come to rescue you!" said Colleen in a strained and hurt voice.

Tears rolled down her face, but now they had turned from tears of joy to tears of bewilderment. Didn't her mother know her? What had the Witch and these goblins done to her?

Ellie moved sideways along the wall deeper into the shadows, and then said, "No, you are an illusion, like all the others. Leave me now! You are not real!"

"Mother!" cried Colleen. "I've come for you! I've been searching for you for weeks! Now I've found you, and we are going to get out of here and go home!"

Ellie glanced at Nous, then back at Colleen. "You are a mind trick – a mirage of this goblin. I will not listen to you or tell you anything!"

"It is the Pwca killer!" rasped Nous. "See, Nous told the Colleen about it! It is mad!"

"Mad!" shouted Ellie. "Mad! Yes! And madness haunts these dank caverns like night shades! Be gone from me! You are nothing but a fantasy of my madness!"

Colleen was weeping openly now. "Mother!" she cried. "It's not true! I am your daughter! I came through the mirror in the woods, just like you did! Frederick and I both came!"

"No!" cried Ellie.

Suddenly, there was a noise from some distance down the cavern, and loud, angry voices could be heard.

"Goblins come!" hissed Nous. "The Colleen must hide!"

"Mother!" whispered Colleen.

But Nous was pulling on her arm now, and he dragged her behind a mound of broken stone, and Oracle, still bearing the Wigglepox family in his pockets, quickly followed behind.

"Hush!" whispered Nous as they stooped low.

A moment later, three ugly goblins bearing torches and clubs, and a fourth goblin handling a wicked-looking whip, barged into the room.

"What's going on here!" he growled, cracking his whip in the air. "What's all the shouting about?"

Colleen contained her sobs, threw her hood up over her head, and then peeked over the pile of debris.

"Where's that big ugly one hiding? There it is! Come on out of the shadows and tell us what you've been yammering about this time," it said.

Colleen watched with dread as her mother shuffled forward into the torch light, her head down in an attitude of defeat and submission.

"That's right," said the big goblin in a mocking tone. "Come on and grovel for us a bit."

"It's gone loony," said another goblin. "I've always said it."

The other goblins laughed, and the big goblin said, "They all go mad."

He cracked his whip above Ellie's head, and she shrank down to the ground. All of the goblins laughed hysterically.

Colleen very nearly cried out, and would have run to her mother's side that very moment, had not the goblins' laughter quite suddenly ceased. The air of the chamber seemed to grow thick, the ground trembled, and the acrid smell of sulfur filled the chamber. The goblins backed against a wall, Ellie crawled back into the shadows, and all the little people scattered.

The atmosphere grew hot, and with a sudden roar that sounded like the beating of great wings, a black choking smoke filled the room, and then with a terrible resounding *SNAP*, it seemed to come together and form, for an instant, a gigantic shadow of some terrifying lizard-like creature with huge black wings. The smoke swirled, carrying the horrible vision with it, and in its place stood a hooded black figure bearing a black staff whose end burned with a red fire.

Colleen knew instantly who this was. The Witch had come.

Chapter 10 – The Waking of the Little People

Adol McGunnegal was exhausted. He had followed the trail as long as the light of the moon had held, but that had not been for long, and he dared not wander aimlessly in the dark and risk losing it. He had climbed a huge tree, gripping the massive ridges and knobs in its bark until he reached the lowest branches some thirty feet above the ground.

The tree was so massive that the first branch he came to was easily four feet across. He had hauled himself up and onto it and found that a good-sized hole was right there above the limb. He cautiously had felt inside and, to his amazement, found it smooth and clean, not at all rotten and full of insects as he had expected. He had crawled in, feeling his way inch by inch in the dark. Once inside, he had laid down with his head near the entrance, listening for anything else that might try to climb after him.

It had not been long before the baying of the night creatures came close, and then stopped. They had lost his scent at the tree, had run around and around, and then had run off into the night, howling in frustration. But he lay listening hour after hour, forcing himself to remain awake, but from time to time, some wave of weariness would sweep over him, until finally he fell into a deep sleep.

Morning came, but Adol did not wake. Rather, with every wave of the Spell, his sleep deepened. His dreams drew him further and further into a land of forgetfulness, and there he found himself searching, searching for Colleen and Ellie, all the while close on their trail, and ever pursued by beasts that he would fight off, only to face more and more of them. His dreams exhausted him further, and he fell deeper under the Spell until his dreams became his reality, and he could no longer distinguish one from another. He had fallen into the dream world of the sleeping forest, from which few had escaped in thousands of years.

In his dream, Adol crouched low to the ground, following an old trail – a dried hoof print about a week old. He lifted his eyes to look ahead for more signs, when suddenly, the air around him quivered, and the ground trembled. The world began to blur and, without warning, it vanished, and then Adol was suddenly and truly awake. He shook himself and sat up. How long had he been sleeping? It was morning, and he could see by the dim light that the inside of this tree was smooth, even polished, and the hollow space in which he sat ran upward into the darkness.

Several small openings like little doors were placed on either side of the hollow.

He wondered where he was. Was it last night he had climbed up here? Or two nights ago? He could not remember. But he was terribly hungry and thirsty. He felt his face and was surprised to find nearly a week's growth of beard. How long had he slept? Crawling over to the entrance, he cautiously poked his head out and looked about. Nothing stirred. It was a nearly dead forest, devoid of life – except, of course, for those things that he had met in the night.

He was about to crawl out on the limb and make his way down when he heard a distant sound coming from far off. At first, it was very faint, but within moments, it grew in intensity and power. It sounded like a great wind blowing, and he could hear the creaking and snapping of trees as it approached. Adol's eyes went wide as he sucked in air through clenched teeth. He knew that sound. He had heard it once before when a freak gale had swept across the coast of Ireland. It had sounded like a train coming, and it had nearly torn the roof from their house as it battered their farm. But this was far bigger. So big that he could not imagine what it must be.

He scrambled out on the branch, clipped the hammer to his belt, and with as much speed as he dared, climbed down the big tree's trunk, with the distant rumble growing closer. It was coming fast.

He was ten feet from the ground when it hit him with such force that he was torn from the tree. He went flying through the forest – trees, branches, leaves, and dirt racing around him and scouring his face and arms like sandpaper.

He slammed hard into a tree, and the wind was knocked out of him. Then he was carried on, hitting another, then another, and he was sure that he was going to die.

Then, just as suddenly as it had come, the wind passed. He tumbled over and over and came to a halt. Leaves and dust fluttered to the ground, and all was still.

Blood trickled from his mouth and his eyes flickered open for one moment. He knew that he was hallucinating, for he thought that in front of his face fluttered a tiny, shining young woman with silver wings and a green dress. He groaned and tried to raise his head. But the vision faded to black, and he collapsed in the leaves and knew no more.

* * *

All around Adol's unconscious form, something began to happen. The air was lighter now, as though in the passing of the storm some great heaviness had been blown completely away, leaving both ruin and, somehow, relief in its passing. The green fairy fluttered away, flying high above the trees, surveying the forest. The ruin was disastrous. Fallen trees were everywhere, some two or three feet across, and the forest floor was littered with branches and leaves and debris. Dead and dying trees lay prostrate, having fallen toward the north, blown down for as far as her eyes could see. And farther north, the blast wave continued on, mile after mile, beyond her sight. She lingered there for a moment, astonished and in shock. Then she sped down into the forest. It was waking now, and its wrath would be great.

She sped on through the stretching and yawning trees, searching for anyone who was there. And one by one, she found them – gnomes, leprechauns, pixies, fairies – all who had fallen asleep under the Spell were now awakening. Some, she knew, would never awake now, and they would find their final resting place beneath their fallen trees. But those who emerged, bleary-eyed and unsure, she gathered together, and told them of the man in the forest who lay dying also. Within an hour, some fifty of them had gathered themselves together and held a council.

"He doesn't look like a Witch's Man," said one gnome, opening one of Adol's eyes and peering in.

"No, no Witch's Man," said the green fairy. "But where did he come from?"

"Is he a wizard then?" asked a leprechaun.

"Did he cast a spell that went all wrong? Look at our forest!" said another.

"There's some magic about him," said a yellow pixie. "It's in his blood for sure."

"But it's not little people magic," said a gnome.

"I'd want to say elvish," said a blue fairy who was fluttering over him. "But he looks like a man to me."

"Something has happened, and not just to the forest," said the leprechaun. "We are… we are awake!"

"Is the Spell broken?" asked another.

An old gnome sniffed at the air. "Blown away, at least for a time," he said.

"What shall we do with the man?" asked a fairy. "Do you think he blew the Spell away?"

"Who knows? I say we take him to the Dwarf," said another old gnome with a white beard and red pointed hat. "If he's still alive, that is."

"Aye, to the Dwarf!" called another.

"Leave it to us!" said the green fairy.

"Yes, leave it to us!" said the yellow pixie.

A pink fairy joined them, and together they zoomed round Adol in a circle and sprinkled fairy and pixie dust all over him. Then each hovered over him, and as the other little people watched, Adol began to float in the air. They drew him by their magic up and over the forest and southward to the only place where they thought a bigger person might still live – to the house of Doc the Dwarf.

Chapter 11 – The Last Island

Frederick gagged and coughed violently, expelling water from his lungs as his mind struggled back to consciousness. He was lying on a sandy beach, and the sun was rising in incredible colors and hues over a deep blue ocean. *My, how beautiful!* was his first thought.

Then he remembered the night before. *The wave!* It had carried them for a long, long time – just how long, he had no idea. Had it been hours or days? How long had they struggled to keep their heads above water, hoping beyond hope that the rope that bound them together would not break? And how long had he been lying on the beach? He wiped his eyes and looked around. The rope had broken or had slipped off of him. It was nowhere to be seen.

Slowly, he stood and began to brush wet sand and seaweed off of his soaked clothes. He smelled of the sea. It was not an unpleasant smell, he thought – but the grit and stickiness of the salt made him wish he could find a fresh pool of water to bathe in.

Fresh water, he thought. *I'll be needing that soon.*

He was amazed to find that the sword was still at his side. He drew it out and emptied water from the sheath. It glittered golden in the morning sun, as if it were aflame. Frederick gazed at it for a moment, thinking that it looked different somehow – brighter and keener than he remembered. But thoughts of his friends quickly came to him, so he sheathed it and looked up and down the beach. Quiet waves washed peacefully on the sand in odd contrast with the violence of the tidal wave that had carried him here.

The beach stretched away in both directions, disappearing around a distant bend, and some distance inland, he could see a mound or ridge of rock of some sort, like a broken spire. It looked almost man-made, rising dark against the deep blue of the eastern sky.

He started walking north along the shore, looking for any signs that another human being had come this way. The beach was bare of any footprints, and the only life he saw were scuttling crabs and stranded starfish. The light gradually grew with the rising sun, and he walked for about a quarter of an hour before he saw something lying up ahead on the beach. He paused, straining his eyes for a moment, then began to run – someone was there, lying in the sand. A large wave washed ashore, momentarily lapping around the body. Running to the prone figure, he dropped down on his knees beside it and carefully rolled it over.

"Helga!" he shouted.

She did not move, and did not appear to be breathing. He frantically felt for a pulse in her wrist, a trick a doctor had showed him once. He could feel nothing. Quickly, he turned her head to one side, then scrambled around to her feet and began to bend her knees up to her chest and back again. Water poured from her lungs. He continued doing this until the water stopped flowing from her mouth.

Another large wave washed up the beach, soaking both of them again. Frederick grabbed her arms and tried to pull her up the beach. But she was heavy, and her soaked clothes made her even more so. He hauled and heaved, but was getting nowhere. Desperately, he knelt beside her and untied her life vest. Placing both hands on the center of her chest, he pushed down, then let go, pushed down and let go. But Helga lay limply, unresponsive to his efforts.

"*Helga!*" he screamed.

Unsure of what else to do, he desperately he breathed into her mouth, forcing air into her lungs. Again, he pumped her heart. He was desperate now, and tears were streaming down his face. Another wave lapped at Helga's feet.

"*Come on!*" he cried. "*Breathe!*"

Again, he breathed air into her lungs. He tried to pump her legs again. "*Breathe!*" he shouted angrily. "*Please, Helga, breathe!*"

Again and again, he tried, but at last, exhausted, he collapsed on top of her prone body and lay sobbing. He cradled her head in his arms as another wave threatened to roll over them. Somehow, he pushed her into a semi-seated position and got his arms under hers from behind. He heaved with all his might and dragged her a few inches up the beach. Again, he pulled, and again he gained a few inches. Then again. More water spurted from her mouth each time he hauled her a few inches inland.

Soon, he was totally spent, and all of his efforts were getting them no further. He laid her back down again and beat on her chest frantically, breathed into her mouth, pumped her legs. But she did not respond. Exhausted, he collapsed beside her and wept.

"I'm sorry, Helga!" he cried. "I'm so sorry! I tried! I really tried!"

He stood after some minutes, still crying and wiping his eyes, wondering what he should do.

"I'm sorry!" he whispered. "I have to find the others. I promise I'll come back for you, Helga. I won't leave you here! But the others could be hurt too... I have to find them! The professor will know what to do!"

He began to run down the beach the way he had come, desperately calling for help, praying he would not find the others dead as well.

* * *

As he fled with sorrow and grief from Helga's seemingly lifeless form, a hint of pink suddenly blushed on her cheeks. Her chest rose and fell once, then again. Her eyes fluttered open, and she began to gag violently. Weakly, she rolled to one side and vomited seawater. She gasped for air, and a spasm of coughing took her for several minutes. She was alive. But Frederick saw none of this. He was far down the beach now, still weeping and calling for the McGunnegals and Professor McPherson.

Chapter 12 – Helga's Awakening

When Helga's body finally calmed from its terrible coughing and gagging, and as her mind slowly cleared, she looked about, and memories of the terrifying night in the sea came flooding back to her. She shuddered, remembering only darkness, the rushing of water, and the straining of the rope for hour after hour as they were propelled forward by the wave.

Where were the others? Had they survived? She sat up slowly, wiping her limp and sticky hair out of her face. A wave broke on the beach and lapped at her knees. Unsteadily, she rose to her feet and coughed again. A large wave rolled in, knocking her down and wiping away Frederick's footprints from the sand. She crawled on until the waves were behind her, then she rose unsteadily and stumbled up the beach toward a line of trees.

Then she noticed it – a piece of the ship. It was lying just beyond the tree line where the wave must have dashed it ashore. It appeared to be the bow of the ship, broken off from the rest of the vessel. The wall and lower door that had separated the cargo bay from the rest of the ship's lower deck was, amazingly, still intact. The big iron sliding bolt locks that held the door in place were still secure. This piece of the ship must have remained afloat and survived the ride all the way to the island. She hurried up to it as fast as her wobbly legs would carry her, then slowly walked about the wreckage.

"It is still intact!" she said aloud. "That means that the food and water and the car are still inside!"

But she was weak and needed to rest. She sat down in the shade of the wreck and looked about. Had the others survived? Had they been washed ashore as well? Or simply swept away in the sea, still stranded out there somewhere? Was she alone? Fear rose up in her, but she steeled herself and, gathering her wits, decided that, in spite of her weakness, she needed to do something.

Looking about, she found a long bamboo stick. It was just barely long enough for her to reach up to the bolts and attempt to unlock them. The first one gave her no trouble, sliding with some ease to one side, but the second one was stuck, and it took her some minutes to finally dislodge it. She stepped quickly back, for as she finally knocked the bolt to one side, the door groaned and came flying downward, smacking into the jungle floor with a crash, forming a steep ramp.

A wall of water several feet deep came pouring out of the hold and nearly knocked her to the ground. But as the last of it drained, Helga carefully climbed up the ready-made ramp and into the cargo bay. It was a total wreck, with boxes and barrels strewn about, many broken open and having spilled out their contents. But the car was still intact and tied to the floor. She climbed up into it and inspected its interior. To her surprise, it was almost completely undamaged. Climbing out, she carefully released the ropes that held the car to the floor and then climbed back in. She then found the parking brake and released it.

Slowly the car rolled forward, and Helga grabbed hold of the brake handle, ready to slow the car as it rolled down the ramp. Down it went, picking up speed, and Helga pulled the brake. There was an audible *PING* as something snapped, and the car continued down the ramp, out of the woods and down the sandy beach faster and faster.

"Eeeahhh!" screamed Helga and she pulled the brake lever again and again while trying the steer the out-of-control car. Just before driving right into the ocean, she turned the wheel hard, and the car stopped in the sand.

Breathing a sigh of relief, she climbed out and inspected the auto. She was not very familiar with these new steam engines, but had ridden in them enough times, and had watched the driver start and drive and steer, so she felt confident that she could do the same.

After several unsuccessful attempts, she finally managed to start the boiler and went back to the ship to rummage through the supplies. She returned to the car with an armload of food and a flask of water, along with a knife, a pistol, and a pouch of gun powder, and found that the boiler had built up a good head of steam, and the interior of the car had dried considerably in the sun. She loaded her goods into the back and climbed aboard.

When she engaged the drive chain, the car rolled down the beach on the wet, packed sand with a white puff of smoke. Waves lapped at the wheels as she drove away in the opposite direction that Frederick had gone. Soon she was out of sight, and once again, the never-ending ocean wiped away all trace that she had ever been there.

Chapter 13 – Reunion

When Aonghus woke, he found himself lying at the edge of a beach among palm trees. Henny was sitting in the sand next to him.

"I was watching you sleep," she said calmly.

"You okay?" he said, sitting up and looking her over.

"Yes. That was some ride. We washed all the way up to the trees last night and got plopped right here. You were so tired that you fell right to sleep. Do you remember?" replied Henny.

The memories rushed back. He did remember. The wave had begun to grow higher, and then broke on something. The last he remembered were the ropes snapping and him gripping Henny as they tumbled over and over beneath the waves until they hit sand and were tossed ashore.

"Have you seen the others?" he asked urgently.

"No," she replied. "I guess we should go look for them. They're all right, though. I just know."

Henny did have ways of *seeing* things. She had always been like that. She could find things that were lost, somehow knowing just where to look.

"Come on then, lass," he said, standing. "Can you walk all right?"

Henny stretched and rubbed her arms and legs.

"Just a bit scratched up, that's all," she said. "But you look a bit bruised on your chest."

Aonghus looked down. His shirt had been torn off in the storm, revealing his tightly muscled chest and abdomen. There was a wicked-looking bruise across his pectoral muscles. He touched it and winced.

"Oh, it's nothing, Sprout. I'll be fine. Come on, then, let's get to looking. Which way do you think we ought to go?" he replied.

Henny looked down the beach in both directions and then back into the woods.

"Well, there's Bib right there," she said, pointing into the underbrush.

Aonghus rushed to where Henny was pointing and saw a foot protruding from a matted pile of weeds.

He ran over, pushed the brush aside, and found Bib lying on her side. She was breathing easily and appeared to be asleep.

"Bib?" he said quietly.

Her eyes fluttered open, and she looked up at him. A frown crossed her face, then a look of dismay. Then she reached up, grabbed his neck, and hugged him.

"Oh, Aonghus, what happened to us? Is everyone okay?" she said.

"Henny says she thinks the others are okay. But we haven't found them yet. Can you walk? Here, let me help you up," he answered.

Slowly she stood, and felt a pain in her ribs and right leg.

"I'm all right," she said. "But I could use a little rest. How about I just stay here for a bit and check on this stretch of jungle?"

"No way," said Aonghus. "We stick together. And I can see that you're not all right. Your leg is hurt, and I'll bet those ribs are mighty sore. You were nearly crushed by that kraken, you know."

"True," said Bib, gingerly touching her side. "It's not every day you have these sorts of adventures. All right, then, can you find me a stick or something to support me?"

Henny walked to a pile of bamboo and pulled out a sturdy cane.

"How's this?" she asked.

Bib took it and leaned on it.

"That should do," she said. "I think I can limp along with this. Just no marathons, please."

"Down the beach that way," said Henny, pointing. "Look, there's Frederick."

They waved to him and shouted, but as he drew near, they saw that he was in great distress, and was crying.

"Oh, Aonghus, she's dead! I tried to save her, but I couldn't!" he wailed as he ran up to them.

"Who?" said Aonghus urgently, "Who are you talking about?"

"Helga," he said through his tears. "I found her on the beach. She wasn't breathing. I tried to save her, but I couldn't."

"Hold on, lad. Are you sure? Can you take me to her?" he said.

"She's way up the beach," he said, pointing back the way he came.

Aonghus was about to run in that direction when a call from behind stopped him.

He turned to see Professor McPherson, Abbe, and Bran coming up the beach, looking ragged and worn, and supporting one another, but alive.

"Thank God you're all safe!" said McPherson as they hurried to meet them. "We were so worried! But we were all still tied together when the wave broke, and the three of us tumbled ashore at the same time. Knocked clean out by the landing. Frederick, are you all right?"

Quickly, Frederick told the three of them what had happened.

"Come quickly," said McPherson.

"Aonghus, please stay with everyone and come along as quickly as you can. Bran, you come with Frederick and me," said McPherson.

"Yes, sir," said Aonghus, and he carefully picked up Bib and said, "Let's go. Sorry, Bib, we need to hurry."

Frederick, Bran, and the professor ran down the beach, but when they reached the place where Helga had been, she was nowhere in sight.

Frederick looked about and said, "I'm sure this was the place. She was lying right here. The waves were washing around her!"

A fearful look washed over him, and he grew pale.

"What if she's washed out to sea?" he said in horror.

They looked out at the ocean, then up and down the beach, but could see nothing.

"Are you sure this was the spot?" asked Bran. "Maybe it was a bit further on?"

"I'm pretty sure," said Frederick, looking about desperately.

Just then, he noticed the wreckage of the ship and pointed, his mouth dropping open.

"Would you look at that!" said Bran. "Do you think she revived and went over there?"

They ran up the beach to the wreck and immediately noticed footprints near the wreck.

"Someone has been here," said McPherson. "And look – tire tracks. But they disappear down the beach – no doubt washed away by the waves."

"Do you think that someone has taken the car?" asked Bran. "Maybe it was Helga."

"Perhaps," said McPherson. "Or someone else took the car and Helga, as well. It could be that someone else found her and has taken her away to care for her."

"Or bury her," said Frederick, still distressed.

"There are many possibilities," said McPherson.

"Well, we can't go after them now, not with the others back the other way. I say we stick together and follow this beach," said Bran.

"Look here," said Frederick, gaining some hope that Helga was, in fact, not dead, but had been rescued. "Someone has gotten into the food crates. Maybe we ought to make this our base camp for the day. The cargo hold there will give us some shelter if a storm comes."

"An excellent and practical idea," said McPherson, smiling at Frederick. "Not everyone would think clearly in a desperate situation like this. That is the mark of someone who knows how to survive."

Frederick wiped his eyes and tried to smile.

"Thank you, sir," he said. "Shouldn't we go back for the others, though?"

"Aonghus will bring them along shortly. Come now, we need to rest for a few moments, and then sort out what we can here."

They began to go through the supplies, and found some of the crates of food and water were broken and spoiled by the ocean water, but a good many were still intact and even dry inside.

Bran began to gather wood outside for a fire while Frederick and Professor McPherson organized the inside of the ship.

"Frederick," said McPherson as they were moving barrels about. "I see that you still have that sword. How did you manage that?"

"I'm not sure, Professor. I woke up, and it was still fastened to me. It is a magic sword, you know. It must be. The Lady Danu gave me the sheath to put it in. It's actually the *second* magic sword I've held. But I left the other one back in the Land of the Little People. I hope that Colleen still has it. It was quite amazing too."

Professor McPherson looked at him. "Son, you have had, in the last month, more adventures than most of the population on the planet Earth will have in their entire lifetimes."

"Do you really believe me, Professor? Do you really believe that I was there and did all that stuff and came back?" he asked, a little afraid of what the answer would be.

Professor McPherson paused from his work, put a hand on Frederick's shoulder, and said, "If I were any other man, I would call you a foolish child and a liar, or gone mad. But I have had an adventure or two in my time, as well. One day, I will tell you more about those adventures. But for now, I will just say this – you and I and all these amazing McGunnegals, and maybe Helga too, God willing, are about to do something so astonishing that no one will believe any of us if we ever get back home."

"Really, Professor? And what is that?" he asked.

"Don't you know where we are?" McPherson asked.

"Well, on some remote island in the middle of the Atlantic, I suppose. Near to Bermuda, I would guess," replied Frederick.

Professor McPherson reached into his pocket and pulled out the compass that he had rescued from the ship. He held it in his hand for Frederick to see.

The arrow was spinning round and round.

"I thought it always pointed somewhere – like north," said Frederick.

"Ah, yes, most do. But this compass always points to where you want to go.

And when you get there, then it does this."

"It spins?" asked Frederick.

"Yes. It spins," he replied.

"You mean this is it? This is where we've been trying to get to for the past week? This is … *Atlantis?*" said Frederick incredulously.

"Well, we have arrived at the place we intended. Whether it is the last remnant of Atlantis – I cannot yet say. And how we survived this journey to this point, I cannot say. We should have died out there in the ocean. But by some Providence, we are here."

Bran walked in just then and said, "Well, there's no lack of firewood. Do you suppose we ought to build a signal fire to attract a rescue vessel? Oh! The others are coming up the beach!" he said, and sped away to meet them.

McPherson and Frederick walked down the ramp and onto the beach to see Aonghus, Bib, Abbe, and Henny drawing near.

"Well," said Aonghus as they drew near, "at least we'll have shelter tonight. And I would dearly love to get out of these clothes."

"We all would," said Abbe. "Were any of the clothing crates saved?"

"It looks like everything was still in here except two very important things – the car and Helga," said McPherson.

"She took the car," said Henny, looking down the beach. "She's a long way away now."

"Well, that's a fine thing," said Bib. "Frederick tries to rescue her, she plays dead, and then goes off with the only transportation on this forsaken island. Just where are we anyway? We must be somewhere near Bermuda, don't you think?"

"Now, now," replied the professor. "We don't know what has happened to the car or Helga. I pray that she's all right, but I think that we should not go after her right yet, nor make a fire. We don't know what else a fire might attract – good or ill. But we must change and get into dry things. Look – here in the cargo hold, we packed extra clothes for all of us, and they're dryer than what we are wearing now. You ladies come in here and find what will fit you. We men will go out and gather more wood, for later, of course, when we do light a fire, and scout the immediate area for any more signs of Helga."

Aonghus walked up the ramp and put Bib carefully down. She limped over to a crate and sat on it. The girls then busied themselves looking through the boxes and found some decent britches and shirts that fit them, and these they gladly put on and then took their sticky sea-soaked clothes outside to dry.

"There are some blankets here too," said Abbe, opening a crate.

"All the comforts of home!" joked Bib.

Henny found a comb among the wreckage and began combing out her long golden hair, then passed it on to Bib when she was done.

Abbe looked at her two sisters and smiled. "We sure are in a fix, aren't we?" she said. "What tales we'll have to tell when we get home! And there's more to come, I'll wager. Why, there's this whole island to explore. Come on, then, let's see where the men are."

As the girls walked down the ramp, Frederick and Aonghus were coming through the jungle with armloads of sticks, and Bran and the professor were examining something down on the beach. Bran reached down, picked it up, and they walked back toward them together.

"Look here, Frederick," he said as they approached. "It's that tooth or whatever it is from the kraken."

He handed it to Frederick, who took it and said, "Thanks, Bran, I forgot all about this!"

Then he took a deep breath, remembering nearly being eaten alive.

"That was something else, wasn't it?" he said.

Professor McPherson looked at all of them with admiration and affection.

"You children are truly remarkable people," he said. "You have left your home, gone on a sea journey, survived a hurricane, were attacked by a sea monster, were nearly struck by a meteor, have ridden a wave in the open ocean for who knows how long, been shipwrecked, washed up on a seemingly deserted island, and you stand here talking about how adventurous it all is! Your parents truly raised you well."

His eyes lingered on Frederick for a moment and then he said, "Well, we have been through quite a bit together. I only wish you...."

"Professor," interrupted Abbe, "please, stop apologizing to us. We're in this

605

all together. We're all safe and sound – just a few bruises here and there, and I'm sure Helga is fine too. Stop blaming yourself for it all."

"That's right," said Aonghus. "It does no good to blame anyone."

The professor looked at them with even greater respect and replied, "Well said, my friends! Let's set up camp here and rest. I think we all need it."

After the boys and the professor had also changed their clothes, they set about organizing all of the supplies and cleaning and drying the wreckage of the ship so that they could use it as a shelter. When they were finally done, the inside had dried, thanks to a warm breeze blowing in from the sea, and they stretched out blankets on the floor.

"You all rest for a while, children. I will keep watch," said McPherson, and he sat down at the door and gazed out over the ocean.

In spite of the hardness of the floor of the wrecked ship, all six of them were almost instantly asleep. It was many hours later that Aonghus was awakened by the professor gently shaking him. The sun had nearly set, and McPherson whispered, "Aonghus, I'm afraid I can't keep my eyes open any longer. Would you mind watching for a while, and wake Bran if you grow weary?"

Aonghus sat up and yawned. "Of course," he whispered, and crept to the doorway, while the professor took his spot and immediately fell into a deep sleep.

* * *

Aonghus stared out over the water, watching the gentle waves wash in and out against the beach. It was peaceful here on this island, and if it had been just himself and Bran here, he would think it great fun. But the thought of his three sisters and young Frederick stranded here with him brought their situation into sharp focus in his mind. He was responsible for their safety, and he would do all he could to get them home as quickly as possible.

But they had come so far, and they had arrived. The professor had shown him the compass, and said that this was the island they had aimed for. He could not help but want to explore it and see what secrets it might hold.

And could this place hold the key – the doorway into another world, where Colleen was still trapped? Hours more rolled by, and still everyone slept. The sun disappeared, blackness filled the night, and the stars winked in one by one, until they blazed in the heavens like a million fiery diamonds.

Around midnight, Bran woke and came and sat next to him.

"Isn't it amazing?" whispered Aonghus, waving at the night sky.

Bran gazed in silence at the incredible wonder illuminating the heavens.

"You know," he whispered, "every time I think I've seen the most amazing thing in God's Creation, it's not long before I find something even grander. Do you think it will always be like that?"

Aonghus thought for a while and said, "I imagine so. It's a big, big universe, or so they say."

Bib woke, hearing their quiet words, and limped over to her brothers and sat down with them.

"Brilliant!" she whispered. "They say the universe is so big that even if you could walk to the nearest star, you would go and go all your life long and never get anywhere near it."

Now the other children woke, and they quietly moved down the ramp and, arm in arm, went and sat on the beach, leaving the professor to rest.

"I made a wish a few days ago," said Frederick quietly.

"What did you wish for?" asked Abbe.

"I was out on the deck of the ship – Henny was with me. And the sky was like this, except that it was reflecting in the sea that night. It was so still! I wished that I could sail out there in the sky – into space. I wonder what's out there?" he said.

They all sat staring up for some time before Henny answered.

"You wished on a star, didn't you?" she asked.

Frederick looked over at her. Her hair shimmered in the starlight and her innocent face seemed for a moment to have a light of its own.

"I did," he said simply.

"Then your wish will come true," she replied.

None of the others snickered at this or thought that she was just being a child with such simple faith. The events of the past month had begun to change their way of thinking about things. Once, they might have played along fondly with Henny's little-girl games. Now they were beginning to think that anything might be possible.

After a long time, Bran spoke. "It's so quiet up there."

"What do you mean, Bran?" asked Abbe.

"I mean, here we have our voices and the voice of the sea. But up there – I can *feel* the silence. It seems so vast! I feel as though if I contemplate it any longer, it will just swallow me up," he whispered in awe.

Again, they sat for some time without speaking, until Frederick said, "Maybe silence is the language of eternity."

His young face was turned upward, and the brilliant stars sparkled in his wide eyes. In that moment, the statement seemed fitting and profound.

With that thought, they simply stared into the unfathomable depths of space, giving themselves over to the profound vision.

Chapter 14 – The King in the Sea

Sunrise came, and they had all drifted off to sleep except for Bran, who had remained alert, but had neither seen nor heard anything except the steady wash of the waves.

Frederick was the first of the others to open his eyes and sit up. The sky was clear and the air warm, and the presence of the sea filled his senses. His mind was clear, and he felt more rested than he could ever remember. He stretched and stood, looking around. Bran put a finger to his lips, indicating that they should let the others rest as long as they needed to. But it was not long before the sun woke them as well, and each one of them opened their eyes and felt that same sense of calm and peace deep within them.

"There's something really special about this place," said Abbe. "I can feel it."

"It's a magic place," said Henny.

"Yes, I believe you're right," said Frederick. "And it's mighty good magic. I've been to magic places, but they didn't feel like this. Not nearly so... wholesome."

"Well, good morning," said a voice from behind them.

They turned to see the professor coming down the beach toward them. He too appeared to be well rested.

"Did you sleep well?" he asked.

"Wonderful, Professor," said Frederick, and they all agreed.

"Good," he replied. "Then let's have some breakfast. Bib, how are you feeling this morning?"

Bib gently prodded her ribs and then carefully put weight on her injured leg.

"It's so strange – I feel almost completely well this morning. It's almost as though I was not even injured," she said, amazed.

"Aonghus – look at your chest," said Bran.

Aonghus looked down and touched the place where the terrible bruises had been. They were nearly gone.

"I told you it's a magic place," said Henny.

"Come." The professor laughed. "There are no doubt more surprises waiting for us today."

As they gathered together supplies, Professor McPherson said that the only thing he could recollect from his visit to this island several decades ago was that there was a rocky outcropping that stretched from some distance inland to the shore, and that it was in a tall spire of rock that he had found the cave.

"That is what we must search for," he said.

The day was clear and beautiful as they set out, and they made their way along the beach. Crabs danced and fought among driftwood and shells and seaweed, and gulls called and soared.

They had walked for about an hour when they rounded a corner on the shore, and could see a rocky outcropping in the distance. It extended from some distance inland and went out beyond the beach, ending in jagged rock formations that protruded from the sea floor like rough and broken black teeth.

There, inland about a quarter mile, was the spire of rock that they had seen earlier. In the clear light of day, they could see that it was actually an ancient tower surrounded by broken stone buildings, all overgrown with vines and moss and ferns.

"Do you remember any of this?" Aonghus asked McPherson.

"Not like this," he said in a hushed voice. "It was night when I stumbled upon it, and when I left, I was out of my mind. The memories are like a dream that I can't quite remember."

They continued along the beach until they came to the rocky outcropping, and could see that it was actually a great broken stretch of wall that spread outward into the sea and disappeared among the jagged spires that still protruded from the ocean floor.

"This must have been incredible before it was abandoned," said Abbe. "Look at the size of the blocks of stone – they must be twenty feet across!"

As they approached the barnacle and slime-covered blocks, they saw that there was a paved path some thirty feet wide that ran along its length, and although largely overgrown with grasses and fern, it was still fairly visible.

"This must have been a road of sorts," said Frederick. "Look, it runs right into the ocean. I wonder how much of this place is under water?"

"Who can say?" answered the professor. "But it would seem that we must follow this path inland to reach the tower. Come."

The shattered length of wall gradually became less broken as they followed it inland and, before long, they came to an intact arch that was completely covered with thick, green vegetation, and through which the road continued on toward the tower. They went through this archway, looking about at ancient stone buildings that stood in silence along the way.

The path led them to the right and around the base of the great tower, and as they looked back toward the ocean, they could see that, at high tide, the waves washed even to the very place they were walking, for mollusks, seaweed and barnacles covered much of the walkway. The land sloped gently down some quarter mile to where low tide now splashed against fallen stone.

They looked up at the tower. At its base, broken stone led to a gaping hole in the seaward side, giving the appearance of a jagged maw held open in a silent moan, a last testament to whatever disaster had brought ruin upon this place and its people. A chill ran down Frederick's spine, and he shuddered. He looked at Professor McPherson and saw that he too was staring with wide eyes at the gaping mouth.

"This is it," McPherson whispered.

Slowly, they made their way among the slick rocks and cautiously entered the open passage. The light was dim inside, and Bib kicked something hollow, sending it rolling away. She screamed, and the sound of her voice echoed in the chamber. She put her hand over her mouth as she looked down at what she had kicked. A grotesquely shaped skull lay there next to a twisted skeleton. As their eyes adjusted, they drew close together, for before them stretched a field of bones – dozens of them, and all in some way deformed or misshapen.

"This is a tomb," whispered Aonghus.

"No," said Bran. "It's a battlefield."

He reached down and lifted a black shaft from the bony hand of one of the fallen skeletons. What had once been a spear crumbled to dust at his touch. Now they noticed bits of weapons and armor among the bones, and as they made their way inward, a sense of foreboding filled their minds.

"What are these things?" whispered Bib. "Many of them are small, like children. But they are so disfigured! Some barely seem human. Look at their skulls!"

Indeed, many of the skulls were elongated or twisted or had bulbous protrusions of bone sticking from them.

Suddenly, Frederick realized what they reminded him of.

"These are goblins!" he said.

"Goblins!" said Aonghus. "Frederick, keep that sword ready."

The sword rang as Frederick drew it from its sheath, and it flashed in the dim light. A strange feeling came over him, and he said, "It's angry..."

"What's angry, Frederick?" asked Abbe.

But he only looked at the sword, which now seemed to be glowing ever so faintly. Then the memory of the Lady Danu filled his mind, and he knew without a shadow of a doubt what he must do next.

"*He* is here!" he whispered, and he began to move slowly forward.

"What are you talking about, Frederick?" asked Aonghus. "And where are you going?"

But he did not hear them. There was another voice in his mind now, a voice bidding him forward, a voice whispering to him.

"*Come!*" it said in his mind.

Frederick held the sword before him, and with every step, it began to shine brighter and brighter, until it illumined the whole chamber around them. Now they saw clearly what was all around the room – bones upon bones – some broken and smashed, and others whole and seemingly undamaged by the ravages of time. But what gripped them all and tore their eyes from the shades around them was a raised dais at the end of the room. Steps led upward, decorated with more of the fallen dead. At its top was a magnificent throne of gold and gems, and seated upon that throne was the form of a man clad in silver and gold armor. His head was bowed, and they could not see his face.

Henny gave a cry and hid behind Aonghus. They moved slowly forward, Frederick leading the way. He reached the bottom step and the sword burned brighter.

"Wait, Frederick!" warned the professor.

But he did not wait. Slowly, he climbed the steps, making his way through the bones. He could see the man clearly now, and he half expected to find the bare face of a skeleton wrapped in armor and seated there. But it was no grinning skull that greeted him as he reached the top of the dais and stood before the seated form, but the grim, pale face of one who appeared to be sleeping. His armor was tattered and caked in sea salt, and his golden hair hung in limp strands from beneath a silver crown that sat on his noble head. The man's hands lay limply, palm upward in his lap, as though he were waiting to be handed something.

The sword was blazing so brightly now that it hurt Frederick's eyes. But he knew that he had found the king in the sea that the Lady had spoken of, and now he knew what he must do. Slowly he raised the sword high in the air, and said in a clear voice words that seemed to come to his mind from far, far away, "Rise, oh king of the sea. I return to you what is your own. Rise and fight the good fight one last time."

Then, as the McGunnegals and Professor McPherson watched in silent wonder, Frederick laid the handle of the sword in the upturned right hand of the king and the blade in his left, and released it. The sword flared to a blinding intensity, making them all shield their eyes. But Frederick, standing before the throne, saw the right hand of the king slowly curl its fingers around the handle of the sword.

Frederick stepped back. The man's chest heaved, he breathed deeply, and his eyes fluttered open. He slowly raised his head and stared at Frederick. A look of wonder washed over his face, and then, as though some dreadful memory came to him, his expression hardened, and he looked about the room.

Slowly, he rose from his throne and layers of salt cracked and fell from his body. He was tall – as tall as Bran – and looked to be just as powerfully built as Aonghus, but he nearly collapsed, and Frederick rushed forward, taking him by the arm and lowering him back to his throne. He tried to speak, but no words came. He licked his lips dryly.

"Bring water!" called Frederick, but Abbe was already on her way up the steps with a water sack. The others quickly followed behind her.

She gently held the water to his lips, and he drank deeply, his deep green eyes moving from one face to the next. After drinking for several moments, he held up his left hand and Abbe took a step back.

The man looked at them, then at the blazing sword in his hand, then beyond them to the bones that littered the room. Frederick unbuckled the sheath around his waist and handed it to him. He took it and gazed at it for a moment. Then slowly, he rose once again from the throne, towering above all but Bran and Aonghus. He steadied himself and slipped the sheath around his own waist. He looked at each of them, shifted the sword to his left hand, and took a step toward Frederick.

Aonghus and Bran immediately stepped forward, ready to defend the young boy, but the tall king paused and only held out his right hand to Frederick. Frederick hesitated for a moment, noticing for the first time that he wore a green ring on his ring finger that now seemed to have some light swirling in its depths. Frederick extended his own and took the outstretched hand of the king. Instantly, a torrent of images flashed through Frederick's mind, and he gasped. The king held his grip for several moments and then released it.

Frederick reeled, and his vision began to fade, but Aonghus steadied him and said to the tall man with a hint of anger in his voice, "What did you do to him?"

The king took a deep breath, and then said in a raspy deep voice that seemed only to come with effort, "Frederick is not harmed."

"I'm all right," said Frederick, steadying himself now. "That's the second time a dead man has done that to me!"

"Who are you?" asked Bran. "And what were you doing sitting on that throne? Were you shipwrecked here like us?"

The man licked his lips and whispered harshly, "Please, may I drink again? And I must sit."

Abbe handed him the water sack, and he sat carefully down on his crusty throne and drank deeply.

He drained the entire container, sighed, and looked at the group around him and said in a clearer voice, "Thank you."

Then he stood once again and stretched as one waking out of a long sleep. The sword continued to flash, as though it were joyful at being in his hand. He looked at the bones that littered the steps leading down from the dais and the floor of the room all about them, and a hard expression crossed his face once again and he looked deep in thought. Then, before anyone could stop her, Henny stepped forward, reached up, and tugged on the man's silver armor. He looked down at her in surprise.

"Please, sir," she said. "Who are you?"

"Who am I?" he replied.

He looked thoughtfully at the little girl before him and then at the others. Finally, he drew himself up to his full height, stretching his arms wide, and with a clear voice that seemed to command their attention, and even their devotion, he cried out, "I am Atlantis!"

Chapter 15 – The Witch

A sense of dread and fear swept over Colleen as she peered over the rock pile at the Witch. She had heard so many dreadful stories and had come so far hoping never to face this creature that lived in legend and myth, but which now stood not twenty feet from her. The black hood slowly surveyed the chamber. Colleen could see no face, and even the Witch's hands were shrouded by the long, black sleeves of the robe. No one moved. No one dared even to breathe. The urge to run and hide was almost overpowering.

But she glanced over at her mother, who was sitting in a dark corner with her arms wrapped around her knees, and this brought her back to her senses. She had come for Ellie. She would not abandon her now.

The goblin with the whip fell down at the Witch's feet, groveling like a dog.

"We're sorry for the disturbance, Your Grace!" whined the goblin. "The human woman is mad, and she was shouting at the air. We were just going to teach her..."

"Silence!" came a rasping voice from under the Witch's hood.

Colleen shivered. It was an alien-sounding voice – neither human nor animal, but something *other.* And yet that sound invoked a feeling, or perhaps a memory, of something that she had experienced before, but which was like a long faded dream. The goblin backed away and was silent. The Witch raised her staff, and the red flame at its tip grew hotter. It lit the room, but only seemed to deepen the oppressive, dark feelings that smothered their minds.

"There is a power here..." said the Witch.

Colleen dared not move, but the gaze of the Witch was slowly turning in her direction. It moved past the cowering goblins, fell and lingered for a moment on Ellie, past the little people who trembled behind rocks and boulders, and as those invisible eyes slowly crept toward them, fear and dread overwhelmed her, and she shrunk down, sending rocks tumbling down the pile. The Witch's flame blazed to a terrible furnace, and Colleen knew that she had doomed them all.

At that moment, Oracle quickly placed the Wigglepox family on the ground, scrambled up the stone pile, picked up a rock, and with a *"hump!"* threw it right at the Witch. But the stone never reached her, for fire shot from her staff, incinerating it in midair. Oracle threw himself down and went tumbling behind the stone pile as the flames roared over their heads. Colleen's hair would have been singed had the hood of her cloak not protected her.

"Seize it!" hissed the Witch, and instantly the goblins were on their feet and ran toward them.

There was no time to think or act, and Colleen knew that they were undone, and all of their plans and hopes were dashed. But Oracle rolled down the pile of stone, leaped to his feet and ran right out into the open with speed and agility that surprised Colleen. The goblins were on him instantly, shouting as they tackled him to the ground and drove his face into the rough gravel.

Nous restrained Colleen as she tried to run after him, and he whispered harshly in her ear, "The leprechaun sacrificed himself for us! Stay!"

Tears rolled again down her face as she watched the goblins kick Oracle again and again, until at last the Witch said, *"That will do."*

The goblins dragged Oracle to the Witch and threw him down before her. He looked up, and his face was bleeding and dirty, but bore a calm expression.

A hiss came from beneath the Witch's hood as Oracle gazed up at her, and for the briefest moment, she seemed to hesitate, and the flame on her staff dimmed. Then she seemed to regain her composure and stepped forward, towering over the prone and beaten little leprechaun.

"You!" she crowed. *"You dare to enter my domain?"*

She shook with rage at the sight of him, and for a moment raised her staff, as if to strike, but then she seemed to think better of it.

"So, you have come at last. I had wondered if you had abandoned these pitiful creatures that haunt my dungeons and sleep in my forest," she crowed.

Oracle said nothing, but pushed himself up and stood facing the Witch.

"Now, Dian, dear," she said in a softer, kinder voice. "You see these little people all around?"

She waved her staff and, on the far wall, a window seemed to open, and a vision of dungeons came into focus. One dark room after another appeared, showing hundreds of little people digging with tiny picks and shovels, mining gems and gold and iron, or laboring to make the rough shoes that the goblins wore. Goblins were everywhere, bearing whips and prods and clubs, ever forcing the little people to slave away in the dark pits.

Then the image changed, and the forest came into view. The scene moved from tree to tree, from hollow to hollow, and there, hidden beneath root and stone, hundreds, even thousands of little people slept with fitful dreams, never waking to the reality of the dying forest all around them.

The scene shifted again to chamber after chamber of tormented souls, little people chained or sitting with their heads in their hands, some weeping, others beyond tears, and all without hope. Among them stalked a translucent gray figure, ghost-like, as if its nature was uncertain – real yet unreal. But fear and despair followed after it, smothering the minds and hearts of those in its dark domain.

"You see, Dian, they are all under *my* command, and under *my* Spell that walks among them. I have embodied despair and the fear of death in the Gray Man, and it haunts their deepest nightmares. I have the power to wake them and call them into *my* service," she said. "This is their only reality now."

She paused and walked slowly around the leprechaun.

"But!" she continued, "I will give *you* that power, and I will give you the key to these dungeons."

The Witch reached into her robe and pulled out a black key.

"This is the key to the deepest dungeons – the key to the domain of the Gray Man. It will lock and unlock the magic that binds the forest. Do you desire to have it?" she crooned, dangling the key before his eyes.

Oracle said nothing, but only stared into the black hood.

"I will give this to you if you will pledge yourself to serve me. Give *me* your pot of gold, Dian, and in exchange, I will give you this key, and you may do with these pitiful creatures as you wish. Come, Dian, surely that is a fair exchange?" she said in an almost loving voice.

Colleen turned to Nous, dismayed. Either the Witch didn't know that they had broken the chamber, or its destruction hadn't truly broken the Spell. The terrible fear swept over her that they had done nothing at all, or worse, maybe they had spread the Spell out over the land to such an extent that now it would never be broken. Perhaps the chamber had only been a place where the Spell collected and was spread – an artificial amplifier of the true source – this Gray Man that Nous, and now the Witch, had spoken of. What was this creature that held such terrible power? Was it a being like the Lady, only her opposite – a thing of great power gone terribly wrong, spreading death instead of life? Was it a creature at all? And how had the Witch gained power over such a thing?

But Oracle was smiling now and, looking deeply into the Witch's face, he said, "The Spell of the Gray Man is about to do the last of its damage in this world. The little people are about to be free of it, and will waken back to the light of day and reclaim what they have lost. And," he said in a somewhat louder voice, as though he wanted everyone in the chamber to hear him, "the key to your dungeons shall not be yours for long."

"*Lies!*" shouted the Witch, and her shoulders heaved with hot anger.

She raised her staff, whipping it in a great circle over her head. As she did, a whirlwind of fire surged above her, and with sudden fury, she brought it down. The goblins scattered as the swirling flames slammed down upon Oracle, completely enveloping him. But no cry came from the leprechaun's lips, although gleeful and shrill laughter came from the hooded figure of the Witch. At last, she released her spell, and the flames flickered and went out.

Colleen opened her eyes, for she had shut them tight when the flames had been unleashed. She fully expected to see Oracle's seared and blackened body lying dead before the terrible power of this merciless creature. Indeed, where Oracle had been, there was nothing but a blackened husk in the shape of a little man. The ground around it was glowing red-hot. A wave of fear and sorrow and hopelessness swept over Colleen as she stared at the burned stump where Oracle had once stood. Tears welled up in her eyes once again, and she put her hand over her mouth to stifle a cry.

But to her astonishment, the charred statue cracked and crumbled and fell to the ground, and out of it stepped Oracle, dusting soot from his gray robe as if he had just been cleaning the fireplace.

Nous crouched, wide-eyed beside her.

Oracle looked into the face of the Witch and said nothing, did nothing, but only stood waiting.

The Witch paused for a moment as if she were unsure what to do next, and then howled in frustration. Then she seemed to contain herself once again and, with an obvious effort, said, "Ah, Dian, I have been merciful. I only wished to show you my power and that I am fully able to destroy my enemies. But I am not willing to do so needlessly. Come, let me get you something – you look tired and thirsty."

She waved her staff and before the image of the forest on the wall appeared a banquet table that was laden with all sorts of wonderful foods. The aroma of the meal filled the room and made Colleen's mouth water. Then the room itself changed, and became a beautiful hall, brightly decorated with wonderful tapestries and paintings. A rich red carpet covered the floor, and carved pillars reached upward to an ornately painted ceiling that depicted the struggles and victories of the little people.

"Please, Dian, sit and dine with me, and we shall discuss the plight of your people. Surely we can come to some agreement together and revive this perishing world?" she said pleadingly.

Oracle did not even glance at the table spread before him, but sighed heavily and shut his eyes. The vision changed, the lights went out, and the table of delicate foods was transformed into a cold gray slab of stone with rough bowls of Ooze dripping upon it. A fetid smell filled the room and nearly made Colleen gag.

"Fool!" raged the Witch and, waving her staff once again, her form began to change. Her body and staff merged and elongated into a huge serpent with fiery red eyes, yellow fangs, a tongue of fire, and a body of dense black smoke.

The Serpent-Witch surged forward, coiling itself around Oracle again and again, completely smothering and hiding him from their sight. Then it began to squeeze. Smoke rose from the coiled body like a furnace, and the great fanged head struck down the center of its own coils. Down the black gullet they saw something go, swallowed whole into the fiery gut of the monster. Colleen knew that Oracle was gone. Nothing could have survived such a vicious attack.

But suddenly, the great serpent lurched, and right out through the side of the creature popped Oracle, coughing and waving the smoke away from his face as though it were a mere nuisance.

The creature hissed a terrifying sound, and seemed to uncoil, reshaping itself back into the form of the Witch.

Oracle spoke. His voice was clear, and his words held no mysterious meaning.

"Put away your staff and come, child. Come. Let us speak of better things. There is hope for you yet. Do not be afraid. I will not harm you," he said.

Colleen was shocked and perplexed. Who was this leprechaun? She had suspected that there was more to him than he let on. But why the ruse? Why had he acted like a fool so many times? He obviously held a great hidden power beneath his antics and jokes.

"Come? COME?" she screamed. "I have held power here for thousands of years, and you wish *ME* to come with *YOU?* You forget where you are. Perhaps you forget that it was the Elders themselves who handed the power of the Gray Man to me in their betrayal! I have been patient with you, hoping that your pitiful self would come to its senses and join me in this noble struggle against weakness and poverty that lies on this land like a stinking fog. These *little people* have no sense or desire to better themselves, and I have taught them that – brought them out of a deeper sleep than the Spell that I laid upon them – and that for their own good. I offer them greatness! Do you remember Lugh, grandson of the leprechaun elder? Do you even know what power and authority he gained from *me?* I offer you that greatness, Dian, but this is the last time I offer it. Join me, or I shall utterly destroy you and all of your useless *little people* too!"

"Your reign is coming to an end, child. Today, even in this room, is a power that will bring about the end of your dark night, and break the Spell of the Gray Man that you have spread, although you do not understand that of which I speak," replied Oracle calmly.

Colleen was amazed at the courage of this little man, standing face to face with the menacing power of the Witch, and surrounded by her goblins. His old face was calm, almost unconcerned. But she had no time for such pondering, for the Witch rushed forward and, for the first time, her hood slipped slightly back and, for just a moment, Colleen glimpsed two yellow eyes, reptilian, or perhaps cat-like in appearance, with black slits for pupils. The dark fire of her staff seemed to snuff out the dim light of the torch on the wall, and Colleen fell back, muffling a cry, for all around Oracle fearful apparitions took shape – figures blacker than night, but burning with the same non-light of the Witch's staff. Like giant bats, they seemed, but a menacing fear flowed from them like liquid evil.

Colleen could barely see the horrid face of one of them now. It seemed to waver between form and void – now a pig, now a bat, now an emptiness that revealed its true essence. From its open mouth dripped some foul saliva that steamed like acid as it struck the ground at its goat-hoof feet. Its eye sockets were pits, revealing nothing in its soulless face.

Oracle glanced about at the six huge monstrous forms that now surrounded him. But still, his own face was quiet, and in a calm voice, he spoke to the Witch. "Even these have no authority here, child. This is my world, not theirs. Send them back to their lonely haunts. Or shall I?"

"Your world? *YOUR WORLD!*" shrieked the Witch. "I rule here! I am the goddess of this world, and *I* rule. These servants of mine shall take you into torment, where you will pay for your insolence and the insolence of your people! Destroy him!"

The black forms swooped upon Oracle with howls that made Colleen want to scream in terror. She knew that he could never stand against their evil power, so overwhelming was their terrible presence. But as they fell upon him, there was a sudden flash of golden light that formed, it seemed, around the little man's head, and the creatures fell back in despair, howling now in fear and rage, shielding their eyes as if the light hurt them. To Colleen, it was the most beautiful light she had ever seen, though it was almost frightening in its beauty.

The Witch took a step backward, a look of astonishment on her face. Then her eyes narrowed, and she hissed, "Kill them all! Throw everyone in this dungeon into the Pit!"

The goblins and dark creatures swept about the room, grabbing little people, and rushed for the door, ready to do their master's bidding, when Oracle cried out, "Stop!"

His command was so urgent, and the power in his voice so great, that all of them froze in their tracks and looked back.

"You shall not take them!" he said.

"They are mine, *elder*," said the Witch. The last word came out with a sneer. "They have *all* given themselves to *me!* They no longer want you."

"Then take me instead," he said.

The Witch cocked her head to one side as if considering what Oracle had just said. "Do you mean that you would take their place in these pits? Would you become *small,* for *them?*"

"Yes," said Oracle. "I know that you have stolen all of their magic and that they are no threat to you anymore. The pitiful shoes that they make and the tiny bit of mining they do does nothing to serve you. You hold them only out of spite. But my magic is beyond theirs. Do you dare to see if you can contain *it?*"

"Contain it? *Contain* it? Ha! I shall possess it and make it mine! The Ooze shall drain you of all that you are and then I shall drink of it and have all of your power for myself! And you shall be my miserable slave for what few days you may have left." She laughed a hideous laugh and then said, "Very well! Spare the wretches. But take him to the Great Pit!"

The six black figures rushed in with wicked grunts and snarls, and their shadowy forms seemed to blend and merge into one great darkness that threatened to envelop Oracle. But they could not take him. The light coming from him held them at bay.

"I will go of my own will," he said. "These shall not take me."

"Leave your gold!" demanded the Witch.

Oracle drew out his pot and placed it on the ground. Then he walked from the room, followed by the whirling darkness, and was gone.

One of the goblins slunk forward and slid the shaft of its club through the handle of Oracle's fallen pot of gold, not daring to touch it.

"Bring the human woman!" demanded the Witch.

The other goblins rushed over to Ellie, seized her by the arms, and dragged her to her feet.

The Witch glanced about the room, and then followed the line of goblins as they took their prisoners away.

"Escort our dear Ellie to the king, then come back and kill all the little people in this dungeon. They are of no use to me anymore. The rat has taken the bait at last," she sneered.

Her form changed, grew huge and menacing, swirled into black smoke and whisked through the door and out of sight. The goblins marched away, pushing Ellie roughly before them.

No one moved. They were too stunned by what had just happened to say or do anything. Finally, Colleen shook herself and said, "Mother! Oracle!"

"Colleen!" said Mrs. Wigglepox in a strained voice, "Oh, Colleen, how could we not have known?"

"Known?" said Colleen, wiping tears from her face.

"Oracle... I should have known. He is Dian, the Elder of Elders! He was there when the Seven awoke within the Waking Tree!" said Mrs. Wigglepox.

"What?" exclaimed Colleen. "All this time... I thought he was just deranged from the Spell. I think he must have been pretending. But why?"

"It is said in the legends that he was always humble – and powerful. Did you see how he walked away from the Witch's magic? It didn't even harm him!" said Mrs. Wigglepox.

"But those things... those black demon things... they took him," replied Colleen with a shiver. "And the goblins took my mother! We've got to do something!"

"Yes," replied Mrs. Wigglepox. "Now you just stay here for a moment."

Around the room she went, pulling little people out from behind rocks and boulders, and gathering them together. Soon six shabby-looking gnomes, three leprechauns, and one wingless fairy stood gazing up in wonder at Colleen and cowering at the sight of Nous.

"Now listen to me, everyone," said Mrs. Wigglepox to the little people. "You heard the Witch. Those goblins are coming back in a few minutes and then we're all goners. We've come here to set you free, and that's just what we intend to do. Now quickly, is there anywhere in this place to hide or run to?"

But the little people said nothing and only bowed their heads.

"What's wrong with you all?" said Mrs. Wigglepox. "Didn't you hear?"

Then one of the gnomes stepped forward and said, "We heard. But there's no hope for any of us. No one escapes from this place. No one."

"There's always hope," said Colleen, looking down with pity on them. "Come on, now, pick up your chins. We're here to help you!"

"A lot of good your friend did," said the wingless fairy.

"Didn't you see what happened?" remarked one of the leprechauns. "The Witch's fire didn't even singe his beard! And did you see how *big* he was!"

"His name is Oracle... or Dian," said Colleen. "And we must try to help him. He sacrificed himself to save us. Do you know where the king's chamber is? And what about this Great Pit?"

"They will have taken the human woman up the main passage and through the locked gate. That's the only way out," said another gnome. "As for the Pit – yes, we know it. No one who goes in there ever comes out. It leads down – down to the Gray Man and past him to the Worm, or so they say."

"Are there more goblins down here besides those that just left?" asked Colleen.

"There are always more goblins," said the fairy, glancing up at Nous. "But who is this?"

"His name is Nous," answered Colleen, "and he is a friend. He has helped us many times. He is not like the other goblins."

Nous leaned down toward the huddled group of little people, and they quickly backed away.

Nous frowned.

"They don't trust Nous," he said.

"Oh, Nous, don't worry. You can hardly blame them. After all, look at where they are," replied Colleen. "But come, we must get out of here quickly."

"Wait, there's one thing I have to ask," said Mrs. Wigglepox to the other little people. "Have you seen anyone here named Bhrogan Wigglepox? He is my husband."

"We're not allowed to use our names here," said another leprechaun. "We're only numbers. And we either mine or make shoes. Nothing more."

Suddenly, there was the sound of a gate clanging in the distance.

"They are coming!" cried Mrs. Wigglepox.

"Hide!" whispered one of the gnomes, and they all ran into the shadows.

A moment later, the goblin with the whip walked into the chamber and began to call mockingly to the little people, "Come out, come out, wherever you are! We'll have a little fun before we send you to Mr. Gray!"

Colleen crouched behind the rock pile and peered out from the shadows as the goblin went about the room kicking over stones and searching. A moment later, he found one of the gnomes, scooped him up in one rough hand, and peered greedily into his face.

"I wonder what a gnome pie would taste like?" sneered the goblin, licking his lips. "Or maybe I'll just dip 'em in a bit of Ooze and eat 'em raw!"

The goblin roared with laughter at the look of horror on the gnome's face. Then it held the gnome by its feet and opened its huge mouth wide, dangling its victim over its stinking gullet.

Colleen had had enough. She had watched as Oracle was taken away, watched while her mother was marched off by goblins, and now something snapped inside her. She could stand it no longer. The words of the Lady Danu came to her mind, and her vision cleared. Was there help even here in this place of darkness and despair? She closed her eyes and listened with her heart.

In an instant, she could see beyond the stark walls of the cavern, beyond the misery and moans and fear, and into hidden places where no goblin had gone. There she saw them – secret creatures that lived within the rock itself. They were unlike anything she had ever encountered before. And they were ancient – older than the rocks and cracks and crevices that they inhabited.

As she became aware of them, they were aware of her as well, and somehow, in a way she could not explain or understand, they spoke with her. It was not with her ears, or even her mind that she heard them, but with that deeper sense that was steadily awakening within her. They moved and flowed with that piece of the music of the Song that the earth sang, and where they passed, they left that Song somehow richer, deeper, and healed of the dissidence made by the corruption of this place. She could also sense that they were no friends of the Witch.

"We know of your plight. We will help," they said.

Colleen now leaped up, ran toward the goblin, and shouted, "You put him down *NOW!*"

The goblin, taken by surprise, jumped backward against the wall and dropped the gnome, who went running away into the shadows.

"Who are you?" was all the goblin got out, before there was a grinding sound of stone against stone, and something seized him from behind.

The goblin screamed, for the stone of the wall itself seemed to have come to life, and was now forming around his body, pulling him in, until nothing but his face, belly, fingers, and the tips of its shoes protruded from the rock.

"Thank you," said Colleen, not to the goblin, but to the wall. "I appreciate your help."

"Make it stop, make it stop!" howled the goblin.

"First, you will tell me how to get to the king's chamber," said Colleen.

"What are you?" breathed the goblin. "Are you the Sorceress?"

Colleen was not sure what to say, but decided to play along.

"It may be. But you will answer my questions now, or I shall leave you here with this wall. It is most upset with the way you've forced these little people to mine it," replied Colleen coolly.

"All right!" whimpered the goblin. "You go straight out the main gate, up three flights of stairs, straight on for about three halls, up six more flights, past two guard posts, and there you are!"

"Do you really expect me to believe that you got all that way and delivered my Mo... Ellie to the king in so short a time?" replied Colleen. "Now tell me the truth!"

"It's true!" whined the goblin through its pinched cheeks. "I sent the others on ahead so that I could come back and have a bit of fun, that's all."

"Fun! You nearly ate that gnome!" replied Colleen.

"Ah, what's one little gnome anyway? It wouldn't be missed. Plenty more down here for you to have for yourself if you like. See here, I'll help you round them up and make a stew, just let me go!" said the goblin.

"Make a stew!" said Colleen angrily. "Why, you evil brute! We do *not* eat other people! I think you had better just hang there for a while before... what?"

Colleen was about to scold the goblin further, but an evil smile had crept onto its face, and it appeared to be looking past her, behind her.

Colleen spun around. Nous was creeping forward, carrying the Wigglepox family.

"Grab her, mate!" howled the goblin who was stuck in the wall. "Now's our chance!"

But Nous slowly came forward and handed Mrs. Wigglepox, Lily, and Rose to Colleen, who put them into her pocket.

He then walked up to the dangling goblin and began to poke him in the belly.

"Hey! See here! What are you up to? Hey! Stop!" cried the trapped goblin.

But Nous ignored him and kept on prodding him until something jingled, and he reached into the goblin's robe and pulled out a set of keys.

"Dungeon cell keys," said Nous, and handed them to Colleen.

"Traitor!" howled the other goblin. "Wicked traitor! You'll boil for this!"

"Time for you to be still," said Colleen. A neat piece of rock slid over his mouth like a gag, and he was silent.

"Now you just hang there a while and think about how rotten you've been. Maybe my friend will let you go if you behave yourself," said Colleen to the trapped goblin.

The little people in the room were now gathering around Colleen and gazing up at her in amazement.

"Are you the Sorceress?" asked the wingless fairy. "You look like the descriptions of her that I've heard."

"No," replied Colleen. "I'm only a girl. But I would surely like to meet this Sorceress if she's fighting against the Witch. Do you know how to find her?"

"We've never seen her," said one of the leprechauns. "It's just a rumor. Some poor fellows in the cells next door said they saw her once. She appeared and rescued some pixies who were about to have their wings pulled off by the goblins. They say she summoned the very rocks to fight off the goblins... just as you did..."

"Well, we better get moving here. Come, let's open the doors down here and see how many prisoners we can find. It's time to raise up the little people!" said Colleen. "First, though, we have two people to rescue, so we must be quick. But who should we save first?"

Chapter 16 – The Sorceresses

Ellie McGunnegal was pushed roughly by three goblins up several flights of stairs. The fourth goblin had left the others a few minutes before. Had she really seen Colleen? Or was this just another trick of the Witch, or of her own imagination? Was she going mad? And who was the big leprechaun who had walked away from the Witch's spells so easily? Surely this was just some mind game that the dark mistress of the Goblin King was playing on her. But she couldn't be sure.

Whatever the case, the Witch was angry – very angry, and she felt in her heart that it would not be another simple questioning that she would undergo this time. She feared that she would not be walking back to her cell to mine for gems – or going anywhere ever again. She had to escape, but it had to be before they reached the guard station – sooner than that – for the walls and floors and rock above were enchanted and impregnable.

Her only chance was a strange group of beings that lived in the very rock itself. The first time she had met them, she thought she truly was going mad. She had been in the darkness for an entire week and was starving and dying of thirst. But the solitude and deprivation had awakened some deeper sight inside her, and she became aware of them, and they of her. There, in the darkness, they spoke mind to mind.

Now the goblins were taking her up, beyond their realm. She needed their help now. She shut her eyes and reached out with her thoughts – or with that sense that is beyond the mind, probing into the rock beneath her feet, in the walls, and deep, deep into layer upon layer of foundation stone that these halls had been carved through. There she found them, lazily moving along their private paths, doing what, she could not understand. But her call to them was desperate, and they stirred. Ellie stopped walking and concentrated.

"Hey, you!" shouted a goblin. "What do you think you're doing – get moving!"

It shoved her hard so that she fell to the ground. The goblins laughed. But Ellie was focused elsewhere.

"Help me," she pleaded.

One of the goblins gave her a hard kick in the ribs, sending her sprawling on her back. She groaned in pain and looked up at it.

"Good-bye," she said, her dirty face splitting into a grin.

Confusion and fear darkened the faces of the perplexed goblins, for Ellie McGunnegal simply sank into the stone steps and was gone. The goblins looked about, then at each other.

"I didn't see a thing," said one.

"Me either," said the other.

Both turned and fled in different directions.

Ellie, however, felt herself in the grip of one of the rock creatures. In its "soft" form, as she called it, it surrounded her like a bubble, and moved her through the bedrock as easily as she would walk through air. She had done this before, unknown to both her captors and fellow prisoners, but it was still new to her, and was rather unsettling. But she urged on this creature to greater speed, to take her to the hiding place where she had been once before.

In a few moments, they arrived, and the rock creature, whom she had nicknamed Richie after her cousin, gently deposited her into a large square chamber that was filled with all sorts of beautiful green, orange, and white rock formations.

"Thank you so much, my friend," she said to the amorphous blob that now sat on the floor next to the wall where it had emerged.

She sensed its own gratitude toward her, for she had also rescued it once not long ago. It had been captive to the terrible mind of the Witch, and she had wrestled it free of that shackle. That encounter had nearly undone her, and she had barely hidden her true identity.

Now, from time to time, she called on this rock creature and its two companions to rescue the little people who were being tormented by the goblins. In the last several months, they had freed a dozen or more and had brought them here to these caves, far below the dungeons of the Witch. Ellie turned to see a group of them coming toward her now. Their clothes were disheveled and their bodies thin and worn, but they were smiling and greeted her heartily.

"Ellie!" said one gnome, and he ran forward to greet her.

"Digger! How are you today?" she said and sat down on the floor before him.

"Well as can be," he said. "Any news from the pits?"

The other little people gathered around her, and she looked at them with pity.

Four fairies, two pixies, three gnomes, six leprechauns – all she and the rock creatures had been able to spirit away without drawing too much attention to their efforts.

"I don't know," she replied. "I thought I saw – I thought I saw my daughter today. But it must have been an illusion. Another tormenting phantom from the Witch."

She sighed and then continued, "The goblins were taking me to the old crow. I was afraid she would keep me for good this time, so I had to ask Richie for help. The goblins saw me, though, and word is sure to get back to her."

"Then now's the time," replied Digger. "We've been busy down here with Richie and his friends."

The gnome signaled to one of the leprechauns, and from behind his back he produced a golden ring on which were mounted three brilliant gems – a sapphire, a ruby, and a diamond.

"Richie got us some gold and gems!" said one of them. "We've been working on this for you. It isn't a proper Wishing Ring, mind you, what with our own strength nearly all gone, but between the lot of us, and with these rock creatures helping, we've managed to put a bit of magic in it."

Ellie took the ring and looked at it in the orange light of the cavern. It was marvelously made, and she wondered at the skill and resourcefulness of these little people.

"Put it on, put it on!" said one of the fairies, leaping into the air and flapping her broken wings.

She slipped the ring onto her right ring finger, and instantly she was keenly aware of the three rock creatures around them, and could almost see with their strange sight the courses and flows of the stone and earth that stretched for leagues above and around them. She also suddenly knew that Richie, and his companions, Willie and Harvey, as she called them, had somehow joined themselves to these three gems.

"With this, you bear the power of the rock people," said Digger. "And we've been able to, well, extend that a bit. You'll see."

Richie spoke to her now, and the voice of his mind was clearer than she had ever heard it before. "Take us with you when you go," he said. "We too are prisoners on this isle."

She nodded and touched the gems of the ring to the floor. All three of them flowed effortlessly into them, their forms not constrained by the smallness of their new homes. Somehow, the remnant power of the fairies and pixies and gnomes and leprechauns, and the native abilities of these strange creatures now lay within this ring, and she knew that it was now in her hands. The realization of it stunned her, and she wondered what would become of it.

"Thank you, my friends," she said to them all. "I'll do my best to bear this well, and I'm humbled and honored. I think it's time for the rumored Sorceress to make an appearance, and to free all of the little people!"

Cheers went up, and Ellie, with a wave, vanished into the rock.

She arrived at her old cell and found it empty, except for one rather disturbed goblin who was stuck in the wall. Its eyes bulged as it saw yet another human, a larger and very stern human, rise right out of the rock before it.

"Richie?" she thought.

"The other human child asked our help," he replied in her mind.

"The other... then she was no phantom!" said Ellie.

"Where is the human child?" Ellie said in a commanding tone to the goblin, and the rock gag across its mouth withdrew.

"Don't know," said the goblin. "She left some minutes ago, leaving poor Mucus hanging here. Help m..."

The goblin was silenced, for she touched the wall, and the gag was replaced, and Ellie strode through the wall of the chamber and into the main hall of the dungeons. She sprinted down the length of it, searching as she ran, but no little people remained. Only dank pits of bubbling Ooze greeted her, their putrid odor filling every chamber. Signs of the tormented life of the little people lay everywhere – abandoned picks and shovels, tiny chains strewn about, and wretched piles of broken debris. Signs of the eternal labor of the pits were everywhere, but no one was to be found.

Fear rose up within her – she was too late! On she ran, down deeper into the pits to where the most foul of the Witch's torments were done. She stopped, for here a great pool of Ooze slowly swirled in a massive hole. The dreadful sight of chain after chain dangling from the vaulted ceiling met her eyes. There, the living remains of many little people hung, their last desperate hopes dashed. One fairy, chained by its tattered wings, looked up, and said in a weak voice, "Help them..." and looked across the bubbling lake.

There, crowded together, stood at least a hundred little people, and in front of them stood Colleen, her arms wide with a sword in one hand and a staff in the other, as if trying to protect them. And crouched at her feet was a single goblin, bearing its yellow fangs. But it was not threatening Colleen. Instead, it was standing with her, face to face with ten other goblins, all of them bearing wicked-looking prods and clubs.

"Now we've got 'em all!" sneered a particularly large and ugly goblin. "Trapped them all like rats!"

Ellie burst into a run and rounded the bubbling lake. "I think not!" she shouted.

All of the goblins spun about, startled and alarmed. There stood Ellie, seemingly all alone. But the ring on her finger seemed to shine with its own light.

"Grab her!" shouted the leader of the goblins, and five of their number surged forward. But Ellie only smiled, and they instantly sank down to their ears in the very rock beneath them and were held fast.

The other five, seeing so formidable a foe before them, and only a child and little people behind them, turned to attack Colleen and her group, thinking to take hostages. But she sprinted forward, and with a wave of her hand, all five of them simply dropped into the stone floor and were gone.

Now the five goblins' heads squirmed and shouted. Ellie strode up to them, knelt down, and said, "Now, my dear goblins, before I send you to the same fate as your friends, I want you to know that the reign of your Witch is about to come to an end." She blinked, and the goblins, wide-eyed, vanished beneath the stone.

Colleen had been spellbound by all of this, but as soon as the goblins were gone, she ran forward and threw herself into her mother's arms.

"Mother! Do you know me?" she cried.

"Oh, Colleen, forgive me! I am so happy to see you! But how? How did you get here?" said Ellie, tears running down her own cheeks now as she held her daughter in her arms.

Colleen hugged her tightly for several long moments and let the tears flow. She sniffed, looked up into her mother's face, and said, "It's a long story, Mom. Do you know how much I've missed you?"

She hugged her tightly once again and took a deep breath. "But I'm afraid the goblins will come back soon, and maybe the Witch too. We've got to get out of here," she said. "But... Mom, are *you* the Sorceress?"

Ellie laughed. "It seems that I am! And *that* is largely due to my friends."

She held up the ring, and Colleen could see the three rock creatures that now dwelt in the gems.

"Let me look at you!" said Ellie, holding Colleen at arm's distance. "My, how you have grown! And you... you're dressed as a sorceress yourself, with a staff, and a sword!"

"Oh! It's Frederick's sword," she replied. "He was here too, but he had to go back for help. My, I do hope he brings some soon!"

"Frederick?" inquired Ellie. "What of your father, and your brothers and sisters? Are they here too?"

"Frederick Buttersmouth. But no, no one else is here. He and I came alone. Oh, there *is* so much to tell!" replied Colleen.

She looked about at the crowd of little people now gathered around them, and then a thought struck her.

"What did you do to the goblins?" asked Colleen. "You didn't...."

"Seal them in solid rock?" asked Ellie, an amused look on her face. "No, although they might deserve that for all the mistreatment and murder they've done in these wretched pits! But no, I sent them to one of their own dungeon cells. They should keep there for a while. But quickly, we must free everyone."

"But where will we take them?" asked Colleen.

"Well, I presumed that since you found a way *in*, you have also found a way *out*?" said Ellie.

"Mrs. Wigglepox made a wish and brought us here," replied Colleen. "We jumped into the wishing well... it's a long story."

Ellie raised an inquiring eyebrow.

"Oh!" said Colleen. "I have not introduced you yet. Mrs. Wigglepox, Lily, Rose, this is my mother, Ellie McGunnegal."

The Wigglepox family stepped forward.

"Mother, this is the Wigglepox family, and this," she said, turning and placing a hand on Nous' shoulder, "is my dear friend, Nous. He has proved himself faithful many times. He is a good goblin!"

Nous had crouched behind Colleen, but now shuffled forward beside her.

"A good goblin? I've not heard of such a thing before. I'm most pleased to make all of your acquaintances," replied Ellie, inclining her head to them. "But if you please, we really should be getting on with the task at hand. The Witch may be here soon, and I dare say we do not wish to meet her unprepared."

"Mom, they took Oracle, our friend. We have to rescue him! He gave himself up to save us!" said Colleen.

Ellie looked down into her daughter's distraught face.

"The rock beneath the fortress is enchanted, Colleen. We cannot pass that way, and we dare not face the Witch on her own terms," she said. "But I think we are not discovered yet. Come, we must gather together as many of the little people as we can and take them to safety. I think if we...."

"What is this?" Ellie's voice was cut off by another that sounded strangely like her own, and came from across the cavern. But this voice was harsher, darker, and full of malice.

They all turned, and there, surrounded by the shifting void of the six black creatures stood the Witch, and a host of goblins was quickly filling in behind her.

"So, you have all come to watch the execution of the first and last Elder of the Little People, have you? And what have we here – a human child. Ah, a daughter, no doubt – I see the family resemblance," said the Witch in a mocking tone.

She reached into the bodily void of one of the creatures and pulled Oracle out of it. He sagged heavily, and they could see that he had been beaten and terribly mistreated.

"Leave them be," whispered Oracle. "You have me."

The Witch laughed. "Yes... but you seem to have lost your pot of gold, dear Dian. What will you do if I refuse?"

She slapped him across the face, and he stumbled and fell backward. The goblins and dark creatures laughed.

Oracle slowly stood and braced himself for another blow as the Witch drew back her hand to strike. But Colleen could stand it no longer.

"No!" she cried, and brandishing her sword and staff, she rushed forward, forgetting the danger and the growing number of goblins that were still coming into the chamber.

Ellie was right behind her, and she raised her hand, willing the stone beneath Oracle to soften and receive the little leprechaun and whisk him away to safety. But the Witch sensed her power, and with a wave of her staff, the Great Pit erupted, and out of it leaped a great dripping creatures of slime and ooze, roughly man-shaped, but huge and towering – a horrid golem that stank and exuded fear.

Ellie involuntarily backed away, and her concentration was broken. The terrible apparition loomed before them, bearing down on their entire company.

"Stop!" cried Oracle, and the monster paused, looking over its massive shoulder at him. "Stop," he said in a quieter voice.

It stood frozen, teetering on the edge of the Great Pit for a moment, then, ever so slowly, it tipped over and, with a great rush and splash, it fell back into the Ooze and was gone. Time seemed to stand still, and they all stood in a hush.

"No more," said Oracle after a moment. He was speaking now to Colleen and Ellie and the others in their band. "Do you think that even if you defeat this Witch, these dark Orogim, and all of the goblins, you can destroy the Great Pit as well? Can you rescue all of the little people who have gone down to its uttermost depths? Can you reach into its source and uproot its dark power? Can you bind the Gray Man and crush the Spell that the Witch, through him, has unleashed on my world?"

Colleen had no idea what he was talking about, so she only said, "Oracle, we can't leave you here, not with *her*, not with *them!*"

"You must. There is no time. You must go! There will be a moment when you can escape. Take that moment when it comes. You cannot follow me!" he said. Then, weakly, he dropped to his knees.

Time seemed to resume, and the Witch looked from side to side, as if a moment of confusion had taken her. Then she seized Oracle by his tattered robe and held him up before her.

"Now you will all see what happens to the enemies of the Witch!" she cried out.

The goblins cheered, and at a wave of her hand, the six black creatures, the Orogim, as Oracle had called them, swooped upon him and carried him high into the air and over the Pit.

"Send him!" she shrieked.

They watched in horror as, with hideous laughter, the Orogim released Oracle from their dark hands.

"No!" cried Colleen, and Ellie held her back as she tried to rush forward toward the Pit. It seemed to her that he fell, as if in slow motion, down, down, until he hit the swirling Ooze, and it washed over him.

Then his face came to the surface. The dark slime began to swirl and bubble, and Oracle was swept by its ever quickening current down into its center, which began to form a vortex, drawing him toward a black maw that seemed to stretch down into endless depths.

Yet, something else seemed to be happening as well. The Ooze within the Great Pit seemed to be emptying away, even vanishing as it carried Oracle downward. For the briefest moment, his eyes met Colleen's, and on his face was a strange look of peace. Then a gray form appeared. It reached out of the dark pool with its translucent arm, took Oracle beneath the frothing muck, and was gone.

She looked on in disbelief for a moment as the last vestiges of Ooze in the Great Pit drained away into a black chasm whose depths stretched down, down, far beyond the sight of any human eyes.

"Oracle!" she cried, but her voice only echoed down into the darkness and back again. She dropped to her knees, buried her face in her hands, and wept.

But she was given no time to mourn his loss, for the barks and laughter of the creatures of the night filled her ears once again. Anger blazed within her heart, and she turned to face them. She felt as though she would explode with rage and sorrow, and unleash it all at her enemies, when a still small voice, as if from far, far away, whispered to her mind, "This is not your battle. Not yet. Go!"

Colleen looked up, and saw that the Witch had now turned her attention to the little group of people on the other side of the Pit and began to walk toward them, her staff raised, its tip hot with dark red fire. She began to speak an incantation, when suddenly the room began to shake, only a little a first, and then with growing violence.

The little people who had been hanging suspended above the Ooze suddenly found their chains swinging wildly, then shaking loose and falling to the ground next to the empty Pit. Chunks of rock began to tumble from the ceiling, shattering as they crashed around them, and cracks ripped through the walls.

"We must go, now!" said Ellie urgently.

Colleen suddenly had the strange sensation of falling *into* the rock beneath her feet. She found herself standing inside an egg-shaped pocket that seemed to be moving swiftly downward. In a few moments, her motion slowed, the air opened before her, and she stepped out of the wall and into a beautifully illumined chamber.

Nous looked around nervously and drew close to Colleen. Little people began to be deposited into the room. They rose from the floors and tumbled out of the walls by the dozens.

The ground around them still trembled, and as Ellie stepped from the wall, she said, "I think this whole island is shaking apart. We need to get to the surface quickly."

"But what about Oracle?" said Colleen, tears streaming down her cheeks.

Ellie closed her eyes, as if concentrating. "I don't know," she said after a moment. "Something is happening far below." She paused, furrowing her brow. "It is not something of the Witch's doing, but..." Her eyes flew wide, and she gasped.

"What is it, Mother?" said Colleen, wiping her tears.

Ellie closed her eyes again, and then took a long, deep breath. "There are so many of them, Colleen!"

"Who?" whispered Colleen nervously.

"Look!" she said breathlessly. Removing the ring, she took Colleen's hand and put it on her finger. "Look deep!"

Colleen remembered how Oracle had led her to see far beneath the ground when Dvalenn the dwarf had left them. Now her mind raced downward, guided by the rock creatures until she perceived dark and gloomy rooms far, far below.

Then she saw them – thousands and thousands of leprechauns, pixies, fairies, gnomes, and many others that she could place no name to, were pouring into the corridors through smashed and shattered doors. A shining figure, whose face she could not see for its brightness, larger than all of them, stepped up to a closed rock door that was wrapped in iron bands, and, reaching through the rock, ripped the door in two and cast down their shattered halves, which fell across one another. The ground under Colleen's feet trembled as the doors toppled. She steadied herself and continued to watch. The bright figure stood upon the broken shards of the doors and, reaching down into the darkness, lifted a small fallen form that was bound in tiny chains. It seemed lifeless. He cradled it in his arms for a moment, and there was a blinding flash of colors. The chains that bound it broke and fell to the ground. The limp form sat up and was gently placed with the other little people. The bright figure moved on to the next door. The whole island of the Witch reeled as, again and again, the brilliant power demolished the ancient prison and set its captives free.

"Something strange is going on down there!" said Colleen. "Someone, or *something*, is tearing the dungeons apart!"

The ground trembled again, and a large crack appeared in the wall.

"Well, whatever it is, it's tearing up more than the dungeons. We need to get away soon," said Ellie.

"What about Daddy?" said Rose suddenly, a worried look on her face.

"And all the others, as well," said Mrs. Wigglepox. "We must do something to help them!"

"There are hundreds of little people still down in the dungeons," said Colleen. "They're being freed by... by whatever it is, but how will they get out? It's much too far for them to just walk out, and I suspect the halls and chambers of this place are all breaking apart. Shouldn't we go and get them before this place collapses in on itself?"

"And there are more in the fortress," said Ellie. "What are we to do for them?"

They were silent for a moment, unsure of what to do next, when the ground shook so violently that they feared the ceiling would collapse.

"Everyone join hands *now!*" said Colleen, and when they had done so, they all vanished in a flash, flying upward through stone until they popped out of the ground and stood on the surface of the island. A hot wind blew on their faces through the dark night air. They were on a hilltop, overlooking a rough harbor.

A single winding road that twisted like a distorted tongue ran from the dark mouth of the fortress gates along a spiny ridge with sheer vertical sides down to the shore, where it opened to the smaller walled docks and rat holes of a goblin town. There, rocking upon the waves in a rough harbor, they saw the fleet of the Witch. A hundred ships at least were docked or anchored there, with one great black ship that dwarfed all others.

"Ships," whispered Nous. "The Colleen and all the rest must get aboard the ships."

"And just how are we going to do that?" asked Colleen.

"Nous will take you," he said slyly. "Nous will take you as prisoners. Then we will capture the ship and run."

Colleen thought for a moment, and then said, "Yes, but first we need more prisoners. I have an idea."

Chapter 17 – The Rescue of Bhrogan

Nous led Ellie along the dungeon passageway toward the main gate. With her worn and dirty clothing, dirty face, and messy hair, she looked every bit a prisoner. Colleen walked beside her, covered head to toe in a goblin robe that hid her face, hands, and feet. The Wigglepox family had stayed on the surface to care for the other little people.

"This robe stinks and itches!" whispered Colleen from beneath the black hood.

"Just don't let anyone see the ring," said Ellie.

Colleen fingered the ring on her hand. Her mother had told her to wear it, and to use it at the right moment to whisk them all away as soon as they found the remaining little people. Their plan was to walk right into the Goblin King's chambers, on the pretense of bringing Ellie as their prisoner.

"The humans must be silent!" hissed Nous. "Only Nous must speak!"

Colleen nodded and walked on, trying not to be too graceful in her stride, and pretending to be a goblin.

They reached the main dungeon gate and Nous slipped a key into the lock. It clicked, and he pushed the iron gate open.

The dungeons shook again, and the open gate broke and fell from its hinges, barely missing Colleen, and sending up a cloud of dust that filled the hall.

Upward they ran, with Ellie before them, her hands seemingly tied. They passed a number of running goblins, who glanced at them, but sped on their way. It seemed to take forever, and with every goblin they passed, Colleen feared that they would be found out. But Nous led them to the very chamber of the king, where two huge goblins stood nervously with great spears.

"We have captured the human," said Nous to the guards. "Let us in to see the king."

One guard slipped through the door and emerged a moment later. "Get in!" he said roughly.

Into the king's royal chambers they went, and Colleen bowed her head a little lower to be sure no light from the torches that lined the walls revealed her face. But she looked up enough to see at the far end of the room a stair of three steps that led up to a dais and a great iron throne studded with many gems and inlaid with gold. On the throne sat the largest goblin she had ever seen. It was easily as big as Aonghus, and across its lap sat a great black broadsword from which a thin stream of smoke seemed to rise. Colleen suddenly realized that she had seen this goblin before – in the courtyard of the castle – it was the one that had been fighting with the wizard.

To the right of the throne stood a black-robed figure holding a staff with a flaming tip. Fear and despair radiated from her, adding an oppressive air to the room.

As they entered, the Witch pointed at Ellie and said, "So, your power has run out, has it? And captured by mere goblins! Oh, I am disappointed in you!"

Ellie said nothing.

The Witch stepped down from the dais and moved toward them.

Colleen felt her heart racing, but she quickly looked about the room. Little people stood with their heads bowed, humiliated and broken, slaves of the Witch and the Goblin King. What could they possibly want such slaves for, she wondered. They were too tiny – surely they could do nothing worthwhile as servants.

"Keep your mind in your heart," warned Richie through the ring. *"There the Witch cannot see you. Do not grapple with your fear or any images that come to your mind. Ignore them, and focus on your task at hand."*

Colleen did her best not to let her mind reach outward to all the things that her eyes were seeing: The goblin guards, the Witch, the massive Goblin King, the poor little people, some of whom were chained to the wall, others that were standing meekly by waiting for some instruction. And all the while, the floor trembled, was quiet, then trembled again. There was also the distant blowing of horns and beating of drums that dimly reverberated through the rock walls of the fortress, and the oppressive fear that threatened to well up within her.

"The throne dais, Colleen," whispered Richie in her mind. *"It is not enchanted. That is our way out."*

Colleen inched away from Ellie, toward several of the little people, and closer to the dais.

"So, we have you at last!" crooned the Witch. "I do not know what you have done to cause these tremors in the ground, but you shall stop it now, or I will destroy all of these little people before your eyes, and then kill you as well!"

Nous pushed Ellie forward, and she stumbled, almost falling. Colleen slipped over to the wall as she did, using the moment of distraction to move out of the center of attention. She was now just a few feet from the nearest of the chained little people – a wretched looking pixie. Just a little closer...

"Speak!" roared the Witch, and the flame of her staff blazed a deeper red. "What have you done?"

"I... I have done nothing," Ellie said weakly.

"Lies!" cried the Witch, moving toward her threateningly.

Colleen slid forward a few more inches.

"Please, Your Majesty," said Ellie, extending a hand toward the Goblin King.

"You shall not speak to the king unless he speaks to you!" hissed the Witch.

Nous jabbed Ellie in the ribs with his club, and Ellie groaned and fell to her knees.

Colleen inched forward.

"You will tell me *NOW*," screamed the Witch. "What have you done?"

The Witch strode over toward Ellie, her flame deepening to almost black. Colleen knew that she had to act quickly, while her back was turned. The Witch raised her staff as if to strike Ellie. Colleen stepped over to one dangling chain and seized it. It sprang to life, leaping from the wall and carrying the pixie with it. Then she ran, touching each chain in turn as she sped toward the dais, and scooped up every one of the little people who had been standing in a line, waiting for their orders.

The Witch, staff still raised high, spun around. A shriek escaped her lips as she saw a human girl's hand protruding from a goblin's robe, and holding four little people. A word of dark command leaped from the Witch's lips, and Colleen felt the goblin robe ripped from her. She stood there, momentarily frozen in fear, for she was standing exposed, her green robe with a sword strapped at her side and her staff tucked in her belt at her back

"What is this!" screamed the Witch, and she swung her staff about, a whirlwind of flames suddenly billowing above her. The goblin guard sprang to life and came running forward.

But suddenly, to her complete surprise, Ellie McGunnegal leaped from the ground and onto the Witch's back, sending them both sprawling to the floor.

For an instant, there was a confusion of black robe and worn work dress, and then the hood of the witch fell back, and everyone in the room – goblins, little people, Colleen, and Ellie herself – froze in utter astonishment. For Ellie was staring face to face with what seemed to be a mirror image of herself. The Witch bore the same facial features – the same golden-red hair, the same delicate nose and cheekbones, the same lips. They would have been near identical twins except for the dreadful eyes of the Witch, which were yellow, with reptilian slits for pupils.

Ellie pushed the Witch away and yelled, "Run, Colleen!"

But Colleen did not run. She had not come all this way to abandon her mother to some dreadful fate at the hands of this Witch.

"Mom, Nous, here – to the dais!" she yelled.

But to her complete horror, the huge muscled body of the king of the goblins stepped down from his throne and blocked her path. The Witch began to laugh and rose to her feet. Ellie too rose and backed away as the Witch reached to pick up her staff, which had fallen. Colleen knew there was only one moment in which to act. The chain that had held the pixie sprang to life once again, leaped upon the Goblin King, wrapped itself about his legs, and sent him crashing to the ground.

Both Ellie and Nous dashed for the dais. Ellie reached Colleen first, and Nous stepped on the fallen king and would have leaped, but the big goblin reached up and tripped him, sending him flying right onto the throne.

"Now!" cried Ellie, and she and Colleen and the little people, and the entire throne upon which Nous sat, sank into the floor of the dais while a bewildered group of goblins and an enraged Witch watched. Her last sight of the room was a wall of dark red flames smothering the dais in searing heat. They had escaped, for the moment.

Colleen found herself suspended in a semi-real world of thick gray that seemed to hang about her like an impenetrable mist. But the sensation only lasted a moment before her vision cleared, and Richie led them through a maze of un-enchanted stone. It was rather like flying, and the rock through which they soared passed by easily, and it felt as though a light breeze were blowing against her face.

"There is a passage here," said Richie, and their course changed. They stepped from the rock and all of them – Colleen, Ellie, and half a dozen little people – found themselves standing in a roughly cut tunnel, the only light coming from the gems on the ring. The little people collapsed to the floor as Colleen sat them down.

"What just happened? The Witch – she looked just like you, Mom," said Colleen.

"I don't know, Colleen. I think it was a trick of some kind – an illusion to confuse us. She is a master of mind games," replied Ellie.

"Did you see her eyes?" said Colleen.

"Another trick, I think. No time to ponder it now, though."

Ellie thought for a moment and said to the little people, "Quickly – you must tell me where the other little people are in the fortress."

A thin leprechaun picked himself up unsteadily and said, "Who are you?"

"Friends," said Ellie. "We've come to rescue you. But we need to know where the others are. Quickly!"

"There are no others," he replied. "We six are all that remain. All of the others have either died or worse."

"What do you mean by that?" asked Colleen.

"Gone. Sent to the pits," he replied, hanging his head. "We were kept only to tickle the fancy of the king. He enjoyed tormenting us. But how did you bring us here? Who are you?"

"There's no time to explain," said Colleen. "My name is Colleen McGunnegal, this here is my mother, Ellie, and Nous – no, don't be afraid of him – he's a friend. We came here with the Wigglepoxes and Oracle. But it would all take too long to tell the tale."

"Who did you say you came with?" asked the leprechaun.

"The Wigglepox family – Edna, Lily and Rose. They're waiting for us. But we lost Oracle," she said sadly.

"Edna Wigglepox? Lily? Rose? They're here? I'm Bhrogan Wigglepox! They're my family!"

"Bhrogan!" cried Colleen, and bent low to have a look at him. "We've been searching for you! Your wife and children have been terribly worried. But you'll be with them soon!"

"I don't mean to rush things," said Ellie. "But if you are all that is left, then we will take you to the others. Come!" said Ellie, taking the extra robe from Nous and slipping it on. It barely covered her feet, and she had to tuck her hands into the sleeves to hide them.

"We will have to walk back to the dungeons from here. You all will need to hide in our pockets. Hold your breath. These robes don't smell the best."

Chapter 18 – Son of Atlantis

"Atlantis!" said McPherson. "But how?"

Atlantis looked at each of them and then at the sword in his hand.

"There is much to tell," he said simply. "But I have told you my name. Now you shall tell me yours."

"But you know my name already," said Frederick. "You... you read my mind when you took my hand, didn't you?"

The king smiled. "You are quick to learn, child," he said. "We have much in common. Please, will you tell me your names and how it is you came here? And what is the year? And have you any word of my people and my sister? And are the goblins defeated? And what of the dragon? There are so many questions!" he said.

"Well," said McPherson, "as to the rest of our names, I am Professor Atlas McPherson, and I am the teacher of these young people – Aonghus, Bran, Abbe, Bib, and Henny McGunnegal, and somehow, you know Frederick's name."

At the mention of the name McGunnegal, Atlantis' eyes widened and he stood a bit straighter. But then, his expression returned to its kingly state, and he said, "Come. Please help me down these stairs. Let us leave this place of death."

"Yes," piped up Henny. "And, Mr. Atlantis, you need a bath very badly."

The king look at her in surprise, and then at himself. "Truly!" he said. "I seem to have been sitting on my throne for some time! Please, let us go down to the beach."

Atlantis sheathed his sword, and Aonghus and Bran helped him down the stairs of the dais, past the many bones, and out into the sunshine. Professor McPherson quietly placed the stone chest he had been discretely hiding behind his back next to the throne, and then followed.

They made their way down to the beach and, as they went, Atlantis looked around him, surveying all that remained of his kingdom. They all saw that he hid his emotions, but his face was grim. When they reached the beach, they helped the king remove his salt-caked armor. He stripped down to the leather shorts he wore beneath his armored skirt, and then stretched hugely in the sun. "Frederick – you shall be my sword bearer. Guard it well," he said, handing him the sword.

His body was thickly muscled and obviously athletic, and as he plunged himself into the waves and swam far out into the breakers, the children talked among themselves, wondering what fate or providence had revived this legend from ages long past. They busied themselves washing the salt from his armor while they waited for him, and when he finally returned, he strode up on the beach like a sea god coming up out of the waves. His long golden hair and beard hung down his chest and back, and he now bore no sign of having been sitting on that throne for untold years.

"There should be fresh water nearby," he said. "Follow me."

He looked about, getting his bearings, and led them a short way into the jungle. Indeed, there a greatly weathered and overgrown fountain still sat. A trickle of water spilled down what had once been a statue of some sort into a deep pool some twenty feet wide, and then ran away in a stream into the jungle.

Atlantis sat on the edge of the pool and sipped the water, tasting it. He splashed himself, washing the salt water from his body, then plunged in, swimming down to its depths, and there he rubbed his arms and hair, until at last he pushed off the bottom and shot to the surface.

"Ah, the water in the Fountain of Summer was always sweet! Although I admit this is the first time I have swum in it!" said the king, smiling as he pulled himself out and sat on the edge again.

"Please, give me my shirt and armor so that I might wash the salt from them," he said.

They did, and he rinsed them in the stream and laid them in the sun on the side of the fountain.

"You look as though you are a bit crusty yourselves. Might you wish to bathe as well?" asked Atlantis. "But no, that can wait. First, we have tales to tell one another, and you must answer my questions. Come, sit here in the sun with me while I dry, and speak with me. What year is this?"

"Your Majesty," said McPherson, "you are the second person of great antiquity who has awakened to us and asked that question. It is the year of our Lord, 1846."

"You have a king then?" asked Atlantis. "And how do you reckon this date? Does it mark the beginning of his kingdom?"

"The date marks the year of his birth," replied Bib. "He's called the King of kings."

"Remarkable!" replied Atlantis. "I should like to meet this King of kings and speak with him of his dominion and compare it with my own."

The McGunnegals all looked at one another.

"Well, yes, I suppose one day you will," said Aonghus. "But I think your kingdom may predate his birth by a good many years."

"Yes," said Bib. "The earliest account we have of the Kingdom of Atlantis is by a philosopher named Plato. He said that it existed some 9600 years BC – that is, before Christ – the King of kings we spoke of. And that it had conquered many lands, but after some failed war, it was destroyed in a single day and night of misfortune."

Atlantis looked down into the pool.

"Misfortune," he murmured. "Is that the only word that history has left of my nation and my people? Did none of them escape to tell the true tale?"

Again, they all looked at each other.

"We think some of them did survive," said Aonghus.

He looked at the professor, and then said, "We *think* that *we* are their descendants."

Atlantis stood, looked at them slowly one by one, and said, "There is a test."

"What sort of test?" asked the professor. "I will not have these children harmed. They are in my care."

"No, this test will not harm them, or you, Atlas McPherson. But before I speak further of myself and my people – and of my doomed kingdom - I must know for sure who you are. Will you trust me?" asked the king.

After a moment, Aonghus and Bran both stepped forward and stood before Atlantis, and Aonghus spoke. "Nothing, sir, is going to happen to our sisters or anyone else here without our approval. The professor says that we are in his care, and that is true. But Bran and I are also responsible for their care, and we will not allow *anything* to happen to them."

Atlantis raised an eyebrow and looked up and down at these two brash young men, as though measuring their strength and abilities.

"Indeed!" he said and laughed. "I would not dare to allow harm to come to any of your sisters, or to you. I perceive that you have the strength of giants in your blood, good Aonghus. I should not wish to rouse it! But come with me and I will show you the test. I myself will undergo it first, and you, no doubt, will wish to go second before you will allow anyone else to do so."

He was nearly dry now from the hot sun, as were his clothes, and he put them on, but only buckled his sword around his waist, allowing the others to carry his armor for him.

"We must return to the throne room, I fear," he said. "It is there that we shall perform the test."

They made their way back, and when they reached the room of bones, Bran said, "These skeletons do not look human. What are they?"

Atlantis paused, looking down at the bones that littered the room.

"They are my... *misfortune*," he said. "Although not all of it." Then he climbed the stairs to his throne.

"This was my throne room – the center of my kingdom," said Atlantis. "From here, I ruled, I judged, I conquered... and I died – or perhaps I did not?"

He paused and, for a few moments, his gaze grew distant, as though he were remembering some distant and terrible event.

"But here also I built the seat of my power – for me and my descendants forever. Only someone of my own lineage can unlock the secrets of my throne and cause the powers that I have laid hidden in this place to be unleashed. For all others, this is nothing but a golden throne of cold, dead metal and stone. Behold!"

Atlantis sat on his throne, placing his hands on its ornate, golden, gem-studded arms, and as he did, the gems began to radiate light, and on the wall in front of him, a silver door began to shine like the moon.

It captivated their minds, drawing their thoughts toward it like a hypnotist's coin.

All except Frederick stared, spellbound by the door's magic.

"Right, then," said Frederick, climbing the steps of the dais and standing before the king.

"Turn that off, please Your Majesty. I've seen this sort of thing before, and so has the professor, or so he says. I know exactly what that is. It's a door into Anastazi the Great's Timeless Hall. But, please – they don't know their peril by staring at it. Please, do turn it off."

Atlantis looked in wonder at Frederick. "You know of Anastazi, and of the Timeless Hall?"

"Yes, I heard all about them in the Land of the Little People. I saw one of these Gates there. Colleen got all mesmerized by it too, and nearly took a swim in a big river," he said.

Atlantis raised an eyebrow again. "Oh, do tell more, Frederick," he said.

"I don't suppose I should have even said that. But see here, if you're a wise and fair king, turn that off before they lose themselves in it. They weren't ready for it."

Atlantis thought for a moment, and then said, "No, Frederick. You must turn it off." He rose from his throne and stepped aside.

Frederick looked at Atlantis and then at the throne. He swallowed hard and then slowly slid into the seat.

"Place your hands on the two great gems on either arm of the chair," said Atlantis. "And then *will* the door to be silent."

Frederick placed his hands on two smooth white stones that were embedded in the arms of the throne, stared at the door and, with all his strength, mentally willed the doorway to go dark – to be still – to silence its siren call to every eye that beheld it. Instantly, the doorway flashed and went out. All of the McGunnegals and the professor gasped and looked about. Then they looked up, and seeing Frederick sitting on the throne with Atlantis standing beside him, were amazed.

"What happened?" asked Aonghus.

"You shouldn't have stared at the door," said Frederick. "That seems to happen to first-timers."

"First-timers?" said Bib. "What does that mean? And what are you doing, sitting on that throne?"

"I asked him to be seated," said Atlantis.

Frederick quickly got up, feeling embarrassed. He also felt both awkward and thrilled at what Atlantis had just said. Could it be that *he* was truly a direct descendant of this dead, and now living, king of the ancient island of Atlantis? It was just too incredible. He felt that he had never been much of anything – just a boy. His only real talent was that he seemed to have a limitless capacity to *remember* things. In fact, he didn't ever seem to forget anything that he learned or read or saw. But there, in the Land of the Little People, strange things had begun to happen to him. Had that land somehow awakened something in him – something deep in his ancestry? He wondered.

"Please, sir," said Frederick to Atlantis, "might these others also sit on your throne and, well, try it out?"

"Of course, please do. You all have begun to interest me a great deal," he replied.

One by one, the McGunnegals sat down on the great throne, and instructed by King Atlantis, they placed their hands on the white gems and willed the door to come to life. But although the white gems glowed softly, the door remained dark.

Finally, Professor McPherson was the only one who had not sat on the throne.

"No, no," he replied. "I think that I shall not sit in that great seat, Your Majesty. It is yours and yours alone. It is not fitting for another grown man to even rest in it while the true king still lives, unless there should be great need."

Atlantis raised an eyebrow and inclined his head toward the professor.

"As you wish," he replied, and he seated himself in his great chair. He gazed at them, a thoughtful expression on his face.

Frederick could see the disappointment on the faces of the McGunnegals. All of the clues that they had found back in Ireland – the writing on the stones around their farm, and the same writing on Professor McPherson's stone, and on the sword that he had found, and all of their strange abilities that other people did not seem to have – these all pointed to some amazing connection for them in the distant past – some connection with a people like themselves who had lived long, long ago, and from whom they had descended. If they did not come from the people of Atlantis, then where did they come from? Who had been the people that built the castle on their farm?

It was Bib who spoke the words that Frederick knew they all must be thinking and feeling.

"Sir," she said, "we were so sure that this place must be the answer to our own family riddles. We thought surely we must have some Atlantian blood in us. What else could it be? We all have strange abilities, and our family has always been long lived – most live well over a hundred years. If we are not your descendants, then... *what are we?*"

Frederick was thinking not only this, but the incredible ramifications of what had just happened were beginning to sink in. *He* was Atlantian!

Atlantis looked deeply at Bib, as if peering into her mind through her blue-lavender eyes. Then, a thought seemed to take hold of him, and he looked one by one into their faces.

"Your eyes..." he said, and then paused. He began to say more, but stopped, shook his head, and changed the subject.

"Perhaps time will answer all of these riddles. There is some power in your bloodline – did you not see the crystals on my throne glow at your touch? Simply because you are not my descendants does not mean that there is not some connection between us. But now, how is it that you have you come here?" he asked them. "Was it an accident that shipwrecked you on this husk of what is left of my kingdom? And how is it that my sword has returned to me? I remember..."

He grew silent, and his face was grave once again as long ago memories came back to him.

"I brought your sword to you, sir," replied Frederick. "I found it stuck in a tree in a cave. The Lady Danu told me to find the king in the sea. We found you, and when I put the sword in your hands, you awoke!"

"It is as she said!" whispered Atlantis.

"*You* know the Lady?" asked Frederick in amazement.

Atlantis saw the questioning look on their faces and said, "I believe you deserve to hear the tale. Sit here on my dais – or what is left of it, and I will tell it to you, and perhaps it will answer some of your questions as well."

They all sat, and as he glanced about his throne room once again, a light flashed in his emerald green eyes. He surveyed the scattered bones, the broken wall, and looked into each of their faces as they waited expectantly.

"Once," he began in his deep rich voice, "my kingdom stretched far and wide, beyond my own land here, and covered much of the lands to the east, northeast, and southeast, and to the coasts of the western lands as well.

"I conquered many peoples, and they gave me homage and gold and riches. And in return, I and my people taught them many things – the secrets of the earth and sky and sea – of mathematics and philosophy and astronomy. We taught them how to build and grow, and many of them grew great, and their kings were wise and strong.

"There was no place on earth that I did not go – from the icy lands of the north and south to the strange countries of the far east and west. I sought wisdom and knowledge through the wide world and, most of all, I sought one grand prize – the wealth of all wealth, and treasure of all treasures."

"What was that?" asked Henny, who was sitting at his feet.

"Eternal life!" replied Atlantis. "What more is there to gain, when one has conquered the world?

"In my journeys, I found that all peoples of the earth were seeking this selfsame treasure. All men desired it, and all feared death – that final vanity that strips us naked of all that we have hoarded to ourselves.

"There were hints! Yes, there were stories and legends and myths that stretched back in time to a place where there was no death, and *that* place I longed to reach, for I felt the creep of mortality's shadow beginning to cast itself over my soul.

"For some people, this prize was a fountain. For some, a tree. For some, a river. For some, a valley. For others, a mountain. But I became convinced that somewhere that place or that thing that gave unending life must still exist, for there was one place – a place that my father had found – where time did not seem to pass! I was convinced that *that* place was somehow, someway, connected to that ultimate treasure."

"Who was your father?" asked Frederick.

"My father?" said Atlantis. He paused for a moment, considering how to answer. Then he straightened and said, "My father was named Anastazi."

"*Anastazi?* Anastazi the Great?" said Frederick. "But... wasn't he a great Elven Lord? Didn't he create the Timeless Hall?"

"Yes! He was *the* Elven Lord in this world, come here from his ancient home with great hopes and aspirations through the Timeless Hall. No, he did not create the Timeless Hall – he found it, and it was there he constructed the

Gates," replied Atlantis. "And *that* is the place that I was speaking of – that place I am sure must be linked to the secret of eternal life."

"But if this Anastazi was your father, wouldn't that make *you* elven as well?" asked Bib.

Atlantis smiled. "I am half elven. My mother was Branna, a human woman."

"But I thought that all the stories said that the elves lived forever," said Bran.

"It is true that they do not naturally die like the race of men, although their bodies can be destroyed, and their spirits go on to another place. But although my life was long – much longer than that of others, I felt *age* coming upon me. I had inherited the doom of men. I was mortal. My sister, Mor-Fae, however, took after my father and showed no signs or inclinations toward her human, mortal side. She was, it seemed, immortal, and was free to follow after other pursuits, and not this maddening search that I had embarked on.

"But, as I said, I knew that all of these legends of a time and place where people had once had immortality must have some common source. I traveled not only across the face of this world, but to others as well, and I sought more and more for ways to reach outward. *What of the skies and the deep oceans?* I wondered. *Is this secret in the deep places of those realms?* I sought power and for ways to extend my search farther and deeper than before. I made great ships, and one ship – the Ship of ships! The *Atlantis* I named her, for she would be the greatest vessel ever made – made with the cunning and wisdom and magic of all the races and peoples I had encountered in my journeys – and *she* would carry me beyond the Eight Worlds to hidden realms that even my father and sister did not know of!"

"What happened to your ship?" asked Frederick excitedly.

"That, my friends, is a question that we shall soon answer, for she was hidden away when my... *misfortune*... took hold, and I kept the key to sailing her with me at all times."

He paused, and a look almost of fear flashed across his face. He looked down beside his throne. But seeing the stone chest there, he seemed to relax, and a puzzled expression came over him for a moment. He reached down and opened it. Then, he sighed with relief, closed the lid, and looked back at his audience.

"But first, allow me to complete my story, and then we shall come to the matter of the good ship *Atlantis*," he replied.

"In my ship, I did indeed travel to other worlds. On long, perilous journeys I went, and some of these I will not speak of. But it was on one of them I found what I believed to be one who knew the secret, but he demanded a price for such knowledge."

"What did he want?" asked Henny.

"To be free!" replied Atlantis. "He was trapped on a lonely, barren world. Marooned there long, long ago, by whom he would not say."

"Did you set him free? Did you rescue him?" asked Henny.

"No!" replied Atlantis, a flash of anger in his voice.

"No," he said again, more quietly. "It was not I who set him free."

The king paused again, some inner turmoil reflected on his face.

"I will say no more of him except that *he*, or perhaps I should say *it* was the cause of my downfall and the loss of all that you see and all that you do not see." Atlantis sighed and looked weary, then continued.

"But alas, he was set free! And here, to my kingdom – to my very throne room he came. Yes, through that mystical door that you have now seen, he came with his armies. And here, in the end, I fought him."

Atlantis stood then and looked about. He gazed upon the mangled bones of a hundred skeletons that littered his once-glorious palace. Then he unsheathed his sword and held it before him.

"One by one, I slew his guards, until at last I faced him alone, although I was weary from the long battle. The huge, undulating body of my foe came upon me! Again and again, I drove my bright sword into his bloated flesh, and again and again, I leaped away from his thrashing form. But in my mind, he showed me the doom of my kingdom, and his dark hordes pillaging my fair cities. It was this that proved my doom, for I paused in the battle, overwhelmed with grief for my people. The Worm, for a worm he was, then swept his bulk upon me. I was hurled to my throne and I felt death at hand. The Worm laughed at me and said, 'So shall be all of your kind, and this world shall be my own!' I knew there was but one thing to do – one last desperate measure. I would unleash the doom of my own kingdom, but in so doing, put an end to this dread threat to all humanity. With my dying strength, I summoned what I had long hidden, and when it came, Atlantis was destroyed, and all the armies of the Great Worm sank beneath the waves of the sea. The Worm itself, seeing its own end, would have devoured me in its wrath, but lo, the Lady Danu, on that dread last day of my kingdom, came walking out of the sea, and the brightness of her coming dissolved the nightmares that my foe had spun about my mind as we battled. He, wounded and weak, was thrown down and, with the last of his power, escaped through the Gate that you have seen.

"The Lady came to me as the waves of destruction lapped on the steps of my palace and said *'Sleep, O king of the sea! Sleep until the son of your unborn son comes to waken you!'* She then took my fallen sword, and my last vision was to see her fair form carry it away beneath the waves.

"Alas for my people!" he cried out, "Alas for my kingdom! Alas for the life that once I sought and have lost! But I foretell that I shall not leave this life until my sword has pierced the heart of my ancient foe, and then that Great Worm and I together shall go down into the bitter dust of death! And you, Frederick, son of my son, you shall inherit the remains of my shattered kingdom!"

Chapter 19 – A Light in the Dungeons

"Richie says there's no passage through the rock to the outside from here," said Colleen. "We have to get back to the dungeons."

"It is not far," said Nous. "We are in the goblin quarters. Nous has been here once. He knows the way."

Colleen handed the ring to her mother, but she gave it back. "You keep it, Colleen," she said, and put a finger to her lips when her daughter tried to protest. "You've shown yourself stronger than I with this. Wear it well."

Colleen nodded and touched the three stones. "I will, Mom," she replied.

Nous led the way. There was a great deal of bustling about in the goblin quarters, and as they hurried along, they were jostled about as the forces of the Witch were called to arms. The goblin holes stank horribly, and more than once, they passed foul pools that Colleen guessed must be ponds of Ooze. Somehow, they managed to make it out into the main corridor, and then down into an empty one.

"This way to the dungeons," said Nous.

They soon found the broken door that led down, but it was guarded by a big goblin bearing a spear.

As they approached, he held the spear ready and said, "No one goes down. Orders. There's something going on – something or someone has escaped, and orders are that no one comes in or out of the Pits."

Nous stepped forward and said, "New orders have been given now. We are to go down and round up those little people and make sure they're all accounted for."

"Whose orders are those?" demanded the guard. "I've not heard it."

Nous paused for a moment and then said, "There!" and pointed down the hall.

The guard turned to look, and Nous jumped at him, knocking the spear from his hand.

The goblin struck the wall and rebounded with a roar, leaping for Nous, but he dodged aside and, with a quickness that amazed Colleen, was behind the other goblin with one arm around his throat and the other locking his arm behind his head.

There was a great deal of thrashing for several moments, and then the guard lay still.

Nous got up, breathing heavily. "He's not dead," he said.

"Neat trick," said Ellie. "Where did you learn that?"

"The Frederick," replied Nous, grinning.

They pulled the unconscious guard in and went as quickly as they could down into the dungeons. Soon they passed the magical barrier, and Richie informed Colleen that they could now move through the stone.

"Hold on to me, Nous," said Colleen, and he took her hand with a grin.

Immediately, they fell through the floor as the rock creatures carried them with lightning speed back to the surface where all the rescued little people were waiting, hiding among the boulders. They were greeted with whispered cheers as they appeared, and Ellie and Colleen carefully put those they had rescued down in their midst.

Mrs. Wigglepox, Lily, and Rose made their way over, and as Bhrogan turned, their eyes met. Mrs. Wigglepox gasped, and Lily and Rose cried out for joy. They ran to each other and embraced, and wept tears of great joy.

"I thought we had lost you for good," cried Mrs. Wigglepox.

"It was the thought of you all that kept me going," he said weakly, and he sat on the ground, embracing them.

Colleen grinned from ear to ear, watching their joyful reunion, until Mrs. Wigglepox said, "Bhrogan, I suppose you have met my good friend, Colleen McGunnegal."

"Yes!" said Bhrogan. "She is elvish, is she not?"

"That's what I thought, but she says she is human, as is her mother," replied Mrs. Wigglepox.

"Human!" replied Bhrogan. "I did not know that they possessed such powers! Pleased to meet you. Edna, how is the Wigglepox Tree?"

"It lives," she replied. "At least when we last saw it."

Bhrogan embraced them all again, and their conversation would have gone on except that Colleen began to sense a need for haste.

"Right!" said Colleen. "Now, how are we going to get all these little people safely stowed onto a goblin ship? There's no way we can carry them all. And there are many more down in the deep dungeons, aren't there?"

Suddenly, the earth shook so violently that they all tumbled to the ground. With a terrifying sound of cracking and shattering rock, a great tower of the Witch's fortress split down the middle and crashed into rubble.

Colleen closed her eyes and focused her senses underground. Down she searched, looking through layer after layer of rock and stone, through passage after passage her mind swept, but to her astonishment, they were all empty. There was no sign of life.

"They... they're all gone!" she gasped. "All of them. I can't see any of the little people! But there is something... Could it be...? I must go see!"

"Colleen, wait!" said her mother, but too late. Colleen had slipped into the rock and was gone.

Downward she sped, deeper and deeper until she came to the place where she had seen the bright figure tearing down doors and freeing the prisoners.

The hall into which she emerged was ominously silent. The shattered remains of the dungeon lay everywhere in the darkness. The sense of *emptiness* was thick around her.

She made her way down the passage, past the broken remains of the Witch's deepest dungeons until she came to the very end of the great hall. There, a huge iron gate with thick bars and massive doors lay twisted and wrecked. Great locks and keys and chains were broken and scattered across the floor as if someone had snapped them into pieces and cast them aside. Where the gate had once stood, a gaping black hole loomed before her.

Out of the darkness came a deep, eerie moan, then there was a distant flash, and a sound like great thunder rolling in the depths. The ground shook and all was still. Colleen crept forward, and a chill ran down her spine.

"Beware," whispered Richie to her mind.

She crept through the rubble that had been the door and peered into the darkness. Down she gazed, and knew that a deep abyss lay before her. One step more and she would tumble in. But whether by virtue of the ring that she wore or by that deeper sense that had awakened within her, she perceived far, far below what appeared to be an old gray man, bound hand and foot in chains. He wore nothing except a tattered loincloth about his waist. But he was falling downward, farther and farther into the pit, and with him rained down the broken remnants of chains and locks and keys, as though they had all been thrown into this abyss like so much refuse.

Colleen's first thought that he was yet another prisoner of the Witch who was in need of rescue, and had fallen over the edge and would soon be lost. But even as he tumbled deeper into the endless darkness, somehow, he sensed her searching mind, and his own thought caught hers and tried to seize it, clinging to her as though it were his lifeline. His hatred of all living things raked at her soul, reaching upward even as he fell, seeking to pull her in after him, to fall with him forever into the blackness. She knew at once that this was the Gray Man – that apparition only spoken of in fearful whispers by both little people and goblins alike.

A haunting voice whispered in her mind, "Colleen McGunnegal, one day we shall meet face to face. But I shall pass through many worlds in my fall. Join me now, and in the end taste the Final Darkness with me!"

For a moment, a strange vertigo took hold of her, confusion and fear gripped her, and she nearly pitched forward into the gaping maw. Then far, far above came another flash of lightning that pierced the darkness and struck with terrific power at the falling form. Colleen steadied herself and watched, as, with vain, threatening gestures, the Gray Man slipped further and further into oblivion, his power fading away as he vanished beyond her sight.

Colleen looked up. The pit rose to unknown heights and, just at the edge of her vision, she thought that she saw a great crowd of tiny figures flying upward, all of them wreathed in rainbows and light, dancing and swirling about a shining figure. They were flying upward, upward and out of the black pit that once held them.

"You may join us if you wish," came a distant voice to her mind. "We will wait for you! But first, remember your task at hand! Remember the Island of the Waking Tree! Remember the waters of light!"

Then it seemed that they rose to a great height, shouted for joy, and were gone.

All was silent now, and Colleen stared into the void that lay between the two visions she had just experienced. She was unsure of what to make of it, but it seemed to her as though two great choices had been offered, and she was free to take either path – to tumble headlong into the darkness, alone with the

Gray Man, or to soar upward with a great company of bright companions to an incredible adventure that would never end.

A freakish allure whispered in a tiny corner of her mind, as though a last echo of the Gray Man's power still tugged at her. "Leap into the darkness!" it crooned. She hesitated. Then the last words she had heard from the bright cloud of little people re-echoed in her mind. "Remember your task at hand..."

"Well, don't just stand here in the middle, staring," she said aloud. "Move in one direction or the other!"

She looked up, took a deep breath, then turned and ran back the way she had come. Speeding back to her waiting mother and friends, she realized that she had been a single step away from disaster.

"I suppose all of life is like that," she whispered to herself.

Chapter 20 – The Waking Tree

Colleen and Ellie knew that they had only moments before word of their escape reached the goblins, and that they had to act quickly. Crouching on the hill above the docks, Colleen put on the spare goblin robe, and she and Nous led the entire group of little people and Ellie down the hill.

Goblins were rushing this way and that, some shouting and others looking utterly confused. Horns blared, drums beat, tremors shook the ground, and general pandemonium had taken hold.

Right up to the largest ship they went, and only then, a big, burly goblin stopped them.

"Where are you taking these prisoners?" he barked.

"The whole island is coming apart!" hissed Nous. "We're evacuating. Prisoners are to be put aboard ship."

Another quake shook the ground, and a section of wall around the fortress fell with a resounding crash.

Fear filled the big goblin's eyes, and then he said, "Get 'em on board and take 'em to the brig." Then he ran off shouting, "Get aboard, you swine, the island is sinking. Get aboard if you don't want to sink with it!"

Colleen, Ellie, Nous, and the little people hurried aboard, and Nous neatly lifted the gangplank and dropped it into the water. He grinned hugely, revealing his brown teeth, and said, "Oops."

There were still at least half a dozen goblins on the ship that they could see, so Nous led them all below deck.

"Wait here," he said and ran back out onto the deck. Colleen peered out after him and saw that he was untying the ropes that bound the ship to the docks.

"Hey, you!" shouted one of the goblins, "What do you think you're doing?"

"Get the ship ready to launch!" Nous hissed back. "The island is crumbling to pieces!"

"I haven't gotten those orders," growled the goblin as he came near.

Nous bent down, grabbed the goblin's leg, and neatly flipped him over the side of the ship. There was a yell and a splash, and two other goblins came running to see what had happened.

"The oaf went over the side," said Nous.

The two bent over the railing, looking down at the goblin who was now flailing in the water. Nous did the same to both of them, and there were two more splashes, followed by a good deal of yelling coming from the sea below.

Nous finished untying the ropes, and then saw that there were at least three goblins up in the sails.

"Let down the sails!" he called. "Orders!"

Black sails were lowered and tied, and the goblins descended the masts. A seaward wind caught in the sails and the ship began to drift slowly away from the docks.

"Where's the captain and crew? Are they below?" asked one of the goblins, looking about suspiciously.

"They fell in the water," said Nous, pointing.

The three goblins gaped over the side, and this time, the struggling goblins yelled up, "Grab him!"

Nous leaped on the first goblin and tried to throw him over as well, but the others joined in the brawl. It would have gone badly for Nous, except that there was a sudden *thump* and one of the goblins that was on top of him went limp. The other two spun about and found themselves face to face with Colleen and Ellie. Colleen held her staff in her right hand. She had given the goblin a good whack on its head, stunning it, but even now, it was waking, rubbing its head. Ellie stood by her side, Colleen's sword in her hand, held threateningly before her.

Nous took advantage of the distraction and grappled with one of the other goblins, attempting to wrestle it to the ground. The last one, seeing the wicked-looking sword in Ellie's hand, and facing two opponents, dove over the side of the ship and was gone.

There was quite a tussle for several moments before Nous and the goblin broke apart and then it too jumped overboard and vanished with a splash.

The last goblin was fully awake now, glaring at Ellie's sword with mixed hatred and surprise. Then it too fled, leaping over the rail with a cry.

Goblins were now gathering on the docks and shouting warnings and curses. An arrow *zinged* over Colleen's head, and she ducked.

"Get below!" yelled Ellie as more arrows followed the first.

Colleen and Nous ran for the door that led to the cabins, but Ellie climbed to the upper deck and, taking the wheel, turned the ship out to sea. An arrow stuck in the decking beside her, but she held her course and, in a few moments, the cries and darts of the goblins began to slip away behind them.

After some time, Colleen, Nous, and the little people emerged from below and looked at the dark island behind them. Then one of them gave a cry – other ships were lowering their sails now. The chase would be on very soon.

Colleen ran to the bow of the ship and looked out over the ocean. The sun was just peeking over the horizon to their right.

"We're going the wrong way!" cried Colleen. "Mother! Take the wheel and head west, away from the sun!" she called.

"But why, Colleen? The nearest land is to the north, isn't it?" she called back.

"No, not the nearest," she replied. "There is one other island we must go to. The Island of the Waking Tree!"

Then she closed her eyes and began to sing. For a moment, the wind died, and the sails fell limp. She concentrated harder and sang, and a wind from the east sprang up and filled the sails. The ship leaped forward and they were off, leaving the Witch's fortress far behind.

But what they did not see was a great black, winged creature rise from the deck of the foremost of the ships that were now leaving the harbor. Like a foul red meteor, a dark flame circled higher and higher into the air, and then, with dreadful speed, made its way west until it hovered far above them, watching with greedy reptilian eyes to see where its prey would go.

* * *

The wind that Colleen had summoned blew like a gale even after she stopped singing. It propelled them forward for hours, threatening to rip the sails apart and causing the ship to creak and groan as it barreled through the waves. But Nous stayed with the wheel, and at Colleen's instruction, he held their course westward.

For the first time since they had been reunited, Colleen and Ellie had time to talk and become reacquainted with one another. It had been nearly a year since Ellie had fallen through the mirror, and they had a great deal of catching up to do. They talked mostly about the family, and Ellie asked question after question about Adol and the other children, and she grew very concerned when Colleen told her of the potato famine and how things were going so badly for the farm and all of Ireland.

The noon sun was high, and they were still discussing all these things when Ellie squinted, pointed ahead, and said, "Land!"

Indeed, directly ahead of them, they could see the top of a high plateau rising from the ocean. All the little people gathered to watch as it drew near. Tall cliffs of dark rock rose up from scant sandy shores, and towering high into the air for easily five hundred feet stood an amazing, huge tree.

"It's the Waking Tree!" whispered Mrs. Wigglepox. "My heart tells me we have found it!"

At Colleen's bidding, the wind slowed, and as they drew into shallower water, it stopped altogether, and they let down the anchor. Lowering two of the lifeboats from the ship, Nous and Colleen took one with half of the little people, and Ellie took the other with the rest. Once ashore, they found a fairly smooth slope that ran up the cliff side to the plateau above. They followed this to the top and came out on a grassy plain.

There, about fifty yards from the cliff edge, towering high into the sky, was the tree. It was easily fifty feet across at the base, and its smooth brown trunk rose far into the air. A rich green canopy of leaves spread outward over the plateau. A wholesome feeling seemed to radiate from it, and as they walked forward, there was a sense that it was *aware* of them. The magic all about it was so potent that all weariness and despair and fear melted away, as though its power was just the opposite of the Witch's Spell that had afflicted the forest and its people for so long.

They stared in wonder for several long moments, gazing up into its fabulous branches that spread out over the plateau. Then, all at once, the little people ran through the grass toward the massive tree, tears of joy streaming down their faces. They shouted and danced and clapped their hands, their years of torment in the dungeons of the Witch forgotten. It had been too long since they had lost this great relic of their civilization – the source of the life of the forest, and the birthplace of their first ancestors.

But suddenly, from behind them, came the concussive sound of an explosion. They wheeled around, and, looking out at the ship, saw that it was burning. Great billows of smoke rose up from it as its entire deck was consumed in flames. Then they saw what had happened, for out of the sky a ball of fire fell upon the ship and, with a tremendous *BOOM*, it exploded as it struck the deck, cracking it completely in two. They watched in helpless horror as both halves of their ship sank beneath the waves, leaving nothing but smoke and steam.

Then a small black speck in the sky appeared and grew larger and larger, until, with terrible speed, it wheeled down upon them, and landed beside the Waking Tree. Whether it was a great bat or a featherless bird, or some flying reptile, Colleen could not tell, but it was hideous, and it croaked like a sickly frog. From its back a black robed figure dismounted, bearing a staff whose end burned with red fire. The Witch had found them.

Her laugh floated across the grassy plain, and she cried out, "Thank you, my dears, for leading me to this marvelous tree! I allowed you to escape me for this very reason. It was said that only one pure of heart could find it. How kind of you to lead me straight here! And now, my little friends, see your world die!"

Her staff blazed, and its searing fire struck at the roots of the tree, enveloping the massive trunk in hot flames.

"No!" cried all the little people at once.

The Witch leaped onto the back of her beast and soared skyward, flames roaring from her staff as she circled round and round the tree, igniting its fair trunk, branches, and leaves in a deadly inferno. The Waking Tree seemed to come to life, writhing in agony as it burned and, all the while, the Witch laughed her hideous laugh as she rained down more and more flames upon it. Then, with a final wicked laugh, she wheeled over their heads and said, "Farewell, my simple ones. My fleet sails now to burn the rest of your pitiful forest to the ground! Sit here on the ruin of your life and ponder what tomorrow will bring your world!"

One last blast of fire fell upon the beach with a sickening, splintering detonation, and they knew that their boats had been destroyed as well.

Colleen watched as she flew northward, and there, far on the horizon, she could see the tiny outlines of black sails.

The horror at hand brought her attention around again. Mrs. Wigglepox and the others ran forward, but Colleen and Ellie ran after them, calling for them to stop. Bits of burning leaves and branches were beginning to rain down from above. Nous stayed back, not knowing what to say or do.

Mrs. Wigglepox, tears streaking her face, cried out, "Colleen! Call the waves!"

"The waves?" said Colleen. Then she realized what she was saying.

She ran to the cliff's edge and looked out over the ocean. She focused, and there she saw one of the great beings of the deep that lazily made the waves its home. She called to it in her heart, and immediately it responded, feeling her desperation. Then she called again upon the wind, and it whipped upon the water in a frenzied gale, picking it up and forming a great waterspout.

Toward them it came, and Colleen ran back crying, "Everyone, hold onto one another *now!*"

They looked behind her at the great water as it rose high into the sky. Just as it was about to reach them, she grabbed her mother's hand, and together they sank down into the thick soil beneath their feet, the power of the rock people saving them once again.

Colleen could sense the incredible roots of the Waking Tree all about them. But they also seemed to be writhing in agony, and she knew that this was not a safe place for them to be.

"Back!" she called in her mind, and up to the surface they rose again, just as the water spout lashed its wet fury past the island and then fell back into the sea on the other side.

They looked up, and there before them were the smoking remains of what had once been the most magnificent tree in all the Eight Worlds. All of the leaves were gone, and its smaller branches fell like so many sticks of charcoal to the ground. A shudder passed over the tree, and the ground beneath them writhed. Then, a sweet smell like rose incense filled the air, and all was still.

All of them stood in shocked silence before the magnitude of the tragedy that had just occurred.

Colleen could hardly believe it. In a few moments, they had gone from utter joy to absolute shock and a sense of loss too deep for words. Then she remembered something and reached into her cloak.

"The Lady's gift! It can heal all wounds!" she thought.

She searched her pockets for it, but it was gone. Then she remembered – she had lost it when she had gone back in time – it had fallen from her cloak, and it was no doubt buried beneath the ruins of the Wizards Castle, far, far away amid the Burning Sands. She had failed.

She fell to her knees beside Mrs. Wigglepox and together they wept.

Chapter 21 – The Dwarf and the Man

When Adol woke, it was to the smell of stuffed mushrooms. He thought that he had been dreaming some dreadful nightmare and that when he opened his eyes he would be back in his own bed at home, but instead, he found himself lying in a very strange room. Sunlight was streaming through one window, and very old tapestries and curtains hung from bronze rings fastened to the walls. Someone was humming a tune in an adjacent room and occasionally hammering on something metal.

Adol tried to sit up, but the world began to spin. He quickly lay down again and waited for the dizziness to pass. Then, more slowly this time, he pulled himself up. His ribs were sore and bandaged, and he was much thinner than he had been. His shoes and shirt were neatly placed on a small chair beside his bed.

The humming grew louder, and into the room stepped the smallest man that he had ever seen. He was not more than four and a half feet tall and sported a long white beard that nearly touched the ground.

"Well!" he said, looking surprised and rather happy. "Welcome back to the land of the living!"

"Who are you? Where am I?" asked Adol, running his fingers through his hair.

"My name is Doc," he replied. "And I am a dwarf. And you are Adol McGunnegal, father of Colleen McGunnegal, and you have been searching for her."

"How..." Adol began, but Doc raised a hand and cut him off.

"You've talked quite a bit in your sleep. I was quite concerned. But you do heal quickly! Quite astonishing, actually," replied Doc.

"What happened to me? I remember waking up in a tree, and then there was a terrible storm," said Adol.

"Yes, you nearly died in it. I'm quite surprised that you didn't. The little people found you and brought you to me," said Doc.

Adol tried to rise.

"Now you just lie down there!" said Doc, rushing to his side. "I'm too old to catch you if you fall, and you are much too big regardless. But see here, Mr.

McGunnegal, I have news of your daughter, Colleen."

"Colleen!" said Adol, lying back down. "What news? Have you seen her?"

"Yes, indeed. She and my brother and a young lad named Frederick, and a family of little people, all went south some days ago. They were traveling by horse and wagon, so I suspect there's no chance of you catching them now, even if you tried. They will have passed into the desert by now, and nothing leaves a trail in that place," replied Doc.

"But why?" asked Adol. "Where were they going?"

Doc looked at him with compassion and said, "She was determined. I could not talk her out of it, although I told her the journey would be perilous."

"What do you mean? Where did they go?" demanded Adol, sitting up again with difficulty.

"They went to the Witch's fortress, Mr. McGunnegal," replied Doc. "She went to find her mother."

"Ellie?" said Adol, amazed. "Ellie is here?"

"Colleen believed it to be so," replied the dwarf.

"Then I must go to them!" he said, and pulled himself to his feet, swaying slightly.

"Now, Adol McGunnegal, do sit down. You can no more follow them than you can stand on your own two feet at the moment. Come now, I've prepared a bite for you to eat. You'll be well soon enough, eating my fare, and then we will discuss how we might find your daughter. Come and sit," said Doc.

Adol swayed for a moment, then nodded, and seated himself at a none-too-clean table. Doc unceremoniously blew off the dust, blushed, and said "Sorry about that. It's rare that I have guests."

He placed a large plate of stuffed mushrooms and some other dish, along with a mug of a strong-smelling drink in front of him. Adol paused, whispered thanks, and then voraciously downed every scrap of food that was set before him.

He asked for and received seconds, and then thirds, before finally placing his hands on his stomach and saying, "Thank you."

"You are quite welcome," Doc replied. "I rarely have guests who enjoy their food so much! In fact, I rarely have guests! But now that the Spell seems to have been broken, I've had them every day! The forest is coming to life again, and the goblins and stalkers and such evil things seem to have fled south, but we fear that they are gathering for an assault. The Witch will not be idle. She will come, and we must all be prepared. I think the final battle of our time is about to take place. We are in the calm before the storm."

"Please tell me," said Adol. "What is this place? Where am I?"

"You are in the Land of the Little People," Doc replied.

"The Land of the Little People?" Adol said, unsure whether to believe him or not.

"Here, let me show you. They brought you to me, you know, and they have been quite concerned for you. The fairies that bore you here have stayed by your side night and day, casting their blessings upon you for good health, and the yellow pixie has been here as well. They're buzzing about here somewhere."

"I don't understand," said Adol, shaking his head.

"Well, that is a good start – not pretending to understand something that you don't, that is. You are a wise man to possess such power and strength, yet be humble. Do not lose that. Ah, here they are now," said the dwarf, and into the room flew four tiny women - green, blue, pink, and yellow.

"He's awake!" cried the green fairy, and she and her fellow fairies joined hands and danced in the air over his head while the yellow pixie spun about, raining pixie dust down on them all.

Adol crossed himself, his eyes wide with uncertainty, but he immediately felt health pouring into him as the fairy dust rained down on him.

"What wonders I have seen today!" he said. "I have met goblins and giant wolves and a dwarf, and now the fairy people... what else does this land wait to show me?" he said.

"Much!" said Doc. "And much that you may not wish to see."

The green fairy settled in the air before Adol's face.

"I saw you, didn't I – before I fell unconscious in the forest?" said Adol.

"Yes, that was me. But listen carefully, Adol McGunnegal. We do not have much time. The dark scouts of the Witch have been arriving in greater and greater numbers. Far to the south of the forest, the goblins have rallied. Dark creatures roam the south border in great packs. And the night skies are a terror, haunted by great winged creatures. There are so few of us left, Adol McGunnegal. We need your help."

The green fairy's voice was pleading, and Adol looked into her young face and felt pity for her.

"My strength has not yet returned, dear lady," he said. "But I will do what I can. I must find my daughter and wife! I cannot stay for long."

"The Lady Danu sends you greetings, Adol," said the blue fairy. "She says to tell you that Colleen and Frederick passed her shores safely, and that Frederick has gone home for help. He may return in an unexpected way."

"Who is this Lady Danu?" asked Adol, more questions than ever rising to his mind.

"She is the Lady and guardian of our land, sir," said the pink fairy. "With the washing away of the Spell, her power is growing, and our springs are once again flowing with her blessed waters. The forest is reawakening! You must come and see!"

"Yes, I shall, and I would like to speak to this Lady Danu about Colleen and Frederick. Is she nearby?"

"No, she is some days distant, in the Valley of the Fairies, by her lake," replied the pink fairy.

Adol rose slowly from his chair.

"I must say that Doc's food and drink have revived me considerably. Another day of such vittles and I'll be good as new," said Adol, stretching. "I think that I would like to see your forest."

The pink fairy clapped her hands with girlish delight and spun about in the air.

"Take it slow, Mr. McGunnegal. But when you're ready, come back here. I have something for you," said Doc.

Adol looked about and saw his hammer and belt lying by his bed. He picked them up and strapped on the belt. Strength surged through his body anew.

"Take care of those," said Doc. "A fine dwarven hammer and belt they are."

"Dwarven!" replied Adol. "It is a marvelous weapon. I would very much like to discuss its make with you. But first, the forest."

Adol followed the pink fairy out of the room and into a long hall. They turned left and came to an open door that led them to a large porch. As they stepped out, Adol breathed deeply. The air was clear and the sun was shining.

"It looks and feels like Spring," said Adol.

"Not Spring," said the fairy, "for we never had a Winter. Only the long and lonely Sleep. Now the forest is waking once again, and it stretches its limbs."

The fairy led him down the steps of the porch and behind the house. Grass and flowers were beginning to peek up through the leaves that littered the ground, and a bird sang in the branch of a nearby tree. They went on, and Adol could hear the brook bubbling on its way along a rocky bed. He knelt down by the stream and drank deeply. He sighed contentedly, then rose and looked about. There were still fallen trees lying everywhere, all facing north. Yet there were also signs that the forest was indeed awake now, and making its consciousness *felt*.

"You see, Adol McGunnegal," said the fairy, "we have begun our work of rebuilding, but much remains to be done. We only hope that it is not all in vain. We greatly fear that the Witch will come and bring her fire. Then who will save us?"

"I need time to think. So much has happened to me in so short a time," he replied. "Please, let me walk in your forest and think."

"Walk, then," replied the fairy, "and rest your mind and body. Perhaps we will have peace for a while. But my heart tells me it will not be so."

She flew away and joined her companions, and Adol began to stroll along the edge of the wood, looking at all that the little people were doing and at the marvelous construction of the old house where Doc the Dwarf lived.

He walked for nearly an hour, and was just turning to go back when a sudden tremor ran through every tree in the forest. Adol began to run back to the house, for a terrible foreboding came over him. The trees began to creak and groan all about him, and their new blossoms and leaves began to fall to the ground. He was halfway back when the green and blue and pink fairies all came flying at breakneck speed to meet him.

"What's happening?" he said.

"We don't know, but the forest is afraid. Something is happening, but the trees say nothing. They only moan! And we all have a terrible fear. Adol, we think the forest is dying!"

"Dying! But how? Why? I thought it was just beginning to revive!" he said.

He ran back to the house, with fairies zipping about through the trees around him, and found Doc out on the front porch, gazing out at the woods, a worried look on his face.

"Doc," said Adol, "do you know what's happening?"

The dwarf shook his head. "No, but I think we will find out very soon."

The sound of the forest was growing to a crescendo now, a violent moaning and twisting of a million trees across hundreds of square miles. The clamor rose to such a pitch that Adol and Doc covered their ears. Yet still the groans of the forest rose to the heavens. Suddenly, there was a wild frenzy and the trees whipped their branches, and some uprooted themselves and actually moved, crawling with their roots, dragging themselves toward the south. And then, with a great cry, the tumult ceased. The trees stood for a moment, frozen in their agony, and then one by one, seemed to sag, drooping their branches down, and a deep, low moan could be heard, and then all was silent.

Slowly, one by one, little people began to emerge from the forest. Their eyes were cast down, and they hung their heads. They gathered in front of the porch where Adol and Doc stood, and an ancient gnome made his way forward. Tears were streaming down his face.

"What has happened, Eliot?" asked Doc quietly.

"It's the Waking Tree," he cried. "It is no more."

The little people fell to their knees or on their faces and, with cries of despair, began a great and heartrending lament that filled the wretched wood.

Chapter 22 – The Last Ship of Atlantis

Frederick didn't know what to say. The others all stared at him. *He* was to be the heir of Atlantis?

At last, he broke the silence and said, "I don't know about all this, sir, but I do know that I made a promise to return to the Land of the Little People, where there is a witch who is causing great harm, and where Colleen is stranded and needs help, and where Mrs. McGunnegal may be. Will you help us get there? Will you help us to find them and bring them home again?"

Atlantis looked keenly at him and said, "I will make an agreement with you, Frederick. I will help you if you will help me. I will take you to the Land of the Little People and help you find this Colleen if you will allow me to teach you all that I know, and you must become the heir I never knew I had."

"Now one moment, sir," said Professor McPherson, rising from the step on which he was sitting. "I am responsible for these children, and I cannot allow them to agree to anything without their parents' approval."

"Indeed?" said Atlantis. "Then grant your approval."

McPherson paused, looking at Frederick.

"But my father is at home in England," said Frederick. "Or perhaps in Ireland."

"Is he?" asked Atlantis, still looking at McPherson.

The professor was silent for a moment, and then said, "Perhaps if you prove yourself worthy of trust, O king, this lad's father would be willing to grant such approval."

"Very well, then," said Atlantis, rising from his throne. "So be it. Come with me."

"Are we going to the Land of the Little People?" asked Frederick.

"We shall. And there I will show myself honorable," replied Atlantis.

He reached down and picked up the stone chest that the professor had placed by his throne and strode down the steps of the dais. Out of the palace he led them, and through the jungle for some ways until they came to a vine-covered wall. The sound of the ocean could be heard not far ahead. Atlantis searched along the wall until he found something, then, tearing away the vines, he placed his hand over a symbol on the stonework. The entire section of wall moved inward.

Down an ancient flight of steps they went, into a vast chamber that was filled with water. There, floating silently beside a white marble dock, was the most beautiful ship that Frederick had ever seen. It was sleek, with delicate curves along its gold-trimmed white hull. Its bow ended in the head of a great eagle, and it bore two golden masts with silver sails.

"She is still here!" whispered Atlantis, and he ran down to the dock and went aboard, caressing the ship's golden railing as he did.

Frederick ran down as well, his love of ships overcoming any caution he might have.

The others followed more slowly, talking among themselves about this strange new turn of events.

"Come aboard, my boy," said Atlantis as he placed the stone chest by the ship's wheel and opened it.

Frederick carefully climbed aboard and watched as the king removed something from the chest. It was the compass that Professor McPherson had used to get them there.

"Frederick," called the professor. "Wait..."

Atlantis untied the tethers that held the ship and ran to the wheel.

"Atlantis!" called the professor, and began to run down to the dock. The others followed, not sure what was happening.

Then they saw. The ship, seemingly of its own accord, pulled away from the dock and headed straight toward a stone wall some hundred feet away. Atlantis touched something on the front of the ship's wheel and the stone wall slid apart like a great door.

"Stop!" called the professor. "Where are you going?"

"To prove myself honorable!" cried Atlantis, and the ship sailed smoothly out of the doors.

"To the shore!" cried the professor. "Perhaps we can catch them!"

Aonghus scooped up Henny in his arms, and they all ran from the room, out into the jungle, and down to the shore.

There they could see the white ship moving effortlessly, parallel to the shore, heading straight for the spiked teeth of the breakers.

"Stop!" cried the professor again, waving his arms.

They could see Atlantis at the wheel, and Frederick gripping the railing, looking out at them as they ran in vain along the beach.

"We will see you again, McGunnegals, I promise you!" cried Atlantis over the waves. "And I will bring Frederick back and prove myself honorable, McPherson!"

The silver sails of the *Atlantis* unfurled, the ship shot forward and, with a flash, vanished.

* * *

The McGunnegals stood gazing out at the ocean. For a moment, no one spoke.

Then Henny looked up into the sky and said, "Where are they going?"

"I believe," replied the professor, "that they are going to the Land of the Little People. And now it is time for us to go there as well. Follow me."

Chapter 23 – Rebirth

The world flashed around Frederick. One moment, he was staring at the six figures on the beach, waving and shouting to them, and in the next moment, they and the entire island became a blur and sped away behind. The blue ocean raced past, and then away. Then, a round blue marble fell away behind them, and he found himself floating in a sea of stars. Was he dreaming? Was he back aboard the professor's ship and just waking up out on the deck? Frederick closed his eyes and rubbed them, then opened them again, but the stars still blazed about him.

"Have you never dreamed of sailing between the stars, Frederick?" said a voice behind him.

He wheeled around and there stood Atlantis at the ship's wheel, steering it as though they were still floating on the ocean.

"Come! Stand with me!" he said. "Your dreams have come true!"

Frederick leaned out over the edge of the ship and looked down. Nothing but stars met his eyes. Frederick grew dizzy and gripped the railing, and Atlantis laughed.

"My experience exactly the first time I sailed her!" he said.

"Are we..." began Frederick. "Are we... out there?"

"Among the stars themselves? Who can say?" answered Atlantis. "She is a magic ship, after all. The pixies might know. They helped me build her. But hold fast, my friend, we have left the world of Men. Come here now. I need you to set the next course."

Frederick relaxed his grip on the railing and made his way quickly to Atlantis' side.

"Do you see my compass, Frederick?" asked Atlantis.

Frederick had, of course, seen Professor McPherson use this very compass on their journey, but he only nodded, seeing that Atlantis had placed it in a small frame to the right of the ship's wheel.

"It will lead us anywhere that we wish to go. Now, I do not know this Colleen McGunnegal that you seek, but you do. You must set our course to her. Take hold of the dial and set Colleen firmly in your thoughts," he said.

Frederick reached down to the compass and touched the outer edge of the device. He shut his eyes, trying to block out the incredible sights all around him, and then he focused on Colleen. There was a sudden sense of acceleration, and the stars began to move by slowly.

"It will be some hours before we arrive," said Atlantis. "Perhaps we might talk as we sail?"

"Why didn't you bring the others with us?" asked Frederick. "I'm quite sure they do not trust you now."

"They would not have allowed you to come with me alone," he replied. "And there are many things I wish to know and many things that you must learn. Some things are for your ears only, my son. First, please, tell me of the world and its people. What has happened while Atlantis has lain hidden beneath the waves?"

For a long time, they stood and talked about many things – the world, Atlantis, the ancient past, the elves, the goblins. Some of the things of which Atlantis spoke, Frederick had already heard about by those he had met in the Land of the Little People. But Atlantis was a master storyteller, and he told of many of his adventures, and also learned many things from Frederick, even more than Frederick's words told.

At length, Frederick asked the question that had been on his mind for some time.

"King Atlantis, tell me about your kingdom. There are legends of an island called Atlantis that have been handed down for hundreds – or perhaps thousands of years. They say it was a wondrous place. Its loss was a terrible thing to the world, I would think."

Atlantis looked out into the sea of stars, his gaze distant. "Yes, it was a wondrous place – a place of happiness and health for everyone. I considered it the height of moral perfection – a land where no one was unhappy or sick. Ultimately, I wished to make Atlantis a land without death. Can you imagine, Frederick, a place where no one ever dies, and where all are happy?"

"It would be amazing," he replied, and for some time, they spoke no more, each absorbed in his own private meditations. The vast field of the galaxies did that to a man – drew his heart and mind outward into that vast void, there to wander and think deeply on many things, or just to be absolutely still and ponder nothing.

Frederick thought hard about this mythical land of health and happiness that

Atlantis had sought to create. It seemed to make sense on one level, that such a place would be the height of what was moral and perfect, but something else didn't seem quite right. Did happiness and health, or even living forever, sum up what made life good and right? He thought about Colleen's family – so poor, but possessing something that he had never known in his own rich family. The McGunnegals were willing to sacrifice everything for each other and their neighbors – neither lack of health or happiness would stop them from loving and being so devoted. Colleen had even cared for that goblin that had bitten him. There must be more to live for than just health and happiness. It seemed to him that Colleen, who was willing to sacrifice her very life to save others, even her enemies, had showed him what real living was all about. It had nothing to do with her personal health or happiness. He knew that was how he wanted to live too.

These deep thoughts were interrupted as Atlantis began another story of his fabled land, and so their journey went on.

After some hours, a chime sounded from the compass. "See, our destination approaches," said the king.

Frederick looked and, for a moment, a round sphere zoomed into view, and then became a blue ocean again beneath then. Then they were there, sailing on the waves of the sea and, just ahead, dark smoke rose high into the sky from a small island. The sails of the Atlantis withdrew and the ship splashed along on the waves, drawing nearer and nearer to the column of rising smoke.

"That was some ride! But look - do you suppose Colleen is there?" asked Frederick. "Is that the island of the Witch's fortress?"

"We shall soon see," replied Atlantis. "But I have no doubt that your Colleen is there."

The sun was lowering in the western sky as they approached the island, and they found that it had sheer cliffs and no beaches except on one side. There they drew the ship in close to shore, for the *Atlantis* sat marvelously light in the water and had almost no keel. In fact, they needed no dingy to get to the beach, and simply waded through a few feet of water some fifty feet from shore.

There they found the remains of two shattered boats that appeared to have been blown to bits, and many footprints, large and small, leading up to a path that climbed up the side of the cliff toward the top of the bluff. This they followed and, as they neared the summit, they became aware of a most amazing smell that filled the air. It was the smell of a campfire, of flowers, and of incense, such as Frederick had once smelled in a church he had visited as a young child.

But as they climbed over the edge, it was no pleasant sight that greeted their eyes. A gigantic blackened stump of a tree sending up a mixture of smoke and steam stood not far from them, and kneeling in the wet grass near its base sat huddled an odd assortment of figures holding one another. Scores of little people were there as well, and off to one side, standing aloof from the rest, was what was obviously a goblin. Frederick immediately tensed, and Atlantis whipped out his sword and began striding toward the goblin, a fierce look of rage on his face. The goblin turned and saw them and hissed, causing the others to turn, first toward him, and then toward Frederick and Atlantis. Colleen rose and, seeing Frederick, cried out, "Frederick! You've come back!" and began to run toward him.

"Colleen!" he shouted, and he also ran forward to her.

When they met, they hugged one another for a long moment, and then Frederick said, "What has happened here? That's not..."

She nodded, and tears rolled down her soot-darkened face.

"We led her right to it, Frederick. It's all my fault," she said. "The Witch followed us here, and she burned down the Waking Tree. And now she and her goblins are on their way to the forest to burn it down too! Oh, Frederick, we've got to do something! Have you brought us help?"

Colleen look at Atlantis, who had now stopped his advance on the goblin and was now staring at Ellie.

A look of shocked amazement was on his face, and he said, "Mor-Fae? You are here?"

Ellie did not know what to say, but upon seeing this tall warrior with a bright sword in his hand, moved to Colleen and Frederick's side and stood in front of them, as though protecting them.

 Nous crouched, unsure of what was going to happen next, and all the little people stood expectantly. Tension filled the air.

But Atlantis continued to stare at Ellie, and again said, "Mor-Fae? Sister, do you not know me? It is I, your brother, Atlantis. I have returned!"

"Nous, come over here," called Ellie.

The goblin obeyed, making a wide circle around Atlantis, and crouched behind Colleen.

"What is this?" said Atlantis, his face growing hard. "Has my own sister allied with my enemies? And what has become of this Tree? I know this Tree – it was the heart of this world, and now it stands burned. What has happened here? Is this goblin responsible?"

Atlantis' sword blazed, and all the little people gathered close. Things might have gone badly if Frederick had not stepped forward and said, "Now hold on a minute. Something is mighty wrong here, but let's not be hasty. See here, now – Colleen, this is Atlantis – he's the son of Anastazi the Great. We found him on the Island of Atlantis, and I woke him with this sword that I found in... well, never mind that. But he seems a decent enough fellow. Mrs. McGunnegal, I'm mighty glad to see you alive and well, and all these little people too. But I'm not sure why you have a goblin hanging on your coattails and – say – isn't that..."

"This is Nous," cut in Colleen. "And yes, he is the very same goblin who bit you. I see that you are quite recovered from it. He has changed his ways, and has been faithful to me through many hardships, and even in the very court of the Goblin King, he showed himself true. He must not be harmed in any way."

She turned toward Atlantis and said, "I am pleased to meet you, Atlantis. I spoke with your father not long ago... or, well, it was a very long time ago... but, anyway, you do look like him... sir?"

But Atlantis only stared at Ellie, then at Colleen, then back at Ellie again. Then he slowly sheathed his sword and his face relaxed, but still an expression of wonder was on it. He came forward and stood towering over them with his six-foot-six muscular frame. "Please, forgive me," he said. "A multitude of wonders has greeted me this day, and I am sorely beset to understand them all. I am, as Frederick said, Atlantis. Frederick and I have come to rescue you."

"Why, sir," said Ellie, "did you call me 'Mor-Fae'? She is your sister?"

Atlantis paused, looking Ellie up and down.

"Because," he replied, "you could be her twin. I see her reflected in you almost perfectly. Only now that I gaze deeper into your eyes do I see that you are not her. But there is a mystery here to unravel – that I should awake after so long – how long I do not know – and find the image of my sister walking in the Land of the Little People. And you, Colleen McGunnegal – you are the image of my sister as a child. I remember her well! Surely you are both of her lineage. And, Frederick, this is the solution to the riddle of the other McGunnegals. They are surely the descendants of my sister, Mor-Fae."

Ellie and Colleen looked at one another, and a sudden fear crept over them. The Witch looked almost exactly like Ellie. That could only mean...

Mrs. Wigglepox suddenly interrupted their thoughts by coming up to them and saying, "Please excuse me, but time is slipping away! The Witch..."

"She's right," said Colleen. "There's nothing we can do here now. The Waking Tree is gone beyond recovery, but if we can only get back, maybe we can stop the Witch. We've got to try. How did you get here, Frederick?"

A sudden thought struck Frederick, and he said, "Colleen – what about the gift that the Lady Danu gave you? She said you would know when to use it. Might that be now?"

Colleen bowed her head. "Oh, Frederick, I've lost it. I lost it, well, a very long time ago and there's no time to look for it now. If only I had not been so careless, we could have saved the Waking Tree."

Frederick reached into his tunic and drew out two things – a cloth in which was wrapped something round, and a shining vial of bright blue liquid.

"Frederick! Where did you find it? How?" cried Colleen. "And is that cloth...."

"That's my scarf!" said Ellie.

"Time! Time!" said Mrs. Wigglepox.

"Come on," said Colleen, and ran over to the smoldering husk of the Waking Tree.

A sweet fragrance rose from the black trunk and a great crack had opened, allowing them to enter. Frederick felt as though he were entering a burned-out church or walking onto sacred ground.

A single ray of sunlight streamed in, falling on the very center of the tree, and there he saw that a thin line of unburned wood remained.

"I think that's where we need to pour it," whispered Frederick. "But, Colleen, wait – there's something else."

As they approached the tree's heart, Frederick handed Colleen the Lady's vial and carefully unfolded the small round fruit that he had carried with him for so long and held it in his hand.

They stood in silent reverence for a moment, and Frederick could not help but imagine how thousands of years ago the first seven Elders of the Little People and their wives opened their eyes for the first time right here. This was where their world began, where they lived and grew as a people, and this was the father of all the trees in this world. He looked at the fruit in his hand, and carefully placed it on the ground next to the unburned heartwood.

"I think it's time to use the Lady's water. Maybe we should pour the whole thing over it, Colleen," he said.

She nodded, removed the lid, and slowly poured out the shining waters of light over the yellow fruit. Only a single drop remained in the vial. It flowed over the last uncharred wood of the tree and soaked down into the ground.

For a moment, nothing happened, and then the fruit split in half, and out from it crept a single stem bearing a green leaf. Then from the heartwood of the old tree, a leaf sprouted.

"Let's go!" said Colleen, and they quickly left the tree trunk.

"Everyone move back!" said Frederick. "Something is happening!"

Indeed, the very ground seemed to be rippling, as though something were moving beneath them, and the great stump of the Waking Tree began to creak and groan.

Suddenly, there was a violent *CRACK,* and the entire tree split in two, and out from its heart a new tree emerged, indeed two trees. Together, they pushed apart the burned shell, and, as though they were one, they sprouted upward, their branches filled with buds and small leaves. They intertwined into one single great trunk until they could no longer be distinguished from one another, but were truly one.

The huge halves of the burned trunk fell with a resounding crash to either side, and crumbled into great heaps of charcoal. The new tree grew ever wider and taller as they watched, until it surpassed the width and height of the old one, and continued to grow. Its leaves were large and full and green, and a million blossoming flowers burst into bloom across the great canopy that was now spreading over the entire island. The little people shouted and danced, embracing one another and weeping tears of joy, seeing the rebirth and renewal of the tree that was the source of their life and civilization. All were filled with new hope.

They stood in silent wonder for a long time, simply watching as the great tree grew and expanded and flowered. How long they watched, Colleen could not remember, so amazing was the sight.

At length, Frederick broke the awed silence and said, "I think it is time for us to leave. There'll be no room on this island soon."

"Yes," said Atlantis, gazing at the incredible sight. "But today, I have beheld something that in all my years and travels I have not seen the likes of. Truly, this is a miraculous day! Come, there is room for all on my ship. But, I am loath to allow a goblin to step foot on the *Atlantis*. Never has such a creature defiled her with its touch!"

Nous shrank away from the king, a hurt and grim look on his face.

"If Nous doesn't go, then neither do I," said Colleen.

"Nor I," said Ellie.

Frederick gave Atlantis a pleading look, and then said, "I'm with Colleen. I go where she goes."

Atlantis considered them all for a moment and then said, "A chance to prove myself honorable seems to have arrived. Very well then, the goblin may come. But you, Colleen McGunnegal, shall be responsible for him. If he performs any mischief, I shall hold you responsible."

"I trust him with my very life," said Colleen. "Thank you."

They turned to go, but strange sounds coming from the new Waking Tree made them stop and turn. A door was opening at its base, out of which a light began to shine. Brighter and brighter it grew, until they had to shield their eyes.

Suddenly, to all their amazement, a brilliant figure stepped out, followed by one, then two, then hundreds of smaller figures, all shining with the same radiance.

After a moment, the light began to dim, and Colleen's eyes went wide and she gasped. Then she clapped her hands and ran forward, shouting, "Oracle!"

But she stopped before reaching him and, seeing him fully now, she said, "Oracle – is it really you?"

"Don't be afraid, Colleen," he said. "Yes, it is me."

"But you've changed – you aren't old anymore, and you're speaking clearly now," she said.

Frederick and the others now came up behind her and stared at the leprechaun. Indeed, he had changed, and appeared to be a younger version of himself, although his eyes were deep and filled with hidden wisdom, and there was a power about him.

"Did you call him Oracle?" asked Atlantis. "Why, this is none other than Dian, the Eldest, and Elder of Elders, the very one who greeted the Seven who first woke in this Waking Tree, or I am a fool. Your Majesty!" Atlantis fell to one knee, bowing in reverence.

"Why it *is* Oracle!" said Frederick. "And you are... you are the king of this world?"

He was feeling very embarrassed at how he had treated Oracle during their journey, and now wished he could take back many of his words.

"Ah, Frederick," said Oracle, seeming to know his thoughts. "I forgive you. Your words were said in ignorance, not malice. However, I think you have learned not to judge by mere appearances. But come friends, today is a day of rebirth and new life for our world!"

The little people all round him cheered, and Colleen knelt down and gave him a huge hug, which he returned.

After a moment, Ellie spoke. "What of the Witch? She flies north with her fleet to burn the forest."

"Yes," said Oracle. "Already the forest burns. Will you go and stop her?"

"You're not coming with us?" she said. "But you have a power over the Witch. We need you!"

"The Waking Tree lives! Here the little people began, and here they must begin again. They must stay and begin a new work, and for now, I must stay with them. Be fearless, Colligal! We need you still. Will you go for me and do this great work?"

"Yes, Oracle, I will go, as long as I have my mother with me. But Mrs. Wigglepox? Lily? Rose? Won't you be coming with us?" Colleen said, feeling suddenly sad.

They looked at Oracle, and he nodded.

"We've been with you this far," she said, "and we're not about to abandon you now. If we survive all of this, then we may return here. But I would dearly love to see the Wigglepox Tree again."

"I'm so glad!" replied Colleen. "I've grown quite fond of you all, and I would so miss your company."

Thus it was that they all watched as Oracle led the little people over to the growing tree. They gathered in a great circle around it and, one by one, they placed their hands upon it and bowed their heads. As they did, they began to change. The leprechauns sprouted up to a full two feet in height, all of the wingless fairies and pixies began to shine, and new wings appeared on their backs. The gnomes grew plump, and all of them were clothed in bright new red outfits with pointed hats, the leprechauns with shiny brass buckles on their shoes and belts, and the fairies in gossamer silks. They all began to twirl and sing, and then with a wave from Oracle, they joyously danced their way through the door and into the new Waking Tree. Last of all, Oracle looked out at them, winked, and with a final wave of his hand, followed his people into their new home.

Now the tree was growing quite near, and they hurried down the cliff trail to the beach and, wading out through the shallow water, boarded the *Atlantis*, and looked back at the island. Soon, the entire plateau was filled with the gigantic trunk, and its great roots twisted and gripped the edges of the cliff and sank down deep into the earth. It was as though the tree had sprouted from the ocean itself.

As they sailed away, the setting sun shone magnificently through the massive canopy of leaves, surrounding it in a great golden halo.

"I wonder why Oracle isn't coming with us," said Colleen to Mrs. Wigglepox. "He could help us. He's the leader of your people."

"I think he's preparing something for us, Colleen," she replied. "Who knows? We may see him come unexpectedly with some new help. But for now, he's given us the task of saving our world, and we need to get to doing it."

"I could take you all home now," said Atlantis from his wheel. "No need to stay in this land if you do not wish to."

"You mean you could take us all home to Ireland?" asked Colleen.

"In a flash," he said. "We could drop these little people off on the northern shore and have you all home in time for supper. Or they could come with us. Just say the word."

"But, the forest!" said Lily.

The Wigglepox family looked up at Colleen, and she hesitated for a moment.

Home? She could actually go home with her mother and be with her family again? She could leave this land of sorrow and hurt behind? But no, she had come too far and learned too much. She felt a great responsibility had been given to her, and she would not neglect it now.

"Take us back to the forest," she said.

"Very well," said Atlantis. "It seems that more than one of us is proving to be honorable. But the forest is vast. Where shall we go? I cannot sail the *Atlantis* through the air. She was only made to go into the two great Deeps."

"But we will never get there in time," said Colleen. "The Witch has that flying beast, and her ships are far ahead of us. And Oracle says that the forest is already burning!"

"We can catch this goblin fleet, and I would be happy to do so. But we must also rest and prepare ourselves for the day ahead. It will be a day of battle," said Atlantis, grinning. "Come, I will set our course, and we shall take a meal and rest while we may."

He touched the compass and the ship turned and headed north. Then he led them down a short flight of steps to a small cabin. There he found water and dried cakes in his stores that by some magic had been preserved over the long years. They ate in silence, although Atlantis occasionally gazed at Ellie and Colleen and shook his head. After this, he led them to two cabins, where they found comfortable beds. Colleen, Ellie, and Nous took one cabin, and Atlantis and Frederick the other.

When they were all in bed, Colleen could feel the weight of sleep coming heavily upon her. She said, "Mom, do you think that the Witch is really Atlantis' sister, Mor-Fae?"

"I don't know," said Ellie. "But I don't think we should speak of that to him just yet. He is a man obsessed with something. I haven't quite figured him out yet."

"But he's all the help that we have right now," said Colleen.

"Yes," replied Ellie. "I don't think he'll do us harm, but he may forget his noble intentions if the object of his passion comes before him."

With these thoughts, they fell into a deep sleep, and had such rest as they had not had for a very long time.

Chapter 24 – The Timeless Hall

Professor McPherson led the McGunnegals back to the throne room, but as they entered, he seemed to change his mind about something.

"Perhaps I am being rash," he said. "I think that we should wait for a while and see if Atlantis and Frederick return. We will wait until morning, and then decide what to do."

"What else can we do, Professor?" asked Abbe. "We've no way off this island that we know of, not unless we can open that door or find another boat."

"I suggest we do a bit of exploring," said Aonghus. "I'm feeling quite up to it. How about you, Bib?"

"I'm completely well," she said. "No pain at all!"

"Right then," said McPherson. "Let's see what is left of the city of Atlantis."

They spent the remainder of the afternoon searching among the ruins of the ancient city. There were walls and houses and buildings, all overtaken by the jungle. Occasionally, they saw a bone protruding from the ground, but these they did not disturb. The vines and trees of the jungle were so thick that, after searching for a time, they decided to make their way back to the shipwreck and spend the night where they would have food and shelter.

The next morning dawned bright and fair, and they packed some supplies in two side-bags that they had found in the cargo hold and headed back to the throne room. It was decided that if Atlantis and Frederick had not returned already, they would wait for them there at least until the evening. They set off, and before mid-morning were once again making their way along the ancient road that led to the throne room. But Atlantis and Frederick had not returned, and so they sat on the steps and waited.

An hour passed. Bran decided to explore the room and examine the many bones that lay scattered about. All seemed to be of the same misshapen sort, but as he made his way along the wall in the darkest corner of the room, he came upon what appeared to be a fully clothed skeleton crouched in the corner. In fact, it was dressed in modern day clothing, with brown britches and a white tunic and a brown overcoat. In its skeletal hand lay a rolled parchment.

"Have a look at this," he called to the others, and they hurried over.

"This is no Atlantian," said Bran. "Look at the clothes. Someone else got here, but didn't make it off the island."

Professor McPherson stooped down and examined the skeleton. Suddenly, he stood and backed away.

"What's wrong, Professor?" said Abbe, alarmed at the professor's reaction.

But he said nothing and slowly inched his way forward again. Then he slid the parchment from the bony hand and carefully unrolled it.

A look of distress and disbelief flooded his face as he read, and then tears filled his eyes.

"Professor?" said Bib.

Aonghus moved to his side and read the parchment.

"*Forgive me, Father. I found ...*" but the rest was blurred and unreadable. It was signed simply, "*Charlie.*"

"It is my son," breathed the professor.

Then he knelt down beside him and, with great sobs, he wept. After several minutes, Henny quietly knelt down next to him and put her little hand on his shoulder. He looked up into her sad, innocent eyes and somehow seemed to draw strength from them. He took a deep breath and wiped his face on his sleeve. Then he looked at the rest of them and said, "I am sorry, children. This, I am sure, was my son. He left three years ago to search for this place. Would to God he had never found it!"

His voice broke, but he steadied himself, sighed heavily, and looked at the remains of his boy. It was then that he noticed that his hand was resting inside his ragged overcoat. The professor, with the greatest care, reached inside where his boy's hand lay, and pulled something from the inside pocket of the coat. He held it up for all of them to see – a golden brooch bearing a large blue sapphire and a second parchment. He unfolded the second paper, and there was a map that appeared to be a detailed drawing of the lost island of Atlantis itself. A small "X" was drawn on one place some distance from a box labeled "*Dead King.*"

The professor refolded the paper, slipped the brooch into his pocket along with Charlie's note, sighed once again, and then said, "Aonghus, will you help me take him outside and bury him?"

Aonghus nodded, and with as much care as they could, they lifted Charlie from his resting place and took him outside. The others followed in silence.

"We have nothing to dig with," said Aonghus. "But perhaps we could build a cairn of rocks for him."

"That will have to do for now," replied the professor.

They all set out and gathered as many rocks as they could find, and gently arranged them over Charlie's body. Then Henny picked a yellow flower and placed it on top of the cairn.

They stood in silence for some time, and then the professor said, "Charlie was much like me – adventurous and impetuous, full of wild ideas and schemes. This was his last. He loved to hear me tell the tale of when I had found this place once before. And he became obsessed with the idea of finding it again and discovering some amazing treasure from its long lost civilization. Oh, that I had never told that tale!"

Professor McPherson wiped his eyes once again and said, "Farewell, my son. May you find rest on these ancient shores. I forgive you."

Then he turned and walked into the jungle.

"Let him go," whispered Aonghus. "He needs some time alone. Let's go back to the throne room and see if we've missed anything else."

With heavy hearts, they slowly walked back, and this time thoroughly searched the room, but no more surprises were found, so they gathered on the steps again, and sat and talked quietly about all that had happened to them. About an hour later, the professor came in. His face was washed clean, and he had a sad but resolute look about him.

"Thank you, children, for giving me time alone. But time presses and I feel that we must do something and wait no longer," he said.

He climbed up to the throne and hesitated. Then he sat down upon it, and slowly placed both hands on the white gems and shut his eyes.

A light sprang into their depths and, on the opposite wall, the silver glow of the door began to shine. The McGunnegals all looked at him, amazed. He focused his thoughts, and to their complete astonishment, the double doors of the Gate swung silently open.

"Now!" he cried. "Follow me!"

He sprang from the throne, dashed down the dais steps, and they followed. They crossed the threshold, and as they did, they felt time and space slip away behind them. They stopped, and found themselves standing in a towering chamber of eight gigantic double doors that were each at least forty feet tall. The room was an octagon, cathedral-like in its architecture, and the peaks of the arched door frames met in a great pinnacle in the ceiling far above their heads. The chamber was illumined, but how, they could not tell. All of the doors were shut, and there was no sign of which one they had entered through.

They stood gazing at the incredible gates all about them, and somehow, they knew that they were both ancient and ageless and that here they themselves were ageless as well. Time passed, but did not pass. Moments came and went, yet there was no sense of their passing. Aonghus picked up Henny and held her close, and they instinctively gathered in the middle of the room.

Bran slowly walked from door to door and, seeing symbols on them, he said, "Do you remember these symbols? They're the same as the ones on the stones back home. That's the key to that riddle – these must be the doors to the eight worlds, and one of them goes to the Land of the Little People."

"Under the hill lay eight doors ..." began Bib.

"The riddle on the map back home that Helga stole," said Abbe. "Colleen told us about it. How did the rest of it go?"

"She didn't say," replied Bib. "But each of them led to some other place – lands of elves and dwarves and giants... and to very bad places."

"But which is which, and how do we open them, anyway?" said Aonghus.

"There do not appear to be any handles on them," said McPherson. "There must be some secret way."

They tried pushing, touching certain symbols, saying different words, even knocking. But nothing seemed to work.

Soon the realization took hold – they were trapped in the Timeless Hall with no way out, and they might very well be here a long, long time.

Chapter 25 – Flight of the *Atlantis*

The next morning, Colleen awoke to the sound of the king calling, "Land ho!"

She rose and climbed up to the deck where everyone else was already awake and standing next to Atlantis. She peered ahead, and there on the horizon was a brown strip of land. But there was no sign of the black fleet of the goblins.

It was a jutting piece of land with high cliffs at least a hundred feet high. As they drew near, they could see that a wide river flowed from an inlet, and, seeing no black ships on any horizon, they sailed into the inlet to gain some shelter from watching eyes and to get their bearings.

The river flowed from an enormous cave at the far end of a bowl-shaped canyon surrounded by high cliffs.

"Well, no sailing further up river, it would seem," said Atlantis.

But Colleen was thinking of the old map that they had seen back at Doc the Dwarf's house. He had mentioned that the river that flowed beneath the forest ran all the way to the sea and that, at one time, there had been an underground road beside it, and his folk had sailed small boats along its channel regularly.

These thoughts, however, were interrupted when Rose pointed up to the top of the cliff line and said, "Mother, what are those black birds?"

They all turned their eyes upward to where she was pointing and, to their great dismay, on the entire surrounding cliff edge, great black shapes began to lift skyward. Within moments, hundreds of them filled the air and were swiftly descending upon them.

"Hold fast!" cried Atlantis. "There's no time to plot a course off this world and raise the sail to escape. We'll have the gain some distance from them first!"

He wheeled the ship around, and Frederick carefully scooped up the Wigglepox family and put them in his pocket. As they turned, their apprehension turned to dismay as into the inlet sailed a dozen black ships, and a dozen more were following behind. Atlantis turned the ship hard once again, and as he did, a cackling laugh came from the sky, and a ball of fire fell right where their ship had been a moment before.

"The Witch!" cried Mrs. Wigglepox.

Atlantis touched something on the front of his wheel, and the *Atlantis* surged forward, just in time to miss another explosion of fire that plunged into the river, sending up a great spout of steam.

"King Atlantis, head for the cave! It's our only hope!" cried Colleen.

"The cave! We may be dashed on unseen rocks!" he called back.

"No, sir, I remember Doc the Dwarf saying that his people used to sail there. We've got to risk it," cried Frederick as another blast barely missed them.

Now the great black shapes were more clearly visible, and Nous said, "Wyverns! The Goblin King's First Guard rides them!"

Atlantis steered his ship first one way, then another as he headed for the cave entrance. Closer and closer it came, until with tremendous speed they rocketed in just as a tremendous detonation exploded at the entrance, nearly singeing their hair. The river was several hundred feet wide at the mouth of the cave and flowed in a deep and lazy channel. Atlantis sped his magical craft upstream, and as the light faded, he once again touched his wheel, and great lights shone out from the ship in all directions, illuminating the underworld into which they had plunged. At the mouth of the cave, they could see the bat-like flying lizards wheel in, and three of the smaller black ships following them in pursuit.

"Frederick!" called Colleen. "Take this!" And she handed him the old sword.

"Thanks," he said, strapping it around his waist and then drawing it out.

As he did, its blade flickered in the dark.

"Ellie!" called Atlantis. "Come here, quickly. Can you steer the ship?"

"Certainly," she said and took the wheel.

Atlantis unsheathed his sword and said, "Frederick, give the little people to Colleen and ask her to take them below. We shall give these goblins a fight they shall not forget!"

His sword burst into green flame, and as it did, Frederick's own sword seemed to vibrate with an unexpected joy, and it too shone like a brilliant shaft of white light.

"Take the port side, son!" said Atlantis.

"What about Nous?" said Frederick. "He can help us."

"If he will, then I shall truly believe that he is trustworthy. But he has no weapon to defend himself with," said Atlantis.

Nous, however, followed Colleen down into the hold, and Atlantis said, "That's what I thought. Goblins are cowards," and he braced himself for the first flying creature that was bearing down upon them from behind.

The winged beast was a hideous creature, resembling a cross between a great bat and a flying reptile. And upon its back, sitting in a leather saddle, was a great goblin bearing a crossbow in his hands and a spear strapped to the creature's side.

"Look out!" cried Atlantis as the bolt from the crossbow sang, straight at Frederick.

Frederick had seen the goblin raise its weapon, and had already leaped to one side. The bolt missed him by an inch and splashed into the river. The leading wyvern soared past them and swung around, and they could see its rider readying another bolt, and two more riders were now upon them, also bearing crossbows. More bolts zinged through the air, one at each of them this time, and again, they barely missed, both of them glancing off the decking, into the waters that rushed past.

"This is no good!" called Atlantis. "If only we had a bow!"

"Wait a second," said Frederick, dodging another bolt. "Colleen can..."

Suddenly, Nous appeared, leading Colleen out of the hold. She saw their plight and knew what she had to do. She began to sing.

Behind them, a wave began to take shape, riding on their wake for a moment, and then rising higher and higher until it bore the shape of a stallion running on the water behind them. Out from its body stretched two watery wings and, with these, it took flight. Then a second watery Pegasus reared up, then a third, and these engaged the sweeping wyverns in a flying and wheeling dance over their heads in the narrowing channel.

The bolts of the wyvern riders sang, splashing straight through the watery horses, and doing them no harm. Then the first horseman galloped down his foe, and both fell with a great cry into the river and were swept away. The second beast was driven into the cavern wall and fell, stunned, into the water, its liquid pursuer thundering after it. The last tried desperately to flee, but the watery elemental charged after it and burst in a tremendous clap of thunder just as the creature winged out of the cave.

But the black ships continued to follow, and more of the flying creatures had now settled on their decks, waiting for their opportunity. They knew that their prey was trapped and it could go nowhere.

Atlantis sheathed his sword and strode back to the wheel where Colleen, Nous, and Ellie were now standing.

"Nous came down and said you needed help," said Colleen. "He asked for my staff so that he could fight, but I thought I should come up as well."

"You summoned the elementals?" asked the king. "You have a power in your voice, my lady!"

Colleen blushed. "It's nothing."

"Nothing!" cried Atlantis. "Few wizards of the world I once knew had such power. To control the elements is no small thing!"

"I don't control them," answered Colleen. "I just sing, that's all. I can hear their song, and when I sing with that song, they seem to respond."

"You speak as if the wind and waves were living things," said Atlantis, amazed. "Do you see their souls?"

"I don't think it's like that," she replied. "Plants and trees and water don't have souls. But there are some creatures that have chosen to live in the hills and wind and waves. They are all around in this world, and they seem to have become quite active. It wasn't like when we first came. But, now that the Spell seems to have broken…" she replied.

"You broke the Spell?" interrupted Frederick. "But how?"

"Not me. It's quite a story," said Colleen, "but I don't know if now is the time for its telling. We ought to keep a lookout for more of those flying things that might try to sneak up on us. The black ships do seem to be keeping pace."

"Dark magic drives them," said the king. "No ship has ever kept pace with the *Atlantis*. But I dare not take us faster for fear of rocks. I pray that this dwarf of yours was right. But how far can we go? We will have to stop somewhere."

"I say we make for the Gate of Anastazi. At least there, we can get out of the ship and get up into the forest. Maybe Doc will be able to help," said Frederick.

"The Gate of Anastazi!" said Atlantis. "The wizards built their castles around the places where they entered the Eight Worlds."

"But this one has moved," said Colleen. "The Cataclysm shifted the whole landscape of the Land of the Little People."

"Then pray we may open it, or find some refuge. I would not wish to surrender the *Atlantis* to these goblins or their Witch," replied Atlantis.

Nous said nothing, but only looked back at the following ships, the lamps on their decks glowing dully in the dark.

"How do they come on with no light?" asked Frederick. "Surely they should be crashing into the walls or something."

"The wyverns guide them," said Nous quietly. "They see and hear like bats in the dark, and they speak to their masters."

Then, among the yellow lights that bobbed in the darkness, a red flicker appeared, floating for a moment, and then settling in among the others.

"I think the Witch has joined the chase!" said Colleen.

They all looked back, only to see a red eye staring at them from the darkness.

"They are coming closer!" shouted Frederick.

The bouncing lights were steadily growing larger and brighter.

"Then the race is on," said Atlantis. "Hold fast to something!"

The *Atlantis* shot forward at her captain's touch, and their hair and clothes began to fly in the wind as they reached breakneck speeds. Atlantis swerved suddenly to the right and then to the left again, avoiding a pillar that jutted up from the riverbed to reach the ceiling. Fortunately, the river was wide, at least a hundred feet, and they were able to navigate around with ease. But now they were wary, and Frederick moved to the bow to keep watch for other obstacles that might present themselves.

For a few moments, the lights of their pursuers dimmed as they outdistanced them, but then Colleen saw that they were coming again and shouted a warning.

"We dare not go faster!" shouted Atlantis above the wind that whistled in their ears.

Ellie made her way to the wheel and stood next to Atlantis.

She looked up at him with a stern look in her eyes, placed her fists on her hips, and shouted, "Let me steer then, and push this ship to her limit!"

Atlantis glanced at her briefly and shouted back, "You are either foolhardy or fearless! Your husband is a lucky man to have such a woman! But see here, have you no magic about you? Can you do nothing to slow down this Witch's ships?"

Ellie looked at him for a moment and then a thought struck her. She ran back to the rear of the ship and said, "Colleen, you are more gifted than I am, and you have deeper sight. Use the ring. Stop those goblin ships."

"I don't know, Mom. I think you should do this," she replied.

"Colleen, you have been given a gift. Don't be afraid to use it. Back in the dungeons, I found that, with the help of the rock people, I could move things through solid rock, but I suspect that, with your keener sight, you may be able to move the rock itself. Try, Colleen," she said.

"Do you mean the things that the rock creatures can do, I might be able to do?"

"Try," said Ellie.

Colleen remembered the wind and waves, and now called upon the rock creatures. Behind them, a pillar of rock shot into the air, directly in the path of the first oncoming ship.

But there was a terrific explosion, and red fire filled the chamber, momentarily blinding them with its sudden brightness, forcing them to cover their faces. As their eyes adjusted, they saw that the goblin ship still came on, and was now only a few hundred feet behind them. On its bow stood a black-robed figure bearing a staff with a flaming tip, and beside her hunched a great, black winged beast on one side, and a gigantic goblin on the other.

"The Goblin King comes with the Witch!" hissed Nous. "We are doomed!"

Colleen raised her hand again, and again, a pillar of rock shot upward, sending water spraying everywhere. Again, a fiery blast from the Witch obliterated it, and still they came on. Again and again, Colleen raised pillars of stone in their path, and again and again, they were blown to dust.

Desperately, she concentrated, raised both hands in the air, and suddenly, an entire wall erupted from the river floor, forming a solid barrier between them and the onrushing ships. The water of the river immediately piled high against it like a dam, and the *Atlantis* was thrown forward. But within a second, with a detonation like a bomb, a huge gaping hole was blown in the rock, sending debris flying over their heads and raining down on the *Atlantis'* deck.

"It's no good," shouted Atlantis. "You might end up sinking us both!"

"We need something else, Colleen," said Ellie.

"I will try," she replied, and shut her eyes, looking inward to see what her physical eyes could not.

"This place is empty," she said. "Nothing lives here. Only fish and crawling things."

"We need more speed!" called Ellie to Atlantis.

He looked over his shoulder at her and scowled. "Hold on, then!" he called. "This will be the last of it. I will dare what I have never attempted before!"

A terrific blast of wind struck them as the *Atlantis* rocketed forward. The rock walls were now flying past them at such speed that they came and went in a great streaking rush. It seemed to Colleen as though they were fading in and out, blended into one surreal blur.

"Pray to God we encounter no more islands or pillars and that the river's course does not dip!" yelled Atlantis. "This is insane!"

Onward they shot, and Colleen felt as if they were flying, for the ship skipped over the waves as though she were barely touching them, and they all had to hold fast to the railings or be blown overboard. They stared back into the darkness behind them, and now, at last, the lights of their pursuers began to fade once again into the distance, winking in and out, until they vanished altogether and were lost.

Colleen and Ellie pulled themselves forward along the railing of the ship, their hair blowing behind them like golden flames in the wind. Nous remained at the stern, holding tight and staring into the darkness.

"We are outracing them!" said Colleen to Atlantis when they reached the ship's wheel.

"Yes," he replied, "but we have not lost them. We have nowhere to go but forward, and they know it."

They raced on, and Ellie and Colleen joined Frederick at the bow of the ship to keep watch for any hazards in their path. But it seemed to Colleen that they would not be able to warn Atlantis of anything they saw coming, for they were traveling far too fast, and the spotlights that shone forward from the ship only illuminated the cavern a few hundred feet in front of them.

After a time, she glanced back at Atlantis and then decided to broach a subject that had been growing on her mind.

"Mom, who do you think this Witch is? She, well, looks exactly like you," she said. "Do you really think she's this Mor-Fae, Atlantis' sister?"

Ellie stared ahead into the blackness.

"I am afraid of the answer to that," she replied after a moment.

Colleen lowered her voice and leaned closer to her mother.

"But what will he do if he sees her and finds out?" asked Frederick, who had scooted himself closer to hear the conversation.

"I don't know," replied Ellie. "He's a good man. But he is old – very old. He comes from a different age of this world and once ruled a good bit of it. Who can say what secrets he keeps to himself? There's some mystery about him."

"And what does it all mean for us, Mom?" asked Colleen. "If we're her descendants...?"

Before she could answer, Frederick pointed forward into the distance and shouted, "Look! There is a silver light ahead!"

Indeed, approaching was a distant glow that reminded them of a full moon.

"I know that light," said Colleen. "It's the light from the Gate of Anastazi the Great!"

Atlantis began to slow the ship and, within a few moments, they could distinctly see the shining outline of the Gate in the distance, standing against the wall on the shore to their left.

"Looks like we made it, but how could we have gotten here so quickly?" asked Frederick.

Atlantis, still standing at the wheel, laughed and said, "Magic, my dear Frederick, magic! I dared to push my ship to do what she had never done before, and she did not fail us! The Witch may not have matched her speed, but she is no doubt close behind."

Soon they were so near that the brilliant light of the Gate illuminated the entire chamber.

"Don't look at it too long, Mom," said Colleen. "Mom?"

Ellie shook herself and looked away from the Gate. "It... I can read it," she said.

"Amazing!" said Atlantis. "The wizards of old could read the inscriptions on the Gates of Anastazi, but few others. Surely you have the blood of the Ancients in you! But take care – such things as these hold a power that can draw the unpracticed mind into them."

As they reached the gate, its brilliant sheen flooded over the *Atlantis*, making the ship seem to glow. Colleen glanced at it for a moment, but then looked away, and peered across to the opposite bank, half expecting to see Doc the Dwarf standing there, waving at them. But the shore was silent and empty, and the river before them flowed out from under a low roof that the *Atlantis'* mast would not clear.

"So, this is the end of the line," said Atlantis gravely. "We must prepare ourselves quickly."

"Doc's tunnels are just on the other side, across the river from the Gate. They are rather hidden, but maybe we could find them, and go find Doc."

"Yes," said Atlantis. "We will need all the help we can get. If we can't open this Gate, we'll need an escape route. Secret tunnels would serve us well. But I'm loath to leave the *Atlantis* without a fight."

"Maybe some of us should look for the tunnels," said Colleen, "while the rest of us see if we can open the Gate."

"We must keep all of our options open," he replied. "But I advise we stay together. We must not be separated when the Witch arrives. Come, we're on this side of the river. Let's see what might be done with the Gate of Anastazi the Great first."

Frederick jumped to shore and secured two lines that the king tossed to him around stalagmite pillars.

Colleen ran below and emerged, bearing the Wigglepox family in her pocket. Atlantis put the gangplank out, and they all quickly went ashore.

Colleen had never been so close to the Gate before, and she felt it tugging at her mind, calling her to lose herself in its magical magnificence. Atlantis touched the seam between the two doors.

"It's slightly ajar," he said, and tried to pull it open with his fingers. But try as he might, the door held fast.

"Doc said that it was leaking timelessness," said Frederick. "He thought it was damaged in the Cataclysm."

Atlantis paused for a moment as if pondering this, and then returned to his inspection of the door. He tried taking the blade of his sword and prying the doors apart, but they would not budge.

"My father had the key to these doors. I wonder whatever happened to it," he said.

"Who can say?" said Colleen. "When I saw him last, I think he was on his way to do battle with the Witch. But she's here, and he isn't."

There was a moment of awkward silence as they considered what this might mean.

"But the stories of the people in this land say that he had defeated her, but when he pulled off her hood, he backed away, and left the battleground without killing her. No one knew why," said Frederick.

Colleen wanted to say, "Until now," but she remained silent. She knew why Anastazi had not destroyed the Witch. It was because she was his daughter. And now Atlantis was surely going to discover that she was his sister. What would he do? Would he do the same? Would he board his magical ship and speed away down the river, leaving them alone to face her terrible might?

Frederick felt the tension too and decided to change the subject.

"We might as well try the other side of the river. Maybe we can find Doc's tunnels," he said.

"Mother, why don't we use the ring again?" said Colleen.

But at that instant, their hearts sank as the great black shape of a ship emerged from the river cavern and, standing on its bow, was the now familiar black-robed figure of the Witch.

She laughed as she saw them gathered on the shore, frozen like statues before her, and cried out, "At last! The Gate of Anastazi is mine!"

With a wave of her staff, she became a column of black smoke. The shapeless cloud seemed to mount the flying beast crouching next to her and took flight. As the ship neared the shore, scores of goblins poured out, leaping from its deck and running toward the little group on shore.

"Get back!" yelled Atlantis, and charged at the onrushing goblins, his sword bursting into flame as he drew it.

He met them head on, crying out some ancient war cry that rose above the din of the goblins as they rushed to meet him. His sword rose and fell, and three of the foremost goblins fell. Heedless, into their midst he ran, and his blade was a blur of green fire as it felled goblins all about him. For a brief moment, they all stared, and then Frederick seemed to come to himself, and, whipping out his own sword, he cried out and charged forward. Now his own blade burst into a shaft of white light, and the brightness of it struck the eyes of the goblins, and they backed away. Atlantis and Frederick met in the midst of them, and they stood back to back, their swords held aloft. The horde of goblins circled around them.

"Colleen!" said a voice. It was Mrs. Wigglepox. "Get us to the Crystal Chamber! If ever there was a time for wishing, it's now!"

Ellie touched Colleen's and Nous' hands, and they melted into the rock beneath them just as a great goblin threw its spear their way. Inside the solid rock of the cave, they could sense the gate of Anastazi as an impenetrable barrier that they could not pass. It was like the enchanted stones of the Witch's fortress, but denser somehow, of a different nature, and even more impregnable than those dark halls had been. In a flash, they moved through the ceiling and over to the other shore, and there they emerged and found themselves in Doc's tunnel.

"I know the way from here," said Lily. "I remember it."

Colleen quickly put them on the ground and, together, they ran down the hallway.

"Nous," said Colleen urgently. "Follow this tunnel and find the dwarf called Doc. Tell him I'm here, and we need him. Tell him the Witch has come!"

Nous paused only a moment, then nodded and ran up the hall. Ellie took Colleen's hand, and they vanished through the rock again.

"Do you think you can do that wave trick again, Colleen, like you did on the ship back in the tunnel?" asked Ellie quickly.

Colleen shut her eyes. "Yes," she said.

Immediately, Colleen took them through the wall, and they found themselves on the far shore beside the river. Although they had not been gone more than thirty seconds, when they emerged, the opposite shore by the Gate was filled with goblins, and they had ringed in Atlantis and Frederick. They had fallen back and now stood against the Gate of Anastazi, their blazing swords held high.

* * *

Suddenly, the sea of goblins parted and, from above, a great, winged creature bearing a swirling column of smoke descended.

The smoke slid from the creature and solidified into the form of the Witch.

She slowly walked forward, her staff flaming. The goblins grew silent.

"Where will you flee now?" crooned the Witch as she stood before them. "Give me your swords, and I will spare you. More than that, I will give you your deepest desires."

"What do you know of my deepest desires?" retorted Atlantis. "You do not know me, or you would know that your life is in peril. I say to you, surrender your staff to me, and I will spare you. But all of your goblin host, I shall slay, in recompense for what they have done."

The Witch laughed and said, "Do I not know you? I see your mind. Your desire is to cheat death. That still gnaws at your soul, does it not? But I have found what you have been seeking. Behold!"

She pulled from beneath her robe a black vial. All of the goblins around her chortled as though they found it to be something very precious.

"Here, in this elixir, is life eternal. Do you not desire it?" she said, her voice softer.

The tip of Atlantis' sword dropped down an almost imperceptible amount, but the Witch seemed to notice. She pulled the stopper from the bottle and said, "See what this can do for my goblins...."

The Witch motioned with her staff and through the pack of goblins, a truly gigantic form came. It was a goblin, without doubt, but it stood easily as tall as Atlantis, and much broader. In its great fist, it bore a long, black sword.

The other goblins fell back before it.

"Behold our king!" said the Witch, inclining her head. "He is the oldest and most powerful of his people, and he has been preserved all these years through this elixir. See!"

The Goblin King stood beside the Witch and pulled back his hood.

He was more hideous than any goblin Frederick had ever seen. His face was a swollen mass of tumorous growths, and his great ears hung down to his shoulders. Huge yellow fangs shot upward from his bottom jaw, and his nose was the size of a grapefruit.

But his eyes were small and had a distant look, as though he was not truly present, but walked in a fog.

"See!" said the Witch, and the Goblin King took the vial from her, placed it to his massive lips, took a sip from it, and then threw the container to the ground, smashing it to pieces.

A black oily liquid splashed on the rocks where the vessel had been broken.

Frederick knew exactly what it was.

"Don't listen to her, Atlantis!" said Frederick. "That's the goblin ooze! It's a trick!"

"A trick, my boy?" said the Witch with vehemence. "No, it is life! See!"

As they watched, the face of the Goblin King seemed to twist and contort with some inner agony, and then, as though he had been awakened out of the fog of his mind, he spat, growled, and spoke.

"Yes!" he said, and his voice was deep and thunderous. "Yes! It is the goblin ooze. And long I have drunk it. And for over five thousand years, I have not known death. Now, bow down to me, and I will tell my witch to give this fountain of youth to you!"

Atlantis looked at the king of the goblins, at the Witch, and at the black liquid that was now fairly *squirming* on the rock, as though many worms writhed within it. Frederick could not believe that Atlantis was actually *considering* this offer. Or was he just buying time? Far on the other shore, Frederick could see Colleen and Ellie – they were standing in the shadows, and it appeared that they were whispering to one another. He hoped they had a plan. But now the Witch was speaking to him.

"And you, my young lad, what are you doing in this strange land? A human, like those two pitiful ladies across the river. Yes, I see them, and I have spared them so far so that I might make you an offer as well. I see in you greatness, and I could teach you to wield power that you have never dreamed of before. And riches – gold and silver and magic gems – this world is full of them, and I have gathered them to myself. You, dear boy, can have them all at your disposal. And then I shall send you back to your own land, there to be an ambassador for me, to gather the wizards there together once again, and you and I shall become a great power in the Eight Worlds and beyond!"

Images of himself seated on a throne and commanding goblins and men danced across his mind. He froze for a moment, considering. Could such a thing be possible? His father would be proud... The thought seemed to dangle tantalizingly before him. *Frederick the Conqueror.* He could do such good if he just had the power...

Suddenly, he shook himself and the vision burst like a bubble popping.

"I thought about that once. I used to think that I might get rich and powerful and that people would look up to me. But I've found something greater here. I've found that things like being faithful and trustworthy are better than all the gold and gems in the world. You can keep your riches and your magic. I'm doing just fine without them."

"Shame," said the Witch. "And you, Atlantis? Do you desire to live forever, or shall we speed you along your mortal way toward death this day?" she crowed.

Atlantis looked about at the sea of goblins around him, and at the king of the goblins, standing staring at him and brandishing his great black sword, then at the Witch, the fire on her staff tumbling upward like a nauseating and fetid tongue.

"I am not ready to die today," he said after a moment. "There is one final battle that I wish to fight. But if this be the day of my death, then I shall make such a slaughter that shall not be forgotten, and it shall begin with you!"

He leaped through the air so fast that everyone was taken by surprise. He came down, his sword flashing in a great arc of green fire, and slicing right through the body of the Witch. But his eyes grew wide as, in her place, nothing but smoke stood, and this solidified again into her laughing form.

Now, however, the Goblin King sprang into action, and his great black sword came to life. Black fumes rose from its blade as he attacked Atlantis. Barely in time, Atlantis blocked the goblin's stroke, and now they battled in earnest. Again and again, green fire met black, and the clash of their steel filled the chamber. The goblins howled and shouted as they ringed in the two combatants.

* * *

"We've got to do something!" cried Colleen.

She shut her eyes and, a moment later, the waters of the river began to seethe and writhe, and up from its depths the form of two great stallions rose. They neighed, and their voices were like waterfalls. Then they stampeded forward into the midst of the goblins.

She raised her hands in the air, and down from the ceiling a great spike of rock came plunging down, piercing the black ship, and sending its remaining crew of goblins screaming as water began to fill the hold.

The Witch whirled around and, with a wave of her staff, two fiery apparitions appeared. They were dragon-like in appearance, and they sprang forward through the goblins, sending them screaming and bursting into flames at their touch. Many dove into the river to extinguish themselves, while others thrashed about wildly. But the fire and water creatures collided with a terrific concussion, sending steam and smoke everywhere, and blinding everyone for a moment.

"Now," said Ellie, "let's get across and get Frederick and Atlantis out of there."

They vanished just as a ball of fire detonated in the place where they had stood a moment before. As they emerged beside Frederick, the Witch once again waved her staff, and this time, the walls and ceiling and floor all about them began to grow hot.

"She's enchanted the rock!" said Ellie. "We can't pass through it without burning ourselves!"

Now Atlantis and the king of the goblins were battling so fiercely that goblins fled in every direction to avoid being swept away in the fray.

Colleen looked around desperately, but could see no other creatures in the river or the rock. She pulled her staff from where it was strapped on her back and held it ready. Ellie stood tensely beside her and Frederick.

Then, at a signal from the Witch, the goblins charged.

* * *

Nous ran up the hall as quickly as he could. He did not know how he was going to find this dwarf, or how he would convince him to follow him, but he would try. Why he was doing this was still something of a mystery to him. He was a goblin, and yet there was something different about this human girl that stirred something inside him. He *cared* for her. Never before in his life had he actually cared for anyone other than himself. It was a new sensation, and it felt... *right.* He emerged from the tunnel and found himself standing in a hallway. Down the hall was an open door leading outside. He began down the hall when behind him something like stone against stone began to grate and move. He spun around, and there stood a huge statue of a centaur, and it was coming to life.

He cried out and sped down the hallway, the centaur galloping behind. Out the door, he sped, and there, standing on the porch, was a huge man and a very short one with a long beard. Both looked shocked to see a goblin run *out* of the house and onto the lawn. Little people screamed and scattered, and the short, bearded fellow on the porch gave a bellowing yell and hefted a golden ax. The big man pulled a great hammer from his belt and hefted it high over his head, as if to throw it.

"Wait! Wait!" cried Nous. "Nous has come with the Colleen and the Frederick and the Ellie and the king!"

"What?" cried Adol. "Speak now or you will die where you stand, goblin!"

"I am with the Colleen – the Colleen McGunnegal! She is by the river! The Witch... she is there too! The Colleen asked me to come to get help!" said Nous desperately.

"If you lie..." said Adol.

"No, no, no lies!" said Nous. "Come with Nous. He will show you!"

"He's a goblin, Adol," said Doc. "I have a hard time believing him. But how he got in the house..."

"No time," said Adol. "We will follow you... Nous... and if you are lying..."

"Follow, quick!" said Nous, and ran up the steps. But he stopped at the door at the sight of the stone centaur standing there with his spear.

"Go back and guard!" said Doc, and immediately, the centaur galloped back down the hall and returned to its post.

Nous ran in, with Adol and Doc behind.

* * *

As they ran, Adol wondered what was happening. They had been standing on the porch one moment, watching the little people beginning to rebuild their world, when suddenly, it had all gone bad. The forest had come alive and then seemed to fall, as though it suddenly began to fade and die. The little people said that they sensed that the Waking Tree had died. Then, when everyone was crying, and all seemed lost, something had changed again. There was a sense of both death and new life. The forest had stirred once more, and the little people said that something was happening. There was hope.

Adol put the thought of that behind him as they ran down the long passageway. Doc struggled to keep up, and fell behind, but when he finally came to the end of the passage, he placed his hands against the wall and the secret door swung open.

There before them was a scene of pandemonium.

* * *

Mr. and Mrs. Wigglepox, Lily, and Rose ran down the hall and found themselves suddenly in the Crystal Chamber. Its red-gold roof and thousands of crystals sparkled with rainbows.

Bhrogan looked about the room in amazement. "Is this..."

"Yes," replied his wife. "No time to explain."

They ran to the middle of the room and pulled out their pots of gold. But Lily's was empty, as was Mrs. Wigglepox's. Rose had a single piece, that she looked at for a moment, then pulled out.

"Rose, you mustn't ..." began her father, but his wife put her hand on his arm. "We have all learned that sacrifice and love have greater power than the old laws given to the leprechauns. Let her give her last and best wish for our world."

"But the rest of us have no gold," said Mr. Wigglepox.

"No matter," said his wife. "This room shall be our pot of gold. We will wish together with Rose. Perhaps we will be granted one last wish here in this place. May we wish well!"

They hugged one another, and then Rose held out her last piece of gold to her father. "You should have this, Father."

"No, Rose. It is yours and your wish to make," he replied.

Rose took a deep breath and looked at her beloved family one more time.

Then she cried out, "We wish for help to come to rescue us from the Witch and expel her from our land forever!"

"May it be so!" wished Mr. Wigglepox.

"May it be so!" wished Mrs. Wigglepox.

"May it be so!" wished Lily.

The room flashed with rainbows.

* * *

Aonghus stood staring at the doors with Bran, Abbe, Bib, Henny, and Professor McPherson. Something was happening, for all of a sudden, there was a series of eight distinct *CLANG* sounds, as though great bolts of locks were being thrown back and, as they watched, all eight of the huge Gates of Anastazi swung silently open.

But he had no time to wonder what was happening, for out of one, a great clamor rose, and to his absolute and complete astonishment, he saw the most unexpected group of people that he could ever have imagined. For there was not only Atlantis, battling some huge creature, with a swarm of smaller creatures all about him, but Frederick as well, swinging a blazing sword, and wonder of all wonders, there was Colleen... and their mother.

Colleen was fighting with one of the black creatures, wielding a staff like a fighting stick, and Ellie was wrestling with another.

Aonghus roared and charged through the door, with Bran right behind him. They threw themselves at the goblins that were attacking Colleen and their mother, and in an instant, those goblins knew no more.

"Mother!" he cried. "How?"

But suddenly five, then ten more goblins took their place, and they found themselves fighting for their lives.

* * *

Adol stood for one moment as he saw, to his shock and great joy, Colleen and Ellie, along with Frederick Buttersmouth and a tall stranger.

"Ellie!" he cried out.

She was alive! But they were in grave danger – and too far away! How could he reach them?

Suddenly, a great black shape swooped down upon them. Adol let fly his hammer! It struck the beast, sending it crashing into the river. The hammer flew back to his hand.

"Come!" shouted Doc over the noise of battle. "I have a passageway over the river!"

He ran back into his tunnel and led Adol and Nous through a second secret door. Up a climbing passage they ran, and down again, through a third door, and then they were out, in the midst of it all.

Adol bellowed as he saw a goblin grapple with Ellie. He ran forward through the pack, tossing goblins aside like rag dolls.

Then, without warning, the great double Gate that was directly behind them began to swing inward, and a moment later, out ran the last two people he would have ever expected – Aonghus and Bran.

Adol cried out again and bolted forward, his hammer swinging in great, mighty blows. Doc was behind him, although giving him plenty of room, and his golden ax flashed as he followed in the big man's wake.

Nous kept his distance, not wishing to be mistaken for one of the witch's goblins, and he blended into the mass.

A goblin came round to one side of Doc and would have had him with its spear, but Nous tripped him, and the goblin fell on its face with a shout. Nous quickly stepped away as the other goblin looked about for his attacker.

Aonghus and Bran saw their father, and with shouts of joy and astonishment, they met and formed a wall, with Adol in the middle swinging his great hammer, and his boys on either side, their fists flailing, and short Doc the Dwarf wielding his golden ax, his white beard whipping to and fro. Professor McPherson joined them as well, and showed himself to be quite a fighter.

For a moment, the goblins retreated, and Abbe, Bib, and Henny came through the gate.

"Mother!" cried the girls, and ran forward to embrace her.

"Ellie!" cried Adol, and with tears of joy running down his face, he kissed her on the lips.

She laughed then and gently pushed him away.

"No time!" she said with glee, and then grew serious. "Bib, stay with Henny! Abbe, stay with me. The goblins have a weak place – their eyes and ears. Hit them there if you must!"

"I'm right beside you, Mom," Abbe said.

But the pause did not last, and now the battle between Atlantis and the Goblin King pressed against them, and they retreated back through the Gate of Anastazi and into the Timeless Hall.

Goblins poured through the open doorway, and they look about, wondering if they should make their escape through one open passage or another. Most of the doorways were dark, but a few looked lighter, and one opened to what appeared to be a bright courtyard.

Suddenly, two goblins leaped onto Atlantis' back, throwing him off balance. The Goblin King roared in triumph, and would have dealt him a deathblow, but Adol, seeing the man's peril, leaped to his side and, with a terrific blow right to the great nose of the goblin, sent him tumbling backward. The goblin fell to the ground in front of a dark door and lay still.

At that moment, the Witch walked in and cried out, "Enough!" and sent a great bolt of fire roaring over their heads.

The goblins retreated, circling around the room and blocking every exit.

The McGunnegals, Frederick, Professor McPherson, Doc, and Atlantis were forced into the center of the room. The men pushed the women behind them, forming a protective circle.

The Witch walked over to the unconscious body of the Goblin King and glanced down at it. She then gazed about the room at the scores of fallen goblins, and then looked up at the twelve people who stood in the middle of the room.

"So here it ends," she said. "You have all done well, my friends. Rarely have I enjoyed such a chase and contest of wills! But see here, things need not go badly for you. Will you not reason with me for one moment?"

Her voice was crooning and somehow powerfully persuasive. They all hesitated, as if a question had somehow formed in their minds, but they could not put it into words.

"Yes," she said. "I see in your hearts that you do not desire bloodshed. And there need be none! You think me a witch, an evil in this land. But I tell you it is not so! I was trapped here by traitorous men long ago, and these *little people*, through their black arts, wounded me deeply. I was forced to defend myself, as were these folk that you see with me – these that you call *goblins*."

A vision formed in their minds of a fair woman being chased through the woods by angry gnomes riding on stalkers. Pity and doubt rose up in them, and they began to wonder how one maiden could possibly take on and defeat a world of magic peoples. For a moment, no one moved.

It was Doc who first shook himself free of the spell. He spat and said, "I think not, witch. I've been here as long as you, longer, in fact, and none of these little folk went bad until you came along. It was a pure and good world, and its people were the same. You're the one who brought them goblins and that there Ooze. That's what started all the ills of this place. It was you!"

Doc's words seemed to break the spell, and the vision shattered. But the witch began her weaving again and said, "Poor old dwarf. I do not blame you. No doubt, these fairies and pixies have fed you many lies through these long years. Do not believe them! I have only defended myself, and sided with the less evil of two fallen races. But see here, Colleen McGunnegal..."

* * *

Colleen's mind snapped to attention as the Witch focused the full power of her spell on her. "Did not the *Lady* tell you that you need someone of your own kind to teach you how to use your powers? Let *me* teach you, girl. Let *me* teach you what your real destiny is. Let *me* show you how to truly sing this *song* that you hear – oh, yes, I have heard the *song* – it can be changed for the better! As a great musician can alter a piece to her own liking and shape it to move her audience, you can do the same with this song. But only *I* can teach you. That pitiful woman at her little lake could only show you tricks. What you have experienced so far is like a child beating a drum with a stick. Come with me, Colleen, and I will teach you the true symphony of power and freedom that is available to anyone who has the strength to seize it!"

Suddenly, Colleen heard the song again, not with her physical ears, but with that inner ear that was beyond her senses. The lives of those all around her sang it, the river sang it, and the rocks, and the forest far above. All the little

715

creatures that dug and moved through the earth sang with it. It flowed through everything, even through her. She watched as the Witch raised her staff. The room began to tremble, and they had to steady themselves to keep from falling. A sense of tremendous power filled the chamber, and all were struck with a sense of dread.

For a moment, the power of the witch mesmerized Colleen. *Could I do this too?* she thought. Was this *song* simply a part of the world that could be harnessed, like a steam engine used steam, or electricity could be used to send a telegraph?

Try it... whispered a voice in her mind. *The power is so sweet...*

She stood still for a moment, and the temptation to seize the song and make it her own, to use it for her own purposes, tugged at her mind.

Then another voice seemed to whisper deep in her soul. She remembered the Lady Danu and the peace of her lake, and all she had experienced there. She smiled at the memory, and the spell of the Witch shattered like a falling mirror striking the ground. Her inner sight returned, and now she heard the notes of the Song that played in concord with one another were broken and fragmented all about the Witch and goblins. It was as if the notes of creation's music faltered as they tried to penetrate the living essences of the dark creatures, and all of its power and beauty and strength, and the fabric of existence itself warped around the dark hooded figure of the Witch. It was sucked into the flaming staff and emerged again as a screech of discord that threatened to undo everything around her.

Colleen covered her ears and shut her eyes.

"No!" she shouted. "No! I see what you are doing! I'll have no part in *that!*"

The Witch lowered her staff and the discord faded.

"A shame you will not join me," she said quietly. "You could have been great. But now, it is time for you to die!"

She lifted her staff, and its tip began to flame. Again, Colleen saw the universe around them begin to shift and buckle. Destruction was coming. The Witch's spell grew, mounting and folding and warping upon itself.

Suddenly, Colleen realized what was happening. "We've got to stop her!" she cried. "It's happening again! She's going to unleash a second Cataclysm!"

The huddled group of defenders braced themselves, sensing, but not seeing what she saw. Colleen began to focus her thoughts, preparing to summon all of her strength to heal the rift that she knew was about to occur. The ring was shining, and the magic of the little people and the rock creatures flowed into her. She reached out with her hand, and touched Aonghus on the arm, remembering what Anastazi had done with her. Aonghus' eyes widened as she drew strength from him, but he understood, and put his other hand on Bran's shoulder. Instinctively, all of the McGunnegals made contact, and Colleen was astonished at what she found. The force of their combined strength of heart nearly bowled her over, but she steadied herself and allowed it to fill her, preparing to send it all against the onslaught of the Witch. Power was about to clash with power, and Colleen felt as though she would burst unless she unleashed it.

Then the Witch struck. The detonation of power that exploded around them knocked them to the ground. Colleen watched with her inner eye as the Witch's power caused the very fabric of existence around them to buckle. The Great Song faltered in her mind, becoming a clamor and shrieking of unbearable noise.

She pulled herself to her knees, holding on to Aonghus' arm. Fighting against the chaos, she tried to remember the Song she had heard at the Lake, tried to summon it back and stop the rending of time and space that was about to occur.

Slowly, at first around Colleen, and then expanding outward, a white light appeared. Like a shield against the raging tide of black-red destruction, it grew and spread outward, a protective wall, which the cacophony of the Witch's noise could not penetrate.

The others around her stood, their strength returning. Colleen drew on that strength, and her resolve firmed. The protective barrier began to expand, pushing outward and toward the Witch and the goblins.

But their enemy sensed their strength growing and her own attack faltering. With a scream of rage, the Witch raised her staff high over her head. The goblin nearest her cried out and, to Colleen's horror, it seemed to *dissolve* into a black mist and was sucked into the flame of the staff. All at once, the power of the Witch erupted outward again, redoubled, and pounded upon them with fresh fury. A second goblin's life was snatched away, and the darkness in the hall deepened.

Colleen fell to one knee, her strength nearly spent. How could she fight against such savagery and brutality? How could she summon any healing against this Witch's terrible might? She felt herself faltering, their shield weakening.

Suddenly, just as the world about them was about to detonate in unimaginable ruin, something very odd happened – there was the sound of a horn. Not a trumpet blast, or a war horn, but the duck-like beeping of a car horn. And, without warning, in through one of the gates – indeed, the very gate that the McGunnegal children had come through – drove a steam car, and at its wheel was Helga Von Faust. She was dirty and haggard looking, and her hair hung in tangled clumps about her face. Her eyes were wild, and her mouth was open.

"Look out! Look out!" she shouted. "The brakes are gone, and I cannot stop it!"

Goblins dove out of the way as the car, horn beeping, bore down upon them and directly into the Timeless Hall.

She swerved this way and that, barely missing the group gathered in the center of the room, and the car sent steam puffing about in great clouds.

"A demon from hell!" shouted Atlantis, gripping his sword with both hands.

Goblins screamed and began to run about, jostling one another. Their panic grew as the car mowed several of them down, and complete pandemonium took over. The Witch stopped her attack, taken by surprise. The atmosphere around them boiled with angry clouds of dark power and confusion.

Colleen seized her chance. With all her might, she willed herself to fight the impending doom. She summoned the Song in her heart and, with all her strength, sent it outward, a healing power that strove mightily against the deceit and death that roiled about them. An explosive concussion of thunder rocked the Timeless Hall as the power of the Witch was thrown down. The world snapped back to reality, the impending disaster momentarily averted. But the Maiden of the Night quickly raised her staff once again to send a blast of destroying fire to annihilate this terrible apparition that had suddenly appeared and stolen away her victory.

But as she prepared to do so, a goblin, who had been quietly moving around the periphery of the room, suddenly leaped, and performed an act that no other goblin in five thousand years had dared to do. It grabbed the Witch's staff, snatched it from her hands, and went rolling away with it. He sprang to his feet, and with all his might, brought the staff down across his knee, and broke it with a *snap!* There was a terrible eruption of fire, and the goblin was enveloped in flame. The Witch shrieked with rage. But as she turned to fall upon the traitorous goblin who had dared to do this thing, the horn of the car blew a long continuous *BEEEEEEP!* Above the clamor came the voice of Helga screaming, *"Look out!"*

With a *THUMP*, the car ran directly into the huge fallen body of the Goblin King. It stopped abruptly, its back wheels rising up into the air. The horn also ceased, and Helga, screaming, went flying over the steering wheel, out of the car, and hit the Witch squarely in the back. Her arms flew out to her sides, and both she and Helga went tumbling over and over, and rolled right out one of the open gates.

Instantly, all eight doors began to close.

Helga had, in her flight over the steering wheel, knocked the car out of gear and into reverse, and it was now rolling backwards. They all watched as it drifted through a gate and out of the Timeless Hall, puffed out one last cloud of steam, and vanished into the darkness beyond.

"Everyone, out!" shouted Atlantis. "Back through the gate, run!"

They all moved, releasing their link with each other and Colleen. But now the gift of their combined powers was in her. She felt as though she had to send it somewhere or be overwhelmed by it, and so she directed it all into the ring. It blazed like the sun and then faded to a moon-like glow.

Everyone headed for the gate after Atlantis – all except Doc, who was staring at the door through which the car had rolled.

"Home..." he whispered.

"Doc!" called Frederick, and the dwarf came to himself, glanced longingly at the door, and then joined them.

Atlantis, Adol, and Doc led the way back through the Gate through which they had come, their weapons ready, but the goblins were now in no mood to fight, seeing both their king and the Witch defeated or gone. Instead, they dashed through the nearest door, vanishing into the darkness beyond.

Just then, Colleen realized that Nous was missing and that it must have been he who had broken the Witch's staff.

"Wait!" she yelled, and dashed back to where he lay.

Frederick ran after her and, together, they knelt down beside him. His black robe smoldered, and she desperately patted it out, burning her hands as she did. She gasped in horror as she saw that his hands and arms had been sickeningly burned, and almost no flesh remained on them, and his body and face were horribly blistered.

"Colleen!" shouted Adol, running back to them, his hammer ready.

"We've got to get him out of there!" she cried. "He's hurt!"

Adol picked up the goblin with as much care as he could and laid him over one of his great shoulders.

"Now hurry!" he said, and they rushed back to join the others.

Colleen glanced back once and saw the Goblin King begin to stir. He rose, picking up his sword, and, seeing her, rushed forward.

Just before the Gate closed, they all slipped through, back into the Land of the Little People. The Goblin King gave a roar and cried out, *"I shall find you, girl, if I wait until the end of time, I shall…"* The Gates closed with a *CLANG,* and their familiar moonlit glow filled the room.

Now the goblins that remained began to rally together, for two other ships had sailed the perilous river course, guided by the black magic of the Witch, and their captains were no cowards. Although the first ship had now sunk, these latter two had now moved forward, one beside the other, and goblins were flooding the banks, with half a dozen wyverns circling about in the air.

Adol laid Nous down on the shore, readied his hammer, and turned to face their enemies, but Colleen and Frederick knelt down beside the goblin.

"Nous," cried Colleen. "Don't die. Please don't die."

Nous' burned eyelids fluttered open, and his gaze found hers.

"Nous… wishes…" he began, but his breathing became ragged and he could not speak further.

"Don't talk, Nous," said Colleen. "You saved us. Now we're going to save you."

With great effort, he raised a hand and reached out to touch her face.

"Never said it …" he began, but his face twisted in agony, and his hand dropped. "Nous loves …."

He glanced at Frederick, his eyes grew distant and, with his final breath, he whispered, "Forgive me…."

Then his eyes closed, and he grew still.

"No, no!" cried Colleen. "Nous, don't go!"

She shut her eyes, ignoring the rising clamor around them, and she willed herself to find him – to find the life force of his spirit within the Great Song, to listen for the pulse of his being. And there he was. She watched as his heart beat one last note in perfect harmony with the Music, and then the song of his life began to lift away.

With all the power that was in her, she pursued him, trying to catch the fleeting notes that he played, willing them to stay. They paused for a moment, echoing in the chamber, then with a sound that seemed to smile, they flew upward into unfathomable heights and vanished away.

Colleen sat on her knees and sobbed. Frederick put his arm around her, and tears fell down his own face.

"He's gone, Frederick," she said. "He's gone."

But their sorrow was interrupted by Adol's voice.

"Prepare yourselves, children," he said. "They are coming."

Frederick stood, his sword in his hand, and joined the others. They formed a circle around Colleen and Nous and watched as the hordes of goblins gathered around them. The foremost of the goblins came at them in a great rush.

Just as it seemed they would have to fight for their lives once again, a cry went up from the goblins on the ships. Something was coming up the river, and they were terrified by it.

All stood tense, expecting some new horror, but a moment later, their hearts lifted, and a great white shining light blazed through the darkness, and a sweeping flood of bright water poured into the cavern.

Riding upon a great, white, foaming stallion of waves came the Lady Danu, and where her steed's hooves trod, the water burst into a brilliant blue. Hundreds of fairies and pixies flew all around her, their green and blue and pink and yellow bodies radiant with an inner glory.

The goblins screamed in agony, covering their eyes and fleeing back to their black ships. The shining waves crashed over the banks of the river in a great flood, knocking goblins from their feet and causing them to writhe like slugs upon which salt had been thrown. Some were swept away and lost in the river, and others, like rats, leaped aboard their ships and cut the ropes that held them. The wave of shining water washed back, and the black ships began to drift down river, carried now by the strong current.

As the flood rose knee deep to where Colleen and the others stood, they felt refreshed and renewed, and all weariness and fear left them. What remained of the dark magic of the Witch broke with a concussion of sound like thunder, and the flying wyverns fled down the passage after the ships.

The radiance of the Lady filled the room. Everything grew sharp and clear, and all shadows fled away.

Chapter 26 – The Final Meeting

The shining waters receded as the Lady Danu stepped onto the shore and approached the little group. Most of them stood with wide eyes and open mouths, amazed, and even a bit fearful at the splendor and power and beauty of this being that approached.

"Lady Danu!" said Doc, bowing.

"It has been a very long time, Sindri. And longer for you, my good Atlantis," she said.

Atlantis bowed and said, "When I last saw you, it was the death of me. I hope our meeting on this occasion shall be different!"

Colleen still knelt next to Nous. The waves had momentarily covered him, burying him in their terrible brightness. He lay still in death.

Frederick approached the Lady. She placed her hands on his shoulders and said, "You did not fail, young Frederick. You brought the help that was needed, and revived the king in the sea. You have grown, my young friend, and shall grow further. I foresee that many dangers and great deeds lie before your path, but you are equal to them so long as you stay true and humble."

Frederick grinned and said, "I suppose everyone is wondering just who you are. This is the McGunnegal family and my teacher, Professor McPherson. Apparently, you know Doc and Atlantis. Everyone – this is the Lady Danu. She helped us in our journey, and she's the one who sent me back home."

The Lady curtsied to them in her shining white dress.

"You can close your mouth now," whispered Aonghus to Bran, and he immediately did so, blushing.

"But, Colleen – why are you weeping?" said the Lady, looking beyond them to where she knelt. "The Witch has been banished. The Waking Tree is renewed. And one long waited for is returning to the forest. Indeed, he is waiting for you."

Colleen did not look up, but knelt on the wet ground beside Nous.

"He's gone, Lady," she said through her tears. "He sacrificed himself to save us, and now he's gone."

They all gathered around Colleen and Nous and looked down with sad faces.

The goblin lay very still. His chest did not move, and his burned black hood covered his face, washed there by the waves.

"Colleen, such sacrifices are never in vain. Do you not know that you have saved him as well?" asked the Lady. "See!"

Colleen gently pushed aside the tattered hood of the cloak that hid him, and gasped. Where once had been an ugly, bulbous, and burned and blistered face, was smooth violet skin, a perfect nose, small pointed ears, and long, deep purple, almost black hair. The Lady went to him, knelt down, and touched him on his head.

For a brief moment, Colleen thought she heard the faint sound of joyful singing, as though a distant door had opened, and a breeze had carried the sounds of festival to her from far, far away. Then the door was shut, the music echoed in her mind for a moment, and then was gone.

Nous' eyes fluttered open, and he slowly sat up. The burned husk of his old garment fell away, and they saw his smooth, muscled body, free of all deformity, and no worms remained.

He looked in amazement at his new hands, felt his chest and perfect violet feet, and then touched his face. Then he turned to Colleen and smiled, and perfect white teeth were there where his old yellow and brown fangs had once been. She gave a squeal of delight and threw her arms around him, and he, hesitantly, embraced her back.

"Nous does not... I mean... I do not understand," said Nous. "How is it that... that the worms... and the Ooze... they are gone from me!"

"Nous, the worms have been burned away by the fire of your self-sacrifice, and the Ooze has been washed away by the waters of light. You have learned that life only finds its true meaning in love. All else is worms and Ooze," said the Lady.

She then nodded toward the goblin and the last vestiges of his old rags fell to dust and, in their place, appeared a white robe with a deep purple belt. He rose and stood before the Lady Danu, straight and strong.

"You saved us, Nous," said Colleen. "The Witch is gone!"

She hugged him for a long moment, and then backed away, and he gazed back, a look of wonder on his face. Then his expression grew serious, and he bowed his head.

"Where shall I go now, Lady?" he said. "My people still wallow in the Ooze, though the Witch may be banished."

"Ah, there is still much for you to do, Nous, and I think I know what your first task will be. Look, there is someone here to meet you," she replied.

Another white stallion of waves came thundering up the river, and on it rode Evchi, the good goblin they had met in the desert. She dismounted the watery steed and gracefully walked over to Nous. He blushed, and his cheeks turned a deeper shade of purple. Evchi took him by the hand and smiled, and then they embraced.

The Lady laughed, and her voice was like the sound of pure rain on a spring day.

"Ah, you two shall one day be partners in this great struggle for your people," she said, "for there are still goblins in this land and in other lands as well, and a whole world of them that lies under the dominion of the Great Worm. There is much for you both to do."

Nous then let go of Evchi's hand and turned to Frederick.

"I am sorry to have bitten you," he said and held out a hand to him.

Frederick shook it, and said, "Oh, it turned out all right, didn't it? I think that almost becoming a goblin helped me realize how much I want to be truly human. I suppose I've still got a ways to go. But look at you – you're clean and handsome, and you don't stink anymore. I guess you're becoming what a goblin ought to be as well."

Nous' gaze turned inward, and he looked thoughtful.

"*Becoming*," he said. "Yes, that's the word for it. The journey goes on."

Frederick nodded, marveling at how much the goblin had changed. Then he lowered his voice and said, "Nous, is that a goblin girl? She's very beautiful."

"Her name is Evchi," whispered Nous near his ear. "And yes, she is beautiful, isn't she?"

Frederick grinned, and Nous went over to Colleen.

She still had tears in her eyes, and Nous said, "Why does the Colleen cry?"

"I'm going to miss you calling me that, Nous," she said. "But I think you have to go now, and I do as well. I only wish that we could stay together for a while and talk, now that things are looking up, and we're not running from one danger to the next."

Nous looked sad and said, "The Colleen will have more dangers to deal with at home, Nous thinks. Pwca is there in your world, is he not? Beware him. He wields dark magic. I wish I could… could…"

"Hush, now," said Colleen. "I've become quite fond of you, you know. But I think someone else has as well."

She glanced at Evchi and said, "You have something terribly important to do here. I'm sure we will see each other again."

He paused and cocked his head as if listening, then gave Colleen another hug and said, "Nous thinks that as long as we sing in the Great Song together, we will never be far apart, although all the worlds lie between us."

Then he let Colleen go, walked back to Evchi, and took her hand.

"It is time," said the Lady. "There is more for you to do before you depart from this land. I bid you all go up to the forest and see what awaits you."

"One moment," said Colleen. "I had nearly forgotten! Where is the Wigglepox family?"

"They were running down a hall on the other shore when I left them," said Nous. "I do not know what became of them."

"I shall see you once more before you leave," said the Lady. "I must go now. There is still work to be done."

She vanished beneath the river, and as she went, the shining waters dimmed and the river resumed its course. Now only the moon-like silver glow of the Gate of Anastazi illuminated the chamber.

"Come with me," said Doc, and he led them to his secret passage in the wall.

They followed him up and through the climbing passageway, down again, and then onward to the Crystal Cavern.

There, to their great surprise, were four short figures seated back to back in the middle of the room. They were about the size that Oracle had been, although two of them were smaller and were obviously children. They were all holding hands, and appeared to be asleep.

"Mrs. Wigglepox! Lily! Rose! Mr. Wigglepox!" cried Colleen, and ran forward.

Lily yawned hugely, smacked her lips, and batted her eyes.

"What a dream that was!" she said, "Mother, I..."

And then she stopped, seeing all the big people gathered in the room and Doc the Dwarf by their side. Then she looked at herself, and at her little sister, Rose, who now stood beside her, and then at her mother and father.

"We've grown!" she said.

Then she spotted Frederick, and with a giggle, ran toward him and leaped up into his arms.

He spun her around, laughing, and said, "Wow, Lily, you sure have grown! Did you all make a big wish again in here?"

"We did!" she said, laughing. Then she grew serious. "But it was our Last Wish. And now our pots of gold are..."

But as she pulled out her pot from the satchel at her side, she found it filled to the brim with shining, perfect gold nuggets.

"Mother!" she cried, "Look!"

Mrs. Wigglepox found her pot filled as well, and even Mr. Wigglepox, who did not even have a pot of gold when he went into the chamber, found that he now had one.

"And mine is full too!" said Rose.

"Something wonderful has happened," said Mrs. Wigglepox, coming up to Colleen and holding out her hands to her.

"Yes," she replied. "I think your world has a chance to be made new again. The Spell is broken, the Witch is gone, the Gray Man is banished, the goblins are fleeing, there is a new Waking Tree, and the Lady Danu is free again to help you bring your forest back to life. And look at yourselves – you are not small anymore!"

"Each of us has grown, haven't we?" she said.

"Glory be, glory be!" said Doc. "In all my days, I've not seen the like of it! But come, come! The Lady bade us go upstairs. Follow me now. Let's all be quick about it."

Doc led them at a quick pace up the long hall, into the house, past the stone centaur, and out onto the front porch of the House of Mysteries. Out on the lawn, a great many little people were gathered, and all of them had grown to their proper size. Leprechauns were no longer a few inches tall, but stood at their proper height of about two feet. And the gnomes were no longer skinny and wretched looking, but were properly plump, and all of the fairies and pixies shone with an inner light that made them what they ought to be.

All of them were looking up expectantly, as though waiting for something. There, off in the distance, in the fluffy white clouds that dotted the blue sky, a ray of sunlight shone through and pierced the forest canopy, and through that ray, a tiny flying figure appeared. It came closer, and Colleen could see that it was one of the little people dressed in bright green trousers and a dark green jacket. All about him pixies and fairies flew, sprinkling him with magic dust as he soared through the air.

"Oracle!" shouted Colleen, and they all moved out into the grass to see him arrive.

He waved and called to them as he descended in a shower of golden pixie dust that floated down upon them all.

"Oracle!" said Colleen again, and ran over to him and knelt down to hug him. Frederick was right behind her.

"Colligal! Fredersmouth!" he said with a huge grin. "You have finished your task here at last. Your family is saved, and our world is free of the Witch."

"But I really didn't do anything," replied Colleen. "It was everyone else who did so much and sacrificed themselves for your world."

"Right," said Frederick. "In the end, it was Nous who broke the Witch's staff and Helga who sent the Witch, well, rather tumbling out of this world."

"Nous? Helga? Well, you both did more than you know," he said, and then bowed to them. "Thank you all for what you have done for us," he said. "Colligal, would you introduce me to the rest of your family?"

"Oh! Of course!" she replied. "Well, you know my mother, Ellie, and this is my father, Adol, and my brothers Aonghus and Bran, and my sisters Abbe, Bib, and Henny. And you know Evchi and Nous. Oracle, look at Nous! Isn't he handsome now? And you know Atlantis."

"And this is..." began Frederick.

"Professor McPherson," cut in the professor.

Oracle looked hard at the professor for a long moment and then smiled.

"McPherson," he said slowly, and then nodded and said, "It is a joy to meet you all. Please, come for a moment into one of our Great Trees, and see what is happening."

As he led them through the forest toward a huge tree, Bib whispered to Abbe, "Did you see that back there? McPherson and this Oracle fellow have met before."

"It's your imagination, Bib," she whispered back. "How could that be?"

"Don't know," she whispered. "But it was weird how Oracle stopped and looked at him."

When they arrived at the tree, it opened for them, revealing a spiraling staircase that led upward in low steps. They followed these until they emerged to an opening that looked out to the south. Off in the distance, they could see the shining waters of the Lady's Lake, but far, far to the south was something that they did not expect on this happy occasion, for there a line of smoke was rising.

"The goblins had begun to burn the forest," said Oracle. "But the Lady has stopped them, and they have fled into the desert. Much harm was done, but behold!"

They watched as the columns of smoke grew white, as though they had turned to steam, and Henny said, "There's a river flowing down there."

"You have sharp eyes, young one," said Oracle. "Indeed, the Lady Danu, even now, is sending the underground river waters up and through the forest. The flames are being extinguished, and the desert watered. Soon we will plant at the edge of the desert, and foot by foot, we will turn it once again into a green and growing place."

"What will you do when you reach the Wizard's Castle?" asked Colleen. "The crack in time is still there, and the ghost of Lugh as well."

"We shall see, we shall see," said the leprechaun.

"Oracle," said Frederick, "why is it that all that time we were with you, you acted like a fool, with all that crazy talk and the pranks – what was the point of all that?"

Oracle smiled, but said nothing.

Now the canopy of the great wood was bursting into green and white and pink and yellow as far as the eye could see. It was truly coming to life, and wherever the fairies and pixies showered their fairy dust, flowers burst from the ground. All across the forest, trees and ferns and flowers and meadows and moss were shining and growing, and seemed to be singing a new song of life and happiness.

"The New Waking Tree is calling to the forest, my friends. You have planted and watered it, and in the very shadow of our world's death, new life has come. Thank you. We are forever in your debt," said Oracle, and he bowed low to them again.

"But I have a final task for you all. There are many in our world besides the goblins who sided with the Witch. They could still do a great deal of mischief if left alone. A rotten fruit left in the barrel will eventually spoil the whole lot. Indeed, they are like fallen fruit, and the time to save them from themselves is now. They are trying to hide under root and stone, but the forest will not have them any longer. We are gathering them together for their judgment. Would you come with me one more time to the Island of the Waking Tree, and there see what their fate shall be?" asked Oracle.

Colleen walked over to Adol and Ellie and said, "I think we should. I'd like to see this through to the end."

Her parents nodded, and Ellie said, "If the good Atlantis will take us, we shall meet you there in the morning."

"Of course," said Atlantis.

"Then rest, my friends, in the shade of the New Forest! Eat of its fruit and find strength for your journey ahead," Oracle said. "Meet me at the rising of the sun on the Island of the Waking Tree!"

Then, surrounded by four shining fairies, he pulled out his pot of gold, which was now filled to the brim, took out a nugget, winked at Colleen and Frederick, and vanished in a flash of rainbows.

"Well!" said Frederick after a moment. "He sure has changed."

"I don't think he's changed at all," replied Colleen. "I think he's always been just that way, only we didn't see it. Remember how things always seemed to work out whenever he was around? The Elder of Elders of the leprechauns! Who would have thought it? And oh, I've not told you what he did in the dungeons of the Witch! What a tale!"

"Well," said Doc. "I think we ought to have a feast and you can tell us the story proper. Then some rest! Tomorrow will be a new day for this world!"

"A feast!" said Atlantis. "Aye, I could use that. I feel as if I have not eaten in ages! But I think that we must set sail tonight if we are to meet your friend back at his Island."

And so they feasted on the lawn in front of the House of Mysteries. Doc produced a great spread of mushrooms and herbs and roots, and the little people gathered berries and greens and fruit, for already the harvest of the fruit trees in the wood was ripening.

Colleen and Frederick and all the rest of them were amazed at all of the little people who gathered together – fairies and pixies of all sorts, and gnomes and leprechauns all dressed now in their finest apparel. They ate and drank Doc's draft and sang and danced and laughed and told many stories until the stars shone over their heads, and Henny was fast asleep in her mother's arms.

Nous and Evchi were especially of interest to the little people, for they had never seen good goblins before, and a great many of them sat in a circle around the two, asking them questions, most of which Evchi answered as Nous sat quietly and listened.

Soon the midnight hour came and went, and still their celebration went on until Colleen yawned and rubbed her eyes.

Frederick came and sat next to her and, together, they looked up at the fairies who were now dancing in the air while a group of gnomes sang a song of the earth and its Creator as they sat in the grass.

"It all feels so... so primeval," said Frederick after a moment. "Like we're seeing something that's really, really old. Something that has been lost back home."

"I know what you mean," said Colleen. "I wonder what it was like all those thousands of years ago when those Gates were open, and these people walked into the World of Men. Do you think there are any of them left – back home, I mean?"

"Who knows," he replied. "I'd sure like to find out. I don't think life will ever be the same for us, now that we've been here, I mean. Something has happened to us. I feel so different now."

"You are different, Frederick. The little people aren't the only ones who have grown," she replied.

"Well now, you two," said a voice behind them.

They turned to see Adol towering over them.

"It's time we headed out. You might want to say your farewells to these good folk," he said.

They stood and walked over to the porch where the others had already gathered. The little people had also all re-assembled on the lawn and had grown quiet. Out of the crowd, a leprechaun came and made his way to the front.

"Cian!" shouted Frederick and Colleen together, and they both ran down to greet him.

"My friends!" he said, and embraced them both as they knelt down next to him. "My, but you have come a long way. And I see, Frederick, that you are quite cured of that goblin bite."

"Yes, sir," he replied, looking down at his arm. Indeed, there were no longer any signs that he had been bitten at all. "And I will always remember what you told me."

Cian smiled and said, "You are well on your way, my boy, to being truly human. Fare you well. Fare you all well!"

He began to sing a song, and all of the little people that were gathered there began to sing with him, and Colleen thought that she had never in all her days heard such a beautiful chorus as on that night under the stars of the Land of the Little People.

"May you rise each day
Through the strength of heaven:
Through light of sun,
Through radiance of moon,
Through splendor of fire,
Through swiftness of wind,
Through depth of sea,
Through stability of earth,
Through firmness of rock,
Through the strength of heaven
May you rise each day."

Their song ended, and they all waved and said many good-byes, and then slowly turned and, still waving, disappeared into the night forest, returning to their homes among the trees and roots, free at last from all fear.

Now only four little people remained on the lawn – the Wigglepox family.

"It is time," said Atlantis.

"And we are coming with you," said Mr. Wigglepox. "With your permission, that is."

"Of course!" said Colleen. "I'm sure Mr. Atlantis here would not mind, would you?"

"Not at all!" he replied. "There is plenty of room on my ship. And this time, you need not spend the entire journey down in the hold!"

They all made their way back down to the ship, and Doc said he too would be going with them to the Island, and gathered together a great bundle of things as big as himself.

"Oh, one thing I forgot to do! Would you wait a moment for me? Colleen, Frederick, would you come and lend me a hand?" asked Doc.

"Sure," they said, and they walked back to the secret door and to the Crystal Cavern.

To Colleen and Frederick's surprise, there was Cian waiting for them. He was standing in the middle of the shining room, gazing up at the multitude of shining crystals and the rainbows that lazily floated among them.

He smiled as they came in, and said, "The Hall of Sindri! It shall do much to transform our world. Never before have we had a place such as this to make our wishes come true. We are in your debt, good dwarf. You have kept your charge well."

Doc bowed low and said, "It was a labor of love. And it gave me something to do for all these years. But I think my time here has ended."

"You are welcome to stay with us, of course," replied Cian. "But whether you stay or go, I foresee that the Hall of Sindri will help to heal our world and others as well. It shall endure to the end of days and, in the end, will seal the fate of many."

Doc looked about and sighed. "Who knows? I may be back one day. I hope this house will serve once again as a meeting place for the peoples of all worlds. But for now, I return it to your care."

He pulled a large key from his pocket and handed it to Cian.

"The key to the house," he said.

"We shall take good care of it," replied Cian. "Thank you once again."

Doc bowed and then said, "Well, just one more thing to do – one last stop in the old workshop."

Colleen and Frederick followed the dwarf to his shop, and there he produced several things – a new blue robe for Frederick, and a new green one for Colleen.

"Yours are getting a bit dingy, you know, and I thought you might find these useful. And one other thing..." he said, and produced a rather large sack and gave it to Frederick.

"I made this for you, Frederick. Wear it well with that sword and chain mail shirt of yours."

Frederick looked inside and found a marvelous outfit of armor with a silver shield that bore the symbol of a dwarven hammer emblazoned on it.

He pulled out the helmet and slipped it on. It fit perfectly.

"You'll find the rest fits just as nicely – and always will," said Doc.

"And for you, Colleen," he said, producing a smaller package.

Colleen looked inside and found a silver belt of tiny, intricately woven chain links.

"It is very, very old, lass," he said. "Comes from the days of the wizards, and was worn by an elven lady. What happened to her, I do not know. But it possesses some virtue of that lordly people. Wear it well."

"Thank you, Doc. I shall," she replied.

"Come now. We must be going," he said, and they made their way back to the ship, where they found the others waiting.

"All aboard!" called Atlantis.

The three of them climbed aboard, and they cast off down the river, their company now numbering seventeen.

"We shall not take the *Atlantis* on that harrowing ride that we did last time!" said the king. "We have some hours yet, but still, we must go fast. Go below and get some rest. The professor and I shall sail her."

This they agreed to, although Frederick decided that he too would stay on deck and learn more about this marvelous ship and her mysterious captain. For some hours, they sped down the river, and down below, the crowded but happy crew nestled in together.

Mr. and Mrs. McGunnegal sat side by side and were soon fast asleep in each other's arms. The McGunnegal children smiled as they too dozed off, exhausted but happy to be with their parents. Nous and Evchi too sat beside one another in silence, and the Wigglepox family snuggled contentedly in one corner.

* * *

Doc looked about the room and smiled. He was glad for them all – glad that they had found each other and were together now. But what about himself? There had been a moment in the Timeless Hall when he could have gone home – gone home to be with his own people through that Gate where that strange contraption had rolled. But he had chosen to stay and defend these people.

He sighed and closed his eyes and was soon snoring away, dreaming of his long lost home in the Land of the Dwarves.

Chapter 27 – The Shrunken

The *Atlantis* sailed out of the cave and into the inlet that led to the sea. Frederic had fallen asleep listening to him tell tales of his ancient and lost homeland. The sky was just beginning to brighten in the east, and the sun would be rising soon. Professor McPherson was at the wheel now, and Atlantis was telling him about some aspect of the ship's design, when they saw Frederick sit up.

"Well, good morning, Frederick," said McPherson. "The king and I have had some marvelous conversations these past few hours. How about going below and waking up the rest of our crew?"

Frederick stretched and yawned, then got up and made his way down into the hold. Soon he returned with the others, and they gazed out across the sea.

"Well, there were no signs of those goblin ships on the river," said Atlantis. "They must still possess some magic about them to travel so far so fast."

"Yes," said Nous. "The Witch was not the only one among us with magic. But hers was the strongest by far."

"Well, the sun is about to rise on a new day, in a new world without a Witch to burden it. Come. Let's go to the Island of the Waking Tree. Hold on now!" said the king.

The silver sails of the *Atlantis* unfurled, and the ship sped forward across the sea, dancing on the waves with grace and ease. As the first rays of the sun peeked over the eastern horizon, the Island came into view, the great Waking Tree towering hundreds of feet into the air. The land around it seemed to have grown somehow, for instead of the steep rocky cliffs that had surrounded it when they had left, now a white sandy shore stretched outward from a great green hillock on which the Tree sat.

Soon they were drawn up to its shores and anchored there, and they easily climbed from the ship and waded through knee-deep water to the beach. Only the Wigglepox family needed a bit of help, which the McGunnegals and Frederick gladly gave them. Up the hill they climbed, with the sun rising behind them, and as they reached the summit, they saw that a great grassy field now stretched in all directions from the gigantic tree, and a great many little people were gathered there.

As they drew near, they saw that Oracle was seated on a big knob of a large root that formed a kind of chair for him. At the base of this, a spring of shining fiery blue water bubbled up from the ground, forming a great pool before him, and from there ran in a swiftly flowing stream across the green field and tumbled in a bright waterfall down the hillside and into the sea. And, sitting on the grass with her bare feet in the water, was the Lady Danu.

To Oracle's left, cringing away from the bright flowing stream, and huddling in the shadow of the tree, were a great many dark and shrunken figures. A brown smoke seemed to drift among them, like a living shadow that writhed and struggled against the light of the waters. But on the right side, standing in the glorious rays of the rising sun, were many little people, all healed and made whole, and shining with an inner illumination. But they were all somber as they stood, waiting in silence.

"Cluricauns and gremlins!" whispered Mrs. Wigglepox as they approached. "Those black creatures over there are the fallen little people. But... they are so small now!"

Indeed, just as the other little people had grown, the little people who had gone over to the Witch had shrunken, and now stood only about two inches high.

"What is that smoke that crawls among them?" Colleen whispered to a leprechaun who wore a bright green jacket. "It seems to move in and out of them."

"That is the foul smoke of self-esteem and the stench of boasting," he whispered. "It drives away the light of the waters that could heal them and make them grow again, but I fear they do not desire such healing. But look, the Elder is beckoning to you!"

They turned, and Oracle nodded to them, and they made their way over to where he was sitting. When they had drawn near, he stood on the knob and said in a loud voice, "The sun rises today on a new world. Today, those of you who have served the Witch are called to give a reckoning for your deeds. As witnesses, we have called those of what races may be assembled – of little people, of human, of half-elven, of goblin, and of dwarven kinds. And here also are those of earth and heaven – the rock people and the Lady Danu."

There was a murmur of fear among the cluricauns and gremlins.

"You have no right to judge us!" came one voice from the tiny black figures.

"That's right!" shouted another. "We were doing just fine without you!"

"Our world was dying, and you with it," replied Oracle quietly. "Do you think that the Spell and the Ooze and the worms of the goblins and the Witch were making our world into a better place? No, friends, our world would have become one great Ooze pit, and you would have become its worms, swimming within it until you were taken down to its uttermost depths, there to become food for the Great Worm. Is that what you desire?"

"Better the Ooze than that burning river of fire!" called back someone from the crowd. "Better the Witch than this Lady Danu's burning waters!"

The Lady Danu looked up at Oracle, and he nodded to her. She rose, tall and beautiful, and full of light and love.

"I bring my first witnesses before you, friends," she said, and she turned to Nous and Evchi and beckoned for them to come forward.

Shyly, they came and stood before the assembly.

"These two were once in the service of the Witch. They were once goblins who bathed in the Ooze, covered with its worms. They brought many of you to the Witch, and there you were turned to her service. But they have turned away from her and have been washed in this water of light. See! They are well and whole and strong! The Ooze and worms that deformed them are gone!" she said.

This produced a good deal of whispers among the cluricauns until one of them shouted, "Well, what of it?"

"Come!" said the Lady to them. "Come, taste and see that these waters are good! See, even now you are shrinking with the rising of the sun. But if you will only come and drink and wash yourselves clean of the Ooze, you will grow again and become true little people and no longer The Shrunken."

"That's good and fine for goblins," shouted another. "But we're not like them. That river is a river of fire! It would burn us up!"

"It only burns two things – that which you cast into it, and that which you cling to. The first it will free you of forever. The latter will become a fire in itself that ever burns and ever melds itself to your soul," she replied. "All else is healed by it. Come and wash away the Ooze from yourselves while you have time! See! Already these waters of light flow into the great ocean of your world. Already, it begins to shine, and it shall increase forever and forever, and all those here shall shine brighter and brighter with it."

Again, there was a murmur of fear that spread through the cluricauns and gremlins.

"But we don't want your shiny waters. They hurt our eyes and burn our flesh! Send us away. Send us to the Pits of the Witch's Fortress! We can hide from it there!" cried one of the little figures, and even as he did so, he shrank even smaller.

"The waves of the sea beat on every shore," said Oracle. "Even the Pits of the Witch cannot keep out the waters of light forever. Even now, those dark shores are crumbling, what remains of the black fortress will utterly fall, and the Pits will become a great lake of bright and shining light. Do you still wish to go there?"

"I'd rather cast myself into the Witch's Pits than into that river of fire you've got there!" cried one of the cluricauns.

Colleen could stand it no longer. She felt as though she had to say something to convince these shrunken little people that they could be big and whole again, just like Oracle and all the others.

She climbed up next to Oracle and looked at him. He nodded to her, and she gazed out over the hundreds and hundreds of shrunken figures before her.

"Listen to me!" she said. "The Lady Danu and Oracle are right – you're all shrinking away to nothing – that's what the Spell of the Witch and the Goblin Ooze has given you. The Spell is broken, but now it's stuck inside you. If you don't give it up, it's going to shrink you right down to nothing! Please, you can be made into what you should be – just look across the stream at the other little people. Can't you see what each of you is and what you can become?"

"Shut it up, girl!" shouted one of them.

"If we can't have the world, at least give us the Pits. Let us be!" said another.

"Will none of you come to your senses?" said Colleen pleadingly.

"You don't get it, do you?" sneered one. "We don't want your light and all your *goodness*. I say, send me back to the pits of the Witch!"

"Send us to the Pits!" they began to shout, and soon the whole group of them was chanting, "To the Pits! To the Pits!"

Oracle looked very sad. Slowly, he pulled out his pot of gold.

"Are you certain? I will grant you to go there if you wish," he said, but they shouted all the louder, "Let us cast ourselves in if you won't do it! To the Pits! We wish for the Pits!"

He sighed heavily, and a tear ran down his cheek. Slowly, he took a piece of gold from his pot and held it up.

"To the Pits!" came the chant. "We wish for the pits!"

There was a flash of rainbows and, one by one, the cluricauns and gremlins began to disappear, carrying the brown smoke with them. Faster and faster, the rainbows rained down on the field as they continued to shout until there was only one cluricaun left.

"To the Pits! I don't need you. I'll be my own Elder!" he shouted.

Oracle closed his eyes, and one final rainbow fell upon the field. The last of the dark smoke swirled around the cluricaun, entered into him, and then he too disappeared.

The field was silent now, and Oracle sighed heavily.

After a moment, Colleen said, "Did you really send them to the Pits?"

"I did not send them anywhere," replied Oracle. "They wished themselves to go there. And there they shall remain until the Ocean of Light beats that last bastion of darkness to oblivion. Then let us hope that all these Shrunken Ones will, in the end, desire to come home."

"But will they?" asked Frederick.

"We shall see," replied Oracle. "We shall see. But what is this?"

From behind a root of the Waking Tree, three small figures emerged. They were obviously pixies, but one had completely lost her wings and the other two were dull and drab, and their wings hung in shreds behind them.

Colleen's eyes went wide, and she cried, "It's them! Intelli, Irassi, and Apetti! The pixies we met in the forest!"

Oracle looked on the three pixies with pity. Their eyes were downcast, and they stayed in the shadow of the great root, clinging to one another.

"It would seem that we have a few more little people to grant wishes to," said Oracle, and he slid down from his seat and walked over to them.

"Do you also wish for the Pits of the Witch?" he asked them gently. "You need not, you know. You may wish to have your wings back, and to shine again with the light that is natural to you, a light that lingers on inside you like the last glow of a coal from a fire that has long died away."

Intelli stared at her feet and said, "If I could only believe it all. I want to believe."

Then Irassi said, "If I only had the will power left – I would go with you."

"Oh, if I could desire something more than pleasure – something truly meaningful! Is there really such a thing?" asked Apetti.

"Such wishes cannot go unanswered," said Oracle, and he pulled another piece of gold from his pot.

The three pixies stared at the shining lump of gold in Oracle's hand for a long time, then at each other with worried faces.

Finally, they seemed to come to some silent agreement, and they slowly came forward.

"We wish to be what we should be," they said in unison.

A rainbow descended upon them, hiding them for a moment, and then, with a joyous laugh, they burst into the air, sending a multitude of colors scattering in all directions like fireworks. Joined hand in hand, they flew upward, sending a shower of twinkling pixie dust down upon the field and everyone in it. Higher and higher, they spiraled, dancing and laughing, their bodies shining brightly in the sun.

Colleen giggled and held up her arms, dancing on the green grass as pixie dust floated down upon her. Suddenly, with a *FLASH* of golden light, they winked out and vanished.

"Where did they go?" she asked Oracle. "Surely not to the Pits of the Witch!"

"No, no," he replied. "Not them. They have regained their natural powers and can see into the worlds, and move between them. Do not be surprised if you see them again, my friend."

"How marvelous!" said Colleen.

But then a thought struck her, and she grew more serious. "Oracle, what's to become of all the goblins that are still here in the Land of the Little People?"

"Ah," he replied. "The goblin ships seem to have disappeared. They were last seen sailing past a strange island that no one had encountered before. A fog rose up from the sea, and when it lifted, both the island and the ships were gone. Who knows where they went? But there were some goblins who were not on the ships, and for them, I have a very special gift. If Evchi is willing, I would like to send her back to the Burning Sands – to her oasis, and there she will wait for them to come to her, and she shall teach them how to be rid of the Ooze. In the meantime, the desert shall be flowering, for we shall be planting, and the waters of light shall be flowing. These goblins too will one day have to make a final choice."

At this, Nous looked distressed, and Evchi looked sad as well. But Oracle smiled and said, "I see that Nous and Evchi would not be parted from one another. What is your desire, my friends?"

Nous blushed and leaned over to Evchi and whispered in her ear. She grinned, looked sheepishly at him, and whispered something back to him.

"Nous and Evchi wish to be wed!" said Nous.

"That was quick," whispered Frederick to Colleen, at which she elbowed him in the ribs.

"Then let it be so!" said Oracle. "For I am Dian, Elder of the Little People, and this privilege has been given to me. And what joy it would bring us, on the eve of our new world, to wed these, the first of the New Goblins, in the shade of the New Waking Tree, with these witnesses here present!"

Thus it was that very hour, on the Island of the Waking Tree, as a warm breeze blew and flower petals and pixie dust floated down through the sweet-smelling air, Nous and Evchi were wed.

It was a glorious wedding, with the little people singing, the sun shining, the waters of light flowing, the Waking Tree growing, and all the world waking and coming to life. It was as though everything in every place had a new start, and Nous and Evchi looked like a prince and princess in a fairytale, for indeed they were.

Chapter 28 – Leave Taking

Colleen spent the rest of the day walking and talking with the strange and wonderful group of people she had come to be so fond of. The whole Island of the Waking Tree still seemed to be expanding outward and blossoming with bright flowers and plush green grass.

As she and Frederick and Nous walked with Oracle through a blooming meadow, she listened to the Great Song all around them. Everything sang in perfect harmony, and the Waking Tree was like a centerpiece of the grand orchestra of this world. Somehow, she sensed that the little leprechaun walking beside her was the conductor of it all. Or was there even more than that about him?

Suddenly, a thought struck her, and she said, "Oracle, is the Gate of Anastazi still leaking timelessness?"

"Indeed it is," he replied.

"Does that mean that people here will live on forever?" she asked.

"Yes," he said, "but death is not a natural thing to the little people anyway. When others come here, however, they will cease to age. You are in a land of eternal life for all who dwell in this world."

Frederick whistled. "Wow, this place was pretty bad not so long ago," he said. "I think it's turned into Paradise instead. Should we tell Atlantis? He told me once that he was trying to make his own country into something like this. I guess his dreams all got dashed when the goblins and that Great Worm invaded."

Oracle frowned at the mention of the Worm, then said, "He may stay if he wishes, but I think that the bitterness in his soul would drive him out. His heart is bent on revenge, and he would find no rest with us, although we shall indeed make our world into a paradise, and he could live on forever here."

"Well, he doesn't seem like such a bad fellow," said Frederick.

"No," said Oracle. "There is hope for him, and he has much to offer your world if he wishes."

* * *

They walked on for some time, and at last, Oracle led Frederick a short ways away as Colleen, Nous, and Evchi ran into a field of orange flowers. The leprechaun looked up, and Frederick followed his gaze skyward at the towering heights of the Waking Tree.

"Frederick, I want to tell you something," he said. "Do you know that the Gate of Anastazi is not the only doorway leading from our world?"

"There are others as well?" he replied.

"Yes," said Oracle. "The Waking Tree is such a door."

"Where does it go?" asked Frederick, growing curious.

"Into the Great Beyond," replied Oracle. "Into realms of mystery and adventure that no one has ever imagined. There are worlds beyond worlds where even the fairies have never gone, and the Waking Tree opens into all of them."

A great longing welled up in Frederick's heart to run into the great tree and see where it might lead him. The desire to venture into the unknown and discover the wonders that were waiting out there was almost overwhelming. For a moment, he could barely breathe, so strong was his desire simply to go – to taste and see.

Oracle smiled.

"The day is coming, my friend," he said. "The day is coming. Only be patient and true. Through every day of your life, remember that the Waking Tree is here and is waiting for you. When you are ready, come. Remember."

* * *

Colleen, Nous, and Evchi ran back to Frederick and Oracle, laughing as pixies raced them across the field. They continued on down the trail, talking on for a time until Colleen began to think about Nous as he walked beside her. She was amazed at how much he had changed. It was as though his entire outlook on life had been transformed.

"Nous," she said as they came back to the shining stream, "you've become so *handsome,* both inside and out. You've changed so much, I can hardly believe it."

He blushed and said, "The Witch always said that these waters of the Lady were evil – that they were like fire that would burn us. She lied to all of us. She never told us that we could be different – that we could be new, like the goblins of old."

"I was wondering," asked Colleen. "Back there in the Timeless Hall, why did you do it? Why did you turn on the Witch?"

He looked thoughtful, then said, "In the midst of that battle, when you and your family were facing the Witch, I remembered something you said once about the Great Song. I needed, then and there, to be sure you were right, and the Witch was wrong. I thought I would burst if I didn't find out. In my heart, I cried out for help – for ears to hear and eyes to see what you had heard and seen. It was then that I saw it – the Witch's power rending and tearing at the world, and your power mending and healing it. Her way seemed all wrong, and yours was right. I made my choice. I'm still making that choice."

They walked on in silence, marveling at the awakening world around them, and both Colleen and Nous listened, hearing with a sense beyond hearing, the Great Song that whispered in every bit of life around them.

The time finally came for them to depart, and they headed down the hill to the white beach. One by one, they all embraced, and tears flowed down their faces, for they knew that they might never see one another again.

"Oh, how I wish there was time for us to wander through the woods together, my dear friends," said Mrs. Wigglepox. "But if you are ever in the Land of the Little People again, come to the Wigglepox Tree."

"We will," said Colleen.

Colleen then knelt down and embraced Mrs. Wigglepox. "Thank you so much for helping me rescue my mother," she said. "I could not have done it without you. I will never forget you."

Lily then pulled on Frederick's sleeve. He bent down, and she whispered something in his ear. His face turned red, and he smiled, and she went back and held her daddy's hand.

"Thank you all so much," said Mr. Wigglepox to them. "We will be forever grateful for what you have done. And thank you, Sorceress Ellie McGunnegal."

"Sorceress?" said Adol.

But she only grinned up at him and said, "I'll tell you that story later."

He put his great arm around her and pulled her close.

"Goodbye, Nous. Farewell, Evchi," said Colleen. "If ever we get that crystal ball back from Pwca, I will try to come and see you again, or perhaps we might find a ride here again one day."

She gave them each a great hug, and tears of sorrow and joy ran down her face.

"Goodbye, Doc," said Frederick. "Thank you again for the armor and sword."

"Keep it well, lad," he replied, "and use it only as a man should."

"I will," he said.

"But didn't you know," said Doc. "I've decided to come with you!"

"You're coming with us?" Frederick said. "Back to the World of Men?"

"Yes," he replied. "I believe you youngsters need someone who's your elder to keep you all in line. And since I'm just about the eldest here, that would be me."

"That's wonderful!" said Colleen.

Last of all, Colleen turned to Oracle. The little leprechaun smiled up at her, then waved her to bend down closer.

"We will meet again, Colligal," he said, "although you may not recognize me. Remember that things are not always as they appear."

"That's for sure," she said. "We had no idea who you really were. The Elder of Elders! Tell me, Oracle, what is your real name?"

"Well now, a name is a thing not easily given. I just am what I am. Remember me from time to time, and I will always remember you," he replied.

She looked at his mysterious face, and he winked at her, and then gave her a hug.

"Oh, there's something I've just remembered," said Colleen. "What about Mal? Is she still back in her cave?"

"Ah, Mal," said Oracle. "Yes, and what are we to do with her? She will not like our new world, and already she is disheartened by her lair. It no longer closes itself up for her, and its darkness has given way to light and beauty. What shall we do with Mal?"

"Father, Mother," said Colleen, calling her parents over. "We met an old woman here named Mal. She was a bit of a hag, and had it not been for Cian and Oracle rescuing us from her, we might have been taken by the goblins. But she is a pitiable old thing. Could we take her with us?"

"Mal, is it?" said Ellie. "That's an interesting name. I remember my great grandfather telling me stories about his Aunt Mal. *Malorie* was her real name. She was always bothering him about the family secret and wanting to see it. Finally, he gave in and showed it to her one day. She was never heard from again. I wonder… Oracle, might we meet this Mal?"

Oracle turned to find Cian, waved to him, and said, "Cian, could you fetch Mal for us?"

Cian nodded, went back up to the Waking Tree, and walked into its gigantic trunk. There was a flash of golden light and, a few moments later, he re-emerged with an old haggardly woman in a ragged brown dress. Her hair was wilder than ever, and she looked up in wonder and fear at the towering tree, the shining river, and at all of the little people who laughed and danced on the green lawn.

Cian led her down to the beach and said, "May I introduce Mal, Hag of the Wood."

The McGunnegals gathered around her, but she shied away fearfully.

Ellie looked into her eyes, and there, in those gray depths, were tiny flecks of lavender.

"Aunt Malorie?" she said.

Mal stiffened, as if the words brought back some distant memory. She looked Ellie up and down, poked her in the ribs, frowned, and said, "You need to fatten up, dearie. Here, let Aunt Mal fix some gingerbread cookies for you."

She looked about, but seeing no tiny little people, sighed.

"They're getting harder to catch, you know," she said, "and I never did get to make cookies out of them. Somehow, they always got away."

"Aunt Malorie, it is you!" said Ellie. "Come. We're going to take you home and help you get better."

"Home?" said Mal. "Why, I'm afraid the old cave is getting shabby, and all my cages are broken. Ever since that last night that Cian visited, and my best catch in ages escaped."

"No, not back to your cave. We're taking you back to Ireland – back to the farm," said Ellie.

"Back to … to Ireland?" said Mal. She screwed up her face at the thought. "Well, I've a mind to do just that, and tell William that it's all gone wrong, that whole *family secret* thing. Ha! But maybe another place would do better. I would so love to make some gingerbread again."

"Come along, then," said Ellie. "We're going home."

With one last round of hugs and goodbyes, they boarded the ship, and the Lady Danu rose from the water, illuminating the already shining sea further.

"Fare you well, friends. Remember us, and remember all who still suffer under the dominion of darkness," she said.

And so they boarded the ship, and Atlantis raised the silver sails.

"Take her out, mate," he said to Frederick.

Frederick gripped the wheel of the ship and shut his eyes.

The world flashed around them, and there was a momentary "Oh!" from everyone as they watched the world shrink away. It was a green world, with a vast blue sea, but they could see that the forests were bursting into color and light that radiated out from the Island of the Waking Tree. The Land of the Little People was returning to its former grandeur and would soon be filled with the light of fairies and magic.

Then they were among the stars. They all gazed in wonder at the awe-inspiring spectacle that surrounded them. But after a moment, Colleen walked over and stood beside Frederick.

"Do you think we'll ever see them again?" she asked.

"Oh, I think so," he said. "Just think of it, here we are sailing between the worlds on a magic ship and, back home, you have your mirror that you can step through. Back on the Island of Atlantis, there is a magic Gate that leads to the Timeless Hall, and who knows how many other ways one might go from world to world."

"But what if we're not supposed to do that?" said Colleen. "What if our time is over?"

"You can't be serious," he replied. "I dare say this adventure has just begun."

He paused and looked about at the millions of stars around them.

"After all, Helga is out there somewhere, and the Witch," he said. "Something's got to be done about all that. We can't just leave poor old Helga with *her*."

"I suppose you are right," she replied. "But I will be glad to get home."

"Home then!" said Atlantis and nodded to Frederick.

Again, he shut his eyes, and willed the compass to point to home, back to the World of Men. Then he released the wheel, giving it back to Atlantis, and he and Colleen went and stood with the others. There were no words to be said as they watched in wonder as the galaxy rolled by.

Chapter 29 – Home

Some hours had passed before Atlantis spoke again. "We are almost there, friends. And on the way, I will show you what few other men have seen."

Suddenly, a great blue sphere loomed before them, and slipped silently by, followed by its sister world. A great banded planet followed, and then one with massive rings. Within moments, they passed through a field of great stones the size of mountains. Atlantis paused the ship for a moment, looking sad.

"They were great once," he said, and then willed his ship on.

"Mars should be next!" whispered Bib to Colleen.

Indeed, the red planet zoomed by them, and then their home came into view. It grew from a tiny marble to a brilliant blue sphere, larger and larger, and then suddenly, they were bouncing along on the sea, and the coast of Ireland and their little town's port came into view. It was dusk, and the warm lights of shops and houses shone brightly on the shore.

"One last thing to do," said Atlantis, and he touched a series of gems, and the ship began to change. Its bright white decks were transformed into dark, old, wooden sea-worn planks, the silver sails faded to a dirty gray, and she took on the appearance of a weather-beaten old schooner.

"Best put our swords away, mate," said the king. "Run below and bring up a sheet to wrap them in."

Frederick did so, and also brought up blankets that they could wrap themselves in since some of their garb was hardly fitting for the Ireland of 1846.

Atlantis brought her in, and they tied up to the dock.

Many a townsman's eyes followed the odd-looking crew as they went ashore and walked down the dock toward the old Inn.

"Does anyone have any money?" asked Bran. "I'm afraid I lost all mine at sea, and I would dearly love to stop and get something to eat. It is dinner time, after all."

"Bran!" scolded Abbe. "After all we've been through, you're thinking of food? Just like a boy!"

They all laughed and headed down the road.

At the main intersection, they came across a thin, gruff-looking old man leaning against a lamppost.

"Well, bless my soul!" he said. "I ear'd you 'ad done sent 'em all to England, Adol. And 'oo's this? Why, it's the Missus! It's been plum a year since I seen you last! But I'm right glad to see you again! And 'oo's these folk? Relatives maybe?"

They paused for a moment as Adol greeted the old man and tried to give an explanation of where Ellie had been.

"It's a long story, Barley," he said. "And we're right tired. Stop by sometime, and I'll tell it proper."

They chatted on for a moment, and Colleen stood just outside of the circle of light cast by the street lamp, removing her blanket for a moment to cool down. She listened impatiently, wanting to get home, and did not see a sleek shadow slip from house to house, drawing nearer and nearer until it was hidden in the growing darkness just behind her.

A gray-green hand slipped from beneath a black cloak, reaching until it silently slipped its fingers into Colleen's cloak pocket, and stealthily withdrew the golden key that Doc had given her.

In a flash, it dashed away and was gone. Colleen sensed something and spun about, peering into the gloom. But only the sounds of the town greeted her, and she turned back as her father and the old man finished their conversation.

Adol waved and said a final farewell, and they walked on down the street toward their home.

It was nearly dark when they arrived, and to all appearances, nothing had changed, except that there, sitting on their front porch, was an old man with a long beard.

"Oh, Father, Mother," said Aonghus, "we completely forgot to tell you – we have a guest at home."

"A guest?" said Adol. "Who?"

They all looked at one another and Frederick spoke.

"He's a wizard, sir," he said. "I found him when I came back the first time.

His name is Gwydion."

They walked through the gate, and the old man stood.

"Well! I see you've come back at last. And if you haven't brought a figure of renown! If it isn't Atlantis himself!"

"Gwydion, my old friend!" said Atlantis, and the two gripped hands and then embraced.

"Well, it's plain that you two know each other," said Adol. "But might I introduce myself. I am Adol McGunnegal, and this is Ellie, my wife, and these are my children, who apparently you know, and Frederick, who says that he found you, and Professor McPherson, who perhaps you know? And this is ... our Aunt Malorie."

When Ellie stepped forward and extended her hand, the wizard's eyes grew wide.

"No," said Atlantis, "she is not Mor-Fae, although she could be her twin."

"Ah, so many tales to be told!" said the wizard. "Pleased to meet you, Ellie. And this must be Colleen. I *am* pleased to see you safely home. And who is this? But no, it couldn't be – Doc the Dwarf himself? How long has it been? Bless my soul, bless my soul! But please, come in, come in, and oh, do forgive me."

"Forgive you?" asked Ellie. "For what?"

"Well, you see, while you were gone I did a bit of... rearranging," he replied.

"Rearranging?" asked Adol, cocking an eyebrow.

"The house was a wreck when we left, Dad," said Bib. "Literally a wreck. Something had gotten in... or out."

"Yes," said Adol. "Something – one of those goblins, is here."

"It was bigger than that, Dad," said Abbe. "It nearly took out the side of the house."

"It was a troll," said Bran. "We saw it."

"A troll!" he replied. "This gets stranger all the time!"

"Well, you best come in and see for yourselves," said Gwydion.

They followed him through the same old squeaky door and into the living room. Nothing seemed to have changed, except that the wreckage that had been there was no more.

"I thought it best to keep appearances as normal as possible," said Gwydion. "No sense in attracting a load of attention to ourselves. It's really in the cellar that I've, well, fixed things up a bit. Come, I'll show you."

Down into the cellar they went, and at first, they could see no difference except that it was considerably smaller. Gwydion had constructed a rough wooden wall with a dilapidated doorway, and he led them through this, down a creaky set of stairs, and through another doorway.

As soon as they crossed the threshold of the old wooden door, everything changed. They walked into a large room with a green and white tiled floor, and twelve-foot-high walls of great white blocks of stone, covered in the familiar runes that they had seen so often now – the runes of a Wizard's Castle.

A round table was there, situated in the center with eight chairs set about it. The light of a blue-white chandelier illuminated the room, and there were various square tables spread out along the walls that hosted sealed glass jars and containers of odd liquids, strange devices, wands, and other things that seemed to glow, float, or wink. In a fireplace on one wall crackled a smokeless fire.

"I've been scavenging," said Gwydion. "Amazing how much survived all these years. No doubt there's more to find in the tunnels I've dug."

"Tunnels?" asked Ellie.

"Oh, yes, Mrs. McGunnegal. See these doors about the room?" He pointed to four side doors, one on each side. "They open into the digging I've been doing. The original Wizard's Castle stretched out all over this area, you know."

"Wizard's Castle?" she replied questioningly.

"Oh, there is so much to tell!" said Gwydion.

"Indeed there is," said Adol. "This is incredible, and we must see it all! But come, it has truly been a long and eventful day. Let's go upstairs to the living room and have some good old Irish tea."

Long into the evening, they spoke, and Colleen and Frederick and all the others in turn shared story after story of their adventures. Gwydion told them of the strange things that had come to the bog, and that he had cast spells of protection along all the walls around the farm. At least for a time, the goblin and its creatures could not pass over that enchanted barrier. But the dark things there in the bog had multiplied, and he dared not cross the fence alone.

Now the conversation was turning to what might be done with the dark forces that were gathering in that dismal place.

"I think that it is time for a new Council of Wizards and Heroes," said Gwydion. "And each of you must have a part in it. But the world outside must not know. To all appearances, we must be poor farmers, or the curious and meddlers will pry their way in and cause trouble."

This idea was discussed at great length, and it was proposed that Professor McPherson open a new branch of his boarding school in Ireland – a House of Special Studies, and that the McGunnegals would "rent" a piece of land to him for this purpose. This rent would pay their taxes, and they would not need to send the children to Wales, after all. In fact, the professor would recommend that Frederick be transferred to the Irish School for the remainder of the year to participate in a foreign exchange program. The new Professor Gwydion would be the school's principal, with McPherson as the dean, and Doc as the teacher of architecture.

"There may be others that we can find and invite to this special school," said McPherson. "Others like you all – who have the blood of, well, *other peoples* in their veins. They no doubt know that they are different, but they likely do not know why, or what to do with their extraordinary abilities, unless someone takes them in and gives them direction for their life."

"Yes," said Gwydion. "And you may be sure that the goblin will not hesitate to seek out such allies as well, and corrupt them to its desires. We must find them first."

On the conversation went, with many such ideas discussed. Bib insisted that the school must also be a place of scientific discovery, since the world around them was being shaped by it.

It was intriguing to Frederick to think that a new age that mingled science and magic and heroes was dawning. Soon, however, he began to grow tired of the details of it all, and his mind began to wander, thinking of all the amazing things that had happened to them. Slipping from the room, he went out on the front porch, and there found Colleen and Mal.

"Hello," she said. "I needed some air. What do you say - shall we take a walk? Aunt Mal, would you like to come?"

"Oh, no dearie," she replied. "I'll just stay here and bake some cookies and pies." Then she cackled hysterically.

"She'd make a good match for your Great Grandpa, I'd say," whispered Frederick.

Colleen smiled and then walked down into the yard. For a moment, Frederick hesitated, wondering if it were safe. But he had his sword, and she had her staff, and the magic ring was still on her finger, and Gwydion said that the goblin could no longer get across the wall. So he shrugged, and they headed across the farm toward the Hill. They walked mostly in silence, and when they got there, they climbed to its summit and sat down.

"This is where it all began, Frederick, back on that day that you followed me here," she said as they watched the sun sinking in the west.

He looked thoughtful, then said, "Yeah, I remember. I'm sorry that I was such a sneak back then."

Then he paused again and said, "Say, whatever happened to Badger? I just realized that he wasn't with you there at the end."

She sighed, then told him the tale.

"I'm sorry to hear that," he said. "Maybe someday you'll be able to visit that old Wizard's Castle again and try to get him back."

"Maybe so," she said. "I remember riding him that day we went through the mirror. How long ago was it?"

"I've lost track," he said. "But somehow, I think it hasn't been that long. Maybe a month? Or two?"

"I feel as though it's been years," she replied.

They were silent for a while longer, and then Colleen said, "Well, thank goodness we're home now."

"Isn't it so strange, Colleen? Can it really be?" Frederick said. "My family, descended from King Atlantis?"

"And mine from... from his sister," said Colleen gravely. "And here we are, what, five thousand years later, and we meet them both! You do have his eyes, you know."

Frederick grunted and said, "I'm glad you don't have hers."

Colleen laughed, but then grew serious.

"Do you think Atlantis knows?" she asked. "That the Witch is Mor-Fae, his sister? Or is she another long lost relative – another look-alike?"

"I don't know," he replied. "But I hope I never meet her again. Sheesh, Colleen, she's like your mom's evil twin!"

Colleen looked up at the sky. "She's out there somewhere, you know, and poor Helga is with her. I do hope Helga is all right. Grandpa is still missing too. I still wonder if he hobbled off into some strange land that first night. Remember that?"

"Do I!" said Frederick.

She thought for a moment and then said, "You know we have to do something. We have to find him and Helga, and we have to get the crystal and the mirror back from the goblin. I mean, what if he brings the Witch here, or that awful Goblin King. Did you hear what *he* said in the Timeless Hall? There's so much to do and learn!"

"I've been thinking about that, Colleen. Now that we're all together – your mom and dad, and Atlantis and Gwydion, and well, we'll have a good chance at doing something about it all. Isn't it just so amazing? It's like a whole bunch of heroes from legends past have sprung to life again! And you and I and your brothers and sisters are with them! Who knows? Maybe we're part of a new legend in the making. I saw some pretty amazing things that you did back in the Land of the Little People. Do you think you can do that stuff here at home, in the World of Men?" said Frederick.

"I'm not sure," she replied and looked about. "Our own world seems to be pretty sleepy too. If there were any spirits of trees and rivers and such here, I don't see them."

Then she gazed up at the big oak.

"Except maybe..." But then she shook her head and said, "I don't know."

Frederick nodded, and they sat in silence and watched the moon rise. After a while, they rose and returned to the house. The others were still deep in conversation, and Frederick joined them.

Colleen said goodnight, and went up to her familiar old room and lay down.

After a few moments, Ellie came in and sat down beside her.

"I'm so glad you're home, Mom," she said.

Ellie sighed a huge contented sigh. "So am I, Colleen. So am I."

Epilogue

Pwca the goblin sat hunched before the broken door that led to the secret chamber he had found.

It was in there. The *Presence.* The ancient *thing* that drew him and all others of his kind to itself. Even now, he felt its subliminal call, urging him on, demanding that he come closer.

In one hand, he held a burning torch, and in the other, he nervously fingered a golden key. He sensed that it was a magical key, and now he was gathering the courage to try what he was being driven to do – what *it* was driving him to do.

The urge to crawl through the broken door became too great, and he slipped in. There it was - its great bulk of a body lay in the darkness, black upon black. How long it had lain there, who could say? Its huge eyes were shut – always shut. Yet it was somehow aware, as though it were in some twilight sleep that kept its body frozen and still, but allowed its vast mind to send out tendrils of thought and compulsion, drawing all things wicked to itself. But it was chained - chained with great silver chains and locked with magical locks to blocks of stone set deep in the floor.

Pwca silently edged his way forward, past the vast head of the creature, and to the first shackle that bound the massive front left leg. Carefully, almost reverently, he slipped the key into the lock of the shackle. The urge to turn it – to release this abomination became almost unbearable.

But then he hesitated, seeing something curious, and his own greed overcame the thing's almost overpowering call. There, on the clawed forefinger, was a shiny black ring, easily as big around as his own waist. Pwca reached out a hand and touched it, and as he did, his eyes shot wide open in astonishment, and he jerked his hand away. He had never sensed such magic and power before.

An urgency hammered upon his mind. *Release me!* He knew it came from the chained menace. He staggered in place, holding his head with his hands. *Release me! NOW!*

Pwca trembled, and his hand involuntarily reached out to the key, but with a terrible effort of will, he pulled it back and, with a suddenness that surprised even himself, he grasped the great black ring with both hands and pulled with all of his might.

Nothing happened. It was bound to the great finger through some magic and untold years of wear. *RELEASE ME, it commanded.*

Pwca reached for the key. The key! Perhaps it could release the ring – if it were shaped a bit...

Quickly, the goblin pulled the key from the lock and set it on the ground before him. Then he pulled up his sleeve and plucked a single worm from his arm. He stared at it briefly as it writhed in the torch light, and then placed it on top of the key and began an incantation.

The worm and the key began to merge into one, and soon a golden worm wriggled on the ground before him. He picked it up, and stepping next to the great claw, placed it between the ring and the scaly finger, and began his spell again. The worm slithered around the edge of the ring, round and round and then vanished into a small space between two scales.

Pwca waved his hands once more, and his chant rose to a feverish pitch. Then he let drop his torch and grasped the black band with both hands and pulled with all his might.

Slowly, it slid over the vast middle knuckle of the claw, then over the first knuckle, and with a sound like a great gong, it fell to the floor.

Pwca snatched up the torch and held it before him, but screamed and hastily backed away, for as the great ring fell from the armored finger, the vast black body of the horror before him began to twist and writhe, as though it were withdrawing into itself, shrinking and becoming misshapen.

He pressed himself against the wall, watching with fascination and fear as the massive wall of scales dwindled down, down, shrinking into the shadows. The great silver chains and locks clanged to the floor as the monstrous body vanished. Then all was still, except that from the darkness of one corner came the sound of ragged breathing.

Pwca hesitated, his heart beating wildly, and then inched his way forward, his torch held before him. The chains and shackles and locks lay strewn upon the floor, empty of their former prisoner.

Then he saw it – the ring that he had pulled from the claw! But it had shrunken as well, and now lay upon the floor, small as any normal ring. Slowly, he edged forward and reached down, picking up the smooth circlet between his thumb and forefinger. The same sense of power and magic flooded over him, and he held it up to the light of his torch to see it more clearly.

Suddenly, without warning, there was a scream and a hiss, and out of the darkness before him sprang a small creature, about his own size, but with long, wild black hair that covered its head and face and tumbled down to its knees. So quickly did it spring upon him that Pwca had no time to react, and his torch was knocked from his hand to the floor, and the ring rolled away next to it, landing in its circle of orange light.

The hairy creature struck Pwca, then dove for the ring, but now the goblin knew what it was after, and also knew it must not get it. He dove after the creature, grappling with its bare legs. It fell, shrieked wildly, twisting and turning and reaching for its prize, which now lay inches from its knobby hand.

The two combatants rolled over and over, tumbling against the silver chains, and suddenly, they were apart. Both scrambled for the torch, and both reached it together. Both grabbed for the ring, both touched it, and now they were face to face. The goblin found himself looking into dark, malevolent eyes that stared into his own from behind a tangled mat of black hair that hung about its naked body like a garment.

But they were not the eyes of a beast, but of a small man – no, of a dwarf! Pwca hissed and bared his fangs, but the dwarf bellowed in return and struggled mightily to gain control of the ring. For a moment, there was a blur of motion, and then Pwca had it. He slipped it onto his forefinger.

"NOOOOOOOOO!" screamed the dwarf as the form of the goblin began to twist and grow. He watched in terror as the goblin's body became bloated, and gray-green scales burst from his mottled skin. His neck stretched and grew, and his strands of hair burst into horns on a massive fanged head.

Suddenly, a small glass ball rolled away from the growing monster and stopped at the dwarf's feet. He hesitated only a moment, seized the torch and the crystal, then turned and dove through the broken door just as great jaws snapped closed behind him, barely missing their prey. Cursing and screaming, he fled from the chamber, up a long flight of stairs, and out into the starlit world.

He stood on the hill, breathing heavily, and looked about him. Dense fog and curling mist surrounded him like a sea. There, silhouetted against the rising moon, his long, wild hair and beard splayed all about him, he shook his fist at the sky, then at the earth beneath him, howled like a wild beast, and then collapsed to the ground and lay beating the stone with his fist and trembling.

Suddenly, a terrifying roar came from deep beneath the earth. The dwarf leaped to his feet, his eyes filled with rage and terror, and fled into the night, the crystal ball gripped in his boney fist. The sound echoed across the Dismal Bog and was carried on the wind to the peacefully sleeping farmhouse.

All at once, everyone in the McGunnegal house awoke. Colleen and Frederick both rushed into the hall, only to be met by the others. With worried faces, they crept down the stairs and were met by their parents.

"What was that?" whispered Colleen.

No one spoke. Gwydion and Atlantis emerged from the cellar, Atlantis with his sword drawn and Gwydion with staff in hand.

"What has happened?" asked Adol, a fierce look on his usually kind face.

"It has awakened," said the wizard grimly. "The terror that we buried so long ago has awakened."

* * *

To Be Continued...

Author's Note

I hope you have enjoyed reading *The Strange Land Trilogy,* a compilation of books 1-3 of *The McGunnegal Chronicles.* My goal has been and always will be to provide great clean adventure stories for all ages that also whisper of deep things.

Please consider giving these books a review on Amazon. I would really appreciate it.

Look for more books to come in *The McGunnegal Chronicles*, and check Audible.com for availability of the audio book version of the series.

Thanks,

Ben Anderson

Made in the USA
Columbia, SC
08 December 2017